The Domino Coincidence

The Domino Coincidence

Roger Weston

iUniverse, Inc.
Bloomington

The Domino Coincidence

iUniverse books may be ordered through booksellers or by contacting:

iUniverse
1663 Liberty Drive
Bloomington, IN 47403
www.iuniverse.com
1-800-Authors (1-800-288-4677)

ISBN: 978-1-4759-6235-2 (sc)
ISBN: 978-1-4759-6237-6 (hc)
ISBN: 978-1-4759-6236-9 (e)

Library of Congress Control Number: 2012921592

Printed in the United States of America

iUniverse rev. date: 11/29/2012

For
Betty-Anne

If the mind can stray into its own dark places - can it also stray back into the light without a guide?

If nothing is as it seems – it seems that there is nothing. If nothing is as it was – then is there still nothing?

Is the mind
the guardian
Of the soul
Is the beat
of the heart
the only way
blood can flow?

Calder – Rory: Age 38 University Lecturer, Criminologist, Profiler and Investigative Advisor to CIB. Prior to taking up a position at the University of Cardiff in Wales, Rory had been working for the Police, and SIS, in an investigation into Industrial and Research Espionage, that appeared to have its roots in a large Tertiary Institution. While on a vacation in Scotland he is informed of the deaths of his estranged wife Serena, and his three children. Rory is traumatised, and sinks into deep erratic depressions, and travels to the verge of a cerebral breakdown. This dramatically affects his judgement of himself, his life, his work, and of others....Was it an accident – or was it murder? And if it was – why? Or were the circumstances of weather and excess speed, and possible mechanical faults the factors? Or was everything – just coincidence? Does his search for the truth, and his distrust of himself and others become part of the mystery? Is he consumed by his inability to grasp the tragic devastating loss of his children? As well as dealing with who and what he really is?

Marguriette Bronson: Age 36. Detective Superintendent. Previously involved with Calder, at a professional and on a personal level. She passes information to her Superior CIB Officer – Colin Moorhead regarding Rory Calder, his previous involvement with the Bureau, and specific information about the circumstances that could be behind the deaths of his children and ex-wife. To seek him out in Britain, and manoeuvre him to come back to work on a sensitive investigation involving a past colleague. However, when further information, is provided by Bronson to her Senior Officer, he is manipulated, and persuaded. Bronson does not disclose to her Superiors how she has known of Calder's whereabouts, or how she has the information regarding his family tragedy, does she have her own hidden agenda?

But the calls from Moorhead provide the impetus for him to return home and assist in the investigation of a Criminal Consortium operating out of an unlikely small coastal town. And to investigate further, a part of his deceased wifes life that was unknown to him. None of this is known to Calder, until he returns, and then travels to a small incestuous coastal village.

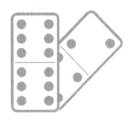

THE BEGINNING –
Plymouth April 23rd 2010

ory Calder, stood at the apartments window, his head throbbing, aching, as if a steel band were around it. His body felt no better, it was being wracked – as if the torture instruments of the Middle ages, were being slowly tightened. Stretching every nerve fibre! Appropriate considering not only his present situation, but the City that he was in.

Outside cold bitter rain laced with hail and snow flurries, sleeted down from the north – swirling and smashing onto the glass, thick rivulets running to the wide stone sill, the streets below awash. Out across to the sea, black thick clouds were cut with vivid lightning flashes, and rolls of thunder shook the windows.

Rory's mind bounced from one thought to another – back again and then sideways over the events of the last weeks. He leant his head against the glass, and looked out across the park, past Smeaton's Tower and the Plymouth Dome, towards The Sound.

The reflection from the window against the dark sky beyond reflected his haggard image.

Calder was above average height, an inch under six feet. He was well built, with a strong muscled frame, his features under his long dark wavy hair were slightly too rugged to be called handsome, but he was considered by some of his former female companions, to be unusually attractive. His deep blue penetrating eyes had drawn him a considerable number of admirers, as did his personality – one that always took and interest – and he always listened, and rarely talked of himself. But at this present moment his face was tired – drawn – the eyes dark, sunken, the brow furrowed, the last thing on his mind was how he looked, but the thoughts – they were another matter.

Off to his right, he could just glimpse in the distance churning black water, with waves crested with white, cris-crossed by the stark frames of cranes. Beyond that, the Naval base, it's cold grey mass rose from the water - matching the stark cold of the morning – adding to his dark mood.

Away to the left the uncompromising Royal Citadel, the fortress constructed in 1666 to intimidate the population of the only town in the south west to be held by the Parliamentarians in the Civil War, another reminder of the bleakness of his situation.

Rory looked down into the street below, where early ants of cars, and fleas of people, scurried to and fro in the wet dawn light. He had been standing staring now for two hours, he'd watched the darkness fade to drizzled grey. But his mind, mulling over – at first slowly, then rushing through the turmoil of the previous days events, didn't lighten or enlighten any more than the skies would that morning.

It was fifteen days since the bodies of his wife and three children had been found, but only three days since he'd been contacted, requested to attend an interview, as it was first referred to, by the British Police in Plymouth.

Rory had been on holiday in Scotland, when the shock news reached him. It had numbed every fibre of his body and brain. It had taken several hours and a half a bottle of brandy to help alleviate the initial pain, stop the tears, the shaking, and the bile and vomit that was wrenched from his body.

He had taken a flight from Glasgow to Heathrow, this had been draining, as it had been delayed six hours because of the weather, and despite his being in the VIP lounge and virtually alone, the hours couped up had been extremely taxing – mentally. He had considered a rental car and driving down, but had rejected that and opted to fly. A decision he now regretted.

Then the journey, firstly from London to Bournemouth in a small uncomfortable underpowered hire car, (Hertz unusually, had not been helpful) had added further to his frustration. The traffic was unbelievably tight and heavy – and – the countryside that he loved as much as that back home took on a dark and sinister veneer.

Very tired and irritable, Rory stayed a night at a moderately priced, and very pleasant, comfortable Guest-house – Eartham Lodge, on Alumhurst Road.

It was in a pleasant area near the shoreline, and normally he would have found it a good place to stroll the town before dinner and the seaside later. But, after an adequate meal and several glasses of wine, he went to his room, threw himself onto the four-poster bed and looked out the window at the darkening sky. For some time he went over and over the previous days, then the weeks before – but his tired brain could come to no conclusions.

Eventually he shrugged of his clothes and crawled into the soft bed. He didn't sleep well, and after a restless night, he discarded the idea of breakfast and had left early, before six am.

Rory's aim was hopefully to avoid the choking traffic, but unfortunately not. All through the slow drive to Plymouth he wondered how and why? The 'how' – how had the police even known where he was? It wasn't as if he had been involved in anything to do with Serena for many months – that is – apart from the 'lawyers letters' that flowed from one side of the world to the other – and all around Britain – and the why. Why Plymouth for this meeting? If the accident had occurred near the Torbay area, surely Torquay, Brixham or Dartmouth, would have been one hell of a lot more convenient? He had suggested this, but had been cut short and he was just told – be in Plymouth – contact us as soon as you have settled in. He had considered ignoring their request – but had thought better of it considering the circumstances.

Now – nearly twelve hours, after leaving Dunoon in Scotland, Rory was in Plymouth. He'd been summoned for an Inquest – questioning, regarding Serena and his children's deaths. Rory supposed he could have refused, as he saw that there was little point in pursuing the matter as the accident had nothing to do with him. They had been estranged for a long time, more than two years. But it was his children – and he loved them dearly – deeply - he too needed answers as plainly the Police did. Yes the death of Serena was tragic – and in many ways produced deep sadness in him, but the loss of his children– this pain, the agony of that loss would not leave him – now – ever. He needed answers to all the 'whys and wherefores'. Whether he or they would get any, could be another story.

He'd booked into a Hotel – The Beeches, opposite Hoe Park – an easy stroll to the Barbican, the Mayflower steps and Sutton Harbour. An area, once again near the water, it was a quirk of his nature that wherever he went he had to be as close as possible to the sea – or a lake, and he loved this part of the old town the History that oozed from it fascinated him. This sometimes over fertile imagination, as he walked the old streets and wandered into the taverns and bars, took him back to the era of Drake and Spanish Armadas!

However this visit was nothing to do with fantasy or day dreaming – it was deadly serious - about death. He called the police and informed them that he'd arrived in the town and where he was staying.

The Police had – surprisingly – and somewhat strangely, he thought, adding to their already unusual previous requests – opted to interview him in a private room at the back of the Hotel – an area that was used for small conferences.

Their interrogation had begun with accusations and innuendo – questions to which he had no answers. He just had no idea what they were talking about, this didn't help the mood of the enquiry. Rory knew he had no information other than what they had been telling him and he had nothing that he could add in anyway.

In actual fact – apart from the fact that the tragedy touched him – more because of the children – yes and the loss of Serena, despite the antagonism over the last years, also touched sensitive nerves – there was in his opinion, no reason for him to be questioned at all.

Frustrating mind games had been played – by the Police, and by his own frustrated confused state, and these were taking an even greater toll on his nerves.

The Police had originally questioned him on the phone, for nearly an hour, immediately after they had rung to inform him of the accident. But it went much further this time – and he continued to be frustrated and puzzled as to why did they feel he may a suspect? They didn't answer this question and continued to ignore his pleas for answers to his 'whys'.

It crossed Rory's mind several times, as to why they hadn't asked him to accompany them to a Station or any other Police facility, or suggested he call his lawyer. They had talked, twisted words and phrases, delved, asked obscure yet wildly suggestive questions, often hardly waiting for an answer before going to their next point. But they really had nothing to go by – nothing at all to connect him to the accident. However an 'accident' was also becoming even more unlikely – so what and where was the truth?

Seemingly it appeared now, from the little he gleaned from them, that someone had deliberately set out to kill her, planned it all – and had 'they' – whoever this 'they' were, had also set out to kill the children - deliberately, or was that an unknown equation, and that the children were not expected to be in the car with Serena? The word 'deliberately' raged in his mind.

Rory had been tempted a number of times, to alter the direction of the questioning, and to inform them of his real occupation, and he wouldn't have been talking about his work at the University. But he refrained, it may have only served to complicate matters further – and that wouldn't be a wise move – and would not benefit anyone at this stage.

Serena's car had been found in the Dart river, near a caravan park outside the country town of Galmpton, about twenty miles south east of Torbay on the fringes of Dartmouth. There was evidently little damage to the car. All had drowned, all were still inside the vehicle, all the car's windows were partly open. This was strange, considering the time of day that the accident was said to have occurred. The weather conditions had been wet and cold, the road slippery, which may have been a factor. It appeared the car had skidded, rolled down a bank, and sunk into the slow moving waters where the river curved deeply into the side of the road.

In this instance, at this point of the investigation, excessive speed didn't appear to be a factor. Which Rory also found a fraction unusual.

Serena was more than 'quite a fast driver'. He'd often commented about the speed she drove, the risks she took. Particularly when she had the children in the car. Serena had never appreciated his comments and they'd often argued over the matter. In fact they had argued over a considerable number of matters, including his work and the hours that it involved, and the secrecy.

The Police had questioned acquaintances, and professional colleagues – as to perhaps the reasons she'd been in the area. They had found an appointment diary in her briefcase, and an entry indicating that she was to have a meeting with her solicitor in Southampton around the time of the accident, also quite a large sum of money. The notation, 'Peterson and Waltham: Solicitors -- James coming down from London -- meet, Elizabeth House, The Avenue 3:30.' So why was she near Dartmouth?

Serena was travelling in the opposite direction and was miles away from where she perhaps was supposed to be. Why were the children with her? They should've been in their Boarding School.

The Police mentioned this to Rory early in the interview. He was completely unable to shed light on anything to do with it – nor did the names mean anything, they were not the names of the people that he had thought were representing her, and were definitely not the names on letters he had previously received from Serena's Lawyers.

The interrogation continued. The Detective Sergeant's voice had droning on. 'Where have you been for the last four months, Mr. Calder? Who have you seen? Have you been near your wife's car or her house? Why did you split up? The neighbours told us about your continual rows. They also gave us a description of a man coming to the house several times – it matches your description very closely!' over and over - continually repeating the same line.

Rory was stunned 'I've no idea where Serena's been living since she moved to England.' He shot back. 'I've never been to her house – I don't even have her phone number! I don't know who she was arguing with - it certainly wasn't me!'

They ignored his requests for information and repeated their same questions over and over again, occasionally rephrasing them, but they were still the same. All connected in some way – all had to do with their individual lives, and their marital problems.

Rory tried to answer sensibly - calmly, but their line of questioning and arrogant attitude eventually touched too many nerves, and he called his lawyer in London. He was advised to take it all quietly, to just follow the path they were trying to lead him down. Later they would discuss matters. The brief conversation had left him feeling helpless, out of the loop – whatever loop they were in! And of that he wasn't at all sure. It seemed from the tone of his legal eagle, to just say as little as possible and then forget it. That thought didn't sit well in Rory's mind.

This was another factor that had baffled him for a moment, until he realised what their angle may be - but he'd done some damage with one or two of his outbursts – damage that in the end would be of no significance at all.

'If you are accusing me of involvement in this accident – you can bloody well forget it!' It was more his tone and some of the adjectives, that hadn't helped his cause and that his voice had now risen in volume. Their glances and aside comments only served to increase his aggravation.

The fact that Rory had now, after nearly two hours, since he made his call to his legal advisor in London, that he demanded a lawyer present. That had produced satisfied smirks, and the Police suggested a local firm that may help. The Police Sergeant gave Rory the name of a supposedly reputable firm in Plymouth. He made his call, and was able to briefly 'brief' the solicitor he was put through to, about the situation.

When the Lawyer finally arrived around forty minutes later, and the interview continued, the Police told them of – "suspected tampering with the vehicle" - brake lines appeared to have been partially severed, and the steering was also suspect..

'Well it sure as hell wouldn't have been me – I wouldn't have a bloody clue how to do that – and as I was fucking long damned miles away – what are you suggesting, that I had a hit man on the job? Get a bloody life – you're living in fucking TV land!' Rory's outburst and deep anger didn't help the temper of the meeting – but it was quietly acknowledged that they weren't insinuating anything, as to whether or not that he had any involvement with the accident. More puzzles 'Why then – why am I here – being put through this 'third degree'?'

His outburst did nothing to improve the flavour of the moment, and the police carried on. The Sergeant's bland look the tone of his comment - 'You're just helping with our enquiries sir,' was more acidic than before.

Rory admonished himself for being such an emotional twerp, it was not his normal behaviour or his character.

An inspection had been carried out within hours of the removal of the vehicle from the river. They'd obviously been extremely fast off the mark in their investigation of the scene and the removal of the car from the river.

He thought later about that, that it was possibly far too soon, under normal circumstances, but what were the circumstances for them to have investigated the vehicle?

After the interview, Rory spoke to the Lawyer regarding who he was, his occupation, and what he'd been doing in Australia, then the States, before he'd returned to Scotland for the last few days of his holiday. Also - apart from this business of his estranged family, he should have been back in Cardiff at the University - getting organised for the next Semester. So this whole episode was causing a considerable inconvenience.

He suggested that it might now be a good idea to give that information to the Police. The Solicitor agreed, and said that he would do so, and that he would be in touch in a few days. He took down Rory's mobile number, asking also where he could be contacted. But, as they left the building with them, he said nothing and turned away in the opposite direction.

Rory had taken the Solicitors card, and put it in his wallet. He would call him as soon as he had stopped somewhere where he would be for more than a few days. Where that was at that point he was not sure. Probably back in Cardiff.

These arrangements never came to fruition.

When he was alone Rory began his own analysis of the last hours. Firstly – why was he reacting the way that he was? Why was his intuition not working as it normally should? – Why was his own internal initiative not taking control of situations? – Why was his training – years of training and experience, not helping him deal with this situation? Was the whole emotional turmoil taking control – was he feeling guilty about any of the occurrences – could he have prevented them? The answers to all the queries came up blank. And there was one other thing nagging at the back of his mind. 'How the hell did they know he was in Scotland anyway?'

What was it that they knew but weren't revealing? Why was it that they had tracked him down and called him to the interview, and then been in so bloody unhelpful – giving little, if any information? The car, the inspection the initial insinuations.

Unless - unless they had information that it had been interfered with, from another source? The whole scenario didn't fit – it was a rental van - so where did they get this information? He hadn't known why they were on that road, or where they were going.

Rory hadn't seen Serena or his children, had any contact – not even phone calls - for months. It had been an agreement between them – it would serve no useful purpose – but that was according to her, and he had said at the time - 'of course' – and he had concurred – reluctantly.

Lately, as he had told the Police, and the 'duty' solicitor, he had been in Australia – in Melbourne for a short time visiting friends – then to the States - San Francisco – a conference. Then to where his Mother had been born – that last part of the vacation period had just been a whim. So Rory hadn't been near her for well over a year – and their children for months, he had certainly not touched her car.

Rory reflected on the situation, the time leading to 'now'. They had been living in separate apartments for over two years. Initially, seeing each other regularly, and spending at least one, sometimes two nights a week together. It appeared to be working, repairing bridges and extending communication.

That had continued for three months. Then out of the blue - she had said that there was no longer any need to carry on the situation, and didn't want to continue with that arrangement. She wanted more space, to just see him occasionally, and not sleeping together. He could still see and have the children every two weeks.

The new arrangement worked for two months then Serena decided that she didn't want to see him at all – ever – and that his access to the children would be reduced to once a month – but no sleep overs – just day visits. She had handed him a letter from her lawyers setting out the terms.

Serena had not said why - they had of course, had their usual argument and it had been heated, he had stormed out and driven away at a ridiculous rate. No doubt the neighbours had been witnesses to that as well.

Later he had calmed and tried to talk to her on the phone, but she had just hung up each time that he tried. Rory thought of fighting it but then – after a talk with his legal advisors, and friends, with the consideration of more tension and upset for the children, he had concurred – in the mean time.

It was two days after that heated discussion, that Rory had received a further letter from her lawyers. It had been forwarded to him from his own legal advisor, Euan McGillveray. The were only two people who he thought knew his exact whereabouts. Euan, was one, the other, was his friend in Cardiff - Rebekka.

This letter informed him of her move to Britain. It wasn't that she wanted to move to England, that, even to Rory was not unreasonable, that was where her original roots were. Her parents lived in Whitstable, in Kent. Originally from Chesterfield, they had always wanted to retire in their home County. They had returned there three years before. It fact was she had already gone. More than a month prior to the letter being passed on. That, was the point of his anger, and contributed to another bout of deep depression. He hadn't had any opportunity to be with with his children , and to say goodbye to them! There was nothing he could do – but fume!

Serena was also threatening legal action against him, if he did not refrain from continually trying to contact her. Arrangements could – would be made for him to have reasonable access to the children - in time. Though of course this would be extremely difficult! It appeared that she must have been working on this agenda for some time, Rory was at a complete loss as to why the secrecy? There was something that he didn't understand – an underlying sense of 'who else is tied into this and why? Apart from the – what some would call the inevitable, because of their complete opposite personalities and ambitions. They were both intelligent and most of the time sensible so why were they not able to communicate in a sensible adult way? It was beyond his understanding of human nature, but was his understanding quite the same as others?

It was then he decided to take leave – and also to take up the offer of the work and study in Cardiff. Perhaps from that point he could resolve a number of matters?

Why was Serena in the south west – why was she on her way to Cornwall and where in Cornwall? Who was she going to meet? The diary in her bag said she was meeting some lawyer – or was it a lawyer – would he ever know the truth?

As the storm moved out to sea, skies began to clear, the sun began its slant across the Sound – the park – over the Fort and through the buildings, shafts of bright light began to penetrate through his window. Rory pushed himself away from the sill, and moved back to the bed, lying down on the top of the rumpled covers. He felt tired, worn, drained, emotions that had once been high, were now low.

But the brain kept at him – why – and why should he have these feelings about himself, and the vindictiveness towards Serena – he'd done nothing wrong, what had she done?

That was – apart from the personal nature of their break-up, there wasn't anything that Rory could see that should be niggling at him, or niggling at the bloody coppers – but then – he did actually understand that.

The phone shrilled, he jumped at the sound as it cut into his thoughts, by the fourth ring he had composed himself and picked up the receiver. He wasn't expecting a call from anyone, particularly at this time of the morning, how could he – no-one knew where he was - apart from the Police, and the Solicitor. His location to anyone else right this moment was unknown. As far as his future movements, he had only given 'them' a vague itinerary, and Rory himself was now not entirely sure himself of his next move.

'Hello - Calder speaking.'

'Mr. Rory Calder?' The voice had a slight accent that he couldn't immediately place.

'Yes, this is Rory Calder, who is this?'

'My name is Moorhead, Colin Moorhead, but that's not really important, not at this moment. You don't know me, but I know you, - well of you may be more accurate, and quite a bit about you and your present situation. Very - very unfortunate, you have my - and my associates commiserations.'

Rory's confusion escalated, he became suspicious - cautious. 'Who are you? Why are you calling me? If you don't know me? And, why isn't your name important - at the moment? What do you want? And further more, how did you find out where I am?' The caller did not reply, Rory went on, 'This information how did you get that? Not that I suppose it would be relevant if you don't actually know me.' God - he thought, that sounded so bloody stupid. 'What's going on, how do you know of my position as you call it, are you referring to, my wife my children? Is that what you're talking about? The only people who know are the police, and my lawyer, so who the hell are you? What do you want?' Rory had an extremely uneasy feeling in the pit of his stomach. His voice, he knew sounded shaky.

'Yes, that is what I am referring to, some news in some circles, travels very quickly. Do you know a James Peter Sullivan or have heard of him?' The man's voice quiet.

'No, should I? But, well yes, I have recently heard the name, or one that sounds – um – similar, though -- no, it was Peterson, not Peter Sullivan, yes Peterson -- James Peterson, he's a Lawyer. Who's this other person? Is he a Lawyer – why do you want to know?' Rory frowned into the phone. A knot that had been building in his stomach, he could feel his hand holding the phone receiver begin to sweat. He became angry, he began shouting. 'How the hell did you get this number – of this Hotel – how did you know I was here – what's going on – who are you?' There was silence on the other end of the line.

Rory could feel his tension and agitation building. Moorhead's tone irritated, but there was something else, something about it, that increased his pulse rate and brought perspiration to Rory's face. The man's voice had very little expression to it. Rory sighed 'Look I'm very tired, and quite frankly I'm fed up with being asked questions - so either tell me who you are and what this is about or get off the bloody line and leave me alone!'

'Calm Mr. Calder – please be calm, there's no need for you to be so – antagonistic – at least not yet, and not with me. Let us, just for the moment say that - you should know the name, remember the name and try to find out more of who and what he is. But, be careful - very careful in the way that you do it. I suggest that you retrace your steps - back a long way to where you think that you belong. Do this in your mind first – and then do it physically – if you are really seeking answers to your unanswered questions. . After all Mr. Calder, it's your job – to find the answers to the unanswered – to inquire – delve - solve– is it not? We'll be in touch again Mr. Calder. And – it may well be advantageous for us to meet but then – it might not. Though we will – eventually.'

Rory hung up. He sat on the edge of the bed, not moving, just thinking. Minutes passed into what seemed hours.

'What the hell is going on? Who's this Moorhead, and how the hell did he know where to contact me? And for gods sake - and mine - how does he know so much – about what? Things I don't even know about!' Rory got up from the bed and paced the room – stopping in front of the window he stared out at the grey day. 'Should I call the Police? Tell them about the call, or just ignore it? Ignore it – don't be such a bloody moron – you can't ignore it! But the Police? Where would that lead after that last interlude, how would it be viewed?' Rory sat on the windowsill, his chin sagged on to his chest as he rubbed his eyes and forehead

'For Christ's sake – remember who and what you are! Stop this – this self pity – this crap – get a grip and get off your arse! Find the answers!' Rory stood up – and looked at his watch. It was one thirty, he'd been mulling his morose thoughts for over four hours. He decided that there were several alternatives, but only one appealed and the decision was 'unanimous' – get off your arse get into a hot shower, change and leave. He would go back home, although he had no real reason to listen to the man, and he had little idea of what he was talking about, he would take on board the 'mystery man's' suggestions. He would think about it.

Rory wasn't sure why he felt that the advice was even remotely sound – would even be of any assistance, there was just something in the man's tone. It was as if he knew him – but in strange unconnected was. He wondered whether Moorhead would call him again – or whether that was just a way of saying – if I need to or you want me to? But how would he contact him anyway? No number - no caller ID on his phone - a complete communication blank! The only way would be if the man contacted him again – but how would he know where he was? All conjecture and all unsubstantiated and all at this moment too bloody mystifying.

'Don't be such a stupid bloody fart Calder.' Rory berated himself, 'if he could find you here he will know your every fucking move you are making anyway! And – he's probably got your cell number as well!'

'I'll call the University later, give an 'explanation' sort out a few things and where to head with this next.'

Rory would have to look into their affairs, and review everything that had happened. There was a lot to do – to organise – to cope with, and there would be the funerals. The thought of that sent a chill through him. Later he would try to make some sense from it all, though he doubted that he would be able to, at least not at this time - but he would try.

With that he packed his bags, went down to reception, paid his account, tried a smile with an unconvincing thank you. The Clerk, a sullen young man, took no notice at all and didn't even thank him in return – pleasantly or otherwise. It was – Rory thought, of no bloody consequence anyway. He left the hotel, he'd hoped that it may have been 'respite accommodation' and that he could've put other matters aside and spent some time enjoying a city with so much History, to him almost a home place – but for what reason he could never quite fathom.

Right now he didn't want to return to his environment. What had been essentially work – and little more. He had grave doubts with his present demeanour about his ability to cope with general conversation with colleagues, never mind explanations. Then his living quarters – a third floor apartment in Cardiff close to the University, was small – dull – claustrophobic. Not an ideal place with his mind in turmoil it had no appeal. Rory left the lobby and went down to the Hotel's garage to his rental and deposited his luggage. He was now pleased that it was the small Ford, as he wanted to be as inconspicuous as possible. This had nothing to do with the police interviews. It was another feeling – a feeling that since the conversation with 'Moorhead', that he was being watched - even followed! But that begged the question again – why - what for?

Rory sat in the vehicle, but didn't move to start – he just sat – was it ten minutes – twenty?

He lost track of the time, as now other thoughts encroached. "Go back to where you think you belong -- go there first mentally, then go there physically". Where – and what exactly, was the man referring to? It gradually began sinking in. Rory realised that the advice was somehow, for reasons still unknown - going to be sound and of high importance, but yet, still leaving far too many unanswered questions.

Calder started the car and drove out from the shadowed garage into the early afternoon light. He headed across the city, traffic was moderately heavy, but as he moved out of the town into the countryside, it was extremely heavy, fortunately in the opposite direction. He relaxed a little and accelerated past the speed limit.

Now past Waterlooville, and heading for Petersfield, he thought of taking the coast road back to London through Chichester, Worthing and Brighton, flying out from Gatwick. But in the end he opted for the slightly lesser congested route.

His original idea, faded. Going one of his favourite drives, taking a couple of days to go down to Truro, then back up the coast. Padstow, Bridgewater, Weston-super-mare, on into Bristol, where he could have visited friends for a night. Before heading around the Severn, and back down to Cardiff.

There now seemed very little point, his mind clearly made up as to his next move. The fact that – in a sense, it had been made for him irritated. Moor head – if that was his name, had set the path.

Rory felt that he had no choice, but to return home. He would arrange for his belongings - those that he needed, to be sent on by friends on the staff at the University. Rebekka - suddenly came into his mind. He was sure that she wouldn't mind, she was one person who he could rely on and trust. Though it would also be sad that he would more than likely never see her again. She could also look after his apartment, use it as a 'close to work' refuge. Something that they had discussed – if? She was privy to much of Rory's life – and knew him very well.

The concentration, between the small under powered Ford, and the hectic frenetic motorway frenzy, now distracted him from the previous days, and the last night he had spent in the Hotel. Rory decided he would stay the night in St. Albans, it was a long drive, but it had been one of his and Rebecca's favourite haunts. It was close to Watford, then down the M25 to the airport. He could organise his arrangements from the Hotel. It was just a small pub in Abbey Mill Lane. They had stayed there on quite a number of occasions, and each time had had extremely enjoyable evenings.

"Ye Olde fighting Cocks" was small, ancient, Medieval tiny rooms, with an atmosphere and History that Rory found both relaxing and fascinating. It was not important to do so, but he would also arrange for the Rental to be picked up at Heathrow the next morning, he could have just left it – but he was particular about 'service' – giving and receiving.

New plans were galvanising in his tired brain – but he preferred that feeling – it made him become more alert and aware of 'a situation' and this one required that..

Rory began to review the last twelve months. A trait that he had first begun and continued from when he was in his first years at University, it gave him better understanding and focus on what was going on around him and where he may be headed. Only this time – where he may be 'headed' was rather more blurred than he would have liked.

He had recently for a period of three Semesters, been working as a lecturer of Criminology at the University in Cardiff, a position arranged for him by his 'employer' – to expand and explore his areas of expertise, to feed off the 'intellect of others in a new and different environment'. Actually, it was more involved with the psychology of the Criminal mind. He had also been considered quite a proficient Profiler, and the Welsh Police had used him on a number of occasions.

For this period, he'd been supposedly on Sabbatical leave, that he had been recommended to take. Along side this the employment had provided remuneration that was reasonably lucrative, but he had found it irritating and quite boring. He knew he should be going back up to the University and discussing the 'situation' and what he intended to do about it. There was also the matter that he had been asked politely to be available if needed for further questions and answers.

There were only two weeks left in the vacation period, and although he'd prepared most of what he needed for the final term, there was still more to do.

However, with what had happened what would be the point? When the news broke, he would have the questions - the probing of colleagues. The "What are you doing here under the circumstances, shouldn't you be --" and - "how did you cope with the Funeral" – and so on – and on. And besides, he knew that he was far from indispensable – others better qualified could pick up the ball where he had dropped it and many with better ideas to expand and carry through what he had prepared. Besides the work had only been arranged for the most part to give him a bit more to live. The work – along with the friendship that had blossomed with Rebekka had also helped him out of a very depressed period that had stemmed from his lack of contact with his children.

'Yes, they'll be fine, I shouldn't even be thinking of being there, I just had the fleeting thought that it could've been a helpful distraction. Now, I've decided that the refuge of the coast, the sea – away from everyone I knew and all the questions is a better option.' I'll head across to Padstow!

For the next half hour he felt comfortable with his decision. But his mind wouldn't let go. He began to work through the minefield that had been laid out in front of him over the last weeks.

The internal turmoil of the shock hadn't yet reached him. It had been strange that the police had not immediately taken him to identify the bodies. That had only happened after the solicitor had intervened, brought the point up, that they had been taken into the morgue at the hospital. He was to ponder that for some time to come.

Rory's children and their Mother, had been laid out in the cold stark white room, side by side, three small bodies and Serena, there was no visible damage apart from the grey swollen bloated corpses.

They had been in the water for nearly two days before the car had been found. (One of the 'small matters' that had the Police had neglected to mention, another was the type of vehicle, a Toyota people mover. Not at all what Serena would have normally been driving. Why wasn't she in her Audi? Considering the area and the amount of traffic, the close proximity to the road where the Van had slid into the river, why had it taken so long for it to be reported? Again a big why?– This also seemed extremely, strange.

There had to be arrangements made, Rory's legal friend would - he said - take care of this initially, but Rory would have to complete them. A dull chilling numbness contracted around his heart - as he had looked at his children, for a brief second he saw them as he had the last time they were together. Then his eyes blurred and the tears flowed, every fibre of his body and mind sent screaming pain through him, but apart from the water coursing down his face there was no other expression no other sign of his fear.

Rory drove on the country opened up and the roads, although less congested, were still flowing with traffic, twisting like snakes through rolling hill country, through gorges with swift boulder filled streams churning and chattering alongside, on through small villages and hamlets. The pretty quaint sites that he passed said little to him. Instead Rory's mind was now racing – as the water in the streams – around and across and around again so many areas -but one kept surfacing then disappearing in the mind currents, coming back again and again - "Do you know Mr. James Peter Sullivan". What was it about that name – that person that was eating into him, there was a dark shadow forming – a black cloud closing above his head – and it wasn't to do with the approaching weather. Rory could see and feel the black fist of evil clutching at him.

It began to rain. Sheeting down, blotting out every part of the country side. But nothing, not the wind, the pouring rain, or the long jet lagging journey that he would be making, would blot out the mind games. Like many other games he had been caught in over the years - he could see the dice rolling and he keep landing on the wrong 'square of life', he kept missing his turn.

Rory's muddled musings were cut off by the muffled sound of his Cellphone, he pulled the Ford to the shoulder of the road, dug out the phone and pressed the receive key.

It was the same quiet voice -- Moorhead!

'Take your time, think and act with great care – but you don't have forever – no-one does Mr. Calder, no-one does.' There was nothing more.

'How the hell does he know my cell number now!' But this time there was no anger in Rory's thoughts about the man's intrusion. He placed the cellphone back in his pocket, he sat thinking about the words the man had murmured.

'Perhaps I'm over reacting – being too hasty – perhaps appearing to have 'something to hide'? Perhaps finalising my time here in the proper and correct manner would be more sensible and you are at times Rory Calder prone to 'over-reaction'. Settle down – go and sort out your affairs in Cardiff, it won't take long and could be of advantage – may not be – but could be.'

But later, as he turned north from Salisbury and headed towards Bristol, he knew that there wasn't a satisfactory answer to any of the swirling questions racing in his mind. And, he knew that meeting with Rebekka and telling her of what had happened, and was going to happen, wouldn't be easy.

Rory pulled the car to the side of the road and waited until it was clear of traffic before he turned and returned to his original idea. 'Cut the ties Rory, cut the ties and get on with the next part of this bloody mess called your life – just do it!'

However – sometimes quickly laid plans can lead to delays. It had been suggested to him. 'Take your time – think carefully, act with great care'

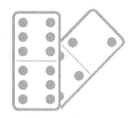

ONE
February 2011

Over six months passed before Rory finally extricated himself from Britain. In that time he dealt with intermittent calls from the Police – still questions – still no answers. There was the funeral, held in Whitstable, where he felt like a complete stranger, Serena's parents and close family were polite – almost sympathetic – but very distant.

After – he had returned to Cardiff and continued his work at the request of the Chancellor. Then he dealt with his relationship with Rebecca, this had not been at all easy and she had pleaded to allow her to come with him. He had hurt her deeply with his rejection. She was intelligent, beautiful, thoughtful and supportive, and as he withdrew from the relationship his bouts of depression increased. He spent long periods thinking, as walked alone in the hills near Pontypridd, and the coast at Penarth. But he knew he was procrastinating over the inevitable.

He had eventually finalised his arrangements and departed – a black cloud of disappointment at so many 'failures' hanging over his head.

* *

It was now eight weeks since Rory had arrived back in New Zealand, and matters now had taken a quite different, and unexpected course.

The journey back had been exhausting - five hard days of travel. After leaving London – two hours late, the flight delayed in New York – extraordinary early winter weather grounding everything on the Eastern seaboard for three days. A night in L.A, followed by an engine problem, then an Aircraft change after fifteen hours sitting and waiting in LA. International. That flight to diverted to Hawaii – why that delay and detour he never ever found out, and by that time, he really didn't give a damn. He was washed out.

However, on his eventual arrival in Auckland there was to be no respite, he was to be thrown back into 'the lions den' almost immediately.

After settling into – for the time being, a good Hotel, The Waterfront on Quay. He had been subjected to an intensive 'debrief'. This had been partly instigated by his employers, but mostly by himself – he needed to clear up a number of matters pertaining to the deaths of his ex-wife and his children. But he got none, they couldn't – or perhaps wouldn't shed any light on any of the events – or the actions of the British Police.

Rory felt that he should still feel more than he did – more emotion – but all he was feeling now was 'numb', and a sense of frustration and bitterness. The love between himself and his wife had evaporated a long time ago, though of course his feelings towards his little ones was intense, and this, he was finding extraordinarily difficult to reconcile.

During the meetings with the Superintendent and the Commissioner, matters had been cordial and frank. The frustrations of the last days and fatigue, had taken their toll, but their directives were clear, concise – and the "sabbatical" was over – there was work to be done.

Rory felt though that at least one 'nagging thing' had been partially addressed - the questions that he had regarding a certain 'Lawyer' – if that is what the 'Mr. Sullivan' indeed was - had in part been answered, but there were many questions yet to be satisfied. His Senior Officers had been extremely interested regarding this person being mentioned to him when he was in Britain – extremely interested, but gave initially, no indication as to why their interest was so strong.

Now, after another two weeks – partly because of the de-brief and partly for several other reasons that had been discussed - he was driving the narrow winding coast road that ran along the edge of this spectacular jutting peninsula.

Rory was ostensibly on another holiday, this time with quite different agendas than previously. His brief, a manila folder in a manila envelope. It would be clear only to him, and inexplicably, not to be opened for at least twenty four hours! What sort of silly game were they playing? He had muttered to himself as he had taken the large bulky envelope. -- 'I suppose this is more bloody cloak and fucking dagger crap'! And – 'Why down to one of his favourite old holiday areas – what the hell sort intrigue could be there?'

Extensive heavy rain had fallen through the night and into the morning, in some parts, the road was covered with deep surface flooding. Water ran in torrents from sheer cliffs that boarded the road on one side, across to the rocky foreshore.

But now Rory could see that it was beginning to clear, and in the distance he could see that the sky was blue, bright sunlight was beginning to bathe the countryside in golden lights.

As he took in the scenery - the steep terrain, bush covered hills, the sea sitting close to the road, Rory was reminded in part of the scenery back in Cornwall and Devon, a place that he had thought may have become home. Now – he was back in New Zealand, and this road clung into tall rugged cliff faces. Pohutukawa gripped tenuously on the rugged seaward ledges, their strong inter-woven roots binding them tightly to the banks that dropped onto small beaches, rocky points and jutting headlands.

As the scent of salt spray and seaweed wafted into the car, Rory began to think for a moment, that, 'This could be where I belong, well may belong, at least somewhere by the sea' And, despite the ill winds of fate that had driven him back here, he began to feel the security blanket of home territory. He hoped that feeling was a good omen.

Rory Calder had been driving for nearly an hour on this coastal stretch when it began to climb. The tar seal ended and the surface became rough – metal strewn, winding steeply inland, then turning back on itself, back towards the sea.

At the top of this winding stretch he pulled off the road, stopping at the edge of a viewing lay by, he sat for several minutes waiting for swirls of brown dust to settle. There was no wind, and the sun was now staring from a cloudless sky, burnishing the land and setting the sea below afire with purple and blue lights, the bush lower towards the waters edge hung in a thousand greens. Nestled into the waters edge a small town looked quiet and sleepy.

It was now a morning of summer glory as he remembered them from when he was young, and for a moment the darkness of the past months evaporated – but just for a moment – then it distilled into the deeper reaches of his mind to begin its fester

* *

Rory Calder had grown up on the fringes of the city of Auckland. From the lookout point high on the jutting promontory, he could see its vague outline in the summer haze, as he looked back across the water.

It wasn't that far from this rugged beautiful coastline, with its brilliant deep red flowered bows that draped the roadside, dipping towards blue clear water. Just a matter of two hours, it was an area that he had visited often in the past – but not for quite a number of years now – it was a good feeling to be back – no matter what the reason or circumstances.

He had lived with summers by the sea, sand, and surf, small and large boats, were part of life from a very young age as were fishing rods and nets, seaweed and seashells. Although for much of his early life they had not actually lived by the sea, his family had never been far from it, and as many weekends and holidays as possible had been spent there, they had been fortunate. Then in his early teens they moved to the coast – there - his mood changed.

Rory felt at home near the sea and the times that he had been unable to be near it, and there had been a number, when his work and life had taken him away from coastal areas. He had felt there was something missing. The sounds and the movement of life were different. The 'inland world' lacked the right colours, not quite the right light. This was not to say that he hadn't enjoyed many of the places he'd lived, he had, for different reasons - and they often had held deep beauty for him.

Rory got out of the car and stretched, turned his neck to left and right, taking out the 'kinks and creases' of the drive. His Chevrolet Coupe had seen better days. It wasn't the easiest car to drive on the twisting narrow roads, the steering was heavy and the tyres wide, the actual steering wheel felt as if he was driving a bus. But at least it was reliable.

He'd sold some of his old possessions and a couple of prized vehicles. This had helped provide extra cash for extraneous expenses, assisting with furnishing an inner city apartment he'd rented – and replacing a number of items and clothing left in England. Items not covered by his Salary or his expense account. But Rory had kept his 1967 Corvette, (and of course his 1948 Chev!) he'd owned both cars for nearly fifteen years. Both mementos of particular times in his life. Particularly pleasant and loving times, before and during those with his now deceased wife Serena. But they were just possessions, he didn't want the previous memories - but he kept the cars anyway. The rest was just bitter sweet.

However, apart from the apartment expenses he had some additional cash – certain bank accounts could be left alone. Perhaps for his dreams, whatever they were? They may be pursued, now that he was completely alone, they may not.

At the edge of the road side rest area, Rory looked down into a small seaside village, seemingly not too far - by the eyes view, but still a little way from this point, through the winding road. A wide shallow stream flowed through the settlement, it was right on a tidal coastal shelf, and flanked on each side between arms of high buttress cliffs, and behind by the steep slopes of this isolated peninsula. Where the steep sides nudged into the sea, rocky outcrops were washed by surging tide flows. From here on the hill, he could see the sun glinting on a few cars moving slowly around the narrow streets.

A wharf jutted into the bay, a few old fishing boats lay clinging to their rope lifelines, and further out on the flat sandy mud, several pleasure craft and yachts lay, some on their sides, others propped on twin keels. Several more were leaning on stands near the beach, erected to assist in cleaning of hulls – weed, green slime and barnacles.

The bay was protected by two smaller points, their arms curving closer around, an almost estuary. Memories of the coasts of Devon and Cornwall were vivid, different but the same.

Crouching, Rory picked up a few pebbles and flicked them from one hand to hand as he rested his eyes on the symmetry of the scene, a peacefulness that seemed to exude from it. He shifted his sight, to the north of the wharf - under the shade of the hills, a number of cottages, and a few larger holiday homes, more palatial, dotted the shore. A tiny access track running behind them to a dead end and what appeared to be the beginning of a walking track around the rocky jutting point.

To the south, in the bright sunlight, two flat grassy areas, each with an old bungalow in their centre, each plot was quite large – giving a sense of space. At some time the houses may have been separated by a line of trees, now just odd old trunks twisted into a partial barrier. Both houses in need of paint and love, the one on the most southern side, had its own rickety jetty, a clinker dinghy pulled beside, clinging to a tired rope.

Rory stood - stretched and yawned, not from boredom or tiredness, from a sudden sense of peace, his whole body relaxed. It was a long time, so many years since any feelings of this nature had touched him. But the feeling was fleeting – in and out of his mind – like the rapid rattle of type writers keys - as the reasons he was here - at this familiar place returned. It had been many many years, and he hoped that no-one remained that may recognise – or know him. No - that was ridiculous. He had only ever passed by – never stopping for more than a few minutes – on his way elsewhere.

Now he was alone, a new journey? A new adventure? A new direction? He doubted that. The relaxed quiet was shadowed by, 'there is another purpose' in being here – and it cast dark clouds. But right now, not enough to take away his relaxed sense of self. Though he knew that it would not last!

'Can I keep my focus - feet on the ground, walk on this path? Can I, this time, not allow myself to wander off the bloody track?' It was a habit to talk to himself - aloud - and at times - he allowed himself the liberty of answering - as long as there was no one else in earshot!

Rory was about to turn back to the car when he thought he saw something – something puzzled him. He stopped and walked closer to the edge of the lay-by and looked down at the coast below. He saw another scene – a vision of a village on the Devon coast – another almost enclosed harbour – quaint cottages – the three hundred year old Pub where they had stayed for two nights, drank with the locals – sang and laughed. The high protective cliffs, calling gulls and the fishing boats – the sight of that scenery – and a girl – no a young beautiful woman, standing on the edge of the cliff road with him – almost the same as now – but different – now - here he was alone – then he was not! His mind stared at the frame of the film that played in his mind - set what seemed so long ago and he wondered if that 'scene' would ever leave him. And – could it be relived – with – someone?

While the imagery and memory was in most of its respects something that he wished to remain – he knew that it wasn't to be, and that it's only pain of this recollection that would stay with him – but for how long? He knew that it had to go, for his life to move – and it must move – his problem at this moment was 'where to move it to!'

Rory attempted to shrug off the thoughts and ambled back to the car. He slid behind the wheel but didn't immediately begin the journey down the hill to the village. He sat watching the slow circling of two hawks as they peered for prey, their movements graceful, the only movement in a still azure sky. They disappeared below the line of the hill and were gone.

He started the car and headed back out onto the dusty road, even driving as slow as he did, the fine dust swirled up behind, and seeped in through the windows and doors, filming the interior with a fine haze. He drove very slowly, it took nearly thirty more minutes to negotiate the winding and twisting of the steep road before he reached the bottom.

A sign at a junction just over a bridge that crossed the river, pointed the way to the village, or away up the coast, he swung the large heavy wheels to the left and headed onto a sealed road.

'So? What interesting facts, fantasy and fictions will I find as I look into this sleepy hollow?' The temptation to turn away and travel further - seek somewhere else for a time, had passed. He knew what he had to do. 'And if I don't look – delve here - will I ever know?' Indecision, he drove slowly, watching – was he procrastinating in this search for answers? Or was it something else, was it a fear of what he actually may discover.

'You've been required to go and have a look – delve – inquire search – look for answers to the unanswered – not quite the phrasing used but it will do – and that – in part is why I am here!' A disturbing realisation that he had heard those words not so long ago – a telephone call. And they had been repeated – very recently!

Rory turned the car at the intersection of the main road, and headed down a narrower street that led into the village. As he did so, one of his 'haunts' from his past much younger days filtered back, it was a recurring nightmare and appeared at different times, often when his mind was clouded and his thoughts were not as straight and clear as he wanted them to be.

*   *

Rory remembered the mud clinging to his legs, sucking, pulling, dragging him down. He struggled to free each one. Each time that he removed it he would totter sideways and fall on one hand or the other. He was covered in the sticky smelly muck, each arm coated to the armpit, his face spattered, his clothes wet inside, drying hard on the outer, each time that he stopped to rest, the sun quickly baked him.

The far side of the mud flat seemed a thousand miles, but today he was determined that it wouldn't beat him. This was the fifth time he had tried. The first was three years ago when he was seven, now at ten, he would win. His birthday had been four months ago, at the end of the winter, that had been his fourth attempt, two days after the birthday.

Halfway, and the trickle creek ran out to sea just ahead, about fifty yards. 'If I can get past that, if I can get past the barrier of the creek - I will win!' Rory had never made it past that point before, he had always fallen at the 'last mental hurdle', lain and cried and crawled back. So the journey was the same - he achieved the half, and then returned, so in a way he had won, covered the distance - but not won the prize. 'At least,' he told himself, 'if I get to the other side I can walk back on the road, and feel that I haven't been beaten.'

'Do as I say,' his mother would tell him, 'And you will be alright, I know best. And remember everything that you do reflects on your Father and me.'

Then, 'Whatever you don't know - ask.' Every morning that he left for school. But he had great difficulty doing that, the fear of asking a stupid question, and being laughed at by the other children, and the teacher, disabled him, he would rather struggle with it himself. Rory had been shy and withdrawn, and laid himself open to bullying – sometimes physically, sometimes mentally. His name often became a great game for the meaner rougher boys – and girls in his school and neighbourhood. His parents were very religious, solid members of the church, and he, his older brother and sister, were 'always being dragged into it'. The area was heavily industrialised working 'class'. His parents felt they were above most of 'them'. Rory felt isolated from many of his age group, isolated by prejudice.

On the odd occasion that he had been brave enough to put up his hand in class and to ask, how to attempt, or go about something - he had been told. 'Use you initiative Boy!' But Rory didn't know what 'it' was or where that was. That produced another fear, the fear of asking, then being ridiculed, but sometimes he did.

'Please Sir what's my Initiative, where is it – where do I look for it?' The teachers always thought he was being cheeky and facetious – but in fact he wasn't, and he felt quite ashamed and lost. The class would laugh at him – 'Stupid Stewed head Stewart' they would chant, and the teachers would laugh, before quietening the class.

His family, because of his solitary ways, and personal determination to be himself, found him 'odd'. They continually attempted to put him on what they considered - the right track. 'Why can't you be like the other boys in your class? Why are you being difficult – not fitting in?'

In fact he did fit in, for the most part – outside the classroom – by being himself – most of his classmates and school friends accepted him and they played together – whether in the play ground or at cricket or football. Though he was not allowed to 'join clubs' as a lot of them did. There were yes, some who bullied him, calling - pushing, that 'Little Churchy, goody good creep!' Was the chant.

It was not long after this period of his life that Stewart decided that he would call himself by his middle name – Rory – he thought that it was a bit more manly – stronger.

But despite that change – nothing else changed and it was back into his shell, and the shadow of the super confident outgoing parents - who yes, he could not deny, gave him affection, and all the necessities - but not his confidence. So - it was easier to be alone when he could, and live in his own private world.

So the trek across the mud was a personal challenge to establish in his our mind that he was capable of achievement a strange challenge, for in fact despite the problems encountered and compounded by his quiet withdrawn nature, was in the high IQ bracket, and in most exams he topped or nearly topped the class. Later in High School his teachers despaired at the amount of work 'not done' – that didn't reflect in the extremely high marks and calibre of his work and presentation. He was labelled a number of things – few complimentary – to most he was an enigma. It was many years later – after he had left home and later still when both his parents died that he came out of himself and into the life and person he was now – but sometimes the past still invaded his spirit.

*   *

As Rory drove into the main street of the village, many of these and other thoughts of his childhood and his teenage years, returned. Every new beginning, had brought back the same fears, every new job, new career moves. The fear of being seen as different - not that he looked different, and inside he probably wasn't any different from anyone else, on the outside -

confident, on the inside - churning, stuttering, "internally spewing" that he wouldn't succeed, not reach the other side of the mud.

But Rory remembered that December day - three months after his tenth birthday – when he finally reached the other side of the mud. He thought he had turned the corner to success, but the mud clung to him, he couldn't, wash it off. Had all the slimy squirming effort been worth the repercussions that he knew would follow? He hadn't won a prize, except in his mind - unless you consider a leather strap, and the tongue lashing to follow, later that day - a prize.

Now he had another opportunity to achieve an aim, he had been set a goal, in fact there were two – the one set from the demands of his work, and his personal one. To work out and reconstruct his own life and direction. Rory must now work out how the best way was to complete them both to his satisfaction - mind - the goal that was in the foremost of his mind was to rebuild himself. Rebuild after another disappointing disaster - caused yes, partly through his own folly of allowing others influence once more to distract.

It would and must be back to the lonely path. Go out and seek the truth, but don't allow anything or anyone in – nobody, to get too close. He was used to being remote and keeping people at arms length or further, and it had been one of the contributing factors in his marriage failure.

Rory slowed the big car edging into the curb, with the engine still running, he sat for several minutes looking over the scene that shimmered through the heat rising from the black melting tarmac.

Near the far end of the narrow, deep guttered street there was a Hotel, a curved corrugated verandah curling out over the pavement.

'That looks a likely place to start.' Rory muttered as he pulled the car into gear and drove slowly along pulling back into the curb opposite the old building. He was about a hundred yards from the waterfront and the end of the narrow jetty. The road went off to both sides at the corner and he could see a granite wall that ran along its edge. Behind to his left a Garage workshop, two fairly out of date petrol pumps. It was a rough fibros plaster and corrugated iron building, large, unpainted, open at the front, several cars with bonnets raised, were inside. Two grease covered men, had their heads together under one of them.

Rory Calder looked around the rest of the street. Three dogs ambled down by the harbour wall, noses to the ground, and a tall young woman pushed a baby carriage up the other side past the Hotel. Her long black hair swinging behind her straight back, head held high, her stride purposeful. Her brown face had an almost regal air, a straight nose, and full mouth, strong chin - although her dress was jeans and T-shirt, sandals on bare feet, she seemed to wear them with a certain confident style.

'That,' he said, 'looks a very interesting person - I wonder what she has in the there, a baby - or groceries?' Rory's thought rankled as ridiculous! He shook his head at his silly ideas and watched the girl stop to talk to another woman. Older, the other woman didn't look into the carriage.

It wasn't normally his nature or way to be forward, and approach strangers, especially attractive young women with a child carriage, for no real apparent reason. But something about her that drew him from the car. Rory crossed the street. He was almost beside her when she turned as if she hadn't seen him, and began to walk down an alleyway between two old shops, closed and shuttered, their paint faded and peeling.

'Excuse me, could I have a moment, I need a bit of help.' Rory called after her.

The young woman looked around at the sound of his voice, she was even more interesting to look at up close. Her eyes were dark brown pools, penetrating, deep.

'I have ah – um,' Rory stammered out, taken off guard by the girl's attractiveness, and her slightly hostile stare. 'I – I've just arrived, just driven into town, and I'm - um - I'm looking for somewhere to stay tonight. Or perhaps for a couple of days - to have a look around, here and up the coast, the --,' Rory hesitated again the dark eyes were troubled and looked at him with a hint of suspicion. 'Is there a camping ground, or cabins - some kind of accommodation - doesn't have to be flash.' His voice trailed lacking any expression or the enthusiasm he had felt when he had first seen her.

Rory felt a bit foolish, he could have easily asked at the garage, or the hotel - the obvious place. He glanced into the baby carriage, he was right on both counts, there was a baby, and groceries, just a few piled at the child's feet, the little face smiled up at him.

'Sorry - I hope I'm not being a nuisance, but I saw you walk past and -.' he trailed off and waited as she looked first at him, inspecting him up and down, then at his car, tatty and dusty behind him.

'There's a camping ground around on the water front - to the right at the end of this street, a few cabins - pretty run down now, used to be good - and there is the Hotel - which of course you've seen from your car, when you stopped and parked - there.' She waved her hand in the direction of the vehicle. Then with a slight twisted smirk. 'You could have asked there. It's okay, clean, tidy, nice people, not to noisy, try them, that's about it. Now I must be going. Good luck, I hope you enjoy your stay - but there's not much here to see or do - it isn't the exciting city life - like you're used to. Still I suppose that to some – and maybe you, might be an attraction.'

This time the girl's voice hadn't been unfriendly, pleasant, but not too welcoming, just helpful. It was well modulated, an educated tone, as if she may have been to a private school and from a 'good' upbringing. Which posed another question in Rory's mind. 'What was she doing here in a small seaside village?'

'None of your damned business!' he replied to himself. 'Yet.'

As the girl turned to leave she smiled - this time, with a bit more warmth and she said with a bright smile, 'Yes, I think the hotel would suit you better, much better.'

Rory watched her walk away up the narrow alley, then disappear down another side street, before he turned and went down to the door of the Hotel's Public bar. He rejected the idea, and went to the front door.

'God Rory, settle down, think before you speak – what the fuck have you been trained for! It's bloody obvious that I'm not from around here! Of course I'm not, idiot – you asked about a camping ground – accommodation, and that doesn't take an Einstein to work out, I may look scruffy, but maybe it's my after shave?' He shook his head at the stupid thoughts that entered his brain. As he talked to himself he pushed open the double glass doors and went into the dim interior. The entrance hall was dark, a single lamp with a cheap plastic shade, the only light, hung from the high ceiling, doors to the left the right and the centre - no labels to indicate what they were or where they led. But the place was, as the woman had said clean, it smelt clean, not even the tinge of stale beer and smoke that he had anticipated.

'Can I help you with something?' A voice behind him.

Rory swung round at the sound behind him. It was the woman he had seen talking to the girl with the baby. She was standing inside the doorway near the Office in the dim light. Rory hadn't been taking a lot of notice of his surroundings and hadn't noticed that someone had been watching him.

'Shit, where did you spring from, you gave me a heart attack!' Rory almost shouted, he was always, despite his experience, nervous in new situations.

'Sorry - thought you'd heard me. Let's start again.'

'Start again what?' Puzzled by her comment, was the question that entered Rory's mind.

The woman gave him a wide smile. 'I'm Cheryl, Cheryl Brown the owner, Publican, and general dog's body, - how can I help - do you want a room, a drink, food, directions or the lot? And I'm a nosey bitch and talk far too much!' She thrust out a hand and gave him a wide smile.

Rory shook the proffered hand. He hadn't taken a great deal of notice of her in the street, as his fascination with the other person had blocked out most else.

Cheryl Brown had a pleasant pretty face, and wasn't as old as Rory first imagined. The woman was short, but very nicely proportioned! She had fair hair, not blonde, cut short, stylish, and although he couldn't see her eyes in the dullness of the hall, he imagined them a vibrant lively blue.

'Strangers stick out a bit like bloody sore thumbs around here, and now the holidays are over, even more, and we don't get as many of them as we used to either. Times change, and ah well, there ain't too many people passing through - great weather eh? Now what can we do for you? I saw you out on the street before, come on through here, can't see much of you in this dull hall - must get a bigger lamp.' Cheryl led the way through the next door on the left, he followed her into what probably had been the

Public bar, but now was a mixture of that, and a lounge, immaculately tidy and clean.

Cheryl saw his look at her décor, and smiled. 'Yes I know, it's hodge podge. But I didn't like the old Public bar concept, and the locals didn't want a posh lounge. We had a bit of a battle, so I came up with this - it sort works, for them. Mind I'm used to it now, and I'm used to them, and them me, been here six years now, thirty-four to go to become an honorary local. She went behind the bar. 'What's your poison?'

Rory looked at his watch, it was just past twelve, it had been late morning when he had stopped at the top of the hill, and looked down at the town.

'A half of lager will be fine thanks, do you have anything to eat, I'm getting a bit on the hungry side - haven't eaten since early this morning.'

'Don't do proper meals until tonight, so we have the obligatory Pub pie, with chips and peas - or I could do you fish and chips, nice fresh stuff brought in this morning by one of the local guys.'

'Sounds fine, the fish and chips if it's not a bother, you don't seem to have anyone else coming in at the moment - but yes that would be great.' Rory could see that the woman was pleased he had decided to stay. She but seemed nervous and lonely.

Cheryl pulled the half-pint and went out the back of the bar, leaving him to wander about and look at the photos on the wall, they showed the history of the Hotel and the town. Some had a commentary, about the activities that used to take place, others were old and faded, dating as far back as the 1860's. Rory enjoyed looking into the past, and more so now as he was wanting to walk a path into the future.

It was ten minutes before she returned with a plate heaped with two large golden fillets a pile of fries, a small bottle of vinegar, a dish of tomato sauce, and two wedges of lemon.

Cheryl watched him eye the display. 'Just covering all tastes,' she said placing it on the bar and without asking, took his glass for a refill. As she put it back in front of him. 'I'll leave you in peace to eat, nothing worse than a nosy barmaid interrupting eating time - I hate it and so do my patrons, and I've been told about it too.' The woman laughed as she went out of the room.

Rory began the process of demolishing the food. It was excellent, the batter light and crisp, the fish delicate and moist, the fries were coated with a seasoning that hinted of garlic and spices, delicious. For some reason Rory had expected that it would be good, but this was exceptional. The cool lager was the perfect complement to it. Although the meal was large, he'd soon eaten it, he'd been hungry, he pushed the plate away, and on cue, Cheryl came back into the bar.

'That didn't take long, now, where are you headed for? Or will you stay around here for a day or two,? The questions kept coming, The next one surprised him. 'Are you here for some purpose, some reason? Just get a funny feeling about you. I told you I'm nosy, goes with the trade, particularly in a place like this.' Cheryl's smile was warm but had a tinge of irony, there was a wariness in the way she looked at him.

'And you talk and ask questions as if they were fired from a machine gun - I hardly get time to draw breath to answer!' He grinned at her.

She laughed in reply.'Yes I do a bit don't I, sorry, you carry on.'

'I would like to have a look around, I'm looking for a place on the coast, perhaps buy, maybe just rent long term. Sort of getting away from the rat race. I used to do a bit of composing of sorts, music, poetry, bits of writing, and want to, well, a shall we say, re-establish myself - then my crafts.' There was some truth in his explanation. The reality he would keep deeply hidden, but that story would do – even if a just a bit far fetched!

What Rory said next though was the exact truth, his voice was quieter, and the meanings, the images, of his words, were not lost on the woman behind the bar.

'I need the sea, the bush and plenty of peace and quiet. I haven't been into this village before, but I have passed by it, I've been on this coast, plenty of times, but never stopped to look closely. I also picked it out on the map, studied it, found its sheltered, closeted location, and this time when I actually stopped and looked at it from the top of the hill, I thought – 'yes - this could be it'. But, I would like to spy out the lay of the land before I make any final decisions, whether or not to stay a while.' Rory felt his tone was weak, but there was no indication on the woman's face to indicate that she did not believe him.

Cheryl pointed to his empty glass, and raised an eyebrow, he nodded, she went to fill it.

Rory had not realised that he had finished his second beer. 'Watch it boy, you're talking too much and drinking too much – slow down – in fact after this one stop!' But his warning was only in his head and he didn't make a sound as he watched the woman refill his glass. There was something about her, she didn't quite fit the image, too neat and tidy -what? He couldn't as yet quite work out, but he would.

He was standing at the far end of the curved bar, looking towards the door where he had first come in. Not only was there something about Cheryl that puzzled him, but the whole set up, the decoration mingled with old photos and dated furnishings. When she came back to him he went on. 'Which brings up the next question, I asked the young lady with the baby about accommodation, she said there wasn't a lot, and suggested here may be best for me. I saw you talking to her - does she get commission for sending you guests? I gather from the way that you were talking in the street you may be good friends?'

Cheryl gave a short uneasy laugh. She was about to comment that he was a bit too bloody observant for a holiday maker, but decided it was not a wise move. 'No - no commission, but yes, she's a good friend. I've known her from almost the first day I got here. In a way I came for a similar reason that you're talking about. Get away from something, find whatever in life you're looking for. I did, in a way find it. I had my eye on this pub, saw it advertised, came and looked at it, and decided to give it a shot. It was then owned by her Grandfather. He had died seven or eight months before I came down here, his wife was getting on and couldn't handle it. The rest of Miranda's family hated it - even before the old guy chucked it in, so they weren't interested. That helped make the price right – a bit of luck really.'Cheryl saw no harm in spinning the story, she didn't think this guy would hang around long.

'Miranda? Is that her name, unusual. Don't hear of many Mirandas. Is she local or an import?' Rory smiled to himself at his comment, trying to be something that he wasn't, but it seemed to work.

'An Import! That's one way of describing people who weren't born and raised here, not that there are many young ones left, they all head off up to the big smoke. Yes they, her family were imports as you call them, mind you – most in the beginning were, one way or another although you'd think that some were quarried here from the local rocks the way they go on. Anyway they, Miranda's family came here - oh - some fifteen or sixteen years ago. Her husband did as well, sort of, although he's more from this part of the world. A fisherman, though not all that flash at it, gets sidetracked. His lot come from the coast, you know, the other side, they're still there, but when he married her, he moved, she wouldn't. But he liked it better, he said, quieter, not so many loopies over summer.'

'Loopies? What the hell are they?' Rory asked, then rapidly went on. 'Was her husband the one that brought you the fish today? It was by the way a really great meal. Thank you.'

'No problem, glad to help, and Loopies, they're holiday-makers from the city, drive us all mad, and we probably drive them mad too. But they certainly help the bank balance, but as I said, we don't have as many coming down as we used to, don't have the same attraction as the other side of the hills. The beaches there has far more to offer, but you probably know that, – plus the big game fishing, still we make do. Now do you want to see the rooms? I'm not trying to be pushy mind, but a girl's got to try to make a buck when she can, and no, it wasn't Miranda's husband.'

'Okay, that's filled in a couple of gaps, quite irrelevant ones too I might add,' Rory's eyebrows raised a fraction in query, 'now back to the accommodation, so let's have a look, your friend also said that there was a motor camp and cabins, somewhere nearby, but they weren't great, just nearer the shoreline.'

Rory drained the last of the lager and as he pushed himself away from the bar he went on. 'I think she may have said a backpackers too, but I'm not sure I heard it right, the thing is I like, well to be separate, private, quiet. And don't like imposing or being imposed on - if you get my drift?'

Cheryl watched him as he spoke, noticing a nervous shyness, wondering who this man was. Why was he really here - "searching for self"? No – she felt that there was another agenda – but what and why? She may well have to watch her tongue, it tended at times to divulge too much 'information', and that wouldn't be wise, but she would definitely be delving herself, she would need to know a lot more for a lot more reasons!

'That's fine, I'll show you around here. Then point you in the direction of the others. Miranda was probably trying to put you off, she likes to see me have guests, says it makes the place, or perhaps me, more sane if I have people to look after. Not entirely sure what she means by that.' Cheryl laughed quietly, and stole a side glance at Rory as they went out the Bar door, and back into the dark hall. At the end, was a large ornate staircase.

'Weird eh?' she spoke over her shoulder, 'The original hotel was quite a fancy affair, back about a hundred and ten years ago, this is one of the remaining original bits. Alterations and additions – modernised, though with what was done I'm not sure that's the right word, several times, and the odd fire changed appearances. So not only is my bar a hodgepodge, so' s the rest of it. But I like it, it's a bit like me, strange and erratic, so are a few of the characters that hang out here, as you'll see if you stay awhile.'

They progressed up the stairs to the accommodation, a long corridor with rooms off each side. Old oak wood panelling half way up, dark stained and highly polished, the cream embossed paper above that had seen better days, a picture rail, with oak framed prints of old masters. With all the doors shut and only one window at the far end, it was dim, two lonely unshaded bulbs hung from the ceiling, trying their best to illuminate the eeriness.

'Keep meaning to get brighter lights and some decent shades, but never get around to it. Means a trip to town, and doesn't seem worth the hassle for the number that stay, particularly now.' Cheryl had kept up a torrent of information about the Pub and the Village, then suddenly fell silent and looked thoughtful, she shook her head as if to clear it.

Rory thought that she was going to continue, but 'the particularly now' seemed to hang in the air, as if something should follow, but decided it didn't want to. As they reached the door at the end he asked. 'Do you live here on your own, run it on your own - or -.'

Cheryl interrupted, 'My husband walked out two years ago, the old story - the younger barmaid. He thought she was something, she thought he was 'a good money bet' - wrong. The funds were all mine in the place. I actually bought it with an inheritance - my Grandfather liked me. So it was Granddaughter buys from Granddaughter in a way. Mind you, I was the only Grandchild, so that helped too. When she found out that he was all talk, and bugger all else, she ditched him. About three months later, he came crawling back, he never was much, actually lazy son of a bitch, shouldn't say that - his mother was a really good type, and not a bitch. His father was like son and vica versa. So I told him to not bother with his sad sob story and to piss off - and he did. So the short answer is - yes. I gave you the long one, or part of it, first, sorry.'

Cheryl opened the door and went in. 'This is the best room, well rooms. It used to be for staff, so it's got a sitting room, a bedroom, of course, and a bathroom of it's own. I did it up a bit awhile ago, and it has a view over the top of the other buildings down to the water - when it's there.'

Rory stared around the 'plush' surroundings. It was a complete contrast to all that he had seen so far, deep rich wall covering and drapes, the furnishings dark solid timber. The carpet was almost plain in comparison, a deep bluey purple, with a dull red running through it. The whole appearance was 'over the top' weird.

She took in his reactions to the rooms as he walked through them.

'I did it for us, the man of the house and me. He hated it, and after he took off I moved out, and did another one right down the corridor at the far end, not the same view, and not the same decor either. Similar I suppose, might show you sometime if you're interested. I do realise that the style and colours aren't exactly everyone's cup of tea!' A faint smile shimmered across her lips.

'Who stays in here - do you really have guests that would stay in here?' Rory tone was incredulous, it seemed extremely unlikely, it wasn't exactly his taste, and he thought, 'not many others either'.

'No, in fact you're the only stranger I've shown it to, in some considerable time. All the other rooms are pretty basic to say the least, like most of the people who come to the village and stay here, sorry that's not very nice,' Cheryl sighed, 'I just have a feeling that you may not possibly be - basic. Not that there is anything wrong with being basic, depending on the way you use the term. Oh look sorry I'm blabbing on, I do that when I have someone new to talk to - maybe that's why not many people stay here.' Her face flushed.

'It's, well, um, probably a bit much for me and it looks a bit pricey. Could, as I'm here, have a look at another room, then I'd better have a look around the town.' Rory smiled wryly. It wasn't just the room, although he thought it could do, but Cheryl was also a 'bit much' friendly, pleasant, helpful, but - a bit much.

'I could let you have it at a special rate, much cheaper than the normal. And they really aren't you, the other rooms or the Camp ground, honestly, pretty bloody grotty, you know, old and run down, smelly! Presumptuous I know, but how about - no worries - sixty five a night, and if you wanted it for a week or so, I would bring that back to an even fifty, no pressure, go and check out the rest. Come on I'll point you in the right direction.' Cheryl went out and waited for him, then closed the door and locked it.

Cheryl didn't show him the other rooms, and as they went down the stairs she chatted about some of the characters of the town - like Old Jim Bland.

'Nothing like his name, a real hard shot. Used to be Mayor here maybe forty - fifty odd years ago, they reckon he's near a hundred. He says he doesn't know, I think he does, just likes to be mysterious, and he's no where near that. Comes in every night at five twenty sharp, why five twenty we have no idea, has three good whiskies and talks at ninety to the dozen for half an hour then off he goes - fit as a fiddle, looks after himself, clean as a whisker.'

She stopped at the front door, and put her hand on his arm. 'Sorry - look I do go on a bit, like I said, I must be boring you to tears - and I don't even know your name!'

Rory held out his hand, there was a look in the girl's eyes – despair. 'Rory, Rory Calder. There are other bits in between but we won't bother with those, and no you haven't bored me. I'm not much of a talker myself, not at the moment, can be though, so watch out. I may want to bore you sometime.' Rory realised how he had put that comment and metaphorically but his tongue! 'It's been said that I often use ten words when one would do. A bit unfair, though it does at times have a ring of truth to it. Anyway, if I stick around long enough you might find out. Now - where am I headed?'

Cheryl shook his hand, with a considerable amount of warmth, then ushered Rory out the front door onto the footpath.

'Right, great, now, if you go down to the wharf and turn right that'll take you to the Camping ground. Then about a hundred yards past that, you'll see a narrow road. Well, more a track, just wide enough for a car, that goes up to the old Boarding house. It's up in the bush a little way, very private and quiet, full of creepy things, and the odd mouse. The back packers don't mind, it's cheap, and they get a reasonable feed, for the money. Down the other way about a quarter of a mile from the wharf, up on the other bluff, is another B and B, bit more classy, cleaner and not too badly priced. Good luck and enjoy the walk.'

'Who said I was going to walk?' he asked smiling at her, 'I might be a lazy sod and drive.'

'I think you'll walk,' Cheryl pointed across at his car, it had a flat front right tyre. 'Unless you want to change the tyre first. You must have punctured on the way in - get the guys at the garage to fix it for you while you look around, it will only cost you a couple of bucks. Good guys but slow, but who cares in this weather! See you later?' She waved and went to go back into the pub.

'Yes - I'll see you later, thanks Cheryl, I'll let you know what I decide to do. Might pop in for a drink later.' He went over to the garage and asked them to fix the tyre. It wouldn't be a problem, leave it to them. Rory gave them the keys and set off down to the wharf. 'No wonder the old bus felt heavier than usual, though, I don't remember,----' Rory shrugged and walked on.

Approaching the jetty he glanced at his watch. 'Two thirty!' he said aloud, a couple walking by glanced at him with raised eyebrow as if to say - "So what?" He decided to talk inside the head. 'Exactly - so what, I'm not in a hurry, I don't want to go anywhere else - so slow down - chill out - relax! I know you didn't come here to get away from the pressure you apply to time, and there are other things to worry about, leave the time alone. Let it flow by and go with that flow. Or your reason for being here will become plain bloody obvious!'

Rory stopped at the stone wall that flanked the shoreline, sat on the top and looked around. The road in each direction was bordered by odd shops, a convenience store, and a couple of cafes. Each side almost a clone of the other in their style, some empty, dilapidated, long passed their used by date, others spruced up and clean, painted in the tradition of their age, verandahs arching over the footpath, nothing new interfered.

Several small stores, one each side of the jetty, a dairy, a bookshop, a bakery, and a butcher, a drapery, and a pottery gift shop, an odd collection for such a small village. Then two cafes separated only by the bookshop, tables scattered across the pavement, and onto the other side of the road by the water's edge - umbrellas bright.

All the business's names clearly sign-written, pride shown. He wondered how they made a living, as the only people on the street in the heat, were himself two old men - and a dog.

The sun was warming and pleasant, no breeze moved the air. Rory turned and looked out over the flat of the muddy sand bay, the tide still out beyond the boats that lay like stranded whales waiting for the water to re-float them, to turn them back into living creatures. They (the boats) he thought, always looked unhappy when they were not floating, swinging on moorings, or pushing through calm or rough seas. But their life-blood – the seeping tide, was on its way back, creeping slowly, devouring the dried sandbanks near the outer edges. The crackling sounds of the heat on the empty bay, shells opening, crabs crawling, gulls swooping and rising, picking off an odd snack on their way. And on the land, - virtually no movement. The sleepy hollow of an afternoon siesta and dreams of better things – but who was dreaming?

Looking at the scene, Rory contemplated his next move. Check out the flea-pit boarding house, the Camping ground, or the upmarket Bed and Breakfast, in the other direction. 'Another direction' were pertinent words. And what of Cheryl and her offer, of the 'plush flat', incongruous with its other surroundings, and the owner. The owner too didn't fit or fit in the surroundings. There were anomalies. Her manner, her speech, one moment educated, the next into the vernacular of the out-country.

Rory hadn't asked where she was originally from, but he would lay odds it wasn't where she had said, or did she say? There was a brogue, a lilt to her voice - but not distinguishable. She was like the Hotel a strange mixture – but a mixture of what?

Her continual out pouring of information, or lack of it – was it nervousness? If so – about what? For all of that, she was likeable, friendly, not wanting something in return – except perhaps, some recognition?

Rory chose, as he thought this, to walk to the Camping ground, he inspected each small shop and the Cafes on the way. He began to feel an unusual peacefulness, even in the short that he had been here. Was it real or false, was it a precursor of unknowns?

The camping ground loomed on his right, it was, as Cheryl had described, a sorry sight, a shambolic mess of tangled broken fences, iron gates twisted, rusting. The long overgrown grass was dotted with gorse and Broome, and strewn with old timbers and rubbish, further back beyond derelict cabins, vines and unkempt trees covered what had once could have been a park.

'How, why it has got to this state? Who the hell would bother staying here?Perhaps someone may be able to enlighten me, or perhaps not. But really, do I need to know?' Rory, thinking about, 'the already peculiars', walked further along the road.

Just past the grounds the track that Cheryl had mentioned, that led up to a Boarding house. It too was overgrown, with blackberry, yellow Broome and gorse bushes shadowing the pathway, tangled grasses matted the middle. No 'traffic' had passed for some time.

But unlike the camping ground, inquisitiveness conquered this time. Rory pushed past the overgrowth. The track became steeper the further he went, then opened into a parking area, tall weeds and, as with the Camping ground, rubbish scattered around. To one side, a flight of rickety steps lead up through native bush. He decided to explore further.

As he ascended, the growth became thicker, and the thought that he may be on the wrong path crossed his mind. 'That's nothing unusual is it!' He muttered. The stairs stopped at a cross path - one left the other right, both clearer and cleaner than the ones he had come up so far. Sunlight filtered through larger trees creating shadowy patterns and light shafts. He took the path to the right.

The bush began to thin out and he could see the shape of a large two storied wooden structure. He came to the end of the path, it opened onto a spreading lawn, he was surprised, after what he had been told, and what he had seen on the way, that it was so neatly trimmed, dotted with flower beds and shrubs, well cared for. The house imposed itself over the scene, it was very large and very white, green sills and frames around deep red doors, the roof was a deep grey, the guttering, was the red of the doors. Yet the scene seemed impassive – the house disinterested in it's position.

'This can't be the place that Cheryl told me about,' he said, 'doesn't fit the run down crappy description at all.'

'The description of what? And what are you doing here, this is Private land.' There was a strong emphasis on the 'you'!

The voice from behind him, he turn sharply, startled. 'I'm sorry, I didn't see anyone about, I didn't mean to intrude.' His face turned scarlet, he hated being caught out, and put in embarrassing situations. He stammered on. 'I - I'm um, I'm - looking for - looking for a boarding house that I was told - um, was up, up the a road just past - the camping ground - and -'.

Rory stopped talking and took a bit more notice of the person standing in front of him. It was Cheryl's friend with the baby carriage. He calmed, 'This is certainly not the place that was described to me by your friend from the Hotel. Cheryl said it was a run down flea pit, and this is definitely not, is this where you live?'

Miranda took in his embarrassment. 'No - it belongs to my parents, actually my Father, I'm just up here visiting. You should have taken the left path. Not that you would have known that. We don't really use that way up and down, as it does actually belong to the boarding house - I mean the paths do. We just use it as a bush walk, so if you go back the way you've just come, and keep going along the other way, you will find the "flea pit". But as I said, the Hotel would suit you better, I really don't think this Boarding house will, but who knows I could be wrong - have been about people before - perhaps you should listen to instructions better and watch where you're going in future.'

Before Rory could reply, the girl, Miranda turned on her heel and strode off towards the house. 'I don't think she takes to me too well somehow.' As he spoke to himself, turned and went back into the bush.

TWO

I t was as Rory had been told, the Bush Boarding house was similar to the camping ground, tired, run down, untidy, the people though friendly, were the same. There was evidence that there were some guests, but apart from the owners there was no-one in sight. He trekked back down the rough path and steps and came back out onto road to town.

As he got to the village, Rory looked back to see if he could see the large white house, it was invisible. He thought back to when he had been up at the top of the hill road looking down into the valley, he had no recollection of seeing anything in that area. 'It must be very well concealed in the bush, or the angle that I was looking, did not quite bring it into the line of sight.' He shrugged, 'Why do I do this, does it even fucking matter, so why am I interested? Why indeed – but there's something that makes it – but what is it?'

Rory stood for a few moments, his intuition doing overtime. He reflected on his analysis of his position. Shook his head at the notions, that there was more to what he had seen and heard, and walked on. At the corner of the main street he stopped, contemplating whether to go further down the sea wall path and inspect the other Bed and Breakfast or go and see if his car was ready, he opted for the latter and went to the Garage.

'It's all ready,' the Older of the two men in overalls said, pointing to the car at the side of the forecourt, 'That'll be five bucks thanks, it was just a minor problem with the valve, somehow it had given up the ghost

- who knows why, it wasn't very old, but these things happen. Great old bus there – had it long?'

'Yes quite a while. Thanks for helping out.' Was all he said as he paid, he didn't want to get into another long dissertation with local right this moment. He was about to continue his exploring for accommodation in the car, but as he opened the door, the heat build up while parked in the sun, hit him. He was already warm from his walk and could feel the film of sweat on his forehead and back, he decided to continue on foot! He asked the garage proprietor if he could leave the car for an hour or so, if it wasn't a problem. The man readily agreed that it wouldn't be, so leaving the windows down to let in an airflow, Rory set off back down the street to the wharf.

The tide was now creeping quickly over the flats, lapping around the boats. Some, further out, were just beginning to float. There wasn't a breath of breeze, a bronze haze had settled over the afternoon. A few shops had closed - he supposed - earlier than usual, to enjoy the summer warmth, and the tables over the road from the Cafes now had a number of people perching under the umbrellas, food and wine being consumed.

Instead of going in search of the B & B, Rory walked out onto the jetty, it protruded over a one hundred metres into the bay. Several children lay on their stomachs peering over the end, rods and lines dangled into the shallow water, anticipation of a catch as the water rose.

Rory looked at the time and saw that it was now past three, he sat on a bollard and watched. The excitement in their voices as they discussed the merits of their tackle and bait, and who would catch the biggest fish, gave a good indication that this was a favourite pastime of the local young boys after school.

Rory remembered his own childhood, fishing from rocks or small boat, while enjoyable, it hadn't been his favourite way to pass indolent days.

Long walks, mostly alone, but at times with a friend, usually a girl, someone that he could share thoughts with. While he had male 'buddies', Rory found the company of the opposite sex more in keeping with his sensitivity. He also found that he enjoyed - other aspects about them, and from quite young had been sexually attracted. This had led often into areas that for his age, he shouldn't have been venturing, and in later life to complications. Some that haunted him, causing depression and anger. Anger that for the most part he controlled, hid in the deeper reaches of his subconscious. But – not always.

There was one who he had wanted more than anyone else, to really develop a life with. And for some time they did. They had worked together – lived together, planned so many things, but for some reason after months of what seemed to be an idyllic life, it had fallen apart. Outside interference, and jealousy. Later, he married Serena.

Rory knew where she was – he knew he could contact her – but he hadn't, and he wouldn't.

His thoughts were and reminiscing were shattered by -------

'Great afternoon for nothing' eh?' a voice nearby. Rory looked up, it came from the shade of the wharf shed a few feet from him. As his eyes adjusted to the change of light from staring into the bright sun, he could see who the voice belonged to.

A tall thin man, of indeterminate age moved out of the shadow. He was dressed in an old faded khaki shirt, baggy trousers, well worn sandles. Although the clothing looked about as old as their occupant, they were clean and pressed, an equally tattered straw hat perched on his head, tilted to the side, long straggly grey hair hung beneath, framing a deep tanned face and hawkish, bright blue and inquisitive eyes.

'Hello,' replied Rory, 'didn't see you there when I came by, yes, a great day for nothing, a real lazy one, if one has the time to be that way.'

The old man smiled at him, showing even, but slightly stained teeth. 'You weren't meant to see me. Stranger in town eh? I always know when one arrives, feel the vibes in the air, he smile widened and he chuckled, 'but also, to be honest, I saw you drive in a couple of hours back.' He held out his hand. 'Jim Bland, ex-mayor and extraordinary nosey old bastard to boot. Watcha doin' in these parts - holiday maker, or, lookin' for something? And if lookin', what you lookin' for? As I said I'm nosey and I like to know why people come here – particularly someone who looks like you and sticks out like a sore bloody thumb.' The old man's eyes narrowed, as he sat on one of the bollards, – suspicious.

Before answering Rory examined the man, that Cheryl mentioned to him. He spoke casually, with a friendly smile, which he hoped hid his own cautiousness. 'Not exactly a holiday, no, probably more looking for something or somewhere, I'm running away from home, need a place to hide for a while, somewhere to,' he decided elaboration was not a good idea, 'this may be the place, it may not.' As he spoke Rory wondered. 'Why the hell am I saying this!' But he continued. 'To sort of renew the mind body and soul. Anyway – I'm having a look around for a place for a night or two. Perhaps you have a bright suggestion - not the camping ground, not the Boarding house in the bush - the Hotel is a maybe?'

Bland didn't comment on Rory's explanation, then. 'The Hotel is good, Cheryl is a wonderful friendly host. Good, clean, not fancy mind, that's the Hotel not Cheryl, and actually not too noisy, and this time I mean the Hotel and the host.' Bland grinned at Rory. 'The locals usually go home quite early, not that there's many, maybe a dozen a night, you know the old five to six thirty bit, then off to Mum and tea. You could do worse, and it'll give you an intro to a few people. Up to you of course, don't want to stick my nose in - much, then there's the posh B and B.'

Rory didn't mention that he'd already been to the Hotel, and had a look around. He thought about what the old chap said, and wondered if he was being a bit picky, after all it would only be for a night or two, until he found something else, somewhere where he would be a little less conspicuous. He felt he did stand out a little like a 'sore thumb' But that couldn't now be helped – he'd already plainly been observed by quite a few people..

'I'll think about it, you may be right, and I don't know that I can be all that bothered looking further today.' Rory glanced at his watch, the time was heading towards four o'clock. The afternoon had melted, with the quiet and the heat. He thought about that, and realised it could be thought of in a few different ways.

'Well, as I said, not my business, but may see you later, do you like a drink?' before he could answer, 'yes you do, right I'll get going - see you about five twenty.' The old man stood up and set off back down the wharf at a fast walk.

Rory shook his head. 'Yes, as Cheryl said, a character, could be an interesting evening after all, but watch your tongue, don't let it get away on you.' He stood from his bollard perch and watched the boys fishing for a few more minutes, then set off to the garage for his car. There were a more people wandering around now, most greeted him as he passed, either with a word, or a nod, one or two, with a wary glances.

Back at the garage he spent a few minutes with the men. A brief discussion on the weather, and the merits of a rather nice red BMW sports convertible, that they were servicing.

They told Rory it belonged to, 'The guy that lives up in the big house on the point'.

The Mechanic explained, 'Lawyer fella, been here quite a long time, some fifteen or sixteen years, works mostly up in the city.' That was all that was said. Rory put the information into his file in the back of his mind. And, 'must be that girl Miranda's Father'. He would enquire more, later – but why? That thought puzzled even his over inquisitive mind. Until, 'You idiot – find out his name – what the hell do you think that you're here for!'

Rory didn't have to wait long for the information. 'That girl, the one with the pram, you were chatting to her earlier. Miranda Sullivan – he's her father, names Peter.' It was just a casual comment but the alarm bells went off with a huge clanging! But he kept his expression impassive, but inside he certainly was not! Things had suddenly changed their complexion. 'It couldn't just be a strange coincidence could it – to have that information so early after getting here? Keep calm and get yourself organised, and watch your back, and keep your mouth shut!'

It was only about fifty yards to the Pub. Rory could see a driveway down the far side, a sign on the fence pointing to a Car parking area. He drove across the street, down the unsealed alleyway into the metalled area at the back of the building, a cloud of dust following close behind, the crunching of the gravel, and the deep rumble of the old V8, giving away his arrival.

Cheryl appeared at a back door, she called to him. 'Heard you were on your way here, lanky Jim's been on the blower, said you'd decided to put up here for awhile.' She came over to the car. 'I've got the place ready for you. Here, let me give you a hand with your bags.'

Rory opened the boot and extracted a couple of battered leather carry alls, a shoulder satchel and a suit bag. He handed her, the smaller ones, and picked up the rest, slinging the shoulder bag, he followed her into the dim interior.

'God,' Rory thought, 'news travels extremely bloody fast. I'd only just made up my mind, almost, but not quite, when I was talking to him. But that information at the Garage was interesting and may help a lot!'

'You want the flat I showed you don't you,' before he could answer, 'I'll tell you what, I'll let you have it for the rate of an ordinary room - Forty bucks – okay?' Cheryl's smile was pleading.

Too friendly, Rory thought, he hesitated, but only a moment, thinking. 'God - she must be desperate! And desperate in what ways? And for what else – or am I now really over reacting? But I guess it's a bit late to change my mind now.'

'Right, yes - that is very generous of you, I'd prefer the bigger space, don't like being shut in, but the normal rate is fine.' Rory followed her up the stairs.

'No - I said it, and I do what I say - forty bucks a night, for as long as you like.' Cheryl said over her shoulder. She placed the bags on the floor. As she opened the door, she turned and looked at him, questions in her eyes.

'It will probably be for only a couple of days. Then I may either try to find something more permanent. Maybe I might even go over the other side. I'll see how it goes. I'm not really sure what I want to do. Now, would you like me to pay something in advance?'

'Forget it, I can run a tab for you, an account when you leave, put everything on it, booze, food, the lot, - how would that be?' An even wider smile. 'And what would be the reason go over there – or even being here now? You sound mysterious.'

Rory frowned as he considered, all the comments and questions, then agreed, 'That would be fine – thank you.' But he didn't elaborate on the other queries.

They'd been standing outside the open door for several minutes, then Cheryl bent, picked up the bags she had been carrying, and went into the room, chattering over her shoulder as she went, about the towns Grapevine info service. It was plain to Rory that not a lot went unnoticed.

Inside he put his bags down, as she handed him the key. 'I was presumptuous, I did think that after our conversation before, that you'd be back, at least for a few days - call it my spooky intuition.' Cheryl had a mischievous glint flicker in her eyes, 'And, a few other thoughts.' She turned away quickly to avoid further scrutiny. 'There you go, I'll leave you to sort yourself out, catch you when you come down, you know where the rooms are, and you'll find all you need in the bathroom and the kitchen.' She gave him another smile and went out, pulling the door shut behind her.

Rory stood looking around at the bazaar surroundings. As he had thought before - unusual, strange - but they sort of worked, although he was not sure why, in many ways they offended his artistic colour sense, but was he or anyone else right? Rory shrugged off the inconsequential notions, and took his bags into the bedroom and dumped them on the luggage rack.

The room looked out the back across the car park to the steep bush that curved around the town. The sun was lowering and casting lights and shadows amongst the thick growth, creating a palette of colour, picking out the myriads of greens, yellows, and reds that mingled together on the slopes.

For a few minutes he wandered the rooms checked the bathroom and kitchen, it was stocked with some breakfast foods, milk, eggs, butter and bread, the fridge also had a few beers, a half bottle of gin and a full one of brandy, several small bottles of ginger ale and tonic water.

'If the place hasn't been used - why the bits and pieces and alcohol supplies?' he queried, then realised that Cheryl had obviously stocked it for him – yes presumptuous. 'Then again, if Mayor Jim had clued her up, but she didn't have the time – or did she? 'I was talking to the men across the road for a while.' Rory mulled the thought again - 'Perhaps she had been presumed that he was actually going to stay, and she knew he would take the flat. 'Why the hell I am even thinking about this - it's pathetic - who cares - I'm here now!' He wandered back into the living area. He stood looking at the view down to the sea. The tide was quite high now, right up against the wall. A shiny blue grey mirror reflecting the shapes of the small ships, and the surrounding bush, the sounds of cicadas echoed across the bay, sending their buzz into the village.

'What am I doing here, this all looks so idyllic, so serene, but, what am I doing here?' Rory mouthed the words, but their sound though quiet, seemed to fill the room. He leant his head on the glass. 'Is it the paranoia of my work that has to be dealt with playing it's part already, will it produce all the answers to all the questions I am supposed to ask. About myself and about that 'portfolio' in my bags. My masters tasks for me to investigate – coincidence or design?' But it's already begun – and begun in a rather unexpected way!' Rory suddenly wanted silence, remoteness, yet was afraid of it, he wanted his solitude - but should he let the outside in? Yet he knew he had to, that his 'brief' was extremely explicit. There was no coincidence – it'd been planned – yes - definitely designed, but what was their theory? If there was one at all?'

'Remember your other goals, you may be wanting to rebuild yourself – your life and your esteem – or whatever you want to call it, but you are committed and are – under orders.' The voice, in the back of his head.

'Yes,' Rory replied to the empty room, 'yes I am – and I have – I haven't forgotten.

In months since, Serena, Nicholas, Jodie and Kathleen had died, he had kept himself apart from others, almost monastic, yet together within himself. He had this craving to leave the "city rat race" was this and his 'commission' one of the answers?

The questions, the sympathy, the suspicion, and more questions - for more than three months the police had been relentless, they hadn't believed him - they'd known of their problems through "kind concerned neighbours". The arguments the tension. His instability and his nervous breakdown.

To get away as much as he could from the prying eyes and gossip – the innuendo of even some of his friends and family, he had sold the house, and the small apartment in the central city high rise, for when he needed to be nearer his work. He had rented another house in another part of the city, on the fringes, few houses and surrounded by bush.

It wasn't that they hadn't had a 'type' love for each other, and their children, but their interests, and life directions changed, in fact they'd never been the same, or even similar. So why had he been 'there'? That question that had always puzzled Rory. As would another. 'Why had it been so totally different, with Marguriette? So connected and uncomplicated? – until ------.'

He'd wanted to give up his career at the University, and the CIB, and live in the country, devote time and energy to his creative passions - not too isolated, close enough to the city for Serena to still pursue her dreams, her desire for a career in Law. He understood that part of her, she didn't understand or even want to understand, his dreams and feelings. The gaps had widened.

The eventual Coroner's verdict - that of suicide or accidental death. They couldn't decide completely which! So all of the investigation's results were inconclusive. But that's how it had been, the whole thing - inconclusive. He suspected, that the Police still believed that he contrived the whole thing, and a few people, "that he did not get on with" hadn't helped. He had no real enemies, but there'd been professional jealousy, and there were also two particular gentlemen, who had had desires and designs on Serena. And Rory knew that it hadn't just been - just looking thanks!

In the end, the Police had given up their line of investigation, into whether he was involved or not, and started to look in other directions. They had stepped back, and sideways allowing him to pass.

But what did he believe about her death, was it an accident? A tragedy that took his children as well, was there something deeper, more sinister? And if so - why? He really didn't know, didn't have answers -- was that the reason he was here, or was it - the isolation in the country for his own sake? To find that elusive Rory? He smiled at that thought – it was really a pipe dream. But then – sometimes even pipe dreams come true.

However Rory knew that right at this moment it was neither. Though who knew? In time it may be the pipe dreams that would prevail?

The old grandfather clock chimed down in the hallway, the half-hour, bringing him out of the near past back into this strange room. He looked at his watch, it was five thirty, the thought of a shower and fresh clothes crossed his mind, but he rejected the idea, and went down to the bar.

As he came down the stairs he remembered it was Friday, he'd forgotten the day - each one seemed to roll into the next.

'A Friday night in a semi-public bar, God it's been a bloody long time since I did that -- particularly in a strange town!' He went in through the double glass doors, the chatter of the customers stopped, all turned to look at the new comer, all but one went back to their conversation. Jim Bland came and took him by the arm, leading him to a group of five standing near the open windows on the far side of the bar.

'Come and meet some of me local cobbers, been telling them about the stranger in town, Cheryl's been adding her bit too. Now they're interested, want to get something they can gossip about. Cheryl told us your name, but I've forgotten it, what was it? -- Rolly, Ron?'

'Rory, Rory Calder.' He shook hands with the men, their names went in one ear and out the other. 'I might pick them up later.' He thought amongst the chatter and tried to sized up each man, and he felt himself underwhelmed, 'I'm not a snob, at least I don't think I am,' he looked around the bar, 'Hmm,' he thought, 'but maybe I am -- I wouldn't usually choose to have a drink with these chaps, but then maybe I'm judging the book by it's cover, so wait and see.

'What's you poison young man?' It was Jim again. 'I'll get one in for you.'

He would've liked a good wine, but decided he would do "what the Romans do" and have a beer.

'A lager thanks Mr. Bland, a half will be fine.' Even opting for lager instead of the heavy draught, raised eyebrows. 'Bugger them,' he muttered, 'I'm making an exception anyway, but don't want stand out too much! Be careful.' He warned himself.

Jim Bland came back with the drink. 'Well, you didn't really give me much of clue to why you've called on our fair village. Just some rubbish about running away, we've all done, and you look a bit old to have had a row with Mum and Dad. What do you do for a crust?'

'I used to lecture at the University, Psychology, and a bit of Art History, a strange mix, that's up to a few months ago. Got a bit fed up' It wasn't a complete fabrication, and he was about to continue, when another person entered the bar..

'Well this is a turn up, Mr. Peter Sullivan, he doesn't come in here much, a very rare occurrence, I wonder what he wants.' Jim's eyes narrowed, a frown creased his weathered face.

'Peter Sullivan? The lawyer bloke with the Red BMW? The guys at the garage mentioned him. Owns the big white house on the bluff.' added Rory. He looked at the man. He was short, stocky, heavily built, but he looked 'hard', powerful, a shock of curly grey hair, his complexion tanned. He was smartly dressed, a tailored dark grey pin stripe suit, white shirt, no tie. He didn't greet anyone, and went straight to the bar, and began talking to Cheryl. Sullivan's presence, and dress, stood him out, even more than himself. Calder and Sullivan, weren't dressed in the rough, casual way of the other patrons.

Rory hadn't seen the look on Bland's face when he'd mentioned the information he'd already obtained. The older man though expanded. 'That's right he's a Lawyer. And yes, he owns the big white house on the point, his daughter's married to that guy over in that corner,' He waved a hand at the far side of the bar. 'And she's a friend of Cheryl's, you spoke to her earlier. Sullivan keeps to himself, mostly, but occasionally pokes his nose into local affairs, and the affairs of others, if you get my drift. You're already well informed aren't you Rory, interesting that.' Bland continued his stare at the 'Lawyer at the Bar', as he spoke.

Rory went to the window and looked into the street. The red BMW was parked across the street. A girl was sitting in the passenger seat. He glanced across at the man deep in conversation with Cheryl. He went back to Jim Bland, who was still watching the man as well. He wanted to ask how the hell Bland knew that he'd spoken to Miranda, but instead, 'So that's his daughter in the BMW?.'

Rory watched the old man's face as he answered, a veil fell over his eyes.

'Uh, yes - that would be right, tall good looking girl, not like her old man, both good lookers though, although he's not exactly my type, her mother was a stunner.' Bland grinned at Rory. 'He doesn't approve of the husband, thinks he's a bit of a layabout, actually he's not wrong, and he tends to hang around with the slightly rougher element in the village, fishermen and others, that make their living by more dubious means.'

Rory thought of questioning further, particularly after a rather different story by Cheryl. There was obviously more to this scene than met the eye, and Miranda hadn't been too friendly, when he had strayed onto their land. He turned back to the group of men and listened to their chatter about races, and oncoming Rugby season. But his eyes were on the man at the bar, there was something about him that seemed familiar, but he couldn't put a finger on what it was. But it was the name, and the occupation, he had been given by Mr. Moorhead!

The conversation held no interest. He excused himself and went to the bar to get another drink. The men he'd been with, were 'school drinking', each shouting a round. Rory had no desire to become involved, it was not his scene, nor was the conversation. He'd played Rugby, played it very well, and he occasionally drank beer, but had no interest in Horse Racing.

'Well, I wanted time on my own, so I suppose if I'm not going to mix with the locals, I might be able to have it. However at the same time I don't want them to feel that I am a bloody stuck up snob, it is important to keep the lines of communication open! After all that's the main purpose you twerp! Communicate – investigate!' He muttered to himself as he threaded his way to the bar. The room had filled considerably since he'd come in, it had been a fine hot day, and he could see these were thirsty people.

Cheryl glanced down the bar at him. He was the only one waiting to be served. She excused herself from Sullivan and came to where he was standing.

'How's it going stranger?' she smiled at him, 'how've you been finding the locals? A few more than we usually get on a Friday, must be the hot weather, -- would you like another Lager?'

'No, I am not really, I'd like a wine please. One or two beers is my limit, and only on a hot day, or,' he smiled warmly at her, 'with excellent fish and chips. So what do you have, something white and crisp, or would that be asking too much in this lovely little town?' Rory's mind swirled round his words, 'Why the hell am I talking like this, all I want is a bloody reasonable glass of wine!'

'Ooo! I hope we're not being sarcy! You've only been here ten minutes, and we're getting picky!' Cheryl chuckled and smiled though, she knew that he was only joking. 'We have a good selection, partly because we do have people coming through and asking, and partly because I myself, and a few discerning patrons, who enjoy a reasonable glass, most days in fact. I don't suppose that you'd want a whole bottle? So by the glass we have,' she turned and looked at the fridge, 'A good Riesling, a good Chardonnay, a good Sav Blanc, and a very good Pinot gris! Or you can have the cardboard if you wish.' She knew very well that he wouldn't be having that!

Rory became aware of the man watching him from the other end of the room. He had moved there when Rory had come up to the bar. Although he was in conversation with someone in the corner, Rory could feel his eyes on him. He kept his own slightly averted, and concentrated on what Cheryl was saying.

'Is the Riesling a dry one?' He asked quietly

On her acknowledgement he ordered a glass. As Cheryl poured, he commented on the man she had been in conversation with.

'Oh yes, Sullivan, lawyer guy - works from his house on the point, not sure what he does from there, goes to the city about once or twice a month, big wheeler dealer they tell me.' Cheryl seemed suddenly off hand, not wanting to talk.

Rory watched her closely, he suddenly knew there was something here in this town that he didn't like the smell of, and it wasn't the fish. Why was he being fed a load of shit, one story here, another there. They had from each teller of the tale, a different tone. While it appeared none of it was any of his business, he felt that it very well might be.

He didn't see any point in the deception -- the stories of a few people to a stranger were of no consequence, unless "they" whoever they were, didn't want him or anyone else, to come in, feel comfortable – accepted. But why should they feel that way? What threat did they think his presence imposed on the people in this small community? Even though he knew that it may well do so – how would they know at this stage? Rory could feel Sullivan's eyes on him, as he moved from the bar to an open window. He leant on the sill and gazed casually out into the street. The girl, Miranda was no longer in the car.

'Looking for something or someone Calder – or is it something else these days, something more incognito?' A voice behind him.

Rory turned to find Sullivan standing close to him, the chatter in the bar stilled as everyone watched them.

'No not really,' Rory ignored the piece about his name and kept his voice even, friendly. He smiled at the stocky man. 'I'm just enjoying the evening air, gets a bit stuffy over by the bar don't you find?'

'I hear that you have been wandering around, looking into places that are none of your business - private property. I also know who you are, and why you're here, and,

I'm not sure that I, or some other people like the idea. Perhaps you might be better to move on - to somewhere else.' Sullivan's tone was friendly, he was smiling as he spoke, but so quiet that what he said, was not heard by the rest in the bar.

Rory didn't answer immediately, he listened to the silence in the room, but didn't take his eyes off the man. After a minute he replied.

'I don't see that it's any of your business what I'm doing here. Do you own the town? The big lawyer man in the big white house with the pretty red car. But no, you may think you do, and some other's here may let you think that. However, as far as I have noticed, this is a country where one is relatively free to go to where one wishes. As long as they're not breaking any law, they may stay and do whatever. As a lawyer you should be aware of that. Besides, I was following the directions, I must have taken a turning in error. Now if you will excuse me I'd like another glass of wine.' Rory walked past him to the bar. The patrons returned to their drinks, but voices were more muted than before, it was obvious that the topic of conversation had altered.

Sullivan made to follow and continue, but he knew he had lost round one. The look back from Rory said - 'I wouldn't bother if I was you'. He turned and left the bar.

'What was that all about?' asked Cheryl.

'I thought you might know, you were talking to him long enough, he seemed to know an awful lot about me.' Rory's tone was cool.

'Yes, he did, didn't he, in fact he told me a lot about you. It seems he feels you're an undesirable in this town – why? He said something about your wife and family, and that you could be trouble. What's this all about Rory?' Cheryl's tone seemed to indicate genuine concern.

'Could I have another wine please, in fact I'll take the rest of the bottle.' He ignored her questioning.

'Yeah, sure fine, look I know it's none of my business, or for that matter anyone else's, but perhaps you'd better watch him. He really doesn't like you, and before you ask,' Cheryl looked a little embarrased. And well - yes, I told you a load of crap and rubbish about Miranda's parents, and her Grandparents. Sorry, that's what she likes me to tell any nosy people, not that I think you are, and yes that guy is her father. And be careful, Bland really is her Grandfather. If you really want the low down the truth, I'll tell you, later. That's if you decide to stay around, and from the look on your face I'd say that you don't like being told what to do, and where to do it - right?'

Rory took the bottle, nodded, and grinned. He went back over to the table where Jim Bland was still talking to his friends.

'I thought you had two whiskies and went on your way - at least that the story I've been told, must be a load of rot, like some other's I've heard today, is it okay if I rejoin this merry band of men?

Jim looked at him as he spoke. 'Most definitely, you're already a celebrity here, not in town a day and you've annoyed the man on the hill - or perhaps as the song goes - "The fool on the hill" - what's this all about young fella - want to tell us the guts, or don't you know either?'

'There are suddenly a lot of questions, and not many answers, and I have no idea why, or what they're about. But I will in time find out. As with most people I have a past - not all that bad. But my wife and three children were killed in an accident not quite two years ago. It hasn't been an easy time, and the Police tended to think I had something to do with it. I was cleared - and no, I didn't have anything to do with it. I don't know what

Mr. Sullivan's agenda is, but this too I will find out. I have probably told you too much anyway. Anyway, I am staying around for a while, despite what the short grey haired gent has to say! Oh yes – Jim – when did you talk to your Granddaughter last? This afternoon was it?'

Bland didn't respond to the last question, his face was as his name. 'Good for you, and you didn't need to bear your soul quite so much - so soon - but you did,' the old man drained his glass. 'Must be off, if you feel like a cuppa tomorrow come and see me. I live down the end of the bay. Take the road to the left of the wharf, it's the second to last house, can't miss it - say about eleven, if you feel like a chat, some local colour and gossip – and maybe more.' He didn't wait for Rory to answer, just patted him on the shoulder as he left.

The bar had emptied over the last ten minutes, there was only the group that he had been talking with, and two others. It was just on seven o'clock. The rest of Jim's mates excused themselves. Rory had at least one glass of wine left in the bottle, he poured it and went back to the bar.

'Is there an eatery in town open this evening? I saw the two Cafes down on the water front, are they open at night?' Rory asked Cheryl.

Before she could answer he went on 'And I know that you probably wouldn't mind cooking for me, but I have already bothered you once today, and it doesn't look as if there will be anyone else wanting a meal.'

'At this time of the year they're usually not so busy, they stay open until nine or so, later if there are people around, earlier if not. You could give them a try, both have pretty good food. But I'm more than happy to get you something, one or two quite often stroll in here for a drink and a nosh, often after eight, so it's up to you.'

'Thanks, I need some air, I'll wander down, see what's going on. Is it safe to walk the streets after dark here?' Rory smiled rather "lopsidedly" half-serious - half not, after the confrontation with Sullivan.

'Oh I think you'll be okay Rory, don't take that bastard too seriously, I know I was chatting and being sociable with him, but he cuts no ice with me, despite Miranda being my friend. Forget him, go out and relax. Sometimes they have a bit of live music, not sure about tonight though, couple of yanks that hang around here play guitar and sing, they're pretty good too.'

Rory thanked her and went into the warm evening air, and walked down to the wharf.

There were a few couples strolling the water front, along the road he could see the cafes were indeed open. A number of people were sitting at the tables by the sea wall. The sun was just lowering behind the hills flanking the village, but it was still touching the water front road. He walked along and asked at the first one to have a look at the menu, it wasn't extensive, but looked interestingly innovative, he asked for an outside table. The waitress said there was only one left. 'On the pavement, on the this side of the road.'

'That'll be fine, thank you,' Rory replied and seated himself, checking the menu, then the wine list on the back.

The girl came back, he ordered a glass of Chardonnay, and told her that he should be ready to order shortly. She appeared efficient, pleasant and attentive, not overbearing, and didn't try to be too chatty. It wasn't that he minded talking to people, it was just at present - tonight, he wanted to be left alone, he needed to think, though this may not be the best place for that!

When the waitress came back with the wine, he asked about the "House Special" salad.

'It's like a Caesar salad, but with extras, the Chef tends to pop in all sorts of different goodies. Always popular. And, you can have a choice of Smoked Salmon, Barbecued fresh local catch, or char grilled Cajun spiced chicken in it, or the whole lot – if you're adventurous. Would you like to order or shall I pop back in a few minutes?'

Because the waitress seemed friendly, helpful, and as there were enough people to keep her occupied, Rory didn't want to bother keeping her waiting.

'Sounds interesting – the smoked salmon sounds good, that'll do fine thank you.' He muttered quietly, not thinking whether the waitress had heard or understood. After the girl had gone, Rory sat back and watched the other diners, all couples, except for one group of four. It was difficult to tell if they were visitors or residents, but after a few moments he decided - most were visitors.

He continued to chat silently to himself. 'You do like playing these ridiculous games! If you were talking aloud – you would attract attention, they may send for men in white coats, bringing straight jackets!' As Rory watched the scene it reminded him of the painting "Party at the Boat house" by Renoir, there was just something about the arrangement of tables umbrellas, the way the people were dressed. It was a content relaxed scene, and for the time being took his mind away from the events in the Hotel.

The waitress came back to the table with his meal. 'You forgot to tell me what you wanted as the additive for your salad, so Chef just put in a bit of each, I decided that you looked adventurous enough to cope, and told him to go for it. Like me - he is also a bit cheeky like that, as well we thought we would treat you – sorry, hope you don't mind, we wont charge you any more.'

Rory was about to retort that she hadn't listened but it was as much his fault, and just smiled. She placed the large plate in front of him, with a plate of crisp French bread, and bowl of Olive dipping oil.

'Would you like another wine?'

'Thank you, I would.' Rory eyed the mountain of food. 'This looks pretty good, but it's bloody big! I hope I can do it justice.'

The waitress picked up his glass, 'I'm sure you will, I wont be a second.' she smiled back at him – showing very even white teeth.

As Rory watched her go back into the building, then glanced around, there were more people arriving. Then he saw, a hundred yards away, coming towards the cafes, four people, he felt himself go cold and prickles ran down his spine. It was Sullivan, his daughter Miranda, Cheryl, and another woman.. They didn't appear to see him, and went into the other Cafe, The Boring Bull.

The waitress came back with his wine. 'There you go,' the girl hesitated, and looked down at him, 'Are you alright, you seem to have suddenly gone very pale, seen a ghost or too much sun today?' She laughed softly, 'That seems a bit of a contradiction does it not too as well? Which is about as silly!'

Rory stammered back at her, also with a half grin, 'Yes, um -- but n - no -- I'm fine thank you, just saw some people that I thought I recognised

- from a long time ago. And, didn't really want them to see me, I know that might sound a bit strange but I just want to be alone, not have to be bothered talking to anyone. I'm fine – really. Oh sorry that sounded rude. I didn't mean you!' It wasn't important that she believed the lie, and he didn't feel he had to say anything, but he had.

As she'd left Rory heard the girl's cellphone buzzing in her pocket, he watched her stop and answer the call. She didn't speak, but several times glanced quickly back in his direction. She frowned and nodded a couple of times before she clicked off and slipped the phone back into her pocket.

He sipped the wine, and took a mouthful of the salad. It was very good, but his appetite had deserted him. Rory picked around it for a few minutes before giving up. He sat back watching the groups of people. His mind ran through the last hours – the conversations, the questions, the answered, the unanswered. What is it -- what is it about this place? The people who are they? The assignment – what is it? They'd given him little background, and of course, he hadn't read the contents of the bulky brown envelope, his 'brief'. But he had enough to make his mind super suspicious! The powers that be are definitely not concerned with my health and well being, but they know that I should, even in my disturbed state, be able to delve and find answers. And am I actually all that disturbed? Am I just making feeble excuses about myself?

'God, I've only been here a few hours, in what appeared to be an idyllic sleepy village, that now does seem to have a dark and sinister side after all. But, was that unexpected? Plainly, and plainly I'm not unknown here. That seems too much of a coincidence, I think that I need to ask a few more questions, subtly of course, perhaps my Mr. Jim the Mayor, may have some answers?'

He hadn't noticed the waitress returning, and he hadn't realised he was doing his "chat out loud" routine. The girl had an odd look on her face.

'Are you sure that every thing's alright. You've hardly touched your meal. I know it's none of my business, but you were talking to yourself. Quietly, but talking, I confess that I do it too,' the waitress smiled at him, 'but it did sound a bit – odd. I don't think anyone else noticed. I really shouldn't say this, but I get off my shift in about half an hour. I know you said that you didn't want company, but the guys who play here start about then, and I like listening to them, I don't have anyone else to share the music with. How about it? I won't be offended if you say no.'

For the first time, Rory took a closer look at the waitress, she was older than he'd thought, in fact, she wasn't much younger than himself. She was of medium height and slim build, with dark brown hair, cut in a bob that framed her oval face, deep brown eyes, a straight nose over very pleasant lips that set off almost perfect white teeth with their red. 'Really rather attractive,' He thought.

The girl watched him closely -- questioningly. 'Well Mr. Mutterer, I might be taking a chance here, you could be an axe murderer, or a rampant rapist, but I've decided that I want to find out! So what about it, can I join you – please?'

They were interrupted, the waitress saw that someone was trying to attract her attention from another table. 'I'll come back in a minute for an answer, which does not alter the fact that I will be staying, having a drink and listening to Rick and Rob.' She went to the other table, apologising for keeping them waiting.

Rory thought about her invitation. Cheryl wasn't at the pub, not that he wanted to spend the evening talking to her, although a question did cross his mind. 'Who was running the place, surely it should be open?' And she was with Sullivan. An odd thing? Or was it? Anyway, there appeared not a lot else to do. Besides, who knows, perhaps the waitress may be able to give a different perspective of this place. She may be local, or she may not. His mind jumped from one thought to another – few of them making any sense. He decided to stay, and began to pick at the food again, his feeling for it grew, the flavours were indeed very good.

The attractive waitress came back past his table, her head at a quizzical angle, he nodded to her with a smile and held up his empty glass. She came over and took it from him.

'Do you like Chardonnay?' Rory asked, she nodded. 'Oyster Bay?' The girl nodded again, now smiling warmly. 'Right then, you had better bring a bottle, then you can share it with me.'

'Great!' she exclaimed, 'I always wanted to spend a night with an Axe murderer!'

The people at the next table looked up at them - rather in quizzical shock, at her loud comment. She grinned at him and disappeared inside, returning in a few moments with the bottle, and fresh glasses.

'I'll be about another twenty or thirty minutes, don't drink it all.' She was off again, bouncing around the tables, attending to customers arriving looking for a table. In fact, as he looked around, there were quite a lot of new comers arriving, some going to tables, others perching on the rock wall, some brought their own camp stools, it looked like a popular place. Rory saw the musicians arrive and go down a side path to the back of the building.

His mood in the last ten minutes had lightened, and he pushed the incident with Sullivan to the back of his mind, and shut a door on it. Not forgotten, just for the moment, out of sight. Rory turned his mind to the waitress, he didn't know her name – at this point, unimportant. He wondered now, what the night would bring.

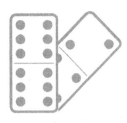

THREE

Sullivan put the phone down. For the second time in the last half-hour. His eyes wandered to the view out of his office window. It faced out to the curves of the bush covered arms that framed the tiny harbour. His thoughts on the man he had confronted in the bar. He'd certainly not expected him to come here, it had been a complete surprise when his daughter had told him that she'd talked to him in the street, and then his appearance on their property. After his questioning her, and her description of the stranger in town, he had checked it with Cheryl.

Peter Sullivan had never actually met Calder, didn't know him personally at all. But he knew a considerable amount about the man – from other sources. He also didn't think Calder knew him or anything about him, but he couldn't be completely certain on that point. Calder, because of his occupation, may know something about his business connections, and those with his wife, Serena. Either way, he regretted now confronting the man. He had uncharacteristically panicked. The first phone call had been from Cheryl at the Hotel, informing him that Calder had gone out to find somewhere to eat, one of the Cafes on the water front. She wanted to get out and had arranged for one of her casual staff to fill in for a few hours.

'Can we meet for dinner, we haven't been able to get out for some time together,' was Cheryl's request. Sullivan had agreed that they could meet a little later. He didn't however, want Calder to see him with Cheryl. They would have to be cautious, it was a very small town. He asked her to keep an eye, when she had located Calder, then to meet him at the Yacht club around 7:00. They could decide then, what they'd do.

The second call had been his P.A. Andrea, she'd called from her car, and was only twenty minutes from the village. Sullivan had been expecting her, but not until the following morning, he told her come up straight to the house, hoping he hadn't sounded too surprised that she was arriving tonight, instead of the morning. This threw another light on the evening.

Sullivan picked up the phone and dialled his daughter's house. Miranda answered immediately. 'Is that husband of yours there with you?' Was his first question, the second was, 'Can you get organised to deal with Andrea, she's arriving in about twenty minutes, I didn't expect her until tomorrow, and Cheryl is meeting me at the Club!'

Miranda's reply was what he'd hoped. 'He's not, he's gone over the other side, you would of course know, with some of his less reputable friends, and wont be back until Tuesday. As for Andrea, what do you want me to do? God, you get yourself into some situations. Did you know about this at the Pub? And, what's this I heard about you talking to this Calder guy? No bloody doubt there's something I don't know, and I am not sure that I want to.'

'Who told you? Shit, news travels fast around here - anyway, never mind that, I might talk about that later, I may not. Just disorganise Andrea's brain, sort her out – you know how, we can all meet for dinner later. Cheryl, at the moment is just looking out for something for me. I'm sure you can square things with Andrea, I'll worry about Cheryl. Now, I'll be meeting her about 7:00, be back home around 8:00, and we will take it from there, is that alright?'

Miranda was silent for a moment. 'Okay, I guess. I'll see what I can do, but what's all the bloody mystery about? And what am I supposed to do with Suzanne, I haven't arranged anyone to look after her.'

'I'll get Francis to come over, she likes looking after her. I'll call her mother in a minute, you just get up here as quickly as possible, I'll leave when you get here, hurry up.' He hung up.

Peter Sullivan made the call, and arranged the sitter for his Granddaughter Suzanne. With that task completed, he dialled another number. It was quite a long time before it was answered.

'Mangus Macmillan, I'm out of office and therefore can't talk to you on this phone. If you need to contact me urgently, please use my mobile number 021 839029 - or just leave me a message and your number. I'll get back to you when I can.'

'Bugger, I thought that may be the case, he would have gone by now.' Sullivan realised he was already leaving a message, 'Okay Mangus, it's me, I guess it's not that urgent, although we'll need to talk, soon. Rory Calder is in the village! Don't ask how or why - I don't damned well know! Why, I've no idea and as yet not found out. I think complete coincidence, get back to me when you can - thanks.'

Sullivan put the phone down and frowned. 'What the hell am I saying! It's only the message machine and I'm raving on like a lunatic! Am I making too much of this? Possibly, now I have another problem to deal with, but then, Andrea knows the story as well.' He sighed, stood up from his desk and went through to the lounge. In the corner near the large bay window was a bar, small inconspicuous, but very well stocked. He opened the fridge and took out a bottle of Iced Finlandia. Poured a good measure over some lemon cubes in a crystal stemmed goblet, added a dash of bitters and a splash of tonic, then went to the window and looked down into the curve of the bay. His mind running back, dwelling on the events of nearly three years ago.

Peter Sullivan had met Serena Calder at a Law Society lecture he'd been giving. She'd asked sensible intelligent questions during the lecture, and he sought her at the function that followed. They had talked for quite a length of time. However his interest was not purely of a professional nature, although initially hers was, and she continued to pick his brains over the gin and tonic. They talked for over an hour and the room had begun to empty, her eyes never left his face as he answered her probing queries. He took what he thought was an opportunity, and asked if she would like to continue the discussion over dinner. To his surprise, and pleasure, she had readily accepted.

That evening had progressed well, they got on well, and had more in common than he had imagined. He was extremely charming, she, extremely interesting and was, was stunningly attractive. His mind started down the track - the track that had led to them beginning what seemed to be a very close liaison in the all the senses of that word.

A sound behind Sullivan brought him back to his present dilemma.

Miranda came over to him and took the drink from his hand. 'I'll finish this - you get out of here. Call me from the club in about half an hour, and arrange to meet us, I'll have Andrea primed, with a couple of drinks and some sort of information, not as yet sure as to what, but something about what's going on tonight. What is going on tonight?' Miranda looked at her father quizzically.

Peter Sullivan nodded and kissed her on the cheek. 'Thanks, good girl that will be fine, and no - not a lot I would think, and I will probably try to keep it that way - I'll talk to you soon.' He left the room, and a moment later Miranda heard his car speed off down the front driveway.

Andrea would come into the property other way from the top road, and wouldn't be aware that Peter had just left.

It was a matter of only a few minutes when Miranda heard another car crunch in on the gravel drive at the back of the house. She opened a bottle of wine and took a couple of glasses from the bar and went out the French doors onto the lawn where a garden table and chairs sat amongst the flower beds. Although the sun was lowering on the horizon it was a pleasantly warm evening, and despite a few large dark clouds gathering above the hills the weather looked settled. Miranda could hear Andrea calling from the other side of the house, and went back through the study to the kitchen door to let her in.

'God, where is everyone, I thought I'd been abandoned! I rang and told his Lordship that I was almost here, where is that rotten slave driving bastard anyway?' Andrea was a tall blue eyed blonde, with an exceptional figure - a fashion plate, with an incredibly sharp brain. She was as efficient at her job as she was loud, but she did work hard, and had the best interests of her employer at heart, in more ways than one!

It's a shame thought Miranda, that the feeling wasn't quite so mutual, her father only used Andrea's abilities to suit his own ends. As he did with most people, including herself.

'He's gone down to the village to the Club, we were down there earlier, but he forgot something or other, he shouldn't be long, that's what he said anyway. Come on I've just opened some wine, and it's rather nice out on the lawn looking down to the bay, it's still warm enough, we can wait out there and catch up. Haven't seen you for ages, you can give me all the dirt from the office and beyond.'

Andrea had a large overnight bag in her hand, she dumped it on the kitchen floor and followed Miranda through the house into the garden.

'So, what brings you down from town Andrea, just to get away, or has father summoned you for a weekend of work. He doesn't seem to be going up to the office as much lately, in fact very rarely. He does however, spend a lot of time in his office here, and doesn't talk to me as much about work as he used to. I guess, this places more of a load on you, and the rest of the office staff.' Miranda was deliberately probing. She had for quite a while, been concerned over her father's activities - or lack of them. He had to a large extent of late, shut her out, and she had always been his closest confidant.

Andrea took a sip of her wine and was silent for a few minutes, staring out over the bay at the last of the sun's rays disappearing below the far land horizon. When she spoke her voice was quiet, thoughtful, as she weighed each word carefully, as if not sure whether she should actually reply.

'I'm not sure what he is doing Miranda, to be honest I too used to be party to his closest thoughts and confidences, but over the last year, I suppose it would be, yes at least that, he has become remote, detached, from his work and the people around him, and the last few months even more so. You are right, he hardly comes up at all, although he does spend a lot of time on the phone to me, it is generally just well - nothing really, I can't explain it, when I get off the phone, it is as if he hasn't really said anything!'

Miranda decided to change the subject. 'About the only gossip here is that there's a new face arrived in town today, some guy looking to live here or something. Cheryl said he's an artist, or musician, something arty farty, name's Rory Calder – you're sort of up on the Artistic, and music world - you ever heard of anyone by that name? I spoke to him on the street, then found him sort of lost, nosing around up here. He said he was looking for accommodation and had taken the wrong turning, I didn't know his name then. He's now staying at the pub. Dad's already had a run in with him, he doesn't like new people - even visitors actually. Mind you, even some of the locals tend to upset him, even more these days than they used to. That's the only excitement around here in weeks!'

Miranda looked across at the other woman and was about to pour her some more wine when she saw her face, behind her tan and make-up she had gone deathly white, as she held her glass out for the wine her hand was shaking.

'What the hell is the matter Andrea - you have gone as white as a sheet - are you feeling alright?'

Andrea steadied her hand and took a long pull at the drink. 'No, nothing, I think that I'm just tired after the week at work. It's been pretty hectic, with his Lordship never bloody there, then the drive down. I should've left it until tomorrow as I'd planned, no it's okay I'll be fine in a minute, and no never. Nobody by that name rings a bell, but then I don't walk within those hallowed halls, and farty circles any more.' She took another drink and the colour started to return. The phone began to ring in the house.

'Excuse me, I won't be a moment, it's probably his Lordship, with some scheme for the evening - or to say he isn't coming back because he's met some mates at the club, help yourself to more wine.' Miranda ran across the lawn and into the house, she picked up the phone as it was about to go into the answering machine. Before she could speak her father's voice boomed through over the noise of the crowd in the Yacht Club. It was always busy with a particular group on a Friday evening, most of them had nothing to do with yachting, that part of the club's function had long since ceased.

'Took your bloody time didn't you, is she there and what are you doing? I need a bit more time here, a few people that I need to speak to.' Sullivan's voice gruff. Miranda could tell he'd already consumed a good few drinks. Before she could reply, Peter Sullivan went on.

'I explained to Cheryl about Andrea, she was none too impressed, but that's too bad, we can't do anything about that. So, you two meet me at the Boring Bull in about half an hour, actually we will meet you along the road a bit, that Calder guy is at the Cow, it shouldn't be a problem to avoid him. Get Andrea well primed, but not drunk.' Sullivan didn't wait for Miranda to answer and hung up.

Miranda stared at the phone, before placing the receiver slowly back onto the cradle. 'What,' she thought, 'is all the tension and fuss about? Surely it's not all to do with this Calder fellow. So a stranger, Artist or whatever the fuck he is, comes to the village, big deal, who cares - I don't,' - she hesitated, 'but some people do – why?' She went back into the lounge, stopping at the window and watched Andrea. The girl was talking intently on her cell phone. Miranda waited until she had finished and put the phone away before getting another bottle of wine from the fridge and going back out onto the lawn. 'And, why does he want Andrea "primed", that's odd too.'

'You okay out here, or would you like to go into the house.' Miranda asked. It was getting darker, but the bay were still quite visible, and it wasn't cold.

'No fine - it's fine out here. Oh, good some more wine, I feel like a bit more. What's going on, was that Peter?' Her voice was calm, composed, now despite the obvious intensity of the phone call and her previous agitation at the mention of this man Calder.

Miranda wanted to delve further, question as to whether Andrea knew Calder, but resisted the temptation.

'Yes, he's at the Boat Club with a few people, and Cheryl, you know, from the Pub. He said that we might as well come down for dinner and to meet them near the Boring Bull in about a half hour. Some reason or other he wants to go there, he usually much prefers the Cow, they have live music Friday and Saturday - oh shit what am I telling you this for - you know anyway, have another glass of wine. Do you want to change and freshen up before we go?'

'No, I'm fine, it's not exactly going to the Ritz is it, and most of the locals don't make an effort to --- ' she didn't finish, 'we'd better not stand out too much had we.' Andrea gave a wry smile, knowing she would stand out anyway.

'Besides I wouldn't want to put Cheryl in the shade would I, and I promise, I will behave in front of her, I remember the last time. She certainly has designs on him, I wouldn't want her to get the wrong impression of me - would I?' Andrea giggled into her glass.

Miranda noticed the affect the wine was beginning to have on the other woman.

'No, and anyway, I think that it went over her head, but it probably would be an idea to be reasonably low key. You know what he's like - he can be a pompous ass, and the moods he's been in lately, well, do we want the volcano to erupt?'

The pair smiled, and chuckled at the thought. Then Andrea became serious. 'He is pretty hard on you, isn't he. You put up with a fair bit, and he hates Warren, his friends and family, so how do you cope with it, his moods? In fact I must admit I couldn't, not long term, despite my feelings, and working for him, those periods of time are enough. Anyway, how is your Dark Warrior Warren, he's not about?'

'Let's not go there Andrea, and we'd better go to that somewhere else, where the smoking volcano may be waiting. Finish up that glass, we can walk down the track to the village, they will probably be waiting for us by now.'

They drained the last of their wine. Miranda went and turned on a few lights in the house and the floodlights over the garden. Then set off down into the bush track. Andrea tried again to discuss Miranda's husband, but was ignored, the other girl walking ahead, only making warning noises about snags on the track. At the bottom, before they went along the water front road, Miranda stopped and turned to the tall girl.

'Sorry, I shouldn't ignore you or your questions, and I shouldn't ignore the fact that Warren is a lazy bludging bastard, who conned myself, and Dad, with his greasy smarmy charm. It got him what he wanted, and now somehow, he has a hold over Dad, I don't know what it is or how he did it, but he does. All he seems to do is hang out with his old group from the other side of the Peninsula, but they never have a shortage of money, and never seem to do anything. I think I know what he gets up to, and that he has at least one, if not two other women. We don't have a relationship any more, in fact since well before Suzanne was born, not that he wouldn't, given half a chance, but I don't give him that half or any other encouragement. I want rid of him, but despite Dad's loathing, I can't get any sense out of him when I try to talk about it. To be really honest - I am worried, very bloody worried.'

Miranda turned away and looked out through the fading light over the bay. 'Now I have got part off my chest let's drop it - for now. But I will admit, I need someone to talk to, and I can't talk to Cheryl about this, because, well because I think that she has a thing for Warren as well. Christ what a tangled evil complicated web! And I wonder too, whose the bloody spider is in the middle of it!'

They continued their walk in silence. About fifty yards along the path from them they could see the figures of Sullivan and Cheryl standing at the side of the road by the rock wall above the water, deep in conversation. They saw Sullivan put his cell phone away in his pocket.

Just as they were about to meet with them, Andrea made one more comment. 'Your father really controls your life doesn't he. I know how he works on people damn it, including me, but he really has you under his thumb. Why don't you break away from here, and him, get away, start a new life. There are a lot of places, interesting places and, interesting people out there, in the big bad world beyond this village. But heh - I know you know that, just reminding you - that's all.' Andrea knew that Miranda wouldn't have time for a reply. She hoped that what she said would have an impact when she had time to think about it, and perhaps respond.

The words did though, strike a chord, penetrating Miranda's mind. She glanced at Andrea, then at her father and Cheryl standing under the tree. She began to wonder how many other people saw the situation the same way, the way this man controlled situations and others, to his own ends, with little or no regard for those peoples feelings - at all.

'He wanted me to organise Andrea and dull her brain, so that she wouldn't see what was supposedly going on with Cheryl, I think he vastly underestimates this lady beside me, and that's unusual.'

They arrived under the tree and they all exchanged the usual pleasantries and greetings.

Peter Sullivan butted in over the babble and forced laughter.

'Right, I've booked the table, it should be ready now, they were a bit busier earlier, and said they were going to be having a busy night. It's quite amazing where everyone appears from on a Friday. I think that a lot must come in from the country, and some up from town, always seems the same. Still I suppose it's good for business, even if they are a bit of a nuisance around the place over the weekend.'

'Stop acting as if you own the place Peter, you've already been told once tonight that you don't, so let's forget it and have a good time, I haven't been out of the Hotel for weeks.' Cheryl looked at the other two as they exchanged glances at the comment.

'Who accused you of that - not that I'm surprised - you do act on the high and mighty side sometimes Peter, whether you do intentionally or not, one of your local mates?' Andrea smiled at him as she said it, trying to make light of it, although deep down she was serious.

'No, it was that guy whose staying at the Pub, Peter tried to warn him off for some reason or other, obviously didn't like the cut of him. Mr. Calder didn't take too kindly to it, and I don't blame him. He seems a pleasant sort of bloke if you ask me.'

The look that she got for her from Sullivan was not exactly friendly, he took her arm roughly. 'Come on, I said enough about that, and you said to forget it and let's have a good evening, so let's do it.' He pushed Cheryl in front of him, and set off across the road, Andrea and Miranda followed a few paces behind, both with concern creasing their faces. Particularly Andrea's, she knew more of this man Calder than anyone, apart from Sullivan.

As they walked to the crowded tables, they could see the "Crazy Cow" (the owners had collaborated on the names) was buzzing with patrons, every table full. Cheryl could see Rory sitting outside the front window, talking to a waitress, who partially obscured him. Besides, she knew from her prior investigation, on Sullivan's instructions, of his whereabouts, and who the waitress would be! She hoped that the girl would keep her normally gabby mouth shut! But as she'd now been warned, she more than likely would.

They went and asked for their table, which as requested, was just inside the door next to the deep bay window, it had a good view of the street, and the wharf. The waiter brought their menus and wine list. Without consultation, Sullivan ordered two bottles of red, his favourite, Merlot. There was no complaint however, they trusted his judgement, and he was paying. After the waiter brought the wine, they toasted, "to a good fun evening", then busied themselves in their selection of food.

This wasn't Sullivan's favourite eating place in the village, he preferred the 'Crazy Cow'. The food was of an equal standard, it was, that here, the staff were male, and at the Crazy Cow, they were of course, female. Although Sullivan certainly enjoyed female variety and company, he preferred the males to 'serve him', they did not gibber and interrupt in quite the same way or frequency, at least not here. There was another matter too - he could see Jenny 'Wilson' working the tables.

Within a few minutes they had all made their choices. Sullivan, as usual selected the fillet steak with fresh asparagus, warm pickled mushrooms and caramelised baby sweet potato. The women both ordered "the catch of the day", pan fried with fresh herbs and lemon butter, garlic paprika potatoes, and a feta and cucumber salad.

It was after the orders had been placed, and the waiter had retreated to the kitchen, that Andrea decided to broach the subject of Calder.

'What's the problem with this new man in town, I believe from what Miranda has told me, that he only arrived here today, that he is some sort of arty type or other, and is looking at settling somewhere on the coast. So how has he got on your wick Peter? You don't usually let people that you don't even know get to you.' She knew that she was treading on very thin ice, and the look that she got from Sullivan was sharp and annoyed.

Peter Sullivan tried to brush it off. 'Oh, I don't know, just something about these types that come down here and think that they can take over with their self sufficient, self possessed ways. Too many of them, getting the area a reputation as an alternative life style place, I just find them irritating and boring, just thought I would have my say, that's all.'

'But,' interjected Miranda, 'he doesn't look like one of "those", he's pretty clean cut, good looking, well built, nice eyes, and seems friendly, even perhaps a little uncertain and shy, and his beard and hair aren't even long and scruffy - so how do you know he's "one of those"?' She suspected that her out spoken ways would bring some repercussion later, but for some reason tonight she didn't care. Some of what Andrea had said had hit a nerve.

'Yes,' continued Cheryl, 'If that's what he looks like, and it is, I don't see that you even have a point about him, not in that respect, he actually does seem, from first impressions quite a decent bloke, intelligent too, and that would be a change to have some more of that around here.'

Sullivan could see that he would be better to get this conversation dropped, so shrugged it of with, 'I suppose so, maybe I over reacted, you could be right.'

Andrea's eyebrows raised a fraction, this was not like him to back down, she had the inside running on this man, and she knew something of the one that had been under discussion. She knew of Calder's wife, and Peter's involvement with her, but not the full story, the details! There was something very uneasy about Sullivan's behaviour. She had noticed it for some time, longer than she had let on to Miranda. Did he realise that all was not as it should appear, was he suspicious of more than he was letting on? She would not let this lie, and would do some delving over the next two days, if the opportunity arose.

The meal continued for the next ten minutes in silence. Miranda had pushed the food around her plate, her appetite dwindled as she thought about the evenings conversations. She became pre-occupied with the activity in both parts of the street. She watched the customers and staff from both establishments. Suddenly she found that she was looking straight at Rory Calder, a group had just left and a woman had, at the same time, stood up from another table beyond them.

'Well,' Miranda muttered she thought to herself, 'he is still around, and appears not to have taken any notice of father here, interesting.'

The others at the table heard her quiet talking and turned to her.

'What was that Miranda?' asked Cheryl, 'I couldn't quite hear you over the noise.' She started to follow her gaze, but Miranda stood up and excused herself.

'Nothing, I've just go to the loo, sorry, won't be a minute.' Miranda pushed past the others and manoeuvred her way around the other tables to the toilets at the back of the building. She locked herself in a cubicle and sat on the seat, she didn't want to go to the toilet at all, she just wanted to get away from the three of them.

The discussion, though brief, with Andrea on the walk down, and other comments that had been made before and since, had disturbed her. She, as with Andrea, felt the tension, and that something, whatever it was, needed to be sorted, but Miranda had no idea what it was exactly, or how to go about it.

FOUR

The musicians came out the alley between the buildings, and went across the to a small raised platform under the trees. Rory noticed the street had been blocked off, as tables were now spread right across the road, from both Cafes. For the first time as he looked around, he actually took notice of the names of them. When his waitress returned to sit with him, he asked whether it was coincidence that they were named the way they were.

'They're actually owned by the same person, although that's generally not known, not publicised, a few may not appreciate their entrepreneurial skills. They work quite independently, and the owner doesn't actually work in them, just manages and organises, and she doesn't live in the village. It seems to work okay.' The girl, as she spoke, kept her eyes and face averted.

'Sounds sort of sensible – I guess. What about the street being blocked off – doesn't that cause a problem? Inconvenience anyone wanting to get through?' Rory was looking around as he spoke, and although what he'd been told about the ownership it seemed not to ring true, but decided, – 'What the hell does it matter, and why should I even want to know?'

'There are ways around the back street, so it's never been a problem. Besides, it looks like as usual, most of the village are here – at least they're supportive – even if some don't spend as much as I'd like – I mean the owner, but most have a few drinks.' She realised that the boys are about to start. The girl sat down and they both concentrated on the wine and the music.

The 'musos' played acoustic guitar, unplugged. Their voices were strong and harmonised well. Old favourite folk, mixed with Beatles, Simon and Garfunkel, Waylon Jennings and Willie Nelson, made up their first bracket. Even though customers continued with their conversations, the singers could be heard clearly above them. When each song was completed the patrons showed their appreciation with generous applause. It was clear that they were very popular, and enjoyed their entertaining.

Opposite Rory the girl was listening intently, when she suddenly turned to him. 'These guys are from - of all places Boston, University boys, just doing a stint around the world in strange places like here! Rick and Rob. I guess they're from pretty wealthy homes to be able to --- Oh – hell, sorry, I don't know your name? And – how rude of me! I haven't introduced myself! I usually tell people my name when I seat them, – you know the routine - "Good evening, I'm Jennifer, and I'll be looking after your table tonight." Bit bloody poncy for here, – so I just say," Hi I'm Jenny", so before I go and get another bottle, that's if you'd like to stay longer, my name is Jenny, Jenny Wilson.' She held out her hand, he took it,. Her grip warm, as was her smile. It hid the darkness that was lurking behind her eyes.

'Rory Calder,' he replied, 'yes, I'd like to stay, and yes, why not more wine?' He dug in his pocket, taking out a hundred dollar bill. 'If you don't mind fixing up my account, and get the other bottle with that as well, if that's enough?'

Jenny nodded. 'More than! Good grief I don't see many of those around here!' She jumped up, and went to the building. As she moved away a group of four from the next table also moved. He looked up, across to the people along the road. Miranda Sullivan was looking straight back at him, then quickly away, a moment later she disappeared.

Rory went back to concentrating on the music, but made a mental note to question Jenny about "the Sullivan's and co". At the right moment. It could be likely, considering her work, she may know something about them, then again, she may not.

'Are you enjoying your evening now? You weren't all that happy before.' Jenny arrived back with a new bottle, refilling their glasses while still standing.

'Yes, I am, thank you, a lot more. Do you always finish half way through the busy part of the evening, seems a bit strange, thought somebody of your efficiency would be needed right through.' Rory looked puzzled through his smile.

'Sorry, I should have said – I – well - I'm actually the Manager. I told you a sort of – well a bit of a 'white lie' before. So – well it's me who makes the rules, well some of them. And I also have a bit to do with the other one, The Boring Bull, I keep a close eye on proceedings, at both places. And if I'm needed or someone is not quite coping, I'm back into it. It all becomes pretty laid back and casual once the boys start their show, most have eaten, and it's just a matter of getting the booze out.' Jenny sipped her wine, watching his reaction to her statement over the rim of the glass.

Having told him not many minutes before, a little about the "set up" of the ownership, she wondered if he would make a connection between herself and the two Cafes - not that it mattered with this man – he wouldn't be here for 'that long' to be a worry in that direction.. She gauged him to be a bit older than herself, she was thirty-one, he, she thought in his later thirties, and quite easy on the eyes.

Jenny would question – she wanted to find out more, but her thoughts were interrupted by one of the staff who needed help. A group of eight who had arrived, they wanted drinks and to eat. It would need a couple of tables pushed together. Jenny raised her eyebrows at him, and as she got up, leant over to him.

'I don't like big groups much, we don't get them often, but we do get them. This lot appear a bit demanding, already 'well on the way'. demanding and obnoxious, and of they're course not locals!. The kitchen closes in a half an hour, apart from desserts. Anyway, sorry about this, I hope I wont be long.' Jenny went off with the other waitress.

Rory settled back in his chair, feeling a little more euphoric, the wine had started to take effect. He returned to people watching. It was certainly an eclectic mix, but it was interesting to observe that people from different tables, and groups were mixing and conversing. His feeling that the place may suit him returned, 'If I've got to be here I may as well feel as if I can enjoy part of it!' But in the back of his mind the confrontation with

Sullivan simmered, and he hoped that it wouldn't colour his feelings too much, but then there was - "that other matter of his assignment – vague and intrusive as it may be" - it had to be considered – seriously – very seriously.

Over the next few days he'd talk to more people, and have a good look around the town. Not just the main street, and the scene he was watching, but check out what else may lurk in the shadows. Was this place a unassuming as it seemed right now?

It was a good half-hour before Jenny came rushing back. Rory had had glimpses of her during that time as she helped around the tables, it appeared that they needed more assistance than she'd expected. He could see that she wasn't in the same mood as when she'd left.

'Sorry, it doesn't look as if I am going to get back. One of the kitchen staff has suddenly gone home sick and one of the waitress's has tripped on a customers foot that was sticking out and twisted her ankle, shit happens usually in threes, and when it does I have to clean it up, and be there for everyone else to moan to that they are getting stressed! Perhaps we could catch up tomorrow, would that be okay? What about lunch?' A voice called out to her, a panicked tinge to it. 'Sorry got to go, call in here if you want to, about twelve thirty - please?'

Before he could even think of an answer she was gone.

Rory thought, 'I could wait until things quieten down – I've nothing else to bloody do'. He sighed and started to feel the fatigue of the day, and the wine. He decided to pack it in and go back to his room at the Hotel. He stood up and walked a little way away from his table, listening the musicians for a few more minutes, still casting his eye around for Jenny – but there was no sign of her – which he found strange if she was having to fill in.

After ten minutes Rory turned away and walked back up the road to the wharf.

The evening was fine and warm, a gentle breeze wafted in off the water carrying the smells of the sea, and night scents of the bush. At the end of the jetty, Rory decided to prolong his walk, and wandered slowly out to the end, where one or two couples sat on the seats talking, several boys were still trying their luck on the ebbing tide, they'd each caught a number of sprats and piper that wriggled in a bucket.

As the music and chatter from the Cafes crept out over the bay. Rory made small talk with the boys, and the couples about the weather and the beautiful evening, but as he turned to walk back to the village, he felt what could only be described as an uneasy sense of peace. It just seemed to be too good to be true, a good meal, good wine, what appeared on the surface – not withstanding Sullivan – to be idyllic. And a very attractive young woman, who seemed to want to get to know him and had invited him to lunch! All close to perfect? But Rory knew from the unease and churning in the pit of his stomach – that it was too good to be true and he was here to find out why it was not. But for the moment he would enjoy the first feelings.

Rory ambled back to the end of the main street, and sat on the rock wall. For the second time in a few minutes, he reflected on the evening. How it had started and ended, the query from the girl Jenny - to perhaps have lunch - if he wanted to - please. Did he want to? He'd only been here a matter of hours, fleeting hours, in some ways. In another, it seemed much longer. He had certainly not expected what had happened, he had hoped for anonymity - complete anonymity. What he did have though was, 'what has fate dealt me this time'? Was his idealistic dream out of reach - and perhaps this wasn't the place to find it, and this wasn't why he was here anyway! Work first, his direction second - or even a distant fourth?

'Forget your dreams and ideals for another life Calder – just do your job!' It was if Rory could actually hear what his Chief would say if he could read his thoughts at the moment, and he would be right. Despite his attempt to get away – it was just a pipe dream. 'Just do your job – just do your job and forget the air-fairy crap!' He stood up and set off up the road to the Hotel.

Rory reached the old building, and went in through the doors of the Public Bar. There were a few people, maybe a half dozen, but none he recognised from earlier. Most were men engaged in loud conversation, all with their pints perched in front of them, two women sat in a corner nursing glasses of wine. There was no sign of anyone tending Bar. Rory left and went up stairs to his room. The hallway at the top dim, shadowy, with only one of the bare hanging bulbs lit. He opened the door of the flat, went in, closed the door and locked it, an attempt to shut out the chatter and laughter from below. But he opened the two sash windows in the lounge. Soft strains of the music from the water front filtered over the trees and roof tops, but that wouldn't be intrusive.

An old television was on a table in the corner, Rory turned it on, as it flickered into life the first pictures were fuzzy, snow covered, he changed the channel and picked up a better signal, even a touch of colour, he adjusted a couple of the knobs, and managed an acceptable reception. It was an old John Wayne classic, Rio Bravo. He stood and watched for a few moments, then a series of adverts arrived. He looked at his watch, it was nearly half past nine. His mind said - 'I want another drink' his body said - 'No you don't' - his mind won. He went to the kitchen and constructed a gin and tonic, knowing that the combination on top of the wine was probably not wise, but he proceeded with "mind" anyway.

Back in the lounge he sank into an armchair and nursed the drink as the film returned to the screen. He had finished the drink by the next adverts, but before the film restarted his head sank forward and the glass dropped from his hand onto the carpet.

Loud voices and doors banging woke him. Rory felt stiff and uncomfortable from falling asleep in the chair, he checked his watch. It was twelve thirty. Rory got up and stretched, and went over to the door and listened. The noise was coming up the stairs, there seemed to be quite a lot of people attached to it, he edged the door open a fraction as Cheryl, Sullivan, and the other woman he had seen with them, came onto the landing and headed to Cheryl's apartment. He closed the door silently and re-locked it, he turned off the T.V.

Through in the bedroom he discarded his clothes and crept into the bed, the sheets were cool, crisp and clean. He was soon asleep, despite a sense of disquiet over the sight of the people going down the corridor.

Rory was woken by the noises of the morning, the birds in the nearby bush, a few cars and trucks moving through the streets, and the sound of movement down stairs, clanking and banging. When his head registered, he supposed it would be someone cleaning from the night before. There was the knock on his door. He struggled out of the bed, feeling a little seedy, but considering the previous day and evenings activities, he wasn't too bad, he pulled on a robe and went to the door.

As he opened it he was greeted by a bleary eyed Cheryl. 'Hi, how are you this morning, hope we didn't disturb you last night, I had a few friends back after we went out – um – got back - dinner. I thought I heard your TV as we came upstairs, thought that you were still up – and ah – well.' Cheryl fell silent for a moment, then. ' Would you like some breakfast? It'll only take a moment to do you something, fried eggs and bacon – whatever sort of thing - you know, toast and such, if you like. I'm doing some for myself, and the left overs from supper last night, with – they - who um – are – um still - but we won't talk about them.'

Rory ran his hand through his dishevelled hair, first wondering about "those other people" then the thought of food. 'No, well, yes maybe, that might be good, thank you, shall I get organised and come down to your place? Say in about fifteen - twenty minutes?'

'No,' Cheryl smiled at him, 'I'll bring it along to you, I'll be only ten minutes okay?'

He nodded, 'Yes fine, I'll have a quick shower and try to sort out my brain, I think I may have indulged a bit too much yesterday and last night.'Rory closed the door as she went back down the hall. He went into the bathroom and turned on the shower, then spent the next five minutes letting the water refresh and cleanse. By the time he had finished, and dressed there was the knock on the door.

Cheryl stood there with a tray laden with food, fruit, cereal, juice, toast, eggs and a plunger of coffee.

Rory received the tray with an enthusiastic "Thanks", and took it back into the room, placing it on the small dining table.

Cheryl smiled 'Not a problem only too happy to do that for you.' As she pulled the door shut he could hear the voice at the far end of the corridor. They were raised and more than a little heated.

Rory sat down to the breakfast, he frowned with thoughts of, 'those people'. The disquiet of the previous day returned, and the feeling that possibly he was in the wrong place at the right time, invaded. 'But was he?'

'I must give myself, and them more time. I'm being completely paranoid, theirs, and particularly Sullivan's attitudes, probably have nothing at all to do with me personally now - or my past. Every time that anything happens, reactions and interactions, are not what you think that they should be. You dive back, and delve into the incidents of the last two to three years. Forget it - get on with what you have to do and where you want to go. If it's not here, does that matter? You, as usual, are not giving yourself or anyone else, the space for the mind to expand and absorb what is around. Then it absorbs all the wrong signals - or does it?'

During this "mind talk" he'd been staring down at the food, he shook himself out of it, and picked up the orange juice, drank it down and poured a cup of the coffee. He began on the of the breakfast.

As he finished there was a knock at his door, he went over and opened it to find Cheryl there. 'I just thought I'd see how you're getting on, and take away the bits and pieces if you had finished. Was everything alright?'

'Yes, excellent thank you, I'll get the tray for you.' Rory went back to the table and stacked the dishes. As he handed it to her he could see over her shoulder down to her open door. Sullivan and the woman that had come up with them, were standing back from it, but in clear view, they were watching him as he handed Cheryl the tray.

'Still got your guests I see, must be good friends to still be around at this time of the morning.' Rory couldn't resist the next comment. 'I thought you said that fellow who berated me in the bar last night, wasn't a friend of yours. I must have been mistaken. Anyway, thanks again, that's set me up for a while. I think I'll have a really good wander around today, try to get a different feel for the place, if you get my meaning.' He placed especial emphasis on the last two words.

Cheryl flushed slightly, stammering. 'Um, well, yes, I may have - um given the wrong impression, I suppose, I well, I um, I'm sorry if I did, not intentional, I probably - well you're a stranger and --.' Her voice trailed off with the embarrassed blush.

'Will I see you later in the bar?' Cheryl's face reddened more. Almost a plea of - "Please, I would like to explain and start again".

'I might pop in, don't know really, I'll just see how the day goes. There are some things that I like about the place in the short time, other's well - I will just wait and see.' Rory smiled, but not with his eyes. Cheryl went back down the hall with the tray. The others in her room, had continued to watch the whole proceedings. As he closed the door Rory made a decision to find other accommodation. If he was going to stay around here for any length of time, this would not suit, and it appeared that he would very much have to. He wondered whether Cheryl would relate his last comments to her friends.

'What do you mean "wonder if" you bloody fool, of course she will. But why had she played this little game. It was now quite plain that she was - "A very good close friend of Sullivan's".'

Rory went to the bedroom tidied bits that he had left around, and made the bed, and collected his wallet. He went into the bathroom and cleaned his teeth, then brought out his toilet bag, placing it against the end of the large bag. He took his robe, folded carefully, putting it exactly half way up the the bed.

Back in the lounge, he opened the window to let fresh air in. Although the place was clean, it still had a rather peculiar perfume, he presumed that it may have been left over odour from when Cheryl had last lived there, or residue from the bar smells from below, it didn't matter what it was, he didn't like it. But he had another reason too for leaving it open, the fire escape was right outside it. His suspicious mind was beginning to work over time.

Rory left the flat and locked the door, there was no sign of anyone and there was only the sound of a radio, coming from the bar. He went down the stairs and out the back door to his car. He hadn't locked the old car the previous night, now realising that he should have, but when Cheryl had helped with his bags he'd forgotten, and hadn't returned, still, what was there to steal - apart from his cellphone.

There was certainly nothing to indicate who he was, why he was there and what he intended to be doing – whether he wanted to or not. Rory rummaged amongst the glove box debris and retrieved the phone. The thought struck him – 'Nothing to steal' - except – the numbers in his phone! For some reason, he thought he wasn't going to need it! It was a strange and ridiculous notion! Even if he disliked the small instrument and the way it was changing life, but he wasn't completely stupid, he knew it was a very necessary piece of equipment.

Perhaps his 'cover' idea of supposedly to be 'getting away from it all – the past and the future', had muddled his thinking about the phone? But that high flying idealistic crap had dissipated. He dropped it into the pocket of his shirt. He didn't, as he locked the car, see the three pairs of eyes watching him from behind the sheer curtain of Cheryl's apartment.

At the back of the Hotel was a gate. An old arrowed sign, faded and partially rotten indicating a track. "To Botanic Gardens". He headed out it, thinking what an odd place this was to have Botanic Gardens, that they must be a relic from when the area was first settled, someone with grand ideas of what this town could become? Rory pushed open the old pickets, it creaked on rusty hinges, threatening to fall off, but somehow held together. He disappeared into densely packed trees, and bushy under growth, an old cobbled path almost invisible.

It was his idea that it would lead him back out someway to the waterfront, then he would double back, down to the far end of the bay to where Jim Bland had directed him to come for a morning cup of tea?

From what he had seen of Mr. Jim 'the mayor' Bland, he doubted that it would be tea, but there he could be wrong. After a couple of hundred yards he emerged into an open area. In the middle of the long grass stood a fountain, or what would have been one once, now grey and moss covered, it had been, he could see, at some stage quite grand. About fifteen or so feet tall, with horses and lions Rampant, around what he supposed was a Warrior of some sort, unfortunately not too recognisable now, the head had gone!

As Rory walked over the old broken paths to the far side, he could see the planting's of the past. Some were rotten and broken, others, still robust and flowering. It was difficult to make out the overall plan, as overgrown trees growing into each other, with vines, and creepers now covering most of the area. Where there had been beds of flowers and hedges now only weeds prevailed. It was a sad sorry sight, and he wondered – why?

Rory took a path to his left, it appeared that it would go towards the water. It lead between high native trees and wound beside a small stream that must also have been a feature of the grounds. Shortly he emerged at the back of the camping ground. A War Memorial, in better, though not much, repair than the fountain, the names of the fallen of two wars stood beside the path. It seemed that the whole place, including the camp, had been part of this Botanic park.

A deep sense of melancholy swept over him, and he decided that after his visits to Jim Bland, and then lunch with Jenny, he'd drive up the coast for a few days, he needed to reflect, sort out a few whys and wherefores! There were more reasons than he cared to think about right this moment - what he was investigating – and where it would lead? Why he'd actually been sent, and what he may actually find? He then realised that he still had not taken the time to read the brief dossier!

He shook his head to clear a space. Would a couple of days away then back to business, be the best call. Even in the short time he'd been here, too many questions had been asked, and not enough of them from him! And certainly not enough answers!

A brisk sea breeze had sprung up and was rippling the water of the Bay into tiny white caps, on the far horizon beyond the pincers of the points, dark clouds were gathering. Rory could feel the warmth of a northerly wind as he walked across the camping ground. It was even in a worse state than he had imagined when he had walked past the previous day. A continuing feeling of decaying dread, and despite the warm air, he felt a shiver run down his back.

Rory gained the road, and crossed to the far side near the sea, and headed back towards the town. As he came to the end of the Jetty he turned onto and ambled to the end. Seating himself on the same bollard he had the day before. He looked at his watch, it was just before eleven, he slipped the cell from his pocket, and pressed a pre-set number. It was answered straight away, by a young, well-spoken female.

McGillveray and McGillveray, you're speaking with Sarah, how may we help you?

'Hello Sarah, doing your Saturday morning legal stint again? How very civil of you. How are you? It's Rory, is Euan in?' His friend was the only lawyer he knew who opened his office on a weekend. He always had so much work, he found that he had to go in anyway, so dragged everyone else with him. He paid very well, so they didn't grumble.

'I'm good thank you Rory. Yes he is, just hold a sec, he isn't in his office, but he's not far away. Hell, it's good to hear from you – seems ages! Do you want to hold, or shall I get him to call you - wait on, he's just come through the door, didn't tell me he was going out for food, the mean bugger, I'll put you through. Perhaps we can catch up sometime soon?' Sarah's voice bubbled.

Euan McGillveray was Rory's close friend and solicitor. He hadn't spoken to him for several weeks. There had up to now - been no need. Sarah was his secretary, personal assistant, and step daughter. Rory had known her since she was seven, he was he thought, like an honorary Uncle, though sometimes, he thought that she didn't see him in quite that way. He was very fond of Sarah, and after Serena had been killed she'd been a great personal help to him. They'd spent hours on the phone, consumed many coffees while in conversation in Cafe's, and had had a number of 'long lunch' engagements, and dinners – where they had substituted wine for the coffee!

Rory heard the phone in Euan's office ringing, a moment later it was picked up. 'Who are you? Where are you and what do you want? Very busy can't help, try another sucker.' It was typical of Euan, he knew who was on the line, as Sarah would've informed him.

'Hello you miserable stingy bastard, and how are you too.' Rory heard the chuckle on the other end, then a door close. 'Can you talk now that you've removed that wanton woman from your office?' Euan's business partner, Maxine was his close friend and business associate, and his long time lover. They had lived together for eighteen years, and had then married. Euan's first wife had died very young, some twenty years previously from cancer. Sarah was Maxine's daughter, and had become

Euan's by adoption after Maxine's first husband had simply disappeared, walked out on them, when Sarah was three. He was never seen, or heard from again – despite vigorous investigations by Police and Private sources. They were still extremely protective of her.

'Yes, it's good to talk to you to, where the hell are you, you sound like you are in a cave a thousand miles away, and what's that squawking noise, are you killing something or someone?' Euan queried good naturedly.

'No, they're seagulls, I'm down 'Coro' way, and I don't mean the street! I'm out of town for a while, not sure how long really. I'm looking for a place to semi-settle, you may remember all the years I've talked about it, now I'm looking. But that's not what this is about. The main reason is - I also have an assignment bugger it. But that's not what I have called about, though – um – well it might be – anyway firstly – it's about the past, an unpleasant part of it.' Rory hesitated, he knew he was hedging – beating around the bush - he wasn't sure how to explain it.

'Something or more to the point someone, has cropped up, a weird coincidence perhaps, I'm not sure, it's possible it does has something to do with work, but I'm unclear as yet. You know when Serena was killed, and I got those funny crank phone calls warning me about someone named Sullivan, I took no notice at the time, other things took priority. Anyway I'd like you to do a bit of Dick Tracey for me, are you over worked at the moment or could you spare me a few hours, I'll even pay you for a change, I feel that it's almost that important.'

'Yes, I am – always, no you don't have to pay and yes, I remember. So as I'm not over the top this coming week. Just preparing a lot of court crap, that's coming up over the next couple of months, so how can I help? I can let you have a hour or two, are you coming back to talk to me about it, or are you giving me my instructions now?'

'No, I don't know when I'll be back, in a few days a week or whatever, who knows, you know me, can never make up my mind these days. Look, just to start off - get me any gen you can on a Peter Sullivan. He's supposedly in your profession according to sources, it may be so, it may not, and I guess could be more than one. The name that weird-o caller gave me was James Peter Sullivan, very close but who knows? But, there's a Peter

Sullivan here, and he seems to know a lot about me, and doesn't appear to like me, at all.' Rory stopped talking expecting an instant reply.

There was a long silence before McGillveray spoke again. His tone of voice changed and had a strange suspicious note of distrust in it.'I don't know – well, yes, possibly, okay ---- I'll ---- see what I can do,' a long pause, 'really he doesn't sound familiar, he could be one of us, mind - I don't know everyone.' Another pause. 'Got to go, someone's knocking on the door. I've an eleven o'clock appointment. Call me Monday. If you are still able.' The line went dead.

Rory stared at his phone. 'What the bloody fucking hell got into him, that was not - well - wasn't what I expected? He sounded agitated, strange – not his usual self at all.' He frowned at the phone, then shrugged. 'He must've become preoccupied with his client's arrival. I'll call him first thing Monday, perhaps I shouldn't have bothered about this until I got back. But when will that be? Also should've asked him to do a search on Moorhead, that should've been done that a long time ago. What the hell did he mean – 'If I'm still able'? What a bloody peculiar remark!'

The sound of a horn blaring at the end of the wharf tore him out of his thoughts. An old battered Land Rover was parked across the end. Jim Bland was waving at him. He stood up and jogged to where the old man was parked.

'Are you on your way to my place or just in a bollard sitting competition?' Bland gave the younger man a wide smile. 'Well, now you are on your way to see me, like it or not, get in, and I'll show you a few of the sights on the way.'

Jim Bland turned up the main street, then took a left just past the Hotel, into a narrow windy unsealed road, it quickly rose up into the bush. The old man expertly manipulated the rattling vehicle over the potholes and ruts. 'Thought I might take you to see the lie of the land from another vantage point, not many go up here now, actually not many know about it, and the locals neglect it. Used to be a favourite evening spot for couples years ago but we don't have many of them left either, at least not ones that can be bothered coming up here.'

After five minutes of bouncing and swerving around sharp corners, they came out onto a plateau, the metalled surface over grown with weeds and small scrubby bushes. At the back of this, old falling down corrugated iron buildings, and rusty rail wagons lying beside a narrow gauged line.

'Used to be a 'coal mine here, yonks back,' Bland explained, 'they thought there could be a lot of gold, actually there was for a while, 'til the seams ran out. Kids used to play here, then one fell down an old shaft, they never found the body, it seems it disappeared into an underground stream, now people get a bit spooked about the place, silly buggers.' He'd parked right up at the edge, there was an old barrier, but it didn't look as if it would stop a tricycle, never mind a Land Rover.

They got out and looked out at the view across the valley. It was not as high as the road he had come in from on the other side, but it gave a different perspective of the area. The sun was still shining strongly on the town, but the clouds that had begun to build earlier were now beginning to tower and blacken, and the wind now westerly was strengthening.

'Looks like a good blow on the way, bit of thunder and heavy rain I would reckon. Often get that around here this time of the year, but then, I guess you know that.'

'Yes, I've spent a bit of time down here over the years, and besides, the whole of this part of the world from west to east gets it from time to time. Can be quite exciting - if you like that sort of thing, can rev a few people up though, cats and dogs aren't so fond of it.' Rory felt that he was gibbering and fell silent, but he didn't remember saying to the old man that he had been here before – strange.

The old man waved his arm and pointed down to the far end of the bay, where Rory had noticed the two old houses the day before, when he had stopped on the far hill top.

'That's my little burg down there, been there a long time, and it looks like it, but I enjoy the place. Mind, I keep pretty much to myself these days, since my wife passed away twenty five odd years ago. And I gave up my civic duties, such as they were. It's not a difficult place to administer, or it wasn't, now it's controlled by the District Council, and we, for the size of us, get a reasonable deal, so nobody really worries much.'

Bland spent the next ten minutes talking about what he considered points of interest, old historic sights, buildings, farms and so on, and talked about some of the towns past and present personalities.

Rory was about to ask about the Botanic Gardens and camping ground, but Bland interrupted his thoughts. 'So how about we go down now, and have a look at my empire, I hope you don't mind me poking my nose into your time, but, I just find strangers in town quite interesting, and you know I can still learn a thing or two, about life and people. Okay? Shall we get going.' They climbed into the old vehicle, and Jim set it off back down the road to town.

As they bounced their way back, Rory decided to broach the subject of the run down parts of the town he had discovered.

'Why has the town gone back so much Jim, you say the Council gives you a reasonable deal, but I had a walk around, the botanic gardens then past the Memorial, and the camping ground, it's all so run down, yet the hospitality scene seems buoyant. I know it's the weekend and people are still coming down for a break away, but with what you just showed me, and the other things I've seen, it all seems a pretty sad sight.'

'The original settlers, if you could call them that, they were a mixed bunch – from all walks of life – all types from many different countries and backgrounds. Anyway to cut a long boring story – with the mining looking viable, and the fishing looked promising, they had some big ideas for the town. For a while they made some progress, then the bum fell out of the mine, and the fishing turned out to be better elsewhere. Some tried to turn their hand to forestry and farming, but they had little knowledge or skill, and the land was a bit on the unyielding side. Gradually people drifted away, most of the banks closed, and foreclosed as well, but a few hung on. Though we don't have one now – just a bloody money machine! Then it became a bit of a holiday destination, and things picked up for a while. There is talk of a tourist boom on the coast, but who know these days. Things aren't as stable as some would think. But to answer the question regarding the old gardens – the Council say they haven't the money and the locals don't give a damn.'

They had arrived at his gate, or where it had once been, the big posts were still there but that was all, even the fence had fallen over. 'So with no money to complete tasks begun and enthusiasm by the remaining residents rather low, a lot of the grand ideas were shelved and no maintenance done on what had already been started, and as I said - it doesn't look as if it will change.'

Jim Bland looked at his companion. 'Yes, I know it looks pretty tatty and run down too! That's cos it is, I'm a bit like the town - on the outside. Going back to that It's a long time ago, shame really, but no one seems interested or has the money or energy. We've lobbied Council, even the local M.P – but nothing ever comes out of the rhetoric. Sorry, I'm repeating myself – comes with the age!' Jim Bland sighed and fell silent – seeming reluctant to continue. He drove up the driveway and swept around stopping outside the front door.

'Can't change the past. Only can hope that the future brings better. Come on enough philosophising, it's getting hot and sticky, let's wet the whistle.' The men got out, and Jim led Rory onto the front porch, and pushed the door open ushering him in.

Although the clouds were darkening the sky it was still brighter out than the interior of the house, it took a moment for Rory's eyes to adjust. The old man's comment that - "he was a bit like the town" suddenly became relevant.

The bungalow was immaculate. Furnished, decorated and 'ornamented' in the era it was built, the furnishing beautifully kept and arranged. Lamps and vases, statures, all manner of memorabilia. Gilt-framed etchings depicting battles scenes from the Napoleonic era, and a number of original oils, hung on oak panelled walls. Jim's knowledge of antiques and art, appeared to be extensive.

Rory stopped in his stride and stared, taking in all that was laid out before him, Jim's voice from behind cut in.

'Thought it might surprise you,' he chuckled, 'Yes, I know I should make the outside presentable, but I like the old notion - "don't judge a book by it's cover", so my cover's as obtuse as possible. No I'm kidding, I just don't have the energy, the inclination, or the money, so I find it easier to look after the inside.'

Rory regarded the old man, 'No,' he thought to himself, 'I think that perhaps his first explanation is more probable, there's much more to this old gentleman than meets the eye.' He followed him through a door to their left, and found they were in a lounge, decorated in the same way as the hall, and just as, if not more, immaculately presented.

'Take a pew, now what would you like, it's getting near midday, so I think morning tea is out, what about a G and T, that's always good before lunch, or would you prefer something else, something soft?'

'G and T would be fine, thanks,' Rory thought of the gin he'd had after all the wine the night before, and almost changed his choice, but shrugged it off. 'I'm supposedly on vacation, so why not vacate the mind, which reminds me. I've had a kind of invitation, for lunch, twelve thirty, Jenny at the Crazy Cow.' As he finished speaking the room became very dark, a loud clap of thunder shook the old house, the sounds of heavy raindrops smacking on the iron roof made them both stand and look out the window.

'You're going to be late, one, because you're here, having a drink with me, and secondly we are in for a down pour, while I get the drinks call the Cow, and I don't mean Jenny, tell her you'll be a bit late.' Bland paused at the door, 'She's a nice girl, even if rather weird at times. How come you are having lunch with her? You've only been here five minutes, and you get an invitation to have a drink, with an old codger, and lunch with an attractive young woman, you don't waste time do you. The phones on the hall table, the numbers in the little book by it.' He went into the hall.

Rory followed and saw him go down to a door on the right and disappear. He found the number and dialled, as he listened to the ring. He mused, 'I wonder what he meant by "weird".'

Jenny answered the phone. 'Hi, the Crazy Cow, Jenny speaking".

'That doesn't sound terribly complimentary to yourself, are you the Crazy Cow, or are you Jenny speaking, or both.' Rory's voice was light and friendly, he laughed quietly.

'I could be mistaken, but that sounds very much like the muttering axe murderer, have you murdered any axes today?' Jenny's tone was similar.

He was silent for a moment, then decided to tease further, changing his voice to "serious". 'I'm sorry, I think you must have the wrong person,

I would like to make a booking for tonight please, ten people, six o'clock, and have you got two high chairs?'

The pause, on the other end, didn't make him think he'd fooled her. 'Certainly Sir, is that smoking or non-smoking, and can I please have a hundred dollar deposit dropped in, just in case of cancellation and inconvenience, and if it's smoking you will have to be outside under the trees on the far side of the road in the rain,' she paused again, but before he could think of a reply to that. 'And what time do you think that you will turn up to lunch? It was a good try, but besides that, your voice is very distinctive. I saw you go past with Jim Bland, I know when people get caught up with him, time and the people, tend to - well vanish.'

Rory laughed, this girl had a knack of making him feel good, even though they'd only just met, and didn't know her. 'I'll be about half an hour later than you suggested, is that okay, or do you want to leave it to another time?'

'No, I would still like you to come, it's quiet, so I will be able to spend some uninterrupted time with you, it will though be busy again tonight. So I'll see you in a bit over an hour, no more side tracking.' Jenny hung up, and as Rory put the phone down Jim came back down the hall with the drinks on a tray, plus the bottle, tonic, and a bucket of ice.

'God all bloody mighty,' Rory said to himself, 'I hope he doesn't think I'm here for a session!'

As they went back into the lounge the heavens opened and the rain came down in torrents, driven by a very strong northerly wind. The noise on the roof with the huge raindrops, laced with hail was deafening. Jim handed Rory his drink. They stood at the window and watched the ground fill with spreading wide deep puddles, the thunder became more intense and the lightning brilliant against the black sky, the horizon was slashed with the dancing forks, and the bay churned white with water smashing into water.

'How long have you lived here Jim?' Rory had to raise his voice to be heard over the din of the weather. 'I've heard rumours already that you've been here over a hundred years, which is plainly rubbish, so what's the truth, you do seem in the brief moment I've known you, to have an attachment to the place.' Rory's tone was serious.

Jim Bland, ignored the question and drained his glass. 'Come on young fella, you can't fly on one wing, get that down you. Don't forget you have an appointment with a young lady, and from what I know of her, she can be a bit of a fire brand, in the nicest fun sort of a way of course.'

Rory finished his drink, it was just the right strength, a good amount of gin, not too drowned in the tonic, sharp yet palatable, he handed the glass to Jim.

'Well that was not exactly a clear answer was it, you avoiding my question?' Rory raised an inquisitive eyebrow,

'Let's just say for the moment that I don't have enough time to tell you the story.' Bland changed the subject again.'God this is some storm, the worst, or best we have had for a couple of years.' After the first five minutes the thunder and lightning had lessened, but the rain hadn't let up, eased as it often does after an initial onslaught.

Rory looked at his older companion as he took the second drink from him. 'Fair enough,' he tried a change of tack, 'There's another old place next to you, on the other side of that line old trees, who lives there?'

'Nobody any more, haven't for over twenty years, it's been empty, well almost, and locked up for that time.'Bland's face matched his name.

He took another sip of his drink as they lapsed into another silence.

Rory was beginning to wonder about the old man, he'd been very chatty and outgoing, up to a few minutes ago. Until he had asked about the time he'd lived there. He ventured another question. 'Who owns the old place, I see it's got a bit of a jetty out front, is that part of it or is it there by accident?'

Jim looked at the clock on the mantle. 'God the times moving on isn't it. What time did you say that you had to meet Jenny for lunch, one o'clock was it. It's quarter to now, with this storm I had better run you along the road. Come on drink up we have time for one more, then we'll have the two wings and the tail.' He took Rory's glass from his hand almost before he had drained it, and set about making two more drinks. As he handed him the glass, he sat on the arm of one of the big chairs by the window, his shoulders sagged and he suddenly did look a very old man.

'Look sorry – yes – I avoided the questions - as I said before Rory, it is a long story. And that house is part of that story. As I'm the owner of it and all the land at this end of the bay, we, my wife and I, lived in that one for most of the time that we were here together, when she went, well I couldn't stay there, I found it too difficult. One day, if you stay around I may tell you the story, and a lot more about a lot of other things too, but now, let's get these down, and get you into town.'

Rory looked at the man, he saw the beginnings of the tears in the corners of his eyes. He turned back to the window.

The wind had increased and was now blowing the rain against the front of the house, the streams of water on the panes blurred both their eyes. They finished their drinks in silence, Jim Bland took their empty glasses and placed then on the tray, then with a hand on the younger man's shoulder he guided him from the room and together they went out into the storm.

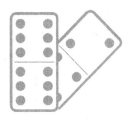

FIVE

Miranda didn't come back to the table after she had told them that she was going to the toilet. She left by the back door, she knew the staff well, and used a pretext of having a chat with them, to get out that way. She hadn't enjoyed the evening, and for some time now, had not enjoyed being her Father's pawn. Andrea was right, he controlled her, and what she was doing, how she lived her life. She had allowed this, and now, she would have to find a way to extricate herself, from him and her husband. It wasn't going to be an easy task. But she would find a way.

When she left the building, she'd walked back through the little alleyways that led to the main street. Down a side road opposite the hotel, running parallel to the water front road, across the football grounds, then through a gate into the back of the towns disused stockyards. It took her about ten minutes before she was at the old house. She knocked on the door, it wasn't that late, just a bit after nine thirty, and the lights were on in several of the rooms.

The door opened, the old man lifted his eyebrows in surprise. 'What on earth are you doing here, I haven't seen you in ages, thought you would be out on the town with your father and your friends, isn't that your usual routine?' The last part of the comments, were slightly sarcastic.

'Can I come in, or do you just chat on the verandah?' Miranda pushed passed her Grandfather into the hall. 'I'm sorry I haven't been to see you. You know it's difficult to talk in town, and how he hates me seeing you, the repercussions – well?' She shrugged and shook her head at that thought.

Bland had stepped aside, and watched her as she walked in through to the lounge, flopping into one of the large leather armchairs.

'I see that you're still looking after yourself, the house is looking great as usual, it really is lovely in here. Why don't you do something with the outside, or get someone to do some work on it, you said you were going to. And despite what you tell people – you can more than afford it! But it never seems to happen.' Miranda caressed the furnishing with her eyes.

'You know why, it would destroy my image. There are few people who know what it's like in here, and the fewer the better, besides I don't really have my heart in all those notions that we have talked about over the years. I think that now, I'm too old too worry. I'm okay, and exterior images aren't that important, you know that, although I know that you find it difficult to live with it - or them - the images I mean.' But the old man was smiling as he followed the gaze of his lovely young granddaughter.

'I know what you mean, sorry, I'm being a pest and a nag. I guess I worry too much about you, but do nothing to help. I also do know that you're more than capable of looking after yourself, and that you should be able to be what you want and do what you think is best for yourself. As I should be doing and don't. Have you got any wine, I had a few glasses with Andrea at the house before dinner, well not as much as her, and at dinner I wasn't in the mood, and left after eating. They were well away and probably haven't realised that I've gone.' Miranda shrugged, 'And – I don't care if they bloody well have noticed!'

'Hmm. I sense one of your deep moods developing,' Jim Bland smiled at his granddaughter. 'I always keep a few bottles around, just in case you come over. Mostly wishful thinking, since you haven't been here since Suzanne was born, and that was what, eighteen months ago?' He stopped in the doorway.

'I admit it hurts me, not seeing you for so long,' the old man sighed. 'Why does this ridiculous feud have to continue? You used to come over a lot when you were expecting. I enjoyed those times, and I know you did too.' His words hung in the air as Miranda nodded, not meeting his eyes. He left the room in search of wine.

Miranda felt the emptiness that her Grandfather felt. She got up from the chair and wandered around looking at the paintings and antiques.

She enjoyed looking at them, and touching, lovingly caressing them, they brought back better memories. Tears began to form, but she brushed them away, closed her eyes and took several deep breaths. Miranda thought back over those past better times, and that she was again in the company of her Grandfather, she started to feel the tension of the evening fall away. She continued to wander the room before coming to a painting that she didn't remember seeing, one, that wasn't in the style of the rest of the old man's collection.

When Jim Bland came back into the room with the bottle and glasses Miranda commented on the work, an oil, hanging over the carved desk beside the fire place, it was an abstracted, impressionistic style landscape. 'I haven't seen this before, I like it, but it's not the usual sort of stuff you have, when did you get that?' Miranda tilted her head to one side and narrowed her eyes. 'She peered closer – can't decipher the signature – whose it by?'

Her Grandfather ignored the question. 'I've had it for a few years. Liked it, but didn't. Had it in the store room. Then a few weeks ago for some reason, I decided to give it a chance to impress me, and hung it. It's starting to grow on me, there is something about it, quite intricate, detailed work when you study it.' He poured their wine, and raised his glass, Miranda lifted hers against it. 'Here's to you and your baby, and to whatever you want to do, but I think you should begin to make a start on that "whatever" soon!. You're wasting your life here with Warren, but you know that, but I guess it's up to you, when, and if you do anything.'

Miranda didn't reply, just looked into his sad eyes and sipped her wine, she turned and looked at the painting again. Her Grandfather sat on the sofa and watched her. They wrapped themselves in their own silence, then she came and sat on the couch beside him. The wine bottle was on the table in front of them, she picked it up and refilled their glasses.

'I believe you were drinking with that guy that's in town, the one staying at the Hotel. Did you hear the comments that Dad made about him?'Miranda kept her tone off hand.

'Yes, but I don't know or understand what it's about. The chap told me a little of himself, but nothing that I thought warranted, or why, the comments that were made to him, does Peter actually know him?' Bland asked.

'He claims not. That he's just tired of down and out arty types, alternative life-stylers coming down here and - as he put it - taking over. But I think that's rubbish. The man doesn't even remotely fit that description anyway. I've spoken to him twice although briefly, he seems alright, what do you think?' Miranda's brow creased , puzzled – worried. There was something definitely strange about the incidents of the last eight or so hours.

'I think I wonder why you're even interested? Don't you think you've enough things to sort out, without worrying about a stranger in town, or why your father's picking on him. He's only just got here, he's probably only be visiting anyway.' Jim Bland became conciliatory – sympathetic.

'That's one of the things that's worrying. Why is he picking on him, if he knows nothing about him? He was having dinner at the Crazy, we were in the Bull. I noticed Jenny paying him a lot of attention. But there's nothing unusual in that! She's like the name of her Cafe – A crazy cow – maybe you should warn the poor man! She can be a real strange and dangerous bitch! And I know, as you do! But yes, I wish things could be different - and we could be more - well together – though I can't really see that ever happening, can you? Not that it's any concern of mine either, so why the hell am I talking about it!' Miranda's voice was tense, an aggravated edge to it. 'And I'm being unfair and unkind – but heh – that's me sometimes these days. But it's more than sometimes, it's just about all the damned time!' She went silent. Her Grandfather didn't comment as she went on.

'No - it's more what Dad is like, he's got himself caught up in something, not that that's unusual is it, but I don't know if it's to do with Warren's activities, or something more. Cheryl and Andrea commented on it too. As well as telling me that he and Warren are controlling my life, but don't really give a shit about me at the same time. Andrea says that for well over a year he has been acting, differently, strangely, not occupied with his work the way he used to be. She's having to take more and more responsibility at the office, and there is of course his other activities with her, and with Cheryl, and who knows who else! Personally I haven't noticed a great deal of real difference. He's always been the same with me – yes controlling – but never without affection, caring. But at the same time, just as disinterested in my personal life as ever – yes – I guess it's all confusing.'

'Have you come here tonight for a specific reason, to see me, for us to renew what we're losing, or to ask advice? Or, just to let out something that's bothering you, and you don't want me to comment. I don't see you for months apart from a brief hello in the street, and now you turn up out of the blue. What's it all about, or is it about everything, and nothing? Has this bloke – this Calder got something to do with Peter? Something from the past? You just never know with that Father of yours would you.' Jim Bland's expression was sad, bemused. But beneath, his mind was moving, scanning all he'd heard - sharp as a razor.

'I'm sorry,' Miranda put her hand on his arm. 'I realise that I should come and talk to you more often, but you know what he's like. In fact both of them, I don't know, Andrea is probably right, I am under their control, at their beck and call, like tonight. I was ordered to look after Andrea, prime her, while he was out priming Cheryl, then the baby sitter is organised and I follow the instructions.' She suddenly got to her feet. 'I'd better get going, I'm not making a lot of sense of this and I have I think, had enough wine.' Miranda swallowed the remainder in her glass. 'Well, I have now. I'll walk home, it's not very late, then Francis won't have to sit too long with Suzanne.'

Miranda looked at the painting again, 'I really do like that, but I don't think it quite fits in with the rest, but then I'm not an expert and if you like it, it doesn't matter. Thanks for putting up with me, I really, really, will try to be more in touch. I know you understand, but it's not good enough.' She was about to say some more when he held up his hand to stop her.

'Yes I do, and that's why I don't press the point about things, I'm getting on now, and really it's a bit like the house. I too know that I should make more effort, be more forgiving, but you too understand.' Her Grandfather put his arm around her and led her to the door. 'Just take care, start to make some decisions for yourself, come and see me again soon.'

Miranda kissed the old man's cheek and hugged him. 'I will I promise.' Then she was gone, half walking half jogging into the darkness.

Jim Bland watched his Granddaughter disappear into the night. Then sighing and head bowed he went back into the house.

Back in the lounge he sank back onto the sofa, there was still half the bottle of wine left, he poured another glass and leant back into the soft leather. He found himself staring at the painting, Miranda had commented on. He became pensive, reflecting on her thoughts about it, his own and her situation.

Later, when he had finished the wine, Jim Bland took down the painting and replaced it with the one that had previously hung there, an intense rich still life that he had found in an antique shop many years ago. The new painting he put back into his storeroom, wondering when the next time Miranda returned, what her comment would be. He may, as she had liked the new painting so much, give it to her. Then again, under the circumstances at this time, he may not. He wondered if the young man had noticed it – if he had he certainly had not commented – that in its self was quite strange – how could he have missed it?

'Where the hell has Miranda got to, she was going to the toilet, not China.' Sullivan suddenly realised that she had not returned. He did not like the thought that she was not there - under his eye.

'Well she probably has gone to China, isn't that what the bowls are made of?' Cheryl was becoming quite drunk, and giggled at her attempted joke.

Andrea looked at her, inwardly cringing, she didn't like the other woman, finding her coarse and common. But because of the situation tolerated her, it appeared to be the only way under the circumstances, to keep the peace with Peter.

'Miranda was not feeling all that well earlier, she seemed restless, I think she had a headache, perhaps she has gone home, or for a walk in the fresh air.' After her comments earlier to Miranda about her father and husband, Andrea had felt a tinge of guilt that she was being disloyal to her employer, and part time lover. But, she did also feel some loyalty to Miranda, she knew more of what went on with Peter and Warren than she was supposed to.

Sullivan shrugged. His mind was already well into an alcoholic haze. 'Oh, well I am sure that we can manage without her can't we.' He waved his hand at the waiter and ordered another bottle of wine.

Andrea sighed, 'It was going to be another of those nights, and we just go along with him. Excuse me I too need the loo, but I won't be long, and I will be back.'

She struggled out from behind the table, and negotiated the packed room. Tables were pushed close together, it was going to be a busy night, it took her a few minutes to get to the toilets, there, there was a queue! Andrea leant against the wall and looked back at the crowded room, she could see the corner where they were sitting, and could see Sullivan leaning towards Cheryl, his arm around her shoulder, his lips near her ear. What she would give to be a fly on the wall and hear what he was up to.

Andrea began to mutter to herself. 'What the hell am I doing here, I am no better than Miranda and Cheryl. We just let him have his way, if I only had the guts to talk to somebody about his activities, those with women and men, and with Warren, not that that is sexual, at least I don't think it is, but with him, who knows. But he has some hold over each one of us. He has managed to dig up some dirt, something that he can use if we try to break the chain, except Miranda. I think that maybe the only way he controls her is because he always has, since she was very young. The father daughter thing, can be very strong and often very destructive, and ever since her mother died he seems to increased that control.'

A woman walked passed on her way back to the Restaurant. 'You can stop talking to yourself and go in now, you were last in the line.' She gave Andrea a smile as if to say, well aren't we away with the fairies! Andrea blushed and muttered a thank-you as she went into the tiny smelly room.

'God I'm losing it, I have had far too many drinks tonight.' A few minutes later she was back at the table. The other two were still in close quarters conversation.

Andrea sat down and picked up her glass, sipping it as she watched them over the rim. She shook her head, sighing, she decided to go into the street, where she could better hear the music, and get some relief from the foetid air in the Café. She picked up a half full bottle of wine and took it with her. They took no notice of her leaving. Outside she leant on the front window and propped the bottle on the wide sill.

'Bastard,' she murmured, 'I'll bet you want it from me when you've finished with her, and I'll probably be stupid enough and drunk enough to agree. How the hell he does it I do not know – well he must have some assistance – no doubt!' Andrea fell into a morose mood as she listened to the singers and watched the people at play.

After ten minutes of her leaning she turned and looked back in the window, Sullivan and Cheryl were standing up and waving stupidly at her. Sullivan went over to the desk and paid the bill, Cheryl came outside and stood with her.

'We'll all go back to my place for a nightcap, the night's a bit young to just finish now, and I'm feeling in the mood for fun, but this place here is getting boring now.'

Sullivan came outside and put his arms around both the women. 'Come on - back to the pub - Cheryl's got a good collection of liqueurs, we can have coffee and a few more drinks and listen to some music.'

Andrea had started to object. 'I think I've had enough, I'll just walk back to your place and leave you two to it.'

'Rubbish, you're fine, don't be such a bloody stick in the mud, it's not in your nature, I know you like a good time so let's go and have one or two or three.'

Andrea tried to pull away, but he tightened his grip on her waist and hissed quietly to her.

'Just fucking settle down Andrea, you are coming with us, so don't bloody well argue.' Sullivan's voice was tinged with venom and the pressure in the side of her ribs began to hurt, she walked off with them, letting her mind go numb.

* *

As she went towards the village Miranda decided that she would go back along the water front road. She would be able to walk on the path behind the trees opposite, and be able to see who was still there, what was going on, maybe even stop and listen for a while, and probably not be seen. She did not want to get caught up with her Father and the others again tonight, she knew what he would want Andrea and Cheryl to get up to, and although she had been dragged into their games on more than one drunken occasion, she had no intention tonight, or ever again.

The lights on the wharf and the street reflected out into the shallow water and partly covered muddy sand, and the music from The Crazy Cow echoed around the otherwise still bay. Many of the more relaxed diners joining in with the singers, a party atmosphere that was quite frequent on the weekends at this time of the year. Miranda stood for some minutes in the shadow of the wharf sheds watching and listening to the music. She could see Andrea standing outside leaning on the window, the look on her face told Miranda that she was getting very drunk and did not look at all happy, but from the angle she was looking from she could not see the other two. The table where Calder had been was empty.

Miranda's Cottage was along the track at the bottom of the cliffs, past the camping ground. Her car was still up at her Father's. There was no point in going and collecting it and she continued her walk along the shoreline, pausing now and again as she got further from the music and noise of the Cafes, to take in the peaceful atmosphere of the night. There were few times that she was able to do this without someone wanting to interrupt, even though there was such a small population there seemed to be few places or times that she could be alone.

After she'd passed the camping ground Miranda could see her cottage, the front room lights were on, and she could see that the door was open. Miranda quickened her pace, the house should be closed and locked at this time. Francis had always been given strict instructions about keeping the place locked and secure when she was there alone with the baby. An uneasy feeling flowed through her, and she began to run.

* *

Cheryl and Andrea sat at the garden table on the front lawn over looking the town. It was mid afternoon, and after a morning thunder storm had passed over the weather was now brilliantly fine, but extremely humid. The sun dragged the moisture out of the sodden ground and surrounding soaked trees, from which curls of steam rose in ethereal wisps. Peter Sullivan was inside the house preparing coffee.

It had been a quiet morning in the Hotels Bar, and after Cheryl's return with the empty tray from Calder's breakfast, the three of them had watched him leave. Then Sullivan suggested they go to his house for a late lunch. Cheryl had made arrangements for her relief staff to look after the pub for the afternoon, glad of the chance to get off the premises, and to spend time with Sullivan. Her lie to Calder about her friendship with Sullivan was forgotten, and didn't seem to have any relevance.

Peter had prepared the food, and they had eaten inside watching the torrential rain and the lightning display. He was a competent cook, and had made smoked salmon omelettes and an excellent green salad, they had again, of course consumed more wine, this time, a very good Australian Chablis. For dessert, they had strawberries and kiwi fruit, soaked in Champagne and Franjelico liqueur .

Andrea, after her argument with Sullivan over the previous night's activities back at Cheryl's flat, was feeling tired and disgruntled. They'd all had far too much to drink, after they had got back to the flat in the hotel.

Sullivan had taken advantage, as usual, of the situation, of the two women vying for his attentions, and it had been his suggestion to Cheryl, when they were alone, that the three of them go back to the flat at the Hotel and carry on the evening there. They hadn't seen Calder leave the Crazy Cow, and by the time they actually returned, he and Andrea weren't in any state to remember. She because of her mood, and him, because of his intoxicated state.

In the morning however, Andrea certainly did recall the events that followed their return. She was neither impressed with her own behaviour or that of Sullivan's and Cheryl's, in fact she felt disgusted with herself, and she had expressed these feeling to Sullivan, when Cheryl had gone along to see Calder. Andrea had ranted her objections in a very loud and angry voice, although now far too late to change anything of what had gone on. Sullivan had pushed her roughly, and told her not to be such a bloody stuck up prude, and reminded her that in the past she had not let that type of thing bother her. The fact that he was right did not improve her demeanour.

It was also quite plain from Cheryl's mood that she had enjoyed herself, and that she was probably not going to let anyone, particularly Andrea, forget, and her attentions to her were obvious that she would like to continue with more of those games another time, with or without Sullivan.

Andrea was about to speak when Sullivan's voice came from the French doors. They could also hear the phone ringing behind him.

'One of you come and get this tray of coffee, I will have to answer that phone. He disappeared back inside. Andrea made no effort to move, and gave Cheryl a look to say, get off you arse and do your master's bidding.

Cheryl went over to the door and went inside, returning a few moments later with a large tray laden with a huge coffee pot, cups, saucers, cream and sugar, a bottle of Port, glasses and a bowl of Truffles. Cheryl was struggling with the weight of it, but Andrea made no effort to help her, somehow she managed without mishap to place it on the table. 'Thanks for your help Madam, what's got into you?'

Andrea was about to reply when Sullivan came out of the house, he had an extremely concerned frown on his face, he walked very quickly over to them.

'There is a problem down in the village that I will have to go and see about, you carry on with your coffee, I'll be back as soon as I can.' Sullivan's hands were shaking and he had gone an ashen grey.

'Are you alright Peter, you look terrible!' Andrea got up and went over to him. 'What's the matter, what sort of a problem?'

'The Police want to see me, some legal or technical matter, don't know, but it sounded important, if I am going to be long I'll give you a call.' He had composed himself a little and was getting back in control of himself. 'Enjoy the afternoon sun and leave some of the Port – I may need it.' Sullivan went back through the house and they shortly heard the sound of his car racing out the top driveway.

The two women looked at each other. 'I wonder what the hell is going on – he seemed pretty upset – but – I guess we might as well do as he said and enjoy this, the coffee smells good, the port looks luscious and the truffles among other things - tempting, besides what else can we do on this bright shiny day, -- although there are other possibles as well.' Cheryl smiled slyly at Andrea.

'Forget it Cheryl, I am not getting into that again. Just pour the coffee and port, I'm going to give Miranda a call, see what she's doing. She may like to come up and join us, now that her Father's out of the way.' Andrea got up from the table, walked quickly to the house and went in through the French doors

Andrea went through to the phone in the hallway. The note book with local numbers was open but she had to thumb through before finding the number, she dialled. The phone rang seven times, she was about to hang up when someone picked it up, it wasn't Miranda. It was a man and a voice that she did not at first recognise, it sounded tense and choked.

'Hello, is Miranda there please?' Andrea asked

'I'm sorry she's not, she's not available at the moment.' was the reply, then a brief silence for a moment - then, 'Andrea? is that you, it's Peter here, didn't you recognise my voice?' His voice was shaky his tone – almost desperate.

'No, it didn't sound at all like you. What are you doing there, I thought the Police wanted your help or something, we just thought that Miranda might like to come up for a coffee, we haven't heard from her since last night, what are you doing there?'

'Andrea, look there - there's,' Sullivan's voice broke again, there was tension and emotion in it. 'There's a problem, an accident - Miranda's been hurt, taken to hospital. Police are here - Dougal and Troone, fire brigade, Ambulance, that's gone now - it's been the whole circus! Some people were out for a walk along the track passed her house, after the storm. They found her lying on the rocks, it looks as if she may have slipped and fallen, hit her head.' He stopped his voice choking again, 'I don't know, it all seems a strange, she never - look I have to go, there are things to work out here, there's Suzanne, I'll talk to you later, I really have to go'.

'Do you want me to come down? Maybe I – we can help, bring Suzanne back up here, anyway where is the bloody baby sitter? Where's Francis?'

'I can't talk any more, I have to go.' Sullivan's voice was getting more agitated. 'The Police want more information about Miranda and last night. I don't think they believe that she fell, but there aren't any witness's.' He began to sound even more emotional, which was quite out of Peter Sullivan's character. 'Just stay there and wait for my call, get rid of Cheryl somehow, don't tell her anything, I don't want her poking her nose in or sounding off to anyone, even if she doesn't intentionally mean to, you know what she can be like - okay?' He hung up, without waiting for an answer.

Andrea stared at the receiver, then slowly placed it back on the cradle, she jumped - startled as Cheryl came up behind her.

'What's going on, you're taking ages, is she coming up or do we have all the coffee and port and things - to ourselves.' Cheryl leaned closer to Andrea and stroked the other woman's lower back as she spoke.

It was obvious from a slight slur and burr to her words that over the time that Andrea has been on the phone, she had been sampling more than just a little of the luscious dark liquid.

'No she's not there,' snapped Andrea as she pushed Cheryl's hand away, 'She must have gone out for the afternoon with Suzanne.' She swung around at glared at the other woman.

'Just before I hung up from Peter 's call, he said he's going to be tied up for quite a while, he wants me to do some work for him. He may need to go up to the city tomorrow, at least I think that's what he said. Someone was talking to him in the background, but he wants me to go over papers that he has on his desk. It is actually what I came down for, and with all the partying last night I had not forgotten – but I guess neglected my duty to my esteemed employer. He is not impressed - but - well to a large extent, in fact most of it, it is his own fault! Let's have some of that coffee and port, then you had better toddle off and I had better do some work, whether I am capable or not.'

Andrea looked at the Grandfather clock at the end of the hall. It was nearly three thirty. 'Perhaps we can all meet for dinner later, I didn't realise it was so late did you?'

Cheryl looked rather non-nonplussed, she was looking forward to another night off and another evening with Peter, but it seemed to be falling apart.

'What time do you think he may be back, I could just wait here while you get on with the work, I wouldn't be in the way.'

'He didn't know, he said he may be tied up for quite a long time, and not to wait around. He said he would ring when he thinks he may be free, and then he would call you about meeting up later.' She looked at the clock again. 'I had really better get on with this work, if I don't he may get into one of his moods, and I am not in the mood for that.'

She turned to go to the office but stopped and said to Cheryl. 'Look have another drink if you must, then clear away the tray, that would be a great help - please - I am sure that it won't be all that late when he gets back, and it is Saturday night, so what does it matter if it's another few hours?'

Cheryl shrugged. 'I suppose that you're right, it's just spoilt a rather nice day, I was enjoying myself. I suppose I could do some work at the pub, it does get quite busy about now, yes, I'll do that, you will call me if anything changes won't you.'

Andrea nodded and headed into the office closing and locking the door behind her, she did not want to be disturbed and have to talk to Cheryl again. She went across and picked up the phone on the desk, she dialled a city number, she hoped that there would be an answer. Andrea did not hear the hall phone being picked up.

SIX

Jim and Rory were drenched by the time that they got into the vehicle. The old man started the engine and set the wipers going. They didn't however, have any affect on the windscreen as the rain had become even heavier. The road along the water front was running like a river, and with the side feeder roads sloping slightly down towards it, it was taking the major brunt, the water was more than six inches deep, in some parts even deeper. The old Land Rover ploughed through, sending waves from the heavy tyres, running the water over the gutters onto the footpaths on either side.

'Do you want me to run you to the Hotel so you can change, you look a bit like a drowned rat, and I guess I do too.' Jim smiled wryly.

'Yes, you do a bit, only a slightly older longer haired grey variety!' Replied Rory. They both laughed at their appearance. 'Feel a bit like a naughty kid late home for lunch. Having been playing in the rain and jumping in the puddles, but I had better stop and see Jenny. Then maybe I should go and get changed, although if this keeps up I will be just as soaked by the time I get back, so maybe I'll just see the way the land lies, it's not that far back to the Pub anyway.'

'Righty ho,' Bland turned just past the jutting verandah, swerving back around, driving over the edge of the gutter onto the footpath, up close to the front door. The old spouting on the verandah was not coping with the deluge and was spilling like a water fall onto the road and pavement, it pounded onto the top of the canvas roof, splashing in the sliding windows.

'We didn't get a chance to talk much today, if you are around tomorrow come back late afternoon and I will cook you some dinner. If you aren't there by five I'll know that something else has come up, don't feel obliged or worry if you don't make it, but I would be glad to see you. Think we have a lot in common actually and yep – a lot to chin wag over – chew the fat my old dad used to say, have a think about it.' Jim Bland had a hopeful look in his eyes.

I'll see what happens, if I'm here, I'll be there, and if not I'll try to get a message to you, or give you a call, thanks for the elevenses, and the ride back, I would have had to swim otherwise.' Rory pushed the door open and jumped out through the curtain of water off the roof, and ran up the few steps to the door of the building. Jenny had seen them arrive and had come to the door, opening it as he got there, he almost fell through it.

'Aha, he has changed from a muttering Axe murderer into a staggering drowned ratty – or a crazed Chameleon! Come in I'll get you a towel. Great weather for it, ducks, Swans – fish and whatever "it" is, but not for Cafe's wanting custom, you are the first person through the door today! Follow me and don't leave too many puddles on the floor!' Jenny's smile was wide and warm.

As they went into the room Rory could hear the girl laughing, as she walked quickly in front of him – he felt himself beginning to smile and laugh with her. He followed her, through the dining area, out the back into the kitchen, where she fetched a couple of big towels, he began to try to dry himself off.

'Do you want to dash round to the hotel and change, then come back just as wet, or shall I drive you there, then by the time we get back we will both be soaked, or I could throw your clothes in the dryer. My brother always leaves a few things behind here when he comes and stays, about once every six months. I live in the flat above, so while they're drying you could put something of his on. I think there's a couple a shirts and some shorts, and some jeans, he's about your size.'

'That sounds the most sensible, aren't you expecting customers?' It was, according to the clock on the wall, now nearly the one o'clock..

'Well if there is anyone coming they will have to have me cook, which

I will now do for my one exclusive client.' Jenny's eyes were wide and bright as she continued to smile at him.

'I sent every one else home when the rain started. I just put the closed sign up. Tonight will be busy enough provided the rain stops, and if it doesn't we will have to build an Ark! Go up those stairs over there,' Jenny pointed to the far side of the main room. 'I'll be up in a second, when I've locked the door.'

Rory went up the stairs to the flat, it was far more spacious than he thought it would have been. A large lounge looked out over the bay, a kitchen at the other end, three other doors went off the lounge, to the bedrooms and a bathroom. He stood at the window looking at the rain. The wind had eased and it was now coming straight down. Out towards the horizon the sky was lightening and a thin line of blue could be seen just above the hills on the far side of the firth. He turned as he heard her come up the stairs into the room.

'Come on through here to the bathroom, and let's get those clothes off. Whoops sorry, a Freudian slip, though ---,' She grinned at him, 'I'll find some dry stuff. Throw out your wet gear and I'll get it started in the machine, spin them first.'

Rory followed her into a well appointed modern bathroom. It was almost like something out of a magazine. 'Someone's spent a lot of money in here,' he commented, suitably impressed. 'Also in the kitchen and lounge, it's a pretty smart place you have! I like the decor, you're very comfortable here, but isn't it a bit of a bind living at work? Did you do all this?'

'Yes – and no. Yes it has draw backs. No I didn't do it – done for me – I designed. Enough talk and information! You're dripping water everywhere! Now get out of those clothes,' Jenny spoke, as she went out of the bathroom. 'Hell! That's twice I told you to get undressed in a minute - doesn't sound too good, does it, I could be a woman with evil intent,' she chuckled to herself, 'and maybe I am. I'll just be a moment.'

Rory waited until Jenny came back with the dry gear, before taking off his wet clothes.

'What a shy wee boy we are,' Jenny jibed. She left the bathroom with her arms full of his wet clothing. 'The washer and dryer are downstairs

– shan't be long, modest man, and you can have your own dry clothes back.'

His underwear hadn't suffered, so he didn't remove them. He pulled on the T shirt and jeans that she had given him, the dry clothes fitted well, Rory towelled his hair, and pushed it into what he thought was some semblance of tidy.

Jenny headed off downstairs to deal with his soggy gear. First the washing machine, to spin as much of the water out as possible. As she began to unfold the wet clothes, to put in the machine, she felt in his pockets. Her fingers found his wallet. She looked over her shoulder – no, he had not followed! Gently, with her eyes wide with intrigue and anticipation, she opened the folded leather. Credit cards, a number of hundred dollar bills, and - two ID cards. Jenny's eyes narrowed, and her mind raced as she stared at the those two items. Quickly, she searched through the rest of the wallet for anything else that might tell her more of the man upstairs. Nothing, in any of the other compartments, just old receipts and notes that didn't appear to relate to anything significant. She inspected the Credit cards, then her close attention was back to the ID's!

'So they were right! – He's not what he may appear on the surface at all! And I see that the appearance of the Chameleon can be so deceptive!' She called up to Rory. 'Wont be long – I'll just get some wine, then throw your gear in the dryer!' She put the wallet to one side – she would slip it back into his jeans when they were dry.

While the clothes were spinning, she opened a bottle of Chardonnay, not asking his preference, but remembering what he had enjoyed the night before, and raced back upstairs. Jenny poured two glasses. 'Cheers axe murderer.' They heard the spinner finish moments after she handed him his glass, the whine of it's slow down, sounding loud, even above the pouring rain on the iron roof.

'I'll be back in a second, amuse yourself for a few minutes, you know – talk amongst yourself.' She grinned at him as she put her glass down, and skipped across the room and off downstairs again. As she disappeared. 'I'll get some grub organised in a minute as well, – nothing much – but something to munch with the wine!'

Jenny put the clothes in the dryer, and set the dial. It started its clunky turn. The sound would be loud enough to mask her voice as she went to the phone and quickly dialled. She made three calls. Cheryl – Bland – and Franklin Primmer. Brief and pointed, with confirmation of each of the other's suspicions.

It seemed only moments before she was back in the flat. She grabbed her glass and gulped a mouthful, and began talking at a hundred miles an hour.

'Shit that's good – nice – and all that – oh hell sorry - sorry, I didn't ask you what you wanted, I can be very presumptuous, a bad fault, but who cares. But that's exactly what you ordered last night. So - now something to eat, are you fussy, really hungry or what? I was actually hoping for a fine day, and then I would have left the staff to it, and we could have had a picnic! So, I have French bread, ham, chicken, salami, and salad things, oh – and some bloody nice yummy cheeses! Will that do?' We can sit over at the window watch the rain, and pig out, and you can tell me all about yourself.'

Rory agreed that that would be fine, but to himself he thought. 'I don't know about telling you about myself, at least not at the moment, not yet, and not maybe at all.'

He watched the girl busying herself in the smart designer kitchen. There was something about her that he could not quite fathom, something didn't fit. Yes extremely attractive, yes great bright personality, yes he was definitely attracted to her, physically and mentally – but there was lurking in his mind 'a but' – and it was quite a large one, disturbing, he would be on his guard.

Jenny flipped herself around the kitchen, digging out the food from cupboard and fridge and arranging it on the table. Rory stood at the other end of the room at the window and watched the weather with one eye, and her with the other. She made some very simple food into what resembled a banquet, arranging and decorating the table, that, like the flat, could have been out of a fashionable decorating magazine.

'That looks marvellous, a bit more elaborate than a picnic by the river, you really didn't need to go to so much trouble, although you certainly didn't make it look much of an effort. I am impressed.' Rory smiled at Jenny whose blush at his compliment enhanced her attractiveness.

Glancing at their empty glasses she noted, 'I think that we could do with a refill. Would you be so kind to finish that bottle off,oh ex soggy man? I'll get another one from downstairs. She disappeared down the staircase, calling, 'That didn't last long did it!' He poured the last of the wine, took the empty bottle and put it by the door by the stairs, then went back to the window as the sound of thunder returned, but even in the ten minutes since he had looked at the horizon, the sky had lightened.

The ribbon of blue was now quite wide. The storm was beginning to break out over the sea – but not over the peninsula and the village, it could take another few hours before it lifted from the surrounding steep terrain. The water was getting even deeper on the road, it was banked up quite high behind the rock wall and was cascading out gaps and down the steps onto the narrow beach front, it would not, fortunately, come back far enough across and endanger the cafes and shops. The streets were completely deserted.

Rory picked up a chunk of the bread, just as Jenny came back up, she was carrying two bottles.

'Aren't you getting a bit carried away, I know that it is only sort of um - I thought that you had to work tonight? We aren't going to go over the top are we – or are we?' He said with a smile. 'I hope you don't mind me pinching the bread but I have a need for an internal sponge, Mr. Bland's gins weren't exactly mingy.'

'Don't be smart soggy axe murderer, these were the last two of these, so I decided that they would be mine, and I could share them with you, which idea appealed to me. I do pay for them, well no I don't exactly, but never mind that. Let's have some lunch, sit down you are making the place look untidy, particularly in those clothes, they may fit, but they are not flattering, and I have a feeling that there is more to "flatter" than meets the present eye.'

He glanced down at himself, he had not really taken a lot of notice of the clothes, but she was right they were not exactly his style but what the hell, he was dry, and by the time that they had had lunch, his may well be wearable again.

She sat opposite him and suddenly had a very solemn face. 'Will you say Grace, or shall I?' Jenny watched the expression on his face, his mouth dropped open a few centimetres, as he began to stammer. 'I - um - well, perhaps if you want to, you - could um or --'

'Got cha - sorry I couldn't resist that – but you were being rude about my bottles of wine. I know it's a rotten trick, but you suddenly had such a serious look on your face as you sat down. Now, I hope you enjoy our meagre repast,'

Jenny raised her glass, 'Welcome to my home, and to the village, I don't know if anyone else has said that, but the whisper around is that there have been a few other words said.' She began to break the rest of the French loaf, handing him another large chunk of it, 'How did you get on with Mr. Mayor, so did he ply you with gin for elevenses, he usually does, and if he is on his own, he plies himself, but a pretty good old stick, wouldn't harm a fly and looks out for people – though this too does not necessarily make him popular – with some.'

'Thank you indeed – an unexpected surprise and pleasure.' Rory raised his glass and touched hers across the table. They had been talking quite loudly so that they could hear each other over the thunder and the rain, when they both realised that it was now much quieter, the rain had suddenly eased to drizzle. They looked out the window, a few sun shafts broke through the thinning clouds sending sparkling rainbows through the fine rain and setting the light across the bay afire with colour, they ignored the food, and allowed themselves to be enchanted by the scene.

'That has cleared a lot quicker than it usually does – quite a down pour though - So, now - what brings you here Rory, a small place like this for a city man, are you here for a holiday, if you were wanting peace and quiet you might have come to the right place, but it appears not, and word gets around here mighty fast.'

'So what makes you think that I am a city man - does it stand out or are you guessing, or has the word got around about that too?' Rory raised an eyebrow.

'Oh, come on, of course it sticks out. But, the word also got around, Cheryl at the Pub couldn't keep her mouth shut about anything. And then, there was the incident with Mr. Sullivan, and finally as I am originally a city dweller myself, and work in an industry where one should learn a little of what people are and where they may come from, I sort of worked it out as well. Besides, in this town when someone new arrives it's like a neon sign on top of the hill proclaiming - "watch out for the stranger".'

Jenny stopped talking and began to build herself a sandwich, breaking the crisp French bread and filling it with cold chicken lettuce and pickles.

She topped up their glasses. Jenny's appetite for the wine seemed to far exceed her food intake.

'So having sorted that out, that I'm supposedly a city slicker, a horrible bloody term, almost as bad as Jafa! Just another – well you know the rest.' Rory smiled despite a slight irritation at terminology that he hated. 'So - what brought you down here? I'm not trying to be critical of the local populace, but you seem just a little different from the ones I have come across so far in my short time here. Just a tad more sophisticated, and something else, that I can't quite put my finger on, oh - there is one thing that I am very sure about though, you are very nosy and very cheeky.'

'You're pretty good at that yourself, now really, why are you here?' Jenny leant forward her eyes probing his. 'I am interested for a number of reasons – and yes of course you are right I'm bloody inquisitive – others may use stronger less complimentary words to describe me.'

Rory could see genuine interest in her eyes, and a concern in her face, as she went on with her interrogation.

'Last night I saw your mood change at least three times, and then you disappeared, I thought you may stay even though I got tied up with work. You are staying at the Pub, aren't you, it's not all that private there, if that's what you are looking for, and she, Cheryl that is, is a very close friend of the gentleman, wrong word, but I will be polite, who evidently doesn't like you.'

Jenny's serious face and tone brought a similar reaction from Rory. He looked out the window and thought for a minute about the way that the conversation was going, he had to weigh up whether he wanted this girl to know anything about him or not. She seemed genuinely friendly, and seemed to know quite a bit about the town, and the people. Perhaps he would try to swing the questions more around to be about her again, then, when he knew more and her place in the scheme here, he could decide how much he would tell her, but he knew that it would not be much nor in great depth, no matter how friendly she seemed or how he may feel about her – there he had to tread very carefully.

In the twenty six hours he had been here, the interest he seemed to have generated, and the locals he had met, created something of a challenge, but that was not what he was personally wanting, he may have another agenda for being there but that for the moment was put aside. Rory turned back from the window and picked up his wine, swirling it and watching it spin up the sides of the deep elegant glass.

Rory's face creased in a frown as he asked 'So why are you here Jenny, living in a luxury flat over an ancient building in a town with a base population of less than a thousand people, most of which I would say are retired, and a few of dubious characters. Yes, I can see that at times it may be quite fun running a place like this, although I would admit that it would not be my scene, but it must get extremely quiet. What do you do in the winter, when there is no-one about and the rain continues to fall?'

'You're doing it again. We were not talking about me, we were discussing you, stop changing the subject.' Jenny looked out the window as he had, the sun was now shining and the place was beginning to steam from the warmth of the sun on the drenched street. A few people were venturing out, it was very still and warm. Her voice went soft and her eyes seemed to mist over.

'Okay – you win for the moment. There isn't very much to tell anyway, not at all interesting, I just like it here, and in the winter I close, well the owners close them down to three days and two nights for almost six months, and completely for three weeks in July. I move out, I have a small cottage over the other side of the north point, and I occupy my time there with my - hobbies. I travel a bit during the three weeks closed, usually overseas, and I have friends come and stay now and again. That's about it really, I like being with people and I like my job here, but I also like being alone. I won't stay here forever, but then nothing is forever is it.' She looked back at him. 'We haven't really done a great deal of damage to our picnic have we.'

'No. Okay, you have told me an awful lot of nothing, who are you, where have you been, where are you going, why, what, how, where are you from, what did you do before you came here, and you have not said why you came here.' Rory gave her a piecing look, 'I have gained a little information, that you have a cottage - why - with this place do you need it? I am being really nosy now, what are you running away from Jenny, your eyes told me more than your words.'

Now Jenny changed the tactics. 'Shall we go for a walk, it looks really lovely out there now, and I need to get out for a while. I have to get organised for work in about an hour or so, and I should do something to move the food and wine. We could go along the track under the cliffs at the top of the bay, it's beautiful along there. The track goes up into the bush and down again to the rocks, it won't take us long.' She pushed herself away from the table.

'We can leave this stuff I can deal with it later.' She surveyed his appearance again. 'I think you'll be okay, but you had better put on your trainers, but they will still be wet, does that bother you?'

'No, that's not a problem, but I'm not sure about this gear.' He smiled at the change of approach and her sudden enthusiasm to get out, she was suddenly back to the exuberant girl he had met the night before. 'A good switch of mood, she thinks that she will throw off my inquisition - wrong - I will just delay it.' He kept though, the thought to himself.

Jenny went across to the kitchen taking a couple of plates with her.' She called over her shoulder – 'I'll just go and check your clothes they should be dry by now, so you could change back into them, and I could clear a bit more of the table.' She shot down the stairs returning moments later with his clothes bundled in her arms, she threw him the gear, 'Go and convert yourself back into the axe murderer, instead of the tramp, then we can get going.'

When Rory had gone into the bathroom she looked at the time, it was twenty past two. She could afford to be away until four thirty. The staff would be on at four and begin preparation for that night, there were six bookings so far. All tables of four, it may be as busy as the Friday, but with the storm many of the week-enders may have already headed home, she was not fussed either way. The thought that she might be able to hopefully persuade this person to come and eat again, and to spend some more time with her, was foremost in her mind.

Now that Jenny had seen what was in his wallet, she definitely wanted to find out more about him. There was an air of mystery about him, something that did not fit, so far from what she'd heard – been told, although she felt that may be a little on the dramatic side, there definitely was something. And, that something had begun feelings in the pit of her stomach that she had not felt for some considerable time. Fear and affection – and to her that could be a volatile cocktail.

They left the flat and crossed over the road to the other side by the beach, and stood up on the rock wall. Not that there was much of a beach left after the wind and rain, a narrow strip of rough sand that shelved into a mat of sea grass. The road and paths were spread with puddles and wide pools of water, each one like a mirror reflecting the changing lights from the clearing sky. A light breeze had sprung up but it was still very warm and very humid, on the horizon more dark clouds were building, but they were a long way away, and may not come in their direction. Quite a number of other people were now on the streets, out strolling after the storm and were making the most of the sun, but all seemed to be keeping an eye out on the far building cumulus – sudden storms were frequent at this time of the year.

After a few minutes of observation of the scene Rory and Jenny set off to the far right end of the promenade, she slipped her hand into his as they walked.

'Hope you don't mind,' Jenny smiled up at him, 'Haven't been walking with a handsome man for ages, thought I might take advantage of his good nature. You don't mind do you?'

Rory felt flattered, but also apprehensive, it was the first time any woman for a long time had actually been quite this close. 'No – no I guess not.' He did not let go, until they approached the end of the tar seal road and turned onto the rougher metal where the path narrowed, it was then that they heard from behind the sound of a siren - an Ambulance siren. It seemed to be coming in their direction, they, along with most of the other people on the street, stopped and turned to see where it was going, or coming to. Then, another joined in, a Police car came passed the Ambulance, it was travelling very quickly down towards them. 'I wonder what the hell is going on, we very rarely get this sort of excitement.'Jenny's eyes brightened.

They stood back against the wall at the side of the footpath watching and saw as the police went by that their faces were tense and serious, the car, then the Ambulance came very close to where they were standing and tore along the track that they were about to walk on.

Moments later the vehicles pulled up in front of a two storied cottage, it was about three hundred yards from where they were standing.

'That's Miranda Sullivan's cottage.' Jenny looked up at Rory, 'What on earth has happened, something has happened, I hope not to her little girl, come on let's get nosy.' She grabbed his hand and started to run.

'No, wait,' Rory pulled her to a halt. 'I don't think under the circumstances that it would be a good idea to be in that space.' He looked back down the road as the sound of another vehicle approaching. It was a red BMW coming along the waterfront at high speed. 'Even more particularly with who is now arriving.'

Rory put his arm around Jenny's shoulder and turned her towards the sea. She did not resist his sudden movement, in fact she moved in closer to him.

'Yes, you may be right, and I see that Sullivan is on his way, but what about Jim Bland?' Jenny's voice had taken on a very concerned tone.

'What do you mean, What about Jim Bland, what's he got to do with Miranda and Sullivan, the only comment he made in the bar - was - "How unusual it was for him - Sullivan - to be in there".' Rory looked down at the girl under his arm.

'He's her - Miranda's, - her Grandfather. It's a very long involved story, but I'll bet nobody has told him that something is wrong. There's very little, if any communication between any of them, not because Miranda doesn't want it, because she is forbidden to, both by her husband and her father.' The look on Jenny's face showed that she was very concerned, but for what reasons, this was beginning to look to be a very complicated situation.

'Then, do you think that someone should tell him that there may be a problem?' Rory turned her away from the scene along the track and started them walking back to the village, he left his arm over her shoulder. He could feel the tension in her.

'I don't know. Yes I do, of course someone should, I know that Sullivan won't, and I don't really know who else would. Would you? You've sort of become a bit of a new friend. The trouble is we don't know what is actually wrong, or if it involves Miranda or what. Perhaps we should wait.'

'What's the matter Jenny, you seem very agitated by this, yet you don't know what is wrong back there.' They had been walking quickly when Rory stopped, they were now standing across on the path by the water, but instead of leading them across the road, Rory led her by her hand to the rock wall. He sat down and pulled her down beside him.

'Tell me what you know about these people - I think I need more information. What sort of people are these, who on earth, in this day and age, forbid people to communicate with their family, particularly in such a small confined environment?'

Rory watched Jenny as her face creased in thought for a few minutes before she replied. 'I don't know the whole story, but Miranda's mother was Jim and Molly Bland's daughter, Katherine. They had her very early in their life together, like when he was twenty and she was seventeen. Katherine, was born and grew up in the village until she was thirteen, when she was sent to boarding school. Later of course, she went on to University and met Sullivan. She married Sullivan, against their will, plainly Jim and Molly knew him a lot better than was ever mentioned. They were both, Katherine and Peter studying Law. She was a first year, he was in his Post Grad, she got pregnant you know, the old story. The clever intelligent ones can get just as carried away, in fact probably more so than most.' Jenny's frown deepened. 'The point I think that I am trying to make is that Sullivan somehow seems to have always had something to do with the village. I asked Miranda once about this but she did not seem to have an answer apart from that 'she had always lived here'.

'When Miranda was about seven her mother Katherine, was killed in a car accident. The brakes failed on a trip down here one weekend, she was on her own, Miranda was staying with a friend, and Sullivan evidently, as the story goes, had a lot of work on and couldn't get away. I only have this all third and fourth hand remember, Jim Bland may be able to give you better more accurate details. But I know that there is deep resentment, and he keeps out of Sullivan's way, and visa versa. The whole thing for some reason ruined Jim's ambitions and political career. Although it was just local, he evidently had aspirations for higher things, I am told.'

She hesitated for a moment and looked at Rory, he had gone a very pale and his eyes very dark.

'What's the matter, you look like you did last night, are you alright?' There was genuine concern in Jenny's voice.

Rory nodded his head fractionally. 'Please, go on, what else?' His voice tense. But one comment he would not forget, 'brakes failed – coupled with a phone call in Portsmouth some months ago.' He filed the thoughts together in his 'most important to remember folder'.

Jenny watched his face and eyes, then glanced at her watch, there was still an hour before she would have to be at work. 'Evidently about three months later Sullivan bought the big house on the point, before that they had just owned the one where Miranda lives now, he rented it out for a holiday home. He has been living here ever since, travelling up to the City when he was needed at work. That was originally a lot, but over the last few years he has gone less and less, but as I say, I have not been here all that long in comparison, and only hear all this from others. A small town, sometimes with a small mind, and a lot of in house gossip, some of course true, some well - not.'

'At least what you have told me does set up a picture for me. I don't think though that this is the time for me to go and talk to Jim Bland. What happened to his wife, do you know anything of that, he began to tell me a little of his life, then clammed up, saying it was too long a story - perhaps another time.'

'I think that it would be better left at what he said to you, wait until you know him better, then he may tell you, anyway I don't really know.

I had better go and get ready for work. Will you come and have dinner again tonight, I would really like you to, the Americans are playing again, and the weather looks as if it has settled again, and I will really try to not get interrupted, I have a full staff on. If you want to, you could come a bit later, and we could have dinner together. I know that I shouldn't say this, but I have really enjoyed your company today, not that it has worked out the way I would have liked it, with the weather the way it was, and – well anyway - but it was still fun and I enjoyed it a lot.'

Rory thought about the invitation. He wanted to, but he did not know whether he wanted this new friendship to progress too quickly, if at all, but, she was great company, lively and intelligent. 'Okay, if you would like that.' The sudden decision came as a surprise to him, he had been thinking also about finding other accommodation, perhaps even going up the coast further this evening. After what had transpired over the last day, he wanted even more to be out of the Hotel. And not sure whether staying in the village itself would help either himself or his other matters that he was there to investigate. But much of what he had already discovered gave weight to why he had been sent there.

'Great, how about if you come down at nearer nine, or is that too late, I don't know that you want to hang around the pub, but there isn't much else.'

'I'm actually thinking of getting out of the Hotel, I don't feel that comfortable, but I might leave that until tomorrow, I don't mind sitting and having a drink, as long as I won't be in the way, or take up a table if you need it.' Rory stood up off the wall. He reached out his hand and pulled Jenny up off the rock seat.

'Do you know of a place that would be better, what about the other B and B, I didn't find it yesterday, actually I didn't even look, I believe it's along Jim's end is that right?'

'Up on the hill at the back of the village, tucked into the bush a bit, but with lovely grounds, it's a bit up market and posh, but I'm sure that you could fit in.' Jenny grinned cheekily, 'They are really very nice, if a little conservative.'

'Perhaps I will drive up and have a look before I come tonight, that will give me something to do for the next hour then I might even tidy myself up a bit and surprise you with some of my sartorial splendour. Well no, not exactly – but I may be a bit more presentable.' Rory glanced up at the building opposite.

'Now you had better get going, I can see staff eyes peering out of the front door, I'll see you later, and thanks for the lunch and drying my clothes.'

Jenny crossed to her building, Rory went down the street to the wharf and walked out to the end. He looked back to where the Police and Ambulance had gone, they were still there, as was the Red car of Sullivan's. In the other direction he could see Jim's house and up on the hill behind it, he could make out through trees the Bed and Breakfast that Jenny had told him about. Its access seemed as if it may be up a steep driveway off the second road, back from the waterfront.

Out over the sea the clouds were gathering, darkening the horizon and building high black towers, the air was feeling heavier, damper, heralding the threat of another thunderstorm. The village wanderers that had been out earlier after the rain had stopped had all but disappeared. There were now only a few individuals walking the waterfront. Rory headed back up the main street to the Hotel. As he went in through the front door he could hear Cheryl's voice on the phone in the office. It was raised, angry.

'What do you mean you were here last night! Why didn't you bloody well let me know you were coming back, I could have got away later, not brought them back here.' There was a silence, then, 'You what? You knew about that, where are you now, I am not supposed to know, but how come you do. That bitch Andrea knows that something is going on, that something has happened. Where were you last night, what time did you get back here, you said you were going away for three or four days. ---- What! You've been where today -----. You did what, why? What's he to you?'

Brown's voice was getting louder and was taking on a very worried anxious tone. 'Well where are you now?' Another long pause. 'You know that I would have tried, I could have. What are you going to do now, ----You're going where - now - why?' Cheryl's voice had begun to shake as if she were on the edge of tears.

There was another silence, then the sound of the phone being hung up. He moved up the hallway towards the stairs and started to go up to his room, but the sound of her voice again stopped him.

'The bastard, the rotten stinking selfish bastard!' Cheryl's shouted to no-one.

'Who the hell has she been talking to, listening to only one side of the conversation doesn't exactly give a broad picture, but whoever it is, she obviously knows very well, and she wanted to see.' Rory's mind started to work overtime, with some of the comments he had heard. She would seem to have wanted to be with "this person" last night, more than those that she had been with.

Rory went along to the office door and knocked, he wanted, if he could, to find out what was going on. 'Are you alright Cheryl, I heard some shouting as I went passed, is everything okay?' He tried to sound concerned, and not inquisitive.

Cheryl did not come to the counter, but called out - trying to control herself, but her voice was still shaky. Whoever she had been talking to certainly had upset her.

'I'm okay, thanks, just an irate person wanting a booking for eight people, four rooms and I said I couldn't do it. I was just giving back, as good as I was getting in the aggravated shouting department.'

'Oh, right, sorry to disturb you, I'm just going up to my room. Look I'll pop back down in about ten minutes and have a chat, is that alright?'

'Yes, fine, is everything okay with you, you survive the storm this morning?' Cheryl had now managed to calm herself, and sounded more in control.

Rory muttered an 'Yes – fine – okay – pretty scary though' then went on upstairs to the flat. As he unlocked the door and went in, he knew immediately that someone had been there. He could smell some type of perfume and it was not the one that he had left the window open to clear away when he had gone out that morning. It was a male cologne, and he thought that whoever had been wearing it, had not long been in the room.

The window was still open and the curtains and the carpet were soaked, there was a smudge of mud on the sill, someone had come through it and he was sure that it wasn't a cat! He went into the bedroom and inspected where he had left his toilet bag, it was still leaning in the same place, but on a slightly different angle, and the catch on the big bag was snipped, he had been left it unlocked.

Rory flicked the lock and pulled the zip back, everything appeared as he had left it, nothing however seemed to have been removed, although the clothes had certainly been rummaged through. Rory sat on the edge of the bed and contemplated his next move. Whether to bring it up with Cheryl, that his room had been searched, or after what he had heard on the phone, to carry on as quickly as possible with his move to different accommodation. Rory decided that the latter was the best course. He took some more respectable clothes from the closet and changed into them, then packed the rest of the small amount of gear that he had taken out of the bags, putting them all outside the door.

The sound of another voice at the bottom of the stairs reinforced his notion to move. It was Sullivan's and his tone was not exactly friendly.

'What do you mean, he was in town last night, and that he knows about the accident, anyway, how do you know about it, I didn't tell you and neither did Andrea. And why have you been talking to him, I told you not to contact him. The fact that I deal with him is bad enough. I don't want you mucking things up further by getting involved, and I know that you have been, and what about your friend if she found out, she knows he's a bastard anyway - but something else on top of that - where is that going to place you?' Sullivan was clearly rattled and angry, there was the sound a slap, harsh skin on skin, and a cry of pain from Cheryl.

'I - I - guess - he saw the ambulance at the house, I mean - well - that's how I guessed something was wrong, when I was coming back from your place. Andrea went to do some work - and - I - well - left.' Cheryl stammered the statement out between tears and sobs, she was clearly distraught, frightened, and not at all convincing.

Sullivan was silent for a moment Rory listened and was relieved of both situations when he heard Sullivan say that he was going to the hospital, and wouldn't be back until the next day, and that Andrea would be staying at the house until he got back. Rory could not hear Cheryl's reply as the sound of the office door slamming, covered her voice.

Rory hadn't wanted to go down while Sullivan was there, and while he wanted to hear more he did not want to be caught listening either. This gave him the opportunity. He took the two large bags and went down the stairs and out the back door to the car. He threw them onto the back seat then went back up for the others. As collected them and he reached the bottom of the stairs again, Rory could hear Cheryl talking to someone in the bar. He took the bags out and put them with the others on the back seat, then went back to tell her what he was doing, feeling a bit of a coward that he had waited for Sullivan to leave.

However, after the previous evening in the bar, he didn't want another incident with Sullivan, until he had at the very least, spoken to Euan again. Hopefully he may have information about the man. At the door to the bar Rory stopped and listened. There was just the sounds of bottles and glasses being moved. Rory opened the door an inch and swept his eyes across the room, there did not appear to be anyone apart from Cheryl. He went in.

Cheryl was behind the bar organising the fridges, there was no-one else in the room.

'Hi, I thought that there was someone here with you, thought I heard another voice, didn't want to interrupt, I just wanted a chat for a moment.' Rory looked into the face of the girl behind the bar, her eyes were red and there was a dark mark on her left cheek, she did not look at all happy. 'Are you okay, you look a little upset.'

'No – I'm – fine,' she stammered, 'must be some pollen in the air or something that is making my eyes sore, and maybe the late night,' Cheryl forced a smile. 'What can I do for you, is the room alright?'

'That's actually what I wanted to talk about, it's very good, but I am afraid that it's all a bit non-private and noisy for me, don't be offended but I'm moving out, but I will come and have a drink with you and Mayor Bland. I will probably be moving on in the next few days as well, not sure whether I will go back to town or travel up the road a bit more. I suppose so far my experience here has not really got off on the right foot - I am sure that you know what I mean.' He no intention of taking up either of the options he mentioned – and in time Cheryl would know that, but right at this time it did not matter what she thought or what she knew.

Rory tried not to sound too pointed in the last comment, but her eyes told him that she knew exactly what he meant, and she realised that he knew more of what went on, than she would have liked.

'Oh, I'm sorry that you find it like that, but it has been a lot busier this week than it has been for a while. And I probably didn't help with my friends coming back last night, but that's the way it goes, would you like to fix up the account now, then have a drink with me before you go - have you got a place in mind?' Cheryl led the way back to the Reception desk and drew up his account on the computer. 'With your drinks the food and the room that's eighty eight dollars, and if you change your mind tomorrow or whenever the same deal applies.'

'That's fine and very reasonable and kind of you to give me such a good rate, do you take Credit cards – or cheque?' Rory forced a smile, but there was a troubled look in his eyes and it was really a forced smile that he hoped the girl did not notice.

But Cheryl was smiling and trying very hard to apparently cover her confusion at his sudden departure, although Rory doubted that she was all that confused, at least not with his leaving. 'Sorry Rory – only cash or cheques – I prefer cash, but I'll trust your cheque if that's what you want.

Rory wrote out a cheque, and thanked her for her offer, but declined having a drink. 'I'll go and see if I can get organised. I am told the B and B up on the hill, the more posh one is quiet. I am also told it may be a little pretentious, but I will try them first, I may well come in for a drink later. I will be going to the Crazy Cow later, enjoyed the music there, so could easily pop in here on the way.' He decided to try for a further reaction. 'How's your friend with the baby, haven't seen her around the village today.'

Cheryl looked up quickly from the desk where she was printing off his receipt, taken back and surprised by his question.

'Oh - um - she's away, gone away for the weekend, she didn't say when she was coming back, might be away for a few days, often is.' Cheryl's face had gone red, and she avoided Rory's look, she knew that he knew she was lying. But why was he interested anyway - and why should she have to say anything? 'Well I had better get on with things, people will be starting to wander in soon, good luck with your accommodation. I would have to say up there, would not be my cup of tea, but then everyone's different. So, I might see you later?'

'Yes, more than likely, thanks Cheryl, I'll get on my way – you may be right – but I'll have a look anyway' Rory saw a question in her eyes. 'I've already put my bags in the car,' He hesitated about to ask another question but changed his mind, 'bye for now might catch you later.' As he turned, Rory saw the hurt expression on her face. As he went out the back door and got into the car he had a feeling he was being watched, he glanced casually up at the building but couldn't see anyone.

Rory drove out the alley way and up the main street, taking the next turn on his right.

It was a narrow little road, on one side Plane trees and tiny cottages, the other an expanse of a sports ground. Many of the cottages appeared to be empty, some in poor repair, others as if they were holiday homes, one or two immaculately kept. At the end, the road went up steeply, the tar seal ended, becoming road metal and clay. About two hundred yards up the slope a sign "Wisteria Lodge" Bed and Breakfast for the Discerning.

'Jenny's comment was right - that signs a bit off putting.' Rory turned into the drive, it wound through native and exotic shrubs and trees, many in flower. This soon opened out onto a wide circular area and car park, a rock garden, with a tall white flag pole in the middle. The huge Victorian house stood imposing over the grounds, vines and creepers clung to it, the Wisteria woven across the front veranda.

Rory parked the car where he could see out to the bay, then sat for a minute looking down through the trees over the village, this, his third view, and he obtained another perspective. A noise on the gravel near the car, and the bark of a dog brought him back to why he was there. A black Labrador was circling the car. It was followed, by a woman who looked to him to be in her late sixties. Her straight grey hair was tied back off her face though, belied his first impression, her skin smooth – tanned, her eyes dark blue, penetrating.

She was wearing a straight dark skirt, and dark brown twin set with a double string of pearls around her neck. Thick stockings and heavy sensible shoes, completed the appearance - very – un-summer. He looked at her, trying to decide, from her stern serious expression a number of factors, and concluding none. Except that there was something odd, something, somehow, didn't quite fit. He was almost sure that in a change of clothes and hair style, he would really see a younger – and very attractive woman. So why was she dressed in this way and acting 'matronly'?

'Can I be of any assistance young man, have you lost your way, you aware that this is a Private Residence.' Her voice plummy, syrup covered, she had a stern look on her face, but there was a twinkle in her eyes.

'I am aware, and I am also aware that you are a guest house. I am looking to be a guest - if that is possible, you do have a vacancy sign up.' Rory gave her one of his broad, charming smiles.

The woman looked at his dress, which was very casual, but smart and clean, the she looked at his old Chev car. 'Well, I don't know, we are rather expensive, it's a hundred and eighty dollars a night, that does of course include breakfast.' She was about to continue when he interrupted, politely.

'You were recommended to me by Jenny from the Crazy Cow, she suggested that it would be to my liking, quiet, peaceful, and that the people were indeed extremely charming.' Rory continued his disarming smile.

The dog had started to lean on his leg, turning his face up, tongue lolling, wanting attention, as he put his hand down to pat him another person entered the garden from a path out of the trees..

'If we have been so highly recommended and the dog likes him, I think we should offer him a nice room with a good view, what do you say Amelia?' A deep cultured voice.

The man who approached them across the lawn was tall, rangy, raw boned and bald, he wore a tweed waistcoat, white shirt and a tartan tie, lose cream cotton trousers that had gardener's green knees. His tanned face was creased back in a warm smile. 'Besides, I haven't seen this fellow in quite a while and would like to catch up on what he's been doing, how are you Rory Calder?'

Rory's jaw, dropped, it had been many years since he had seen the tall man, and he had changed considerably. 'Professor Primmer, Franklin, what the hell, are you doing here, and excuse me saying this but I thought you were dead.' Rory blurted,

'You disappeared from the University, people told me you were ill, and that's the last I heard of you! What a small bloody world and an even smaller country – I would never have expected to find you here, in a small village like this! Dead or alive!'

'I was almost – dead that is - I was very ill. Had lot's of bits and pieces removed and then extensive chemotherapy and Radiation, hence the chrome dome, got pretty close to the campus in the sky, but somehow I came through it, then I met this young lady who was then a social worker at the hospital. She, bless her, continued to help with my rehab when I got out into the big bad world again, and now, I feel a million dollars. Three years ago we decided that we were a good team, and that we should exit the old world for a new, and found this place.'

He had moved over and was standing by her, his long arm draped over her shoulder. 'Amelia, I would like to introduce a past student of mine and later a colleague and friend, Professor Rory Calder.'

She held out her hand and shook Rory's. Her grip was warm, firm, but her eyes told a completely different story! 'A pleasure indeed, I am always pleased to meet old friends of Franklin's. Sorry that I was a little – um, brusque. I suppose more than a little judgemental of you, and you car - I still haven't learnt that dusty covers can contain interesting contents.'

'Don't worry about it, I am in an incognito mode, and left my cap and gown at home.' Rory said it with a smile, he did not want to offend the lady, who was obviously embarrassed by her original approach. But wary as ever, despite the presence of his old friend. He did not refer to any other 'cap' that he now wore.

'Come along then, let's get your gear and take you into our parlour.' The tall man looked up at the clouds building on the horizon, which although they were very black didn't look as if they would threaten the town again tonight. 'Look at the time, it's nearly over the yardarm, must be time for gin. Do you still partake Rory, or have you reformed? Unlikely, but who knows.' Franklin Primmer chuckled.

Rory was getting his bags out of the back seat and thought to himself that the people in this village really did like their beverages, and while he too did likewise, the day had seemed to be one long drink, broken with small amounts of drama! But he knew that he would have the drink, just as Primmer said. This was definitely a bonus an unusual one, finding his old friend here.

Franklin helped him with his bags, and the dog did not, by wagging his tail and running in and out of their legs and in front and between them. However when they reached the door he went to one side and flopped down on an old rug in the shade, laying his head between his front paws. 'That's a bit more helpful Devil, now stay there until dinner.' The old man bent and ruffled the black dogs head.

Inside, compared to the warm heavy humid air, the house was cool, the big house shaded by the wide side verandahs.

Franklin and Amelia led the way up the stairs and into a large bright airy room with two huge sash windows on either side of double French doors that were open onto a balcony.

'Will this do you for a few days?' asked the older man, 'it's the one we try to keep for very special guests, and I will make an exception and class you as one.' Franklin laughed and clapped Rory on the shoulder. 'It's damn good to see you, damn good, get yourself organised then come down for that drink. The bathroom is through there.' He pointed to a door in the corner. 'We'll see you in a few minutes.'

Amelia hadn't said anything since they were in the car park, but Rory heard her as Franklin went down stairs. 'Is he really a friend of yours? A Professor? He certainly doesn't look like one, or the sort of person who would be a friend of yours, he's so much younger than you – not your usual at all!.'

'Oh yes, he most definitely is, I guess I haven't told you of all the people I know, and those, some from the past that were special, he was. I suppose I really never expected to see him again. Especially not here, quite a surprise, yes quite a surprise.' The old man's face creased briefly, then,

'Now what time were those others coming, are they going to be here for dinner? I would rather that he didn't see them, that would not be a good idea at all!'

The last part of the conversation was lost as they got further away from Rory's room. He placed his bags neatly on the luggage rack, removed the clothes that needed to be hung, and went into the bathroom to freshen up.

When he'd finished, he came out and stood on the balcony looking over the village, and out to the sea. He could see the rooftop of Jim Bland's house. To his surprise, parked outside was a Red BMW. Why would he be there? From what he'd heard from Bland, and Cheryl anything could be possible. Rory came back into the room, frowning. He didn't see Franklin Primmer in the doorway until he was half way across. He started at the sight of him, his tall gaunt frame filling the space.

'God you gave me a hell of a fright, I didn't hear you come up, I was just about to come down.'

'Just came to see if you had settled in alright and found all you need. But I would have to confess that I've been watching you for a few minutes, when you were on the balcony. You seemed, well, very intent and intense. What are you doing here Rory? this isn't your type of place! This village – or my B & B. Not that I mind, far from it, but my intuition tells me that there's something not quite right in your life, and you being here at my place, not that you knew it was mine - did you?'

'No, I didn't, a real shock as well as a pleasant surprise. I was staying at the Hotel, but it wasn't quite what I needed. There's only a few places to stay here, as I said, Jenny recommended that it would be quiet, if that was what I wanted, she actually said it may be a bit posh for me, or was that Cheryl, doesn't matter, but to have a look,' Rory grinned at his friend, 'And it is. Also I feel that it's not quite where I would've expected to see you again, in a grand place like this! In a small seaside village? I don't think so! So I suppose that we have learnt something new about each other.'

'No Rory, it's not that, there's in your eyes, something that was never there before, it's a good four – no nearly six years since I saw you last, it appears that a lot has happened - or am I mistaken?'

'No, you're not. There's a story and it's quite long and involved and for some reason or other it's followed me here, or I have followed it, and I don't know why. A person who lives here and who drives a red car seems to know a lot about me and is not pleased about my presence. I came to the coast to have a look around with a view to opting out, that may be the expression, or opting into new ideas and feelings about the future. If that sounds confusing to you, you'll be pleased to know that for someone who used to be a clear thinker, with goals and directions in his life, it's also confusing.' Rory watched his old friends face as he spoke – yes there was something that didn't quite fit. And neither was about to elaborate.

'Now how about that drink, and I'll tell you a bit more.' Rory thought of telling his old friend more of the real reason he was there, but there was something that he too couldn't fathom about the situation. Something certainly didn't fit in his own mind about where and why they both appeared in the same place – was it the right – or the wrong time? He thought back to the years in the University and his 'discoveries'.

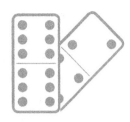

SEVEN

S ullivan left the hotel. When he'd arrived there, from Miranda's cottage, he was already in an extremely foul mood. It was not just what had happened to Miranda, it had been the police's questioning of him, and in particular about his son-in-law, and his whereabouts. He had told them that he had no idea. Now his mood had deepened and was blacker than ever.

Cheryl's actions, and what she had told him, had infuriated him even more, and he had slapped her far too hard, and while he regretted in one sense that he had done so, he felt that he was justified. She had now, information that he did not want her to have, and she had been talking to Warren, something that he had forbidden her to do.

Sullivan knew that Cheryl was playing more than a double game, the fact that he too may be doing so was irrelevant to him. He would not be crossed by her, or anybody for that matter. Also the appearance, admittedly it appeared by chance, of Calder in the town, was doing nothing for his arrogant volatile demeanour.

Outside the building he stood by his car, his mind churning as to what action to take next. He should get down to the hospital and see what the situation was with Miranda, but he also felt a strange sense of duty, (he had none to the man in his eyes, but that was the only word that he could think of) to see Jim Bland. He was very worried, Miranda's husband Warren, had been in the village the previous day, he was supposed to be keeping well away! Blanchard was supposed to be away on business – their business for three or four days.

There were certain tasks that he was to have carried out, and there was, as far as Sullivan knew, no reason for him to have been back here, and, who had seen him. Cheryl hadn't, that is what she had said, and he couldn't work out anyway how she could have, she had been with him almost all of the time from seven thirty on Friday night. There was also now another problem - and this was a particularly serious one - one that the police had questioned him extensively. Where was Miranda's baby? And the baby sitter? He could not shed any light on this at all.

The Police said that they were calling extra staff to assist, that it was a serious matter that required people who had more experience than they, and a team of Detectives were on their way.

Sullivan now had very deep suspicions as to where the Baby Suzanne, and the sitter may be with. He had questioned Cheryl, whether Warren had mentioned anything about them at all, according to her, he had not. But that meant little, he was devious, and not to be trusted.

As Peter Sullivan stood by his car all these thoughts flashed through his mind. The events of the last few hours had been deeply disturbing, and their affect on his business affairs in the area could be devastating.

The final thought as he got into his car was - 'What the hell does Warren Blanchard think he's up to?' Sullivan headed down the road to the wharf, then went left to Jim Bland's house. He would ask the old man if he wanted to come with him down the coast to the hospital. He didn't want to take him, and he doubted he would accept, but it was his Granddaughter, so going against all that he'd said, that he'd never do, he would ask him.

Jim Bland was sitting on the front porch as Sullivan drove up and parked by the steps. The old man stood as the car came to a halt, and came down to meet Sullivan, he was carrying Suzanne.

'Got something on your mind Peter?' Bland spoke quietly, but the timbre of his voice cut through the air. Sullivan was stunned by its tone, and the sight of Miranda' little girl.

'Yes, no, I mean yes - how, where -- what are you doing with Suzanne - here? I don't understand, do you know about Miranda?' Peter was suddenly more confused and he felt at a disadvantage, a feeling he did not like at all.

'Francis and her mother brought her here about thirty minutes ago, and yes, I have heard about, what has been termed an accident, the Police have been here as well, and strangely, I have been expecting you. You had better come in Peter.' Jim's voice was calm – even.

Sullivan followed the old man into the house, they went through into the lounge where Jim Bland put his great granddaughter into a pushchair, and popped a bottle into her mouth, as he stood up he turned to Sullivan.

'Can I get you anything Peter, coffee, tea, something stronger? Or do you just want to give me your version of the story?'

'How many versions have you had so far Jim, because I don't really have one, and yes, please, a whisky, if you don't mind, I shouldn't but I feel I need it.' Sullivan too, spoke quietly, also uncharacteristic in his posture, slumping his shoulders, and tilting his head sideways and slightly forward, he seemed bewildered.

As he went to his dresser to get the drink Bland went on. 'I have two, so far, the Police's and Sandra Conrad's. Which is second hand, in the sense that it's Francis's explanation, relayed by her Mother! I guess that's what you would call it, no not an explanation, an account perhaps may be better, but she seems pretty upset and frightened, and didn't want to say much. So, I think that Sandra tried to fill in the bits in between, with her own version of what she thinks may have happened. What did the Police say to you Peter?' Jim Bland his voice still quiet, even friendly and concerned, he knew this man's temperament.

'They just called and said that there had been an accident and the it appeared that she had tripped and fallen down onto the rocks, they thought that she may have had too much to drink and staggered off the track, I don't actually believe that, do you?' Jim shook his head. 'Well, then they said, that the baby and the baby sitter were missing, which did not seem right, as I am sure that Francis, who has as you probably know looked after Suzanne quite a lot.' Peter Sullivan took a gulp of the neat spirit.

'Miranda was at dinner with Cheryl, Andrea and myself, of course, but she disappeared just after the meal, said she was going to the toilet, didn't come back. We didn't think much about it as all of us had had quite a lot to drink, and just thought she may have gone home, perhaps she wasn't feeling well, it has happened before.' Peter shrugged. 'That's really all I can tell you.'

'She came here, after she left you and the others at dinner.' Jim Bland watched Sullivan's expression, it showed mild surprise and not the anger he had expected. 'She talked to me for about half an hour or so, maybe a bit longer, a bit like old times – but not quite, it was if she wanted to tell me something but couldn't quite bring herself to do so, so I have no idea then what that was. We had a glass or two of wine, general chit chat, then she left, saying that she was going home and that she would let Francis have an early night, that would have been I think about nine thirty, but I am not really sure I didn't look at the clock.'

'So what were these other versions, look do you want to come down to the hospital with me, we could discuss it on the way, I know that we don't get on or even remotely like each other, but perhaps under the circumstances?'

Jim Bland was for a moment quite taken back with the other man's plea for a truce. 'Uh - well I would like to but I have the baby, and I don't think that a journey, of over an hour, would be too good for her, and probably not for our nerves either. Thank you for the thought and the offer, but you may be better on your own. Now before you go would you still like to know what may have occurred? And, it's only at this stage a "may have".

'Yes, okay, yes it might be a good idea. I actually don't know what condition Miranda is in, apart from the fact that she is quite badly hurt. But not life threatening or anything like that, they just said that she had some head injuries, a broken leg and wrist, cuts and bruises.'

'According to the Police, Francis was sitting watching television, she thinks it was about nine thirty, when she heard a sound outside, like footsteps and then a scraping sound. She tried to see out the windows but it was getting too dark, she opened the front door and looked out, she thought she saw someone running away from the front gate. She got frightened and went back in, closed the door and locked it, then pulled down the blinds. A few minutes later there was banging on the back door. Instead of ringing for help she panicked, picked up the baby and ran out the front and along the path that runs up into the bush about fifty yards from the house. She had left the front door open and the light spilled out onto the shore line.'

Jim Bland went and poured himself a whisky and added a dash to Sullivan's.

'She says that she knew that she had done the wrong thing. When she realised that she couldn't get back past the house without, whoever it was seeing her, if there was someone there. Then awhile later she saw Miranda running towards the house, a figure dashed out from the trees beside the house and pushed Miranda over the edge. It all sounds pretty far fetched in some ways. But Francis told me the same story almost word for word that the Police had, except for the interruptions and prompting of her mother.' Bland stopped and sipped his whisky.

'The strange thing is nobody has explained where Francis was for the next twelve hours with the baby, she just says she stayed in the bush too frightened to move, yet Suzanne here seems none the worse for being in the bush unfed and cold for that time. When the Police and then I questioned her she just shook her head and sobbed, and appeared very frightened. Quite a shock for the young girl I imagine' Jim Bland paused for a second, thinking.

'Francis and her Mother and have brought some of the baby's clothes and some food. I won't be able to look after her for long - not too good or experienced these days, so I've arranged for Kate, the Headmaster's wife to look after her. They as you know have a couple of little ones, she was only too happy to help, and of course as we know with Kate, a worrier and very concerned. She will be over in the next half hour to pick her up. That Peter is about it, though I am sure that you know that too. I am also sure that the Police will be making more extensive enquiries over the next few days. Now it's getting on, you had better get down and see Miranda. I would appreciate a call if you don't mind, let me know how she is.'

'Yes, fine, I will, I'll call you from the hospital, thanks for the information, not that it sheds any further light on what has happened. I'll get under way, thanks for the drink.' Sullivan stood up and went out to his car.

Jim Bland walked out to the porch and watched him go, then went back in picked the phone, and dialled the local station.

'Hello Sergeant Mackay please,' He waited for the officer to transfer the call. 'Dougal? Jim Bland, you asked me to let you know if Peter Sullivan came to see me. ---------- Yes we had a chat, ------- no he actually was quite pleasant, not aggressive for a change. He has just left, on his way to the hospital. --- Yes, about two minutes ago,------- no he was not a happy chap, not that you would expect him to be of course. But, I do however think that there was more to his disturbed demeanour than the condition of his daughter. I could be wrong, but I've known him for a long time, anyway that's it for what it is worth.'

The Sergeant thanked him, and he hung up. Just as he did, there was a knock at the door, and the sound of Kate calling out to him.

'Hello Jim, I came over as soon as I could, thought it better to get wee Suzanne and get her fed and settled, have you heard how Miranda is, sounds a nasty fall, strange that she should do that there, she knows the road, and it's not narrow or dangerous.' The young woman had a deep concerned frown as she came into the hallway. Jim led her through to the lounge where the baby had now fallen asleep in the pushchair.

'Yes, strange, I am sure that we will get to the bottom of it, Miranda will remember - she was still unconscious when they took her away in the ambulance, it appeared not to serious, but a nasty crack on the head. When I hear from the hospital. Peter's gone down, he said that he'd call me with any news. I'll let you know how things are, as soon as I hear.'

'Jim, are you and Peter talking, I know that this should override differences, but I would admit to being surprised.' Kate's face certainly did show the surprise that she felt.

'At present it appears so, you know in times of common adversity and trouble even enemies can put aside their weapons and words of war, but I will not hold my breath that it will last, and I am sure that he is not either. Now get on your way with Bub. And, thanks for your help, I really do appreciate it, and I'm sure that Miranda will too.' He wheeled the pushchair to the door and eased it down the few steps to the path. Kate took it from him and set off down the drive to the road. She and her husband lived only five houses away but on the next street back, next to the school. The open grass between was a bit bumpy to wheel across, but there was a sealed track that ran through from this street about a hundred yards along, she was headed for that.

Jim Bland went back into his house, closed the door and went back to his kitchen. He poured a second whisky and returned to the lounge. He stood sipping the drink looking out over the water, wondering and worrying as to what had gone on that day – and the previous night. It was not an accident, by any stretch of the imagination, he knew it and the Police knew it, but who was behind it and why as yet needed to be discovered.

* *

Rory was about to follow his host out of the room, when he decided on a small diversion from the Gin. 'Have you got a second before we go down and join Amelia, I would like to just ask you something.'

'Surely, what is it?' Frank Primmer came back into the room, over to where Rory was back standing by the French doors.

'You see that car down there, in front of Jim Bland's place? You may recall a few minutes ago I mentioned a red car, do you know the person that owns it?'

Primmer looked at his companion quizzically. 'You know Jim Bland and where he lives? You have made good use of your short time here, he's quite an interesting character, but why do you want to know about who owns the red car?'

'No, I know who owns it, I wondered if you did, or anything about him, I have already had an unfortunate encounter with Mr. Sullivan, he seems to be one of the enigma's that I have come across since I arrived yesterday, and his daughter.' Rory's voice was a thoughtful flat monotone.

As they stood looking down at the village, they could see Sullivan come out from the front of the house and get into the car, it turned and headed back up to the wharf, then up the main street. From their high vantage point they could see that it was heading to the bridge and cross roads on the outskirts of the village.

'Looks as if he is going out of town. It may be something to do with the trouble at his daughter's house, earlier the Police and an ambulance, even the Fire Brigade were there. Could you have seen that from here?' Rory queried.

'No, I haven't been looking down at town today, have too much to do to be a watch dog. Heard sirens though, but I was in the bush clearing a wee spot for a Gazebo, and a private guest Barbecue, may even put in a Spa, thinking about it anyway. So what happened, do you know, you seem already to know a fair bit that goes on here.' Primmer sounded matter of fact, almost disinterested.

Rory shook his head. Franklin took his arm and led him back into the room. 'Come on that Gin's getting warm, and Amelia will be wondering what we're talking about. We have two more guests arriving shortly and she'll want to be getting on with the dinner, but will want her spot of courage – mothers ruin, too, depending on your view point, before she begins. Come on, she can be a bit of a Tartar at times, keeps, or tries to keep me in line.' The tall man grinned at his younger friend. 'You can fill me in on some more of what has happened over the last years while she's organising. You will join us won't you?'

'Actually, I've already made arrangements to have dinner later with Jenny from the Crazy Cow, and having not expected to be meeting you. Well – a bit of a quandary now.' The look on Franklin's face stopped him, he stared at him for a moment. 'You don't know do you, I can see that you are shocked by me having dinner with a young woman, when I'm a married man with three children. You don't know that Serena and the children are dead - do you!' Rory went on, 'No – of course you don't – why should you – sorry a bit presumptuous to think that you would be up with all that, after so long out of touch.'

Deep shock appeared on Franklin Primmer's face. 'No, I didn't, you're right nothing. Why should I? I suppose that with everything that was happening to me, and isolating myself, or, ourselves, I didn't, I wouldn't have. Was it in the papers, the news, where was it, when - how did it happen?' It all flooded out, a torrent of words pouring over Rory. He held up both hands to stop his friend, to ward off the onslaught. As he did so he looked into the old man's eyes. There was something behind them, something that Rory could not fathom, almost an 'eerie look' spooky! - And he didn't think that it was anything to do with the man's initial reaction to his statement about Serena.

'I shouldn't have expected you to know Franklin, it was over a year ago, an accident, but it seems, with suspicious circumstances. Come on, I'll give you a brief run down on it all, but it has quite a lot to do with me being down here, in fact it has mostly everything to do with it.' Rory's voice soft, consoling the older man, whose face now was reflecting guilt, at not knowing. That, at least, was how he interpreted it at that moment.

'Come on, we both need that drink. I wont tell you everything tonight, it's all a bit complicated and I can as you know be a trifle long winded! I promised to go down to that Crazy Cow Place, she's been friendly and helpful, particularly recommending here. Look what's occurred just by that! We've met again and that's a wonderful bonus.' This time Rory took the old man by the elbow and shuffled him from the room.

They went down the stairs, to the calling of Amelia, as to, "Where they were and what were they doing, she was getting dehydrated slaving over the hot stove", which in fact she hadn't actually started.

Franklin prepared the drinks, and the three of them sat out on the porch in the lowering sun for half an hour, small talking, mixed with occasional reminiscing. They wandered back into the time that they worked at the University. There was no depth or substance to the conversation, until after her second drink Amelia excused herself and went to arrange the evening meal, she was as yet not aware of the content of the conversation the Rory and Franklin had had upstairs earlier.

* *

Sullivan turned the car out of the town and across the river bridge. It was normally around an hour's trip to the next town and the hospital, but at this time on a Saturday he would make better time. As he drove up the first steep hill his mind started its analysis of the past twenty four hours. Now, not only did he have the problem of the appearance of a man he thought he would never have to deal with. But his daughter had been attacked, and a Police investigation would follow. And, with the story of what had occurred, it would likely be an intense one, unless he could get Miranda to diffuse the situation.

His major concern was as usual not his daughter but himself, while he controlled her life and had deep feelings for her, they were well over shadowed by his own affairs and business interests. He would go on up to the city, after seeing that Miranda was okay, and set into motion a number of contingencies that he hoped could alleviate any problems that may escalate from these events.

Another problem edged into his mind, his son-in-law Warren, where was he, and what was he up to, and the one burning question that he continued to mull over as he drove. What was he doing back in the village on Friday night when he was supposed to be dealing with a particularly important delivery of stock? He would try to deal with that question as soon as he got to his office in town. Perhaps Mangus may be able to shed some light? Although right this moment he couldn't see how.

It was not until he turned through the back streets of the town, into the hospital gates that his thoughts returned to his daughter, and a sad bitter reminder of her mother. The last time he had entered these gates was to identify her body after her accident on the coast road.

There had been much speculation and accusation about her death. Brake failure had been ascertained in the end, but talk of tampering with steering and brakes, had been rife in the village, he was not popular even back all those years, not that he had encouraged popularity, however the finger pointing had not provided any proof.

Yes, they had not been getting on, and their relationship was turbulent and unstable to say the least, but he had not been implicated by the police. However the mud had stuck, much of it had been thrown by Jim Bland, but then he had in other ways given him cause, the way he had treated his daughter during their marriage, and now this with Miranda.

Peter Sullivan's circle of friends in the area was small, but he did maintain some close ones. He had considered selling up the property and moving away, but he liked the house and its isolation from the rest of the community, and after several years and several failed relationships and affairs, he decided he was too tired to bother. The tiredness was not physical, it was mental, and much of it he knew was of his own doing and the way that he lived.

The car park was almost full but he was lucky, another car was pulling out near the entrance. Peter pulled into it and turned off the motor, sitting for a few minutes, he tried to push the blackness from his mind and concentrate on what he had to face now. He took a deep breath, got out of the car and went up the steps into the foyer.

However, his thoughts stayed on the same track, and as he crossed the tiled floor his frown deepened.

At the desk Sullivan made enquiry as to where he could find his daughter, and what was her present state. They directed him to Ward Seven – second floor, but the only comment was that she was conscious now and resting comfortably, the usual, but at least he could see her. He took the stairs to the second floor and went to the duty Nurse at the desk.

'Miranda Sullivan please, may I see her, I know it's outside the visiting time, but I have had a long drive, although I am sure that you know that.' Sullivan assumed they knew he was Miranda's father.

'Yes, you can see her Mr. Sullivan, but only for a few minutes. While she is awake now, she is still in quite deep shock, and quite a lot of pain from the breaks to her wrist and leg, but they are simple fractures and will mend reasonably quickly. She's in Room Ten, just around the corner.' The nurse gave him a smile, 'She'll be okay, I presumed you were her father and not her husband.' Sullivan's assumption had been right - he nodded, muttered a thank you, but was not really amused by that thought.

As he got to the door another panic – an emotion that never had in the past affected him – swept into his mind, he had never really seen her hurt, just the usual childhood scrapes and scratches. Peter looked in, she appeared asleep, her head bandaged, right arm in plaster, and left leg in traction. There were three other beds in the room, two of them occupied, their occupants too, were asleep. He went over and stood by the bed, then pulled the chair that was nearby over and sat down.

Peter Sullivan looked at his daughter and began to reflect on what sort of father he had been. Concluding after some minutes, not a good one, not perhaps the worst either, but he had as she had got older manipulated her into what he had wanted her to be, and to associate with whom he wanted.

She was well educated and had an excellent science degree in marine biology. He had great plans for mussel and oyster farming. Once again there had been a 'but' in the form of her getting involved with and pregnant by Warren Blanchard. Blanchard had initially appeared to be someone who could be extremely useful in his plans, but as it turned out, the young man's interests - lay in other money-making projects .

Sullivan's mind began to wander off again, into his own problems, the figure on the bed disappeared into a mist. His usually clear devious mind, tonight was muddled. All the protracted pondering of the day and the drive to the Hospital filtered back, until quiet words from the bed broke through them.

'Hello Dad, I didn't think you would be here, I didn't know whether you would know where I was.' Miranda reached out her left hand from under the sheet and took her Father's.

It was as if she was a little girl again, and the way she spoke the words it brought back the times of sending her off to boarding school. 'Yes I'm here, how are you feeling?' She pulled a grimaced face at him. 'I know silly question, but, do you know what happened - did you just - make a mistake - and go too close to the edge of the path?'

'I really don't know, I only remember seeing the door of the house open and thinking there was something wrong, I started to run. I do remember that, then - nothing, until I woke up in here about an hour ago. The nurses said I had had an accident, they gave me some pain killers which made me very drowsy, then I just got this feeling a minute ago that someone was here, and I was hoping it was you and not Warren. Does Granddad know?'

Sullivan nodded. 'No Warren doesn't, as far as I know, but, yes I went and saw Jim.' Sullivan saw the shock and surprise on her face. 'I asked him if he wanted to come down with me. But he declined. He also had Suzanne with him. There seem a lot of unanswered questions, are you sure that is all you remember?'

Miranda shook her head. 'Yes, that's all, what do you know?'

'Francis says that she saw a person run out and push you over onto the rocks. She was hiding in the bush with Suzanne. She says, she had been frightened by a prowler she had heard moving around the outside of the house in the garden. They were trying to get in the back door. That's why you saw the front door open, she just ran and hid, not very sensible, but well, who knows what went through her mind. The Police will be talking to her further when she has settled down. Sandra and Francis brought the baby to Jim, the Police I think - brought some of her clothes and things. Kate is going to look after her for a few days until we sort out a few things, and you get home, hopefully soon.'

As he was speaking Miranda closed her eyes, tears pushed their way out from under the lids and trickled down her cheeks. She shook her head, from side to side. When he had finished, she spoke.

'I'm sorry, this is all such a mess and has created problems that none of us need right now, I wish I could remember what happened.' She opened her eyes, and looked up at her father who was now standing closer to the bed.

He could see though from the look that she was giving him that she did know more than she was telling, he was about to ask another question but Miranda shook her head.

'No Dad, no more, I am tired and I can't help you, or anyone, I need to sleep now. Are you going to stay here in town tonight or going back?'

'I'm going up to the city, some things need to be seen to, you understand, business. Andrea is looking after a few things at the house, and she will stay there until I get back. I will be a couple of days, I'll ring the hospital tomorrow.' Peter Sullivan took a cell phone from his pocket and put it on the cabinet by the bed. 'You can use this to call me. You know the number but this one - it's programmed – just press 45 okay?' He squeezed her hand bent and kissed her lightly on the forehead.

As he left the room she tried to smile at him, but it was a frown and a grimace that appeared instead.

Peter Sullivan spoke briefly to the receptionist at the front desk, then went out to his car, settled himself back into the leather and looked at his watch. It was just after seven thirty. It was a little over an hours drive to the city, depending on the weekend traffic, there was plenty of daylight left, he hated driving in the dark, the lights of oncoming traffic had always disturbed and annoyed him, they disrupted his concentration and speed. He was not a reckless driver, but certainly didn't adhere to speed limits. This was testified in the number of speeding tickets he received, most of which had never got to the fine or prosecution stage, friends within had seen to that, for other favours in return - of course. He was, not without influence in the courts and other, legal circles.

Sullivan turned the car out of the parking area and drove down to the main street, swinging left at the intersection he accelerated through the deserted streets. As he reached the outskirts of the town and the main highway, he pulled another cell phone from the glove box and made a call to Andrea. He asked her to contact Jim Bland, and gave her a brief run down on Miranda's condition. What the girl remembered, and what she didn't appear to want to remember. He asked her to be up at the city office on Tuesday morning. He then called Cheryl, but only told her that he had been to the hospital and was on his way to town.

The last call was to Mangus. 'Ha, at last you answer your bloody phone, I've been wanting to talk to you, I thought you may have returned my last message. I'm on my way up to town, can you get a few things for the apartment and drop them round there, about nine thirty, wait for me, would that be okay?'

His partner affirmed that it would not be a problem, and for a few minutes Sullivan gave his instructions, and filled in the position as to what had transpired in the last twenty four hours. When he had finished the call he increased his speed. The road for a change had only light traffic, most heading in the opposite direction and he was able to make excellent time. The motorway too was reasonably clear and he was in the centre, parking under his town apartment well within the time he had anticipated.

Mangus's car was there, he was early, and being well organised, Sullivan hoped he would be preparing a meal. He was, apart from an astute business partner a useful cook, and entertained for his friends at home a lot, rather than going to restaurants.

Sullivan locked his car and took the lift to the fifteenth floor. As he exited directly into the apartment, he saw Mangus by the plate glass windows talking on the phone, and staring into the city night.

At the sound of the lift opening he turned and replaced the phone on its cradle.

Mangus Macmillan was what Sullivan called a "weasel of a man". It was in some respects almost a term of endearment, but he was, a weasel of a man, in more senses than one. Even his physical appearance at times closely resembled the little creature. His small stature, slightly bent posture, thin face and hair, long almost beak like nose, on which he perched his steel framed glasses, and his mind, sharp alert, dangerously so. He was not a person to be trifled with, and this along with his incredibly sharp intellect made him a most valuable ally in their combined business ventures. These were nothing to do with Sullivan's law firm.

'Hello Peter, you are earlier than I expected, I thought rather than going out, or I spending time preparing a meal, we would be better served by time spent discussing - these issues - that have arisen.' His speech was in no respect as his appearance. It was a refined baritone, and reflected his education at Oxford, where he had studies and written his Doctorate thesis on European history, from the Sixth to the Fifteenth century. A broad area, but one in which he became unbelievably knowledgeable - in fact this small man had to a large extent modelled himself on the Florentine Statesman Machiavelli, cunning, amoral and opportunist, and many of his friends seemed to have been cast from that same mould.

'So I have just ordered in, one of my Restaurateur friends as you know often obliges me on when such occasions necessitate, yes of course - as you know.' He smiled at Sullivan.

'That is a very good thought, so how about mixing me one of your famous Martinis, I had some at lunch, but mine are never quite the same.' Peter returned the smile.

The small man preened with the compliment. 'Thank you Peter, I will. Now, while I arrange those, begin to give me the gist of what has transpired, and what our rather reckless friend Warren has been up to.' Mangus went to the cocktail cabinet and began to assemble the jug of Martinis.

'Well, I can't really be sure about anything, it just seems that he went away on the Thursday as we wanted, then for some reason he turns up back in the village. The only one that seemed to know anything at all was Cheryl, and according to her - she didn't know much. But I think that she was expecting, or wanting something more than a phone call. As we can imagine!'

'The delivery wasn't made.' Mangus's tone indicated concern. 'Our friend at the Marina did not see him, or the packages.'

'When did you speak with him, the packages were not going to be arriving until Thursday night, we are now Saturday night, yes, they should have been dropped off to him early this morning, before first light. So where the hell are they and Blanchard?'

'Why you ever brought him into it in the first place, I never trusted him, he is a sleazy little bastard.' Mangus finished making the pitcher of drinks. He carried the jug of Martinis to the table by the window and filled two iced crystal glasses, dropping an olive in one, a twist of lemon and a cocktail onion in the other.

'We could have dealt with that other matter in another way, you know that.'

Both men stood staring out over the darkening city watching the lights flick on. Sullivan thought about that statement, and the knowledge that Warren Blanchard had about him.

'If those packages are missing, and we will have to assume that they are we have a problem that must be dealt with quickly and efficiently. Have you actually tried to contact Blanchard?' Sullivan looked at Mangus.

'No, and until you told me, I thought everything was in order. Now, the more I piece things together, it becomes clear that there's much more to Miranda's accident than meets the eye. Particularly with what we now know, or rather don't know, about Blanchard's whereabouts.' Macmillan sipped his drink, his frown deepening before he went on.

'There were three different types of merchandise in those packages, they should have been on their way to the fishing boat by midnight, they were to be transferred to the freighter by midday tomorrow, if they're not there, there's going to be hell to pay! We had better contact them, they'll be spewing if we don't deliver, and so will we, part payment has already been made, and our credibility will be out the back door, so when ---.' He as about to continue when there was a knock on the door. Mangus went and opened it.

It was the food that he had ordered, two people, a man and a woman, came into the room, each carrying a thermo box. He directed them to leave it on the breakfast bar, paid them, and they left. The couple didn't speak at all, or respond to their 'thank you' - which Sullivan thought rather strange.

'Do you want to eat, or should we try to sort out some of these problems first, the food will keep perfectly in those containers.' Mangus returned to the window. 'Basically and to the point - I think we should make some calls, particularly to our friends at sea, and our contact at the Marina , I think they should be made aware there is a problem, and a serious one. I'll use the private line, you the business.'

Sullivan moved to the bar and poured them another drink, then went back to the window. 'I don't like it, I don't like it at all, put a call in to Warren, then John Mackintosh at the Marina. Let's see what comes from those calls first. Then if we get nowhere, the fishing boat and the Freighter. You handle those, in that order. I think that I'd better have a word with Hans in Joburg.'

'You haven't contacted him for months - have you?' Mangus became agitated, which was very unusual. Sullivan was surprised by the tone of the man, it had a tinge of panic.

'No I haven't, it had not seemed necessary - but does that matter, what's the problem, surely this is one time that he should know that something is not going according to our rules? What's the matter Mangus?' Sullivan gave him an intense questioning look.

'Nothing – no – nothing at all – well that's a stupid statement under the circumstance – but yes you are right, yes, of course, it's just that, wouldn't this action, I mean calling Hans, before we have even ascertained what the problem is, be perhaps a little premature?' Mangus's face was creased with worry.

There was to Sullivan, something extremely odd about his partners behaviour. There was a definite nervousness about him. He changed tack. 'You may be right, perhaps I am over reacting, but still all the same, I will have a chat to him, try not to let him know that we have trouble okay?' He smiled at his colleague. 'It's alright - I won't alarm him – well not too much anyway – not too much, so don't worry about that - now you get on to those others.'

Sullivan had three lines coming into his apartment. There were often occasions that required them to make calls simultaneously, often one of their other associates was there and it saved considerable time if they could all work on a situation at once.

He picked up one of the phones, as Mangus went to a desk on the other side of the room. Sullivan watched the man as he seated himself, and began dialling. As Sullivan began his call he kept his eyes on his friend, he had suddenly had a very very bad feeling.

*   *

Since Amelia had left them to begin her preparations for the other guests arrival, the two men had been silent for nearly five minutes, each caught up in a private world.

Rory, now having to face the demons of the events of two years ago - telling his old friend - who had been a close friend and confidant to himself, and also a friend to Serena and the children. The opening of emotions and wounds was not what he wanted to do, but felt that he must.

The older man pondered his own recent past, of his illness and near death, yet he had escaped, and placed himself in a new life, but he too had thoughts, of - was this what he wanted and needed.

Franklin Primmer turned at looked at his young friend. 'I guess stranger things have happened, than two people who knew each other well thinking that they had lost touch, and that the contact may never return, and neglecting to send out the search messages. Then suddenly for what may appear no reason they walk into each others new world, strange, but, really I think, not so strange, and I don't mean because it is a small country. Like minds I think can often do that, but then again I could be talking a load of stupid waffle. So tell me Rory, what is the story?'

For the next thirty minutes Rory told Franklin everything, from when he and Serena began to have their problems, to when their paths had started to drift in different directions. Then, to the separation and then the accident, he touched on the arguments and bitterness, and the resulting affects on the children, the attempts at reconciling - then the final break. He told him of the accident and the resulting interrogation by the Police. He talked about getting away starting a different life, as he had tried to talk to Serena about, and had decided that that is what he would do, and this was the beginning of that exploration. But again he did not mention that there was another reason he was in this village, and was about to take another tack, when he paused at the sound of a car crunching up the driveway.

'It looks as if we will be interrupted now, but before I go. If you are thinking of a new semi-isolated life style, why here, and why do you want to opt out of the city and the University. You could have the best of both worlds by just cutting down, being more sort of part time, what you have told me so far is tragic, but is it enough to give up what you had in the other part of your life?'

'It was a bit like throwing a dart at a map. I know the area, generally very well. Not this little place though, only passed it by. Which was possibly what attracted me to stop here. I looked at it from on the hill, and thought it could have possibilities, and as far as the other, giving up what I had, my heart wasn't in it, I had no passion for it, no enthusiasm. Oh I can go back, they have said they would always find a spot for me, very flattering and all that - but I want to find another side to life, and to me, but that already seems to have been complicated and compromised.'

He was about to go on about the incident with Sullivan but Amelia's calling stopped him. Franklin stood slowly.

'I had better get on with it, if you are going into town there is a short cut down through the bush, just on the other side of the car park, a little project of mine. Like a tiny cable car, easy to operate, save you driving, and the walk across to the village is pleasant.'

The voice called again, a slightly irritated tone developing. He clapped him on the shoulder. 'I'll catch up on the rest tomorrow, don't worry about what time you get back, the place is never locked and I'm usually still up well after midnight.'

Franklin disappeared in through the French doors just as Amelia came around the corner of the building from the other side of the verandah. 'Oh he's actually got moving at last, God that man likes to talk, but I suppose that you know that. You're not eating with us are you Rory.' It was more a statement rather than a question, tinged with a "hoping that he wasn't tone".

'No, thank you Amelia, I had already made arrangements to go into the village, meeting a friend, in fact I had better get going, Frank told me of his mini-cable car, so I will give it a try.' He stood up hesitating a moment as he wondered whether to go and get a jacket, he decided that it was not necessary, and with a final glance at the horizon sky he set off across the lawn to Franklin's Pride.

Amelia watched him go into the top of the bush track, then turned and went back into find Frank and to see if he was attending to the new guests. She found him mixing them a drink in the lounge.

'Amelia, there you are, would you like to join us in a tipple.' He gave her his widest smile, and she kicked him in the ankle.

'Thank you Frank, that would be lovely. Now,' she looked at the new arrivals, 'has that man taken your bags upstairs and settled you in? Of course he hasn't, but we can attend to that shortly.' She took the tray of drinks from him and went over to where they were seated on the large couch. 'Would you like to come out on the verandah, it's still quite lovely out there. I just have a couple of things to attend to in the kitchen and Frank will take your bags up. Then we can all settle down to a chat, go over a few things before we dine.' She had put back her most syrupy voice again, and was smiling cheerfully. She showed them the seats outside with the view over the bay and then went back in to the kitchen.

Franklin disappeared briefly with the new guests bags. When he came back down a few minutes later he came into the kitchen to see if he could be of any help.

'Sorry about that, got caught up with Rory, bit of an unexpected surprise, and almost a large inconvenience. Now is there anything you would like me to do?' Using his placating charm, but he could see that Amelia was less than charmed.

'No it's alright, you old rogue, go and see to the guests, I guess I'm over reacting, not used to you seeing somebody you know - and obviously liked and respected - what is he doing here, and you are right, but it is slightly more than just a minor inconvenience.'

'Oh just nosing around - think he's on holiday and also looking for a hideaway to buy, wants somewhere to retreat to from the big bad world, can't say I blame him, but apart from that I haven't really got into any depth of anything.'

As Primmer went back outside and collected the already empty glasses from the couple, and went back to refill them, his thoughts transferred to other matters that needed to be addressed. While it was good to see Rory Calder, it may not, as Amelia had said, be the most convenient time.

Rory went about fifty yards down the picturesque track. It was flanked with flowering shrubs, set against the background of the native bush, the path was covered in crushed shell. At the end was the little cart, perched beside a loading platform. An electric motor, winch and large reel covered in heavy wire rope, was housed in a semi-enclosed lean to with the switching gear on a pole beside the platform. The cart had a padded seat and a roof, just enough room for two, the descent looked quite steep, but the structure looked solid and sound, the track running under a canopy of the trees. He read the instructions that were attached to one of the posts on the shelter, and stepped into the cart, reached back around the post and pushed the green button, then released the brake on the fascia of the little vehicle.

It began a quiet and smooth journey down through the bush. Three minutes later it stopped at the bottom. Rory got out and sent the car, as per the instructions back up, he could return it back down if and when he needed later. There was a code, and you could only know that if you had started at the top.

The sky was just beginning to darken with heavy clouds, as he set off along the footpath by the sea wall. Although there was still two hours until it would be completely dark, a sombre shadow hung over the town, and out over the sea. Beyond the points, the occasional flash of lightning lit the horizon. It looked as if the morning's storm could well return, and that could produce a few damp diners.

Rory could see as he came to the wharf, that the Cafes were already quite busy and the outside street tables at both, were almost full. The Musos Rick and Rob were in full swing, and already a few of the patrons, were up dancing and singing, plainly into the mood of the evening. He felt the atmosphere, and was glad he hadn't opted to stay with Frank and Amelia. Though as much as he liked the man, he didn't feel quite as comfortable about his first contact with his new wife, and a thought crossed his mind, then embedded itself in his subconscious. "What a strange place for him to be, what was he really doing here? And – Amelia – not at all what I would expect. Not after Jane!"

As he got close to the Crazy Cow he caught sight of Jenny standing on the steps, she saw him and waved, signally to come over to the door. He negotiated the crowded tables and came to where she was standing.

'I've reserved a table for you, us, for later, the same one as last night - is that okay?' Her smile warm, her eyes bright – happy – infectious.

Before he could answer, she bubbled, 'And, I have a bottle of the Oyster Bay that I removed to upstairs before, for us, I'll sneak a sip or two as I dive around the customers.' She pointed to the table. 'I'll leave you to it, for the time being, it's a lot busier than I expected.' She touched his shoulder and was gone - back into the building. He seated himself, and poured one glass for himself and popped the bottle back in the cooler container, and began to observe the crowd. There were a number that he recognised from the previous night, and across at the Boring Bull, there were also one's who had been there the night before, their regulars as well, he wondered. But for a quiet sleepy hollow, where did all these people spring from at night?

Jenny's voice beside him startled him out of the people-watching trance, he hadn't yet touched his wine.

'Who's a slow boy tonight then, and where's mine, are you not wanting me to stop and pass a merry moment with the you, I may have to let the other customers know that the axe murderer is back.'

'Sorry, just got carried away with the music, let me pour for you Madam.' He picked up the bottle and filled her glass. She sat down beside him, and touched his glass with hers.

'To an exciting, interesting and enjoyable evening - later.' She grinned in a very mischievous way. 'How did you get on at the house of luxury on the hill, is it going to suit the needs - or are they a bit over the top for you?'

'Actually, it will be fine, I think, for a day or so anyway. You wouldn't believe it, but the fellow who owns it is an old friend and colleague of mine from the University. I thought he was dead, he had very bad illness - the big C - but he seems fine now, he too was on the extra surprised list as well, seeing me.'

'At last, a bit more information! So the University, why, what, how, when, I need to know, I have suddenly developed an insatiable appetite for nosiness!' Jenny's smile became even wider.

Rory sat back in his seat and took a sip of his wine. His face became very serious and thoughtful, then he leaned forward again. He placed his glass on the table.

'I was a cleaner in the Physics block, actually, although I did that I was really an undercover security agent - there was someone that was taking research notes, and I had been placed to catch them. It was really quite a dangerous job, as it was thought that the people involved were also tied into an international Industrial espionage ring. I have been doing this type of work for years, different parts of the country, even overseas, other countries. A very specialised type of operation.'

Jenny looked at him wide eyed. 'Really. And it was dangerous? So what did your friend up on the hill do there, was he in the same field, or something else?'

'I shouldn't be telling you this, it's why I never said anything before, it's classified, and I have only just met you, how can I be sure that I can trust you. I had another cover as well, I worked in the Psychology Department and also the Art History as a Professor. I have two degrees a Masters in

Psych. And, a Doctorate in Art History, so it all looked pretty legitimate. Franklin Primmer was a very important Research Fellow, in Chemistry and Physics. That's how we met.'

He had managed to keep his face dead straight as he told the story. There was an amount of truth in it, and also a large amount of fiction! But he didn't see any harm in relating the improvised tale to this girl, who was bound not to take him seriously.

Jenny listened to the story with her mouth slightly open, her tongue flicking across her teeth, her eyes wide. 'Really,' she murmured, 'A cleaner, as a cover, and all those qualifications, and spies - in our Universities, really - a cleaner?' Her voice had started to take on an incredulous tone. 'Really, did you find out who they were?'

Rory was about to answer, he was enjoying his little story, and thought he might embellish it a bit more, when she was called away to deal with a customer who wanted to pay their account. He watched the crowd reacting to the music, and to each other. The lightning was beginning to intensify on the horizon, and the flashes were sending strange lights across the bay.

Jenny came back to the table, she lifted the bottle from the cooler and poured some more wine for them, draining the last of that bottle into their glasses.

'Shall I go and get the other one, then you can tell me the rest of the story.' She was still wide-eyed and a little breathless from her quick exit to the Reception desk and her hurried return.

'No, our glasses are full, we can sip this while we talk, then see how we feel, it's getting very warm, and that lightning is getting more intense, do you think that we will get another downpour like this morning?' Rory sat back in his chair and sipped the wine.

'Stop changing the subject, tell me more about your work, it must have been exciting and fascinating.' Her face was animated and her eyes were sparkling.

'Are you still doing that sort of thing, you sort of said this morning, just a brief comment that you were looking for a new type of lifestyle, so what happened to make you want to leave something as -.' She looked into his eyes and also saw the slight smirk of amusement on his lips. 'You rotten story telling bastard, you made that up!' She gave him a playful, although not soft, punch on the shoulder. 'God you had me really going there, you rat! What do you really do!'

'Oh parts of it are very true, but no not all of it.' Although he had exaggerated some of it, actually most of it was based on fact, but there were only three people, as far as he knew who really knew the truth, himself, and Franklin Primmer. There had been four, but he was dead, and the other - had not been in contact or contacted for sometime.

'I don't do very much at all, I am on extended leave, for a year, I can go back but it is unlikely that I will.' Rory watched her now that she had got over the story telling bit, she too was watching him over the rim of her glass as she sipped her wine.

'Okay, so what's the rest of the story, and this time let's try realism and truth. I am not being nosy any more, I really am interested - genuinely interested.' Jenny's face expressed her feelings. She knew very well how to manipulate a situation to her advantage, and she was going all out to do so.

Rory, put his glass down on the table, and rested his chin on his hands, his head bowed slightly and he closed his eyes. He wondered whether he should reveal anything to this effervescent young woman, who, in the short time he had been with her, he had come to like and enjoy being with. A feeling that had been absent from his life, since he had rejected Rebekka.

'I don't know whether I want to, or should, tell you too much about myself, my work, my past life, not at this stage. Suffice to say that the last two years haven't been easy and I really do want to get away from what I was and what I did, and even perhaps what I am. Pursue a new direction. I don't know if this is the right place, or the right timing. Yes – I know I've only been here a matter of hours, but I like it, so far. He added the 'qualification'! 'Anyway, it's too soon to make any decision, and it may be too small, incestuous, claustrophobic? Particularly, with already this antagonism towards my presence. Sometimes if things happen too quickly they don't not turn out for the best, for anyone. I've learnt that from hard experience, much of it bitter.'

As he had spoke Jenny watched him intently, she could see he'd experienced pain in his life, that he was vulnerable, that he was looking for a new direction. And, she knew that it wasn't that long ago that whatever it was, had happened. But now for a number of reasons, had doubts as to the complete truth of what he had been saying, grave doubts.

'If you want to tell me about yourself that's fine, and if you don't that's fine too.' She was about to say that it didn't matter, she was happy to just enjoy his company, when the village was lit by a huge flash of lightning. The following clap of thunder rumbled straight over head, shaking the tables right to the ground! The skies opened,and the rain pelted down on them. In the darkness, with the music playing, people singing, dancing, enjoying themselves, no-one had noticed another storm moving in from the sea.

The crowd scattered off the street, some running into the buildings, others to their cars, some seemed to just disappear into thin air!

'Shit, most of these bloody people haven't paid!' Jenny leapt out of her chair and ran inside. She breathed a sigh of some relief, the room was crammed with soggy dripping patrons standing by the desk. Others had found spare tables - most had been outside, and only three inside were being used. Rory followed her in, and stood at the back of the reception area, watching as the rain, and sudden strong, swirling gusts of wind, began to devastate the street. Tables, chairs were blown over, bottles, glasses and plates smashing onto the ground. He moved closer to the window, the rain was torrential and was sheeting down across the town. The lightning flashes producing ghostly shapes and the thunder so loud that people were shouting to be heard.

'What a fucking mess,' she whispered, 'how the hell am I going to get cleaned up while the weather's like that!' Jenny after dealing with a few of the customers had followed him to the window and stood with him for a moment, she touched his arm leant on him for a moment – sighed and then went back to the desk.

Jenny dealt with a few more of the customers accounts, and arranged for wine for some others that were not going to brave the storm. While she was doing this, she had seen him move from one window to the other on the other side of the door, she went back and stood very close to him.

This time Rory became more aware of her closeness her perfume. Uneasy feelings stirred in him. He pushed them aside and looked down at her, and smiled ironically. 'You never know, it could be worse, it could have been a hurricane and smashed the windows and torn the roof off as well.' As he spoke another extremely strong gust battered into the front of the building bursting the door open and hurling water that was pouring over the guttering into the entrance.

'Hmm, maybe I spoke too soon!' Rory went to the door and pushed it shut, locking it, so it wouldn't happen again. 'Perhaps you should let the customers exit out the back way, it might be safer and drier!' He came back beside her, this time he put his arm around her shoulder in a gesture of comfort, he could see that she was now getting pretty upset with the situation.

'It certainly doesn't look as if it will let up. I don't suppose your brother left a parka or waterproof coat here. If you have something I could put on his funny clothes and try to get some of that stuff out of the way, can't just stand and look at it.'

Jenny looked up at him, a little bemused for a moment. 'Don't be so bloody stupid, why would you want to go out in this. Besides it's not your problem, and I don't think that anyone is going to come along and steal anything, although you never know, there are some pretty weird people around, and I think I may be standing next to one! Would you really go out and try to clean it up?'

'Standing here isn't going to improve the weather, and going from this morning it could go on all night. Seriously - have you got some gear?'

'Tons of it, my brother is a yachty, he's always leaving stuff behind, it's hanging in the store room by the toilets.'

Rory went out through the kitchen and found the storeroom, he stripped to his underwear and pulled on the bright yellow over pants a jacket and boots. He attracted a few strange looks as he came back through. 'Where do I put the stuff, I can't bring it in here.'

'There's a lean to, around the other side, between the shops, it goes in there, it stacks pretty well.' Jenny's expression was amused at the sight of him.

'Okay, now get me a couple of plastic rubbish sacks, I can put the broken stuff in one and anything that is still intact in the other, oh and a yard broom if you have one.' He waited by the door, she was back quickly with the gear he wanted and a large coal shovel.

'It might be easier to get the rubbish up with this - you really don't have to do this, but I do appreciate it. I would come with you, but I can't leave now with all these people here.'

Rory went out into the storm, the patrons clapped and cheered, many of them were now getting a little worse for wear. As he ran out the door two figures appeared from near the alley between the buildings, two men dressed in shorts T shirts and gum boots, they were already soaked. It was the American boys - Rick and Rob. They all stopped and looked at the sight, and at themselves and all started laughing.

'What a pack of idiots we must look!' commented Rob. They began to sort out the tables and chairs with Rory who after lifting a lot out of the way, got to work with the broom, occasionally picking up an unbroken glass and plate, and fishing the cutlery out of the ever deepening water. Faces of the patrons pressed the windows from both Cafes. Rory got an odd glimpse of Jenny who stopped now and again to view the progress as she and the rest of her staff went about serving drinks and desserts.

The three men were now the floor-show, but within half an hour they had most of it cleared away. They trekked around the side of the building to the back. Jenny had placed a pile of towels for them. As they dried themselves they sat on the back step and watched the continual downpour for a few minutes, then the two Americans got up.

'We had better get going, we have another party, a gig to do up at the Cove Pub,' drawled Rob. 'We are now a bit on the late side, at least it's just us and our guitars, we'll just have to stop for five minutes at get some fresh gear on, still makes a change than everything running smoothly.' They gave Rory a slap on the back and they set off down the little path that ran out to the main street they turned and waved, yelling above the rage of the wind and rain. 'Tell Jen we'll catch up with her next week, okay?' And they were gone.

'It doesn't look like it's going to ease up does it.' Jenny's voice, behind him. 'Why don't you go upstairs and change back into your gear, I put it in the spare bedroom, and there is a glass of wine on the table with some cheese and nibbles for you. I have only a few customers left and they are making going home noises. We haven't had that dinner we were supposed to have, but we could still have another drink and chat, and a snack – I'll throw something together - would that be alright? Not much of a thank you for cleaning up the mess but it's about all I can manage right now. But I think you may well have been very right, by the morning it would be an even bigger shambles.'

Rory lifted himself off the steps, he felt a bit stiff and tired, and although the temperature was not low he felt cold. 'Maybe it's just a reaction to everything that's happened in the last two days.' He muttered as he stood and went over to the stairs to the flat. 'So much in such a short time, when I was looking peace and quiet, and for a place into which to retreat, I find the exact opposite, and yet I suppose, in some ways, it is at least a bit different from I what I normally get thrown at me. Perhaps the powers that be know a bloody site more than I do!' He took off the wet weather gear and threw it in the laundry.

At the top he found the spare room and his clothes neatly laid out for him. This room, as the others, was immaculate. Decorated, in a way though, more Spartan in comparison. Cream walls, a low plain varnished Futon bed, with a black and red bedding. The other furniture too was simple, two bedside tables, black lamps, with shades of the same colour bedding, and a scotch chest. Large stark, abstract paintings, on each of the walls. There were no windows, just a skylight set into the angled ceiling.

Rory sat on the bed, and pulled off the old clothes he had worn under the yellow cloaking. He dressed in his own, folded the discarded clothing and placed them on top of the chest of drawers, then took his shoes and went into the living room, as Jenny had said, there was a glass of wine and a platter of food.

The room was lit by one table lamp, and the refraction, through the still streaming rain, of an orange street light. He stood in the semi darkness by the window and peered out into the storm.

Sounds of Jenny and her staff moving around below came through the floor and up the stairwell. They were obviously now clearing up, the clatter of dishes and glasses being placed on shelves, the noise of chairs being placed on tables and brooms and mops being organised for the final clean of the night.

Rory went over to the couch near the other window and set his glass on the coffee table, then settled back into the deep cushions, watching the rain patterns on the glass. he closed his eyes, and as he had in the hotel room the previous day, he wondered why he was here, what he was doing in this place, and, who was he. It seemed impossible that so much of his past could be here, it may in some respects, or to others, be nothing, but to him - now this moment - it seemed - surreal.

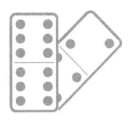

EIGHT

Sullivan stood by the window listening to the ringing of the phone in Hans' office in Johannesburg, it seemed to go on interminably. His mind started to panic.

'He should be there, he is always there at this time on a Saturday morning, what the hell is going on, has someone already tipped him that we have a "situation", and if they have - who could it be? God, now I am becoming paranoid. There could be all sorts of explanations". He was about to hang up when there was an answer, but it was not Hans.

'Hello, may I be of assistance to you?' It was a woman, the accent English, not Afrikaans. Extremely formal.

'Hans Jongejan please, if he's available?' Sullivan tried to keep his voice even, business like, he was getting nervous, he always did when he called Hans, particularly when he had not spoken for some time.

'I am sorry Sir, he's not, he is away on business, and will not be returning for another few weeks. May I take a message and relay it to him when he calls?'

Sullivan thought for a moment, he did not want to set off alarm bells. 'No it's alright, it is a minor business matter, I am an associate, Mr. Peter Sullivan, I can call again when he has returned.'

'Thank you Mr. Sullivan, I have heard Hans speak of you, I will mention that you called, I'm sure he will be interested to hear from you when he returns.' There was a now a suspicious tone in the woman's voice.

He was about to ask where Hans was, when the line went dead.

Sullivan hung up. He felt troubled by the response from his call to Hans. He'd never known him to have anyone 'English' particularly a woman, working for him. He stopped his stare out the window, and turned to see how Mangus was getting on. He hadn't heard anything coming from that side of the room. His partner was sitting at the desk, his head bowed, resting his forehead in his hands.

'What's the problem Mangus? Did you find out what's going on, anything can be helpful?' Sullivan watched his partner with interest.

Mangus shifted uncomfortably, and as he looked at Sullivan, his face seemed to turn grey.

'Yes, I've spoken to Blanchard, I got him on his mobile. He has the merchandise, but he will not be delivering it to the prescribed purchaser.' He hesitated briefly. 'He wants a considerable sum of money - money in exchange for not providing the authorities with information about our operations. It appears that our friend has been feeding - anonymously of course - information to parties that could be damaging to our health, amongst other things, like reputations and so on, and for him to stop doing so, he requires us to come to an amicable agreement, on his terms of course. Also, he says that our agreement may also circumvent any further unfortunate accidents occurring to anyone that may be near and dear. Those are my words Peter, his were not, as you can imagine - quiet so - polite.'

'What about Mackintosh, at the Marina, did you get hold of him?' It hadn't sunk in what Mangus had told him. 'What! - what do you mean - a lot of money - and - accidents occurring - where is the little bastard!'

'I don't know, he said he would be in touch with us in future, and not to bother trying to find him, and of course - don't inform the Police, as if we would, with what we're doing!' Mangus picked up his Martini, and drained the glass. He refilled it, and went to the window.

'So the last consigment of packages from Jongejan are in the wrong hands! What did you say about Mackintosh - What's going on?' Sullivan's brain was jumping from one place to another, he felt panic starting to flow in his veins. He had never lost control of anything before, except his temper, and now - now there were big problems.

'There was no answer, not even the message minder, so what the hell has happened to him I've no idea. But Peter, this is looking serious, we have not been careful enough. From way back I never trusted Blanchard, and now it appears that he's even more of a menace to us than before, it also looks - from what he said - that he's behind what happened to Miranda. Now, what did Hans have to say, did you tell him what's going on?' Mangus looked back at Sullivan – his face ashen. His eyes flicked nervously around the room.

'He wasn't there, which is odd, he usually, although not always, mentions that he's away. An English woman answered, I never knew he had an English lady working for him. Very polite, but cool, almost – icy. It all seems very very bloody strange. Blanchard, Mackintosh, Jongejan, all not available? Well available, may not be the word, because you had contact with Blanchard, it could of course just be a coincidence - couldn't it? No, I don't suppose that it bloody well could! '

Sullivan turned and looked out the window again, the sky was darkening again, as it had that morning, it looked as if another storm was brewing.

'How appropriate,' he thought. Then it occurred to him. "Why had Warren talked to Mangus? Why not him?" He had always been blunt, up front. He certainly wasn't as some, in fact most people, ever been in awe of him - and he'd never had any time for Mangus. He found him weak, obsequious, which in some ways he was, but on the surface only, beneath that lurked that "Machiavellian madness" which as Sullivan knew, could be so very dangerous.'

'Look, I'll just put in a quick call to Euan, you never know – he might have information – something about the situation – and he might know where Han's is! Then maybe we should eat. Later, we'll try to figure out how we can deal with this, before it escalates completely out of our control. What do you say Mangus?'

As he dialled, Sullivan watched his partner standing in the kitchen, there was something not right with his demeanour, he wasn't his usual self at all! The phone was answered after three rings. He quickly asked his questions, then told Euan about his call to Jongejan, and the response from the woman who'd answered. He finished with, 'I have this feeling that she's part of Hans' life. Someone that we've not been for some obscure strange reason we have not been made aware of. You give her a call and see what you can sort out with her. Put on a bit of pressure – you know – it's urgent, we need to contact Hans.' When he finished the call, he looked at Mangus. His thoughts went to the previous conversation regarding Warren Blanchard.

'Don't you find it a bit strange, that Warren told you all this? I mean, he usually avoids talking to you at all costs, he doesn't exactly like you, does he.' Sullivan knew that he was being provocative, and that his partner didn't like being spoken to in the tone he used, but his uneasiness at the whole situation was growing by the minute.

Mangus was busy opening the Poly boxes of food, and didn't look up. He tried to sound offhand about the comment, but there was a nervous stutter to his voice.

'Ye - es, perhaps it - is. I have at times had dialogue with him. N-ot of - ten admitt-edly, but I think that we - um, have - improved our ah - relationship, in that regard, on-ly in that way though, necessary - that - that happened, do-n't you think?'

The way that Mangus had replied, was completely out of character. Sullivan had never heard him like this, and he had known and worked with him a long time.

'What the hell is the problem? Is there something that you aren't telling me? You're as nervous and erratic as a cat on hot bricks. Look I'm just going to the bathroom, I'll be back in a moment – there are things that need sorting!' He went across to the hallway that lead to the bathroom. As he got to the door he glanced back. Mangus was opening the last container.

'I think that we should discuss calling ---.' Sullivan never completed the statement.

The explosion threw Sullivan against the door frame and into the passage, glass fragments and nails followed, along with parts of the kitchen! They slammed into him, slashing his back, arms and neck, part of the left side of his face was lacerated. He didn't see the upper part of his friends body and head disintegrate. Flames and smoke filled the living room, and the huge plate glass windows exploded outwards showering masses of glass into the streets below.

*   *

The pendulum clock on the wall chimed once. Rory opened his eyes and glanced over at it, it was only fifteen past ten. The sounds from the kitchen below were less than before, but someone was still cleaning up, he supposed it may just be Jenny on her own. He thought of her and her vivacious infectious personality, and he thought of the last times, he had been even remotely interested in, or close to anyone.

There had only been two interludes since Serena had walked out on him, taking the children. The first was about seven months later. Strangely she too had been in the same trade as Jenny. She had been the owner of a Restaurant he'd frequented on his way out to his home in the bush up in the Ranges, on the west side of the city.

It had always been a convenient stop, and saved him having to cook every night, not that he minded that, he didn't, and he was very competent. They had talked a lot, it was never a hugely busy place, but it did have atmosphere, and good, reasonably priced food, and a very adequate wine list.. They had often shared more than a glass or two. One thing had led to another, her flat was attached, his home was only another five minutes. They spent time at each others places, but it was too soon, and it was not all that satisfactory for either of them. She, having not long broken up with her husband and business partner. They were better at conversation and friendship, than love making.

Solace, comfort, and the intimacy, that they thought – hoped, that the sex would give them was not provided, and the act was in the end, pure lust and physical release. Then, after a few months, she sold up everything and moved to Australia, that solved the problem of 'where next', completely.

The second 'affair' was with the lovely Rebekka in Cardiff, which was ill fated and ended bitterly, after the deaths of Serena, and the children. His determination to return home, alone, rejecting the girls pleas to go with him, and his depression were also contributing factors.

Rory pushed the thoughts away, they were not relevant, he swung his bare feet up onto the couch and lay his head back on a cushion on the wide soft armrest, he closed his eyes and let the sounds of the night and the rain swim over him. He fell asleep. He didn't hear Jenny come up the stairs, or her come over to the sofa and stand watching. Nor did he feel the light rug being spread over him. The rain was still heavy and lashed the iron roof, the windows, drowning out all but its own sound.

After she had covered up what she referred to later, as the "Soggy Sleeping beauty muttering axe murderer", (she told him he was talking in his sleep, he never ever knew whether to believe her or not). Jenny went to the phone table, and dialled the number of Wisteria Lodge. She glanced over at the clock, it was nearly eleven thirty. It had taken a lot longer to get rid of the hangers on, the die hard customers wanting more wine – and then to clean up, than she had anticipated. 'Shits I hope that I'm calling too late and wake Franklin, and Amelia!' She had, for a specific reason, told Rory that she didn't get on at all well with Amelia. It was part of the game they played. It was Franklin who answered the phone.

'Hello, good evening, Wisteria Lodge, may I help you.' Franklin's cultured voice was clear, but it did have a slightly intoxicated slur to it.

'Hello Franklin, Jenny at the Crazy Cow, sorry I know it's late, but I have your guest, and I believe old friend Rory here. He's asleep on the couch, we had a shambles here after the storm struck, and he helped clean up, we were going to have dinner, but with one thing and another and lot's of boozed patrons sheltering from the weather, well he went upstairs and is now in bye-bye land. And no, I haven't molested him - yet.'

They both laughed, they had always got on well, she had a deep fondness for the old "codger" as she called him. She sent as many people that she could to him, and it was of course reciprocated, as long as she thought the people would would fit in. And that had nothing to do with 'space'! The three had a great number of common interests, interests that went far beyond any 'normal hospitality'.

'The rain's still pelting down, I think he may as well stay where he is, thought I would just let you know that he hasn't been kidnapped – though there's a thought!' She laughed. Okay?'

'Thank you Jenny, I wasn't expecting him back early, now I won't expect him until the morning – sometime. Thanks for your call. Goodnight – and take care, you know what I mean.'

She put the phone down quietly. He hadn't stirred at all during her conversation. Jenny went over closer to the couch and looked at the sleeping man. It had been for her too a long time since someone had got under her skin, and so quickly. She was not sure within herself as to why, it had been her that had made the initial advances if they could be called that. Something had attracted her, an almost instant magnetism. Perhaps it was his reluctance to open up, that made her more impulsive and inquisitive, more determined to find out more, to get - closer. She thought of waking him and suggesting that he use the spare bedroom, but rejected the idea, and thought it may be better to let sleeping axe murderers lie. At least for the moment, just in case of - temptation, and she was not necessarily meaning him!

The girl smiled to herself and pulled the cover up over his shoulders, and feeling comfortable that he was there - and here, she went to her room, closing the door behind her. Jenny removed her clothes and slipped into her bed. She lay watching the street lights and rain, pattern the window, and wondered whether her new 'friend' would stay in the village, she held no expectations, she couldn't, not under the circumstances, and now what she knew about him, but an interesting thought crept into her mind as sleep came to her.

Jenny woke with a start and sat up wondering what the sound was that had disturbed her. She stared around the room and at the window, then got up and went over to it, looking out into the night. It was completely silent, and pitch dark. The street lights were out, and there was not a light to be seen around the town.. Her old fashioned alarm clock with its luminous dial, said it was now a little after two, she went to switch on the lamp, nothing happened, she tried the switch by the door, nothing. Her still half-asleep brain started to wake.

'There must be a power cut, the electrical storm must have shorted a line or transformer.' Taking her gown from the end of the bed, she inched the door open and peered into the blackness of the lounge. She couldn't see across to the other side in the darkness, she inched her way on tiptoe to the middle of the room. The sofa was empty, the rug pushed to the end and half on the floor, she stopped and stared at where he had been, disappointment and sadness swept over her, she had hoped he would have stayed until morning, and spent some more time talking, getting to know why he had come, and what she would read into his words – particularly between the lines. Her thoughts about him were torn in several directions, but all coming back to one conclusion. Caution – be very very careful. Play the part of the person you want him to see – no more no less, until you have to.

'He must have gone back to the Lodge when the rain stopped,' she said quietly.

'What are you doing sneaking around at this time of the morning, checking up to see if I have stolen the silver?' Rory's voice behind her. She leapt about three inches off the floor and swivelled at the same time to see him coming out from the kitchen. Her gown fell open exposing her tanned slim well shaped body. He stopped dead, but did not avert his eyes. She pulled it quickly around herself.

'Sorry about that, should have tied the belt.' She half smiled 'I'm not used to having strange men lurking around in my house. In fact not used to having anyone, strange men or unstrange men - here at all!'

Rory raised his eyebrows and gave a strange look. He was about to mention about her brother staying, but rejected the comment, for the time being.

Jenny could feel the blush rushing through her whole body. 'What are you doing wandering around anyway, I thought for a moment that you had left, gone back to the lodge. I was woken by something. I realise now it was the lack of noise, and the street-light not shining in the window. The eeriness, eeried me!' She grinned up at him.

'There seems to be a power cut, um, and well I got a bit frightened and wondered if you ---.' It all came out in an embarrassed rush, and she could feel the heat of her blush burning through her body, or was it something else, she realised he was standing there in only his briefs. The heat of the blush began to transfer itself to another part of her body.

Rory also suddenly realised and looked down at himself. 'Shit, sorry,

I forgot, I got hot and took of my jeans and shirt, just as well I left my knickers on!' They both began to laugh. 'I was looking for the coffee, I wasn't going to disturb you and was trying to be as quiet as possible, sorry if I woke you, would you, as you are up like to join me?'

'No, you didn't, as I said, it was the silence, the rain stopping and no - it wasn't you, I didn't hear a thing out here, and how do you think you are going to make coffee when the power is off?' She asked, her head cocked to one side and a quizzical look on her face. Their eyes had adjusted to the darkness and they could make out each other now quite well.

'Good point, I hadn't thought of that. So if we can't make a hot drink, we can't see to play cards or read a book. It's just as well it isn't cold or we would freeze, and why the hell are we standing in the middle of the room in the middle of the night having a completely inane half naked conversation. So you could go back to bed and I could crawl back onto the couch and we could get some more sleep - except that now I am wide awake. Do you want to talk. We could, I know it's late and the wrong time and you must be very tired, but we could have that glass of wine we were going to have and nibble on the now sad snacks. Or, I could clothe myself and wander back to the Lodge.'

'You offer so many exciting choices, but first perhaps you should do the clothing bit, seeing you like that, is rather disturbing, I'm not used to looking at - well - rather attractive virtually naked men - and I might get the wrong idea about you.'

She had become, now that the first heat of her blush had subsided, quite light hearted again, and she sensed again her attraction to this strange stranger, yet she felt really that he wasn't as strange as she first thought and certainly now - he was no stranger.

'Yes, right, I will, sorry I forgot.' It was his turn to feel a blush start, and for his age he felt it inappropriate, but could do nothing about it. He went over to his clothes and shrugged them on. His back to her, he didn't want her to see the other reaction he was having, although he had a feeling that it was a bit late.

'Okay now we are both, as you say - wide awake - I'll opt for the suggestion of the wine and stale nibbles, and I will also put on something a little more - covering! If you would be so kind oh ungallant Knight, to get a chilled bottle from the fridge and open it, I will return in a minute.' She disappeared into the bedroom.

Rory found a bottle of Chablis in the fridge, but also spied a good bottle of Shiraz on the shelf above, he went over to her door and tapped on it. 'Would you prefer some red, might be more relaxing at this time of the morning.'

'I think I would prefer so, would that be alright?' She opened the door, she was dressed now in a loose fitting sloppy jogging suit, and she had brushed her hair and applied a small amount of make-up. 'Yes that's a better idea, the Red.'

He nodded and padded back to the kitchen, rummaged for the opener in a drawer that he assumed would house such an implement, found it and opened the wine. Jenny had gone over to the couch and had put the nibbles on the coffee table and tucked herself up in the corner with her feet curled under her. Rory took in the way that she looked, and the way that she looked at him, as he crossed over to her and handed her the wine. They touched glasses, and he sat down at the other end.

'This is really quite ridiculous, I don't entertain people at this time of morning, and certainly not men, well not for a long time anyway, but somehow Rory Calder you bring out the ridiculous in me. I'm not sure whether that is good or bad!' Jenny sipped her wine and looked at him over the rim of her glass, weighing up her next question.

'In the light of that statement being ridiculous. Are you afraid that I might bite or even worse, molest you - you are an awful long way away down there, I feel I will have to shout for you to hear me.' She gave him a very cheeky smile and sipped her wine again. Thinking - "why am I playing this game and saying these things! But unfortunately I really like him! And yes I do want to fuck him – no – I want to make love to him! Then fuck him!"

Rory had been semi-laughing at her first statement, but with the second, his face became serious. 'Yes, and no, I'm more afraid of myself than you,' he managed a weak grin, 'mind you, you are a bit on the scary side, and as with me - you have avoided telling me very much about yourself. I seem to recall at least three occasions in the last two days that our conversations have started to head in one direction, and ended up being really quite innocuous about nothing in particular in another. So what about telling me about yourself.' He took a deep breath and decided to risk it. 'Or better still, so we can both avoid talking about ourselves, tell me what you know about Mr. Peter Sullivan and company.'

'I told you a lot this afternoon, remember, about his wife, and moving here and I recall too, that when I talked about his wife's accident, you went a strange colour and became very tense.'

'As you did, when you started to talk about Jim being Miranda's Grandfather. So there's something that is bothering both of us about this man. What you told me only filled in a couple of gaps - about some of the 'whys' of the situation here. But do you know anything - just about the man?'

Jenny didn't reply and for several minutes she sat staring at him, she sipped her wine, then put the glass down and went and stood by the window. He did not interrupt her thoughts, and waited for her to speak.

At last she did, but again digressed. 'Are you going to be around here tomorrow - I mean today. You spoke of going up the coast, maybe looking at other places to think about staying in, at least I think that's what you said.'

'I may have mentioned it, and whose changing the subject again. You seem very reluctant to talk about yourself or Mr. Sullivan. And before you say it, yes I am just as bad, so what is it that is stopping us opening up and just letting the other person in, just a little bit closer. We seem to get along well, but we are both putting up barriers, I guess we have reasons and yes I do have, and I am, how shall I put it, trying to repair damage, that sounds a bit on the confusing side, I am not very good at that.'

Jenny was watching his face and she could see his struggle with whatever it was that was on his mind. She was about to say that, 'It didn't matter, let's just go with the flow and find what comes along,' when he continued.

'I won't go into details of the whys and wherefores - yet, but when you mentioned his wife being killed in a car accident - brake failure - it was very, very close to home - too close to home. My wife and three children were killed in a similar way, a car with brake failure, ran into a river, and they drowned. I was initially suspected of having something to do with it. We were separated, and there were going to be a few problems sorting it out. But it wasn't me, and they --.'

'Stop Rory, stop it, I know you don't want to talk about it, and I don't want you to, I don't want to know - not tonight anyway, maybe never. I've been prying where I shouldn't. It's too soon for us to get that close - into each other's past, into each other's minds. I'm sorry, I really just want to get to know you slowly, gently, and have some good fun times as well, but I am unsure whether that is what you want, or whether it will ever happen - or if it should even happen. I too have skeletons in the closets of the past, but I think you have gathered that, you are not exactly a dummy, are you.'

'I hope I'm not, but I often wonder. Some situations that I get into would indicate otherwise, and you may be right about not talking about that part of the past – or any of the past - at present.' He looked up at her as she still remained by the window, half turned towards him. 'Why do you want to know if I will be around today. I had as you said thought of adventuring further, but Jim has asked that if I am around later to come in for a meal. Now with coming across Franklin, I will hang about for another day or so maybe more. I guess, even in a small place, like this, one can avoid people. Anyway I'd like to find out a few more things about a few of the people, including the one I just asked about, so don't think you are off the hook there - so yes I will be here, to answer your question in a very roundabout way.'

'Well, it's just that I would like to show you something, and to spend a bit of time with you in a different way. Not here, or the village.' She finished the glass of wine and looked at the clock. 'God it's nearly three thirty, I'm going back to bed.' It was on the tip of her tongue to ask, - "Would you like to join me – feel me – my body against yours". Her body wanted him, but her mind thought better of it and said 'No, it's not the right time – or is it and does it matter if it is – or is not? Because time may be shorter than either of us might think!'

'Would you like the spare bedroom? It's really comfortable, and the light doesn't get into your eyes in the early morning.' Jenny picked up his glass from the table and took them to the kitchen. 'You decide where you would like to try to sleep for the rest of the darkness.' She walked over to him, bent and kissed his forehead, and gently touched his cheek with the tips of her fingers as her mouth moved down over his. But it was a brief kiss, though it held a lot of meaning. 'Goodnight Rory or should I say good morning.' She kissed him again, this time, lingering just long enough to realise that she was putting herself on dangerous ground.

After Jenny had gone to her room, he lay back into the sofa and looked up, out through the window at the sky, it was already showing signs of the approaching dawn. The rain had gone and the dark clouds that had haunted the coast and town for the last seven hours had gone, myriads of bright pin pricks of the morning's stars twinkled, and the sliver of a very new moon hung over the horizon.

Rory stood up from the couch. He had been lying, his mind thinking and churning, for about twenty minutes. He thought about "why am I not wanting to take this further? – I'm most definitely physically attracted to her – or part of my body is telling me lies! - So why?" And, as he analysed those thoughts, he saw that the bottle of wine was still on the table, it had at least a couple of glasses left. He walked silently over to the kitchen bench and retrieved a glass, came back to the table and poured a glass, then returned to the window and rested his head against the cool glass.

'So you can't sleep either, and snuck back into the wine bottle. Aha, so you're not only a soggy sleeping beauty ex axe murdered, but a sneaky wine bottle snuckerer - along with what other vices?'

Rory turned and looked down at her, she was still dressed in her baggy tracks, but her hair was tousled where she had been lying down. 'Yes, you have discovered my secret identity, damn, I will have to change my disguise!' He tried to match her silliness but his tone was not convincing.

Jenny tilted her head to one side then the other. 'Hmm mm, no I think I like the look of the disguise you're using.' Then a change, of mood, and subject.

'This time of the morning when it's still and clear like this, is just so beautiful.' She spoke quietly reverently, and moved close in beside him at the window.

'Seeing that we are both so wide awake, and it is starting to get light, what about me taking you to see this thing that I want to show you. It's the perfect time actually, I think you may be impressed, how about it?'

'Do we walk, drive or fly, and do I need to pack my toothbrush, and if the answer to all of those is yes, well I'm more confused than I thought, but okay, if you like, why not.'

'It's just a short drive and a short walk, and you don't need to bring anything.' To herself she whispered, "no not a thing – you wont be needing anything at all."

She grabbed his hand and dragged him away from the window. 'Come on let's get going, now I have thought of the idea, the more it appeals, no time to waste or we may miss the most exciting part!'

They went downstairs, she led him out the back way to her car. The vehicle surprised him, he had not noticed it tucked under under the old rickety lean to carport when he had come around the back the previous night after putting away all the tables and chairs during the storm. It was a brand new Jeep, black, shiny, with a bright red soft top over the strong frame of roll bars. Jenny sensed his surprise.

'It is rather spectacular and lovely isn't it, would you like to drive?' She held out the keys towards him.

'No, no it's fine you lead the way, this is your show, and I have not the foggiest clue where we are supposed to be going have I, but yes it is rather nice,' he cocked an eyebrow at her, 'And not cheap either.'

Jenny did not answer that statement. She went round and got into the drive side, and waved for him to get in.

'It only takes about ten or so minutes or so driving, then another few minutes walk, you can walk of course all the way, but it's a bit long at this time of the morning, and I don't want to miss the show.' She started the engine, he could feel the power pulse through the body of the car, and through him as she backed out and spun the wheel to turn the car to face down the track that went out to the main street.

'I should blindfold you, to make this more exciting - for me, but that may be a bit unfair, okay are you ready, here we go.' Jenny planted her foot and the vehicle leapt forward, she laughed as she turned out into the roadway. 'Sorry, but I become a wild thing when I get in this black beauty, it brings out the baddy in me.' She laughed, but then, under her breath – 'In more ways than one – many more ways Mr. Axe Murderer!'

Rory watched her as she drove the big wagon expertly. She took the same turning that Jim had the previous morning when he had taken him to the old mine sight, but about half way up the track she veered off into what appeared to be just a dirt track that disappeared into the bush. It was however quite wide enough to accommodate her Jeep with room on each side to spare, and it wasn't rough at all, but a smooth well drained metal road, that had weathered the rain storm well.

The narrow clay road followed the contour of the hill, for about half a mile then it climbed steeply, until it came out on a wide long flat plateau. Although the sky was rapidly lightening the strong headlights highlighted the area sweeping across it and bringing up spectacular features of the bush and steep surrounding landforms.

'This used to be a landing strip for small planes, and helicopters, used mostly by the rich hunting set when there was deer and pigs around here. Before that, years ago, just before the mine closed, by the mining company to bring in overseas experts to see if it was worth continuing to pursue and reopen the diggings, it of course wasn't. It was evidently at times quite a tricky place to get in to, and a few less experienced pilots gave a some of their passengers quite interesting palpitations.'

It was now semi-overgrown with scrub, which Jenny weaved the Jeep between to avoid scratching the paintwork, they were soon across it and heading down another road on the far side that had at some stage been sealed, but was now pitted and rough. She slowed and then eased the car into a wide siding, switching off the lights and the engine. She pointed out through the windscreen. 'This is the first part I want to show you.'

The view was across a wide estuary. It was now light enough to see the water, it reflected the last of the edge of the moon and the stars as they gradually were fading into the paling sky, now tinged on the horizon with morning turquoise, the first bird and insect sounds crackled across the still air.

'Now for the second.' She started the Jeep and swerved it back out onto the road, heading it between the high bush on either side. The road began to slope downwards and became quite steep, she drove with extra care, the lights on again picking up tight curves and pot holes ahead of them. At the bottom of the steep slope the road levelled and another siding appeared about a hundred yards ahead. Jenny headed into it and stopped, she turned off the motor, and got out. Rory followed beginning to sense what she was up to.

'Come on - now the walk begins, into the deep dark jungle.' A track led off from the edge of the parking area. 'I'll lead the way, you'll have to close your eyes, I want this to have an impact and I don't want you peeking, can I trust you to keep them shut - or shall I blindfold you?' Jenny laughed lightly

'I am getting the idea as to what is going on. So, if you really want to make it a surprise and make me go - "Wow, oh gee, man oh man" and so on - you had better, cos I just might cheat, and if you are leading the way you wouldn't know would you.'

Rory was finding, as he had on the other occasions with her, that her enthusiasm and childlike excitement was infectious. She went to the back of the Jeep and took a towel off the back seat and wound it round his head. Then locked the car and took his hand.

'Follow me oh blind one, I won't go too fast it is a bit steep and a little slippery after the rain, but it isn't far.'

They set off into the bush. He had not noticed the Private Property sign that was half concealed in the trees, before she had blindfolded him. But, his feet could tell that this was not, he presumed, from the view from when they had stopped before, just a track to the beach through the bush. He could feel it was well formed and gravelled, with steps and an edging at the sides, not the slippery slope, that she had said it would be. It was interesting, that his other senses seemed heightened, he could smell the bush, the trees, the undergrowth, the rotting leaves. The scents of dampness from the rain, and the sounds of the waking life were so vivid he could imagine the activity in trees, on the ground, then after only a few minutes - the smell of the sea - and mud flats.

Rory sensed that they had come out of the bush, the sounds and the smell of the air had changed, and they were not longer on a slope.

Jenny stopped. For a few moments she was silent then, 'Okay, let's un-bandage the head. I think that you have come far enough in that manner.' She giggled, 'that was fun, I was thinking of leaving it on longer, but decided to have pity.' She came in close to him and he could feel her body gently touching his, the fresh smell of her hair, then her perfume, as she reached up and unwound the towel. He was facing the bush where they had exited from the path, Jenny took his arm and turned him round.

*   *

Sullivan lay against the wall, the pain from the glass and nail fragments burned into his back and neck, his legs felt numb, and his right arm hung loosely from the shoulder socket, the carpet beneath him was soaked with his blood. He tried to roll away from the wall but he couldn't move, he tried to twist his head to see back across the living room, he could only managed a slight movement, all that was visible was the shattered windows, the rest was screened by the smoke.

The pain became more acute. He attempted to move, to see if he could see his friend, he tried to call out. His voice, sounded as if his throat was stuffed with cotton wool, only a very muffled croak issued from it, his head seemed as if it was about to disintegrate. There was no response, he couldn't see him - or very much else - he called again. It seemed he was screaming his lungs out, the only sound in reply was crackling of flame.

Sullivan heard the sirens wailing, the noises below in the street as the fire, police, and ambulances arrived. It seemed an eternity until he heard the door being smashed in, and the calling of the people as they came into the shattered apartment. People rushed past him, fire personal, police. He felt the hands and heard the voices of the para-medic staff. He was lifted onto a stretcher, a needle was forced into his left arm, an oxygen mask pushed over his face, then consciousness departed completely.

*   *

The two men in white coats approached the duty desk of the hospital, they carried clip boards and had stethoscopes around their necks, a third wearing a dark suit walked just behind them. The Duty nurse looked up from the chart she was studying, her eyes flicked across the names on the tags on their coats, it was late and she was very tired.

'Yes can I help?' The names seemed familiar, but not well known to her.

'We would like to see Miranda Sullivan please, said the taller of the Doctors, he had sandy hair and clear pale cold blue eyes. 'We need to give her a check over and this gentleman, needs to ask a few questions, about her accident you understand, it seems that her injuries may not - perhaps not be quite so - accidental.'

'Certainly, Ward Seven second floor – room twelve, please see the Duty Sister before you go to see the patient - we had to move her out into a private room, at the request of the surgeon, he thought that she needed to be isolated, I don't know why, her injuries aren't that bad.' It did not occur to the tired nurse that it was very late, she didn't even know why she volunteered the information about the room change. All she cared was, that she would be off duty in around five minutes, and she didn't give a damn who wanted to see who. She didn't see the three of them exchange glances and smiles as they went down the corridor to the lift, the Nurse went into the office and started to arrange her gear to take home.

At the Ward the men ignored the Nurses station and went straight into the room silently closing the door. They stood at the bedside and looked down at the sleeping form of Miranda Sullivan. No-one spoke. The short dark one in white nodded, and took a syringe from his coat pocket and went over to the stand holding the drip that fed into Miranda' arm. He inserted the needle into the tube and plunged the clear liquid from the syringe into it. As he did this, the man in the suit took an envelope from his pocket. He split the seal and laid it inside the small bedside cupboard ensuring that several of the tiny white pills spilled onto the shelf, then he dropped several of them onto the bed cover.

The third, the one who had spoken to the desk nurse stayed by the door watching the corridor.

When they had finished he nodded that it was clear and they left, heading away from the Nurses station to the fire exit stairs.

At the bottom of the stairway there were three doors, one opened to the outside of the building, the second to a long corridor that led to a service and boiler room area, the third into the main reception area. Each man took a different exit, the tall sandy haired one went out of the building. The one in the suit went through into the hospital and across to the lifts, where he took one to the first floor, the third went down to the boiler room, then out another side door into a loading bay.

The men had not spoken at all since they had been at the Hospital reception on the ground floor. Each had their own transport, and would leave the area at different times in different directions. They would all meet again the next afternoon at the Marina up the coast, about an hours drive, on the far side of the peninsular. From there they would go by boat. A fast luxury cruiser to rendezvous with a freighter in the gulf, one of the trio would go aboard the freighter with a number of large packages, the others would go on into the Gulf, anchoring the launch at an island resort. One of them would remain for three days, the other would go by helicopter to the city.

It would be two days before they would connect again, in that time they had arrangements and contacts to make. They would have to put a great deal of trust on each of the parties, particularly the courier with the packages. They had however put one safeguard in place that linked them all, and connected a number of other people with them as well. A list of names, phone numbers and bank account numbers were, with ID's and signatures of all of them, in a safe deposit box in a Bank in Malaysia.

There were three keys, each with different Security Companies. If these companies were not contacted by each of the three men by the 30th May, a representative of each of these organisations was to contact and arrange to meet together and open the box, and take the information to the appropriate place.

None of the men was to have a key or access to one. It wasn't a completely foolproof safeguard, but, it was a reasonable one, and had been agreed to by all of them. An associate, who had largely organised the security - for a considerable consideration, also felt that under the circumstances with them splitting up for a few days, it would be as safe as probably it could be.

When the two days had passed, it would be the right time for them to meet again for the next stage of the operation. For the planning of that, they would each call the Associate and he would give them the time, place and country that would be the most advantageous, to their projects development.

*   *

Jenny turned Rory around, she tucked herself under his arm. She looked up at him for a brief second, then followed his gaze. Neither said a word for nearly five minutes as they took in the scene. He for the first time, she, although, it had been many, still found it overwhelmingly beautiful.

The sun had just crested the far hills that bordered the northern side of the estuary. Long streaky clouds were burnished, orangey red, backgrounded by a sky tinged with a multitude of blues and mauves. Closer to the hill tops, each colour was reflected in the water of the incoming tide as it crept over the mud. The area coming alive with the sounds of morning.

Stilts, Oyster catchers, and Blue Heron meandered, and the first gulls came in gliding across from small white sanded bays that dotted the bottom of the bush covered slopes. The multitude of colour picked out by the the sun as crept its way up into the day.

Off to their left an old double storied cottage stood, its windows - as with the water - mirrored each colour and shade - the white walls, ruddy, from the main glow of the sunrise.

From where they were, a shell path picked its way along the shoreline, to the Cottage.

At last Jenny broke the silence. 'Was this worth the bumpy journey and the blindfolded bush walk? Did I make the right choice of adventure, with the right adventurous companion, with which to share this dawn?'

'How did you know that it would be as good as this, or was it a guess? But my semi-sarcastic – "wow oh gee man-oh-man" - certainly doesn't do this credit. It most definitely makes up for all the trouble and clearing up after the storm, and no sleep. Who belongs to the cottage, I remember you saying that you had a hideaway, would this be it, and also part of the surprise adventure?'

'Yes, that's it, my retreat from the big bad world of the village, other things, people and places. Come on I'll make us some coffee. Are you any good at chopping wood? There's no electricity so we have to stoke up the range. But, of course you are, I forgot for a moment you were an axe murderer, so you must know how. It doesn't take long and will help build an appetite for breakfast, then maybe a bit of a snooze while the fire heats the hot water for a shower, or a deep luxurious bath,' Jenny's eyes bore into his, and a smile creased her lips. '---- And then, after that, if you would like to, we can explore. Well you can, I've been here before ha ha, but I'll be your kind guide.' She reached out and took his hand. 'Come on it takes about five minutes, but we can make the walk longer, or if you like we can run!'

'It's such a beautiful morning, it makes one feel fresh, clean and alive.' She bounced off dragging him with her. He shook his head and laughed at her exuberance.

The sun was now just above the hills, on the far side of the estuary. Rory looked at his watch as they approached the house, it was still early, just past six. A sudden reflection of the last forty-eight hours flashed through his mind.

'So much so quickly, too bloody quickly?' He frowned and found a dark cloud hover in his mind.

They came to halt, a little breathless from the gallop along the path. Now on the front grass of the cottage he could see that it was actually tucked in behind a steep bush clad bluff, and the ground behind the main house sloped up steeply into it. Another building was at the top of the of this, it hadn't been visible before, being screened by a stand of trees. A type of Bach or shed, but quite a big building, with a deck along in front of large floor to ceiling French doors stretched virtually the whole width of the building.

Jenny saw him looking up at the other structure. 'I'll show you around later, and what's up there, that's another of the mysterious surprises.' She searched amongst some pot plants at the front door and fished out a large old key, which she pushed into the key-hole and twisted it around, the lock clicked quietly and Jenny turned the big brass nob and swung the door open.

'*Entree Monsieur*!' she bowed and waved him through the door with a gallant sweep of the arm.

'You're a crazy person, you really are!' He smiled, laughing at her. He bowed back and went into the house. As at Jim Bland's home, he entered another unexpected world. The comparison to her apartment home in the village, couldn't have been more marked or dramatic. He knew that it would not be a modern renovated interior but it was as if he had stepped back a hundred and fifty years. Everything looked as if it had been placed there, and kept away from time. From a curved wooden hat rack, a boot scraper, to the bare oiled boards of the sarked walls and ceilings. The window at the top of the stairs that ran up from the hallway, with old coloured and white disfigured glass, through which he could see distorted shapes of the bush.

Jenny stood to the side of the passage watching his reaction.

'It was my Great Grandparents retreat, they were early farmers and timber millers in the area, and --,' she hesitated, as if uncertain what to say, her happy exuberant mood faded, it was as if someone had blown out a candle flame in an already dim room.

'They lived near here, and built this with timber from their own mill. The Bach at the back was added much later, they used to come here a lot when they retired, in fact spent most of their time here, they left it to me. They died when I was still a baby. It caused quite a rift in the family, I have offered to share it, and let the others use it when I am not here. But, the feeling about my inheriting what they thought should be theirs has caused pretty deep scars, you know I suppose how families can be.'

The candle was lit again, and her smile returned. 'Anyway enough of that, let me show you the fire wood, and while you chop the wood, I'll hold the lantern, only I will actually be organising some other bits and pieces. The Bach has power, and a fridge where the necessaries are kept, but the cottage I really love to keep as original as possible, it keeps the ghosts happier too. Not even a phone!'

She grinned to herself as she led him down the passage into the kitchen, pointing to what she referred to as Mr. Range over there, as they went through, then out the back door to the wood pile.

'Okay go to it oh Axe man, I'll be back in about five minutes, there is some cut, so you could get the fire started then chop some more.'

'Yes - okay bossy britches, Wicked witch of the forest, I am at your command!' Rory picked up the axe and split several logs into a manageable size for the range then gathered an arm full of kindling, as Jenny headed up the slope to the Bach. He went back in and began to build the fire. Once it was blazing in the firebox he stood back and looked around the room.

The walls and ceiling were timber but they didn't make it feel dark - dingy, it felt warm - homely. A large bare table sat impatiently in the middle, on the high mantle a very old pendulum clocked ticked, sending echoes from the past. From the ceiling hung old kitchen cooking utensils, the sink bench was scrubbed white. A dresser was laden with jars of and china, a cat basket was snuggled into a corner near the range.

He inspected the fire, it was well caught now, and he fed in several larger logs and damped it down, the room was already losing the early morning chill. Rory went to a window, and caught sight of Jenny coming back with a large basket laden with food. He went out into the yard and picked up the axe again.

'Ha! slacking already, you may have to be punished severely for this lazy attitude to your chores.'

'No no please, spare me, I was just chopping more, the fire's a blazing Ma'am.' He tugged at the front of his hair and stooped forward in a mock servitude.

She gave him a wide smile, 'Oh alright, I'll let you off this time, but then again the punishment might have been - fun!'

Rory quickly cut another pile of logs, and taking an armful he followed her a moment later into the house. Jenny was unloading the basket and spreading the goodies across the table, organising them ready to prepare breakfast, she already had a large old black coffee-pot on the stove.

'Come on I'll give you a quick tour then you can assist the Mistress with the cooking!'

They wandered from room to room, although they were quite small, they didn't give that feeling. There was a charm, a quality about the place that reflected the love that must have gone into its creation. Jenny gave him a brief cameo of her Great Grandparents, even though she'd of course never known them. Then her Grandfather, she didn't mention anything about her Grandmother. Her parents had told her all the stories that had happened around their lives and the early years of the area. She didn't though say anything more about them – or their names.

The house was filled with extreme memorabilia, photos of the area and people of the past era, the old mill and farm, even, a few of the Village. It hadn't changed all that much. Jenny didn't talk about many of the photos, but of much of the other items, old books and ornaments, prints etchings and original oils, she touched and spoke of with almost a reverence.

As they returned to the kitchen through the dining room Rory noted some photographs on a Refectory table, against the side wall near the window. The morning sun was stretching across, touching them with soft light. There were three, one was plainly the great grandparents. The other was of another couple, younger, although not young, and the face of the man bore a very close resemblance to someone that Rory had recently met. The third was of a group of six, the four people from the other photos and two others. He was about to call Jenny back to ask about them, when she got in first with new commands to attend. He made his mental note, to, at a suitable time, broach the subject of the pictures.

In the kitchen the coffee was perking and smelling marvellous, eggs and bacon were frying in a large black pan, thick farm house bread was toasting on the top of the stove held in a wire rack. Jenny moved around confidently and competently, setting the table, laying out condiments and complementaries for the meal, several types of jams, marmalades, and chutneys, cereals, and home preserved fruit.

'Where did you manufacture all this from, your secret store in the secret shed - or are you really a wicked witch and can cast spells over the kitchen table, and the poor unsuspecting wood chopper?'

'Which reminds me,' she replied. 'We need some more of that, the water is warming but has a long way to go before it is at the required temperature for baths and showers. And, by the way - what's this wicked witchy bit, I may be a good fairy! But you won't know which I am, unless you go and chop some more wood. Then I might wave my magic wand!'

Rory went back out to the yard, smiling to himself, and laughing at her mock bossiness. At least he hoped it was mock, it was a trait in people that he didn't, if it was real, take too kindly to. He was also thinking, that, this was not a bad way to spent a sunny Sunday morning, and that perhaps the other incidents may have not been as important as he had judged them. Or was that a tired euphoria capturing his imagination?

'Perhaps,' he whispered to himself, "It's just my paranoia, or do I have a guilt complex over wanting to move away from the past, and reject my responsibilities, those of now and the future?' He sighed and picked up the axe, feeling the dark pall form above him. He had come here for several reasons, this was not one that he had planned on.

Rory was fortunately dragged out of those thoughts by the voice from inside the house. 'Hurry up, your breakfast is almost ready, and there is this delicious fruit to devour first.' Her tone light, happy, relaxed. It broke the black spell that had moved into him. He went back with another arm full of firewood.

Jenny was pouring the steaming coffee into large china mugs. 'Sit down at the head and pretend you are the Lord of the Manor, and I am but your humble serving wench.' She gave him a wicked grin as he sat and started to eat the plate of fruit that was in front of him.

'May I sit and have my breakfast with you Sir, I'm but sore tired from slaving over this here hot stove this fine morning and need rest and sustenance.'

He decided he would play along with her games. 'I suppose it would not hurt this once, you have done well wench, but be quick with that fruit, I'm almost ready for my next course, and I don't like, as you know, to be kept waiting.'

They both burst out laughing. 'Do you often bring strange men to your lair - and feed them such a wonderful feast - or am I a privileged soul cos I took pity on your wet soggy furniture?'

The girl didn't answer his question, just got up and filled two plates with the hot food and set it down at each of their places. They set to on the breakfast. For the next fifteen minutes that was the sole occupation of thought and action. When they had both finished, Jenny got up and refilled their coffee.

'Come on let's go out onto the front porch and have this, and watch the rest of the early morning develop, the tide is coming in, and there should be quite a lot of activity out there.' They got up and went out the back door and around the side of the house to the front lawn, two old wooden benches were propped up against the front of the house under the veranda roof. They settled onto one, and looked out over the glassy estuary. 'Sorry about the long walk – the front door has been jammed for years – have no idea why – have tried just about everything and most tradesmen to get it fixed – just does not happen.'

Flocks of sea birds, of many different varieties, were skimming across the surface in search of their morning feed. Out about two or three hundred yards from the tiny strip of white sand at the bottom of the lawn was a shoal of herring being chased by some bigger fish, one of the flocks spied them and began their dive into the midst.

Rory and Jenny sat in silence, sipping their coffee and taking in the action and the serenity. After some minutes it was Jenny who broke the quiet.

'Actually you are the first man I have ever brought here.' She stopped, looked at him and sipped more of the coffee, thoughtful, as if unsure as to carry on, but did.

'I am really a very private person, and apart from the fact of my work, which has to do with dealing with people all the time - I like to be pretty much on my own, and to pursue my personal interests. So you are perhaps not so much privileged, but maybe just seem sort of special. There is something about you Rory Calder that has got to me, and that is very, very rare. I enjoy your company, although it's only been a couple of days that I've had, to get to know very little. I seem to have a developed a trust in you, and that too is very rare for me. I don't trust people, and I have many good reasons for that. I have also the feeling that you may be of a similar nature. You have already opened one of the chapters of your book, and while I said I didn't want or need to know, I probably do. I know you have more questions that you're going to fire at me. You're just waiting for the moment, correct?' Jenny's stare became intense.

He had watched her equally as intently as she spoke. He was more than a little surprised by her sudden change of mood. This was the second time that the light-hearted 'Jenny girl', had vanished, replaced by a much more introspective woman. Rory suspected there was far more to Jenny, than was immediately obvious. Something ethereal - mysterious, disturbingly mysterious. But as yet, he hadn't figured out how to get past her 'fun facade'.

'Well, I might be, then again I might not. I may not want to change what we have developed, a fun light hearted friendship, yes, based, though I think, the same as you, on a type of trust and someone that one can relate to. And, I'm talking a load of bullshit, you are of course right. I'm waiting for the right moment to approach certain subjects that you have so deftly avoided. But, who knows when, or if that time will ever arrive. Now, we were going to do an explore, and you were to be the guide, let's get this cleared up. Thank you it was a most delicious breakfast. It's been a long time since I have enjoyed one as much, and the company, and a very very long time since I have actually had anyone cook for me.'

'That, is another brilliant change of subject, but yes that's right.' She stood up. 'Shall we do that quick clean up? Then you stoke the fire up for the hot water, and we can get on with the expedition into the unknown dangers of the swamp lands.'

It was an attempt to return to the frivolous, but it wasn't so convincing. They went to the kitchen and Jenny did the dishes and tidied up. Rory did his wood chopping, this time making sure that he cut a good supply.

He finished stoking the firebox and damped it down, then stacked the rest of the logs. 'Do we need our jungle gear? I only of course have what I stand up in, you did not exactly give me a chance to pack for trekking and exploring.'

'No, and I don't have the left over supply of brother here, and, actually I lied about those. Sorry, but they're not my brother's, they belonged to an old boyfriend who came down to stay over two years ago, but I would never allow him to come over here. In the end, he left on and under a cloud, sounds a bit strange, just rather unfortunate circumstances. I don't know why I said they were my brother's, we're not on speaking terms, or any other terms for that matter. Because, well, I don't have one.'

Jenny's attempt to look apologetic for the lie fell flat. As did her voice. 'Anyway, I think we will be okay, there is a network of old walking tracks, campers and day trampers use them now and again in the summer, but generally they hardly see a soul these days. Pretty easy going just a fraction overgrown with scrub and long grass. Are you ready?' Her voice had taken on a hollow monotone. Another change.

Rory was about to comment about the 'lie', but decided that it wasn't, like some other queries he had, to be the right time, instead. 'As much as I will ever be, if I fall over exhausted on the track, it'll only be the wood chopping and no sleep syndrome, so just pick me up by the heels and drag me back. Are you sure we shouldn't grab a bit of sleep first?'

She shook her head vigorously. 'No, we may never get this chance again, with a morning like this, and I feel the need to walk, and to contemplate the better things of life.'

Rory saw the cloud flick over her eyes, and his returned briefly. There was much more to this person than initially met the eye.

Jenny went to the front door opened it, he followed. They went and down the lawn as he was talking, 'I thought you said the front door never opened – seemed no problem then – you making up stories again?' They now stood at the edge of the water. There was no reply, Rory went on deciding it wasn't worth pursuing. 'Which way oh kindly guide, lead me on!' He thought about that statement as she went passed him, and wondered if this was in fact so.

The girl swirled past him and turned to the left and headed towards the steep bluff, at the bottom, she pushed aside the drooping branches of some trees to reveal a track that headed up a narrow gully through the rocks. 'Follow me, your Lady Friday, on a Sunday. I will lead you into the unknown, a commentary on the history of this intriguing area will follow - for a small fee, that will be discussed later.'

As they headed up the small ravine Rory watched her, the way she walked, and the way she held her head. She seemed at times so, confident, alive, vibrant, but he was beginning to see that all on the outside, did not reflect the truth of the inside. The lie about her brother, and strangely even the front door, started unsettling thoughts regarding the situation that he was in, or more to the point, he had placed himself in. It might not have been such a huge deal, but his own present lack of confidence in his decision making ability, his mistrust of others, reared it's ugly head. The beauty of the morning, the anticipation of a day, being relaxed and in tune with his companion, was dulled by the dark clouds of doubt that were gathering in his mind.

They came out at the top of the bluff to a cliff edge. Steps was cut into the face, they went steeply down to another strip of beach. The main path carried on along the top, then gradually sloped into stands on Manuka, Toe toe, and Cabbage trees.

Amongst this, secondary growth, of the scrub and low bush, spread over an area, which held the remains of the old mill. Rusty corrugated iron sheds, and the paraphernalia attached to the industry was scattered about the site.

The main Saw room with its huge blades still stood, although its spreading roof, apart from the massive beams, had collapsed in a tangle of rusty iron. On the water's edge, an enormous barge lay rotting, but as if still waiting for it's load, expectant? Nearby, a ramp where huge milled logs were still stacked. No longer to be rafted, towed up the harbour and loaded onto larger ships for transporting to other ports then to foreign countries.

Further back behind the Mill, on a raised plateau they could see what was left of the cottages that had been built for the workers, and behind them a large three storied building that showed the scars of a fire. Most of the roof was gone and the timber scorched and blackened around the windows. Jenny watched his gaze flow over the site, stopping for some time on the big old house.

'That was the home where my Great Grandparents lived,' she intensified her look at him as she continued, 'and died, they were killed in the fire, their three children somehow got out, their bedrooms were on the lower floor, but there was no hope for those on the upper levels.' Tears formed in the corner of Jenny's eyes.

'I can see that this place has great sadness for you, even though you didn't know them.' Rory decided it was time to delve further into her past, while her guard was down. 'So what relation to you is Jim Bland, I saw a photo of him on the table in the dining room, along with other family - is he your Grandfather? As well as Miranda Sullivans? Which actually would make you - sisters?' His voice had taken on an edge an uneasiness, he knew that he was on delicate ground from the look on her face. He had unlocked and opened a door. Now he wondered, as tears began to well in her eyes and began to trace there way down her cheeks, whether it should have remained closed, her body began to shake.

Jenny looked up at him and held his eyes with hers for only a second, but he could see the pain, and the fear. She shook her head vigorously from side to side, her mouth opened as if to speak, but then she pushed passed him, unbalancing him so that he fell into the scrub and gorse at the side of the track.

She ran back along the way that they had come, and disappeared down into the ravine by the bluff. He could hear her wailing cry, it was high pitched and hysterical.

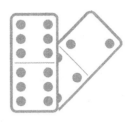

NINE

Jim Bland heard the siren coming down the main street, the sound turned and head onto the water front road that led to his house. He stood up from the arm chair where he had been reading the morning paper and glanced at the mantle clock, it was just after eleven thirty. He walked out from the lounge and down the passage to the front porch as the sound got closer. He frowned at the noise, wondering why it was coming in his direction. As he got to the front door, it stopped, across the front lawn, coming towards the house were two Police Officers, they were not the local men, and although the car was marked they were in plain casual clothes.

'Mr Jim Bland?' asked the Officer who was walking just in front of the other.

'Yes, how can I help you gentlemen?' He did not like the look on their faces, deep concerned frowns creased their brows.

'I'm Inspector John MacDonald, and this is Sergeant Roger Smith.' They both produced their identity wallets, and showed them to Bland. The taller older man continued.

'We would like to have a talk with you please, we are afraid that we are not the bringers of glad tidings, mind you we rarely are, but I think that you may know that, may we come in.' His tone was soft, but troubled.

Jim stood aside and waved them through into the house, directing them down the hall to the lounge, then inviting them to sit down, they declined. He asked them if they wanted a drink of some type, this too they declined.

'I think that we had better get to the point of our visit Mr. Bland. We have - when we have spoken to you, some other persons that we will need to see, but I think that it may be an idea for you to sit down.'

'No, no, I'm fine thanks, now - what is this all about. How can I assist you, or what is it that you want to tell me - has, is this something to do with my Granddaughter. She is in the Hospital down the coast, had an accident yesterday, is she alright, or do you just want to know something of what happened - which if that is the case, I will not be much help, as I have only got the details second and third hand. And I am puzzled – why such – um – such high up Officers for --- um?'

That question was not answered, and the Sergeant who had not spoken at all up to this point, now came forward, he had a folder which he opened and from it extracted a photo which he handed to Jim Bland. 'Never mind that for the moment. Do you recognise, this gentleman, have any knowledge of him?' It was a picture of Mangus Macmillan. Bland shook his head.

'No, never seen him before, who is he?' Bland looked at the photograph with a puzzled expression.

The Inspector produced another. 'What about these fellows, recognise or know any of them?' It was a photo of three men standing near a large launch in a marina. Jim's eyebrows raised a fraction. He hesitated. The movement in his expression, was not missed by the Officers. 'Well Mr. Bland, do you recognise any of these men?'

'Only one, my - um - Granddaughter's husband, why, what's he been up to?'

Another photo was produced. 'You will then know this gentleman.' It was a picture of Peter Sullivan coming out of a high rise apartment building.

'Yes, of course, he's my son-in-law. Miranda's father, now what's this all about? You ask me to look at photographs, you obviously have a reason, now what the hell is it! I'm getting a very bad feeling about this, and your presence - now - I want an explanation.' Jim Bland looked more than puzzled - he was on the verge of being angry.

'Sit down Mr. Bland, and do you mind if we do so as well?' The

Inspector asked politely, ignoring Bland's agitation. He spoke very slowly - quietly, but with a definite tone of authority, as well as concern. 'When did you last see any of these people, and as close to the actual times as well please, if that's possible.'

After the three had sat down, Jim Bland thought for several minutes. 'Warren Blanchard, Miranda's husband. I haven't seen for oh, probably two, maybe three weeks, and I haven't spoken to him for much longer than that, we don't get on. I don't approve of him, nor he I, for that matter. Miranda I saw on Friday night. She had been out with Sullivan – her Father - and two other friends and hadn't wanted to stay with them at the The Boring Bull, where they were having dinner. She came over here. I think it was about ten-ish, possibly a little earlier. I don't see her that often either, her husband, and her father - well none of us get on really - long story, you know relations, jealousy and so on. It was that night that she had this accident, if that is what it was, a mixture of stories about that, the baby sitter and so on, I'm a bit confused about that, but she was taken to hospital.' He stopped, thinking that what he was saying was in many respects quite irrelevant – or was it? Then he went on.

'I saw Sullivan on the Friday evening early, at the Pub, he had a short confrontation with a chap, a visitor, for some reason had a dislike of him, don't know the details, Sullivan didn't speak to me. Then the next afternoon, Saturday, he came over to tell me about Miranda. He was on his way to the hospital, offered to take me, but I had the baby here, was waiting for the Headmaster's wife to come and look after her, a bit much to expect of an old codger like me. Anyway, he was going to let me know how she was, his PA from his work was here for the weekend evidently, and he got her to ring me, told me she – Miranda was okay, a bit battered, but should be fine in a few days – or it might have been weeks – breaks and things. That's all I know.'

Both Policemen leant forward in their chairs at the same time. The one who had shown and asked about the photographs looked intently at him. The other bowed his head and looked at the floor.

'You were, right in your assumption that something is wrong. We are very sorry to inform you that your Granddaughter is dead, and your son-in-law is very seriously injured and is in Intensive Care, it is not known at the moment whether he will pull through, perhaps a fifty fifty chance, probably less.'

'What happened - were they together, was it a car accident, was he bringing her home - I don't understand, why was I not told earlier, when did it happen?' The old man had gone parchment, and his words tumbled out, tears began to well in his eyes, and he began to shake.

'Would you like something to drink Mr. Bland, we know that this is a shock, but we wanted - needed those few answers to our questions first, and we need to ask one or two more now. But firstly, no, they were not together. Mr Sullivan was in his apartment in the City with his associate Mr. Macmillan, there was an explosion, we think it was a bomb, an attempt to kill both of them, Mr. Macmillan is dead, Mr. Sullivan survived but as we said, only just. Your Granddaughter seems to have died of an over dose of drugs, there were pills found in her room, and on the bed. I am sorry to tell you this, this way, but there really is no other. Would you like that drink now?'

Jim Bland nodded. 'Yes thank you, whisky please, it's in the decanter on the dresser, have something yourselves if you would like, I take it just as it is.'

The Sergeant got up and went over and poured the drink, he looked at his superior with raised eyebrows. The Inspector shook his head. He took the glass to Bland. The old man thanked him and took a long pull at the spirit. He sat back in his chair and closed his eyes, hoping that in doing so it would shut out the pain, all the pain of death from the now and the past that was now racing into his mind.

When he spoke again, his voice was tired and husky, the drink had warmed his stomach and cooled his brain, but only slightly.

'What else do you want to know, I can't see that there is anything that I can help you with. What's happening to my Granddaughter - her body, where is it now - can she come back home - here - I would like her to be here with me, just for a while before she is buried, she is really all I have left, apart from -.' He left the statement unfinished, deciding that he did not want to venture into that realm, at least not now.

Both of the other men noted his comment, but did not pursue it. 'They are, performing an autopsy to determine the exact cause and time of the death, then in a day or so she can be brought back here, if that is your wish. Her father is in no state to argue, or help, and it does not appear that he will be, if at all, for some considerable time, and as we don't know the whereabouts of her husband.' He shrugged, 'I guess that you are the one to make the decisions. Now, this argument, if that is what it was, that Mr. Sullivan had with this man in the bar, what was it about, and who actually is this chap, do you have his name?'

'It's Calder, Rory Calder, and all I heard was Sullivan - Peter, saying something about that we - or more to the point he, did not want people like him in our town. Rory has something to do with the University, and Art, and something else, can't remember what that was. I didn't ask him what the problem was with Sullivan, but he said he did not know him, or anything about him. But, he volunteered some information about his wife and family, that they had been killed in an accident two years or so ago, and that he had been - well - sort of a suspect, as there had been a brake problem, and there had been marriage problems. The Police thought he may have been involved - what Peter Sullivan was going on about to him for, I have no idea. Anyway going back to Miranda – you said something about drugs – she never took drugs – was never involved in anything like that – hated them, had a distinct dislike for anyone who had anything to do with them! So I don't understand that at all.'

The two men exchanged glances. And ignored the point that Bland was saying about his Granddaughter. 'Do you know where we can find this fellow, Calder, if he has had any association with Mr. Sullivan we will need to have a talk to him too.'

'Not a clue, he was having dinner last night. I think at one of the cafes, and I think he had been staying at the Hotel. I did ask him to come around for a meal tonight, if he was able, he seemed an interesting friendly fellow, but under the circumstances, that may not be quite what I will be doing.' Bland went back to his thoughts about Miranda. 'This is very difficult, I cannot understand at all why Miranda would do that, she has never taken drugs, and I would know, she would have told me, or if she was depressed or worried about something, she would have come to me, I know she would have. Also, there's Suzanne - her baby daughter, she was devoted to her. No, this is quite out of character, are you sure that she took these - tablets, pills or whatever they were?'

'Nothing is actually positive until the autopsy is completed, it is at this stage, only an assumption.' The Inspector, stood up, the constable followed suit. 'Look is there anyone we can call, someone that you would like to be with you, we know that this is very, very hard on you, and our investigations are only just beginning. Would you like to have someone here with you?' The old man was looking tired and frail, he stood up with them.

'No – no there's no-one – I'll be okay, let me show you to the door. Please, if there is any more news, or news about when I can have her back here, will you let me know?'

'Yes we will do that.' The Inspector produced a card. 'Here is my name and numbers where I can be contacted, if you hear from or see your Granddaughter's husband, or hear anything about him - anything at all, please call me urgently. We have not been able to locate him or the other men in the picture with him. We think that one of them is local to the wider area anyway, the other we think may be foreign - a South African. We would very much like to have a chat with them all, about a number of matters.'

'What about my son-in-law, when will there be news of his condition, can I find out anything, does he know about Miranda?'

'You can call the hospital he is in the Central City, they will help you, and no, of course he doesn't know, and if he doesn't survive, he never will. Sorry that sounds a bit harsh, but what happened to him, and his partner, well there is really very little left of him. Mr. Bland, this is a very serious crime we are investigating, and it may have very far reaching affects. I should not tell you that, and I would appreciate you keeping that as a confidence.'

Jim Bland nodded, this was getting well beyond him, he felt lost, floundering in an area that was beyond his understanding, and the inference was, that his family may in some way be involved.

'Thank you Inspector. Oh – and thank you for the suggestion about calling someone – there is – I had forgotten - I'll call a friend of mine, he may be able to come down and spend a bit of time with me. Someone that I can talk to about the little that I know, but I will stay in tonight and tomorrow, please, call me if there is anything else that you think I can help with. I would as I have said, really appreciate knowing what I can do about getting Miranda home, if you can help or if I can contact anyone.' He stood at the door as they nodded, then went out to their car. He felt himself sag against the door frame, he felt dizzy and bewildered, as he turned and went slowly back in to the house and over to the hall phone, he kept muttering to himself.

'This doesn't happen here, this doesn't happen to me, this cannot have happened to Miranda, what are we going to do with Suzanne, and where is that bastard Warren!'

Jim Bland picked up the phone and dialled, it was only a moment, before it was answered. He spoke quietly but his voice was shaking.

'Franklin, it's Jim, I need some help, I need to talk to someone, can you come down here. It's serious Frank, very serious.' He did not wait for a reply, he hung up and went back into the lounge and poured himself another drink, then sank onto the couch, the tears began to flow and his body shook from his sobs.

* *

Rory got up out of the scrub at the side of the track and began to walk slowly back along the track and down through the bluff. He came out on the tiny beach where the tide was now rippling gently against the edge of the white shell, there was no sign of Jenny. For a few minutes he stood there, thinking of the statement, or at least, the question that he had asked her. Near the waters edge was a large black smooth rock, the water just lapping around its base. He slipped off his shoes, rolled up his jeans and walked out to it, perching on the top, his feet dangling in the coolness.

The scene was so peaceful, the perfect morning - for so many things, and he had, because of impatience, not waiting for the right moment, had fucked it up, and right this second, he was not sure how he would repair it.

'God, things go from bad to worse in this place, either it, or I must be cursed! I think that's a suitably dramatic way of putting the chain of events.' His mouth moved the words in silence. He looked back around the point at the cottage, and had the distinct feeling that he was now being watched, but from where, the windows reflected the sun and the water back at him. Rory sighed, deciding that he must try to repair the bridges that had been blown up. He slipped off the rock and walked towards the house.

Jenny stood in the dormer window of the main bedroom. The tears and the shaking had stopped. Now, she just felt drained, empty. She swore at her stupidity at not checking the photographs. She knew he was an inquisitive swine, and her feelings towards him at this moment were bitter. Yet, when she began to analyse what had transpired in the last hour, she realised that it was not him who was causing the problem, it was her, and her past, her background, what she was. As she stood staring out at the bay, out of the corner of her eye she saw the movement over by the ravine track, Rory emerged from the bush.

The girl watched his body language, his posture and the way he held his head. She thought that she could guess what was going through his mind, and her feeling about him began to revert to what it had been such a short time ago. Someone with who she had wanted to spend time, to share with, to - get close to, or did she - wouldn't that complicate things far too much? She watched him take off his shoes and roll up his pants. Jenny felt feelings flow into her again, and parts of her began to ache, and the anger that had been surging through her started to ebb - but she did not move from the window until he started to walk up from the beach to the cottage.

She left the bedroom and went down the stairs and out the door that led from the old laundry with its ancient copper and massive mangle, that she now used for different purposes. She walked up the sloping grass to the bas, going around the back of it and in the through a stable door, leaving the top part open, she went over and unlocked the fold back doors, clipping back the two larger centre ones. Then she turned and looked around the interior of the Bach.

It was one large room with benches around the walls. In the middle a very large long wooden table, similar to the one in the cottage kitchen, but longer and wider, the corrugated flat roof had three large skylights spaced evenly, giving excellent natural light. Jenny surveyed the room, the equipment and tools that lay about on the benches and the table, she smiled to herself, this, would be interesting to see his reaction. Then a small panic, 'I hope that he's coming up here, or realises that I am here, and doesn't go back up to the car - he may be thoroughly fed up and go!' She turned around and went out onto the decking area sweeping her eyes around, searching the beach and the grounds around the house. There was no sign of him.

Sitting on the edge of the decking, she propped her legs up so that she could rest her head on her knees, placing her forehead on them she tucked herself into a small ball and put her arms around her knees, pulling them in tight. Her mind began it's journey into the reality of what she was going to have to confront, she would have to tell him her story, but only a version of it – and she knew she wouldn't by any means, tell the whole truth.

Within this - the other thought - that he would now have to tell her more of his, and she desperately wanted to know it, and him. In the back of her mind the complications. This was not the right moment, the right timing to bring in someone new, someone that she did not know - and although one part of her wanted to, other parts sent out warning signals. Jenny's mind jumped back and forth between reality and fantasy.

* *

Franklin Primmer put down his phone, his brow creased in a deep frown. Amelia was standing nearby, having come into the house when she had heard the phone ringing. She saw the look on his face.

'Who was that - what's the matter Franklin, you look worried, is there something wrong?' She rarely saw him concerned, as these days he took a very relaxed attitude to affairs, and felt that he was lucky to have the time he has now got, so why burden it with unnecessary worry, but they did have their concerns – but they applied to something quite different.

'It was Jim, he sounded terrible, said he needed to talk, that he needed some help, never heard him like this, I had better pop down. I'll give you a call if I'm going to be there a while.' The frown had not left his face and he suddenly was remote and his mind seemed to Amelia to have gone far away.

'I'll go down in the gondola, it's only a couple of minutes walk from there.' Primmer collected a jacket and his old battered hat from the rack, gave her a perfunctory hug and kiss, and went across the garden to his cable car.

Amelia watched him disappear, then went into the kitchen to get on with preparations for lunch for the special guests. This was not part of normal service, but now – today and tonight - the circumstances were different, from that 'normal'. They had been entertaining company at dinner the evening before, and at breakfast, and they did not seem to fussed about sightseeing, learning about the village, or the surrounding district, instead opting for a day of relaxation. They would, all things being considered, would have plenty of time for that, later The couple seemed very relaxed and also, already very knowledgeable about their home and the area.

Franklin got into the cart and set it in motion. He sat back and admired his handy work, and the bush as it slowly lowered him to the bottom of the hill. For the short time of the journey he forgot his friends plea for help, but as the gondola slid to halt the reason for this descent returned. He got out, and decided that it would be safe enough to leave it there at this time of the day. Thinking - "Besides Rory may come back and it will save him the time of waiting for it to come down - and I wonder what he's up to with that Jenny, I hope not too much". But the thoughts were fleeting and as he set out across the park his mind went back to the task in hand.

Jim Bland was standing on the back porch watching Franklin approach the house, he lifted a hand and waved, then as he came up to the house, he stepped aside to allow him in, placing his hand on the other man's shoulder.

'Thank you for coming down so quickly, I hope I haven't interrupted anything important for you, I know what a tartar at times dear Amelia can be when she has plans a foot for you. Come on through to the front, we can sit out there. Would you like a drink, I am afraid I have already had a couple, when I tell you what has been going on, you may well need one or two as well, so what will you have, I'm having a scotch.'

Franklin decided a Gin and tonic, with a dash would be good. Jim Bland organised the drinks, but said nothing until they were seated on the veranda.

For the next twenty minutes Jim Bland related to his friend the events of the previous couple of days and then what the Police had told him, he managed to keep his voice even and unemotional.

Franklin listened and didn't interrupt, when he had heard it all, he still said nothing, just sipped his drink and stared out to the sea. It was Jim who spoke again, breaking the silence that was hanging like a black cloud over them.

'There seems some very unusual incidents going on. I don't know what to think Franklin, why Miranda? Why would she do such a thing? She spoke to me on Friday night, and although she was unhappy with some of the situations in her life, she was not, in a frame of mind to kill herself, and she doesn't take drugs! Yes, there is that sort of thing going on here and it is increasing, I may be getting on, but I'm not stupid. Then there's this murder of Peter's partner, Mangus. I've heard of him, but never met him, no reason too, Peter had that area under control. But it's plain that whatever went on, was meant to kill Peter as well. I know there's no love lost between us, but I wouldn't wish that on him, he's after all, Miranda's father! And yes - I know there are other factors Franklin, yes I know. Very important factors!' He drained the rest of his whisky in a gulp and stood to go and get another. At the door he stopped.

'The inference by the Police is that Warren and these other two people he was photographed with, may be involved, which makes me think that Miranda was also murdered. Can I get you another Gin Franklin?' Jim Bland suddenly seemed less burdened. Primmer looked at Bland, his face was more relaxed, his eyes not clouded as they'd been when he arrived.

'Perhaps,' he thought, 'It's the whisky, or perhaps he feels better having started to talk about it, to someone he trusts. And he has to trust me.' He nodded and held up his empty glass.

'Yes, thank you Jim, I think I need it too, with what you have told me. To say the least, it is one hell of a shock, and as you know for a number of reasons. It could change a few of our plans. I think we need to give this matter some deep and careful thought. I've some idea about the implications of what you've told me, other bits don't seem to fit, or have relevance. There is much more to this than first meets the eye. It does seem very peculiar that a lot of attention seems centred around our little village, don't you think?' But he was talking to himself, Bland had disappeared into the house.

Primmer sat pondering what Bland had told him. He knew a great deal about Warren Blanchard and Miranda, but that was a different story. The marriage was a sham, and that the girl had been manoeuvred, conned may be a better way of putting it, into it, by Blanchard and her Father. It was not until a few weeks, not even months that she realised it, but she was pregnant. For such an intelligent capable girl this was a tragedy, not that intelligence has a great deal to do with avoiding mistakes, it should help, blended with a bit of common-sense, but who is always so blessed?

There was also one other person in the town that would need to know, although few people knew of the relationship. The only other as far as he was aware about Jenny was himself. Primmer didn't know whether Bland knew how close that he and the young woman were. It was becoming messy and complicated.

A tap on the shoulder brought him back from his wandering mind. Jim stood above him with his drink. 'Sorry I was so long, I rang the hospital in the city to see if I could give any news of Peter, they wouldn't tell me anything until I used the Inspectors name. He is stable, still in intensive care and still unconscious. Although they did say that it was a drug induced state now rather than a cause of the accident as they called it, but they never tell you the truth - do they.'

Franklin sipped his gin, and peered at Bland across the top of his glass, he could see that his friend was deep in thought. He left him alone for a few minutes while he sorted a few files in the brain, when he decided to voice one of them, he did so very quietly, unsure of whether he should or whether what he was thinking was anywhere worth saying.

'Peter, as you know I don't know him really well, but I did know of someone of the same name who used to do a bit of work with the Law Faculty, would it be coincidence if it was the same one? It hadn't occurred to me before, because there was no reason for it to do so, but something that happened a few years back, before I left the University with my problems. It could be mixed up with this, but I could be completely wrong and barking up the wrong tree.' He took another slug at his drink before continuing. He was fabricating the story as he went.

'It had to do with some documents being removed from several departments, research stuff, Government things I think, quite important, his name was in some way linked with it, all supposition I believe. It was information that could be sold, big stink about it, but hushed up in the end. All sorts of security changes happened. I don't know the details, but I know someone who does, and could find out more. What do you think, could it be the same person? Mind you as I said, nothing was proved, but there was also some scandal linking this person with one of the lecturing staff's wife. Not that the fellow ever knew about it, may have been more hearsay than anything, you know how these things are.' Primmer looked thoughtful.

'Well it could be the same man. Yes, because he did have an association with the University Law School, sort of a extra-mural tutor or something like that. I'm not really sure, as I said, we did not communicate or get on at all well. But knowing him the way I do, it would not surprise me in the least. Should we maybe inform our Inspector friend?' Bland thought about what he had just said, a small faux pas, probably not noticed, he smiled inwardly.

'I don't think so, no, not at this stage anyway. Let me see if I can find out more, then we can talk about it further. How are you feeling now Jim, you look a lot better than when I got here, is that the talk, or the whisky?' Primmer suddenly smiled at his friend.

'Yes, I am, thank you. Who is this person that you know that may be able to cast some more light on things, it wouldn't be a local I suppose?'

Franklin decided that the opportunity might be right to bring up the matter of the other person that should know of what had transpired. 'Actually yes - and no, one of them - the one that probably has the most information, is not, but is here, and the other is with him I think at the moment. What are you going to say to Jenny about this Jim, she will have to know.'

Jim Bland looked up from the drink he was nursing and turning around and around in his hands. The initial surprise and shock on his face was fleeting, but the statement had left a mark in his eyes, they glazed and narrowed. When he spoke his voice had slight grating menace to it.

'What! How do you know anything of Jenny, and why she should know anything of this, nobody is supposed to know anything of that, so how do you, and are you saying that this other person is with her? That could only be Rory Calder - I suppose you know him too do you, what the hell is going on here Franklin - who are you, I thought you were a friend, but now there seems something about you that I didn't foresee - who are you, to have this information?'

'I'm not anyone, at least not anyone that is a threat to you, and I am your friend, that's why I mentioned it, and, I am I think, the only one outside you, and Sullivan, and Miranda, who knows that Jenny is your Granddaughter too. I have been a friend and confidant to her for quite a while, sort of came about by accident, we just hit it off, we got to know and trust each other - not even Amelia knows,' he lied, 'and she unfortunately wouldn't be a person to tell. Not a good thing to have to say about one's partner and wife, but it is true. I would never even have told you about it, but with what has happened, well, you can see that she should know, can't you?'

Jim Bland had sagged in his chair his head slumped forward as he listened, when Franklin stopped, he looked up, his eyes had softened again but the deep sadness that had been there earlier when Franklin had arrived had returned.

'I guess you're right, it just opens more old wounds for me, for you, and it will for her. You are aware then of how she leads these two lives. The bright breezy efficient 'Manager', and the solitary lonely soul, who when ever she can, goes to her Cottage. And there is the real schizophrenia, which most of the time is kept under control by medication. Now her suddenly keeping company with this Calder fellow, even stranger, she hasn't even liked the company of men since - well since I can remember, ever since at least that nasty incident with that friend of Blanchard's. Now she will have to face this - too sordid, too complicated. I have not any idea how I can tell her, and who knows how she will react. And how do you think this is going to affect our other plans? You've got the new people up there now, and our associates may not be too impressed if any complications interfere with our Organisation! It seems that we have not been as open with each other over a couple of matter as we should have been.'

'Well perhaps it could be delayed - for a time. Until I've been able to find out more, then we could talk to her, tell her together, she trusts you, I know she does, and she loves you deeply. She may not have told you that for a long time, but she does, she is just afraid to get close to anyone, hence the bossy britches front - mind you, I have seen her in action with that, enough to make some people run a mile! Besides, if she is getting close to Rory, who by the way, I know very well, he's a good man, but he may not actually be all that helpful, he has had---.' Franklin hesitated, and changed tack.

'We lost contact after I became ill. In fact it's – I hope - only by complete accident I think that he's here. And well, he's come up to stay. I digress, let me talk to Rory first, see what light he can shed on things, if any. Then we can go from there. Anyway he and Jenny have only just met, and may not, ever get involved. What do you say?' He had decided not to go into Rory's past or his personal tragedy, he could do that, if it was needed, at another time.

* *

Rory moved away from the rock, he walked slowly to the front of the Cottage, there was no sign of Jenny. 'She may not have come back to the house.' He mused, 'She could have gone back to the car, she was pretty pissed off and angry, but I don't think so much with me as herself - but the way things have been going lately I could be wrong.' He went in the front door and wandered from room to room, he didn't call out until he started up the stairs to the bedrooms, and then he only spoke quietly.

'Jenny, it's me, Rory,' to himself - 'Of course it's you, you silly bugger, who else would it be!'

There was no reply. At the top of the staircase he called again and peered into each room and the bathroom. It was huge. Big enough to accommodate a large old cast iron bath, a separate shower with a brass rose over, a pedestal hand basin, and old leather couch – plus a big carved wardrobe used as storage cupboard. Nobody was there, but he noticed that the bed in the main room had the indentation where she must have thrown herself down and lain for a while.

As he was about to go back down, he passed the little window with the disfigured glass. Rory caught a movement out of the corner of his eye. He had to stoop to see. Jenny was opening the shed at the top of the slope above the Cottage. He watched her until she came out and sat on the edge of the deck. He crouched down by the window, feeling a bit like a peeping tom as he watched her as she curled her legs up, hugging them into herself. The way that she sat and looked was completely childlike.

Rory watched, for several times. He saw her lift head from her knees and swivel her vision around the area. She never once looked at the house, but it seemed pretty obvious that she was looking for him. Was she wanting him to come around to where she sat? He decided after a few minutes that he would go out and talk to her, try to begin the bridge repairs. Yet, he was still reticent, her reactions to his queries, had been, to say the least, disturbing. There seemed to be several personalities emerging, erratic mood swings.

As he walked downstairs into through to the kitchen, he looked at the lonely scrubbed table, the solitary clock tick from the mantle, echoed in the empty room, there was no feelings of the early morning when they had eaten breakfast together. As he went out the back door, he realised, that he too, had presented a number of different sides of himself. Was it time to clear the air, make a fresh start and talk about themselves – their lives?

Half way up the slope he paused and called. 'Hello up there, are you alright now?' His voice was soft, almost a whisper, he hoped it was a gentle caress across the space between them.

She looked down at him as he started up the grassy slope again. She nodded, her eyes though, were still red from crying, and her make-up was streaked.

'Yes, yes, I'm okay, now. I'm sorry that I sent you sprawling, it was silly, I was unfair to run away from you. I should have realised that you, being the nosy sod that you are, you would have noticed the photographs.'

'I'm sorry that my question upset you, and I didn't mean it to come out that way. I know we'd sort of decided that we had to talk, but to find the right time, I guess that then wasn't. How about a truce and we enjoy the day and the sunshine. Maybe later - in a few days, if we last that long,' At that thought he smiled a twisted ironic smile, 'we can arrange our thoughts and talk. That's if we feel that we want to, or even if it's necessary. We've only just met, and it all seems to be very intense, in some ways. There do seem a number of ghosts, gremlins and skeletons in closets that we both need to deal with and set free. We might be able to help each other - who knows - it's possible. Probably not all at once though - just gradually, bit by bit, so that we don't - well - confuse ourselves and each other.'

Jenny nodded again, this time more vigorously, and a small smile started to creep onto her lips, then it disappeared.

'Yes,' she murmured with a serious frown, 'that might really be a good idea, and even some days alone, might be good. I think I need that and I think you might too. In the short time you've been here we've spent quite a bit of time together, and like you said, it's definitely been intense. Like the storms, and we've been struck by lightning!' It could've been a joke, but she didn't smile.

'I know, I instigated that, not the storms of course. But which, by the way is not like me at all - these days. After that, then - no during, I – well, we, can arrange our brains into an order that the other may be able to deal with and understand. So today let's just forget it all, and as you suggested enjoy the day and the sunshine, and just each others company – please?' Her plea seemed genuine this time, but Rory could not see her eyes and the shadows deep within them.

'Right, I - we agree on that then. Now what have you got hidden in that room, some treasures or a torture chamber, full of logs needing to be chopped.'

'Sorry about that too, and that I seemed so bossy. I'm not usually like that, really I'm not.' She could see the grin spreading across his face. 'I think I am rather nervous of you, I have to admit I like you, and enjoy the company, of someone different. But I am not a bossy boots, and I will try to not be again - okay?'

'Okay, but you've not really been that bad, more in fun I thought, now can I come up there or not. I'm getting nosy again, and, I think that you've opened up that shack for a reason, so, let's see what you have in there.' He swung himself up onto the deck. Jenny stood up beside him and took his hand.

'Right, come this way, this is the other surprise I had for you, and you really are very privileged, I've never shown anyone this before, be they friend, relation, and most definitely not, foe!' She pulled him by his hand into the dimness of the room. It took a moment for his eyes to adjust after the bright sunlight.

The room was filled with the paraphernalia of several different forms of art work. On one side of the room she had set up print-making, another for Batik, and a third for sculpture. Lastly in a corner an easel with a large canvas that was partly filled with bright colour, bold strong brush strokes, the beginnings of a form melting through from the background. There was work in progress on a project in each part of the room. Rory stared fascinated by what he saw.

Jenny watched his expression with obvious delight. 'I know it looks a mess, things and everything all over the place, but that's the way I like to work. I like to be able to have several things to think about, and when I have a mental block on one, I can move onto something else. When I have a reasonable collection I take some to markets, and others to a gallery in the city, where I sell it on commission. It's a fair chore to get it out of here, but I have my secret methods. One day I might even show you, as you have so far, been able to wheedle your way into ---. No, that's unfair, it's me that wants you to see it. I'm really quite proud of myself, in what I have been able to achieve, in a part time sort of way. My work really doesn't give me that much spare time, at least not at this time of the year. Still it slows up from now on, as I told you the other day.'

While she had been speaking Rory wandered around the room, looking into her work, and touching some of it, stroking, almost sensually, the materials, the tools, particularly the forms that she was creating in her moulds for the sculptures. She had several almost completed works, in a soft, creamy coloured stone.

'You are indeed a dark horse Jenny Wilson, but, a very talented dark horse. Where did you learn all these skills, and why are you not pursuing this intensely, and doing a bit of part time work to feed yourself in between - or growing you own goodies, there is plenty of fertile land here, doesn't take much, once you get started.'

She was leaning against the frame of the folding doors, her arms folded, now a quiet, almost mystical look on her face, in her eyes.

'I taught myself. When I was quite young I had a fascination with things art, I used to play I suppose you could call it, on my own, in my room with clay, plasticine, paint and paper, cardboard, and so on, just building and fiddling. But I didn't tell anyone, and hid the things that I made. At school, for some dumb reason, I didn't let on to my teachers that I liked art, scared I suppose that the other kids would tease.' Jenny ran her hands over her face and rubbed her eyes. 'I grew up in a pretty tough neighbourhood.' She shrugged and came over to where he was standing, near the easel.

'It's a part of me I keep hidden from prying eyes, critical people. Where I sell, they know nothing about me, not even my real name, and they don't seem to care either. I suppose they make money out of it, and then think-so what! You seemed different, and of course I know that you're interested in similar things - aren't you?'

Rory nodded vaguely, 'Yes, sort of, I suppose, but not quite like this' He was still looking around the room at what he suddenly thought of as displays. There was almost too much for one to take in, or to believe that one person actually did it all, especially as they only worked at it part time. His mind trundled into his cynical - 'what's going on here' mode. But what he saw - the quality, the variety, and the intensity of the work belied to an extent, the earlier feeling.

'You certainly work hard at it all, you must get very involved, and be very organised, when you get your limited opportunity. It's really quite overwhelming, how often did you say you come over?' Rory hoped that his question was not intrusive.

'Every opportunity, but as I said, this time of the year it's difficult. But gradually, away from the holiday season, I have more and more time, business gradually drops, we stop the seven days and nights, and go to just three in the winter. Then we cut out the days, apart from Saturday and Sunday, on the long holiday weekends. So for about six months it's really cruisey, but we keep our heads above water - except in thunder storms of course. I just run it with one other - we manage, very rarely gets too much, and if it does I can call on an odd local to help. So the rest of my time is here, except for my once a year holiday and I don't always do that.' She sounded casual now almost off-hand about her work.

'So what about today, who's running it today, and are you open tonight?' Rory glanced at his watch, it was only just after eleven o'clock, but it seemed later, as they had been up since before first light, yet in some ways too, the time had flown. He suddenly felt very tired, he walked out onto the decking, and took little notice of her next comment.

'This is the first weekend that I'm closing on Sundays. I should've been open today for lunch, but with the storm and - everything else, I wanted out, to get away, I just left the Closed sign up. I did tell the staff though. Besides the Boring Bull is open and the Pub, so if there's anyone around wanting a meal, they can still get something.'

He was standing out leaning on the rail, when what she had said registered.

Rory's first thought was - 'When did she tell the staff – if she did – she was – well most of the time with me – but then I was asleep and she was downstairs and –' He pushed that aside. 'So we don't have to hurry back to the village - can we start our exploring again, if I keep my mouth shut?' Rory felt a load being lifted, he hadn't wanted to head back to town, but he knew that he should contact Franklin at the Lodge. He also remembered he'd said that he would have dinner with Jim Bland, but it all seemed so far away, remote. This was the type of place he'd been looking for - solitude, aloneness, a place to think, sort the mind, the priorities of why he was here. His priority? But then there was the Departments as well, and thoughts rushed back over the strange events, conversations and conflicts. And except, he wasn't alone, and while that bothered him, it didn't bother him too much – as yet.

'No we don't, not if you don't want to, and yes, we could explore again, and we could both keep our mouths shut, and our eyes open, just walk, and not talk, unless we have to.'

'I had better call Franklin. He may be wondering if I'm coming back today, not that he needs to know. I guess I'm just being polite, especially as he was expecting me back last night, but you don't have a phone here do you. But I do have my mobile with me, it's down in the kitchen. He does know I had dinner with you last night, he may think you have kidnapped me, holding me for ransom.' Rory grinned. 'But you would be disappointed, I don't think anyone will pay you!' He laughed, 'I'm not worth much these days dead or alive!'

'He knows you spent the night with me, I rang him and told him, and of your gallantry, also that you slept – unravaged. Didn't bother him at all that you hadn't gone home to Daddy.' He is quite an old friend of mine, ever since he came here, we got to know each other, and yes, we get on well, and with the Amelia, even if she's a bit of a tartar. Bit possessive that one at times, among other things. And, don't put yourself down, you are worth something, alive, everyone, well almost everyone is, - dead - well that might be different.' More shadows passed behind her eyes, 'Memories are strange things and can be dangerous, if they're the wrong ones.'

Rory jumped down from the deck. 'I'll just go and give him a call, do you have a phone book here - or will I have to ring Directory?'

'Of course there isn't a phone book, why have one when there's no phone, what a funny strange fellow you are.'

He smiled up at her, 'Yes, a bit nutty stupid, I'll just pop down to the Cottage and call him on my Mobile! Wont be long. He jogged down the slope to the back door and disappeared inside. Jenny got up and went to the fridge, she took out a bottle of wine and opened it, taking two glasses from the shelf under the sink, she set them down on the deck in the shade of the wall and then leant on the rail, waiting for him to come back out of the cottage.

It was nearly ten minutes before Rory emerged from the house, he didn't look at all happy, his brow furrowed, his posture hunched. He came slowly up the grass. 'Is that some wine I see before me, I feel the need, I'm afraid there's some rather disturbing news.' He levered himself up onto the decking, and sat on the edge as Jenny went and poured the wine and brought the glasses back.

'I tracked Franklin down at Bland's place. I called the Lodge, and Amelia told me that he'd a call from Jim, urgent, needed to see him, to talk to him, she didn't know any more, but she gave me Jim's number and I called them there.' He took the glass from her and drank half of it.

'What's the matter Rory, you look upset, agitated about something, what's wrong with Franklin, or is it Jim? Is there something wrong with Jim?' Her voice started to rise, she put her hand out onto his arm. 'Tell me Rory, what's wrong with Jim!'

'It's not Jim, Jenny, and it's not Franklin, it's Miranda and Peter Sullivan, she is dead, and he's very badly injured. Jim asked me to tell you. I was going to get you to talk to him, but he was getting very emotional. He asked me to tell you about your sister.' Rory suddenly realised the bluntness of what he'd said, but it was too late.

The colour drained completely from Jenny's face, she grabbed the railing for support. She started to shake, as she had earlier that morning on the track, only this time it was worse. Huge sobs and cries wrenched out of her body, the wine glass fell from her hand and smashed on the deck, as she collapsed against Rory.

TEN

A ndrea spoke for several minutes, relating the events of the previous day, the latter part of the afternoon and that evening, she spoke uninterrupted, and when she had finished, she listened to the reply.

'Alright, stay there until you hear from me, then you know where to go and what to do.' The line went dead, but as she was about to replace the receiver she heard the faint click of an extension being hung up. She went quickly over to the door and opened it a tiny crack, enough to see down the hallway, enough to see Cheryl walking quickly down the corridor to the door to the garden. Andrea closed the door and leaned back against it.

'I don't think that she would have any idea who I was talking to, or why, but she will know that something is going on, that she isn't to know about.' Andrea went back over behind the desk and looked out the window towards the back driveway, she kept herself partly obscured behind the curtain in shadow, and unless somebody looked directly at the window, she wouldn't be seen. A few moments later she heard the sound of a car, and saw Cheryl accelerating out of the back gates onto the road to the village. She went to the desk, picked up the phone pressing, the re-dial. Her call was answered immediately.

'She heard the conversation, that's what you wanted wasn't it? It was pretty well read as to what she would do as soon as I said I was having to make a call.'-- -- The voice cut in several times, as Andrea continued. 'Right, --- yes ---- no ---- yes she's gone back, I suppose to the Hotel. So everything else is in order. I'll call you if anything untoward happens, then I will go back up to town in the morning, and meet you at the usual place - is that right?'

Andrea listened for several minutes, making a few scribbled notes on the desk pad. Finally, that she should make one more call. She hung up, and immediately dialled The Crazy Cow. That completed, Andrea left the office, taking with her the heavy brief case that was sitting by the desk. She went up to the main bedroom, and to a tall heavily carved Scotch chest of draws. She opened the largest, the bottom one, and removed a number of flat leather bound boxes, four were approximately eight inches square and one inch deep, a fifth was narrow, long, and two inches wide and deep. She placed them all carefully in the brief case, locked it. Setting a combination, the numbers specifically designed and known only by one other person. Andrea went into the bathroom and turned on the taps over the massive spa bath. As it ran, filling the room with steam, she shrugged off her clothes and sat on the edge, admiring herself in the wall of mirrors opposite.

'I have plenty of time now to relax and enjoy this place, all to myself, and I will - enjoy - myself. No interruptions and no sharing of my mind, or my body, with anyone.'

The bath filled quickly. Andrea stood up and turned off the taps, and again appraised herself in the mirrors, running her long fingered hands down over her breasts, firm belly and thighs. Then gently caressing between them before she stepped into the deep bath and lowered into the warm churning water. She lay back into a corner and closed her eyes, feeling the soothing massaging affect of the water jets on her skin. Her mind turned over the events of the last few hours. The plans that had been laid were beginning to be put into place, and within the next twenty-four hours most, though not all, would have been completed. That smug arrogant using bastard Sullivan would soon be smiling on the wrong side of his face, and a number of people who had been the used, would be in a position to become the users, the ones with the power to make things happen their way.

She lay back, smiling to herself. Nobody really knew that she was here now, apart from that silly bitch Cheryl, and she wouldn't open her mouth, especially when she had a quiet word with her later.

'Yes,' she spoke aloud, 'everything is working out nicely, why didn't I bring a bottle of his best champagne with me, I could celebrate in better style.'

Andrea stood up and stepped out of the water and went through to the bar in the lounge, dripping water across the expensive rugs. She opened the fridge, by luck there was a bottle of her favourite Champagne - Pol Roger. She selected a crystal flute and went back to the bathroom. She opened the wine and poured a glass, then set the bottle on the edge of the spa, she slipped her immaculate body back into the bubbles, of the water, and the wine.

* *

Jim Bland put down the phone and came back to sit with Franklin, who had refreshed their drinks while he'd been talking.

'Who was that Jim? Seemed another serious conversation, some more trouble?'

'Yes I suppose you could say that, though not trouble exactly, it was your friend, Calder. He was calling to tell you that he wouldn't be back at the lodge for awhile. It seems he rang the Lodge, and Amelia enlightened him to your whereabouts, so he called you here. When he told me where he was, and who he was still with, I gave him the information about Miranda and Peter, and - asked him to - relate it all, well, as much as I told him, to Jenny. I guess I'm a coward, he asked me if I wanted to talk to her, and tell her, but I couldn't.' Bland began to fidget.

'How did he sound, react when you told him. Was he surprised - dismayed or what? It would've been a shock to hear of the accidents, particularly after his run in with Peter, and that he had met Mirianda. Also, that Jenny's Miranda's half sister! Or didn't you tell him?' Franklin gave him a piercing look. 'This is becoming more complicated isn't it – the comedy play is turning into a tragedy!' Primmer didn't like the way events were unfolding. His 'friend' Calder could be a very big fly in their ointment. He was unsure whether he should tell Bland of Calder's past occupations.

'No I told him, about most of it, no details, just the facts as they were initially presented to me by the Police. But I didn't say the Jenny was Miranda half sister, I just said sister. Too complicated otherwise, too much to explain, it's, after all, not all that straight forward - is it. These things never are, are they.'

'Yes - I think that would be right, mind Jim, I don't know all that facts, not all the story, and it's none of my business either, and I probably shouldn't have mentioned that I knew - but I did.' But Primmer did have his reasons for his questions, and was wondering whether to enlighten Bland or not. He had brought Jim into his confidence, but had never gone into direct and detailed explanations as to what he was involved in. Too much information could be his undoing, and he needed Jim Bland to help later with some very important details.

The two men sat now in silence, each taking their own thoughts into different places, different dimensions.

Jim Bland's thoughts drifted. He remembered the agony of losing Molly, his wife. Three years later, their younger daughter, Morag, had an affair with Sullivan. She gave birth to Jenny, and shortly after that - she disappeared. Not long after that his oldest daughter, Katherine, Sullivan's wife, died in an accident on the coast road.. The terrible tragedies had set scars deep in his heart and mind, hardening his feelings against Sullivan.

It all seemed so long ago now. Sullivan had been a post graduate student, twenty four years old when he had met Katherine. She had been infatuated with his cunning charm and had become pregnant within several months of meeting him. Then not that long after, he pulled Morag into his evil web, and deep family divisions occurred.

Bland always felt that the depth of the man's evil had also led to the death of Molly, she had actually died of a cancerous brain tumour, but with the sorrow and tensions of the other activities around them, he was sure had contributed. Now, Miranda, but he could not believe it was a suicide. But the web had ensnared many of them, including himself, and there was no escaping the venom of the spider who was building it.

Jim Bland let his head sink forward until his chin rested on his chest, he closed his eyes hoping that that may shut out this world of unbelievable turmoil.

All the fleeting cameos flashed through him. No detail, just the essence of the pain.

Franklin Primmer watched Jim Bland. He sensed the desolation in the man, and the rising fear. Most of his family had died or had been killed. One was missing, and had not been seen or heard of for more than fifteen years, so therefore according to the law was technically dead.

Primmer actually knew far more about the man and the tragedies than he had indicated. Jenny had in fact confided far more than he had told Bland, and had told him much more of the depth of evil (the only word that he thought at this moment fitted) that Sullivan contained.

He was not entirely sure how she knew so much, having been isolated from him, and the rest of the family, for so long. Not all, as she said by her choice. Because of her background - being Morag's child, and being brought up in a number of foster homes, continually changing foster parents, it was only in the last five or six years, that she'd come back and claimed some of her rights. Her place - in some respects, though not all, in the family. But most of the family, including her father and her grandfather, seemed to want to have little, or nothing to do with her. But they definitely saw that she was provided for. Also, through his own necessary research, he had found considerable interesting information about these inter-woven lives.

It was supposedly, according to Jenny, her natural talents for business and art (inherited in some part from her mother), however that carried her, and allowed her the personal recognition, and that of other's from outside the village that she deserved. But, although her isolationism, while initially was from being pushed away by her relations, and the towns people, became her own obsession. To prove that she could survive without them or anyone, and rarely, did she allow anyone inside her lines of defence. Her often bossy abrasive manner assisted her in this task as well. However, Franklin Primmer had discovered that 'her artistic talents' were nothing more than a figment of her warped mind and imagination- a prop for her paranoia!

'If it hadn't been Rory Calder that had suddenly become a friend,' Franklin mused, 'it would be unlikely that anyone - particularly anyone in this district, would ever get close to her. And that would be the best thing for all! His understanding, and unfortunately his fondness of the young man, his talented capabilities, and now the knowledge of the tragedy that had also fallen on him, he felt that they could at least be good for each other, and for a few other things as well, even if for just a short time. Their interests and abilities were similar - their temperaments though, may present another problem. But it could and would, only be – for a short time.'

He didn't realise that his musings had been spoken, not just thought, and they had been loud enough for Bland to hear, he lifted his head up.

'Do you think so Franklin? She is by no means as you have just said, the easiest person to get on with, and I haven't made any attempt for quite some time to communicate with her - I know that I should have, and that I must. I wish that we'd all made more effort now, and that the two girls had been encouraged to get on, but hindsight is a wonderful thing, and is never any bloody help.'

He shook his head. 'Do you suppose that this Mr. Calder will know anything that will be of help, to us, or the Police, or is it just a hope that he might. It all seems such a long shot, and the coincidences of him being here amongst all these events - well just too much chance really, don't you think?'

'What do you think went wrong Jim. I've known you for quite a time now, and we've become pretty good mates. Even if we don't know a great deal about our individual pasts, there has developed a bond. Maybe it's our age, and the grand parts of life are now behind us, but your life, here, in this small village, you have been here a long time - you've left your mark on the place. Now it's leaving its mark on you - so what do you think it is, so much so wrong, for so few? So it's near time that it changed, we changed, moved on, isn't it?'

Bland contemplated the other man's questions, as he did he churned over and over the years that had passed since he had come here. His friend was right, they were close, but they knew very little of each other's backgrounds, where they had been - what they had done - why they had done it.

'I guess if I talk a bit about it, it could begin to make some sense, I don't really know how, but it might. Forty two years ago I was running away, as a lot of us do, although admittedly not many did then as they do now, from life. I was thirty nine. My first marriage had broken down and I had been alone for several years, we, that is my first wife Heather, and I had been together for twenty years, we'd no children and we were both career minded, and those careers were poles apart. It doesn't matter now what they were it's a long time ago. Then on my travels around looking for 'that place to be', I met Molly, she was on holiday - her O.E, she was from Canada. Her mother was Irish, her father Canadian, though I think that he was of Polish extraction. I never met him or her mother. She was eleven years younger, exciting, vibrant, intelligent, and very, very attractive. I thought she was beautiful, and so did a lot of other people, in those days I guess I wasn't too bad looking either, not beautiful, more I think – distinguished. If I am allowed to say so myself.' Bland smiled at the thought of those days.

'We got on extremely well, considering our age difference, fell in love as the saying goes, and she never went back to Canada, her parents - very Catholic - never forgave her, and cut her out of their lives. She tried to talk them round, phone, letters, begged them to come out, they wouldn't, but she was also just as stubborn, she wouldn't go back, and really we couldn't afford in those days to go together, and by the time we could, it was too late. So that was that, very sad, for her, and them, can't quite understand their thinking on that, any of them. But we found this place, bought a little business and settled down. It was a tearooms, where the Crazy Cow is now, and we became part of the community. That was our opting out of society. Then the girls were born, firstly Katherine, then two years later Morag. I think though that Molly's problems with her parents and family had a much greater affect on us and our girls than perhaps we cared to have thought about.' His eyes misted at the memory.

'Another drink I think I need, how about you Franklin?'

Franklin nodded and held out his glass, he didn't look at the other man, he did not want to see the returning pain.

Bland came back shortly with the new drinks, and handed Franklin his glass.

'We may be over indulging a bit, but today I don't really care, and thinking about what I am telling you, well what the hell does it matter? It's not going to change anything. What has happened has happened, and I confess I don't feel any better for dragging it up. So - tell me your story Franklin, what dark secretive past are you hiding behind those spectacles and benign gaze?'

'No, nothing really that you don't already know, not an exciting life, just a fortunate one to still be around to enjoy parts of it. Given another chance, and talking of that, as much as I am inclined that I should stay here with you, I had better get back to Amelia, you know what she's like, and when she sees that we've been drinking - well! And you know about the special guests, we wont talk about them – or why they're here, we both know. I'll give you a call later, see if there've been any more developments, and maybe by then, Rory will've turned up and I can have a talk to him. Though as I said before, that may be a waste of time.'

Primmer finished his drink quickly this time, and stood up, he put his hand on his friend's shoulder. 'I don't suppose it can get any worse - can it? Perhaps I'm being over simplistic and too optimistic, but let's hope not. Our plans are our plans, and they must stay in place no matter what. I'll talk to you later, things may have to move a lot faster than we had originally planned. I juts hope Jenny doesn't rush things and do anything foolish!' He went down off the porch gave the other man a wave and disappeared around the side of the house. He walked quickly, but not too quickly towards the gondola, there were things to be thought about.

*   *

Andrea felt herself relaxing. So much so from the warm water, the wine, and the euphoric sensual thoughts running through her mind, that her eyes started to close. Her hand released the half-full glass into the bath, the plonk of it into the water and the cool spill of it across her breasts snapped her back awake. She looked across at the bottle perched on the side of the bath. It had less than a quarter left.

Andrea picked the glass out of the water and eased herself up into a sitting position, then realised that the combination of wine and hot bubbling water had made her quite light headed. It was time to extricate herself from it, and plan her next move.

She started to get up out of the tub and found that her state was worse than she had anticipated, she staggered and slipped, falling heavily out of the tub and across the tiled floor. Her head cracked against the pedestal base of the hand basin, and the crystal flute smashed on the tiles cutting deeply into her hand and forearm. The gash on the left side of her head oozed blood onto the whiteness as she lost consciousness.

*   *

The two Police Officers gone back to their car, and had driven to the far end of the waterfront road, they got out and went and stood by the rock wall, looking back to the far end where they could see Jim Bland go back into his house.

'Well, what do you think Sergeant, does he know anything or not, from my observation during the conversation I would say not, and his shocked reaction seemed to show genuine distress.' The Inspector cocked an enquiring eye at his younger colleague.

Roger Smith was still looking towards the house, he had watched the now stooped sagging figure of Jim Bland go back inside. 'I may be becoming a sceptic and a cynic - probably from working with you.' He grinned at the older policeman, they had worked as a team in Homicide now for over five years. MacDonald had taught him to not just listen to him, or a suspect, but to observe in many different ways the reactions of people they may be interviewing or were directly or indirectly involved in a case. The fact that he had a Masters degree in Behavioural Psychology, helped a bit.

'But I'm not sure, you could well be right, but we have seen several cases recently where it all seems kosher, and it turns later to be the exact opposite. He seems a reasonable old coot, intelligent, sensitive, and worldly. So let's have a nosy round the town and have a chat to a few of the locals, then track down our friend Mr. Calder - what a coincidence.'

MacDonald nodded, and grinned ironically. 'Life's full of them, it seems, particularly around here, come on let's get on with it.' They got into the car, Smith spun the it around and headed it back towards the village, turning up into the main street and stopping outside the Hotel. They sat for some minutes and watched the few passers-by, and sorted their options of where they would go and who to talk to, then they got out and ambled over to the garage.

For the next hour the two men wandered around the town chatting to the men at the garage, shopkeepers, and people in the street, very casual, very polite, very non-threatening. The information gathered was sketchy and although the persons that they spoke to attempted to be helpful, little was.

Finally they went into the Hotel. The desk was unattended and they went through into the bar. Cheryl was there cleaning and polishing. The two stopped just inside the door and took in the scene. There were two other's apart from her, a couple, middle-aged, perched on stool by an open window each with a pint and a pie, they took no notice of the two men.

Cheryl looked up from her work, and although they were plain clothed and casually dressed for late summer temperatures, her eye of experience immediately alerted her to their occupation.

MacDonald and Smith went over to the bar and ordered two halves of lager, passed the time of day about the weather and the pleasantness of the village. They picked up their glasses and went to one of the high tables by an open window that gave them a good view of the street.

They did not miss the bruising on Cheryl face and upper arms. Even her efforts to cover them with make-up had not been successful, and even though the scrutiny had been brief, it had not been lost on her and she blushed deeply, quickly turning away when she had served them. It was not just that she knew what they were, and that the damage inflicted would not go unnoticed, it was her embarrassment at the condition that Sullivan had left her in.

MacDonald and Smith sat and talked of the progress or lack of it so far. They had no clues as to who placed the explosive device in Sullivan's apartment nor anything to go by as to why his daughter was dead, they did have an inkling as to who may be involved - in someway, but it was all very hypothetical at the moment. One thing they were sure of, this was not a simple matter, and it would have far reaching affects and was not, at all, just to do with a few people in a small seaside village. The photographs of certain people, particularly the South African, Jongejan, brought what they thought, may now be far reaching connotations, a completely different side to it all. Sinister international connections.

They finished their first drink. 'See if the young lady would like to join us for a chat please Mr. Smith, get us another of those, and if she will, something for her, I have a feeling that she may just be able to shed a bit of light on some events around here. Publicans are usually a pretty good source of information - not always mind, but usually - as we well know. Go and use that charming smile of yours young man, I have seen it work before. By the way, you will also have noticed that we haven't fooled her as to what we are, she is as nervous as a kitten in a sack. I wonder why?'

Roger Smith went back to the bar with the glasses. Cheryl had been out in the storeroom behind the bar and heard him coming over. She came out and smiled, hoping that she did not look upset or nervous, but thinking, 'What the hell have I got to be nervous about, it's just two cops off duty having a beer!'

'Two more of the same thank you, that's very good cold lager, some places just can't get it right, you are obviously very experienced - well I presume that it's you. You are Cheryl - the one with the name over the door?' The smile and the flattery worked. Cheryl relaxed and smiled more warmly. 'Thank you, yes I am the owner, and thank you for the compliment, one does try, but often the efforts are not appreciated. What brings you fellows to town, just passing through or some work to do?' She knew it was pointless to pretend that she didn't know what they were, they certainly did not look stupid, and she did not want to appear so either, besides she was wiser about these matters than most knew.

'Both, we have some work to do here, and up on the east coast as well, a few enquiries, actually if you have a moment, how about joining us for a drink. If you wouldn't mind, maybe you could help us with a couple of items. You would notice strangers going through town, particularly this time of the year I suppose, it must be getting a bit quieter. Would you mind?' He didn't wait for the yes or no, and went on, 'what can I get you?'

'I'll have the same as you, thanks, no I don't mind you asking me a few questions, only too glad to help.' She took the money, and pulled another half-pint of lager, then came around out of the bar and over to their table. The couple, sitting down the other end stood up and left.

The Sergeant introduced himself and then the Inspector. They flashed their Id's then settled back on their seats, sipping the beer.

For the next fifteen minutes they talked about the area, the history of the village, Cheryl and the Pub. No-one else came in, and they could see through the window into the street that the place was very quiet.

'Pretty quiet today, I suppose on a Sunday afternoon any visitors head home and the locals go to sleep or work in their gardens, must get a bit on the boring side at times as the summer comes to it's end.' Smith spoke as he was looking away out the window.

'Yes, it can do,' Cheryl replied quietly, she sensed that the small talk was over and they wanted to get to the point of their business. 'How can I help you gentlemen. If it's info about passers through, or the odd one who stops for a night, their haven't been many of late. The couple that just left, and then really the only other one would be the guy that arrived on Friday, but he's looking for a place to buy or rent I think, apart from that I am not much help.'

'Well who we are looking for could have been through any time over the last months, so you may have to wrack the brain. do you mind looking at a couple of photographs - you may recognise someone. It's a long shot, we know, but would you mind?' As he spoke, MacDonald put the folder he had shown Bland, on the table, he opened it but not completely, he had a certain order and agenda that he wanted to follow, and he did not want the girl seeing everything all at once.

There were several shots that he hadn't shown Jim Bland, and he took these out first. They were of individuals, not any of people together. The first, was Mangus Macmillan, she shook her head. Smith watched her closely as the prints were placed in front of her, he would not miss any reactions. The next was Peter Sullivan, her eyes widened a fraction. 'Yes I know him, Peter Sullivan, but he's a local, been here for years, good friend of mine actually.'

The men made no comment, and MacDonald turned over the next one a man, tall, well built, sandy curly hair, standing in front of a large launch moored in a marina.

She again shook her head, but there was a slight hesitation before she answered. 'No, I don't think so, there is something familiar, - no,' she shook her head again, 'no I don't know him.'

Next he brought out one of Blanchard and the same man, standing in the same place, but turned slightly towards each other, seemingly in deep conversation. She stared at it for several seconds.

'Yes I know him, he's a local too, Warren Blanchard, he's married to Peter Sullivan's daughter Miranda - oh, she had an accident the other day, is this to do with that?'

MacDonald shook his head, 'No, not to do with an accident.' He did not at this stage elaborate any further about Miranda. He pointed again to the other man. 'Are you sure you don't know this man.' He watched her reactions closely.

'His name is John Mackintosh. It's just that if you know Peter Sullivan and Warren Blanchard, you might, well, it would seem likely you would have seen him around?'

'No, I am sure, he's quite - distinctive, I would remember.' Again her eyes widened and the pupils dilated a little. Smith took notice.

Lastly, MacDonald took the photo of Jongejan and placed it in front of her. This one was taken at an airport. Here she was very definite. 'No, not at all, never seen him before in my life, certainly doesn't look like anyone who would come through here, he looks a cold hard bastard, who is he?'

MacDonald picked up the look and slight movement of the head from Smith.

'Just an off chance that one, we didn't really think you would have seen him around here. Thank you for your help. But there is one more thing though,' he stood up from the stool and Smith followed suit. 'You will hear this I would imagine pretty soon through press and television, and I am afraid it is not good news, two of the people we have been talking about - one is dead and the other is very seriously injured. Miranda Sullivan committed suicide last night, in the hospital, and Peter Sullivan has been the victim of - well - we believe foul play. There was an explosion in his apartment. His associate Mr Mangus MacMillan, was killed - instantly. Sullivan - is in intensive care, his condition is serious, very serious, he may not recover.'

The men saw the deep shock this news had on her. 'We're very sorry to tell you this, but we would appreciate it, if you see, or have any contact with Mr. Blanchard in particular, anything at all from him, we would really like you to call us. It's very important.' MacDonald gave her, as he had with Bland, his card. 'I know you said they were your friends, will you be alright? Or can we call somebody in, a friend perhaps, to be with you, you are not looking to good. We can arrange counselling if you would like it?'

Cheryl sat on the edge of the stool she had just got up from, she had gone as white as a sheet, but managed to put on a confident voice. 'No it's okay, I'll be fine, really, customers will be coming in soon, I'll be alright, but this is one hell of a shock, so terrible about Miranda so terrible, I wouldn't have thought it possible that she would have done that, no, not at all. Peter - when - if - do you think he will be alright, how serious is he?'

What MacDonald had said had not sunk in. He repeated it. 'It is very serious, he may not recover, his injuries are – most definitely life threatening. It is uncertain at the moment what will transpire. Do you know Jim Bland - silly here of course you would, contact him, he will be calling the hospital, and if you are a friend of his, he could do with a few words of comfort too I would think, perhaps you could help there?' Smith put his hand on her shoulder and gave it a gentle squeeze. 'Call us if we can help, and if you can help us - please, this is a very serious business, as I am sure that you understand.'

Cheryl nodded - numbed by what they had told her.

'One last thing,' asked MacDonald, 'Could you direct us to Mr. Sullivan's house please, we may need to have a bit of a look around. Oh and – yes - sorry there is another, do you know a Rory Calder, and where we might find him?'

'I have no idea, but he's the guy that arrived on Friday. I think I mentioned him, but I wouldn't know where he is - but - wait on. He was staying here, but he went up to Wisteria Lodge to have a look at that, he wanted more quiet, privacy, you could try there. Peter Sullivan's house is up on the bluff at the right end of the town, the far end of the bay. You take the next road back from the esplanade road, it leads right to his gate.'

'Thank you Ms. Brown, you have been very helpful, are you sure now, that you will be alright?'

'Yes, I'll be okay, really, I'm a pretty tough bird, I'll be fine, I may need another drink, probably something stronger than lager though.' But to herself, 'What the fuck is going on - and where is that bloody bastard Blanchard. There are a few things I must do, but – where do I start?'

The two Officers smiled politely and left the Hotel. She watched them from the window go to their car, then she went through to the office and called Sullivan's house, if Andrea was still there, she had better warn her that they were on the way. She had not told them about her being there.

There was no answer Cheryl let the the phone ring twelve times, more than enough for her to hear it and answer. She hung up. 'Andrea must be out or has gone back up to town, she won't know about Sullivan, or Miranda.' She shrugged, 'Too bad, the stuck up bitch will find out soon enough.'

* *

Warren Blanchard walked through the bush track towards the back of the large white house. He had got the helicopter to divert back to the Peninsular. To land at a beach about three miles up the coast from the Village, where he had a Cottage that he used for some of his extra activities, as he called them. When he wanted to be alone or with somebody that he did not want to parade in a crowd. He had there, a fast runabout, and an old Jeep, recreational transport, that he kept strictly for his own use. He had chosen the boat though to get back to the village, and had pulled it into a tiny secluded cove near the end of the bluff. The pilot would wait for him at the Cottage.

From his position at the edge of the bush he watched the house for any sign of activity. He knew that Andrea Jones had been there with Sullivan, but was not sure whether she would still be there, after five minutes he was reasonably satisfied that he could approach the house. There was a number of larger shade trees across the back lawn, and he moved quickly amongst them and up onto the back porch, the door was unlocked he let himself in, stopping just inside, listening, nothing, it appeared that the place was empty.

Blanchard made his way across the kitchen into the hallway, then up to the office. Here he went through the desk draws and the wall cupboards, carefully, methodically, he found nothing, he checked that he had not left anything disturbed, then went through to the bedroom that adjoined the office.

As he entered, he saw immediately the case lying on the bed. He froze, and held his breath. There was no sound, but he detected perfume not strong not overly feminine, more a soapy smell..

He inched his way around the wall until he was by the bathroom door, he put his ear against it, no sound at all, he took the handle and turned it slowly, inching the door open a crack, enough to see part of the interior. The smell of the soapy water, steam and blood came to meet him, he wrenched the door wide open pulling a small automatic from his hip pocket as he swung himself into the room. He looked down at Andrea Jones lying amongst her blood on the white tile floor. She did not appear to be breathing. His grin was twisted, wretched and evil.

'That seems to save me a job.' He pushed at the body with the toe of his shoe, careful not to get any moisture or blood on it. She didn't move, he didn't want to touch her, or leave any evidence on her that might be detected.

'She may be dead, she may not, I'll risk that she is, or is so unconscious that she will not remember what she was doing.' He backed out of the room, his eyes slitted searching for any sign of a struggle, it didn't appear that there had been anyone else involved, he noted the champagne bottle, then looked down at her, and saw the broken crystal cutting deep into her hand.

'Silly bitch, I think she got drunk and fell over, so you're probably not dead.' He raised the pistol, then lowered it. 'Don't be a stupid prick, get the case and get out.'

Blanchard went to the bed and tried to open the brief case, the levers would not move. 'Fuck, she's set a new combination, I hope like hell my instinct is right, that the leather boxes are in there.' He looked quickly around the room, and noticed that the draws of the huge dresser were not closed properly, he nodded.

'Yes, it's possible, they could have been in here, they weren't in the office.' The sound of tyres on gravel shook him back into where he was and why. He ran over to the window in time to see the rear of a Police car swerving around to the back of the house. He grabbed the case and headed to the front of the house, and as he heard the car door bang shut he went out the front door and ran across to the track that led down to the town. Half way down he swung off onto another, slightly overgrown, but clear enough for him to make good time, and within ten minutes he was scrambling his way down to his boat.

Warren Blanchard smiled as he pushed the craft into the bay and climbed aboard. 'All going well, I will be less than two hours behind in the schedule, that will be easy to explain, if and when it is ever queried - and that is unlikely, very unlikely.'

He set the throttle to full and sped out of the cove and around the headland. Fifteen minutes later the chopper took off and headed low and fast across the firth towards the lowering but bright afternoon sun.

MacDonald and Smith saw the sign to Wisteria Lodge on the side road opposite the Hotel. 'There first - or shall we investigate Mr. Sullivan's residence?' Smith asked.

'I think we will try to find out what Rory knows first, if we can find him, mind he may be like everyone else - know nothing - yet. Besides, what do we think we will find at Mr. Peter Sullivan's, if there was anything there, I wouldn't mind betting there isn't now. But, I could be wrong. Come on let's get to it, the incestuous nature of these little places, it starts to get to me, everybody knows everything and nothing. What did you make of our little Ms. Brown. You were doing a pretty good imitation of a spy, the way you were watching her. Though I think she may not have noticed, struck me as a bit thick.'

Smith pulled the car away from the curb and headed up the main street taking the right and went up the road towards the lodge.

'Oh don't be too sure John, I think that she knows a lot more than she was saying, she is a bit of a cunning little witch, and I think she's capable of playing a couple of games of cards at once. She knew Mackintosh alright, and I'd say she's more than chummy with both Sullivan and Blanchard. I know that some of my feelings are hunches, but mostly, I do say mostly, not all, of the time I am right. She didn't mention Sullivan's PA, either, Bland did, I wonder if she is here or up in the big smoke. I'd be interested to know that, might put a call in to Head Office and ask for a check up, what think you?'

Smith saw the sign and the driveway, slowed, then turned into it, driving carefully through the narrow bush lined alley. They came out in front of the house, he pulled the car to a halt by the steps, and cut the motor. They both took in the impressive sight of the house and the view out over the sea.

'So this is where Mr. Franklin Primmer lives, quite nice spot, yes, quite nice.'

'How do you know who the owner is, I don't remember the name being mentioned, how come you are so informed Mr. M?' Smith gave him a quizzical look.

'Let's say I listen and do my homework and not always tell you everything that I hear and know.' He looked up to see a woman coming down off the veranda, and bustle towards the car. He got out, followed closely by the Sergeant.

Amelia Primmer had her best officious frown on. 'I'm sorry but we are full, I should have changed the sign but I can't reach, and Mr. Primmer is away for the moment, you will have try somewhere else, perhaps the Hotel might be more suitable.'

MacDonald and Smith looked at her in almost amazement. They had not had time to open their mouths. MacDonald could hear his partner's under breath comment.

'She wouldn't win a prize for welcoming diplomacy, or a top advertising award for promoting Wisteria Lodge would she! And what makes her think a couple of Cops would be able to afford to stay here – has she not noticed the car!'

'It's alright Ma'am, we are not looking for accommodation, we would like some information. You may be able to help.' They both produced their identification. 'We are looking for a Mr. Rory Calder, it was mentioned that he might be here, and also Mr. Franklin Primmer, we would like, as they say on the - a word.'

'Oh, him, Mr. Calder, yes, he checked in yesterday, but did not come back last night, I believe - he may have stayed at one of the Cafes, the storm was terrible, and he couldn't get back, haven't heard from him since.' Her manner indicated that she didn't appear to like the man.

'How long have you known him - Mr. Calder I mean?' MacDonald asked the question. 'I believe he is an old friend of Mr. Primmers.'

She looked from one to the other, now a bit perplexed that these men knew something about them. 'Um, - well yes, that's right, but I only met him yesterday, Frank had not seen him for a long time he told me, a bit of a shock and surprise that he should turn up here. But I know nothing about him, apart from the point that he used to work at the University some years ago. I don't know anything more than that, and Mr. Primmer isn't here, he's visiting a friend.' Her voice had become even more terse. It was plain that she was not comfortable with the conversation.

'When will Mr. Primmer be back, he may know when Mr. Calder might be, or perhaps you could direct us to this place where he stayed last night? That could be helpful.' Roger Smith, calm polite.

'What do you want this man for, has he done something wrong, I didn't like the way he just turned up out of the blue. The Cafe's on the waterfront road, run by a Jenny Wilson. That's who he stayed with last night, only just met her too.' The acid dripped off her tongue. 'Now I have work to do, if I can't help any further, I must get on.' She turned away from them and went back up the steps.

'Oh - Mrs. Primmer, there is one more thing if it's not a bother, you didn't say when your husband would be back. Do you know where he is?' Smith knew he was walking on eggshells with this woman, he didn't really want to know, they would talk to Primmer later, but he wanted another reaction.

'Well,' she puffed and sighed exaggeratedly, 'If you must know he's visiting a friend who has had some bad news, I have absolutely no idea what it is, and I have no idea when exactly he will be back. Now as I said, I have things to do, good day gentlemen.' She flounced off into the house.

Roger Smith could not hide his grin, and even MacDonald could not hide his amusement.

'Anyone would think she had something to hide, she certainly isn't fond of Rory, and I don't think we endeared ourselves to her either. So where to now Mr. Smith, make a decision, check Wilson's Cafe, or Mr. Sullivan's house. I think we know where Mr. Primmer is, with Mr. Bland, so we can shelve him for the moment. Not that I think that he will be any great help, because perhaps he will not want to be. And I mean that in the nicest possible way of course.'

'I think we just drive passed, have a nosy, if he's there fine, if not, on up to Sullivan's - okay?' MacDonald nodded agreement, they got back into the car, and headed back to the township.

*   *

After she had hung up the phone from calling Sullivan's house, Cheryl Brown sat back in her chair behind the desk in the office. She lay her head onto the high back and closed her eyes.

Her mind then went into turmoil, each piece of the last few days racing past, each bit of information that the Police had given her. The conversation with Warren. Now Miranda's death. Cheryl no more thought it was suicide than flying to Mars, she'd been murdered, but by who –

Warren? Or there was someone else, someone that she completely wouldn't suspect? Somebody who Miranda knew - or not? She couldn't see any answers, apart from Warren Blanchard. Then there was this 'accident' – an explosion they said. Peter was in hospital, badly injured, may not pull through. Though the way he had treated her that afternoon before he left, she felt very bitter about, and she didn't feel all that sympathetic. But she was playing a double, if not, a triple game of chance herself, and had been caught out..

'Bugger,' she muttered, 'Things were going well, I was getting closer to him, why the hell did I have to stuff it up. I didn't even mind sharing him with the Andrea Bitch, if it meant I could get more, still that was fun too. Although, I don't think she thought so as much as me.' Cheryl got up out of the chair as she heard the front door of the Pub open, and went back into the bar, a couple of local fishermen, friends, but not close friends of Blanchard's. She served them their pints, and they went over to a table in the far corner.

Cheryl leant on the bar and closed her eyes again. 'What if some of this stuff comes out, what if those nosy cops keep digging around here. What if they find out what Peter and Warren are really up to, though I don't think that Peter will be taking much notice, so that leaves Blanchard on his own - that could be interesting, now that Miranda is off the scene as well.' Her mind started into somersaults of scheming.

'What do you mean - Miranda's off the scene? - She away on holiday?' It was one of the fishermen, she had not realised that she was talking aloud, her face flushed, and she stammered. 'Um, well, I don't know, it was someone talking the other day, I - really - don't know anything, haven't seen them - you know, her, or Warren for a while.' Her lie wasn't convincing and the young man looked at her sceptically. She pulled two more pints and tried to cover up with talk of the storm, but she could see in his eyes that he knew that there was more to her mutterings, and the high colour from her blush had not subsided.

When he had taken the drinks back to the table she went out into the store room behind the bar. She put her head against the coolness of the back of the bar fridge, and ensuring that she didn't open her mouth this time and verbalise her thoughts, began to try to formulate a way of getting closer to Warren Blanchard.

She had always been jealous that her friend had been with him and married him, even though she knew that Miranda had been coerced into it. Partly because of the pregnancy, but mostly by Blanchard, and his desire for power and money through association with Sullivan. 'Perhaps now, with her out of the way and Sullivan not likely to be around, I might stand a chance.' But first of all, she had to find him.

Smith drove the car slowly through the town, it was very quiet, and only a small number of people were wandering around. On the wharf a few children were fishing. He turned into the esplanade, and stopped opposite the Cafes. Both were closed, there was no sign of life behind the windows. He got out and walked over and peered in the window. Nothing, both were deserted, and the signs on the doors proclaimed the new hours for Autumn. He went back to where MacDonald sat waiting.

'Nobody in sight in either of them.' He pulled the door open and flopped into the drivers seat. 'Let's try the house on the hill.' He started the car and pulled out from the curb, and took the next road on the right, then the left turn shortly after onto the street that led up to the top of the bluff road.

It was less than three minutes drive and he spun the big car in through the imposing blue stone and iron gateway, scrunching it across the red gravel and stopping outside the large garages, enough room for at least four vehicles he observed. The building was a converted stables and barn, and still had the hayloft above, though these days it was used as a guest apartment. They sat staring around at the palatial beautifully manicured garden and the imposing whiteness of the massive house.

'Mr. Sullivan seems to have done alright for himself, for just a - I am told - a small to modest law practice, I believe that he has something similar to this as well as the high rise apartment in the city. Though God knows why he would need so much property for a man alone. He must be a very clever lawyer, and he was. Yet these days we hear little of him, and will probably hear even less. Some of his employees, I am sure do quite well. However, I don't see why that a semi-retired lawyer warrants, and one of his business partners, demands such attention as they received a little earlier. Do you not feel so my dear Mr. Smith?' MacDonald's tone had a modicum of sarcasm running through it.

'Let's see what we can see here. We know that he is not home, but perhaps someone is, maybe his PA, that has been mentioned. I believe that the Andrea Jones is a very capable business manager for him - in more ways than one.'

'You are, for the short time that we have been looking into these affairs, very well informed in quite a number of the different players activities. How so, is there something that I have missed - or is there something that you are not or have not been telling me.'

'Let's just say that I have not told you all that I might of, you see when all this blew up, excuse the pun, I had been looking at a number of these people, under a directive from above. But until today, it did not appear to be leading anywhere. Have no fear, as we progress, I will fill in more detail and in the fullness of time, all will be revealed.' The look on Sergeant Smith's face indicated that he was a bit nonplussed.

'Don't take it personally Roger. I was under orders. I have even now no real reason to understand any of it than you do. But, I will only give you five out of ten marks for today, you didn't even ask where I got all the bloody photos from - very remiss, and I must say not at all like you.'

The younger officer thought about that for a second. 'Yes, I'll admit I was a bit bluffed over those, and yes I should have asked, I guess after the time we have been together, and I know much of the way you work, I suppose I just expected you to have things like that. I will remember in future - and will think and question a bit more for myself. Getting too bloody complacent, and that leads to mistakes. I'll try to get one step ahead instead of walking behind.'

'Don't be too tough on oneself.' He punched him on the arm. 'If you were a clod plod, you wouldn't be with me. There is a hell of a lot that you find out that I miss, you are usually a lot more observant in some areas than I am. So, let's stop this mutual admiration society, and let's see what we can find.'

As they walked over the wide area between the garaging and the house, they heard what sounded like a door bang shut, they could not be certain whether it was an inside door or not.

'It sounds as if somebody is home anyway, that will have to be a plus.' Smith said. At the back door they stopped and knocked, waited in the silence for a minute then knocked again, this time louder, and also called out. 'If there was anyone there.'

Nothing, then the sound again, a breeze had sprung up and was wafting the trees in the surrounding bush to and fro, and a door banged again.

'Pop around the other side Roger, and see what you can see, I'll try again here.' Smith set off at a trot around the side of the house. He was back in less than a minute.

'A door - on the front veranda was open and banging in the wind, couldn't see any sign of anything or anyone else. Have you tried the door, because if this is locked we could - well - wander in the other way.'

MacDonald reached out and turned the handle, the door swung open. 'You go back and come in that other way, I'll go through here, you never know there could be a lurker - unlikely but you just never know.'

Smith nodded and went back the way that he had just come. MacDonald went into the back service area and then into the kitchen. He paused and looked into the room, it was clean and tidy, there were some dishes stacked in the sink, and a few empty glasses on the bench, but no other indication of recent activity or occupation. There were two doors leading off the kitchen, both were open and he could see what was beyond quite clearly, right through a hallway and into a lounge. He could see Smith coming into that room off the front porch, he disappeared to one side. MacDonald noted the wet foot prints then went into the hall and pushed each door open on either side as he went. The second to last one was slightly ajar, it was the one to the office.

Smith's voice came through from another door on the far side of that room.

'I think you had better come in here John, we have another body. A woman, it could be Sullivan's PA.' There was a strong hint of tension in it.

MacDonald went across the office, quickly taking in those surrounding as he went, as he went into the bedroom through the far door he got the hint of steam and a scent. Smith was standing just inside the bathroom door. He turned as MacDonald came over to him.

'In here Mac, I haven't touched her, I am not sure that she's alive. There appears from here that there is no sign of breathing, and a pulse. It could be the PA, anyway it was someone who was staying here. Look.' He pointed to the clothes on the bench against the wall under the window. 'And there's a bottle of wine on the bath.'

'Okay, let's have a closer look.' The two crouched down by the body, and MacDonald felt for a pulse in the neck, then lifted her head very carefully a fraction off the floor inspected the head wound, then checked the pulse again.

'Yes, there is a very faint one, call an Ambulance Roger, I have a feeling this is an accident, if you look at the angle of her fall, and there, there's blood on the basin pedestal. I think she may have been getting out of the bath and slipped. Drunk in charge of a slippery floor perhaps.'

Smith stood up and went into the office to pick up the phone, but was stopped by a sharp call from MacDonald.

'Hold it Roger, just a minute, I think there has been someone else here, has that phone got a redial on it?' Smith acknowledged that it did. 'Okay, push it see who we find at the other end, if there is anyone, don't talk to them, just see if they say who it is, and if not we will see if we can get a trace done.'

As the Sergeant took out his handkerchief and picked up the phone MacDonald went to take a blanket off the bed to drape it over the girl on the bathroom floor, as he bent over the bed, he saw clearly the indentation where the briefcase had been sitting. He left the bed as it was, and went into the bathroom again and found a robe and some large fluffy towels, he used them as a cover instead. Then he went back and began to have a closer look around the bedroom.

MacDonald was inching open the drawers on the dresser with the end of his pen when Smith came in. 'There was a call made to a Euan McGillveray, it went into answer phone, but it shouldn't take too much to check it out. I have called the ambulance, they said about five minutes.' As he spoke the distant sound of the siren was already echoing over the village.

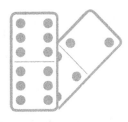

ELEVEN

Jenny choked and sobbed against his chest, her tears soaked the front of his shirt.

Rory felt at a loss as to what to do with her. He could feel, and hear her pain. When he tried to move her, get her to sit down and calm her, she became hysterical. He took her by the shoulders and shook her, trying to get her to look into his eyes, to communicate something of what was going through her.

'Jenny - Jenny stop it, get a grip, get a hold of yourself, calm down, try to tell me what this is all about. What's this about your sister - Miranda, why didn't you say about this before, you've had plenty of bloody the opportunity!' His voice didn't contain a great deal of sympathy. 'Come on, settle down!' He wasn't getting anywhere, he could feel her begin to shake, it became uncontrollable. Jenny tried to break his hold on her, he wrapped one arm around her, pulling her tight against him. He took a deep breath.

'I have never done anything like this before, even on the very odd occasion when Serena had been incredibly hysterical.' He brought his hand back and slapped her, not extremely hard but enough to make a sharp crack on her cheek.

She stopped instantly. Jenny stared at him - but blankly, as if she was looking straight through him.

'Have a sip of the wine Jenny,' he said very softly, picking up his glass and holding it to her lips. She took the glass from his hand and drained it. Then she levered herself up off the deck and went and got the bottle, and refilled the glass, again drinking it down completely, without taking it from her lips. She said nothing as again she poured more wine, almost overflowing the glass, but this time as she went to drink she stopped and stared into the pale liquid.

Her voice was slow - monotone. 'Would you like some, there's another bottle in the fridge, you can open it if you like.' Then she walked into the studio and across and out the back door, she appeared again a few seconds later heading down the sloping grass bank, the wine slopping out and down her shirt as she walked and tried to drink at the same time. She went in through the back door.

Rory stood there watching her, quite dumbfounded by the change in reactions, it was, when she had spoken to him about the other bottle of wine, that he was almost non-existent a stranger. There had been no recognition of who he was, or where they were.

'I know that this is obviously a very big shock to her, so, perhaps she may be better left on her own for a time. I might as well have that wine, some of it anyway, what the bloody hell have I stumbled into. This whole matter is becoming more confused and complicated by the hour!' He went into the room and found the fridge, taking out the bottle of Chardonnay, it had already been opened he noted and was just a little over half full. Rory picked up the other glass and went out to the far end where he could see beyond the side of the house into the estuary, he sat down on the edge of the deck and sipped the wine.

The view was perfect, magnificent, there was still no breath of wind and the water mirrored the surrounding landscape and reflected the mangroves and bird life, but it was tainted by the events that had occurred, firstly Jenny's reaction to the comment about her relationship with Bland, now this. The death of Miranda, and Sullivan being badly injured. All this, over and above, all the other events of the last few days.

'So, what are all the connections, what do all these inter-woven threads mean. As I have said to myself already on several occasions in the last twenty four hours - what the hell are all these coincidences, and I am beginning to think that they are not. This seems to be one bloody great

- no small - incestuous place. Still I am here for a reason, in fact two or three now, and maybe I am going to be able to pull the threads together, then unravel them.' Rory sat shaking his head at these thoughts and his comments about the them.

'I had better go and see how that young lady is, and try to get her to make some sense of all this. I am sure that she has some answers, and I want them - or some of them - now - and I really must stop talking to myself!' He put his glass beside the bottle and jumped down off the deck, then took them with him down to the house. As he went down the bank a new thought trickled into his brain.

'Why aren't any of these supposedly related people anxious to see each other and support each other - they all seem only concerned with themselves - odd - very odd. Or is it – families and relations are very strange animals at times.'

Rory did not expect to find Jenny downstairs, but checked each room and the front porch and lawn. He returned to the kitchen and put his half empty glass on the bench and stoked up the range, it was not completely cold, and there were still hot embers in the fire box, it was soon blazing. He pushed the windows over the sink open and left the back door open, he didn't want the room to get too hot as the day was beautifully mild and still quite sticky humid after the heavy rain. The clock above the mantle told him that the day – with all the drama, had sped by, it was heading past one. It seemed that in some ways though that the time had stood still, that they had been a time warp..

Satisfied that the fire was adequate, he checked the temperature of the hot water, and began his search for Jenny. Going up the stairs he made no effort to move quietly, he wanted her to be aware that he was back in the house, and that she might possibly think he could bring her back into some sort of normality, think things through, although he was sceptical - after the last hours events.

Rory put his head around the door of the main larger bedroom. Jenny was lying in a foetal position, her back to the door, her legs pulled up against her chest, her head tucked down on her knees. Her breathing was heavy but ragged. Her shoulders shook with each breath. He went over to the window and looked out at the bright day, then pulled the drapes across to dim the room. He sat on the edge of the bed and put his hand on her shoulder - the heat of her tension radiated through her clothes into his hand, she did not move under his touch.

'Jenny.' He spoke softly gently. There was no response. He tried again a little louder but still with a soft tone. 'Jenny, it's me, I'm that strange new friend – remember? Come on please, talk to me. I know that this is a hell of a shock, it was to me, and it must be bloody for you. Please Jenny.' He moved his hand to her forehead, it was cold and clammy. He tried gently to pull her onto her back, to make her look at him she tensed and resisted the pressure.

Rory took his hand away and sat back from her. A quilt was spread across the end of the bed. He reached down and pulled it up the bed and spread it over her, then went around the bed and sat where he could see more of her face. Her eyes were tight shut, screwed up as if she was in deep physical pain. He tried again to talk to her.

'Jenny, look - you have got to talk about this. There is very obviously a lot more to all of this, I know that there must be and I know nothing, but you do. You have been avoiding talking about any of your past, any of you family - in fact anything personal, until you showed me your studio. I haven't of course been much better, but I have let out some information, and we agreed that we needed to talk. I have only known you for a couple of days, but we have I think developed a friendship, a closeness of a sort. You said yourself that you did not let people into your life, and didn't let anyone come here. But you could let me in, just a little more anyway. Please Jenny let me help you through this. I think I can.'

He watched her as he talked, hoping to see a response, there still wasn't, and her eyes remained tight shut. After several minutes he got up and went and stood at the window, moving the curtains aside a fraction. His mind went back over the few facts that he had, and the first thing that crossed it was the question "If Miranda is her sister, Sullivan must be her Father!"

'Could you run me a bath please Rory, I would really love to have a deep warm bath, I feel as if I need to try to wash away everything, all these pent up feelings and emotions, all the pain - all of the last ten years - and more.'

He looked back around at her to see that she had pushed herself out of her curled up ball. She was lying "half shut" with her head now on the pillows, her eyes big deep sad pools. Her make-up, the little that she wore, smeared and smudged over her face, the mascara large black smudges under her eyes and over her cheeks.

'Please, can you do that for me, and bring me a cup of coffee, I promise later to talk, how much later, I cannot tell, but I will. The secrets don't matter now, nothing seems to right this minute, but I have to make things matter again - don't I.' Her look was suddenly pleading. She was as a small child, her look frightened, now begging for help. 'I would like you to help me, if you think you can. There isn't anyone else that I think I can talk to, I don't think Grandfather will, and I don't know really why I think that I can talk to you. But I think I can.'

Rory gave her a half smile. 'Okay, I'll run you a bath, and I'll get you a coffee, can I open the curtains now - there is a beautiful day out there wanting to talk to you while I do the chores again. Welcome back, you scared the shit out of me, if you really want to know.' He went out of the room and down the short corridor to the bathroom, turned on the taps, and watched the water start to cover the bottom of the huge old enamel tub.

Jenny did not allow him to see the sly smile that crossed her lips as he left the room. Her eyes took on a distant gleam, and inside her mind her personality began to twist.

The rate that the water was filling the bath would allow plenty of time to make Jenny a coffee and, 'Besides,' he said to himself, 'The kettle should be well hot enough by now.' He chuckled as he went down the stairs, 'I must be a psychic, I must have known she wanted a hot drink, why else would I have put the kettle on the range.' He found the instant coffee, not wanting to experiment with the big old black pot that she had used that morning, and quickly made a large mug, put a small jug of milk and sugar on a tray, then decided that he would have one as well. That done he carried the tray upstairs and went into the bedroom. It was empty.

Rory put the tray down on the table by the side of the bed, then went back out into the hallway and called out to her.

'Jenny, are you alright, where are you?' He felt a sense of panic. 'Where the hell is she now.' He was about to call again when he heard a sound from the bathroom. He went and tapped on the now closed door, he had left it open when he had gone down and made the coffee. 'Are you in there?' He put his ear to the door, and could here the water still running. 'Jenny?'

'Yes, I'm in here, come in and bring the coffee with you, it's alright, I won't bite.' Her voice sounded calm quite relaxed.

'Do you want milk and sugar, or just black with nothing?'

'Just black with nothing thanks will be fine.'

He went back to the bedroom picked up the two mugs, then to the bathroom door.

'Can you open up, I have my hands full of coffee.' He could hear her pad across the floor to the door, she pulled it open, standing behind it as he came in. She pushed it closed behind him and leant against it. The room was full of steam, and the tub was over half full, the water still running slowly into it. It made a pleasant gurgling sound. Rory turned around and looked at her. Jenny was standing with her arms folded tightly across her chest her shoulders hunched up. She was wearing a black towelling robe, it's large soft collar was like a lions mane around her head, she had cleaned the smudged make-up off, and her face looked fresh, her eyes a lot brighter. He handed her one of the mugs, then perched himself on the side of the bath.

'You look a bit better than you did awhile ago, how are you feeling now?' He watched her through the steam, particularly her eyes as he spoke. They flicked nervously to and fro over his face, and around the room.

'I'm - yes - a bit better thank you. But I guess now I feel empty and a bit lost,' Jenny pushed herself off the door and came and sat beside him on the bath, she took a sip of the hot drink, then bending forward she put the mug down on the floor. She turned slightly to face him and put her hand on his arm. 'Thanks Rory, you have been quite amazing to put up with the shit I've thrown at you, and all the other stuff over the last few days, why are you bothering?' Before he could answer she leant over and kissed him, letting her lips linger softly on his, her hand came up gently touching and caressed his cheek. She flicked her tongue across his lips before she pulled away and stared at the floor.

'I often come in here and run the bath, fill the room with steam, and dream. Float off into another world, let myself dissolve in it, the sound of the water, too, it takes away the world outside the door.'

'You seem to live in two - or even three worlds Jenny, I know you have said a little about it, and I mean a little. This is a very small coastal village, yet it seems to have taken on something that is bigger - the people here, at least the ones that I have met, don't seem to fit the mould, don't seem to be part of this little picture post card. Why are they here - really, it's not just the scenery, or the lifestyle, it's something else. What is it?'

'You're not just here looking for a place to hide away are you Rory, you're here for another reason, yes, you are searching, but what is it you are searching for. There was a story you told me, about your work. You made up a story about your work. But it isn't all a story is it.' Her eyes searched his face and bore into him. Once more, she was trying to swing the conversation away from herself, and another change of mood. She reached around behind him and turned off the taps. The bath was only a few inches from the top.

Jenny swirled her hand in the water testing the temperature. The room was now so filled with the steam that he could hardly see the opposite wall. Jenny suddenly stood up, undid the tie on her robe and dropped it to the floor. Rory jumped up from the bath.

'Oh, right, I had better get out and let you have your bath.' He tried to avoid looking at her, but he couldn't, her eyes continued to look deep into his, she stood on tip toe and put her arms around his neck and pulled his face to hers. This time the kiss was not so gentle, her mouth opened over his, and her tongue slid deep in seeking his, she pressed her body against him. His arms went around her, pulling her very close, feeling the smoothness of her skin and the perfect shape of her body. He could feel himself hardening, rising against her. She took her arms from around his neck and put her hands on his chest pushing him away.

Her voice was husky, panting from the breathlessness of the kiss. 'That was just – just a – just – now - would you wash my back for me – please. Then later we might just – extend the just?' She gave him a coy smile stepped into the tub and lowered herself into the deep warm water.

Rory sat back on the side of the tub, he was confused and inquisitive. Her moods swings and now this. Her sudden coming on to him. Not that he minded that, in fact he was flattered and fascinated, he liked her and was attracted to her, but he was also cautious, with all that he knew now or more to the point didn't know. His breathing slowed and he sat on the side of the bath again.

Jenny handed him a large sponge and the soap. 'You can't be my Handmaiden, so you'll just have to be my Handmaster! Attend to my pleasure, but, just this one – for the moment. Maybe more tasks later?' As she looked away from him, the twisted smile returned.

He took the sponge from her filled it with the warm water and rubbed the soap into it, then moved it gently over her back, his finger tips just touching her skin. It was lightly tanned and velvety smooth. Jenny put her head forward and closed her eyes.

'Ah yes, you have just the right touch, I thought you might. I may have to keep you on.'

As he massaged the sponge across her back and shoulders he went back over the last days again, and especially the information about the sister - Miranda. If she was a sister then Sullivan, as he thought a little while ago, must be her father, or - her mother had had her to someone else. He began to wonder how close she was to Sullivan, and whether he had anything to do with her financial situation which did seem fairly comfortable.

The information that he had not given her, partly because he did not want to, and partly because of how she had reacted, that the Police had been to see Jim Bland. He needed to find out more. He stopped and dropped the sponge in front of her. Her head snapped up with the plop of it and as the water splashed onto her.

'You rotten beasty - why did you do that, you've broken our magic!' Jenny looked up at him with an imitation of a hurt expression, but her eyes were laughing. She had switched back, in the last few minutes, to the fun personality that she had when he had first met her.

'Another change,' he thought, 'another alteration of pace and position.'

'I've been thinking as I have been slaving here as you servant. You said

I think that your hours at work were changing, today I think you said, closed a couple of days, is that right?' She nodded agreement.

'Well, perhaps with all this going on, and the upsets. (although now, she seemed far from "upset") You should stay out here for awhile, you know, come to terms with things, re-assess where you are at? What has happened and what it all might – well sort of mean to the future?' He felt he may be getting onto dangerous ground again, but carried on.

'If you like I could borrow the Jeep and go back into the village. You know, find out more of what's happening, and maybe get some bits and pieces - supplies, clothes - and bring them out to you. You could just relax, or even try to take your mind off the happenings, in your studio. That sort of thing can be very therapeutic, what say you oh bathing one?' Rory hoped that he had sounded light-hearted, he wanted the opportunity to get away from her and do some digging on his own.

'Would you come back and spend sometime here with me, not stay at the Lodge, you could bring some of your things back here, would you mind doing that. I don't want to frighten you off. We do have two bedrooms here. It could all be above board couldn't it – well no it couldn't and I would not want it to be – I might have already given you the impression that I want you – your company – and your body. Yes I think it's a good idea, some hours completely on my own to sort my brain could be very good. What a clever Axe murderer you are.'

Rory had observed her and her reactions closely as he had spoken and as she had replied. All above board and two bedrooms, her first comment – then the second – much warmer and meaningful and he knew that was what he wanted to, but he also knew that it could be very dangerous ground – and that feeling he was not sure about where it really came from.' This he mused to himself, and after her actions before she got into the bath and my washing her back! Is this another change of tactic and personality or what?

'The keys to the Jeep are on the mantle in the kitchen. Do you think that you will be long? And you can find your way I suppose, can't you?' Her sudden enthusiasm for this idea took him quite by surprise, and he began to wonder if he had allowed himself to be manipulated into it.

'No - it took less than fifteen minutes, with stops to get here, so I may be away three or four hours, maybe a bit more, I will have to see Franklin, and a I will have to get some clothes, and --.'

'You could get some food - supplies, from my flat and we could spend until Tuesday here - could we? Rory please, I'm sorry about all this – this – thing we can forget it – just – you know what we talked about. We really could explore, have an adventure, some fun, and, we could really talk, and I mean really this time. Can we?' The little girl had reappeared. 'And, when we really get to know each other better we can ------just ---.'

'If I was still working at the Uni. I am beginning to think I could use her as a case study. But I am not, and I'm not here in that capacity.' He thought to himself, then aloud, he replied. 'I guess we could, that might be a good idea, but don't you think under the circumstances maybe after a bit of time on your own to reflect, that you should go back and find out what is going on. I mean, if Miranda and you are sisters - surely --.'

The dark cloud came back over her eyes and face. Her reply was stilted, hesitant, and with a touch of rancour. 'No --- I don't -- need to. We were never close and she - shut me out - we actually - hated each other -- anyway we are only half sisters. Now -- stop spoiling everything,' Her voice softened again, ' - go, go and do what you have to do! And don't take too long or I shall think you have deserted me and stolen my car. Now I am going to relax in this luxury.'

Rory went and found the keys, and set off along the edge of the beach back to the track that led to where they had left the car. He had gone less than fifty metres when he heard her calling out to him. He turned around to see her in her black robe running over the front lawn of the cottage to the shingle path.

As she got closer to him, she panted. 'Sorry I should have told you, when you come back drive another two hundred metres past where we stopped, there is a driveway, it's quite hard to see, but there is a yellow marker opposite it on the left hand bank. It comes down to almost the back of the Studio,' Jenny smiled her childish smile at him. 'You didn't really think that I lugged all my stuff up and down the track that we came down did you.' She was now standing close to him, she lifted her face to him. 'Now kiss me and get on your way.'

He hesitated a moment then obliged her with a simple peck on the cheek. The sudden changes of mood and affections were causing him to revert to his - "reticent Rory character".

She frowned at him, 'What's the matter Rory? You are looking forward to coming back - aren't you?' She reached up and pulled his mouth onto hers, hard searching, but brief, she pulled away with a cheeky grin on her face, letting her hand run down over his chest and down to his lower stomach.

His surprise showed in his eyes, he was thrown off guard. Rory lifted his hand and touched her frowning grinning face. 'Yes, of course,' hoping he sounded at least partly convincing, because he wasn't all that sure that he was, either convincing, or coming back. 'Now go back to your bath or whatever you want to do.' But her look made him ask, 'You will be alright won't you, you don't mind being here alone do you, I mean you are usually always, so is there a problem?'

'No - no I'm fine, it's just that you seem at times troubled and distant, though I suppose that's understandable. Okay I'll see you later.' She waved and skipped off back to the house.

As he got to the bottom of the track Rory looked back, she was standing on the front verandah watching him. He waved and disappeared into the bush. But there was something about the pose that she had, and a chilling shiver went through him. He frowned deeply as he raced up through the canopy of trees.

*　*

MacDonald and Smith watched the Ambulance drive away from the house before they went back in and through to the office and bedroom.

They stood near the door way between the two rooms. 'For a small town it sees plenty of excitement, at least this week anyway. I wonder what it has in store for us next.' Smith's tone was not light, and the deep frown of concern on his face indicated that he was rather perplexed by the events. Although seasoned to the hardships of his work, there were times when he found it very taxing on his nerves. He looked across at the bathroom where the floor was smeared with Andrea's blood.

'Well she is not dead, we may be able to get some information out of her later as to what is or was going on here.'

'They're just taking her up to the little local hospital. It is quite a severe cut to her head and hand, and the knock to her head has given her quite a concussion, but the Ambulance people think that the local crew can handle it. If there is no improvement in twenty four hours they will transfer her to the Base hospital down the coast. Right you do the office, I'll carry on with the bedroom, then if we don't turn anything up, we will have a look around the rest. Well actually we will anyway, but I have the feeling that what we may want to know will be near here.' MacDonald went back to the chest of drawer he had been examining when the Ambulance had arrived. Smith began to work through the desk drawers.

For over an hour they sifted paper, letters, clothes, wardrobes, under beds and in kitchen cupboards. The only clue to anything that may have been removed was that most places were kept in an immaculately tidy state. The exception was the drawers in the dresser that MacDonald had been working on at the beginning. Two drawers were a mess, they had obviously been turned over, something had been removed, but what? Then there was the indentation on the bed where it was plain that some type of quite heavy oblong object had sat for some time, enough time to create the dent in the bed cover, but what was it and where was it. The two men stood looking from the chest of drawers to the bed.

'We could dust them for prints, but my bet would be that we would find a number of sets, including Andrea Jones, Sullivan, and probably his daughter and a house keeper, and who knows who else, maybe even Cheryl Brown's.' MacDonald sighed, disgruntled with the lack of anything to go on. 'However, would you agree that whatever was taken from the drawers, found it's way into the case or box or whatever was on the bed, and now those things have been removed somewhere?'

'That would look like the scenario, but it could also be something quite innocent. Sullivan in a hurry to go up to the City, grabs and quickly packs a few things in an overnight bag, it's sitting on the bed, makes a dent in the duvet, it is quite soft, and off he goes. I think it may be a good idea that we get a couple of men down here to keep an eye on a few people.

Men who can blend in, who can get along side the locals, besides I think we need a bit of dusting around here, I do tend to agree with your theory, but it wouldn't hurt would it.'

Smith gave his superior a "Hmm mm don't you think so look" his head cocked to one side.

'No you're probably right, get on the blower and organise it, I can see that you also have someone in mind, so it's over to you. I'll have a look around for ways of locking this place up, we don't want any more messing with it - you may have to hang around here if I can't find a way, there are a lot of doors. When I have done that and you have done your bit I want to see if we can find our friend Rory, and have another chat with Mr. Bland and Mr. Primmer. Later, when she has recovered somewhat, Ms. Jones. Okay let's get on with it. Oh, and while you're at it, get someone to check out that Lawyer, the McGillveray character.'

Smith nodded went to the office phone and called Central. MacDonald began with the French doors in the bedroom, and worked his way around the house. He was able to lock everything from the inside without any bother, and fortunately the back door had a key in the lock. There was of course the high possibility that others had keys, but they would take that risk, besides, from their search, which had been very thorough - there appeared that there was nothing that could be construed as overly important.

Just as MacDonald was finishing his re-check, he had been back through the house twice, making sure that he had not missed anything, all doors and windows were as secure as he could make them, Smith came through to the kitchen.

'Everything's organised, two of the lads from CIB forensics, they'll be down in about two hours, coming in the Chopper. I told them to land at the sports ground and we would meet them there, and if we are chatting to Bland, we are only a stones throw away, and we will hear them anyway. Should create a bit of excitement. They're going to run a check on McGillveray, but wont probably have anything until tomorrow afternoon. Why so long I'm bloody damned if I know!'

'Alright, we'll head back to the village. There's plenty of time and daylight to achieve something, though I'm not right this second sure what!

And you won't have to spend the night in the haunted mansion - those other two can, if they haven't finished what they need to do, and I don't think they will - not today.'

MacDonald locked the back door, and slipped the key into his pocket. They got into the car and Smith headed them back down to the township.

* *

Rory got to the top of the steep track, and to the Jeep. He unlocked the vehicle, got in and started it up. For a moment, he sat looking over the dusty black bonnet – he looked down at the road, it seemed there may've been another vehicle over it since they'd arrived. But why shouldn't there be? He shrugged at the thought and moved off down the road further, to find the yellow pole that was to guide him to the driveway at the back of Jenny's property. It was as she said, about two hundred metres down from the lay by where they had parked, and she was also correct in telling him that it was not that easy to see.

The entrance was on a long sweeping bend, that appeared to head out to the old timber mill. He carried on for about two kilometres, it climbed gradually until he came to a ridge. The panorama before him was magnificent, and he'd been right, the road continued, winding round to where they'd been that morning.

The view took in estuaries and hills, steep cliff faces that disappeared into deep water, narrow inlets running amongst mangroves and into the bush of the head lands.

'A place to explore, a place of history? I wonder? And somehow, it's all caught up in some tangled web from that village.' To his right he could see the Mill ruins. 'God, coming out here seems a thousand years ago.' He looked at his watch, he'd been without proper sleep for well over twenty-four hours, and it was beginning to tell.

'I'd better get going or it might be another thousand years until I come back.' His earlier reticence of returning had gone, for the moment. He turned the Jeep around.

The drive back took nearly twenty minutes, he recognised the road with ease, even if it was the opposite direction.

When he came down passed the hotel a Police car turning up the street at the back of the sports ground, it heading in the direction of Wisteria Lodge. Rory drove to the wharf, then along to Bland's house.

'I wonder where they're off to? Up to see Franklin? No doubt I'll find out.' But as he headed along the waterfront, he could see that it was slowing, turning into the car park of the clubrooms.

Rory pulled up. Bland's front door was open, and he could see the tall old man standing in the hall talking on the phone. As he got out and walked over, Jim Bland put the phone down and came out onto the porch. He gave him a wave, and called out to him.

'Hello young man, dragged yourself away from the Siren of the Sea, I didn't think it would be long before you came to have a chat, not what after what I told you. How is Jenny? I was only joking about the Siren bit, although thinking about it - maybe she could lure you onto the rocks, she does have a way about her - is she okay, - or not?'

'Let's just say - variable. I think she's alright now, when I left about half an hour ago, but she is a bit like the weather - changeable. A really nice girl - with a big 'but' attached, and I don't mean the one she sits on. She was really upset today about a couple of things. Like to have a chat with you, if it's convenient. Anyway - how are you. It seems that you're the one taking the brunt of everything.' Rory leant on the porch rail.

'It's been - a bad day, yes a very bad day. But Franklin came down, I believe you know him well, he stayed and talked and listened, and drank, and talked some more, drank some more – and he's only just left. Anyway, come in, what is it you want to talk about, as if I can't imagine.' Jim Bland was feeling very mellow. His talk with Primmer, and the amount of alcohol consumed had - for the time being - dulled the pain, the memories, but he wasn't a fool, that they wouldn't be back - with a vengeance. Just as he knew that the Police would be back. Now, for the moment, he had only Rory Calder to worry about, and what he would want to know.

Bland led the way into the living room. 'Can I get you anything, you can have a drink if you like, but I have probably had enough for the time being. I may need more "Anaesthetising" later. I may - you are aware anyway, you're no fool are you Mr. Calder - need some more. I really do want to forget, but that's impossible, completely impossible - isn't it - because you know the pain of it too.'

For the amount that he intimated that he and his friend had consumed, Rory could see that the old man was actually not particularly intoxicated. But that might not be the case later, and what the hell did it matter, hadn't he - from what Rory knew, been through enough?

'Oh okay Jim, I could do with another myself, it has been a trying day, in fact a trying few days for you, and me. I came here to get away from it all - whatever "all or it" is, and I seem to have landed in more of "it". But I'd rather don't feel like sitting and having a drink on my own. Come on you can manage another.'

'I suppose I could stretch to another, the sun's moving closer to the yard arm, but who the hell cares anyway! What'll you have?'

'If you have some wine open that would be fine.' Rory did not actually want the drink, but he did want information, and he didn't want it to appear that that was all he was here for. He liked the old man, but his getting away from it all - had other connotations.

'Not a problem, I'll just be a minute.' Jim Bland went out of the room, and Rory took the opportunity to have a look at the photographs that were displayed on the oak sideboard. He had not taken any notice of them when he was in the room the last time, but with the revelations of the relationships, he was more than interested to see what or who else may come out of the woodwork. As with Jenny's cottage there were a number of very old ones. But, there were also some that were very recent.

'Starting to try to put two and two together are we Rory.' He started at the voice behind him. 'You may be able to, but then again you may end up with five and not four. There appear to be, too many coincidences don't there, like - how you seem to know so many people here, and I don't mean the ones you have met in the last two days - and the few that seem to know something about you. Now I think you came here to see how I was and to have a drink, then to ask me some questions. How would it be if we both did some of that?'

Jim Bland was standing in the middle of the room, a drink in each hand, but no smile on his face. 'Sit down Mr. Calder, if that is your name, and let's have a chat.'

Rory took the glass of wine from the old man, who now seemed extremely sober, and very focused. He sat down in a chair from where he could see Bland, the door and out the window. Jim Bland sat on the couch with his back to the window.

'What makes you think that I am not Rory Calder, and that I am here for other reasons than to find a place to retreat to?'

The older man smiled, the friendly look had returned. 'Oh, it's just a hunch, and something that Franklin said, when I told him about the death of Miranda and Sullivan's injury. Just thought I would throw a scare into you, see if you reacted.' He took a sip of his drink. 'You did, but you didn't. Franklin - when I was telling him about some of the things that had gone on over the years, and he knew a hell of a lot anyway, I think possibly more than he even was telling me. Though when I think about it, he didn't really say much at all - he is quite a close friend of my other Granddaughter, and I have the suspicion that they have had some rather in-depth talks.' Jim Bland watched for reaction from the young man.

'So what did Franklin say that makes you think I am here for other reasons than what I told you.' Rory sipped his wine, it was very good and just the right temperature, almost as if he had been expected. 'I have known him a long time, we worked together, perhaps he was just seeking some other opinion?' Rory, although he seemed to now be quite open, was in fact searching cautiously for an opening - to either divulge further to Bland or to close up - not let the old man in. It was at this moment a delicate balancing act.

'It's just that we were discussing something about Sullivan, and the University came up. Something about some papers, documents being stolen – possibly to be sold. Can't remember all he said really - but obviously Sullivan had something to do with it, at least I think that's what he meant and that - to quote - "I don't know the details, but I know someone who does, and could find out more".' He was watching Rory's face intently. He went on. 'Then I asked him - "Who is this person that you know that may be able to cast some more light on things, it wouldn't be a local I suppose".'

Jim Bland stood up and sipped his drink, he was looking out the window. 'Then Franklin said - "Actually yes - and no, one of them - the one that probably has the most information, is not, but is here, and the other is with him, I think at the moment. What are you going to say to Jenny about this Jim, she will have to know".'

'So,' said Rory, 'You think that I am that person, and that Franklin's statement is about - the person who was with the other person - implied that was me, is that what you are trying to say.'

'That is exactly what he is trying to say Rory, and he got all of it pretty much word for word, quite brilliant for a man who has had as much to drink as he has, that is, if he really was drinking. It could have been ginger ale for all I know, but the Gin's I had were certainly gin, and very nice they were too.'

Franklin Primmer was standing in the doorway of the lounge, behind him were the two Police officers.

* *

As MacDonald and Smith drove back through the town, they made a decision to go back to Wisteria Lodge, and have a chat with Franklin Primmer. The fact that he had spend quite some time talking with Bland - he may have gathered some information that could be useful, in their inquiry. Smith took the car slowly past the Hotel.

It was now a very warm and still afternoon, with none of the threatening thunder clouds that had made their presence felt the previous couple of days. All the windows were pushed up and the double doors onto the side driveway to the car park were open. There did not appear to be much in the way of patronage this time on a Sunday, a couple of heads in the windows and behind the bar Cheryl.

'I wonder what she has been up to since our chat, I'll bet she hasn't been idle in trying to contact somebody for further information, or to pass on that we are about.'

Smith glanced at his partner as he spoke. 'I think that my assumption that she is not quite what she seems will be pretty accurate.'

'You may be right my sharp witted friend, you may be right. Talking of right, it's the next turn that we want, I wonder with what sort of mood Mrs Primmer greeted her husband with when he returned, that is if he has – yet.' MacDonald grinned ironically.

They were heading passed the back of the sports ground when MacDonald put his hand on his driver's arm, and then pointed across the fields. 'That's the back of Bland's house. And, if I'm not mistaken, that's our Mr. Primmer leaving by the back door. Turn in here and go over to the club room car park, we might as well intercept the gentleman, and that way we may be able to have a word with him without interruption.'

Smith slowed and spun the car into the drive to the grounds. The path where Franklin was walking to his gondola cut directly through the car park.

Primmer was half way to the clubhouse when he saw the police car. He slowed momentarily and raised his eyebrows. 'What are they doing there, they weren't there when I came out the back door, so are they looking to have a chat to me, or there for a some other reason?' This query was soon answered as he got closer, the two men got out of the car and walked in his direction.

'Mr. Primmer, Mr Franklin Primmer?' asked MacDonald.

Franklin nodded, 'Yes, what can I do for you gentlemen.'

'We see that you have just come from Mr. Bland's. We will presume you were the friend that he asked to come and see him after we left him.'

Franklin acknowledged with a nod, MacDonald went on. 'How is he, he was pretty upset, and understandably. Do you mind if we ask you a few questions?'

'I suppose not, I don't see though how that I can be of very much help, I am only a friend, I don't know much about what has happened. Just that it seems to be another tragedy in his life. I do know that there have been a few.'

The two Police officers exchanged a quick glance. 'Oh, what other tragedies are these?' It was Smith, he had noticed a slight discomfort in the old man's eyes when they had first spoken to him. 'Look we can't stand here in the middle of nowhere, - the neighbours will get curious. Shall we sit in the car?'

'Is it important, I mean - that you talk to me now? My wife will be wondering where I am, I didn't think I would be very long, and I have been a couple of hours.'

'We spoke to your wife earlier Mr. Primmer, I am sure that a little longer will not cause too much problem.' Smith thought to himself. 'I'll bet the poor bastard gets a grilling and a half when he does get home.'

From the angle that the car was parked they could all see clearly over to the water front road, and the old man's house.

'Now, can you give us any idea of the state of Mr. Bland's mind? And a run down on what he talked to you about?' MacDonald spoke quietly, but there was a depth to his question that was not lost on Franklin.

'Why - do you think he is hiding something - had something to do with what has happened? That would be ridiculous, he may not have like his son-in-law, for many reasons, but he is gentle man, a caring man, and he loved his Granddaughter, he would not harm her. Do you think he knows more than he told you - that he is hiding information from you too? That too I wouldn't believe - why would he do that?'

'We don't know, that is why we are asking the questions Mr. Primmer, we would just perhaps like another opinion - you never know you may shed some light on the affairs from another angle, even a casual comment may mean more than it appears to have.'

For then next fifteen minutes, Primmer talked about the parts of Bland's life that they'd discussed. But he was careful to keep it very general. He hoped that they weren't bright enough to read between the many missing lines! The two Police Officers said little - just asked a few prompting questions to keep the momentum of the dialogue flowing. Then they asked him to repeat what he'd said about Sullivan and Calder.

'Why do you think that this Rory Calder may be able to shed light on some of these occurrences Mr. Primmer? You said you have known him a long time - what actually did you do - together at the University.'

Franklin Primmer went over their respective portfolios, and how they had been connected - particularly in the Psychology Department. Then he talked briefly again about the stolen files.

Smith suddenly clicked. He'd been slow, not thinking outside the square. He realised who they were talking to, and who Calder was. He hadn't remotely expected these men to be here - to be associated in totally different circumstances. Then he connected the names again - Sullivan - Calder - Serena Calder - and several other "accidents". He was about to swing the discussion in that direction, when the Jeep pulled up.

*   *

Jenny watched Rory go into the bush track, then went back into the cottage and up to the bathroom. She looked at the deep tub, sat on the side and wafted her hand through the still warm water, contemplating whether to immerse herself in it again.

'No, I've had enough, and I've lost the magic of those moments when he was here. I wonder why he suddenly wanted to go up to town. Yes - the reasons that he gave seemed quite logical enough - but - there was this big "but" in her mind. Was he afraid of her, was he afraid of women full stop - okay, he has had a traumatic experience with the death of wife and children. No - it's another reason he has gone into the village, it must be to do with this business with Miranda and Peter, and of course Grandfather, should I have gone with him - no - I know he didn't want that.'

Her mind hurtled through all the whys and wherefores and she expressed them aloud, as if trying to convince herself, of which was right and which was not.

'Why has he niggled away, just that every so often, searching delving - no - not intensely but it seems with a purpose, not just a simple enquiring question. To an outsider it may seem innocent, but to me - I don't know, but there is something else to all this and why he is here. I am sure it is not just an innocent - looking for a new life. Am I becoming more paranoid than usual? I really, really like him, and I did come on to him, and - I do want him, more than I have wanted anyone for a long time - and it has been a long time, a very long time., But, what do I want him for? Just sex lust – or am I feeling – feeling what?'

As the girl spoke to herself she realised that her voice was getting louder, her argument with "him and herself", was becoming "real". She stopped, stood up from the bath and looked in the mirror. Her face was flushed and she was panting, and she felt those "sensations", those emotional longings, or were they – as she had thought a moment ago - animal lusts? Jenny shook her head. Puzzled at the feelings that were surging through her.

To be held - touched – caressed, brought to heady heights where her mouth would open and she would scream - and she wanted to call his name. Jenny hugged herself tightly through the towelling gown and ran through to the bedroom, throwing herself on the bed, sliding her hand down over her body - down between her legs. The tears began again and flooded her eyes and cheeks. A while later - she fell into a deep yet disturbed sleep.

Images of her childhood, of her father, of her mother and foster parents all fighting and arguing, screams and terrified faces, fire and people running. Then her standing alone, rain pouring on her, and tears continually flooding.

*   *

The three men watched as Rory got out of the vehicle and crossed to the house. It was Primmer who spoke first, the previous conversation for the moment forgotten.

'That's Rory Calder - and that's Jenny Sullivan's Jeep. She's the Manager of the Crazy Cow, actually she is part owner of them both, not many people know this. She told me one day when we were having a conversation over a couple of drinks. Her father and Grandfather bought the buildings and set them up some five years ago. Just for her - sort of compensation for everything that had happened to her. Actually that's not strictly correct. Bland owned both the buildings – Sullivan provided the finance to develop them.' The information poured from Primmer.

'What did you say? Her name's Jenny Sullivan and her Grandfather is

Bland and Sullivan's her father? And what do you mean - compensation?'
There was confused consternation on the faces of both men. A new light
had been switched on and they could now see a large black curve ball
flying through the air.

The two Officers turned on him with the same question at the same
moment. Franklin was tempted to say - "Snap" - it was the reaction that
he'd expected. He knew that Bland hadn't told the Police about Jenny.

Primmer smiled inwardly, enjoying this intrigue. He suddenly had an
advantage. His mind ran the scenario. 'Not that I need an advantage, they
don't know what I know, and they will have to find out. And that, they
may never do.' He had decided that he would play them around a little,
like trout fishing. If he hadn't had as much to drink, he wouldn't have felt
this way. It was not that he felt any threat or intimidation from them either.
They were pleasant enough and were just doing their job, but he actually
didn't feel like facing Amelia at the moment, he had other things on his
mind, and very few of them to do with Bland, at least not directly, so he
had this alternative.

'Who is her Grandfather – did you say Bland – Jim Bland? And, you
said - Sullivan - Jenny Sullivan - I thought her name was Wilson - who is
she anyway - is she Sullivan's daughter, Miranda Sullivan's sister - which
means that her Grandfather is Bland! How do you know all this anyway -
thought that you were just - "a casual friend"?' MacDonald in a moment
of confusion with the sudden new information, felt and sounded rattled.
'And, what would Rory Calder be doing in her Jeep - where does he fit into
all this?' MacDonald felt a nudge on his leg, and looked across at Smith
who was imperceptibly shaking his head, a tiny warning to - shut up not
say too much until they had taken their talk with Primmer further.

Then Franklin surprised them even more. 'Why don't we toddle over
to Mr. Bland's and ask what's going on? It may save you a lot of time and
energy, asking me, getting my opinion then having to go through it all
again with them.'

'Sounds a good idea to me,' muttered Roger Smith, 'In fact I think
that's a bloody good idea, what do you think Chief?'

MacDonald grimaced. He hated being called "Chief" and he knew that his partner was taking the Mickey out of him. But at the same time trying to relax the situation as Smith could see that he was getting a little more than agitated with this new information - it cast a another light, and another shadow over their investigation.

'Yes, why not, sounds a good scheme, thanks for the suggestion Mr. Primmer, good of you to be so helpful.' He couldn't quite resist a slight touch of sarcasm to his tone.

Franklin grinned to himself and thought. 'I think that you may be in for a few more surprises yet Mr. MacDonald.'

Smith started the car and drove straight over the football grounds, then down a small fenced alley that led out onto the waterfront road. It was just wide enough to allow the car through, but he needed a little caution as the ground was uneven, and he was driving quite quickly. He got a 'jaundiced ' look from his superior as he slid the car to a skidding halt behind the Jeep.

Rory and Jim Bland stared at Primmer - then at the Police Officers. Rory turned and looked at Bland, he had gone very pale. MacDonald interrupted the cameo.

'It seems Mr. Bland that there are a number of blanks in the story, and a number of blanks that have been fired. I think we need to get to the bottom of some bits and pieces that Mr. Primmer here has given us, and is he right, were you drinking ginger ale? I do remember that Mr. Smith poured you a whisky, but did you carry on with that when your friend arrived, or did you have something other than "drinking" on your mind?'

'No I was drinking whisky. It's just that I am quite used to it, and I have a feeling with the shock of everything - I should have been drunk, but it seemed to have the reverse affect. Anyway does any of this trivia matter? I can see gentlemen that you have, from the looks on your faces, much more important things to talk of. I should have known that it would come out in the end, but it's not from the source I expected. I didn't realise that Franklin was privy to so much "private" - information, and I would say that he knows - from his look, that it is more than he has disclosed to me - or to you.'

Franklin Primmer was feeling the scrutiny of all the other's in the room, and the extremely quizzical look from Rory was disturbing.

'Yes, I do Jim, and I am sorry that I wasn't forthright enough to come out with it before. And yes Rory can be helpful, as I said.' He turned to the young man. 'I think you had better tell them what you know Rory, it may help to get things cleared up much faster, even if you don't think that the timing is quite how you wanted it.'

Rory stared at his old friend, then shook his head, glancing as he did from one person to the next, watching their faces.

'I don't know anything Franklin, only what Jim has told me, and what little I have been told by Jenny, what are you referring to?' He gave him a piecing look he would communicate - "This is not the time or place for me to talk" - a look that he also hoped that the others would not see. From the lack of reaction it didn't appear they noticed. Franklin fortunately did.

'Oh, sorry have I got the wrong end of the stick - I had the feeling that when we spoke yesterday that - there was more to your being here than you told me, just with everything that has gone on. These terrible things, that have happened to Jim's family - and you being with Jenny. I guess that my old mind is getting muddled, either that or it's the gin!' He chuckled - in a way that he hoped would indicate that it was indeed old age and gin.

There was silence in the room for about thirty seconds, then MacDonald broke it.

'So this Jenny, where is she now Mr. Calder, are we able to talk to her, I feel that it is quite important that we do so, and do so as soon as possible, you have her Jeep, so you must know where she is. I presume that she knows about her father, and her sister, so why isn't she here with you?'

Roger Smith was now scrutinising Rory's reactions very carefully. He was giving nothing away..

'She, well - she is very distressed by it all of course, she has, according what I have been able the ascertain, had little to do with them, and this.' He stopped and looked from one Policeman to the other. 'Look, I have no idea why she is reacting the way she is, let me say though that she has, over the last twenty four hours been extremely erratic in her behaviour. However, the fact that it is family, despite that they may not appear to be close, there will be emotion, and behaviour that they may not expect in themselves. Barriers can be pushed aside, broken down, at times like this, the trauma even in estranged families or with partners can be severe. But, as I don't know the girl well enough, or have enough insight into the situations surrounding these occurrences I am really not in a position to comment any more than that.'

Smith knew that he was now going to skate on very thin ice, but he couldn't resist it. 'The fact that you are here, here in the village, where Peter Sullivan lives, would have nothing to do with your wife's death two years ago would it Mr. Calder. And the fact that he had been having an affair with her - it's all just coincidence I suppose. Like one thing accidentally leading to another, and that when you came here three days ago, you had no idea that he would be here, and that events such as have happened - would have happened?'

Rory's face went red, then white. MacDonald turned and looked at Smith his mouth open aghast - completely taken aback by his Sergeant remarks. Primmer and Bland looked at each other in astonishment.

'What the hell are you talking about Sergeant - where did you get that information, and what the hell has it --.' He turned and looked at Rory, who was now looking quite ill, and was staring at Smith.

MacDonald became suddenly very formal with his partner. He was extremely angry, for two reasons, - one that Smith had brought out information that he was not aware of, and two this had made him feel and look a fool, and that he was also exposing Rory to scrutiny that was not required or warranted.

'May I have a word with you outside please Sergeant Smith.' He took the younger officer's arm and led him out of the room.

Outside on the front porch, well out of earshot of the other three men, MacDonald turned on his friend and partner. His tone was quiet, but it did not conceal his anger. 'What the bloody fucking hell do you think you are up to! You could blow the whole investigation wide open, ruin all the meagre progress that we have made, what are you playing at?'

Roger Smith held up his hand to slow MacDonald's tirade. 'Hold it John, I know that I should have given you some warning about what I was going to do, but I just felt that we had to try to get things moving. Don't tell me you don't know why Rory is here, he has been working with CIB Special branch for over eighteen months. I also think that Bland knows miles more than he is saying, and this Jenny - I think needs to be brought out into the open.' He stopped to get his breath, he had been speaking hushed, but at a hundred miles an hour.

'What I didn't realise was that Rory didn't know about the affair - that is the mistake - I sure fucked that up, but it may well work to our advantage - and his. Rory was working on this business of the research documents being stolen for ages, he and Primmer. At least he was, until he became ill. And then Rory went away on his Sabbatical. You know all that for Christ's sake. Primmer knew or thought he did that Sullivan was involved, but Rory didn't know who the person was – it's all a bit---. Smith stopped and went on a different tack. 'And there's something else - far bigger - but still evidently to do with those files, that is what we've - I've been told - we are all being bloody far too cagey, as if we are walking on egg shells. Initially, until I realised - only that it was "the real Rory Calder" - when I saw him get out of the Jeep, that I clicked to what was going on with him being here.'

'How do you know that Primmer is in on this – and are you sure that Rory is really aware?' MacDonald's tone had mellowed, and his embarrassment at being caught out had diminished. 'Anyway, how do you know so much about it? You've been accusing me of holding out on you with information, I think that it is much more round the other way!'

'I'll fill you in on both those things - as much as I know anyway - later, but suffice in the mean time that when I was doing my Masters. Calder was taking tutorials, I was in on his, and it was then that I learnt – more than by accident than by whatever - that he was helping in the other investigations - along with Primmer. Although whether he is still part of it I would admit I am not sure - I have to confess that I think there is more to "them" than I know, but that doesn't matter at the moment.'

Primmer and Bland were both looking intently at Rory. 'So there is more to it than you were saying, what the hell is this all about Calder, what do you know about the death of my Granddaughter!' Bland's voice was shaking and very, very angry. 'Have you got something to do with it, - now

I can see why Peter was not at all pleased to see you here on Friday night, he knew why you were here!'

The old man stood up and came and hovered over Rory. 'Get up, look at me, look me in the eye and tell me that what I have said is the truth, you are behind it all, it's revenge - and I suppose the next victim will be Jenny!' He was shouting now.

Franklin came over and took Bland's arm and shook it, hissing at him. 'Stop it Jim, that's not the case at all. Rory knew - knows nothing about this, he knows nothing about Sullivan and Serena - stop it, leave him alone, can't you actually see from his face - look at him - does he look like a man who is bent on revenge.'

Both looked down at the younger man. He was now slumped in the chair, tears welling in his eyes, and his hands were shaking.

'Well!' Bland's voice was still high pitched, but not quite so loud, 'Is that true, what Primmer is saying, or is he just covering for you? Answer me - is he telling the truth?'

'Yes, he is telling the truth Mr. Bland, he knew nothing of the affair between Sullivan and his wife. But he does know an awful lot more than he has told you, or anyone else, about a great deal about other affairs connected with Mr. Peter Sullivan.'

They all looked up to see MacDonald and Smith back in the room. 'I think you had better come with us Mr. Calder, I think we had better have a discussion about the events of the last few days.' Smith looked at Bland. 'I wouldn't worry Mr. Bland, he has nothing to do with the death of your Granddaughter. Or the "accident" to Mr. Sullivan. I think however, that he may be able to assist with a few other bits of our enquiry. Mr. Primmer, if you would be so good as to be available to us in the next day or so, that also would be helpful.'

Rory stood up, and faced the Jim Bland, his face sad, and serious. He was still feeling the shock and pain of the revelation regarding Serena and Sullivan. He had had absolutely no idea about it, he had of course known that things were, or seemed irreparable - but the sudden change when she had filed for divorce - he had been naive, stupid, it had not crossed his mind that there was someone else.

'They are telling the truth Jim, I'm sorry that it appeared otherwise, but none of this was supposed to come out, at least not at the moment. The business with Jenny, well I only found out that she was another Granddaughter by chance, a photograph at the cottage. She'll probably be okay, in time. I think it's the sudden shock, being revealed as Miranda's sister. That's along with her death and Peter - her father - his injuries, that have upset her mental equilibrium. I'll try to get her to come in and see you, perhaps stay with you for a few days, would you find that helpful?' His mind raced off on another tangent as he said this.

'What if - Sullivan was responsible for her death, or an associate of his, my God, what I am involved in, this is getting confused almost irrational - complicated - and am I possibly for the first time for a long time - getting out of my depth!' He did not voice these thoughts to those in the room, but he might to MacDonald and Smith.

Jim Bland nodded, feeling now somewhat contrite over his outburst at Rory.

'I don't know that she will,' He was about to comment further but stopped, 'but yes I would quite like that, we may be able to build some bridges - who knows - sorry Rory, I did sort of fly off a bit then. Are you going to tell Jenny anything of what's gone on - or shall we keep it to ourselves?'

It was MacDonald who replied. 'It may be better left for the time being – in the next day or so we will have to talk to her as well Mr. Bland. We will be discrete, but in the end she will have to know more, the whole story – when and if we actually know that ourselves. So we will wait and see how the next twenty-four hours goes. Come along Mr. Calder, I think we have work to do, some discussion about the events of the last days.'

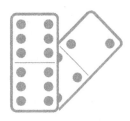

TWELVE

ory sat in the back of the Police car. His thoughts flicked back over the forty eight hours. Each detail had been etched into his brain - most by design, some from coincidence. He remembered so vividly his first impressions from the hilltop, and he remembered his thoughts of childhood and mud walking. It felt now as if he were back in that muddy estuary, struggling, fighting the suction - fighting to achieve a goal, being pulled back and down, being smothered by the grey stickiness. The coldness the wet mud creeping up over his legs then pulling him down.

'How could I have been so stupid, so blind - but why this man - this man that was here, is here - how could I have missed it, he was investigating - "A man called Sullivan" - a Lawyer - a man involved with the University - amongst other things.'

'Then I want out, I want some time away, I want a retreat - a refuge - and I bloody well choose here!' Then he realised that he hadn't chosen – it had been chosen for him – but how – by whom – he had not noticed anything untoward in his discussions with the "Super" and CIB. His train of thought was broken by MacDonald's voice.

'You alright Rory, that was a bit on the unfortunate side back there - Smithy here for all his wonderful brain and ability can be - at times - a complete twit. If it's any consolation, we're sorry about that coming out like it did - but - my dumb colleague and friend here should have informed me first - as I didn't know anything about it either.'

'No, I'm alright thanks, John - now. Yes, it was a hell of a shock, but I guess on top of all the others lately - it's quite minor, and it was a while ago, and it can't be changed.' Rory was back in the work mode.

'Look, there is one hell of a lot to go over, and time is getting short, leads can go cold fucking quickly as you know - I suppose that you are expected back with the Jeep with this Jenny today - would that be right?' MacDonald looked thoughtful.

Rory confirmed that, adding that he was to collect some clothes and some supplies from the girl's flat.

'It isn't the done thing, but under the circumstances. And now we know a bit more about things, and that you have by accident stumbled into and onto what you were working on - mind it's a bloody small world, and we live in an even smaller country, so it's not, I suppose, surprising - well not to surprising, but here – well! What if you go back, and try to get her to come over and stay with her Grandfather as you suggested. It's going to make bugger all difference as and if we try to piece things together today - or tomorrow. We haven't even talked to the local Constabulary yet - yes, very remiss of us I must say.' Rory could see from his expression that he didn't give a bugger, whether they had or not.

'We can set up a controlled environment with them tomorrow. Then the three of us can go over everything that we have compiled. Anyway I want to go back and have another chat with Cheryl Brown. Mr. Smith here feels that there is more to her than is being revealed. Oh and you had better know we have a team coming down from Central – should be here pretty bloody soon.'

'I would go along with that,' Rory commented, 'from what I have seen and heard, and also Mr. Sullivan's PA, she is about somewhere, she may be helpful as well.'

'Not until she wakes up and recovers enough to talk to us - oh yes - you don't know that do you, we went to have a look at Mr. Sullivan's establishment - found her unconscious on the bathroom floor, doesn't look like foul play, but there had been someone else there, something was removed.'

The sound of a Helicopter flying in low over the water interrupted their conversation. 'Ah, about time, they should have been here half an hour ago. They're some of our chaps as I just said - coming down with their fine tooth combs to rake over Sullivan's patch.' They watched the Chopper circle the Sports Ground.

Smith chipped in – and hoped that Rory had gotten over the earlier comments. 'You are, Rory - I assume, quite happy to go back and see the young lady?'

Rory thought about the last bit of news, about the PA, he didn't know who she was, or where she fitted, but he supposed he would in time. He nodded agreement.

'Yes, I think that might be the best, I'll try to get her to come back tonight, but a wouldn't put money on it.' He was going to tell them briefly of the events that occurred just before he left, but decided against it. Things were getting more complicated as it was. He would let them get on with their work without minds working overtime.

Rory got out of the Police car. He leant in through the passenger window. 'Have you got a number that I can contact you, if I can let you know how I am getting on, and when I will have her back in town. I have my mobile with me.'

MacDonald flipped out his card. 'You can either call my mobile, or the Central number - which they will patch through to me, whatever, it doesn't matter. But if you get back tonight, give us a call. We will either be at the Hotel or more likely that Motel, back in the next bay - I wouldn't mind staying at Wisteria Lodge, but not sure now of a welcome - Franklin may be okay, but Mrs P - not so sure. She didn't take too kindly to you either I might add - not from her comments when we spoke to her. Right we will hear from you later. Good luck, see what other info about "the family" you can glean - may not be easy - but you just never know.'

As he watched them head back towards the sports grounds where the helicopter had landed he pondered their last statement. "See what other info about "the family' you can glean".

'What do they mean - the family - am I getting even more paranoid - or is he giving me a hint - about "the family". Surely he doesn't think that they're the Mob - have Mafia links, with this whole affair, that is just carrying things too far - too extreme – isn't it!' But as he whisked his brain through a few of the events and connections he began to wonder. And the thought nagged at him as he got into the Jeep. He started it up and turned around heading back to make his way to Wisteria Lodge - to have a quick talk with Primmer, and collect some gear.

As Rory passed the town market shop, he pulled over. He remembered he was to take back some food, and to pick up wine. If he went back with nothing, a certain person may begin wondering what he had been up to. He jumped down from the Jeep and went into the little store. It was packed with a huge variety of goods, everything from a needle to an anchor type of thing. "A browsing bonanza for a wet day".

He did a quick scout around the shelves and freezers, and despite the selection, found nothing that appealed, but as he came passed the counter it was loaded with fresh French bread, he bought two sticks and went back to the car.

'I'll get other stuff later, now for Franklin and Amelia, then back to the Cottage, and I wonder what will be waiting there - how will her mood have changed this time!' He was back to his muttering. His thinking of "mood changes", took his mind back to his previous call to Euan McGillveray. He reached over to the passenger seat and picked up his phone that he had tossed there when he'd left Jenny's.

Rory sat fiddling with the phone, trying to decide whether to call now, and leave a message at the office – or? He needed to talk to Euan. He searched the phones address book, and pressed the number, it rang seven times – then went into voice mail.

'Euan – it's me again – Rory, please get back to me asap, I need some answers! I need to know if you've dug up anything on Sullivan, especially now I've further disturbing information.' Somehow however, as he switched of, a feeling in his gut, and in the back of his mind, there was a nagging doubt. A doubt that Euan wouldn't have anything of any value to tell him, or more to the point – want to tell him, and he wouldn't receive a reply.

'No, well - I'll wait a bit longer, maybe try again later. I'll have a talk with Franklin, he might shed some more light. The old bastard seems to know more than he is telling as well! Considering he's been away from things for so long - interesting that.' He started the Jeep and headed for the road to the Lodge, he turned into it and sped passed the back of the sports grounds. The Police chopper was just beginning to take off, and Rory could see MacDonald and Smith standing near their car talking to three people, two men – and a woman – all in plain clothes. A number of locals had gathered on the edges of the field in several groups watching the activity.

The group of Police glanced in his direction, as he went passed and up the hill into the bush lined part of the road. Two minutes later he was parked outside the front of the lodge. Franklin Primmer was standing on the far side of the oval lawn a pair of large binoculars pressed to his eyes. He took them away and looked around at the sound of the vehicle on the gravel.

Rory got out and walked across to where the tall man was standing. 'What are you spying on Mr. Franklin Primmer, found something of interest?'

'Was just watching the Helicopter, gather it must be reinforcements - what do you know about it.'

'Forensics - supposed to be a couple of their men to do a once or twice over Sullivan's house, evidently they found his PA unconscious - and feel that there is something missing, have no idea what. There is a third person - a woman with them as well - no idea Franklin, they just want me to go back and try to as you know get Jenny back here. I'm not sure about that. You seem pretty sober now - you alright?' Rory looked closely at the older man. 'Though you seem a bit pale and shaky, what's up, or is it just tiredness, it's been one hell of stressful day.' His own tired mind suddenly realised that he should not have divulged that information no matter how well he knew – or thought he knew Primmer.

'Yes, tired I think Rory,' Primmer's voice, jaded, slow. 'I'm not up to this sort of thing at all, and that bit about Sullivan and Serena - I don't know, I just can't believe it. Just didn't seem her character, not at all. Come on in - can you spare a few minutes with me?'

They went up onto the porch. 'I need a couple of things from my room. Can we talk as I get them, time is getting on, and I have been away longer than I anticipated. And I feel - no sense - that this whole thing is much more than - well anything that we thought it might be, when we began the witch hunt three or was it four years ago. It just has now a much more sinister side to it.'

The two men went up the stairs in silence. Rory began to sort some clean clothes, jeans, a T shirt, and a light jacket, fresh socks, sneakers and underwear. Then he stopped, and looked at what he was doing. 'Oh bugger it, I'll take the lot, who knows when I may get back. I had better give you something for the inconvenience.' He pushed it all back into his bags and pulled out this wallet.

'Another thing - I guess not related to what we are looking in to, but a disturbing "aside" to this small town - or perhaps a trait of it - the amount of alcohol that is consumed. On the surface it appears nothing - just well, recreational, it is the weekend, but everywhere I turn I am handed a glass - or invited to partake. Jenny consumes a lot, Bland - well, at the moment I am not sure, but he seems to. You - you were never a huge drinker - but you seem to have your share.' Franklin said nothing, as Rory went on. 'Look I am not trying to be being a picky critic, you know me, in my time I have been far to far on the wrong side of the bottle - but now I am careful - is it my imagination - and drugs - is that big here too - there's enough grown in the district.'

The old man sat on the side of the bed watching - and listening. He sighed, and rubbed his slightly blood shot eyes. 'Firstly forget the money, not necessary and secondly - yes - there is a lot, and it is more than recreational, it's a habit - for most of them here. Boredom or what, I don't know, and at times I feel myself being caught up in it. Amelia gets very anxious and ratty, she likes her G and T before dinner, and her wine with it, but that's it.' He stared out the window silent for a minute.

'She does not like the local attitude to it, or to her, and she doesn't fit in. Oh we're okay, and okay up here, and really we don't have a huge amount to do with it all down there, or the people, and in fact hardly know anyone - nor they us. But there have been one or two times, mostly with

Jim, or Jenny - and I am not popular. I think that has something to do with people that I have known in the past turning up. Bad influences.

Rory interrupted, 'Okay fine – but anyway - that's not what I wanted to talk about.' He weighed up how to put the next question – then, - 'Is there any local crime, any particular "types" that play on others weaknesses and does this "alcoholic haze" that some live in - lead to problems - trouble, domestic or otherwise? Are there any "bullies" - you know heavies that lean on people – make life difficult – shut people up?'

'Not that I am very aware, of as I said, I have virtually nothing to do with them down there. Look, what has this got to do with all this other business Rory, and are you really here as part of the investigation or is it all an accident - I am getting mighty confused and baffled by it all. It's like a bloody murder mystery. Why would anyone want to blow Sullivan up, even if he is a devious bastard, and who would want to murder Miranda, unless it's her husband that's involved. Now that you talk about local crime - he would be one who I wouldn't trust as far as I could kick him, and that wouldn't be very far these days. There is also the fact that he hated Sullivan - yes, they were involved in some business thing, Miranda told me that as well.'

Franklin Primmer saw a surprised quizzical look on Rory's face. 'Yes, she confided in me as well as Jenny, I think I must have a kind face - like a cow, so people trust me.'

'Who said there was an explosion and he was blown up, well not exactly, but seriously injured, - and who said that Miranda was murdered?' A deep concerned frown crossed his face, then Rory looked at Primmer with raised eyebrows.

'Jim - Jim Bland told me. The Police told him when they first came to see him, although they said that she died of a drug overdose. But he doesn't believe that and neither do I. Didn't he tell you that when he called you, anyway I am sure that they have told you since, seeing that you are now - in on it all.'

'Oh yes, sorry, stupid of me, I am getting paranoid, that word seems to cropping up in my mind rather frequently lately, - sorry Franklin - I guess that I am getting tired too, I haven't slept for nearly thirty six hours and it's starting to tell.' He was even now starting to suspect that everyone was "in" on what had happened - "I am being ridiculous", he thought.

'You had better get going. What I wanted to talk about was this business of Serena and Sullivan. I knew that he was having an affair with somebody connected with the University, but had not a clue who. If I had, I would have told you. Or, at least talked to Serena. I suppose that there is not much that can be done about it now. I don't think he had anything to do with Serena's accident - but then - his wife died in a similar way - brakes failing, a windy road and water.'

Rory stared at the old man his mind going back to that day. That day, when the Police had come to tell him - question him. He flicked his mind into it, then as quickly out, back to the present.

'Jenny told me about that accident, and that he was cleared of that too. It's almost - like a lot of other things around here - too much of a coincidence. I had better get away. I'll talk to you later. There are a number of bits of the past's jigsaw that I haven't talked about. Whether I should drag them up or not - I don't know.' He picked up the bags he had stuffed the clothes into and patted the older man on the shoulder. 'I'll see you tomorrow. Maybe by then we can just relax and forget it all - let the Police handle it.' He raised his eyes to the ceiling. 'Who am I trying to kid.'

Rory left the room and went down to the Jeep. He did not see Amelia, but he could feel eyes on him, watching - had she been listening too?

A few minutes later he pulled up opposite the Pub. He was not sure why, but he felt that he wanted to see how Cheryl was, and to see if she knew anything more, or had heard anything about Sullivan and Miranda.

'This is a small town - if she doesn't by now - there is something wrong with their bush telegraph!' He got out and went over the road - he stopped on the pavement and looked at the building. He had been sure that it had been open when he had come passed it on the way up to the lodge. Now, it was shut, he tried the doors, they were locked. He rang the night bell and waited a couple of minutes, then rang it again. Nothing.

Rory looked up and down the street, it was deserted.

The notice of hours on the door were clear - Sunday 11:30 am to 10:00 pm. There was nothing to say why that it would be closed. He went around the back door car park, it was empty. The door shut, locked tight. The curtains, drawn over the windows. He went back to the Jeep, and drove to the Cafe.

*   *

Smith parked the car at the edge of the paddock as near to where the chopper had landed as he could. The three passengers disembarked quickly, removing there equipment and hurrying away from the slowly churning blades. As soon as they were clear the pilot set the engines back to full power and the machine rose quickly into the sky and hurtled over the field and in moments it was well out over the bay.

MacDonald and Smith got out of the car. Smith opened the boot then went over to meet them. He helped them with the bags and stowed them in the back of the car. The woman approached MacDonald, who was standing with a rather puzzled look on his face.

'Surprised to see me John, just expected the two spook searchers?' She was tall with a lot of fair curly hair that fell to her shoulders. Her lightly tanned face long, her nose thin, her eyes deep piercing blue, striking well-shaped lips. She was wearing faded jeans, a black silk blouse with a bright red waistcoat over.

MacDonald looked at her with a cool stare. 'Yes - I guess I am - didn't really expect the cavalry. How are things with you these days Marguriette? It's been a long time since we've had the pleasure.' He wasn't fond of this woman. She was Senior to him, and worked closely with Customs, Fraud Squad, and Special Intelligence Branch. Somehow she'd got word about their investigation - although, with the incident at Sullivan's Penthouse and the death of his daughter, he wasn't really surprised. It had been several years since their paths had crossed, and the last time he had made a rather unfortunate blunder. And she had made the most of it to leap frog him in the force. Before that they had worked closely for several years and on occasions, had done extremely well together. But Marguriette Bronson was very intelligent, very capable. A hard and ambitious lady, and she didn't tolerate fools, and foolish behaviour.

Smith came over and joined them. The Constables stood a little apart, but close to the car.

'Hello Roger,' she smiled disarmingly at him. 'How's it all going. You two getting to the bottom of this - or is it already becoming a bit to complicated?' She couldn't resist the sarcastic jibe and smirk. She cursed herself, she knew that she shouldn't bait them, they were actually very good men – but, she had always thought – with limitations.

'We seem to be making some progress, in fact I think after today - very good progress. Although there seem to many parts of the puzzle to fit together we are getting there. The unexpected appearance of a Mr. Calder has helped a fraction as well - as it seems that over the last few years he's been doing a lot of delving as well.'

'Calder - the fellow that was involved in the enquiry over the removal of sensitive research material from the University - he was working with another bloke - Primmer - Franklin Primmer if I remember. Well that is a coincidence. What's he doing here?' Marguriette gave no indication that she knew Calder, or that there was a possibility of him being there. This information sent her mind spinning. Rory Calder's presence stirred memories, not all of them unwelcome, but some definitely disturbing!

'Even more of a coincidence,' interjected MacDonald, 'Franklin Primmer lives here, runs a bed and Breakfast - quite a fancy Lodge. He's been retired for some time. But what a strange web we weave around us - both of them being here - on Peter Sullivan's patch. We have uncovered quite a bed of worms – or more correctly a lot of questions – some with answers others with – please fill in the blank at your leisure, that's so far. Hopefully we can fill in these blanks later. Let's get these two gentlemen up to Sullivan's house, they can get set up and maybe make a start. The sooner we begin, the sooner we may wrap it up.'

'Don't be too sure on that John, there is much more to this than meets the eye. You have the photographs that surveillance took of several of our gentlemen friends with you I suppose. I have some more, and I think we need to start to look in much more fine detail at the dossiers of these characters.'

MacDonald was about to lead the way to the car when he stopped and turned to her.

'How come you're here, what have you got to do with this? And you seem, as usual, very well informed. I wouldn't have thought this had such a high priority – though yes, I agree it's important' but you here? Implying that you have information that I don't - well - how about an explanation. And you know about my photographs? Oh silly me of course you do, you don't let much get passed you in the Department do you.' MacDonald knew that she didn't like being questioned, he wanted to irritate her, to throw her off her guard, but it didn't work.

Bronson's supercilious smile and tone, irritated even more, 'I've had - shall we say - an interest in this, and their case for over a year. You've only been called in recently - to do some donkey work - don't take offence though John, it was on my recommendation - we have done some good work, in the past.' Her voice softened and her smile lost the malice, he thought it contained, 'Possibly we could do again, what do you say - bygones - be bygones?'

MacDonald was aware of the scrutiny he was under, from Smith and Bronson. He pulled the frown from his face. 'Why not, you're right, we did good work, until I stuffed up, and I'm being polite about myself. So can we work this through without annoying and aggravating the shit out of each other?'

She smiled at him again this time a genuine warm smile. 'If you can make the effort so can I - yes - of course we can. Come on let's stop yakking and get on with it.'

Ten minutes later they came in the driveway of the big white house on the hill.

'Impressive - our Mr. Sullivan certainly has some nice property, although his apartment needs a bit of a clean and redecorate. Oh and by the way, he is not on the mend, not out of intensive care yet, and not likely to be for some time, the injuries – especially to the brain are worse than first anticipated. He is of course, in a private room with two men on the door, twenty four hours a day. For his protection, of course. At least that's what we will tell him if and when he wakes up. He will be in hospital for quite a long time yet. Plenty of time to let him recover, think, and later for us to ask questions, but as I said, "if and when".' Marguriette got out of the car, the other officers followed. They all stopped at the same time.

The back door of the house was swinging open, and every window along that side of the house was smashed.

*   *

Rory pulled up opposite the Crazy Cow, then swung over the road, parking outside the front door. Around in this part of the village it was quiet, a few strollers walked the waterside path. The sky was still clear blue, and it was pleasantly warm, although he felt the humidity was climbing there was no sign of the heavy thunderous clouds of the last two days. He got out and went to the door, pushing the key in the lock he opened it, went inside and then he turned back, closed and re-locked the door and stood momentarily watching the street. For some reason feeling he had been watched as he went into the building. Apart from the people he had seen walking when he parked the Jeep, there was no-one else, but the feeling as he up to the flat remained. He felt uneasy.

At the top of the stairs his uneasiness increased. He felt his heart beating against his chest, a welling of anxiety. There had been someone here.

Every kitchen cupboard was open, kitchen utensils, pots pans, plates were scattered over the floor, and the small quantities of food that Jenny kept in the upstairs fridge - was scattered onto the floor. It was the same in each room, every one ransacked, her clothes strewn everywhere, her desk containing her paper work, and personal items, cheque books, everything. The bed had been upturned.

Rory went slowly, cautiously to the spare room, it was the same, the bathroom also. Whoever had been here was on a definite mission. What they were looking for, he had no idea. He went back downstairs.

The dining area was untouched, not even the till had been opened. He went into the kitchen area - the same - nothing amiss, the toilets, all in order. He checked the back door, it was locked and bolted on the inside.

'I think perhaps, I had better give our friend Mr. Inspector MacDonald a call.' He spoke - as he often did - aloud to himself.

Rory went to the phone - it was dead, he looked down at the wires, they had been wrenched from the socket.

'What the hell is going on now, who wants something of Jenny or something of hers?' He also began to wonder more about Cheryl, why was she not at the Pub. She could he thought, have gone up to the City to find Sullivan, she seemed very keen on the man, infatuated from what he had observed.

It had been completely contrary to her initial conveyance of her ideas to him about Sullivan. Although - he had beaten her, it was becoming a mishmash mess.

Rory went to the bar fridge and took two bottles of wine, then rummaged in the kitchen finding ham, eggs and some cold chicken. He had the French bread he had bought at the store. 'Not too great - not too much - not too bad, but it will at least look as if I have made the effort. Besides, I think that I should get her back here.' Then the thought struck him. 'Whoever did this may know where she is, and that she may be alone.' He ran to the door and out to the Jeep, bundling the food and wine onto the front seat, he grabbed his cellphone and pulled MacDonald's card from his shirt pocket, dialled the number of the Police Inspector's Mobile. It rang six times before he came on the line.

'MacDonald? It's Rory Calder. We have another problem. Jenny's flat has been ransacked. Someone was definitely looking for something.'

'What do you think they were after?' The inspector asked, 'We have another problem too, Sullivan's house has been broken into as well.'

'How the hell would I know what they were after?' Rory practically shouted. He thought of Jenny at her cottage, and his fear grew. 'Also, the pub is shut up, and Cheryl Brown is not about anywhere. What should I do? Somebody needs to see if Jenny's okay. And --'

MacDonald interrupted, What about the restaurant? Did they hit it too?

'No - that's not been touched – apart from the phone being ripped off the wall.' Rory replied.

'All right, get back over to Jenny Wilson's place and be careful,' MacDonald cautioned. 'Any sign of problems call us, and get both of you the hell out of there. We'll check on the rest of it later. Can you hide the key somewhere?

Rory thought for a second, his eyes sweeping the area. 'I know this sounds stupid - how about under the mat? The place is deserted, so no one will see me, it's the last place anyone looks anyway.'

MacDonald laughed. 'Sure, why not, I'll get one of the "Spook Inspectors" to toddle down and get it, and have a quick shifty while there. We'll go over it in detail later –, there's plenty to do here.' He rang off.

Rory's thoughts, as he got back into the Jeep, started the motor and headed for the road back to Jenny's Cottage, became more jumbled, except for one - "Why didn't they call in the local lads?"

The trip took ten minutes. He was more familiar with the road, and pushed the Jeep as hard as he could -- but that was what it was designed for, and it covered the terrain easily. There wasn't any traffic, and no sign that anyone had been on the road, but that didn't mean there hadn't. As he came passed where they'd parked before, he slowed, so he wouldn't miss the entrance to the property. He drove slowly, cautiously into the track. It opened onto a flat metalled area, the scrunching of the tyres echoed in the trees. He cut the motor, and sat listening.

Silence, broken occasionally by the lazy afternoon chirp of forest birds. The day was still and very warm, the scents of bush flowers and the mulch of fallen leaves filled the air. Rory picked up the supplies, he walked to the path to the cottage. Jenny's studio was open. He gave a quick glance in, she wasn't there and everything appeared to be as when he'd left. He continued down the to the back door, and went into the kitchen. It was cooler, the fire in the range was out.

Rory called. 'Jenny, it's me, Rory, I'm back, where are you?' No reply. Silence – except for the tick of the mantle clock, he glanced up at it.. He frowned, he thought she may be downstairs, or out the front, in the sun. He put the food and wine on the empty table, and went into the front lounge. He called again, and looked out to the water, she did not there.

Standing at the bottom of the stairs he tried again, when there was still no answer he wondered. 'What am I being so damn coy about? I sat on the bath and washed her back!' He set off up the stairs, he looked into her bedroom, the indentation of her body was still there. The bathroom too was empty, but the tub was still filled with water. Rory put his hand in, it was stone cold. 'Why hadn't she let it out?' He reached and pulled the plug, then went back to the bedroom. Her black robe was lying on the floor, as were her clothes that she'd been wearing.

Rory opened the drawers of the dresser, and the wardrobe all was neatly packed nothing appeared to have been touched.

He began muttering. 'The clothes may not appear to be disturbed, but I'm getting that way.' He walked back through all the upstairs rooms. Nothing seemed out of place. He did the same in every room, even the old laundry, he came back into the dining room, and inspected the photographs, searching for faces that he may have seen before, other times -- other places but there was nothing. Last, he picked up the picture of her Grandparents and Great Grandparents. Old Bland was a handsome devil in those days, and the woman, was very attractive, beautiful – elegant, though a regal haughty look about her.

Rory stared at the photograph for a few moments. 'What the hell is going on, why am I standing here staring at a Photo that is obviously a forgery. There is something very amiss. Her flat ransacked, now her not here and this - her Great Grandparents - she said were killed in a fire - at the old house at the mill, - "the three children escaped". Where in God's name is this girl, and what's her game? That may well be Jim Bland - but who are the others, they're not who she said they are!' He put the photo on the scrubbed table, pulled his phone off his belt, pressing redial, he had to talk to MacDonald urgently, with disturbing information.

MacDonald answered. The reception wasn't good, they were only just able to hear. 'We have another problem. Jenny Wilson – or Sullivan, whatever her name is, -- is not here. I've just checked one of the old photos, it's not what it seems. I don't know where she's gone, or if there's anything wrong, but I have a feeling, and it's not a good one. I'd better find her.' Rory listened to MacDonald's reply then rang off.

Rory clipped the phone back on his belt and went out the front door of the cottage, stopping for a second on the beach to decide where to look for her.

He recalled the original settlement, and how her tone had been when she had spoken about the early events, he turned and ran towards the ravine, the track to the old Mill.

* *

They were approaching the house when MacDonald's phone had rung. The conversation took only a minute, when he finished he looked at the other four Officers.

'That was Calder. He's just been into Jenny's flat it's been done over – ransacked, but not the restaurant, there's no evidence of a break in. He called at the Hotel, to see if Brown knew about Peter Sullivan's incident. It was locked up - no sign of anyone. He's now on his way to the girl's cottage. It seems that somebody here is up to no good, we'd better have good a look here. Roger, -- Calder left the key to Jenny Sullivan's in the obvious place, go down and get it, have a quick look, we'll have to think about that later.'

Bronson interrupted. 'There's a strong possibility that these two break-ins are linked, it sounds to me from what I read of the background to Sullivan's life here, and the Brown woman, that actually it's more than a strong possibility. What do you think John, perhaps Smith should take Eton with him? They could have a bit more of a thorough look. There's still the three of us to go over things here.'

MacDonald tried not to show his annoyance, but his expression couldn't hide it. However, he had to agree that it was probably the best move.

'Yes,' he kept his voice even - calm. 'You're right, good idea. Okay you two, get to it, and keep in close contact. If you can't turn anything up, get back here, but get as many prints as you can.'

Smith and Eton took two of the bags and headed to the car. As they went out the driveway the others made their way to the house. Stopping as they approached the back door.

'Have a wander around the outside Thomas, and check the gardens as well. There is a path that runs off down into the bush, leads back down to the water front - don't go all the way, but see if there's anything been disturbed someone using it recently.' As they left, MacDonald turned to Bronson. 'Okay, let's see what's happened on the inside. It's pretty palatial a beautiful home, and while I hold no love for Mr. Sullivan and his money, I hope that we don't find what I fear that we might - and - a lot of possible evidence removed or destroyed.' He led the way through the door and across a bed of broken glass from the back porch windows. They entered the kitchen and the first of the mayhem they were to find.

The kitchen and pantry areas were like a bomb-site, it did at first look like wanton vandalism, but closer examination showed that it was systematic.

Whoever had been here, had it seemed, three reasons - to find whatever it was they were looking for, to destroy anything that could be of use to the Police, and then to destroy whatever they thought Sullivan or his family may have valued.

Thomas came through from the front of the house, his face reflected what he had seen. He too saw it the same way. 'God - It's like a bomb site Sir. I have seen some break-ins and vandalism before but there is something about this that is different - can't actually put my finger as to what it is, but it is.'

The three followed the young Constable out of the kitchen and into the hallway. It was as he had said - a bomb-site.

'How many do you think have done this and when,' MacDonald shook his head at the devastation. 'We have only been away - what two hours, one person couldn't have done this. Not in that time surely.'

They went into the office and bedroom area that they had searched earlier. It was even worse - everything had been smashed - and almost every space of every wall in the bathroom, bedroom and office had been spray painted with threats and obscenities - all aimed at Sullivan, and anyone that had anything to do with him. Any evidence that they may be able to obtain, would be extremely difficult, if not impossible in this part of the house. After examining the other downstairs rooms, they stopped at the bottom of the stairs.

'I'll call Smith and Eton, get them back, quickly. I think we just might need a bit more man power here after all,' MacDonald sighed. 'Maybe I was a bit hasty in sending them off to the other break-in. I know what you're going to say when I tell you that we didn't even look upstairs when we were here before - so don't say it. And I also know that I've cocked up by not having called the local men, and got them to stay and keep an eye on the place. I've been far too complacent about it all, small village, small criminals - stupid, very very stupid.' He pulled out his phone and pressed Smith's number. He answered almost immediately.

The conversation was brief. Smith informed him that it was as Calder had described. He listened to what MacDonald told him about Sullivan's place, and said they would come back straight away. As he was speaking, Bronson and Thomas went upstairs. He clicked off his phone and followed them. At the top they each went in different directions into different rooms, within minutes they were back at the landing.

'Well whoever it was, knew that there was nothing up here to search for, they have been here, but nothing seems to much out of place, and there's no damage. Unless, unless,' Marguriette looked from one to the other. 'They were disturbed before they could do any damage. Our arriving when we did, they may have just had time to get out. Was there any sign of anyone having left the front way, down into the bush?' She looked questioningly at Thomas.

'There had certainly been somebody on that track at some stage. There are prints, going both directions - to and from the house. They show quite clearly in the softer soil of the track, but there are quite a lot of them, there was certainly more than one person. But I would say that they must be pretty recent – the weather here was dreadful I believe over the last day or two – there was no water in the footprints, they are quite sharp.'

They all went back downstairs. 'Thomas, you have some gear, you get started - begin up there, every door and flat surface first, I am sure that we will get several sets of prints, including Peter Sullivan's. Also pick up any hair and other samples from the bathrooms and bedrooms, that may help the DNA lads and lasses, and have a look in the beds - who knows what you may find there.'

The young Policeman nodded and went and collected his bag from the kitchen where MacDonald had left it.

Bronson and MacDonald looked at each other. 'Hopefully we'll turn up something out of this mess.' She said. Her tone sounded dispirited. She felt like berating her colleague for his show of incompetence, but thought right this moment there was no point, it wouldn't solve anything, besides he'd already admitted his stupidity.

'When the other's get here, I think that we should let them get on with this work here, and we should go and set up our command post at the local station. Then we should sit down together and piece together everything that we know. I have quite a large file - and with what you have from your interviews we may be able to put it all together. When we have done that and spoken to this Jenny Sullivan and Calder, we should I think get back up to Headquarters and work from there. I don't think that there is going to be - I may be wrong of course - any more activity of use to us here. I am sure that the main players are now well clear.'

'You are right, absolutely right. And, I apologise again for my mistakes. I've underestimated everything, a small hick town my arse! I should've known, with a player like Sullivan with his money and contacts, this wouldn't be a simple case of – hullo, hullo, hullo what have we here, what do you think you're doing my man?'

His attempt at humour and the apology fell on deaf ears.

'Don't be so bloody stupid and sanctimonious John, it doesn't suit you and I know you don't bloody well mean it, and stop trying to suck up to me. It won't and doesn't help.' But she did manage a twist of a smile.

The sound of a car arriving, stopped the conversation. The two Senior Officers made their way to the back of the house, gave the men their instructions - "To achieve what was needed in the quickest possible time - and that they would arrange for the place to be put under surveillance - as soon as they had completed the work".

Eton and Thomas were to call in the chopper. Get it to come down and pick up their findings first thing in the morning. They needed to get the evidential samples back to the Lab for processing, as quickly as possible. That was if they had anything to process.

'We'll get the Local Police to get a car to you, we'll be needing this one. I think that we're under resourced, just a tiny bit, still it's but only a minor matter, we'll get it sorted..' As the men left, Bronson smiled to herself over MacDonald's remark.

'A lot's happened in a very short time, hasn't it John, an awful lot, quite a frightening amount.' Bronson's voice was concerned.

It was late afternoon when Bronson and MacDonald left the Sullivan house.

*   *

Rory ran up the narrow track that led off the beach, up through the rock shelf. He was breathless and beginning to sweat by the time he reached the top, partly from the exertion and from the anxiety he was feeling from Jenny's absence from the Cottage. If he hadn't found her flat in the shambles it was, he mightn't have been panicking, but he was feeling that there could also be something wrong out here.

At the top of the rise he stopped and looked around the flat plateau. The late sun was starting to cast shadows, and only the gentlest of breezes moved the tops of the short scrub and rippled the shining waters of the estuary. He jogged, slowing from his frantic run, to recover his breath.

Towards the point where that morning they had looked over to the ruins of the old mill, he hesitated, flicking his eyes over the land and the line of tiny beach inlets below the sharp cliff faces.

'Where the hell is she, she could be over in the mill area or passed it, or - she may not have come this was at all.' He crouched down - this time he looked at each portion of the scape in front of him in detail, seeking any movement, any sign of a person - anything that may give a clue to whether she had come this way or not.

Rory stood and stretched out of the crouch and walked down the track. His mind changed from the original rush, to a slower more thorough inspection, of where he was and was headed. "That thought may apply not just to this search but to my life in general - was this narrow track he was on now synonymous to the track that his life was on? He had wanted to change what and who he appeared to be - but what had he fallen into. It was still complicated, still confusing. Now - with the events that had taken place - he knew that he wouldn't be pursuing that ideal."

As his mind took that direction - the path changed, and suddenly veered sharply to his right and headed towards the water. He had been walking head down, searching for any sign of anything that may give him a sign that someone had walked the track. With the change of direction of the path he looked up and could see the shape of the huge blackened derelict barge looming up over the gorse and broom.

Rory thought that the path would have first gone to the settlement and the main part of the mill. He set out - it was clear and easy going for nearly two hundred metres, then it came to a fork. The track to the right, that seemed to still head for the barge was more overgrown, the one that went sharply left was wider, and at sometime been used for some conveyance that needed tracks, as there was still evidence of where rails and sleepers had been laid.

The ground to the right was lighter sandy soil, unlike what he had been over up to now, which was hard packed clay and stone. Then he saw them - the footprints in the sand they were quite clear, and recent.

*   *

Bronson and MacDonald went back to the village. It was now like a ghost town, the streets, apart from two roaming dogs, were deserted. He headed to Bland's house.

'Where are you going? - I thought we were going to set up our operation centre at the local Station - where does this go?' Marguriette queried.

'Just want another word with old Jim Bland - you got anything on your file about him - Miranda Sullivan's Grandfather - want to see if he knows of anyone who would trash Jenny Wilson's flat, and Sullivan's home. I mean - they could be completely unrelated to what we are investigating, but I would bet my last dollar they are not, and the same person or persons did them both. This Warren Blanchard worries me, I think that what people say about him and from what he appears to be - is rubbish, I have a gut feeling that he has much more to do with it all than at first thought.

Someone is not giving us all the info that we would like - not a surprise that though is it.'

He pulled the car over to the curb in front of the Bland house and for the first time he took notice of the house next door. It was virtually identical, and was in a similar exterior state of repair.

The two Police Officers didn't move from the car as they saw Jim Bland come out of the front door of the second house and hurry diagonally across between them, and disappear around the back of his home.

'I think that you may very well be right John, according to my files, Mr. Blanchard casts a far wider fishing net than the one that he supposedly uses around here. When we have had a chat to this fellow and get to the Station - or somewhere perhaps more private may be an idea - I will show you what I have on the man. I actually think that suggestion might be for the best as well, that we find somewhere other than the station - as there could well be eyes and ears that we don't want to know what we are doing.'

MacDonald nodded his agreement to the idea. 'Right - yes I'll go along with that. I think Mr. Bland has had enough time to settle into his armchair. Let's go and have a talk.'

Jim Bland watched the Police get out of their car and wander slowly over to the front porch of his house. He could see them looking towards the house next door, taking a much closer look than he liked. 'Had they seen me come out of it?' He muttered. He hadn't been concentrating on what may have been in the street when he came over the lawn a few minutes ago, and hadn't seen their car.

'What the blazes do they want now. I feel that I have done and said enough for one day, I am sick of this whole bloody business. Now Miranda is dead - people know about Jenny, and Sullivan may not live - not that I really care about him - but it does complicate things.' He watched them from the back of the lounge where he could stand in the shadow, the low slant of the sun cutting a different track now darkened the back part of the room. He listened for the footsteps on the porch and their knock on the door.

'They seem to be taking a long time to get here,' Bland said quietly. He went out into the hall to see if he could see them through the glass at the top of the door. They weren't there. He walked back down the hallway to the kitchen and looked out the window to the back yard, still no sign of them. He went into the small larder off the kitchen, it was a dark panelled room, not touched since the house was built, he hadn't used it in years. It was dim and cobwebby the window was grimy. He seldom came into disused room, but from here he could see the other house. The Police were walking around from the far side now at the back of it. They angled back over the space between the houses to his front door.

'What are they nosing around there for, they must have seen me coming out of there - damn.' He made his way quickly back into the hallway, unlocked the front door, left it slightly ajar, then went into the lounge. He sat in the chair in the corner furthest from the passage door, picked up the newspaper, and stretched out his long legs, hoping to appear that he had been there, relaxing and reading. He heard the knock on the door.

'Hello, come in,' he called loudly, 'I'm in the sitting room.'

The door creaked open and one set of footsteps came down the hall to the lounge door. Jim Bland dropped the newspaper from in front of his face and looked up at the tall woman standing there. 'Oh good heavens, who are you? I thought it was a friend of mine knocking, I was expecting to pop round for tea.'

Marguriette smiled at him. 'Sorry - Mr. Bland isn't it, I'm Detective Superintendent Bronson. I've come down to assist Officers MacDonald and Smith with this little problem we seem to have, with some of your family. Would you mind if we asked you a few more questions - it won't take long.'

John MacDonald was now standing just inside the living room door. 'Hello Mr. Bland - we're back - may we sit down?'

Jim Bland looked from one to the other. Both Police Officers seemed relaxed, and friendly, as if it was just follow up to confirm some of the questions and answers from earlier, but the woman looked hawkish, determined, hard, a person with a purpose – a hunter – and on the hunt. Someone that you would have to be very careful as to how you spoke to her or answered any of her questions. But he did not answer the question as to whether they could sit, and took the opportunity to take the initiative.

'Have you had any word from the hospital - you know about Miranda. Have they sorted anything out, do they know about how or why she died, I know you said a drug overdose but that could – would be wrong, and Peter, surely there is some news of him?' Bland knew that there would not be. He knew that he was being far too premature with this line of inquiry, but he wanted, needed them, to see and feel his concern, whether it was real – or not!. He took several deep breaths and "welled" tears into his eyes.

'Nothing yet Mr. Bland, too soon. We should have an answer on several queries we have on Miranda tomorrow, and the autopsy, and some other aspects of our investigations may well be completed then. I assure you we will let you know when she can come home, and you can make the necessary arrangements for her funeral.' Bronson indicated to the couch. 'May we?'

Jim Bland nodded. 'Yes - sorry - of course.'

The two officers sat on the couch opposite him. Both leant forward at the same time, leaning their arms on their thighs. It was again the woman who spoke.

'Mr. Bland, Jim, may I call you Jim? Your son-in-law. You didn't get on well with him did you? You resented him marrying your daughter. How much did you resent him - enough to be involved in trying to kill him? After all - you felt he was responsible wholly or in part anyway for her death and for the alienation of your Granddaughter Miranda from you. Tell me, did you resent him - hate him enough to - have him removed?'

Both Bland and MacDonald stared at her, astounded by the questions.

'Where the hell had she got that notion from - she must have information that I don't have – and why should I – it seems nobody is telling me very bloody much.' Then he looked at Bronson and thought. 'Unless she's just trying it on! Trying to catch the old bugger out.'

Bland's mouth dropped open. He shouted at her. 'What the hell are you implying, that I'm a murderer, that I had something to do with this, I think you go too far Madam! If you are going to ask questions like that I want my lawyer!'

Bronson watched the old man's reaction. Listening with interest to his tone of voice. While indignant and angry, he didn't have a "guilty"tone, neither did his demeanour or the look in his eyes. She was a very cunning practitioner, and didn't just ask the questions to get an angry response, but to see what was behind the response. His gaze - despite his distress and anger - was strong and steady and didn't waver from her face.

Bronson looked at MacDonald, an eyebrow raised. She turned to him so that Bland couldn't see her mouth or eyes, she spoke very softly. 'Ask him about other persons who might have a grudge, or be confrontationally antagonistic to Sullivan - anyone who he may think would wreck the house. Bring up the girl Jenny's flat last. It' s better we're both involved in the questioning. I don't want him to feel just the new bird on the block, is the bolshie one. We can ease back now, we - you can be conciliatory, get him back, alongside us. The good cop bad cop routine - You are better at that than I.'

MacDonald stood from the sofa and went over to an armchair closer to Jim Bland. He sat, leaning forward, as he had on the couch, but his tone was different from Bronson's.

'We know that this is really tough on you, we know - well we understand to an extent - what this must be doing to you. Of course we aren't you and we can't of course know the deep distress that you must be feeling. But we need to do our job, and we need information to do it. Do you have any idea who may be behind it, anyone that has a grudge, or hated Sullivan, a business acquaintance, anybody? You see Jim, there is much more to this than was first anticipated. We have just come from his home, it has been wrecked, vandalised, and sprayed with foul and degrading graffiti, not just about him, but his family as well. And you were not spared either'

Bland looked up at him his face registering even further shock, he was about to respond, but MacDonald held up a hand to silence him.

'The photographs we showed you earlier. Are you positive you don't know any of them - apart of course from the obvious.'

Jim Bland shook his head. 'No - none - look this is getting beyond me, what is really going on, it's not just a simple - well I don't know the word that I should use - but it's not simple is it - and that's what I feel.

Right out of my depth. The only person I can think of that would do anything like this, is Warren Blanchard. And, well there's Cheryl Brown, Sullivan treats – treated her like shit!' Bland hesitated. 'She also has a thing for Blanchard, I think that you should know that, and the supposed friendship that she has had with Miranda was so that she could get closer to him.'

Bronson then asked, 'What about your other Granddaughter - Jennifer? Does she have any enemies, or friends? Was she good friends with Miranda? Who else knows – or knew about this relationship?' Before Bland could answer she went on, 'however I'm more interested in – enemies, did she have enemies? I mean being Sullivan's daughter too. Not a good situation - particularly if there's some connection between Miranda's death - and - Jenny's flat also being searched, and left in a shambles! Not the Cafe, just the flat.'

This stunned Bland. He thought that she would've still been able to kept immune to all of this, kept apart, but then - she had met Calder. He knew, as these people did, some of her past, and it seemed - that if her flat had been broken into - then there was someone else who did too. And there was the chance that whoever it was may also know something of her present activities!

'Who would break in to her flat? I don't know of her having an enemy in the world. It must just surely be coincidence? Are you suggesting that it may be the same person?'

'The flat wasn't broken into. You know that there's only one way in, it's through downstairs, either the back or the front door, and they weren't forced. Nothing touched broken. except up in her accommodation. No locks, doors or windows have been broken. Whoever went in to Jenny's place had a key, or is a very clever picker of locks.'

MacDonald came and sat back on the sofa. The two sat in silence letting this sink in. The old man started to chew at his fingernails, and his feet fidgeted on the carpet.

'So - Mr. Bland. Tell us about the house next door. Whose is it and why were you coming out of there when we arrived?' Bronson's voice was low, off hand, an excuse to change the subject. But the question was like an electric shock to Jim Bland. They both thought later, that his hair had almost stood on end.

He went a muddy whitish colour, and stammered out a few words. 'What do you mean the house next door, I wasn't there, never go there. Don't know who owns that - I think you must be mistaken, I have been in here, apart from an odd walk in the garden - since Franklin Primmer left, reading the paper and dozing - was expecting him back with Amelia - going to have dinner together - thought I might like the company' He knew that they would see through this, but he went on, 'They didn't want me to spend the evening alone, not after what has happened. They are kind people.' His voice became distraught as he tried to continue with the lie. 'They were bringing down the food and things – they – often – well no – sometimes – occasionally ----' His voice dwindled away.

The Officers stood up, deciding at this point not to pursue the matter any further. There was very plainly something that he didn't want them to know. But with everything else, it would keep for another time. They thanked him for his help, and turned to leave. At the door, Bronson stopped, 'Of course, that's easier said than done. It's a bit of a trek down from the Lodge I imagine, if you're walking – a car of course a totally different matter. Oh, yes, something else. You don't think that there's anybody that would – well, come to see you - anyone that may cause you harm? May be an idea to have someone stay with you, perhaps your friend Mr. Primmer, or perhaps you could stay with them? Go up there – instead. In any case you can get us, - or the local Police, just use the 111, if you need to. Don't hesitate, we are really here to help. We will be in touch tomorrow with any news. Goodbye for now.' They let themselves out.

Back in the car MacDonald looked at his companion. 'What a load of rot. He's not getting company tonight, at least I would bet a month's salary on that. I have met Amelia Primmer, and there's not a snowballs chance in hell of her coming down here, and just about the same for her husband returning - if she has any say - and she does. And, I don't think he is in any danger at all, never mind him even thinking of calling 111!'

I think that you would be correct in that assumption John, but I wonder why he was so nervous and uptight when I mentioned the house next door. I think we will do a little more probing about that. It is probably nothing - but - you just never know. Right let's find our hidey hole and sort out where we go to next.'

MacDonald turned the car and headed back to the main street. The village was deserted, but there was a pair of eyes watching as they drove away. As MacDonald headed for the previous bay, where he had seen the Motel, his phone rang. It was Rory Calder.

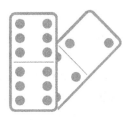

THIRTEEN

Rory followed the track and footprints for nearly a hundred metres before it became more over grown. Gorse, broom and stunted Ti-tree almost completely blocked the way, but the prints still showed in the sand. He could see that whoever it was had had to get down and crawl under some of the bushes, and if he was to continue following he would have to do the same.

The barge and the waters edge was not at all visible now and he began to feel disorientated. He got down on his hands and knees and followed the footprints and scuff-marks. Fifty feet later he came out in a small round clearing, the remains of what he thought may have been a workers hut lay tumbled at one side, and an old wood range lay under a tangle of posts and iron nearby.

Over behind where the hut had been, was a short rise of rock, he scrambled up to see if he could regain his bearings. It became clear that somehow he was now further from the barge and beach than before. But Rory could see the end that was in the water about three hundred metres away. In his scramble, through the scrub, he must have missed something, another track or direction that he should have taken. He looked down at the area below the rocks, there was no sign that anyone else had been in the clearing.

'Where the hell is the bloody girl.' He stared around the clearing looking for another track leading from it. 'Mind you,' He continued his self talk, 'I could be in the completely wrong direction, and she could even be back at the cottage. She might not necessarily see the Jeep as it's up behind bush at the back of her studio.'

As he thought this, his mind went back to what he had seen in the studio, and what she had said about it, and it was what she had said, and hadn't said that suddenly struck him. Nothing married up, and she hadn't actually talked about the work that she was doing, only what happened to it, and that - the people she sent it to - "It's a part of me I keep secret and hidden from prying eyes, and critical people. Where I sell and supply, they know nothing about me, not even my real name, and they don't seem to care either - I suppose they make money out of it all, and then so do I - so what does it matter!" This just added to the muddle of the mystery clinging to the back of his brain.

Jenny, didn't do the work, it was not hers! None of it was finished, there was nothing to even be sent away. If she was supplying and selling, it was more than likely there should have been. "I work on it as much as I can".

Sell and supply to who? If she was so good, the people that she sent it to would be very interested in who she was and where she was from, and the variety and diversity of the work. But she was never there, there was not enough evidence of frequent occupation, even if she was busy with her other work, there would have been more evidence of her being at the cottage and studio, and then there was the photograph.

'You should know better than this Rory Calder. You've been suckered!' What was this, a cover for her insecurities or something more, something more involved, more sinister?

As each of the thoughts raced through him he stared around the place where he stood. He called again loudly. 'Jenny - Jenny! Where are you, are you down here!'

He was replied by the quiet shuffle of the scrub in a light evening breeze that had sprung up.

Rory came down off his rock perch and went back through the track the way he had come. When he was about half the way back, he found what he'd missed before. The scruffing of the sand, off in another direction. 'Christ, this is like a game of hide and seek.' Rory stood up and pushed forward in the new direction, after only a few paces and it opened onto the path that had he had seen earlier, the one that he had thought had been an access way for wagons on rails. He called again, certain now that the footprints were the girls and that she was playing some game with him. Again there was no reply.

Her erratic moods since they had come out here, may not have appeared all that significant to a casual observer. The way that she had reacted to the news of Sullivan and Miranda he had thought odd at the time, but now he saw it as something else. If she had any connection to anyone - including Jim Bland, back at the village, surely she would have wanted to go back - he was now wondering if she was suffering from some form of psychosis, or severe paranoia.

Rory began to jog and then increased his pace to a run, he started to feel fear, for the girl and for himself. There were too many people running down too many roads in too many different directions. He stopped - puffing from the exertion. He was standing right underneath the stern of the derelict barge. 'Unless - all the roads wind back to the same place!'

The footprints had disappeared well before he had arrived at the old vessel, but this time he had been more vigilant regarding whether they had veered off in another direction, or returned back on themselves. He walked around the starboard side of the hulk and looked out to where half of it jutted into the mud and rising tide. There were some old ladders propped against the hull, the first two were rotted and most of the rungs were missing. The third one looked in reasonable condition, he tested the first bars, they seemed sound enough. He began to climb.

* *

Jenny's sleep after the initial deep drugged euphoria, became restless and disturbed. The sleeping pills and the alcohol had not been a good combination. Images of her father and grandfather swirled through mists, their faces white, ghost like, their bodies seemed suspended in the mist - floating, their arms and legs still, their eyes staring.

Miranda would appear laughing and pointing at her, then there were the other men, images she knew well - touching, stroking, holding her, preventing her from moving, doing "things" to her, pushing and pulling at her, laughing - making her scream in pain, and frustration.

Wanting and not wanting, seeking - searching - running and all the time in the mist that became thicker and thicker around her until she was standing on the edge of the bluff staring down into the sea – then a wind whipping and whirling around her. The gulls screeching in her ears. Below her floating in the sea by the rocks the body of Rory Calder.

She began thrashing around the bed as if she were tied to it and was trying to break the bonds, then it was as if a ton weight was pressing her down, down into the mattress as if to fold her in it and suffocate her.

Jenny opened her eyes as she screamed. 'NO! NO! Don't do that - don't touch me, no, no, - let me go let me go let me go!' Then, through her fog of panic, a voice. It seemed to come from a thousand miles away. 'Jenny - stop it - wake up - Jenny - it's me, Cheryl!' Her voice was soft, gentle. She stopped and stared at the form of the woman above her, pinning her arms to the bed, and pressing the rest of her body over her stomach and thighs. She began to struggle violently again. 'No! you're not going to do that to me, not again ever - don't you dare, don't touch me, go away - get away!'

Cheryl took her hand off Jenny's right arm, her expression changed, the quiet calm tone gone, the eyes became hard, cold. She slapped her twice across her face.

'Shut up you stupid little bitch, stop it, you've been having a nightmare - what are you doing lying here with nothing on - what the hell have you been doing - you stink of wine, and where's Calder, he was here with you, where is he?'

Jenny stopped struggling and began sobbing. Cheryl sat back and lifted, almost reluctantly, her body off her. 'What's going on Sullivan, where is Calder, what have you two been up to, you've been warned not to get close, to get involved.'

'Don't call me that - my name is not Sullivan, and I don't know where he is, he took the Jeep, I was in the bath, we didn't do anything. I showed him the studio, he saw the photo of Bland, he started asking questions, but that was before, then he washed my back and then he - left, said he would be back.' Her eyes glazed momentarily, 'why - what's it to you, and anyway what the hell are you doing here?'

'You're not supposed to even be here yourself, you know what's happened, and you are not, you have been told, never ever to bring anyone here.' Cheryl looked into the girl's eyes. Get dressed we had better have a look around. The Jeep isn't here, but that doesn't mean he isn't.'

'What does it matter if he is or isn't, he's just a guy looking for a new life, he told me, he used to work at the University, his wife was killed and.' She saw that from the expression on her face that Brown knew a lot more than she did. 'But you know all this, I can see that you do, what have you got to do with him, how do you know, who is he?'

Cheryl sighed, suddenly appearing tired. 'I don't know Jenny, it's just that Bland told me to find you - and him, I don't know, they don't tell me much, but I do know that things are getting out of hand, with Peter being attacked and Miranda killed. Things are moving fast, too fast for me, I think I may have to get out of here before.' She stopped, realising that her guard had dropped.

'What do you mean get out of here - before, and how did you know that Miranda was killed, she committed suicide, that's what the Police said, what do you know that we all don't Cheryl, and what's the rush to find this Rory guy?'

Cheryl Brown changed her tack, realising that she had made herself vulnerable, this girl was not stupid, and she had a quick mind - although it was a rather warped one.

'Where did you take him, did you go over to the old timber mill, and tell him anything of it, it's history, who used to live there?'

'Yes, and he saw the photo of Bland. He knows about that, and he knows that I'm Miranda's half sister! Do you think he's gone nosing around over there, not gone into town?' She thrust herself off the bed, pushing Cheryl aside. Going to the chest of drawers, Jenny took out some fresh underwear, a pair of denim shorts and a T shirt, then a bright coloured wrap around skirt.

'I think we had better go and have a look. I don't like the feel of all this – not at all!' Her manner had altered in seconds from the frightened uncertain little girl, to someone who appeared extremely lucid and in control.

Cheryl watched as Jenny dressed, she knew she shouldn't, but she couldn't help looking at the girl's body and feeling the stirrings that she tried - most of the time - to suppress. She also thought that she would have to be careful of Jenny's mood swings and psychosis. Cheryl had been wary of these in the past, now she was more than ever before, and particularly after the shock that she must have felt after hearing about Peter and Miranda, and her paranoia regarding the pair.

*   *

MacDonald had pulled the car to the side of the road when his phone had rung. He sat very still after he listened to the click of Calder ringing off.

Bronson saw his troubled expression. 'What's up John, who was that? Is that news of Sullivan? Has he recovered - shown some improvement - enough that we can talk to him?'

'No, you are for a change, up the wrong tree. It was Rory Calder, with - for the second time today - bad news - and not about Sullivan, but about his other daughter. Jenny Wilson or Sullivan, whoever. She's not at the Cottage. There's no evidence of anything wrong, he just has a bad feeling. He's gone to have a look around. This whole affair is becoming stranger and stranger.' He turned and looked at his companion. 'What have you got hidden in your bag of tricks Marguriette? Anything that can throw some sensible light on things? Have you got something that will draw us closer, to being able to sort out some semblance of direction to all that's going on - it's getting quite bizarre!'

'I think if we lay it all out and go through it logically from the beginning - that I have more knowledge of than you - to where we are now, we may be able to put some of the pieces into order and see a pattern. Come on get this thing going and let's get on with it.'

MacDonald took off out of the metal at the side of the road, the car slewing and fish tailing as it came back onto the tar seal. His patience with this case, and the sharpness of Marguerite Bronson -- was wearing thin.

It wasn't just her manner, but also her competence, her ability to see what he could not, and it made him feel inadequate!

'Hey, take it easy John, I know we want to get this sorted, but let's do it in one piece!' She sensed the tension in him and used a light hearted jovial manner, and laughed as she spoke. Bronson had known MacDonald a long time, she knew she annoyed him.

It was in fact that he annoyed and irritated himself. When he had first met her and worked with her, he had found her exciting and interesting but he had made the mistake of - trying to take their working relationship to another level, a personal one, and she had not been interested in that - or him. She had tried to explain about her personal life, but he had not listened and had taken the rejection as a personal affront. Which, she had not intended it to be.

'Sorry,' he took it, fortunately, as a light-hearted comment, and laughed too. 'Got a bit carried away, but - yes, you know anyway - that I am finding the changes in my position and work sometimes - difficult. Sorry.'

They drove in silence for the ten minutes it took them to arrive at the small settlement on the other side of the hill from the village. It was a basic Motel and cabins, with a few camping sites, an office and store. The rest of the bay had a dozen or so, tiny holiday cottages.

MacDonald parked the car in the area outside the Office door. Before he got out he asked. 'Are we going to share, they may have a two bedroom unit, and we will need space to work, I suppose.' He shuffled in his seat. 'I just want us to be sorted in our minds and not look a twit when I go in. You know me, hate looking a fool.'

'I'm sure that we can manage even if they only have a one bedroom. We have a lot of work to do, I don't think sleep is going to be a priority, and anyway I can sleep on the couch - or you can, if we get to be here that long. It's privacy and progress we need' She grinned at him

'Okay, point taken. Let's see what they have.'

They got out and went into the Office, a young woman with a baby on her hip came through from the back. She was attractive, but untidy, dressed in a worn out blue frock, a threadbare cardigan, and bare feet, the chubby baby had a very grubby face. She gave a welcoming smile, as she eyed them up and down. 'How can I help you, would you like a unit, or a cabin.'

It was Marguriette who answered. 'We need a place to work, and get some sleep. Do you have, one with two bedrooms please.' She took out her wallet and flipped her ID.

The young woman eyes widened. 'Um, yes, there is, it's quite roomy and of course quiet. How long will you be needing it?'

'Probably just one night,' MacDonald spoke. 'But it could be two or three, and if it's not a problem - we might need to have a word - nothing serious, just a few questions about the area and the village over the hill. Oh, and there is the possibility that we may need another double as well, some of our staff may need to stay here overnight, they may not, that will depend on - whether they have finished their work here.'

'Yes, well, okay I suppose. My husband knows more about the place, he grew up here, I've only been here since we got married - about a year. He's away fishing for a couple of days with his mates. It goes pretty quiet now the holiday seasons over. You sure you want to stay here, there's some much nicer places in the town, did you have a look there first.'

'Just show us the room, we'll be okay here. As long as it's clean and tidy.' Bronson couldn't resist the remark, as she looked at the girl and baby.

She came out from behind the counter with a key in her hand and at the same time pushed a registration card at MacDonald.

'Oh it's clean alright, not fancy, but clean. Could you fill in the card - sir, while I show - Madam - the rooms - thank you.' She might have looked scruffy but there was nothing scruffy about her sarcasm. Marguriette tried to make amends by talking about the weather, the lovely beach, the nice garden. But it was lead balloon territory. She tried once more, as they went into the room. It was as the girl had said clean - and it was immaculate, the decor was quite unexpected, good quality furnishing and drapery, the carpet new - and all blended beautifully. Fresh flowers were on the table.

'This is wonderful, there's certainly nothing as nice as this in the town.' Marguriette thought to herself, "that's a stupid comment! You haven't even looked, still, she wouldn't know that". 'I guess I'm tired, a lot of travelling and then - well there wasn't anything available in the town.' It was not her style to back down, and despite the fact that she was lying, she did feel disappointed in her previous behaviour. 'I'm sorry I'm not one to judge a book by its cover. You have excellent taste.'

'No you shouldn't should you.' The girl couldn't resist another jibe. But she softened with the compliments, and could see that Bronson was genuinely apologetic. 'Here comes your friend. Is there anything else I can get you?'

She noticed the way that the girl looked at her, then at MacDonald.

'He's not my friend, not in "that" way, he's also a copper, we work together, and yes, you may be able to help, we will want something to eat a bit later, nothing was open in the town. Would you be able to make us something - doesn't have to be much, and anything easy will do, we're really not fussy.'

'I can do that - what about in an hour or so, would that be alright? I'll just get my little one down, then I could arrange it - would that be okay?' She was now really trying to please.

'Fine, about an hour and a half would be good, if that suits, we have to get started,' she hesitated and thought what the hell does it matter. 'We're involved in an enquiry, an accidental death, and someone injured a few days ago, an attempted murder - but they're from around here.'

MacDonald arrived at the door and his surprise at the rooms also showed. 'God this is lovely, have you been doing some renovations?' The girl nodded and smiled. 'You've done a marvellous job, you wouldn't think it from the outside appearance.'

Bronson raised her eyes to the ceiling. But the girl smiled again at the further compliment, seeming to overlook the remark about the exterior condition.

'Thank you,' she said quietly now blushing a little. She left the room and went back to the Office. The thought in her mind - 'Not a bad looker that copper, pity he's with that tall bossy bitch, and not on his own - might be fun while the old man's away, this mouse might've liked to play, with a big cat! I think he had the look in his eye too.' But as soon as the thought was there, it was gone, her baby was restless on her hip and was starting to whimper.

MacDonald drove the car over to the Unit, parking close to the door. They unloaded the brief cases, and there own overnight bags.

There were two large airy bedrooms both with double beds, a bathroom and toilet adjoining between them.

'Well at least we may get a reasonable nights sleep, when or if we get there, these beds look comfortable, and the rooms are really very very nice - surprise surprise.' They put their gear in the bedrooms. As MacDonald went back into the main room, Marguriette heard his comment, 'I hope she ate humble pie after those remarks!'

He didn't think that she would have heard - but her reply came back clear and crisp.

'As a matter of fact - I did - thought you might enjoy me fouling that one up. Now get those cases unpacked.' She came out of her room pushing a pair of thick black rimmed glasses onto her long nose. 'Spread all the ones with photographs, from that brown one - on that table over there. All the folders from that black one, on the servery. Yours for the moment pile on the coffee table.'

John MacDonald sighed in resignation, her brief moment of being a fallible human had passed she was back to her efficient officious best. 'But,' he muttered, 'I at least know that we will achieve something, make some progress.'

'Call Smith and Co, let them know where we are and find out what progress they are making, and see if Roger has organised the local chaps to keep an eye on things, or at least organise some security at Sullivan's house and the girls flat. Then call Calder, see if has turned up anything on Jenny Sullivan.'

'Oh yes, and also get Smith to have another nosy round the pub, I want to know where or what Cheryl Brown is up to.'

'What do you know of her. I don't even recall mentioning her, apart from Rory saying the Pub was locked up and there was no sign of her. But I would like to know what she's up to as well, she seems to have a very strong link to Sullivan, and Blanchard - what do you have?'

'We'll get to that, you will find that I have some rather interesting files, and photographs. Look sorry about this but I have said that I have already been working on this lot for quite a while, it's just now coming to a head, especially with this explosion in Sullivan's apartment, now get the stuff out.' She took her glasses off and placed them on the bench. 'I'm going to the loo.'

MacDonald decided that the phone calls would be best carried out when she was not there to listen and stick her oar in. He called Roger Smith.

Smith, Eton and Thomas, had completed all they could. Considering the state of the house, and their limited resources. But they'd collected many sets of prints, letters and documents that they thought could be helpful - and under the difficult circumstances - had though been fortunate with quite a collection of samples for DNA analysis. He gave MacDonald a succinct clear report on their progress and they had arranged security, for both places, and would carry out the work on the flat first thing in the morning.

MacDonald wanted some control over the work. 'Get it done tonight Roger.' There was still some natural light, and they had artificial light that would assist. 'I'm going to be caught up here, with Bronson all night, and no smart comments. So I'm working here, you can make a pretty good effort getting that flat checked over. It can't be that bloody big and difficult. So I repeat - get it done tonight, I want every sample and piece of evidence from both scenes away first thing, besides you may well have another site to work on - Rory Calder hasn't been able, to this point locate Jenny Sullivan - or Cheryl Brown.'

Next he rang Calder. There was no reply – it went straight into messaging, he did leave one. 'Must be out of range area, or in a dead spot I'll try again later.'

'What will you try again later John?' Marguriette was standing in the doorway pulling up the zip on her jeans. 'Are you usually into talking to yourself - I know Rory does.' He gave her a sharp look. 'Shit - what am I saying - shut up.' She muttered under her breath. She ignored his look and asked again - 'What will you try later - did you get hold of everyone?'

'Smith and Co. have done what they can at Sullivan's, they were going to leave the flat until tomorrow. I said that I wanted it gone over tonight.'

She nodded agreement. 'Good, what about Calder?'

'Nothing - he didn't answer, he could be in a dead area, you know around here that's quite possible.'

'Right, yes - well then - let's hope it's just a dead area and not another body. Now shall we get this show on the road. The girl from the Motel is going to get us something to eat in about an hour, so we should make a good start.'

* *

Rory reached the top of the ladder. The deck, as he expected was empty, it was pitted like the moon's surface, huge craters open where rotten planking had broken and fallen into the holds below. It must at some stage been able to propel itself as there was an old cabin and bridge area still evident, but it looked in the same repair as the rest of the craft, but there was no funnel and from his peering into the hull below no sign of an engine. The skeleton of the framing showed through and appeared like bridges joining the craters. It did, however, look sound enough. He stood on the gunwale's edge, and sorted a route to take to investigate.

'Why am I doing this, I must need my head read, she is probably not even here, or been here!' But, something nagged at his mind. He called again, 'Jenny are you on the barge - Jenny are you here - somewhere, stop playing games - Jenny!'

A gull swooped over head and down to see what he was doing - it's squawk - his only reply.

Rory walked along the gunwale, which was wide enough to move on with ease, he headed towards the bow. Two thirds of the way there his way was blocked by a large chunk of the side missing, rotted out and fallen to the ground below, he selected what he considered the strongest beam and headed into the middle then took another and carried on to the end. Every few steps he would stop and peer into the bowels of the barge where shafts of light from the lowering sun struck through the broken port side of the hull.

The fourth time he stopped and searched the depths he saw her, she was crumpled in the bottom of the barge, her body and head half submerged in a pool of dirty water. The girl was wearing a white Tank top and white jeans, but now they were stained and soiled by the muddy water and blood. It was too shadowy to completely identify who it might be – but he assumed it to be Jenny Sullivan. He stood there staring at her for a minute not knowing what to do to get down there. The only way was to go back to the ladder.

'She must have been wandering around up here as I am, and missed her footing and fallen - how the hell am I going to get her out.' From the way she was lying and the angle of her head, her face mostly covered by the water, he knew that she was dead.

Rory turned himself carefully around on the beam, he had been crouching staring into the depths where the girl lay, and felt stiff and tired as he stood. He began to inch his way back off the centre, to the gunwale, the side where he had made his best progress. He walked carefully until he reached the point from where he had been unable to go any further because of the damage to the side of the barge. Then he made better faster pace to the ladder that he had come up earlier.

As he approached the ladder he thought about Jenny and the time that he had spent with her. His feelings for the dead girl were strangely mixed. He had liked her, and had of course not wished her any harm, in anyway, and that had also to do with his reticence of becoming close to her, he had found her entertaining, interesting, attractive, but an enigma. But the sight of her broken twisted body in the stinking water - now added another dimension. Another aspect to the events of the last forty eight hours in this village. Another domino had been toppled, it didn't seem to connect with another number, but would it begin this chain of coincidence again.

Rory swung himself off the edge of the barge onto the ladder, and began to scale down as quickly as he could, mindful that although it had seemed sound on the way up, he must still be cautious. Half way down a rung snapped under his foot, he fell swinging sideways and gripped at the shaft. He tried desperately to regain balance but with his weight, the state of the ladder and the side of the barge, it began to slip. He looked up to see that it was moving quickly over the slippery old timbers. Seconds later he crashed into the sand and scrub at the base.

The ladder although in poor repair, was made of heavy timber and as he hit the ground it fell across his shoulders, the fall and the blow knocking the breath out of him. He lay there heaving, trying to get his breath back, pain shooting through him. He pushed the remains of the ladder aside and pulled himself to his feet. As he did so he glanced along the hull, none of the other ladders were there, there had been three of them. He stared around - not a sign of them, nor any indication of who or what had moved them.

Rory shook his head, trying to clear the blur of the fall, and as his breath returned he thought of the body inside. 'Missing ladders, footprints, a dead girl - another death, was it not the accident that it appeared?' He regained his breath and composure and began to run down the side of the craft.

There was no way in from this side no damage or rotten areas that would allow him access. At the bow the tide was rising, but it was as yet not deep, the mud was soft wet clinging as he made his way to the other side. Pulling him down, slippery, he fell several times, the brackish water splashing into his face mouth and nostrils, he coughed and wiped it away. He remembered his childhood quest to beat the mud flats, to achieve an aim to reach his goal. There was no prize then, and the prize now was his dead friend.

On the Port side, the mud was deeper thicker more clinging and the mangroves tore at his skin and clothes, he fell twice more before he reached an opening in the thick planks. They may have just rotted away, or they could have been torn off, he stared at the gaping hole and the pool beyond where the body was now being moved to and fro by the incoming water. As he moved inside the hulk, the water movement turned the body over. Her face that had been lying semi-submerged in the stagnant pond looked up at him. Cheryl Brown's eyes stared lifelessly at him.

Rory recoiled from the sight in front of him, not so much at the swollen face and dead staring eyes but at the shock that it was not Jenny. He could hardly describe his feelings as relief. He now realised that the situation here was far more complicated than he had thought, and – the thought - "What the hell was Brown doing out here?" He reached for his phone on his belt. It wasn't there.

'Fuck,' he cursed in frustration more than anger, he was becoming careless, panicky, this was not his style. "Where the hell is it?' He took a deep breath. 'Snap out of it, get yourself sorted and together, it must have come off when I fell off the ladder!' He crouched in the murk and muck of the bottom of the hold and looked more closely at the body. He could not tell without moving her - and even then it may give no indication as to whether she fell or was pushed, or even just put here.

Rory stood up. 'I'd better get that phone and call MacDonald, get an Ambulance here and get her out.' He looked at the tide rippling in through the broken parts of the hull. He had better move quickly. It was a good two hundred metres to get around to where he had fallen whichever way he went, but with the water rising he would have to go back inland down the port side. His initial thought - not to move the body changed. But he couldn't leave her there, not with the tide rising, it may move her body out completely.

'I know I probably shouldn't do this but to hell with the protocol. Besides how the hell would they get a bloody ambulance out here anyway – even a chopper wouldn't be able to get that close either.' He went into the deep pool where she lay, her clothes were of course sodden and the body awkward and heavy, he managed to get under her and lift her onto his shoulder.

Rory waded out and set off through the low mangroves, fortunately the sucking mud soon gave way to the sand and shell of the shoreline and his progress was good, he got back to where he had fallen in five minutes. He put the body down on the dry sand. The ladder was lying where it had fallen, he could see where he had hit the sand. There was no phone.

A prickly feeling ran up the back of his neck, He was now almost certain that Brown had been killed and that her body in the bottom of the boat was not caused by her falling - "by accident". He shook off the feelings and the thoughts that were racing in several directions at once, bringing his thinking back to the clarity that he needed.

'Well - either it has been picked up, or it came off as I went through the scrub and mangroves on my way to the other side. But, I would have thought that if that was the case I would have felt it come off, it's clipped pretty tightly to my hip. So if it was picked up, who is out here watching - who shifted the ladders - and who killed Cheryl Brown, and more to the point if that was the case - why?' He searched around again, around the ladder, where he had fallen. He stood there gaping, 'Now what the hell is going on, I must be going fucking crazy!' Then he saw the marks in the sand.

They were barely perceptible, someone had taken great care to cover footprints and had used - he thought - some of the brush weed as a broom to gently smooth the sand, but not make it appear swept. It had been very well done, but it was the area where his feet had scrunched up the sand when he had levered himself up from where he had fallen off the ladder that drew his attention to it - it had left only half of his body's impression in the soft sand.

'So, I have no phone, a dead body, and someone out there watching me - is it my friend Jenny or another unknown person, but who in hell would that be?' He made his decision, and turned away from the hulk of the barge and headed at a fast walk back to the track that he had followed down from the bluff. Within seconds Cheryl Brown's body was no longer visible, he would have to risk leaving it now. He needed to move quickly.

If he was being followed and if Jenny was part of it or not, he may be able to find out, but he had to get back to town and inform MacDonald and Smith.

*   *

Bronson and MacDonald set about unpacking the briefcases. He was surprised at the amount of paper that they were setting out. He had ten thick files laid out, each with names dates and codes on their covers. She set out the same number of files on the bench, they contained a complex and extensive series of photographs. She quickly sorted them into the order she wanted, then matched the photo file to its partner.

'There's one file that's not here, it's being held back pending some further information that I wanted added to it, and it wont be available until early in the week, possibly tomorrow, but I feel that it may not be for a few days.'

MacDonald was staring at the names on the folders, then he picked up the one headed "Miranda Sullivan" and began to flick through it.

'How long did you say that you had been involved with this? There's one bloody lot of information here. How many have been working on it? You can't have done it all on your little lonesome. I know you're good Marguriette, but not this good.' He picked up the matching photo file on Miranda and quickly looked through them. There were twenty odd shots of her with different people - most of them with the names on the other files.

Bronson interrupted his concentration. 'Try to call Calder again, I have a feeling that there is something wrong. 'He called and said she - Jenny Sullivan - wasn't there, was that right?'

MacDonald nodded watching her closely, there was something about her manner that was sounding warning bells.

'Well by now, I would have thought, he would have called you again with an update, isn't that what you asked him to do?'

Her stare - as usual piecing - made him uncomfortable. 'Yes, of course, but he's only trying to be helpful, and has got caught up in the circumstances here, poor bugger, he probably wonders what he has struck. Do you think he will be able to handle himself if the situation demands it.' He was fishing, he hadn't missed the comment she had made before about the man, it was a familiarity, as if she had known before him, and know him well. He deliberately didn't mention all of what Smith had told him.

'I would have no idea John, what sort of thing do you think he may have to handle, you've spoken to him - talked over some of it with him haven't you, that's what you said, you should have an opinion on him. What do you think?'

'To be honest, I don't know, one minute he seems to be one thing, and the next he surprises. He was certainly surprised when it came out about his wife having an affair with Sullivan, but there again, he bounced back from that pretty well too.'

Bronson didn't even blink at the statement, and went on. 'And the others when they get here,' she smiled lopsidedly at him, 'with my help of course.'

MacDonald tried the call again. There was still no response. He looked up from his phone as he turned it off, to find her still grinning at him.

'You can't let it go can you, even though we have sworn a truce, you don't let up the niggle.' MacDonald sighed. 'I suppose I've only got myself to blame, with what happened between us, and the fact that I am a twit and react to everything you say. Come on - show me what we have here.'

Bronson hid her smile. She didn't really dislike this man, and although he had blundered mightily by her standards, he generally was a competent and respected Officer. It was just that he was one of those people that she seemed to want to "rev up – needle". There were not many, and most of the force that she dealt with she didn't have a problem with, nor they with her. She watched a moment as MacDonald began looking in more depth at Miranda Sullivan's folder. She would try to stem her instinct to needle him and attempt to work with him instead of against him.

'There is nothing in there to indicate that the girl had anything to do with Sullivan's business dealings. If you check the photographs, you will see, after of course you have looked at the others, that the only one apart from her father that we were able to tie her in with is Blanchard.'

'What about these ones with Jones and Brown and Sullivan - just social - as they appear?'

Bronson nodded. 'We found through taps and tapes, that she seemed to have had no connection. So why she was murdered we can only assume that someone, probably Blanchard wanted her out of the way. Look, have a scan of the files. You were sent here to break the bad news, and to see reactions, and to delve a bit into Bland and Primmer.' Marguriette saw his questioning look. 'Oh yes, they need looking into alright. They play their part pretty well - look at them next. Then go back to Sullivan.'

She looked at her watch. 'That girl will be over in about forty five minutes, you might be better to do this unattended and uninterrupted by the wicked witch of the West. I'll go and have a shower. It was a long day before I even got in that helicopter. Try Calder, as I asked, and then give Smithy and the boys a buzz, tell them to get a move on and get over here. They will need to know what the wider ramifications of what we are involved in will be as well. Give Rory another try, you never know, third time lucky?'

MacDonald picked up his phone, dialling Calder. The phone rang six times before this time being answered - at least - he thought it was, as the ringing stopped.

'Hello - Rory - John MacDonald - where are you, what's up, have you found Jenny Sullivan.' At first there was only silence. Then he knew there was somebody on the other end listening - he could hear sounds that he couldn't identify, but there was a sort of swishing sound, like someone breathing, or a breeze. Then nothing. He looked at the phone, then asked himself.

'Why do we do that when we don't get the response from these things that we want? That was strange, somebody definitely answered that, but I don't think it was Calder. Something isn't right, just as Marguriette said.' He called Smith.

Roger Smith informed him that they were almost through. 'Look, there may be a problem with that Sullivan girl and Calder, go and see Bland, and ask him where exactly the place that he went to is. Try to be casual about it, but give the impression that we are not overly pleased with Rory. Then see if you can find the place. Take Thomas and Eton with you. There are evidently things in these files, that are more than just a little disturbing about our two elderly gentleman.'

He was looking at a photo of Bland with Sullivan, Blanchard, Jenny Sullivan (Wilson), and the South African - Jongejan. He became engrossed in what he was reading and seeing. He didn't look up from the files for nearly twenty minutes.

Her voice from the bedroom door broke his concentration, making him look up. 'Surprise surprise, not quite what you expected is it, and when I actually met our Mr. Jim "the Mayor" Bland I will admit that he's a good act, very convincing as the poor old man whose family has been decimated. There isn't anything that points to him being closely associated with Sullivan's business affairs - yet, but he's not what he appears to be - well not entirely anyway. I wonder if he thinks that we've bought his story line? Now, what news of the others progress, and did we get contact with Rory?'

MacDonald's face reflected his concern as he related the phone call incident. He told her that Smith and his two men had finished at the flat and he had asked them to track down this Cottage - hopefully through Bland. But having seen and read some of the file he wondered how hopeful they could be of his assistance.

Bronson thought about this. 'I think he will, if he is involved as much as it now appears, he'll not want to seem to be seen as suddenly unhelpful. When are they going to check in?'

'Shortly I would think, within the next ten or fifteen minutes.' He put down the Bland folder, picking up the one labelled Jongejan. For the next ten minutes he concentrated on his reading.

The phone rang. MacDonald picked up. It was Smith. 'We've seen Mr. Bland, very helpful and concerned. He has given us clear instructions as how to get there, it will take about fifteen minutes, maybe a bit more as we don't know the road.'

'You will call us as soon as you have anything to report, anything at all, even if it seems quite insignificant, alright?'

'Of course, that's what we are here for is it not - now we had better get going, there was a look in our Mr. Bland's eyes that said, "be very careful". That was the way I interpreted it - and I'm not trying to be melodramatic!'

'Right, that's fine, just look out for yourselves, this may be nothing, just a phone failure or such like, but I have a gut feeling that it may well be much more. Perhaps you should report in every thirty minutes, if there is something really urgent or not.'

'I thought Mr. Mayor would be helpful, it put him on side with us - at least that's what he will think and hope. He may not of course even have a bloody clue that we have this information, but he is not at all - a fool.' MacDonald began thumbing through the Jongejan file. This was a man of incredible means, a man with international connections throughout Europe and Asia. He had large resources and interests in gold, and diamonds - and he used these with great affect with people in powerful positions in Governments and in the Justice systems in at least eight countries. Others were less so, but his net of influence was wide, and it appeared dangerous. His family had strong links back to Germany and Holland, but they, for the past hundred and thirty years had been in the Transvaal. He was a noted supporter of white supremacy, but was also cunning enough to see that he must butter his bread on both sides, and had written many articles for newspapers, and a book, on the Integration of the many cultures and majority rule.

While he was reading this dossier, which was one of the largest files - the photographs also giving complete credence to the man's ingratiating influence, being seen with many Government Officials and Prime Ministers, but also with all of the persons that they had in the other Manilas.

'What has such a powerful influential rich bastard got to do with this little town, and our country for that matter. What's his game here - I can see it's not Rugby.' MacDonald tried a little levity, this scene was getting much bigger than he cared for, and from what he was reading it was going to get bigger.

'We are not really sure, why he is going to the lengths that he is. But he is evidently trying to create a new network for the illegal movement of his goodies, namely gold and diamonds of course, but there seems to be another agenda, we are not sure whether he is also now involved in the drug trade. We don't think so - at the moment - but that may be a sideline. We think that he has been buying people here to become part of this trade, I personally think it has to do with the changes in his country and it's Government, particularly now that Mandela is no longer in control. Going back to the "we". If he can set up a network around the world to move what may appear to be only small fry quantities, through business people that are continually on the move then it may not be noticed that billions of Rand are disappearing from their economy. How he is doing it - we do not know. But stumbling on this little crew here is certainly helping.' She stopped, letting what she had said sink in. MacDonald looked a bit out his depth.

'Don't worry John, there is a very large crew in on this, you aren't going to be asked to bust it all up, and neither am I. But it does, evidently, also have a lot to do with those documents that went missing from the University. There has also been talk of someone inside Government, being of assistance to him with sensitive documents. But on that I am vague. Mind you so's everyone else!' She took a deep breath. 'Although somebody we know may not be, and, the other worrying point is this attack on Sullivan, his partner Mangus, and his daughter. It's not, from what I know about him, and I know that it's not a hell of a lot. But maybe enough? - No, well, I've thought enough through this I hope, to have some insight into it. That it's not Hans Jongejan's style to be involved in this type of business. Or is it – and we've missed something, something significant – that has not been obvious – yet, and if there more that we have missed, what the hell is it? But, if he now is, we want to know why! Also what else is tied in, plus of course - who else is behind it? I think, and this is only my personal view, that it's a small fish in a big pond trying to wield a big stick at him. That conjures a funny picture doesn't it - but some form of blackmail comes to mind, and I think it may be our Mr. Warren Blanchard. Look into him next.'

As she finished talking there was a knock at the door. It was their food. The girl brought it in and put it on the kitchen bench. A large tray with home made breads, pickles, cold meats and cheeses.

'I thought that might be the easiest for you as well as me, I hope it's alright. I've got a nice cold bottle of Riesling in the fridge, would you like that, it would go well with this.' As she spoke her eyes roved around the room, taking in all the papers and photographs. Marguriette moved over, between the files and the girl's wandering eyes. Both MacDonald and Bronson were astonished at her sophistication. It didn't fit in with the rest of "the notes in the music!".

Marguriette nodded and looked at MacDonald 'Yes that'd be very nice, thank you, that's very kind and thoughtful of you.' MacDonald said with a slight smile.

The girl beamed at the compliment and hurried off to fetch the wine. MacDonald opened a kitchen cupboard and removed two very good quality glasses, and then dug in the draw and found the corkscrew. 'This place surprises more and more by the minute.'

Then his phone rang.

*   *

Rory made quick time to the plateau above the old mill site, he slowed and looked back over his shoulder as he walked, the sun was now dipping down to the hills on the horizon across the far side of the gulf.

It was at that part of the day when everything seemed to suddenly become very peaceful, the slowing down of time, even the bird-calls changed - became quieter in the still air. He stopped, turning as casually as he could. He did not want to appear to be overly anxious to anyone watching. But even as he did so, his mind told him how stupid that would look given that they would know what he had seen, and they would know that he had moved the body. But who in the hell was they?

His heart was racing, from the fast walk up the hill, and from the tension of the last hour. He looked over what under normal circumstances would have been a beautiful serene evening scene, but he felt only the chilling affect that his discovery had left him with.

There was no sign of anyone following. 'But why should there be, they - if there is a they, would more than likely be in front of me, waiting, or have left the area completely, which he thought the most probable. More to the point where is Jenny, surely it wasn't her that had been involved in Cheryl Brown's death? It seemed improbable, no not impossible, but from what he had seen and learned in the last few days, he couldn't see a connection - or a reason why - yet - there were muddled messages.

Rory set off again towards the track in the ravine that led back down to the cottage. He broke into a jog and found that he had gained his second wind. He was generally in a fairly fit state, and realised that his heart rate and breathing had been from the effect of the trauma of the fall, the sight of the body, and the feeling of being watched. Not that any of these

occurrences were anything new, it was by no means the first time at all
he had been confronted with violent death, or had been in "difficult and
dangerous situations". It was that in this case, and at this moment of it,
they were totally unexpected. But then the thought returned – 'Why was I
sent here? You actually know why – and are just in denial – but why are you
in denial?' He shook his head as he jogged – for Christ's sake get yourself
focused you stupid bastard – focus – as you have been trained to do!'

At the top of the jutting peninsula, as he was approaching the narrow
passage down between the steep rock faces something caught his eye.
Hanging from a gorse bush twenty yards to his left off the beaten path was
a piece of fabric. It was the brightness of it, stark contrast to the greens and
greys of the scrub and rock - a mottled blue red and gold about the size of
a handkerchief, but ragged, torn - swinging in a gentle breeze that wafted
across the top of the cliff.

He stopped and stared at it. It was not anything that he recognised,
but then, there was no reason why he should. Rory changed his direction,
pushing through the low scrub until he could reach over and pick it off
the thorns. It was light, flimsy, like a fabric that would have been used
for a sarong, or wrap around that women would wear over a swimming
costume. It appeared from its condition, that it had not been out in the
weather for very long at all, in fact he thought - "It has been caught on here
very, very recently". There was also a distinct perfume coming from it, he
lifted the cloth to his face and smelt it, it was the same one that Jenny had
been wearing before she had her bath.

'So what is a piece of ripped fabric off some of her clothing doing out
here on a gorse bush?' Rory pushed through the bushes from where the
cloth had been hanging. He felt that if she had the piece torn off she would
have been going towards the end of the bluff, there were no other signs,
no footprints, the ground though was harder, more stable - and the brush
and scrub did not really appear to have been disturbed.

At the edge of the cliff he was able to see back to the bay with Jenny's
cottage clear in view in one direction and in the other as well, the Mill
and barge.

It was the sight of the barge, which brought him rapidly back to earth, the small torn piece of fabric and the perfume had momentarily distracted, sidetracked him, another few minutes lost. He went back, pushing quickly through the brush, he ran down into the gully track and onto the beach. It was then that he heard the sound of the Jeep motor.

*　*

MacDonald answered his phone - it was Jim Bland.

'I have just had your fellow officers here, they seemed to be very concerned about Jenny and that Calder fellow. Wanted to know where they were, where her cottage is. I think that you're all overreacting. But if you must know, it's not far but remote in a way. They said you've had been trying to contact him, there isn't very good reception, it seems to be in a - what you'd call a dead patch, flat area? I'm not up on these modern terms. But I would like her back here. So if they can help, that would be appreciated. She doesn't like people going there, and I was surprised when she took Calder. Just thought I would let you know what I think, I need to worry about her. It's Calder you should be more concerned with.' The old man's voice seemed to be masking something. There was a short silence before he went on.

'Besides, she may want time to reconcile herself what's happened. Perhaps Calder may be helpful, perhaps he won't.' A change came over Bland, 'I don't know why you're so concerned? Why do you want to contact him, what's he got to do with it all? I am getting very confused and a little upset by all this. Especially after what came out the last time he was here!'

'Oh nothing really, he's just trying to be helpful and said that he would - well you know that - you were there when it was discussed.' MacDonald thanked him for the call. He clicked off his phone and looked at Bronson.

'That was a very peculiar call. Why would the old bugger say that he felt that she was fine, when her flat has been done over? Sullivan's house too! As well as her father being blown to pieces, and her half sister probably murdered! He didn't think we needed to worry, but if we could help Rory to persuade her to come back to town that would be fine. Then he sort of implied that we and Rory were interfering. Puzzling, I don't follow.'

Bronson was about to comment, when the girl returned with the wine. From her friendly smile, it seemed she was hoping they would ask her to join them, but they just thanked her. She put it in the fridge. The pair turned back to the table of files.

Marguriette leant on the table. MacDonald picked up another folder. This time, Peter Sullivans. 'Don't want to be telling you what to do, but I think you may find Franklin Primmers, a lot more interesting. Have a look at it next, and sorry – yes I am telling you what to do, hmm, more suggesting perhaps? Besides I don't feel that Peter Sullivan is going to be much bother to us now, if ever. Oh yes, his profile and activities will contribute – but the man himself – no.' her tone was cold, callous.

He looked up in surprise. 'Why, what's it got that's going to interest and excite me. I thought he was an old retired Professor, running a Bed and Breakfast, and that -- I thought you said that Sullivan would --.' MacDonald looked up - her eyes bored into him, 'No - right, yes, of course, I'm doing my stupid assumption crap again - sorry.' He was about to pick up the Primmer folder, when Bronson stopped him, with a rather strange question.

'John, have you ever played Dominoes? You know that game with the tiles with dots on them?'

'No, why do you ask? God, Marguriette, you come out with some bloody funny questions. What the hell has the game of Dominoes suddenly got to do with this. I would have thought that we have a lot more important things to discuss than a game of Dominoes!'

'So you've never played it - well - funnily, it's just occurred to me, why in this case I don't know, but that this damn case has some similarities to it. We have to put one tile - or file next to another, the numbers have to match - like it starts with a double six, each player has these tiles. Look, I'll show you, pass me a piece of paper and a pen I'll draw it, then it might make some sense. Then I'll show you what else I have just noticed, it is just damned weird!'

'Are you sure that you're not suddenly losing it,' John passed her paper and a pen from his case, 'It's not like you to sound so hair-brained!'

'I know it sounds that way but you'll see too, I'm sure. You do believe that coincidence has a cause and affect don't you? No? – well, it does, well at least from my experience it does, now watch what I am doing.'

Marguriette drew twenty-eight oblong shapes on the paper. Then, divided each of them in half with another line, she quickly filled in the dots, from one tile with the two lots of six, then the six five, six four, six three, and so on until she had all of them filled in. John MacDonald watched her as if she had gone off her head. But at the same time with some fascination as to what she was doing and saying.

'In the common form of the game, using twenty eight pieces, the domino tiles are laid face downwards on the table - each player takes seven, the rest being left as a reserve. A player stands his tile hand so the faces of his pieces are not visible to his opponents. The idea of the game is to match the number on one domino half to that of a free half of a tile already played on the table. Pieces are laid end to end, but double pieces are laid transversely, and allow the player an extra turn. The winner is the player who plays all his pieces first.' She looked at him. His expression was one of confusion.

'You'll see - I hope - in a minute what I am driving at. In some games a player who cannot play their tile, simply misses a turn, in others he may draw from the reserve, having, of course, to retain the domino in his hand if he still cannot play.' She paused for a breath, she was becoming very intense. 'Now, do you know the definition of coincidence?'

'Well no, I suppose I don't, not literally, why what's that got to do with it?'

'The definition, if my tiny brain serves me right is - a chance occurrence of events remarkable either for being simultaneous or for apparently being connected. Now you have to have, must have, heard of the Domino Theory?'

MacDonald looked blank for a second then. 'Well yes, I suppose so, but no doubt you are going to tell me and refresh my sagging memory, so?'

'The theory - that an event in one place will influence the occurrence of similar events elsewhere. And, I'm not just talking about stacking up a whole lot of these tiles and pushing them over to see if they will all go in the same direction, you must have heard of people doing that - for fun - you remember what fun is?'

He gave her his impression of what he hoped was a very black look.

'Now, look at the files, look at the numbers on the top left corner, and the bottom right corner.' They were all laid out on the table separate from one another, the numbers were written in black felt pen and were very clear.

'I know you think I am completely balmy, but remember how I showed you how the Domino numbers were played, well, you can actually do that with these files - look.' She took selected two of them and put the first on the floor then placed the next one so that it's number from the top left matched the number of the other file's number on the bottom right. 'Right, let's just see if we can join them all up.'

MacDonald was standing watching her. He shook his head. 'Oh well if you can't beat the insane I guess you have to join them.'

For the next few minutes they matched the numbers, everyone of them was able to be connected to another.

'Now for the next crazy part, take a photo - you pick a card any card type of thing. From a matching file - like Sullivan on Sullivan's number, and place it on top of the corresponding one - it can be any photograph from that file, in fact don't look, just put your hand in and take one - lucky dip. You do the first five and I'll do the rest.'

'This just seems a stupid bloody game, what on earth do you hope to achieve, have we really got time for this?'

'Just stop your whinging John, indulge me, humour me, call me a stupid bitch if you like. But I have done this, once before, and the results were quite a surprise! Now you select from files 6/5 to 6/1, and I'll do the others, you will notice that there is one file missing, - it's not exactly the missing link, but it may hold the final clue. It's the one I told you is still being looked into – and hopefully in a lot more damned depth than some of these were!'

They each slid the photos from each of the files and lay them in the middle of each of the corresponding ones. They crouched beside their collage on the floor, and stared at it for several minutes. It was MacDonald who stood up and spoke first. Bronson had been watching for his reaction to what was in front of them.

'Well I'll be baked, basted and bloody browned! I certainly wouldn't have expected that! How did you know Marguriette, how did you know that it would show us that pattern?'

'I didn't John.' She stood up beside him, and looked at him seriously. 'I hoped that it would, but I didn't know for sure that it would, it's just - coincidence.'

Every photograph they had laid out it formed a strange sequence. In everyone there was at least one if not two common people and every one of them, was linked to everyone else in one way or another. Each of the person's they had been investigating had met with all of the others - and it showed in every second shot.

In all of them there was a man that MacDonald had not seen before, and in five of them there was also a woman, hovering it seemed, partly obscured behind him. He pointed to him. 'Okay, who is the one that doesn't fit in, the one I have never seen before. Who is he, and who is his shadow?'

'That's the one that we are waiting on for the file, his should have the 6/6 numbers on it, if they don't, my game may have been for nothing, but I don't think so, oh - and his shadow is his wife. His name's McGillveray, Euan McGillveray, her's is Maxine. Oh, and there is one – small yet significant detail.' Marguriettes tone was extremely sarcastic. This guy, is Calder's Lawyer, and a supposed close friend – who it seems – I have found out, through admittedly dubious sources, was another, apart from Sullivan, who had passionate designs, on Serena Calder! Now is that a coincidence – or not?'

MacDonald tried to make sense of what Bronson had said, but he felt confused. 'So what's so important about him what influence does he have that we can't or don't know much about him – them? Or have anything on him yet, here? That doesn't make any sense, but I think you know what I mean.' He was still staring at the floor. 'I presume that he is important, but if he's the missing tile, but isn't "exactly" the missing link - who or what is?

If there really is one. And does this "missing link" help us? And – does this also tie Rory Calder in with this 'conspiracy'? If there is such a thing?

'Yes, - no - well I think that it - or more to the point - he - will. Except that he is I believe,completely unaware of McGillveray's involvement and connection to any of this, - activity! That could present a problem. That's if he's still in a position, and who knows about that now, to pass on what he knows – or doesn't!'

MacDonald looked even more perplexed, and shook his head. 'That sounds incredibly, like what one could call 'double Dutch'! Who the hell are you talking about? This missing link – or Calder? If it's not McGillveray – who in the hell is it?' MacDonald looked completely perplexed.

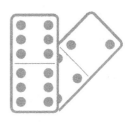

FOURTEEN

The apartment was on the twentieth level of the block, it was high on a ridge amongst large older homes, ten minutes from the City Centre in one of the most expensive suburbs.

Warren Blanchard sat in the deep plush leather couch looking out at the views of the harbour and surrounding city. The sun was sinking into the tops of the Ranges out to the far west, its rays streaking across the partly cloudy sky tingeing it gold and red, and lighting the sails of the yachts winding their way back to their marinas and moorings, after a weekend in the Gulf.

Blanchard had arrived at the heliport on the waterfront, half an hour later than he had anticipated. The driver of the limo was not impressed with the wait, and had been disgruntled and surly. Blanchard had smoothed him over with a hundred dollar note before he got into the car, and an over exaggerated apology,

Now it was his turn to wait. He had been expected, but his associates had been held up with another matter they had said was vital to deal with, and would be at least another hour. The driver had informed him of this as he dropped him off, he also said that he would be back in two hours to take him to the airport, which Blanchard thought strange as it hadn't been mentioned to him as part of the present planned agenda. And the timing made the meant that the meeting would have to be cut short and rushed.

Warren had been let into the building by the apartment block Property

Manager. An officious, middle aged woman who obviously enjoyed her position of power, and made it quite clear - without actually saying so, - that she did no approve of strangers expecting special treatment. Even at the say so of owners, and that she was watching every movement in the corridors and the grounds on the surveillance cameras.

Blanchard had sneered his thank you at her, as he had closed the door. Depositing his bag and the briefcase on the floor in the lounge he looked around the apartment. He had not been here before, and although he had been in some "posh pads" never one that was as palatial and well appointed as this one. Warren inspected every room and carefully went through the drawers in the dressing table and desks, those that were not locked. There was nothing that he felt that he could remove without it being obvious. He then found the liquor cabinet and made himself a drink. A very strong whisky on ice. He was feeling nervous, out of place. He hadn't played for such high stakes before and was beginning to wonder if he had bitten off more than he could chew.

Several gulps of the Chivas stilled his jangling nerves, replacing them with his usual brashness. 'I will not let them control me, I am the one with the upper hand, and the goods. This time they will have to dance to my tune'. He stood up and went to the window. 'This sort of thing will be mine soon. I wont have to bow and scrape to anyone. Nobody, not Sullivan, Miranda', he grinned sardonically, 'well, I certainly wont be worrying about Sullivan and Miranda, or Jongejan, no!' He smiled at the thought of the South African. 'No, particularly that arrogant bullying bastard. I wonder how he's enjoying his trip on the freighter.' He emptied the glass and went back and made another. He glanced at his watch, he had been waiting nearly forty minutes. 'What the hell was keeping them?'

*   *

Rory ran out onto the beach and towards the cottage, but the sound the Jeep was already receding. He came up the slope onto the veranda, to the front door it had not been locked. He went in and up the stairs. The drawers in the dresser were open and empty. Back down the stairs everything looked much as it had before, but for one thing. The photograph with Bland and parents was missing. He went back through each room again, then into the kitchen, he checked that it was as when he had been there earlier, there was nothing different – nothing missing.

Rory stood in the middle of the kitchen, bewildered, and wondering what his next move should be. He had no transport, no phone - but it did appear that the person - presumably Jenny - who had been following him, watching him, had gone in the Jeep. He went out the back and ran up the slope to the path that led around to where he had left the Jeep. It was as he had thought, and heard, it was gone.

'Of course its gone you idiot, what the hell is the game now, it's plain that in some way I have been set up, but what was Brown doing out here. She had connections with Miranda, and Peter Sullivan, who else? Whatever she knew or didn't know, she wouldn't be telling anyway. Jenny must be involved here somewhere, her erratic behaviour, the studio, with so much - that now I see couldn't be hers - but what is it, whose is it?' He looked through the bush back at the Cottage. 'There may be a clue there, there may not, it may be another fucking big red herring - but why would she play games with me, what does she know that she shouldn't, or am I embroiled in "coincidence" and out of touch with the reality of my work – out of touch and out of practice!'

Rory went back down to the studio, the door was still open, inside, was bare. All that had been set out before, was gone, except for the tools that had been on the workbenches. 'What the hell now! Whoever is in that Jeep has stripped out the work that was here. But surely there was too much for that, so where the bloody hell is it all.' Across the room he could see another door, that he had not noticed before. 'Maybe a store room, perhaps some or all is in there?' He went into the room and started to cross to the far side where the doors had been open onto the deck. He had not seen, nor suspected the very fine wire that was stretched across the door, he felt a slight tug on his shin, but took no notice. It was just as he got to the French doors that he heard the faint whirring sound, the soft whirring sound of a timer.

'Shit!' he screamed, 'she's booby trapped the bloody place.' He knew the sound only too well, and that it was set for him to be well inside the building. He grabbed the handle of the glass door, it was locked - he threw himself against it with all the force he could muster, as it gave way the room exploded and erupted in flame.

*   *

Smith, with Constables Eton and Thomas, left Jim Bland's house. They had a feeling of relief at his helpful, friendly cooperation. They were not aware that he was calling MacDonald implying the over zealousness of the Police and that their concern was really unfounded.

Eton had sketched a rough map of how to find Jenny Sullivan's Cottage. Thomas got into the driver's seat, Smith deciding to be the passenger, and let the Constables do the work. They wound their way out of the village and up the narrow roads that Bland had described. The road climbed quite steeply for nearly two kilometres, it was narrow and metalled as the old man had said. They came out on a plateau, a wide flat area well over grown with low scrub and old buildings set back behind most of covered with an overgrowth of scrub and secondary bush cover. There was no way off it but the way they had arrived.

'This can't be the plateau that the old bloke explained.' Thomas looked at the sketch map. 'We must have missed a turning.' He got out of the car and went to the edge off the flat area and looked down. He could see the town, and the peninsula that they were to cross, and he could just see the expanse of water on the far side. Below he could just make out through the trees the dirt road that he presumed that they should have taken.

As he got back into the car he explained their mistake. He whirled the car around and set back off the flat area down the way they had come. He drove slowly so that he would this time not miss the turn. It was plain why they had missed it, the angle that the track ran off into the bush was quite oblique. As they began to turn Thomas found that it was just a fraction tight, and backed up a way to have another attempt, as he did so a vehicle came out of the track at high speed, slewing across the metal and narrowly missing them.

'Shit a brick, that was a bit too bloody close, who the hell is that maniac driving a big Jeep at that speed on these roads, should really follow and find out, but I don't think we have the time or the inclination, right this moment!' Thomas put the car back into gear and edged around into the narrow dirt road, he accelerated, as it became clearer and visibility was better.

Smith had heard the other car go past them but had been looking in the other direction. 'What did you say - did you say it was a Jeep, that's what Calder was driving when he came back into town, a big black bugger, what was this, and did you get a look at the driver?'

Eton answered, 'Yes, it was - as you described so aptly - a big black bugger. But I didn't get a good look at the driver, but I don't think it was Rory, looked more like a woman. But, it was motoring, and I can't be certain. Besides I was watching Thomas's backing manoeuvre, I only glanced up at the last second.'

Smith picked up his phone and called MacDonald. 'We've just, we think, encountered the Jeep that Rory was driving. However we don't think it was him behind the wheel. Thomas didn't see, and Eton only got a quick glance, but he thinks it was a woman. Was the Jeep that he was in Black - a really big one?' He thought he should double check.

'Yes, it was, but if he wasn't driving it must have been the Wilson girl. Carry on and see what you find, he may be out there fishing for all we know and she is coming back to see old man Bland. I might toddle back into town and see if I can spot her, it's only a few minutes or so.' Although MacDonald's manner and tone were quiet , calm, he felt uneasy, alarm bells were ringing. He turned back to Bronson.

'That was Smith and Co. He says that they have just had an almost crunching encounter with a large black Jeep, they think with a woman driving, it seemed to be - similar to the one that Rory was driving, when he came into town - just before you got here. It was travelling fast, recklessly. Well, you heard what I said, to carry on and see what's going on out there. I don't like the feeling I am getting about this. Especially now that I have seen our montage, and that this Jenny Sullivan appears as one of the stars of several of the shows.'

Marguriette had been staring at the photographs while he'd been on the phone. She suddenly bent down and picked up the one that was sitting on the top of Blanchard's file.

'I hadn't noticed this before, maybe because I wasn't taking enough notice of the background.' She placed it on the table, it looked as if it was taken in a very luxurious apartment.

It was Blanchard, with McGillveray, Sullivan, and Primmer. She pointed to the fuzzy slightly out of focus portion, in the background of it.

'Look there, unless I am mistaken, there's Andrea Jones. Talking to Jenny Sullivan, am I mistaken or are their heads together in a rather "conspiratorial pose", and she's pointing towards - Miranda Sullivan. Now, we were led to belief that the two half sisters, didn't speak, and were never seen together in the same place.'

'We were?' MacDonald queried, 'What's this we business, I haven't actually heard that, well not in that way anyway, Bland just intimated that she, Miranda and Sullivan just didn't get on, and that because of the inheritance, things were a bit tense.'

'Are you sure that's what he said, you didn't slightly misinterpret it, and do you know apart from this cottage thing that's talked about in the file, what the rest of it was - or even if this was really the case, is there any inheritance in the normal way at all?. The photographs and the info in the manilas tends to point in quite a different direction.'

MacDonald began to study the print closely. 'That's seems a bit odd, in fact, very peculiar. Do you know who took this?'

Bronson shook her head. 'I would, or can only assume, it was someone we have on the inside, as I said this has been going on for quite some time. And of course we don't always know the identity of our spooks do we.'

MacDonald pointed to a part of the photograph behind Jones and Jenny Sullivan, there was a mirror or something reflective on the wall, and although it wasn't distinct it was unmistakable. The reflection was of Cheryl Brown, with a small camera. 'Now why would she be taking a picture there, and if it is this particular one, how did we get it?'

*   *

Warren Blanchard was on his third whisky. He was now wandering the apartment looking at the very large expensive art collection. He was getting extremely restless and the nerves he had felt earlier - despite the drink - were returning. The thought that he was deliberately being kept waiting was very much to the forefront of his mind. He also was feeling the need to relieve himself, and he made his way to the bathroom. As he did so the door of the apartment opened and the two people he had been waiting for came in.

'Been keeping you waiting a bit long have we Warren.' The man saw the disgruntled look in Blanchard's eyes. 'Sorry about that, but we had a couple of rather important matters to deal with.' He glanced quickly around the room and saw the open liquor cabinet and half empty bottle. 'I see you have been able to make yourself at home though, hope you haven't over done it we have a bit to go over before we go to the airport.'

'You certainly took your time, that surly driver said you would be about an hour, and your Manager bitch wasn't really wanting to let me in, thought I might be an undesirable type and rip you off. Now I have to use your toilet.' As he left the room, the man turned to his companion. 'How perceptive of Gloria, and as for calling Ray surly, it's a bit of the pot calling the kettle black. God he's an arrogant irritating bastard. But I think that we can change that.' He smiled at the woman, she grinned back at him.

'Yes, I am sure we can. Would you like a drink Euan? I'm parched after all the talk, and he doesn't actually improve ones nerves.' Maxine went to the kitchen and opened the fridge. 'What would you like - beer, wine, or a something stronger.'

'I think very clear heads are important, something that our friend here doesn't seem to appreciate, I'll have a beer thanks, you're right about the thirst.'

'What about a thirst - oh good you're having a drink, I don't mind if I have another.' Blanchard had come back into the room, and had only heard the last part of the conversation.

'You don't, I suppose feel that you may have had enough already do you Warren - we do have a number of matters to be discussed and a clear head might help the understanding of it all. And time is now getting short.' In fact McGillveray's concern, was completely false. He didn't give a damn whether the other man understood what they were going to talk about.

'I'll manage, we've been over it all before. I don't think I'm that stupid that I won't understand where we're at, and what to do next.' He smiled to himself. 'If they think that I'm going to continue to be their pawn they can think again.'

But he was beginning to slur his words. He poured himself another whisky and sat in a chair by the window.

The husband and wife looked at each other as Blanchard sank himself down in the seat. Maxine poured a glass of wine, then handed her husband a bottle of Budweiser. They sat on the couch together.

'So Warren, everything's to plan, is it? No hitches so far? McGillveray asked. 'Was it your goons that took care of Sullivan's house, the Wilson girl's flat, and your wife? You and your associates were very thorough – weren't you?' McGillveray was trying to get a reaction from Blanchard, and he wasn't disappointed.

Blanchard looked at him meanly, and his tone was as belligerent as he expected.

'Have I ever stuffed up before? You know bloody well without me even replying to your snide remarks that's been completed - without incident. And, I'm sure that the job we did on the house and flat will keep them baffled for quite some time, I think that it's a very large "red herring" that has swum across the 'oh so clever CIB's path! Of course I had the help of another friend too, but I'm not telling you who that was – so don't ask.'

'And Jenny, has she achieved what we set out for her, or haven't you heard yet?' It was Maxine, her voice was quiet, matter of fact.

'No - we will have to wait until she gets through to Primmer. Provided nothing interferes - I still don't expect that we will know for a few hours as to whether that has been successful, but I am quite confident that it will be, she is very resourceful, and a wonderful actress.' Blanchard suddenly sounded very sober, and very lucid. 'I did not have to take care of Andrea, she had done a pretty good job of it herself. We only want her out of the way for a short period, and by the look of the blood and the split on her head, I think that she will not be bothering us for at least a week.'

'I only want her out of the picture and out of suspicion of being involved with Sullivan - she is too valuable to us, and she knows many of the avenues that we can use, much better than some people.' Euan eyed Blanchard. The man lowered his eyes for a moment, then looked out the window, avoiding both of their stares.

'Now, you have the packages from Sullivan's house?' Euan took a mouthful of the amber liquid, it was cooling - activating. 'What have you done with them, or are they with you now?'

Blanchard suddenly changed the subject. 'This Calder guy, what's he got to do with it, and where did he appear from, is he important or just a nuisance. You asked me to go over his room when he was at the Pub, I did that, as instructed,' his tone very sarcastic. 'There was nothing of any significance, nothing to point to anything that he was anything or anyone out of the ordinary.'

It was Maxine who answered. 'He was there by complete accident, an unfortunate coincidence again, and he is someone of significance – and could have – but hopefully now he will not be able to be of any further nuisance to us. We had no idea that he was there until he rang us. He wanted some information about Sullivan. Euan is – or should I say – was, his Lawyer, and believe it or not, a really good friend!' she laughed ironically. 'But things change, don't they, and sometimes we have to take steps in a direction that we may not expect to. It's unfortunate that he's there and has stumbled into the web. But never mind, and anyway – there are things from the past that are no concern of yours. Now, Euan asked you, where are the packages from Sullivan's house - where are they?' Now a hardness had crept into her voice.

'They're safe, if that's what you mean.' Blanchard said with a very slight nervous tremor. But it did not go unnoticed.

'No - that's not what we meant Warren - we would like to know exactly where they are. And - we'd also like to know where to find another friend, Mr Hans Jongejan? Do you know where he is?' Of course, Euan knew, exactly where *he* was! 'Does he have the merchandise that came in the Diplomatic bags that were to be delivered to Peter and Mangus? Before their unfortunate accidents, of course, or do you? We know where you are, and we know where Mackintosh is. And of course, we know where everyone else, apart from Hans, that is. But we would be quite - keen in fact - to know the whereabouts of the aforementioned packages and person.' The line of questioning really was unimportant – irrelevant, it was a ploy to further unsettle Warren Blanchard, and it was working!

McGillveray's tone hadn't altered, it remained soft, calm. He knew Blanchard was stalling and getting nervous. Euan wanted Blanchard to feel he had control. He knew that he would – with the help of the Whisky, tell them what they wanted to know, if he actually knew anything at all. Or was it all a bloody big attempt at a bluff?

'Jongejan went on the freighter as arranged, but he doesn't have them now. Yes - Hans collected them himself, then passed them on to me, they are - with the other twelve, with Jenny, locked away in her studio. Everything, the drugs, the diamonds and gold, well concealed. Which of course Mr. Sullivan — Peter did have, some of them,' Blanchard grinned maliciously, 'and we may not have found them so easily if Andrea hadn't been on the ball. She doesn't have an awful lot of love left for him, so that was quite easy. The packages as I said are safe.' He pondered for a moment whether to tell the truth about their whereabouts or fabricate something. He went to take another drink and found the glass empty.

Blanchard stood, holding up the glass, he decided to buy a little more time before he made up his mind. 'I need another, sorry, I know you disapprove of my habits, but we do still have over half an hour before we leave.' He sauntered to the liquor cabinet and poured an ample amount of amber liquid, then went to the kitchen and got the ice.

Maxine and Euan glanced at each other. She slid her hand along the couch touching his leg. She gave him a lopsided smile, mouthing the words "he'll tell us".

Blanchard was busy with his drink and didn't see the exchange. He came back and stood at the window with his back to them. 'Hans should be deposited on Norfolk Island the day after tomorrow, then he'll fly to Brisbane.' He glanced over his shoulder. 'Then to Jakarta, after that to Kuala Lumpur. Several days between, and different airlines of course. I'm hoping that my small pieces of titillating seeds of information that I have been planting with a certain Police Inspector will grow and start to bear fruit, and that his journey will end there.' He turned from the window and looked directly at them. They could see that he'd decided that the truth would be the better course, the truth as 'he' understood it! It differed from what they knew, but that was not important!

'The cylinders with the gold rods are in a safe place - in a safe, on the Island in the Gulf, with Mackintosh, but he doesn't know what is the contents of the cylinders. They're to be retrieved and delivered as planned. I was able to arrange the placement of them. Never mind how, the fewer people that know that the better, but they're safe, and accessible - when required. The diamonds are there.' He pointed to a briefcase sitting by the wall near the kitchen. 'Would you like to inspect them, or will you take my word on it?'

'We'll take your word on it Warren, I'm sure that you wouldn't at this stage try to do anything silly and double cross us - would you.' It wasn't a question from Maxine, it was a clear cold statement, and her tone reflected exactly what she meant.

Blanchard also knew precisely what she meant. He coloured as he slurped at his drink. Realising with relief that he'd made the right move by not lying. They were far too cold and clever.

McGillveray stood from the couch and took his empty bottle to the rubbish in the kitchen. As he came back into the room, he went and picked up the case, placing it on the dining table. He inspected the locks. 'Come and open it for us Warren, I think that we should transfer them to a less conspicuous place.'

Blanchard began to protest. 'But I thought we agreed that they would be better to be just well, you said - and I thought that ----.' He stammered out his words.

'Just - come - and open - the bloody case - now.' Although his voice was quiet it seemed to fill the room. His eyes bore into the other man, who put his drink down and hurried to the table.

* *

Rory felt the blast hurling him through the doors, glass and wooden framing exploding out with him. He hit the railing of the deck and went over the top, landing half way down the grass slope, then rolled the rest of the way to lie against the back of the house.

For the second time that evening the breath had been knocked from him, but this time it wasn't that, that brought concern to his mind. It felt as if his right arm and shoulder were broken and his attempts to regain his breath were hampered by what he thought were broken ribs, blood was dripping down the back of his neck from his head. He tried to turn and look up at the Studio, the pain seared through him. He couldn't immediately believe what he saw, and what he had somehow managed to have escaped from. His main thought before he tried to move – 'What in the hell is going on here – what am I caught up in?'

It took several attempts to move himself into a position where he could see up the slope, then a few moments for his eyes to clear enough to take in the fiercely blazing building, a pall of black smoke was billowing high into the evening sky.

Rory tried to lever himself upright but his left legs gave way and he sank onto the grass, he looked down to see that his jeans were torn away around the bottom of the thigh. There was a large gash just above the knee, which was pumping blood, a piece of glass about six or seven centimetres across protruding from it. Rory searched his pockets but didn't have a handkerchief, he pulled the belt out of his jeans and set it around his thigh above the cut, pulling it as tight as he could, then he reached down and slowly and carefully pulled the shard of glass from his leg. Despite the pain and the shock, his mind began to work overtime.

'What the damned hell is going on, my brain and body are getting battered and I have no idea why? If the bitch – or anyone else wanted to kill me – there are a lot easier ways – that was a bit of over kill, but fortunately not successful. So what's the next part of the plan?' He thought back to his conversations with Jenny about his work. Had she must put two and two together and seen through his story – and then what? How had she – how did she find out – what his occupation was? There was no reason that he could see why she would and why this whole affair had got to this point. He knew that he had stumbled into something more than expected in the short time he had been there, but he had hardly begun his in depth investigation of the people he had come to look into - and this part was more than unexpected.

'Now how the hell am I going to get out of here.' He began to pull himself up to his feet again. The leg had gone numb, and he was unable to put any weight on it, but he managed to hop and hobble across the bottom of the grass bank to the back door of the house. He leant against the frame a moment and looked up at the fire. The whole of the shed was now almost completely destroyed, and although there was still a lot of smoke, only the odd skeleton timber remained standing. The whole event had taken less than ten minutes from when he had entered the room.

'I guess I was just a little on the lucky side.' He moved into the porch and pushed open the kitchen door. Using the bench for support he moved along to the sink and pulled a towel out of the draw then turned on the tap, soaking it in cold water. The pain from the shoulder, arm and rib damage was increasing as the original shock decreased and the nerve damage took over. He lifted the wet cloth to the back of his head and held it over where he thought that the blood was coming from.

The cold of the water and the rough cloth stung the wound, but at least it increased his consciousness of the situation. He reached over and took hold of the back of a chair using his left hand to turn it so that he could sit facing the window. As he sank into it he saw three men come around the side of the burning building and run down the path to the cottage. One went to the left, another to the right, the third, who he recognised as MacDonald's side kick partner, Roger Smith, came to the back of the building and in through the kitchen door.

Smith was rushing so much he didn't in the dimness of the kitchen immediately see Calder and almost tripped on his outstretched leg.

'Jesus Christ, what the hell are you doing here, you nearly gave me a heart attack.' Then his eyes adjusted to the light and he sucked in his breath. 'Hell you're a bloody mess, and I mean that in both senses.'

Rory tried a smile but the shock more than the blood loss was now telling, he felt weak and was close to passing out. He managed a whispered reply. 'Thank you for the caring comment I appreciate it. At last the Cavalry, how did you know I was here?'

Smith didn't answer but knelt in front of him and had a quick look at his injuries. He could see the way the Rory was holding his right arm as if it was broken, but after inspecting it, and the leg he found that they weren't, just twisted, bruised and there were probably torn ligaments, there was nothing life threatening, but he looked a mess, and was in obvious a considerable amount of pain, not to mention the shock. 'I know this sounds stupid, but it's what we all say. Wait there, I'll be back in a minute.' He went out and around to the front of the house calling for the others. They were at opposite ends of the beach and turned at his call, running back to the urgency of his voice.

'Eton, get on the blower, to MacDonald and Bronson. Tell them what we've found here, the explosion, the fire, and Rory. Injured, but he'll be alright, tell them though, we'll need paramedics. No sign of anyone else, but we'll have a better scout around - before it gets too dark, we have maybe a bit more than an hour, not much more. Thomas, come with me, I'll see if I can find some first aid stuff in the house, you go and get the kit from the car.' Smith went back into the Cottage through the front door, and after a quick look through the downstairs rooms he went upstairs. He found the bathroom and rummaged in the cupboard. There was little there, some antiseptic and a few gauze bandages, some Codeine tablets. He took what he thought he would need from the cupboard and went back to Rory, arriving only moments before Thomas and Eton came in.

As they began to work on him he mumbled to them. 'MacDonald, tell MacDonald, that the – from the Pub – the - Cheryl Brown from the Hotel, she's out – around the bay further - by a barge, she's dead.' Then he passed out.

* *

MacDonald and Bronson stood at the table. They had disrupted their Domino game, and had taken out sections of the files on each of the ten people, and further photos. It was the same pattern, and the documents began to substantiate that they were moving in the right direction and that every one of them had a link to another.

During their discussion one thing continued to nag at his mind, and the point that John MacDonald kept coming back to was the photo that seemed to have been taken by Brown.

'I don't get it, if she's so deeply involved with this mob, and is it the 'mob'? Particularly Sullivan, why would she take this photo, and it to find it's way into our hands? Once again I ask, and I ask you - wise Detective - what is that there is to know - that I don't? How come we have so many photgraphs of these people – who the hell is the insdier with the camera?'

Marguriette was about to answer, though in a very evasive way, when she was interrupted by MacDonald's cell phone buzzing.

'MacDonald,' his tone curt, irritable at being disturbed, he was wanting some more answers.

'Roger here, John, we have news. We need "para's" and an Ambulance.' The urgency in Smith's voice made MacDonald look up sharply at Bronson. She came and stood near him, leaning her head toward the phone.

'We've found Calder. There has been accident an explosion, a fucking big one – and a studio shed thing out here, has been burnt down, it seems he was caught in it. He's okay, as in alive, but he's pretty battered, though more shaken than stirred, the possibility of a couple of broken bones, and a few cuts.' Smith attempted to make light of the situation but then realised what else Rory had told them. 'But something else – a lot more serious. He just told us before he passed out, I would imagine just from the shock, that Cheryl Brown is out near here - dead.'

'What!' MacDonald shouted into the phone, 'How, where? Has Calder got something to do with it - and where's the other woman - no - oh shit - it must have been her in the Jeep. Okay, we'll get an Ambulance and the local guys out there too, and I'm on my way as well. Send - Eton and Thomas back, as soon as you can. I want them to watch Primmer and Bland, just tell them that's what they are to do. One on each place, anything untoward - let us know. And tell them not to be seen!' He switched off and faced Bronson.

'Did you manage to get the drift of that?' She shook her head - he went on. 'Rory is there, out at that Cottage - hurt, and Brown is somewhere out there – dead. The Wilson girl must have come back into town, and that would've been her the guys saw on their way out there. That's all, at the moment they and we know, I think I had better get out there, you heard what I said to them.'

Marguriette's complexion paled. 'What do you mean she – Brown is dead, what the hell was she doing out there anyway, and Calder, what do you mean he's hurt, how – how badly, and by what - who?'

MacDonald was half way to the door, when he stopped. 'What's the matter Marguriette, you're extremely agitated about this. It's not like you to let this sort of thing get to you, blood, guts and death, I thought were second nature to you.' MacDonald, although he knew that he shouldn't have, enjoyed the hurt, the discomfort in Bronson's eyes. 'I know it's created another problem along with everything else, and it seems obvious that whoever is controlling this operation wants some of his colleagues out of the way, unless this is really just an accident, but there is information that you're holding back isn't there? Unless I'm mistaken and am blind in one eye and have the other stuffed with rags and my ears blocked, but it seems to me to be about Brown and Calder - are they in this too? And if they are, why the hell girl aren't you telling me? Are they part of this Domino game – this group - well we know that Brown is, or was, so Calder - is he the missing tile, the link in your funny game?'

'Put all our gear back into the cases, and put them in the car, we can't leave them here unattended, I'm coming with you.' Bronson sighed with resignation. 'And, oh - alright - okay, - I'll fill in the gaps on the way, this whole thing has now blown right out of proportion – and I don't mean just by the bloody bombs – or whatever they were. Not that it wasn't out of all proportion before - now it's ludicrously so!'

They quickly shuffled the files together and stuffed them back in the briefcases. MacDonald looked out the window to see if there was any sign of the girl in the Motel Office, it was getting well into dusk and nobody was visible in the area. He could see across into the office and she wasn't there. 'I don't think we will bother telling her we are going out, our personal stuff is still here, so if she checks, which I think that she will, she will know that we are coming back. Besides it's none of her business'

They threw the cases into the back seat. 'I'll drive, you direct, I suppose you know where we are going, besides - I'll be able to explain better while I'm driving and you can listen without taking your eyes off the road.' She got in behind the wheel before he could even comment. 'You do know where we are going don't you John?'

'Actually, no.' He sounded sheepish, 'I'll have to call Smith. You had better get on the radio call Central, and also get the Ambulance and locals organised okay?'

Bronson nodded and started the car, turning onto the deserted road. 'Well I guess the first thing is to head to the village, get on to Roger.' She watched out of the corner of her eye as he pulled out his phone. Then she turned on the radio, put on a head set, and called in, asking to be put through to the Senior Officer on duty, which she was relieved to hear was the Chief Superintendent who had assigned her to the case originally. It was very unusual for Colin Moorhead to be in his office on a Sunday, even more unusual - this late. But for some reason he was, and that reason right now didn't matter.

It only took her a couple of minutes to explain the situation, and to ask for a back up to be down there in the chopper at first light. She also asked for an immediate update on McGillveray's activities.

'Forget the file, put him and his wife under continuous surveillance immediately, and if anyone else is with him I want to know who they are straight away, things are hotting up - and not to my liking.' She listened to Moorhead's reply, nodding a couple of times, aware that MacDonald was watching her.

'Okay I have the directions. Take the first road on the right, after you come over the bridge into the town. We go up that for about a K. Then look for a narrow road branching off to the left. A bit tricky to see, and looks very narrow, but opens out to be reasonable, and not too rough. Keep on that until it comes out on a plateau that used to be an airstrip.' She nodded to keep talking as she accelerated.

'The road travels along the side of that, then goes off at an oblique angle and winds down towards a broad estuary. About two k's down, there's a yellow post. I think - opposite the drive way, but we should see the smoke anyway. The Ambulance will be right behind us.'

They wound down the hill towards the village, the sun's direction, lowering into the west changed the light on the narrow road. She flicked on the headlights the top lights and siren. 'That should get a few of the locals going. Where did you tell the Ambulance to go, though I suppose they know the area pretty well.'

'I just said whose place it was and that it was near an old timber mill, I think that the racket we are now making will also be of great assistance! Now - over the noise - what is this all about - what's the story on this Brown woman and Calder, are they connected in some way.'

'I don't suppose now that it going to make a great deal of difference whether you know or not now. The way, in the last forty-eight hours that events have transpired. Besides, this could all lead, I hope, to a much earlier conclusion to the investigation. It will depend on how much Rory can tell us, if he is capable of talking. Also Andrea Jones, when she has recovered from her concussion. Although, I'm not so sure that she will prove very cooperative.'

'For God's sake Marguriette! Will you just get on with it! You can be so bloody obtuse and exasperating!' MacDonald raised his eyes to the roof of the speeding car.

'Rory Calder and Cheryl Brown, that of course isn't her real name, but his actually is. There was not a lot of point in changing it or his identity - just his "Job description". He was seconded from the General Intelligence, to Criminal Intelligence, several years before the whole thing blew up. He had a University background and had worked as a Lecturer a few years before. A bright lad with a bright future that got fucked up, more of the whys and wherefores of that another time.' She was talking extremely fast and with an uncharacteristic nervousness, and MacDonald was finding it hard to follow and keep up.

'They have been working on the case for nearly three years. She did not know him or of him and his work, and of course visa versa. It's as we were talking before a complete coincidence that he was here. I checked, and he really was supposed to be here looking for a retreat, a quiet lifestyle. At least that's what I had initially been led to believe, but who the hell knows when the left hand, never let's the right know that it's on the other side of the body. But, before I came down here, Moorhead told me about the connection, not quite the appropriate term, it applies to someone else, sorry, my warped mind being over active. Anyway an association between Calder's wife - and Peter Sullivan. He'd known about it for some time, and had even contacted Rory when he was still in Britain. It was me that knew where Rory was, and what he'd been doing over there. I told Colin how and where to find him. And ***don't*** ask how I knew – I just did. Anyway, all of this is now really quite irrelevant, what matters is what we do next.' Bronson sighed before she went on.

'She, that's Brown, has been tied into this for a long time. When we found that Sullivan was involved with the removal of sensitive material from Government Departments and Research Programs. He was selling them - as well as other very specialised merchandise, in conjunction with Jongejan. To who, we've no bloody idea! He – that's Sullivan, has lived down here for years. So we thought that if we planted someone in a position that was able to gather information about him, and any others in the area that he was associated with, that could be helpful. We thought a Publican would be ideal, and concocted a story around her, complicating it enough that most of the locals bought it. Very obviously some didn't, and one of them was Bland, but for some reason he's never mentioned it to anyone – well, anyone here. We aren't sure about Sullivan, and Primmer. That doesn't matter now with what has happened to her, but we'll have to find out who murdered her!'

They came out onto the old airstrip. Marguriette spun the car across the where the road veered right, accelerating over the flat ground. Moments later they found where the road started again on the other side. From there it became windy, she concentrated on the drive and fell silent.

MacDonald pondered what she had said. She had turned off the siren and lights five minutes earlier as it had been hard to talk over, and now the sounds of the Ambulance could be heard coming up through the bush.

Bronson saw the yellow post and slowed to a crawl. As she turned the car into the narrow driveway she said quietly to him. 'We are very under resourced right this minute, and we have been caught out. It was too late to bring in people tonight. We will have to rely on the local men, and the few we have, and hope like hell that this mob feel safe and secure and think that we are a bigger pack of bungling idiots, than we actually are looking right now.' She pulled the car to a halt in the car park behind the now smouldering shed, beside Smith's car. The air hung heavy and putrid from the smoke, and whatever accelerates had been used.

She turned and faced her colleague. 'I don't like the feelings that are churning around in my head and my gut, and I don't like what has happened, to some of us, over the last few hours, and like you, I don't like looking a fool, even if I have been one. We were too confident with Sullivan out of the way, and I think that you summed it up John, we thought we were dealing with a pack of hicks i.e. Blanchard and Mackintosh, in a hick town. This is far, - as we now know - from the case.'

MacDonald opened his door to get out. Bronson was about to follow, when the radio broke into their conversation.

'Central to MB, we have located McGillveray. He's with his wife, they're, well I guess the word would be - entertaining. A man called Blanchard - any instructions, you wanted to know any developments.'

Marguriette picked up the microphone. 'Don't let them out of sight. Keep a very close cover, and try to keep ahead of them, I know that'll be hard, but if they leave wherever they are, keep one car in front the other behind and interchange frequently, use three if you have the man power.'

'Roger MB.' The operator disengaged, and she got out of the car.

'We'll have to continue this conversation some other time, there were only three people who know the full details, and now there are four, although as yet you don't have all the details, and may never get them.' She followed him around the side of the burnt building. 'But I guess at least you are not as much in the dark as before, and I will probably have you in on any further interviews, discussions, or interrogations, if we ever get to that. And right at this moment in time I am not a hundred percent sure where the hell we are - except that we know one thing - my theory re coincidences seems to be fairly accurate - if too late for some.'

As they came to the path that led to the Cottage, Eton and Thomas were coming up the steep slope to meet them. MacDonald stopped and gave them instructions as to what he wanted them to do. Bronson carried on to the house and was met at the door by Roger Smith.

'How is he now, has he regained consciousness? The Ambulance is just behind us and should be here any minute.' Bronson's tone conveyed concern.

Smith waved for her to follow him inside. MacDonald had left the others and was just behind them. 'Yes, he's woken up again, I gave him three codeine for the pain, that's all I had, the local lad's kit didn't have any morphine. I've moved him into the front room, it's a bit more comfortable. I think he'll be fine. He thought that his right arm and shoulder may have been broken, but I think it's mainly bruising and a bit of dislocation. The worst thing is the cut on his leg.' Smith went before them and led them through the house into the lounge. Rory was propped up on the couch.

'I'll go and meet the medics, I heard the ambulance arrive as we came inside.' Smith went out of the room. The two other officers went over and stood near Calder.

Rory looked up as they came in, he couldn't hide his surprise when he saw Marguriette. When he was driving up to Primmer's place, and seen the group exiting from the Helicopter, he hadn't seen clearly who the others arriving were. And he hadn't been particularly interested at that moment. He wondered now, why he hadn't stopped and taken a much better look! But, would it have made any difference to the surprise he felt now?

'Well you do look a very pretty sight Rory, been having some fun and games we see. What's the story on Cheryl Brown - and your other friend, she seems to have gone on holiday - and left you behind. Whose been sucked in then?' Marguriette hadn't seen Rory Calder for some considerable time, and a number of emotions churned inside her. She grinned at him, and though her tone was light, her face told of how serious she felt.

'Hello Marguriette, what the hell are you doing here? It's been a long - long time, since - hasn't it! Has everything got so difficult, out of hand here, that they sent you down to clear it all up? I thought that you would've been tied up in your office,' But he had to grin at her through his discomfort, 'now there's a thought.'

They smiled at each other, and MacDonald didn't miss the exchange, and raised an eyebrow, thinking to himself. 'These two are very familiar with each other - very interesting.'

'What are you doing here anyway, I know you took off for a break, and were looking at re-assessing your life, but why did you have to pick here! It's a bit of "out of the frying pan into the fire" isn't it? Or it has become so. Now are you okay to talk about this, I think that the damage is nasty looking but superficial, just give us the bare guts of what has gone on here in the last few hours, then later when we have you properly patched and rested we can get the detail.' Bronson didn't right now, want to mention that she'd known of his deployment on the case.

'I'm not too bad now. I let my guard down, tired I think and stupid, and possibly not wanting to believe what was going on. I should've known better after what happened out near the old mill site. There's an old barge there, that's where I left Brown, why on earth they have knocked her off, and who did it I don't know, but I should've seen it, seen that everything was all wrong, nothing fitted.'

'So, what happened when you got back out here?' MacDonald sat on the arm of a chair, arms folded. He was sceptical that this man, was, or had been, part of Bronson's and Moorhead's investigative team. The mention of - "He was getting away from it all" didn't seem to fit at all.

'I got back out here and searched the house. There was no sign of her, or anything being taken or altered. The bath was still full, she had had a bath before I left, by she I mean Jennifer Sullivan or Wilson or whoever. I went out and searched the foreshore and a couple of tracks, then it occurred to me that with what had happened that morning, with my mentioning Bland being her Grandfather, and talking about the Mill and her Great Grandparents, I thought she may have gone out there. So that's where I went.' He swung round on the sofa so that he was sitting up instead of lounging back. He rubbed his hand over the back of his head and neck, feeling the drying but still sticky blood there.

'I found tracks, signs that people - or at least a person had been out there on the tracks leading to this bloody old wreck of a barge. There'd been no reply to my calls, and when I got to the hulk there were three ladders, two rotten and one sort of okay leaning on it. I went up and searched from up there. That was when I saw the body in the hold, near the bow, well I suppose it's the bow, not that that matters. I went back and started to climb down the ladder, there was no other way to get down, it was one of the rotten ones, I didn't, in my hurry see that it was and that the other two were missing until later. That was also when I lost - or had my phone taken, when I got back there with the body. I didn't know it was Cheryl, until I got inside the hull.' He stopped talking as Smith came in with the Paramedics. There were three, two men and a woman, all young, energetic, serious, very bustley and efficient.

'Right, you stay here Jan, with this bod, see if there is anything more that needs to be before we take him down to the hospital.' He looked at the others in the room, 'I think our little one here can deal with him, anyway he doesn't look all that bad. And she's damned efficient. We'll go with Sergeant Smith and bring back Ms. Brown. Do you know exactly where she is Sir?' He addressed his question to Rory, who gave him quick concise instructions. The three men left, the two medics carrying a stretcher and Smith followed behind

The girl - Jan - went over Rory's injuries asking questions as she checked him out.

'Your men seem to have done a pretty good job on him with their limited gear. Who put the belt tourniquet on, it's done a good job, that cut is very deep and may need internal as well as external stitching I think. Still you'll be okay for the time being - how's the pain now, I can give you a shot if you like.'

Rory shook his head. 'No, I'll be fine, it's actually not too bad at the moment, could be the codeine has done the job, temporarily anyway.' He also wanted to keep as clear a head as possible.

'Alright, point me in the direction that they went and I'll head there and see if I can be of any help, it's better to have four carrying that stretcher.'

Rory re-related the directions and she left. MacDonald, Calder and Bronson sat silent, staring out the windows. Each, for the moment, with their own private thoughts and theories.

'So, you're only here by accident, sorry excuse the pun, just like you said before. You knew nothing of what was going on here, that any of these people that are involved, even lived here. Yet, I'm now told that you've been working on parts of this investigation - which I've only also just discovered - has been going on for some years. I actually find the whole thing quite unbelievable. You both expect me to believe this whole bloody charade? You must think I'm a bloody nutter! But what I can't fathom, is why've I been kept in the dark about it for all this time.' MacDonald sounded aggrieved, disturbed and unhappy, like a child who hadn't been let in on a family secret. 'Marguriette - you said that this guy was undercover. Why not really undercover? Everyone, well almost everyone, apart from me, seems to know him, what he does and did. This seems a nonsense!'

'That's part of his cover. He was too well known to too many people to disappear and be re-invented with a new identity, a new look, it would not have washed, so we just used him where he was. It did, up until three days ago work very well. Unfortunately coincidence has played a mean part.'

'But he didn't know that Sullivan had been having an affair with his wife, and that he could be a suspect in her death. How did that happen, how come he did not know.'

'Because we didn't want him to. We are capable you know John of being quite tricky and devious, not just Security Intelligence people are capable of subterfuge you know. If Rory had known, it may well have coloured his view and perspective of what he was doing. In fact not a lot of people did know. Primmer did, and a couple of others, but as they are all tied in with Sullivan and Blanchard - they didn't let on, and anyway it doesn't matter any more, does it Rory.'

It was not a question, it was a statement, something between them and it was again here that MacDonald saw that there was more than just a professional connection.

'No, not any more. I will admit it was one hell of a shock when it came out that he had been, but it still has never been entirely concluded what happened to the car, or if someone else was involved in it. I personally believe that there were. But that is not going to change anything or bring them back. So Primmer knew - he certainly played a cool part when I told him about it.' Rory looked thoughtful.

'What about Brown then, how much had she been able to pass on from here, she must have been quite a valuable insider, and I can see why now that I have seen those photographs.' MacDonald continued his probing, and when he made this comment he saw Rory's face become quite a study in confusion.

Rory looked at Bronson, the query in his eyes, as well as his voice. It could have been very helpful if I'd known, we could – possibly have worked together! - I thought that she was right in with Sullivan and Blanchard and Co. How long has she been part of it?'

Marguriette sighed. 'She's been an undercover operative now for eight years. This is her third job. The others were in - naturally - other parts of the country. She is, sorry - was one of our best. But in this case I am afraid not good enough. Cheryl - got too close, and over time too personally involved, with Sullivan and others. She had started to like her pleasures too much. Drink, drugs and sex – you know this sort of thing often happens, when 'unders' play the part in the play too well. This I'm sure, you've probably noticed. Someone must have twigged - and I think it may have been both Sullivan, Bland, and more than probably the wayward daughter Jenny,. She's certainly played a brilliant part so far in the damned drama!'

'God, you're a cold hearted bitch at times Marguriette.' MacDonald's voice had a bitter edge to it. 'She may have been just another person doing their job, but she was also a human being, and has died, been killed while on duty, a small amount of thought and compassion would not go astray.'

Bronson gave him a hard stare. 'That may be, but I cannot and will not allow sentiment and emotion to cloud any issues to do with our work. Yes, you are right - she was a human being and actually a very good one, as well as good at her work, and I knew her very well.' Her look became even more intense, but her tone became less severe. 'And - she happened to be a very good friend of mine, a fact that I will recognise at a later time. I will thank you now, to keep your opinions about my character to yourself and to concentrate on your work.'

MacDonald muttered a subdued apology, and sat back in his chair, lapsing again into silence.

Rory glanced from one to the other during the exchange. He'd seen

Bronson at work on many occasions, he knew how she operated. He also
knew that there was another side to her. One that he did not think that
MacDonald had seen, but he could see from the expression on his face
that he had at some stage wanted to see another side to the woman. He
turned and looked out at the estuary and thought of how such a peaceful
beautiful scene could be torn and tarnished by violence and death. As he
watched, the Medics and Smith appeared at the bottom of the ravine track
with the stretcher and the body of Cheryl Brown, or whoever she had really
been strapped to it.

'They're back, they've just come down onto the beach.' Rory watched
them as they came across the sand and shell, up to the front of the cottage.
MacDonald and Bronson went out to meet them. He struggled to his
feet and hobbled after them. As they got to the front door, he reached
across, touching Marguriette's arm. She stopped and turned to face him
as MacDonald continued out the door. 'Never mind the other, Cheryl
played her part extremely well Marguriette. Plainly as you said too well.
I certainly wouldn't have picked her as an Undercover officer. What was
her real name?'

'Helen - Helen Greene, she will be missed Rory. By the force, by her
friends, and by me. Not that over the last few years we have had that much
to do with each other, but we kept in contact, mostly of course through
work. But funnily I only found out recently that she was down here on
this. Her report contact was someone else - you know how these things
work, we don't let our right hand know what the left is doing, God I seem
to be saying that a lot lately. Okay - now let's get her, and us, out of here.
MacDonald and Smithy can have a look around at the bomb site and check
over the house for anything that may help - doubt though that they will
find anything. We can follow the Ambulance, do you want to go in it, or
are you okay enough to come with me?'

'I'll be fine, I'm just a bit sore now. No doubt it will get worse before
it gets better, but apart from this cut in the leg and the arm and shoulder
tightening up, everything else seems to work. Even the brain is starting
to function, that would be a nice change from recent events, and I would
imagine you want to get the run down on what's been going on.'

'Yes, but that can wait until MacDonald and Smith are there. Have you spoken to your friend, McGillveray lately?' She gave Rory a deep questioning look.

'Saturday morning I had a brief conversation with him, asked him if he could get me some information about Peter Sullivan - I had a bit of a run in with the man on Friday night not many hours after I got here - why?'

MacDonald had finished a brief conversation with the Medics and Smith and was coming back over to them. Marguriette stepped away from Rory, speaking quietly as she did. 'I'll talk to you later about that.' She went and intercepted MacDonald. 'How bad are her injuries, is there evidence how she died?'

'Nothing, from appearances it looks like just the fall killed her, now we will have to ascertain whether it was accidental or she was pushed. There are some broken bones and her neck is broken - but until an autopsy is carried out we won't have a final answer.' MacDonald shrugged, and glanced across at Rory. 'Is he alright – shouldn't he go in the Ambulance?

'No – he's fine enough to come with us.' They both walked back to where the stretcher was on the ground. Marguriette knelt down, she removed the cover off the dead girl's face, it was battered almost beyond recognition. Tears began to form, she brushed them away, covered her again and stood up. 'As I knew her and you didn't I will formerly identify the body at the hospital. She has no parents, she was married but was divorced five years ago. Her husband - who was on the force then, didn't like her doing undercover work, she did, she also got a higher ranking than him, that rankled with him too - and the rest is history. But we will let him know, he probably deserves that, in more ways than one!' She stood up. 'Okay you can take her now, we'll follow you to the hospital, have you called for a Doctor to be on duty when we get there?'

The girl Jan answered. 'No, but we will, there are two who we can call, they are very helpful and cooperative. She was a popular lady in town, a lot of fun, and ran a good Pub. She will be missed. What on earth was the silly lady doing wandering all over that derelict barge. And, that building, what were you doing in there Mr. Man, making fireworks? The risks people take.' She shook her head as the four of them picked up the body of Helen Greene and went around the side of the house and went to the Ambulance.

'Smith is going with them, I'll drive the local car back, after I've had a good look around. I think Roger will be more use back in the village, and I won't be long, I don't think so anyway. I'll look into what Eton and Thomas have been up to. Whether they've seen anything worthwhile. Are you taking our friend here?' He nodded over at Calder.

'Yes, I just said that, he could have gone with them, but we have to go to the hospital anyway - he thinks he's okay enough to be a passenger with me driving - he has nerves of steel.' She laughed quietly as they all turned and walked back into the Cottage.

*   *

Blanchard stood in front of the briefcase, he was now sweating and his eyes swivelled from one to the other of the other two in the room.

'What's the matter Warren?' Maxine came and stood by Euan. 'Are you expecting something to happen if you open it? A Goblin to break out and bite your balls off? Or an explosion, like the one that killed Mangus, and put Peter out of the way? And, he won't live, one way or another, so don't worry about him.' Her eyes bore into him and the expression on her face and in her voice conveyed everything that he feared from these two. His original confidence, his bravado had gone.

'I can't, I don't have the combination, the briefcase was already on the bed when I got there. Andrea was unconscious on the bathroom floor. I didn't touch her. I thought she must have put the goods in the case, and was either going to bring them to you - or - take them herself. I checked everywhere else, they weren't in the office or in the bedroom - I didn't want to tamper with it.' He realised he may have backed himself into a corner, now they may trust him even less than before, he could be lying and have already removed them, and he could have booby trapped the case, especially as he had been so reluctant to open it. He swore vehemently at himself.

'Then I think that you should find something Warren and force it open. We are beginning to doubt your sincerity. Andrea would not try to double cross us, and she wouldn't have known that you were coming back to pick them up. Perhaps we have all slipped up in our communications - but - then - how did you know they were there anyway - I didn't tell you, and if Sullivan didn't tell you - who did?'

Blanchard felt there scrutiny, he was being backed even further into a corner, and he knew that his position was becoming even more precarious.

As McGillveray was speaking, he went into the kitchen, opening a draw, and removing a pair of pliers and a screwdriver. He repeated the question. 'Who told you they were there and to go back for them?'

'Nobody told me to go back for them, that was my own idea.' He kept staring at the black leather case as the sweat broke out on his forehead and his neck, it dribbled down his back. He swallowed what felt like a large lump of dry bread stuck in his throat. 'It was Mangus, who told me. I - we were - well, we didn't trust Sullivan to keep his part of the bargain, our agreement. Mangus was nervous - frightened of him. He told me.' He suddenly looked up at them. 'How did you know they were there anyway, unless Sullivan told you, and I don't think he would have, how did you know?'

'Because we tapped the phone Warren, nobody trusts anybody, everyone is after the same thing, they are greedy, we are greedy, we all want money and power - it was us who set up the bomb to be delivered with the food. So everyone is out to cross and double cross everyone else - aren't they.' McGillveray's face impassive – his tone, casual.

Warren Blanchard backed away from the table, his face now contorted with fear. He hadn't seen Maxine move behind him earlier. The blow on the top of his head from the heavy brass statue, fractured his skull and sent him into a jerking spasm, then unconsciousness.

McGillveray caught the body before it hit the floor. Maxine pulled a thick plastic bag from her handbag, and pulled it over Blanchard's head. Together they dragged him out of the apartment, down the hallway to the service elevator shaft. He checked that it was at the bottom, then together they levered Blanchard's body head first into the narrow shaft and let the body fall. They closed the doors before it had reached the bottom, they didn't even hear the muffled thump as it hit the top of the elevator.

Euan picked up Blanchard's jacket, and shrugged it on. He went through to the bathroom and arranged his hair in the manner of the other man.

'Make sure that all prints that he may have left are wiped, the whisky bottle his glass, everything, and that there's no blood on the floor, clean the doors of the lift. Then make the call. I'll go out for twenty or thirty minutes, and will hope that our ever vigilant Manager sees me as Warren!'

Euan put on dark glasses, left the apartment and instead of taking the elevator he went to the stairs. McGillveray and Blanchard were of similar height and build, and he was able to easily imitate Blanchard's walk. On the third landing from the ground floor he exited the stairs and went to the lift, which he took to the basement car park. From there he walked out of the parking entrance and across the street to the taxi rank. He took a cab to the nearby shopping area, about five minutes drive away. There was a small tavern set back from the main street down an alley way.

McGillveray sauntered into the bar, and ordered a beer. He drank two mouthfuls, placed the glass on the counter, and went to the toilet. There, he stuffed the jacket and dark glasses into a laundry trolley that was in the corridor. In the toilets he adjusted his hair back to its normal style, then walked out of the bars other entrance avoiding where he had ordered the beer. Fifteen minutes later he was back at the entrance to the car park under his apartment block. He watched the swivel of the security camera until it was pointing away from the service lift, then he jogged quickly across to it, pushed the button to level twelve then jumped in and closed the doors.

As he ascended he thought of the body on the roof of the lift, he smiled a crooked smile. Forty-five seconds later he was back in the apartment and the lift was on its way back to the basement.

Maxine McGillveray was waiting for him. She was looking out the window at the closing of the day. The last of the suns rays had completely disappeared behind the ranges in the west of the city. Hanging over the back of the chair, were their coats, on the floor, the briefcase with the leather boxes inside. There was no other luggage. They picked up their coats and the case and left the apartment, two table lamps were left burning, the light in their en suite also, the stereo was playing Brahms. Maxine had loaded five CD's into the cassette and set it to play continuously on random.

The couple walked out from the lift into the lobby, waved to the evening Security Guard who had taken over from the Manager a few minutes earlier and went out the front door. They walked down the street two blocks and got into the back of a bright red Ford.

As soon as they were settled and closed their doors the car moved away from the curb. 'Everything in order then, and we are on our way.' The thick Afrikaans accent cut the air. Hans Jongejan glanced over his shoulder at his passengers. 'Now all we have to do is catch our planes. If Mr. Blanchard was able to be, I am sure he would be very very surprised by the recent turn of events.' He turned back to concentrate on his driving, a deep evil chuckle ringing through the car.

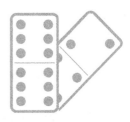

FIFTEEN

After passing the Police car Jenny Sullivan continued down towards the town belt, then swung into a driveway - reversed out, and shot back up the hill to the road to the old mine. There was no sign of the Police car she nearly collided with a few moments ago, she assumed they were heading out to her Cottage. She'd lied to Rory Calder about there being no phone, as she had lied about a considerable number of other things! But that was the nature of the Beast and of her trainers. It had been her Grandfather, Jim Bland who had called her and warned her of Rory returning. She had completed her final preparations for his reception quickly. It was an eventuality that she and "the partners" had always been aware of happening. It was now time to move.

Jenny slowed the big Jeep as she approached the flat area in front of the Mining ruins, driving across to the front edge where she stopped about twenty feet from it. The vehicle would not be able to be seen from there if anyone was looking up from the roads below, or the surrounding area. She got out and taking a powerful pair of binoculars from the glove compartment she walked to the end of the flat, where a stand of trees gave good cover and shelter. She was alert, but tense, however the insecure demeanour, was no longer in evidence. She was back to her most confident and capable. The time for acting was over. They were now preparing for their run home.

She lifted the glasses to her eyes. From this vantage point, she could scan the coast line and the roads that ran to her bay and the Cottage. Below she could see the dust of the Police car travelling quickly over the gravel tracks, then further ahead she could see the curve of the beach below the steep bush covered cliffs - then beyond that the bluff that protruded out from the Cottage. She shifted her line of sight slightly to her right and held her breath. The large circle of the glasses filled with a pillar of flames and smoke that shot into the air out of the bush. Pieces of debris were hurled up with it to float back down and to fall, scattering back into the bush.

Jenny Sullivan let her breath out slowly, she allowed herself a sly smile of satisfaction. She leant against one of the trees and let the binoculars hang by their strap around her neck.

'Well,' she whispered to herself. 'That seems to have been a success, that's two more of the meddling bastards out of the way. Oh yes, they think that they are just oh so clever, well they're not, and wont be again. Pity though he would've been fun, if he hadn't been so hung up on himself and his problems. I fucking didn't want any of them, got enough, or at least had enough of my own. Besides there was plainly more to that man than he was saying – but I'm not that stupid, and can spot a fucking cop a mile away'

Jenny's smile became wider, she started to laugh. She felt elated and aroused by her actions of the last two hours, and could feel the excitement building in her body. She ran her hands down over her breasts and stomach and could feel the heat through the flimsiness of the Tank top and torn cotton wrap. Her breathing began to get rapid and ragged. Then the feeling was shattered by the sound of an Ambulance siren, bringing her back to the reality of what she was doing and still had to do.

* *

Marguriette pulled in to the Village Hospital entrance. They'd arrived about ten minutes after the Ambulance, it was parked out the front, the back doors open, the vehicle empty. She pulled in beside it..

When she had turned off the motor she looked across at Rory Calder. 'We haven't and aren't, making the progress that we should have on this case Rory. You being here - has probably complicated things rather than assisted! Yes – and I know why Moorhead sent you. And I know that you wanted a break and thought there was a possibility of combining that with this assignment – possibly for a short time that may have helped with your cover. It would most definitely seem that Jenny worked out who you were, or at least who you work for, very bloody quickly – I would like to know how? And unfortunate, poor Cheryl - or should I say Helen. When you've got that stitched up and the rest of your damage seen to, I want you out of here. Where's your car?'

'It's up at Primmer's Lodge, with the rest of my gear.' He looked at her questioningly.

'I think that we should let all those that want to think it, that you have been removed from the scene - permanently. We shall have to hope that the people here – as in our crew - can keep their mouths shut, I'll have a word with them. Come on, let's get on with it.' Marguriette smiled and leant across to him, gripping his hand. Her eyes were warm. 'It's good to see you again – and – I want to see you again – and safe – or is that safe and again?'

It was now on just past dusk, and the street lights had come on, and the lights in the hospital and grounds. They got out of the Police car and went in the front of the building. A nurse and a Doctor were standing close together talking, they stopped and looked up at the new comers. Smith came around the corner from a corridor that led off to one side of the reception area.

'Good, here at last, this is the other patient that I was telling you about Doctor, he seems to be holding together quite well after all.' An orderly appeared with a wheel chair, bringing it over to Rory.

'Would you mind hopping in Sir, and we will get you sorted out in no time.'

Rory was about to object, when Marguriette gave him "one of her looks", whispering to him, 'Get in the bloody thing and get it over with. I want to talk to Smith and the Doctor.'

He did what he was told, and was whisked away down the corridor from where Smith had appeared, the Nurse who'd been talking to the Doctor followed.

Marguriette indicated for Smith to join her, as she went up to the Doctor. She held out her hand and introduced herself, taking out her Identification Wallet and flashing it to him. His eyes widened a fraction at the sight of such a senior member of the force being present.

'I want this whole thing, for the present anyway, kept well under wraps, there could be a situation eventuating that requires a considerable amount of delicate handling. Where, are the Ambulance staff, that brought in the body of the woman?'

'They've just taken her down to our tiny inadequate morgue. Perhaps you could be good enough to fill me in on some of what is going on, and I may then be - perhaps of some assistance to you - within the bounds of Patient confidentiality of course, but I might be able to - shall we say - generalise about some things. I would have to admit there have been some activities around this village of late, that have created some rather disturbing feelings.'

The three set off down the corridor. As they passed the room where Rory was being attended. Marguriette could see him propped on a bed, watching what the Doctor was doing, and talking to the nurse.

They carried on another few doorways then turned into the Mortuary. The three Paramedics had moved Cheryl Browns body off the trolley and were about to leave when they saw Bronson, and the men come in.

'Just a word please,' Bronson asked quietly. 'It's very important, and I want to stress that – very! For a few days anyway, that this incident you've have attended stays in the confidential file.' She again exhibited her ID. They all seemed suitably impressed, and nodded, murmuring that they understood.

Bronson reiterated the importance of the request. Mentioning some consequences that might occur if the information happened to leak out. 'We'll take care of any press, if they get wind of anything. And, we will issue information that will hopefully preclude any nosy types who may begin to wonder why the Pub is shut and the Proprietor isn't around - okay?'

They all nodded again, appearing quite overwhelmed by the whole affair. This type of incident wasn't exactly a daily occurrence in the small town.

After they'd left, Marguriette formally identified the body as Helen Greene. She produced evidence of her life and her position in the Police. Smith was rather surprised by this, as he wouldn't have expected her to have such documentation on her. Unless, she had known that it may have been necessary. After the formalities, the body was slotted into one of the four refrigerated drawers, and locked by the Doctor.

'We would not usually deem it necessary to lock up like that, but I think from what you have said, it would not be a good idea for anyone to be having a look at her.'

'I'll arrange for the transfer to the City in a couple of days, when it will not be quite so noticed. There are no very close next of kin, but there is an Aunt, it will have to be her, but it will take me a few days to notify her.' They left the room and went back to where Rory was now sitting on the edge of the bed having his final check over.

The other Doctor who was doing the check spoke as they came in. 'Apart from the stitches in the leg and a couple in the back of his head he's fine. Nothing too untoward happened when he fell, bit bruised, should keep away from glass doors when he's had a few though - I think you can take him away with you. We seem to have had a few of these clumsy types lately, we have a young lady with quite a bad concussion, and serious cuts to her head, right arm and hand, she was it seems, trying to fly out of a hot tub, she came in yesterday. A bloody high alcohol level as well!'

Rory and Marguriette were exchanging glances, when Smith interrupted. 'Oh yes, I'd like a word with her – Andrea Jones? Need to check a couple of things with her. It seemed that she just – well slipped getting out of the bath – but?' He looked questioningly at the Doctor. 'Do you have much crime here? She was found in a house that'd been burgled. Does that happen often in these parts?' He repeated. 'Would it be okay if I had a chat?'

The Doctor didn't answer the first query, but nodded regarding the request to see her, and asked Smith to follow him, he would take him around to her room. As Smith went passed Bronson, he stopped, and spoke to her very quietly.

'Do you want to come in on this, or shall I just do it, see if I can find out if she knows anything. I'm sure she does, but will she talk? I think we should, if she's able move her out of here as soon as possible.' He looked at Bronson questioningly.

'Yes Sergeant Smith,' Bronson became very formal, as she noticed others nearby, taking a close interest in what they were saying. 'I think that you're right, A good idea, you handle it and see what you can do.' Then turning so she could not be heard. 'We don't want it all to look too high powered, news will travel fast here anyway, despite what we have suggested should happen. Get a Rental, they must have something here – try the Garage. I think that should be able to be arranged and get her out of here, you may have to wait until the morning, but try for tonight - the sooner the better with what's been happening. If you can avoid it, don't talk to anyone. If there are any questions, I'll square it with the Doctor.'

Smith headed off after the Doctor to see Andrea Jones. Calder and Bronson watched as they went down the corridor. Then, they left the Hospital. When they were back in the car Rory looked at her inquiringly.

'Where to from here Marguriette, what's our next step? Everyone that we seem to talk to, or at least you do, we come up against a block, a barrier of some kind. I know that I am supposed to not be here, but I am, and all the talk and questions that I have heard, or been told of, does not seem to make anything very much clearer, at least not to me anyway.'

She sat silent for a number of minutes watching to see if anyone came out of the door of the building. 'I don't know either really.' Bronson started the car, driving out of the grounds, and turned away from the village, she headed to the main road, then south, up the winding hill. At the top, she pulled across into the parkway that Rory had stopped three days ago. Below the tiny town's lights flickered in the cooling evening air, the ones lighting the waterfront reflecting on the still incoming tide as it crept across the mud flat. It was the picture of peace, like a small Oasis in the blackening night. But now it seemed that it was far from that. Off on the far horizon an occasional flash of lightning as another of the late summer storms began to build.

The pair sat in the quiet, listening to the last of the bird songs in the surrounding bush, the cicadas give way to crickets. Marguriette broke their silence.

'It doesn't seem possible, when you sit here, to imagine what has happened, what could come out of that sleepy hollow at the bottom of the hill. You've been through a fair bit in the last few years Rory. Your wife and children gone, and then your work with us, the intrigue the subterfuge, and your attempt at an escape, from the reality of life, ends in violence and death. All appearing, as if it is accidental, coincidence. I know that you're not really here just by chance are you. This visit has been part of your investigation – but there are some things that I would never know with you. That's why we brought you in. You are you, but nobody knows really who or what you are. I think that you would be more at home on the stage or in film - or living in the bush disguised as a Chameleon - no - a Chameleon is a master of disguise, you don't no you didn't even need to do that. But lately – things do not seem to be going quite the way that you – or I would like do they?' Her voice was flat, expressionless, frustrated and exhausted.

'How long have you known me - ten, twelve years?' he asked, 'And what have you learned about me over that time - and do you remember how and when we met?'

'It's about that. It's actually was eleven years ago on the 28th Jan. And it will be eleven years and thirty five days to when we first went out together in seven days time, and it will be nine years on May the 6th since you met Serena - would you like to know any other significant dates? As far as what I have learnt about you over the years - a lot and a little - as I said before, are you really here by coincidence - I would never really know with you. And – how long did it take you to work out who Moorhead was? He shook the shit out of you when he called you in Cornwall didn't he. But by the by and by the way, it was on my suggestion. Sorry, but heh – it worked - we needed you back. We'd been watching you for sometime, wondering what to do with you and how to use your skills. You took a bit of tracking – but that's my job. And is supposed to be yours! So I'm wondering when you're going to use them!'

Rory sat for a few moments, his thoughts ranging back to Cornwall, the first call from Moorhead – then to the last few days. He decided to ignore Marguriettes last comments. There was another matter bothering him.

'Why did you ask if I'd spoken to McGillveray?' It was an attempt to change the subject, and he remembered his call, and the reticence of the man, who was usually so lucid and friendly, it had disturbed Rory, that the mention of Sullivan had brought such a negative response. 'I told you, I spoke to him Saturday morning, it was the first time for months. He was quite strange, remote, not his usual self, particularly after I mentioned that I wanted him to see if he could find out anything about this Sullivan character who had verbally attacked me. Rather strong 'verbals' actually, on Friday night in the Pub.'

Bronson looked at him sharply. 'We had better get moving, tell me about it as we go, I'll have to stop and get my gear from the Motel where we set up a base. I think we, you and I, better get out of here. I'll phone MacDonald, he should be on his way back after his look around the Cottage.' She yawned. 'Oh, sorry about that – you're not boring me. He, or one of the others, can go up to Primmers. Spin the spin, with the story of your demise and pick up your gear, and that old jalopy of yours!' A second yawn.

'God, I'm bloody tired. Tired of a lot of things, as well as the physical bit. Anyway, I doubt that he'll find anything. I think that we have been led a merry dance up the garden path by quite a few people. However, I have something that I think you should know, a theory of mine that I think is now coming to fruition. It's all in those files in the back of the car, and I'm sure that it will make little difference if we wait the couple of hours until we're back in town, before we go over it. I was set for a long night of work anyway.'

Bronson reversed out of the park, and sped off down the hill. She picked up the radio, then realised she didn't know the number and frequency of the local car that MacDonald was driving. She pulled her Mobile from her bag. 'I suppose I'll get reception here, it's a bit on the hilly side.' She slowed down as she pushed the buttons with one hand. .

MacDonald's phone buzzed four times before he answered. Bronson explained what had happened, since they'd left the Cottage. He confirmed what they had thought, he had found nothing that was of any help to them. She told him of their plans, and what Smith was doing, and suggested that he stay at the Motel and see that everything they needed to do the next day, was put into operation. That they were to meet up with the backup boys, and wait for instructions on their next move. 'Oh, and could you collect Rory's old car, and his clothes from Primmers? Spin them a line about a deceased Calder.' She rang off before he could answer. They turned into the entrance of the Motel.

Bronson got out and went into the unit. She emerged a few minutes later with her overnight bag and another briefcase, she placed them on the back seat with the rest of the bags, then went to see the Proprietor.

The girl came out of the back of the Office. Marguriette briefly explained the situation, and that MacDonald and some other Officers, could need the room that night, and possibly the following one. But they would be in touch. She seemed happy with the change of arrangements, thanking Bronson for letting her know.

Marguriette smiled, thanked her for helping them, and went back to the car.

As she slid back into the car she watched the girl return to the Office.'I don't know why I said that, I didn't believe that I could be that polite! Anyway, that's sorted for now, let's get out of here.' She didn't start the car, and turned to Rory, 'Look I'm pretty tired, and I know that you must be too, and I realise that I shouldn't ask you to do this, not with what you have been through and the injury to head and leg. But – heh - would you mind driving – just for a while? I need to think and my brain is scrambled enough with the events, to complicate what I want to think about - and listen to what you are saying. It would be better without the added burden of negotiating these roads in the dark. Besides, you know them much better than I do. I haven't been down this way since you and I used to come camping here, and you did the driving then anyway - but I shouldn't bring that up either.'

Rory didn't comment on what she had said, but agreed to drive. They swapped over. 'I don't think anyone will notice, and you know that I don't mind, and I'll be fine. I am a bit tougher than I look - I think.' He started the big car, and took it out onto the highway, the powerful lights lit the road almost like daylight, and with the unlikelihood of meeting anything coming towards them he pushed up to a fast, yet sensible speed for that section of the coastline.

It was ten minutes before Bronson spoke again.

'Okay, I have had a moment to gather my wits and thoughts. What's the guts of this conversation with Sullivan - how did it come about?'

'I arrived in the town, late morning, and wandered around. I talked to Miranda Sullivan, who I'd seen pushing a Pram. I asked about accommodation. I also saw her talking to Cheryl Brown.' He glanced at her. 'Miranda recommended the Pub, she thought that I was a bit too "city slickerish" for anything else. Though, I think she mentioned Primmer's place - but not names. No – yes – she did mention Primmer's Lodge – though as I said, not who owned it. Wasn't sure whether she thought that it would suit me or not, and it doesn't bloody matter now does it? Sorry, I'm rambling. I had a couple of beers and some lunch - fish and chips, they were good too, talked to Cheryl and had a look around at the rooms, then went for a walk. Saw the Camping ground and a run down Boarding house, and arrived by mistake at Sullivan's house, strayed into their garden. I'd taken a wrong turn. She, that's Miranda spoke to me, she wasn't impressed, was very cool. Although when I'd talked to her earlier, she'd seemed friendly enough. She told me to watch my directions in future. I went back to the village. My car had a flat tyre. I'm using the old Chev – but you know that - one of my disguises if you like, but I love the old bomb really - takes me back to when -.' He glanced and saw her expression and stopped that avenue of comment.

'Well anyway, while it was being repaired, I chatted to the garage guys, there was a red BMW being serviced, I asked whose it was, and told that it belonged to the "man" on the hill, the big white house - where I'd seen Miranda. I left the car there and went for a walk, and sat on the wharf - look does all this matter - it really doesn't seem relevant now.'

'You'll see, when I get the story out of you about Sullivan's comments, instead of the "round the houses" that I'm getting now! You always were sometimes one for too many words, ten when one will do, - get to the point man!'

'Okay, I decided on the Pub, I put my things in this apartment that she - Cheryl had shown me - quite nice in a gross sort of way, then I went to the bar to have a drink with Jim Bland.'

'How the hell did you get to meet him, and be invited for a drink, you had only been in the town five minutes. Did you hold up a sign saying I'm an interesting sucker - invite me to drink with you - I've seen you do that before too, but not usually to attract "old geezers".' Her voice laced with gentle sarcasm.

They had come to a more windy piece of road, much narrower, and hadn't been attacked by the council to improve it. He slowed concentrating on the twisting uneven surface. They fell silent until through the three kilometres of metal. It opened onto seal, a straight stretch – still by the water, and flanked with Pohutukawas, their tangled limbs stretching over the road to the rocky shoreline. They looked ghostly in the powerful headlights.

'Back to the saga of Sullivan and Jim Bland please - this silent suspense is killing me - get on with it for God's sake!' But her tone this time gentle, and her hand reached across and rested on his thigh.

'I was approached by the old codger, when I was sitting on the wharf watching kids fishing. I had been told of - or he had been mentioned, as "the Old Mayor" Jim Bland - by Cheryl - Helen, he came up and started chatting. Then he said that if I was in the Pub, to have a drink with him and his cronies - he also suggested that I should stay there. I did as I already mentioned – but somehow although he didn't say it – I suspect now that he already knew. Anyway I did meet him and his friends for a drink. It was then that Sullivan came in, somehow, I had no idea at the time how, but he knew who I was - or wasn't. He started in on me about "we don't want your type around here" and so on. Then after that I guess the litany of lies began, and of course I can see why now. Anyway, then Bland asked me to have a drink with him the next morning, sort of elevenses - and it went on from there.'

'So how did you meet this Jenny character, and then come across Primmer and his wife? Who by the way features in my "Domino file" though only to a minor extent. But she must be in on some - or all of this.'

'What the hell's the Domino file for fucks sake? Is this some new game you've invented?'

'You'll see when we get to my place, I'll explain it all then. We have a long night of talking and planning - a lot has to be in place by first thing in the morning, now what's the rest of the guts of meeting all these people so suddenly, and the roads straightening out now, put the foot down a bit more.'

Rory increased speed and continued to relate the events of the last two days and nights. He covered it all in as much detail as he could, from the meeting with Jenny - to Sullivan, Cheryl and Andrea being together in Brown's flat, the searching of his room, the drinks with Bland, and the meeting with Primmer and Amelia, then dwelt for a time on Primmer and Amelia, the strangeness of them, even just their being there, it didn't fit the mould of the man as he had known him. And then there was her obvious antagonism towards him. 'Somehow the whole thing to me didn't fit – I gather that you have more to say on that later?'

Bronson nodded, muttering, 'Yes'. Her expression as he glanced at her was troubled.

Rory went through in detail the time spent with Jenny Sullivan and the frequent changes of her moods. By the time that he had got through it all they were turning onto the city Motorway system and heading into the built up areas on the outskirts. There was quite a considerable amount of traffic and he slowed the car.

Marguriette reached across him, leaning on his thighs. He flinched from the stab of pain in his leg. 'Whoops, sorry I forgot the damage,' she murmured, but didn't move away. 'I know that this is a bit naughty,but we're in a hurry, and actually we are in an emergency situation.' She flicked the switch to the siren and flashing lights. 'Now get out in the fast lane and boot it my boy.' She saw his grin. 'Thought you might like that - bring out the little boy wanting to play cops and robbers again.' Her hand remained on his thigh, her fingers moving gently across the fabric of his jeans.

Fifteen minutes later, she told him to take the next off ramp exit, then at the top, turn right across the bridge. As they passed over the speeding trafiic below, Marguriette gave him instructions of how to get to her house.

* *

Jenny Sullivan got back into the Jeep, and spun off the flat and down into the access road, heading back to the village. She realised that her time was limited now to carry out the next phase of her plan, before she changed her transport and headed to the airport to meet with Jongejan, and the McGillveray's. She was hoping that they weren't going to have their snotty snooty, insecure daughter with them! She hadn't been a party, as far as Jenny knew, to any of their activities - and had never been mentioned by them - apart from the point that they had said - "she would be alright, and not be a problem". They had told her a long time ago that Sarah was adopted, and that they were making arrangements regarding her future security. Which, when you knew how McGillveray operated, could mean anything.

As she came down the last of the hill and onto the flat at the back of the shopping area, Jenny turned off the road and went through a gap in the wire fence and into the back of the camping ground, then took a right, along a narrow track that ran beside the old Botanic Gardens until she reached the back corner of the Pub car park. She stopped there, and letting the engine still run she got out and walked a few paces into a grove of fruit trees. In the middle was a rickety tin shed, she pushed back the doors. Inside, as arranged was a small blue hatchback - unobtrusive, but modified and very quick.

The keys were in the ignition, she started it up and backed out of the shed and to the side, leaving enough room to drive the Jeep in.

After Jenny put the Jeep in the shed, she removed five boxes from the back, leaving the rest of the other gear she had taken from the Studio. She closed the doors and pulled a chain through the holes, then shut the clasp of the padlock.

Several branches of the shrubs, had been tied back up into the trees, she untied the cords holding them, they fell down and across the doors of the shed, virtually concealing it from view.

Jenny put the cartons in the back luggage area of the hatchback, she got back in and sat for several minutes taking deep breaths and trying to calm her racing heart and nerves. Another small phase completed. She started the car and drove slowly out of the shelter of the trees, the tone of the engine was just a low hum. A narrow track went down on the far side of trees, and came out behind The Crazy Cow. She stopped and stared at the back door, wondering whether she should go in and collect a few personal items but decided that it would be a foolish and unnecessary risk. She turned the car along the back driveway of the shops and came out on the main street. It was deserted. She sat at the end of the drive the engine idling quietly. She watched the street, both ways and took particular time watching the waterfront road. She was about to drive out when her heart jumped. From her right coming past the wharf, heading to Jim Bland's, was a Police car. She was not close enough to it to see who was inside it or how many.

Her supposition was. 'They must be the goons who came down on the Helicopter.' She muttered to herself, as the Police car disappeared from sight. She drove out onto the street and turned left, as she passed the Hotel a twisted grin smirked across her face, and for a second her eyes took on a milky glazed look.

Jenny headed up the road and took the road to the right that ran behind the sports ground, she accelerated past them and up the hill to the driveway that led into Wisteria Lodge.

* *

'So - what do we still have to deal with.' It wasn't a question. Hans Jongejan was reflecting on "where they were at", with their progress to achieving their goals!

'The girl - Jenny Sullivan - she will have completed everything that she has been required to do? You wouldn't have been in contact or spoken to her for sometime. That was the way it was to be, was it not? We wanted as little communication between us as possible.' He saw the looks between his passengers. 'I know there's been an odd complication. But most, if not all should, be out of the way in the next twenty four hours. Mackintosh will be picked up by the Police tomorrow morning - very early. Blanchard organised that, bless the dear dead man, and the cylinders with the gold will be recovered.' 'Except that they're not the real ones. Those are in the trunk of this car. Concealed in the side panels. So the ones with Mr. Mackintosh – are the fool's gold!' His cynical laughter filled the car. 'We shall deal with them later. Our planes don't leave until the morning - late flights. The police haven't made enough progress to even suspect us - yet. They will in time, but by then it will be too late and we will be far to far away, and certainly we'll not be where they may expect!'

McGillveray could feel his throat tighten. He felt intimidated by the South African. The man was arrogant, with an attitude of total superiority.

'She should have everything finished by the morning.' Euan watched the South African's narrowed eyes, in the rear view mirror. 'Then she'll be picked up by hedge hopper, and flown to an airfield out on the south of the city. I've arranged for her to be collected, and take her, and her cargo, to the airport. The cartons will be packed inside others with a special layer of protective insulation around them, that will, if they are inspected, which is extremely unlikely, because of our men inside Customs, will make them appear to be very ordinary and legitimate cargo.'

Jongejan looked over his shoulder as he was talking. 'You don't sound wholly convinced my friend - are we perhaps just a tiny bit nervous, and perhaps not a hundred percent sure about Ms. Sullivan?'

'No not at all - she'll be fine, she has far to much at stake now, money and the risk of life in a not very pleasant environment - but yes you may be right - I think we are all a bit on edge. We've got this far, and now have to disappear - but I am sure Hans that you have everything in order. You do have our new passports and papers don't you?' Nagging doubt crept into Euan.

'Yes, my friends everything is in order - we have got this point with minimum disruption. You have both been such an immense help to me. We are going to be in positions of great power, that only extreme wealth brings, and in the not too distant future. Maybe not in our home lands - but does that matter?'

Euan and Maxine didn't answer him, the comment – 'immense help to me' disturbed both of them.

Jongejan swung the big car onto the motorway and accelerated, weaving in and out of the evening traffic. Fifteen minutes later he exited, driving back in the opposite direction until they came into a small country village, only a small Supermarket, two gift shops, a petrol station, bordered the street. They were all closed. Half a kilometre along from them, a picturesque, boutique Hotel/Tavern, built in pseudo Elizabethan style. A large sign swinging in the evening breeze proclaiming "The Inn Keepers Arms", with a picture of a large ruddy faced man with even larger arms circling a keg of ale.

'We will stay here tonight, it has good rooms, and very good food. They'll look after us well, and they do try to do it properly, in the manner of the era that they are trying to imitate. Not that it matters a damn really what they do! But for what it's worth, it's a nice place.' Jongejan parked as close as he could, to the front doors of the building. On the seat next to him was his briefcase, he opened it, producing two passports. He handed them over the back of the seat.

'You should get used to it tonight, these are the new you, learn all about yourselves and learn it well. We are all booked under our new names, don't forget that.' He waved his at them. 'You are now English but you've been living in Australia prior to South Africa, where you've been for the last ten years. You are tourists of course! Just been here for a couple of weeks. This place was recommended to you by people who have stayed here, some time ago, you spoke to them at the Airport on your way in. Their names were Jane and Michael Flint. The Innkeeper, if we shall call him such, will remember them. They will continue to be useful to us, very useful, later I'll explain why. All our bags are in the back, we can get them a bit later. Let's go and learn about ourselves, and enjoy our last evening here.'

* *

After taking the off ramp Rory drove half a kilometre then took a right, then almost immediately a left turn, and headed down a steep hill flanked on either side by palatial old homes, each surrounded by large elaborate gardens. Two hundred odd yards down the street he took a left into a short Avenue. He drove to the end, then down a long tree lined driveway, stopping the car outside a three level, very contemporary designed house. It was set amongst large exotic deciduous trees scattered through native bush. He switched off the motor, a complete silence enveloped them for a few moments until the sounds of the night crept into the car.

Marguriette stretched, yawning again. 'Right - I'll go and open up, get the lights on, you make a start getting the cases of folders from the back seat. And there's some other gear in the boot. I'll give you a hand with what you can't manage in a second.' Bronson got out and walked quickly up the steps and opened the front door. She turned off the alarm and turned on the vestibule, and outside garden lights. Then she went back and helped Rory pick up the rest of the gear from the car.

They took the load from the car through into the back of the ground floor area into a large room that was set up as an office and library. Two walls were lined from floor to ceiling with books, the third with paintings, the fourth in front of the door they had come through was glass and opened out onto a very private patio with a swimming pool and spa. Marguriette flicked three switches, the concealed lighting illuminated the room, the pool and patio. It was quite spectacular.

'Okay you've admired that, get these things spread out, use that table over there.' She waved her hand at a very long mahogany table, that must have graced an elegant dining room in another time, another place. 'Just put all that other stuff on the floor against the wall. I'll make some coffee, we may feel like something stronger, but that can wait until later, and by then we may need it more than now, particularly you - after I've been through all of this with you, you'll probably be exhausted and the way your brain has been operating lately - more confused than ever.'

Bronson left the room. Rory, after he had another look around, began to move several boxes of papers off the table. Then he opened the briefcases and began to spread out all the Manila folders. He saw the file numbers on them and placed them in order along the table, then the photo folders he put above them. The task was just completed when she came back into the office carrying a silver tray with the coffee and mugs. She put it on the end of the desk and poured their drinks, handing him his, black with no sugar.

'Interesting, you even remember how I have my coffee, you are a clever girl.' There was a very slight tinge of sarcasm, but he was smiling at her.

'Oh I remember that alright, and funnily I also remember quite a lot of other things about you too.' She too smiled for a second. 'Okay we can begin while we drink this stuff, I see that you have already sorted their number order, what did you notice about them, my observant friend?'

'Well there is definitely a sequence to them, that of course is not surprising, but there is one number missing, the six bar six file. I haven't opened any yet, but I am strangely enough able to read, and the names on some of these are to say the least a bit of a surprise. And I see that the photo files have similar numbering – also not surprising'

'Thought you may think that, but - you will be even more surprised when I tell you who file six bar six belongs to. You have I see – good boy - placed the files to match the ones above, which contain photographs. Now, the next trick - push them aside in the middle, make a space and put five on each side, of the gap, pretend that the gap is the missing number six bar six, like its the start tile in a game of Dominoes, then pretend you are playing, you know how, don't you Rory?' When he nodded she went on. 'Right, now put the others in the order that they would be if they were Domino tiles, as I say, the gap being the double six.'

Rory gave her a very strange look as if she had lost her marbles. 'Are you sure that this isn't one of your put ons? It seems even for you - a bit weird.'

'That's just what MacDonald said too, now - please - just do it - humour me, you used to be good at that.' She picked up her coffee and watched him as he began

Calder arranged the folders as requested, then stood back from the table and sipped at his coffee. Bronson put her mug on the table. She opened each folder, and the photo folder above it, then stepped back and watched as Rory moved over to the table and studied the papers and photos spread in front of him. His expression from initial mild interest changed rapidly to deep concern, his face showed the impact that the files were beginning to make, he looked at each files first fact sheet, which was in essence, a summary of the rest of the information. Then he began again -

looking from the written to the pictorial and back again, he moved along the table and started to compare the photos, and began to see the pattern that was unfolding.

Bronson came beside him. Rory looked at her. 'This is not a pretty sight, I had an inkling into a fair amount of this, but these, these take in several years of investigation that I had no idea about, none at all. I did suspect Primmer was much more involved, but we had a friendship and a professional relationship – so I kept quiet – though I did keep delving – perhaps I didn't want to see the truth – that's sometimes not uncommon under certain circumstances. Now I see that he was clearly caught up in the removal of sensitive information - and he has very plainly been trading it for considerable sums of money, and although he wasn't poor on his University salary, he would never have been well off enough, to have bought that property and done what he has to it. But that's – I was going to say irrelevant – but it's not, it's an exceptionally good cover. And of course his illness. I never got to the bottom of that.'

'So, you'd never have been aware then of his association with Bland and Sullivan then - no of course not, you lost touch - and so it's just the coincidence of you coming here that's triggered some of the events of the last few days. Even though you were there to work, it was an unexpected discovery – not just for you I would think. And by the way – if you read further – there was no illness at all.'

Rory didn't answer, and went back to studying the photograph collage.

'So can you see a pattern? Not just my Domino theory - but something else?'

'Domino theory? That's supposed to mean if that you can cause a reaction -- I mean that, the theory says that an event in one place will influence the occurrence of similar events elsewhere. Do you think that everything that has occurred is linked, and that the explosion that killed Sullivan's partner and disabled him is directly linked to the explosion and fire out at Jenny Sullivan's?'

'Look at the photographs Rory, and you know now too, that Sullivan is in some way linked to Serena and the children being killed. Maybe they were murdered - we have now two deaths, there may be others that we have not yet even heard about, no there are three - there's Miranda Sullivan too.'

Rory began his study of the photographs again, then she heard him suck in his breath he went white and turned to face her. 'Euan and Maxine McGillveray? What the hell have they got to do with all this, why are they in just about every one of these photos? Have you had them working undercover as well - nothing you do would surprise me. I did tell you about the strange conversation I had with him, didn't I? Well it's pretty bloody obvious that he knows Sullivan, he's pictured with him enough. What's going on Marguriette - there's something here I don't like the smell of, don't like it at all.' He leant on the table, he was still very white.

'Look I had better sit down, I'm not feeling all that good, I probably shouldn't have driven, with what happened to the body, and the mind. I was being a bit silly, and I sure as hell feel it now.' He went to her desk near the window, and sat in the large swivel chair.

Bronson sat on the corner of the desk. She continued to sip her coffee, sitting silent for several minutes, watching Rory. Trying to gauge what his reaction would be, when she answered his questions about the McGillveray's.

'So we come to the missing file - whose is it - who does it belong to, and how does it fit into my scheme of things. It's all quite incestuous isn't it - considering they all virtually deny knowing each other! Which in its self is quite stupid. They live in a small community – of course they know each other – but it's the way in which they do, they're all tied in together. You know, the Grandfather - Granddaughter thing, the half sister, the disappearing mother of Jenny. Nobody likes or wants anything to do with Sullivan - except some of the additional ladies – like Cheryl and Andrea – to name but two!'

Marguriette was waffling, avoiding answering him directly. She knew he went back a long way with them. This had been one of the reasons he'd been brought in - to give them another insight, an insider, yet that hadn't happened. MacGillveray, had been in their sights for some time. Especially as he had strong connections with Jongejan.

'Okay - so there's some connection - are you saying, in your extremely round about way, that this man, that I trusted with my personal and business affairs for the last ten years, has been a bloody con-man criminal? Or is he working for you? Christ I thought he was a good friend as well!' Rory's anger bubbled to the surface.

'No he's not working for us. But the fact that you were close to him has been useful. And unfortunately Rory, he is file six bar six, and sits right in the middle of them. He - and Jongejan have controlled a network of money laundering, smuggling of gold and diamonds, and people - more correctly slave trading - for the sex industry. And, it's only recently that we have been able to make very significant connections. behind the mask of respectability, lies a very devious and dangerous mind. Sullivan got hooked into it in a half-hearted way six or so years ago, and then became intensely involved in the last three, when he dragged Blanchard into it. Jenny and Andrea followed along with some blackmail – Cheryl of course – Helen - was invaluable, but then she too got caught in the web of deceit. The other facts that you fed in about the removal of files and the connection of Primmer to that, were very useful. But the great stroke of luck - for us, but not Sullivan and Helen, was you coming back and being brought in – though actually you were not completely aware as to why were you, that perhaps in hindsight was a mistake - unfortunate.'

Throughout her discourse of this information Rory stared at her - incredulous that such a small simple town harboured such den of intrigue and crime, and that he appeared to have been dumb enough to not suspect anything. The realisation that he had been used – by both sides, did not enhance his demeanour.

* *

Jenny turned the blue car into the tree-lined drive and slowed to a crawl. Almost inching her way up to the parking area that was to the left of the house, not the front entrance, but a place where guests and trades people could leave their vehicles. She backed it into a marked area near the far side, sheltered from being seen from any other traffic that may come up the drive to the front of the house.

After she had switched off the motor she sat thinking of her next move. To give all the details of what had happened to Franklin and Amelia, or just part of it. She should have gone first to see her Grandfather - but with the Police car heading there that wouldn't have been wise. She watched the grounds for any movement, and any sign, that there may be others at the house. She saw the old Chev parked, tucked away out of sight at the side of the drive, she knew it was Calder's, and that he wouldn't be coming to get it! But it would be useful. Jenny wondered briefly, if everything had been completed successfully. Yet, she was sure that the explosion would have killed him and destroyed any other evidence that could be used, including the sham art show!

There shouldn't have been a hitch, but - you never knew for sure if you were not actually there. She imagined his body - charred and broken – lifeless, lying amongst the smoking ruins of her studio.

'Studio,' she said aloud, 'that's a bloody laugh. The stupid sensitive man bought the whole story.' Then another side of her crept out - the side that had wanted him, wanted his body pressing into her, touching her, entering her - making her feel - everything that she constantly craved, but couldn't allow herself to have - she must be alone. She couldn't let anyone get too close. That might prove her undoing, "they" may discover her - discover her secrets - her personality – her failings, her dual personality. She never ever use the word - "schizophrenic". That would not be right, not right at all. Although she had made no sound, her lips formed every word.

Jenny's body suddenly spasmed. She shook, jerked, her eyes rolled back and a smear of frothing saliva ran from her lips. The attack lasted only thirty seconds, then she was still again. She took several deep breaths, wiped her face, and got out of the car, straightening her clothes. She lifted her head, pulled her shoulders back and sauntered casually across the gravel of the car park and onto the shell path that led to the back door that went into the kitchen. It was getting darker, and the lights were on. She stopped and watched the movement of the woman inside - she was still partly hidden from view by the trees, but she could see clearly enough into the room. She began talking to herself again. 'Stupid old cow, stupid clever old cow, and your brilliant old crow of a husband - what would we have done without you - and of course Grandfather - nobody would think in a million years who you are and what you get up to. No you might look stupid - and old - but you are definitely very, very clever.'

Jenny walked out from behind the shade of the bushes and went over to the kitchen window. Amelia had her back to the her and when Jenny tapped on the glass she visibly jumped in shock, but when she saw who it was a wide smile spread across her face and she bustled to the door to let her in. As she went in the back door and hugged the older woman, she was not at all aware that she was being closely observed. In her own observation of the surrounding area of the house, she hadn't seen anyone, and had not expected to.

*   *

Eton and Thomas sped back to the town. On their way they put a call into the Local station, asking if they could have two men brought in off duty. Sergeant Mackay had been surly, reluctant to do so. He had little time for his "city cousins". Particularly so as he hadn't even been made aware of what was taking place on his patch! He'd gained the information regarding Sullivan and his daughter though, through correct and official channels. However, after some discussion as what had transpired, the alleged murder of Brown, and the explosion that had 'killed' Calder, he agreed. Eton had spun the lie about Rory, in a very convincing manner.

After stopping at the Station house, and collecting the local men, they decided that Eton would take one of the men up into Primmers grounds. Thomas would go with the other and visit Bland, to continue the lie.

MacDonald suggested that after they'd spoken to him, they lay off a distance, keep a very low profile, just keep watch. Place themselves, where they could watch his house and down the road to the waterfront buildings and across to the Hotel.

They talked briefly to Sergeant Mackay when he was picking up the men, giving him some information regarding the situation in the village, and at Jenny Sullivan's Cottage. At last, Mackay became more helpful, telling them about the bush track and steps, that lead up to the far side of the Lodges Gardens. He was sceptical that the people they'd been asked to watch, could be involved in anything of an illegal, criminal nature. 'Far too respectable and respected around here - salt of the earth.' But his tone was far from convincing. A comment that as soon as he uttered it, he regretted, as no-one to that point, had suggested that they were.

'So apparently was Sullivan and his daughter, or as it turns out – daughters.'

Thomas's sarcasm wasn't lost on the Sergeant. In the end he had nodded his agreement. He followed it with platitudes, - "I guess you can't judge a book by it's cover" - and - "I suppose in our job that we should always try to read between the lines".

The two local constables, Troone and Clooney, stood slightly apart from the other men, they listened carefully to the conversation with Mackay. They were both young, but had experienced CIB work, before applying for posting to the coastal village. They had opted to live a more normal life in the country. Both men were strong – fit and had pleasant laid back personalities. They had been close friends since they had joined the force – as were their wives, who had also been in similar employment. Neither had any love or respect for Mackay, and had volunteered for a number of reasons. The main was – they did not trust their Senior Officer, and on a number of occasions had noticed considerable irregularities in his relationships with certain locals of dubious character.

After Eton and Thomas left, Troone said he could work his way round the back of the village. He'd go through the Camping ground and Botanic Gardens, where he could get a good look at the areas to the rear of the Cafes and Hotel. 'There are a couple of good vantage spots, well enough concealed but with a fairly good view.' Troone set off with a walkie-talkie.

The rest set off in the other direction, along the waterfront to Bland's house, Thomas drove well passed it, to the end of the road. Eton and Clooney got out, and headed into the bush track to Primmer's gardens. Thomas drove back, stopping opposite the house. He sat for several minutes thinking about his next move. He watched as Jim Bland pulled down the roller blinds, at the front of the house. The lounge light went on, then the hallway. He could see the shadow of the tall gaunt man, silhouetted against the glass of the front door. Bland appeared to be using the phone. He was about to get out and go over to the road, MacDonald's car came slowly down the road towards him. MacDonald turned, parking just behind him. The men got out and stood looking over at the shadow in the hall. Thomas gave him a brief outline of what they'd done since getting back into town.

'We'll be in contact, if anything crops up that we need to suddenly deal with. But so far we haven't seen anything. Eton and Clooney will have only just got there. Mackay said it would take them a few minutes to get up the track. Funny guy that Mackay, didn't want to be helpful, until he had every detail, still I suppose that's the way he is - don't think he likes other's on his patch. Oh, we didn't give him all the details – but we did say that Brown and Calder were no longer with us. Not in those words of course!'

MacDonald nodded a few times as he listened, 'Okay that's fine, now come on, let's see what Mr. Bland's reaction will be, to what we tell him. If what Bronson told me, and showed me is correct, then I'm going to be very interested in what sort of magic tricks he'll conjure up!'

Thomas looked at him blankly. 'What the hell are you talking about John, what has she got, and knows, that we - or at least I don't? Does Smithy know any of this?'

'No - sorry - long story - in some respects it's too far fetched, a fantasy fairy tale that Bronson's concocted. But, when you read the files and see the photo evidence - it seems to fit - to fall into place. You wouldn't have known that Brown and Calder are both under cover? Well neither did I, until a hour or so ago, and neither Brown or Calder knew about each other either. But someone knew about both of them - or perhaps guessed - which was good luck for the guesser - and not for the other two.' MacDonald allowed himself a wry grin.

Thomas looked quite perplexed. 'So Rory and this Brown girl were working on this. Whatever this is - here - together - is that right? But none of us knew, except Bronson? This is getting more confusing by the bloody second!'

They were almost at the front porch of the house, and they didn't see the shadow of Bland move to the lounge window and peer through the gap in the blind edge. 'No actually they weren't working on it together - I just told you - neither knew of the other's role. But Calder it appears is really here by complete coincidence, if that sort of coincidence is really possible! I think – though I could be wrong – so much bloody stuff has been flying around. Marguriette did sort of mention, that perhaps he wasn't here by complete accident! She vaguely mentioned something about Moorhead and – Cornwall – England, that's though another long story, and now really not important at all.'

As they went up onto the porch and reached to knock on the door the lights went out in the hallway, then in the lounge. 'Round the back Jock quick, I think he's twigged that we're here and is off.'

Thomas took off around the side of the house, as he went between the houses he thought he saw a shape disappear towards the one next door, but it was gone before he could call out. MacDonald banged on the front door.

'Mr. Bland, are you there - it's Inspector MacDonald, could we have a chat please, we have further information. Mr Bland?' He banged again. Nothing.

Thomas arrived back. 'There's no-one there John, I thought I saw someone running between the two houses, but when I had a look around both there wasn't anything or anyone there.'

* *

Rory leaned back in the chair and swivelled it to look out at the garden. 'Where do we go from here, are these people under constant surveillance - now - or are they just checked on occasionally for a photo shoot.' His sarcasm was evident, he had begun to feel tired and out of his depth, he was not a trained Police Officer, and had at times found the work that they had asked him to do - difficult. He turned the chair back to face her, she'd gone back to the table. 'I feel that I haven't been very effective, and looking at what you've shown me I wonder if I could have done more - been more useful. Of course I bloody could have!' Anger in his voice. 'Perhaps being away from it – the cut and thrust of the – whatever you call it – and the business with Serena and – the children.' He felt a lump begin to form and he choked it back.

'You've done the job we wanted. We only wanted you to keep - have a low profile, and up until a short time ago you did that well. Intentionally or not! The information we've received has helped a lot, this last - unexpected effort - has possibly accelerated things to a level where we can wrap it - or part of it up - I hope that's the case anyway.'

'How - I mean - well, where the hell are the main players, do you really think that they are going to be sitting waiting for you, and Primmer and Bland - never mind the little maniacal Jenny Sullivan. Wherever she is - or what she is doing.'

'Like I said earlier, we are under-resourced - right at this moment, but by the morning we should be able to cover all or most eventualities. But we do have all of them under a watch of some type, we will just have to hope that it is enough for now.'

As she finished speaking the phone went, Rory glanced at his watch it was nine twenty five. Marguriette picked up the phone, spoke briefly - then listened.

Rory got up from the desk and went to read through the files. He started on the outside right - Franklin Primmer. Most of what was in it was from his observations and from the interviews with Smith and MacDonald. He felt even more puzzled - "How did that get into a file like that?" He replaced it and picked up the next. He was a peculiarly fast reader, he did not skim - but was able to read and take in every word. Ten minutes later he had read five files. Bronson was still on the phone - a concerned expression creased her classic features.

Thoughts about what he had read, troubled him – and the question persisted – why had he been sent – no, he was asked to go to that Village. He watched Marguriette's conversation, but couldn't make out what she was saying, or who she was talking to. Her back was turned and her voice when she did speak, was very quiet. He went back to the files. They implicated each of the people in the photographs, including Helen Greene – alias Cheryl Brown. 'She must have played a very convincing part - or did she? As with quite a number of personnel who worked in this way, had she got caught up in the whole affair and become a real part of it? The answer to that from his observations was clearly – yes!' He would keep that thought to himself, for the present. Even though it had been alluded to by Marguriette.

Bronson hung up, then stood staring at the wall in front of her.

'What's the problem, you look rather worried about something - just to understate things! What was that all about?' Rory had suddenly got past his tiredness and was feeling extremely alert and focused.

'The tails we had on McGillveray and Blanchard, then with Jongejan, somehow bloody well lost them! They left their apartment nearly two hours ago - and Blanchard - who had turned up there before them, didn't leave with them. He followed for a block then somehow they gave him the slip, he doesn't think that they knew he was following, but I'll bet they did. The the cars that went after them – well – that's another bloody story of incompetent idiots! God knows where we get some of these guys from! Anyway further to that, Blanchard's body has been found on top of a service lift in the building, severe head injuries, and very dead. It appears he fell - like bloody hell he did, he was pushed. Besides he had a bloody thick plastic bag secured over his head! And, I'll bet dollars to doughnuts I know who pushed him.'

Rory's clear head began to work overtime with the information and facts that were beginning to seep in. His friend, lawyer and confidant, was not at all what he had seemed. He'd been fed a lie and lived a lie - for how long? How long had this man been involved in crime? And what sort of criminal activities? He thought of the things that they had done together, the things he'd told him - about himself - and Serena - he felt anger rising. He'd been taken for a 'Muppet and a Puppet'!

'Marguriette - how long have you known that Euan and Maxine were - are what they are? That they've been leading this – this double life? Am I bloody blind or something? Is it only recently, that you've tied this whole thing together. I mean, there is no six bar six file here - does it exist or is a figment of your fertile imagination?'

'It exists, but I would admit I haven't seen all of it. For some reason it was being added to. Look I understand how you feel, at least I think I do – I'm trying to I'm trying to!' There was something in her expression that drew Rory into her anguish as well as his own. 'But, the photographs, and the other files - on Blanchard, Primmer, Sullivan - they all tie them in. Well, more to the point it would seem that McGillveray, and Jongejan, plainly are the leading players, the controllers! With, I would say, Hans Jongejan being the boss! Sullivan may have been - but obviously they decided that he and MacMillan were surplus to requirements.' She hesitated, then let out a long sad sigh. 'There's another thing that I discovered in my research, in a way there's not a lot of point in bringing it up, but it might help you to see a few things differently. Euan had very deep feelings for Serena. He attempted unknown to you, of course, to seduce her – shit that's on old fashioned way of putting that, he wanted to fuck her! He pursued her quite relentlessly while you were married – and after you separated. Sorry, harsh, horrible and harsh, I'm sorry I've thrown more shit in the fan! I'm sorry Rory, but it's true. She did – if it's any consolation, in the end, reject him.'

Rory stood looking at Marguriette, his expression completely blank. Without replying, he turned away and picked up the Jongejan file and began to read through it again. This time there was a deep intensity in his study. He stopped a number of times, selecting pages, studying them more than others, going back and re-reading some pages. He went over it twice, going back and forth, comparing one page of facts with another, then he picked up the pictorial folder and did the same with that. After twenty silent minutes, he placed it back on the table in the place where it had been. Bronson had watched him closely, watching the intensity that he devoted to those words and photos. Finally when he put it down he looked up at her. 'I see, well I guess what you just told me explains quite a few things – yes you're fucking bloody harsh – yes, what you said and the way you said it – well some may say it does you no credit, and that you are a bitch of the first order. But thank you, for your honesty. I can see a bloody lot of things now very very clearly. Shall we get on with our work?

*   *

Franklin Primmer came into the kitchen moments after Jenny arrived. She went to him and hugged him too.

The affectionate greetings over, Primmer summarised. 'So Jenny – you have completed your work on Calder, shame – but necessary, it would not have been long before he worked out everything. The evidence that could have been discovered in the studio has also been dealt with. Excellent!' he gave her another hug around her shoulder. 'It seems that at last we are on our way. Everything that we have planned has gone very much the way that we wanted. I had a call from Hans about half an hour ago. He, Euan and Maxine, will be at the Inn tonight. You will be picked up here by helicopter just on first light and taken through to an airfield south of the city – close to the Airport. Then by car to International, the luggage will be loaded as requested, you will take a different flight to Sydney, then another on to KL, your contact on the chopper will have your new papers and passport. We will leave the country in two days and fly directly to Jakarta.' He indicated for them to follow him through into the living room.

'We have arranged for Managers, they arrived Friday night, and are, how shall we say, close by. It will appear that they have just been away on holiday, and that we don't exist. That we've never lived here or existed.' He smiled crookedly. It doesn't matter if this place doesn't run the way that we have been doing, the new team are being well paid, and have been instructed that they can treat it as their own. They are completely trust worthy, Hans has used them before. By the way, Dougal did an excellent job on your flat, and Peter's house, very thorough! He had a little help from Warren. Who as we know, will not be joining us on the journey.' He gave Amelia a sideways glance and lopsided grin, she raised her eyebrows at him. Jenny Sullivan didn't see the exchange.

'What about Grandfather, has he managed to arrange all that he needed to and when will he be joining us.' Jenny's tone held concern.

'I won't be joining you, at least not in the meantime - there are other matters that have to be dealt with, and they may take more time than some may think.' The old man's voice came from the French doors that led out to the front garden. He sounded tired and breathless. 'The Police are at my house now, I avoided them - just - and was able to make it across to the Gondola. It was MacDonald and one of his young men. I don't know what they want, but I have a pretty good idea that they now suspect that there is more to the events of the last two or three days than was originally apparent.'

The three people in the room looked at him with concern, he was shaking and pale.

'Come and sit down Jim, you look a bit shattered. I'll get you a drink - stay a few minutes - then I think it would be wise if you went and confronted them. I am sure that you will know the right words to use and will put them off their stride. Or at least onto another course - we need at least another ten or eleven hours.' Franklin Primmer handed the other man a good sized scotch.

Jim Bland took the drink and sat on the edge of a chair and took a good pull at the spirit. 'Yes I think I can - I'll surely will try, but I won't hurry too much, I could have been up here visiting - on, shall we say - legitimate affairs, and they are as far as we are concerned. Anyway they may go away - perhaps?' He seemed more nervous and unsettled than usual, and the mood translated to the others in the room.

'It may be a good idea that we get your pick up changed to another venue Jenny.' Primmer had begun pacing. Amelia and Bland, watched him, Jenny had gone over to the French doors and looked out into the now dark garden, the lights of the village spotting through the trees. 'I could call them and get them to go into town. It's only an hours drive and you could go tonight and stay in a motel, very unlikely that you would be spotted in that car, they would be - if they were at all, be looking for you in the Jeep.'

Jenny looked doubtful, but the others all agreed and Primmer made the call. After several minutes on the phone Primmer hung up. 'They see no problem with that at all, in fact they feel that under the circumstances with Plod in such evidence, that the sooner you are out of here, the better. That was your contact, and pilot, Bill Murtrie.'

'Who did you say? You weren't on the phone long, was it Euan or Hans?' Jenny had not been listening, the change in plans, had altered her confidence. She felt she was on a swing - up one minute and down the next - to climb suddenly, expectantly but unexpectedly. 'Can I have a drink - please - I feel the need. Just one - then I'll get away, and Granddad can go back to his house, it should be long enough now.'

Franklin came back from the kitchen with a glass of white wine, it was cold in her hand as she took it. 'No – I said it was your Pilot, Bill Murtrie, you don't know him. He's – well he's an associate of ours, from a long time ago. Always available when needed.'

This time Jenny had listened. 'Oh – right. And thanks for this, it might help, I'm feeling a bit – well you know what I mean by a 'bit'. I had one of my attacks a little while ago. The first bad one for a while, sorry I got the jitters, for just a moment, I'll be fine now.'

The three older people in the room, exchanged looks as the young woman drank half the glass, hesitated, as she swallowed, then drained the rest.

'Alright, my gear and all the boxes of our special cargo are in the car, I may as well get away - as long as you've all that organised Franklin. Where will I meet the chopper?' She could feel the wine coursing through her veins already, she had not eaten any food since breakfast with Calder, and that was now nearly twelve hours ago. She had been acting and reacting on pure adrenalin, the wine reacted with it and her confidence soared.

'At the football grounds down by the old part of the harbour, you know where that is – you've spent enough time there. Murtrie will come in at around six in the morning. Have everything ready to get on board as quickly as you can. We don't want to attract any attention, as you are very well aware, we seem to have attracted far too much already.'

She smiled at the three of them. 'Have no fear friends, all will be well, this should be a real plain sail from here in, the hiccups are over.' Jenny picked up her handbag and slung the long strap over her shoulder. 'Come on - come out and wave me goodbye, you can pretend that I have been a guest - but I would think it unlikely that anyone will be watching - except maybe a possum or two.'

The girls eyes were wide, a maniacal look in them, and her laugh confirmed that her state of mind had altered again. A strained look of concern was on the faces of the three at the door of the lodge.

Rory walked over to the doors that led out to the pool and patio area. He unlocked it and pushed back the heavy sliding glass panels, the sounds of the night bush, and the small waterfall that fell from a rocky fountain into the pool invaded the office. He stepped out into the night and walked around to where a garden seat nestled into a rock wall. For a while he stood with his back to the house and stared into flood lit the trees. Then he turned around and sat on the seat, lowering his head and resting his forehead in his hands.

Marguriette remained where she was, leaning on the table strewn with the folders and photographs. She'd picked up one randomly, as Rory had gone outside. She glanced down, it had been one he'd been studying intently, the last one that he had looked at. She examined the photo, it was large and clear, and showed eight people in close conversation. Hans Jongejan, Maxine and Euan McGillveray, Peter Sullivan, Andrea Jones, Cheryl Brown, Jenny Sullivan, and the last one, standing close between Sullivan and McGillveray, was Serena Calder. Bronson stared at it, she hadn't actually noticed it before, she'd seen it, but no, not actually noticed it. She'd never seen that Serena was in the photograph! Both men were touching her. She turned the photo over to check the date. It was taken only a month before Serena was killed.

SIXTEEN

MacDonald and Thomas returned to the car as Troone arrived, as they got in, he reported. 'Nothing, not a movement, there hasn't been anyone near either of the cafes, they're locked up tight, the Pub as well, nothing. Something very peculiar, I know it's Sunday night, and things do quieten down, but they should all be open, and there should be people milling around, there's nobody about! So I checked with a couple of the neighbours nearby, they hadn't seen anyone near the place all day - but we know that someone must have been there, with the flat being done over, who - well - who knows. I did check the doors and lower windows of the Hotel, it was all very secure, someone may have gone in there as well, but I doubt it. There was only one thing that might be interesting they heard a big powerful vehicle driving slowly through about a half hour or hour ago, they weren't sure. Then some doors being opened and closed, and a sound, like a chain, being dragged through a hole - like through corrugated iron. Then another car, moving away. Not the same one. I looked around the area, searched near the gardens, couldn't find any evidence of what they were talking about.'

MacDonald was about to ask a question when his radio buzzed into life. He picked the microphone and clicked it on. 'MacDonald, over.'

'Eton here Sir. Since Clooney and I've been here, it's been really quite interesting! That girl Jenny Sullivan - arrived, not in the Jeep – but a dark blue hatch. She went into the house and was extremely friendly with Primmer's wife, and Primmer, really well, quite intimate! Then Bland appeared, he came out of the bush. Clooney says there's a sort of cable car, he must have come up in that.'

'So what are they all doing now?' MacDonald asked, 'Are they all still there together - or has anyone left.'

'They went into a lounge at the front. When they left the kitchen, we wandered around in the shadows until we spotted them. This was just before Bland arrived. He - that is the old guy Bland, had a large drink - looked like scotch, he seemed shaky, nervous, then the girl too, she was standing there waving her arms about a bit, then Primmer got her a drink and she calmed down. Buggered if I know what's going on, but it seems in a way a hell of a parley session. Hang on, I think that the girl's leaving, hugs all round and they are heading for the front door.'

'Okay - see what happens. We'll get a car to the end of the road and put a tail on her. Unfortunately we don't seem to have access to an unmarked so whoever does this has to be careful not to be seen, it will depend also on where she is going - it may be nowhere.'

Troone interrupted. 'I could use my own car Sir, it's back at the station. Will only take me just a couple of minutes to get there - if I run. - If you take me she may spot us, if she's as devious and cunning as I have recently been led to believe - the station can be seen clearly from the end of the Sports Ground street.'

'Okay go for it, I'll call ahead and get a new tail for her. If she heads out of the village and we can pick up where she is going we can get another tail and check on her at the next town, until then she can't really get much out of our way.'

Troone got out and ran to the Police Station.

The radio crackled again. 'That's probably the best you can do,' it was Clooney. 'I know that Fred will manage okay. He'll keep a good safe distance, and as you said she can't get off the road from here heading south for about an hour. She is just getting into the car now, it's an easy one - a blue hatch. I wouldn't think there will be much in the traffic line at this time of the evening, so he can sit back a bit and not lose her'

'Right, then she should be going past the Sports grounds in what, two or three minutes?' MacDonald replied.

'Yes about that, I'll hand you back to Eton.'

The young City Detective Constable's voice came back on. 'What now sir?' Before MacDonald could reply, he went on. 'If you want my opinion, we should watch this lot for a while. Then perhaps get some guidance from your mentor Ms. Bronson, to what move we should make next.'

'Thank you for that Eton, but she sure as bloody hell isn't my mentor, you cheeky sod.' MacDonald knew that Eton was joking, but the needle dug in anyway, he sighed. 'But you may be right, I'll get onto her and see what she thinks, I guess as she really is in charge I had better be a good boy and report.' His tone implied that he was none too impressed that he would have to do this. 'Okay keep a good watch on them up there, and let me know if anyone else leaves.'

MacDonald turned off the Radio and reached for his cellphone. As he picked it up it began ringing.

* *

Marguriette placed the photo on the table, left the room and went to the kitchen. She took a bottle of Chardonnay from the fridge, opened it, selected two wine glasses, and put them beside the bottle. She opened the freezer and got two prepared Chicken Curries and put them in the microwave, setting the timer for ten minutes she pressed start. She picked up the wine and glasses and went back to the study. As she came into the room she could see that Rory hadn't moved, but instead of leaning forward head in hands, he was lounging back in the seat staring at the sky.

Bronson went over where Rory was sitting. 'Shove over my good man, I feel that we are in the need of succour and sustenance.' She propped herself on the bench beside him. 'First this to assist our revival, from our last conversation, and for which, though I'm sorry for it, I offer no apology, and you know the reason I say that. Then some food, I've put a couple of my frozen chicken curries in the micro. to heat. They'll be about ten to fifteen minutes, enough time for us to think drink and not be merry. We have a problem don't we Rory. What next to do. Here pour this while I get the phone, I think we need to find out what our friend MacDonald is up to with the little village people.'

Rory poured the wine, Marguriette went back and collected the cordless phone. She was dialling as she came back to the seat.

'Hello, control room? It's 'D S' Bronson. Patch me through to MacDonald's phone, and link the call to the Chief Super. Tell him who it is, that's if he's still there.'

The duty Sergeant assured her that he was. She frowned - she was glad that he was, but why was he? She had never heard of him working at this time on a weekend before. His voice came through.

'I know what you're thinking Bronson, but from the small amount of information that's come in over the last days about this, I feel my fabulous expertise might be useful. I have also been delving into this file on Mr. Euan McGillveray, very interesting. Now, let's have a listen to what you two have dug up in the last twenty four hours. I gather though that the body count is mounting.' His humourless humour wasn't lost on her.

She could hear MacDonald's phone ringing now. She waved her hand at Rory to pass her her glass, she took a couple of mouthfuls of the wine before MacDonald answered.

For the next fifteen minutes the three-way conversation tracked back and forth over the recent events since they had reached the city, and where MacDonald and co. had got to back in the village.

The time seemed to have stood still, yet so much had happened, and yet had not. It had taken Bronson and Calder nearly two hours to get back into the city, and begin work on the files. But the progress down at the Coastal Village appeared to have been at a standstill - yet it hadn't.

Moorhead's voice finally, after the tooing and frowing, broke into the line. 'Okay - now let me just go back over the basic facts of the present situation as I see it - or have heard it - and let's see if we can make some decisive decisions.' He paused, waiting for a comment from either of the others on the line. They were silent. His tone was hard, he had had enough - he wanted it sorted, some positive action. So did Bronson, MacDonald's explanations weren't nearly as satisfactory as she'd hoped. He appeared to be unsure of his next move.

'Right - first - this Sullivan girl has connected with the Primmers and Bland - thus along with the photo evidence etc, they would all seem to be part and party to this - whatever 'this' is! Yes?' Now - do we have any more bloody real clues as yet? NO! Second, she has now left, and has changed cars and is being kept under surveillance. Good – I think. Third - we still have two Officers watching Primmer's house. Fourth - Smith has taken Andrea Jones into custody and removed her from the hospital, and is bringing her up to Central. Fifth - according to what Bronson has said about a photo that she's just - at last, taken notice of, that the connections between these people including our undercover lot, is far greater than anticipated, and includes Rory's deceased wife - Serena! So what the fucking hell are you all doing? Why the hell are you still running around like headless chooks! And, whereabouts are the McGillverays, and this South African bastard Jongejan!' He let his angry tone sink in for a few moments.

Marguriette had managed - throughout all the talk - to consume a glass and a half of the wine. She could feel the tension building in the people - including herself - that were involved in the conversation.

'Look Colin, we have been under staffed right from the beginning of this damn thing, and I know that you will yell at me, and say, "that's no bloody reason for incompetence". Okay, we should have done better, but we possibly wouldn't have even got this far at this time if Rampant Rory here hadn't decided to go bush and by complete accident blunder into this mess - and make it worse.' She glanced down at Rory, 'Well maybe not worse, but it sure as hell has accelerated things a trifle.'

Moorhead cut in, his tone still icy.'If you did, then he is better than I would have given him credit for, and he's not even a sworn fucking officer! The only thing that was an accident, was when he found out that his wife had been involved with Sullivan. And, also now with that photo - with all of them. Though, he didn't click on his mate McGillveray, did he. Which was pretty dumb – though to be fair – I guess understandable - but that's the way it is and was. Also it seems that this little bitch Jenny Sullivan was far more cunning and perceptive than we realised, and far more dangerous.'

'So Sir, what do you suggest, that we pick them all up and bring them in - on suspicion of - what?' MacDonald cut in. He sounded nervous and indecisive. 'I mean we have - well - evidence that they all know each other, but that isn't a reason, they all - or most of them have lived here or had some connection with the place - or have been involved professionally - doesn't seem enough to me.'

'They all have been involved with someone, who is now either dead or injured or in danger. Though, everyone of them - Miranda Sullivan, Peter Sullivan, Helen, the incident with Rory at the Cottage and now Blanchard, I think there is plenty to give us reason to question them further, and more intensely, and we have all this guff here and the photographs. The hard ones to find, are going to be the McGillveray's and Jongejan.' Bronson sounded puzzled and very irritated with MacDonald's weak attitude.

'I agree with Marguriette, pick them up first thing in the morning, when back up arrives. We will send down a couple of cars as well, get hold of that local guy Mackay. Fill him in and this time correctly - as to what is going to happen and what is needed, keep them all under close watch. We will arrange support for Troone to get the Sullivan girl. Now get to it MacDonald. You two, see if there is any clue at all as to where the others may be or where they may be going to. Get some good men onto all the routes out of the city, and the airport, airfields, railways, and the bus stations, I don't think they will use them but who knows. I'll connect up first thing, but if anything turns up get hold of me straight away.' Moorhead rang off.

The line was still open to MacDonald. 'Okay, come on John, show us some of that efficiency that you have, or had, you have some good men there with you, use them, I'll see where and what Smithy is doing.' She rang off, put the phone down on the garden table.

Bronson watched as Rory got up off the seat. His movements were stiff and slow, a pained expression across his features. His face had in the last half hour, become grey and drawn. 'Looks like your adventures are catching up with you. How about you go and finish organising that food. You used to be pretty good in the kitchen, and else where, if I remember rightly. There are some packets of pre-prepared rice in the freezer, the curries will need another five minutes at least, then the rice only takes a few. Go and work some magic for me while I make these last few calls, then I think that you and I can put it away for a while - unless we get a squeak of panic from Mac and his mob.'

As he was about to go past her, she touched his arm, stopping him. 'What's the real truth Rory, I have had one story, probably could call it a 'meal served cold' a bit like revenge – it may be better that way, and yes – I don't deny I've been involved, but you weren't supposed to be here for long at all. that's what I was told - plainly not the truth! I was really surprised when I found you still 'on the case' – or were you? Were you there by accident, coincidence or design?'

'Like the chief said - to quote - "remember - people who work undercover – work undercover". He was partly right, partly wrong, the only things I didn't know, and I am buggered as to why I didn't figure it out a long time ago. I guess I didn't want to know the truth so hid it from myself, a deep psychological fault.' He sighed and shook his head, a deep sadness in his eyes. His shoulders sagged.

'I'll get the food ready.' He stopped, looking back. 'One question – when reading those files I find myself reading conversations that took place in the Village, you were there, you – or anyone else there couldn't have written them – so?' He turned to go out of the study, and find his way to the kitchen. Her voice echoed around him.

'They were taped – there's a wire on everyone of the officers – and yes they knew about it and you didn't. Helen, like you, didn't know – but the 'taps' were in the building – the Hotel – not on her.' Marguriette watched him walk away, she didn't know what to believe, and did it really matter anyway? She went back into the study and sat at her desk, for a few minutes she sat very still staring over at the piles of papers and folders strewn over the table.

* *

Hans Jongejan and Euan McGillveray sat in the private bar at the back of the Inn. Maxine was still up in their room, repairing herself for the evening. An evening of getting to know the people they would become.

Although Hans felt that it may be for a long time, perhaps permanently, that they were unlikely to come to this country again.

'How many years have we been planning this, building to it, and now having all that we require, at present anyway, to move to our next level. It's a long time my friend, many have been involved, most expendable - gone, their use to us at an end. There is now just the eight of us. Andrea wont be joining us, neither will Mackintosh. But for different reasons, and those reasons don't matter, they just will not be. Do you feel any sorrow, no that is the wrong word - perhaps regret, remorse, at anything that we have done?' Jongejan looked intently at him, testing - deep questioning in his dark brooding eyes.

'That is a strange question to ask me Hans? It's been over ten years that we've worked together - the answer is no anyway, none, none at all. But I have a question - why did you bring this English woman into it all so suddenly - I say the English woman because it seems so - if I can use the word, "foreign", and that I don't know her. You must know her and trust her a great deal. I presume that she is the eighth, as you have just referred to eight, as I can only count seven.'

'I do, Susan is, well has been for a long time, what you might call a silent partner. Working for me in some outposts if I can call them that, setting up our new homes, and she shall be a part of it all for the rest as well, she will be joining us in Jakarta ready for the next leg of our travels. Have no fear Euan, you will like her. She is not only very attractive, she is intelligent and has many skills - very efficient in business,' Hans grinned, 'and other ways. Yes – I have kept her secret, how did you find out that she was part of my – sorry our organisation, I wanted to keep her off this scene for as long as I could, until we were away – clear.'

'I made a call to your office, suggested by Peter, he had talked with her, and was I guess, suspicious. I just arranged my questions to her in a different format and got better answers. Probably one of the reasons I'm still here and he's not! Anyway, it doesn't matter now. You do realise that we still are not away - home free - there are still a few, hopefully minor hurdles to jump. But if all goes according to plan we shall be well away before anyone has actually worked it all out, and eventually they will. That is of course provided that all our living associates do their part and don't fuck anything up, as a few other the others have – and have paid for that.' Euan thought for a few seconds, 'Do you really see Jenny as an asset? To be honest, myself, because of her erratic behaviour and psychotic problems, her personality disorders, I see her as a bloody big liability, useful at times and in some situations admittedly, but I have become very nervous of her. Basically, I think she could be a problem.'

Hans listened to McGillveray, noting his nervousness. 'Yes, and no, I think that she may still have some use to us, and we need the delivery that she is handling. I also don't think that we should upset her little apple cart just yet! Possibly never. Anyway, who knows she may settle down when we are all away from here, and could - well, she is - how shall we say, vivacious, infectious and her particular skills may again prove useful.'

Maxine came into the bar and over to their table. They were at the back of the room in an alcove, surrounded by a curved bay window that looked into a floodlit courtyard. Beyond the far fence a silted tidal river could be seen illuminated by the lights that had recently come on in the area. She looked striking, tall, well build, with masses of blonde wavy hair that flowed down onto her shoulders, she was wearing a silver bolero jacket, a black lace blouse and tight trousers. The eye of every man and woman in the room followed her movements to where the men were seated. Both stood as she came up to the table, making room for her to sit between them.

Euan didn't miss the look in the South African's eyes. They held a fanatical lust, slitting half shut, his mouth below the large hooked nose was a twisted leer. Sweat broke out on the back of his neck, and his hands felt clammy. He knew this man well, and he knew his ways, with both men and women. He may be powerful, and he may have helped make their future secure, with immense wealth and the promise of more, but there was always a price. He hated him and what he stood for, and he hated and despised himself for what he had allowed himself to become.

The three sat down. Hans waved over a waiter, and ordered a bottle of Bollinger. 'A celebration, as well as a learning night, we will begin as we mean to go on.' He picked up the whisky glass in front of him and

drained the last of the amber liquid, looking at Maxine as he ran his tongue
suggestively over his thick lips, removing the last drops of the drink from
them.

Euan saw Maxine glance warily at the stocky bald man. Her eyes
betrayed nothing of her feelings. His however did, and he hoped, that they
weren't noticed by either party.

*   *

Jenny drove slowly past the Recreation fields. She could see the Police car
still outside Jim Bland's house. There seemed no movement from them, nor
was there any around the area, it seemed deserted. She increased her speed,
but not enough to attract any attention particularly from the Police station
on the corner, the lights were still on, an unusual occurrence at this time
of evening. But she knew Mackay would be there – watching, listening.
At the corner of the main street she turned right and headed for the bridge
across the river. Now out on the road south she accelerated to just under
the speed limit. She drove the car quickly, and with considerable skill to
the top of the hill above the town, it was not a stretch of road to be taken
carelessly, but she knew it well.

Fred Troone had his car in the shadow on the far side of the Station
house, the engine idling. He saw her come down the street and stop at the
corner, then head out of the town and turn south. He gave her two minutes
before he followed, he could see her tail lights clearly as she wound her way
up the hill. Fred had not done a great deal of surveillance work - of any
type - for sometime. Since he had been in a large Provincial city five years
ago, and then it had only been spasmodic, an occasional "stakeout" where
there had been suspected drug trade going on, or car theft rings.

None of the them had ever come to anything, and he had found the
work tedious and boring. But this was different.

His thoughts briefly went to his personal situation, his wife. He'd
met Jocelyn East, who was also on the force, and worked in the same
department with her. It had been an instant attraction, and they had

married within six months. They had decided to opt for the quiet life and had transferred to the coastal town, they now had two small children, and what they considered an easy pleasant lifestyle - it suited them well.

When he had suggested that he follow the Sullivan girl, he had surprised himself. It was not normally his way to put himself forward, and it hadn't occurred to him immediately, that in this case there was definitely a possibility of some danger. It wasn't until he had started down the other side of the hill and was driving through the next small settlement. It was then that the churning of nerves began in his stomach. There was no sign of the tail-lights of the other car, and he had increased his speed to catch up on it. The road straightened, Troone accelerated further, he started to panic.

'She can't have got that far in front of me. The visibility is good, I should be able to see her tail lights, even if she's three or four k's ahead!'

At the top of the hill Jenny had eased back her speed and pulled across into the parking bay. She turned the car so she could see back down the hill road. A car came over the bridge and start up the hill. 'That's interesting,' she muttered, 'there wasn't a sign of anyone when I came through the village. I wonder who that can be leaving at this time of night - very unusual.' She mused. Jenny hesitated only a few seconds watching the car start it's climb, then drove out and headed down the other side of the hill. The hatch handled extremely well and with the wide tyres and peppy motor she was able to manoeuvre it down the steep winding road very quickly. At the bottom she planted the foot and sped to the Motel at the next Bay. She switched of the lights and engine coasting the car into the driveway and around the back of the high hedge at the side, out of sight of the road. The Motels were in darkness and she hoped that she hadn't disturbed anyone. From where she parked she could see the highway clearly. It was only a couple of minutes for the maroon sedan to come into view, it was travelling fast, but she was unable, as it sped by, to get a glimpse of the driver. But she recognised the car, it was Constable Fred Troone.

'Coincidence, or are they following me? - Or is he on a completely different matter? Nothing to do with anything?' Troone's car was almost out of sight when she made her decision. She started her car and pushed it into gear, moving it as quietly as she could across the front courtyard until she reached the road again. The lights of the Policeman's car were now at least three kilometres away.

'If I'm behind him he just isn't going to know where I am going, but if he isn't looking for me it doesn't matter a damn anyway, so let's just see what happens.'

She took off down the road, building her speed to well over a hundred, but she made little impression on the distance between them. She accelerated further, but she was back in a twisting section of the road again, and had to slow, she got only an occasional glimpse of the car ahead of her.

Troone had been driving for twenty-five minutes when he slowed, pulling to the side of the highway. He turned across the road, and down a slight slope onto a wide grassed area, which bordered between the road and the sea. He swung his car in behind a group of large old gnarled tree trunks and cut the engine, he reached over and took the cellphone from the seat next to him and called MacDonald. 'I saw her leave the village, and head up the hill, I had her in my sights until the we got to the flat on the other side. The road was a bit windy there, so she could have got away on me a bit, but now I'm not sure. I've been moving bloody quickly and nothing, not a sign of a car light - hers or anyone else's. There is the possibility that she slipped off somewhere and let me get ahead of her, but I can't see where. Unless - unless it was at that Motel! Where you and Bronson booked in.'

'Where are you now?' asked MacDonald.

'About thirty five to forty minutes away. Twenty – maybe thirty from the next town, I'm parked down off the road by the water, sheltered by some trees. Thought I might wait here and see if she turns up, if she doesn't I'm stumped. I bloody well don't know where she could be. I suppose she could have doubled back, but she would've had to know that she was being followed, or had a change of mind as to what she was going to do.' Troone's nervousness increased.

'Stay put for ten minutes, if she hasn't come past by then, come back here, if she --.' a sharp exclamation from Troone interrupted.

'Shit! Here she comes now, it's quite moonlight now and I can see the car clearly, she's about a kilometre from me, travelling like a bat out of hell!'

'Well this time don't lose her, stick around and don't let her out of your sight, when or if you can work out where she's headed, let us and Central know, they will send backup. I have a feeling that she will be met somewhere, and that she'll not go through to the city - could be wrong, but I just have a hunch, I hope that it's right. There is nothing happening here, Bland has returned home, the others have stayed put, we have a watch on all of them, and one at the entrance to town, nothing more we can do until the chopper gets here in the morning.'

'She's just going past now!' Troone shouted, 'I've got to get moving!' As he spoke he started the car and drove out from behind the trees, skidding on the dew laden grass. As he headed onto the seal, he suddenly remembered that he hadn't told Jocelyn what he was doing, that he was on surveillance - where, and why he was! He reached for his phone, taking his eyes from the road. His movement flicked the steering wheel a fraction to the left, but at the speed he had reached it was enough, with his momentary inattention to take the car off into the loose metal at the side of the tarmac.

* *

It took Marguriette ten minutes to complete her calls. She knew that with the instructions that she'd left, and the work that the Chief would be doing, they would've covered all the options at their disposal right now. To pick up all the suspects, with the exception of Jongejan and the McGillverays. The operation had to take place as early as possible, with the minimum of fuss, but with the maximum of shock and surprise, and she wanted all of them to be kept separate, not to have an opportunity for any of them to be able to talk at all. She had organised road blocks and at first light a Helicopter for air surveillance – a local top dressing machine, that she thought wouldn't create any suspicion.

Then she made last call - to Roger Smith. To inform him of the arrangements that she was making. She trusted his descretion more than

MacDonald's, and knew if she gave him instructions, they would be carried out efficiently.

Before she could say anything, Smith thanked her for her assistance. 'Thanks for your help Marguriette!You said you'd talk to the Doctor about removing Jones, but I guess at the last instance you bloody forgot! But – heh – guess what – I coped!' His sarcasm wasn't missed, she apologised to him. Something that she didn't do often.

Smith went on. 'That's now not important. However, with what the Doc had seen and heard from us, it wasn't a particularly difficult task to convince him that the Patient – Andrea, would be safer in custody. He even sedated her. So I was able to get Jones out of the hospital with a minimum amount of effort and fuss - with the assistance of the Doctor. I had a talk to John and he filled me in on what was happening with the Sullivan girl, Primmer and co. I'm leaving the area now, and should have her up there in the hospital in about two or so hours. I've arranged for two plain clothes to be on her ward, one on the door of the room the other wandering. Now what about the other three - or four - or however many it is.'

'We have no idea at the moment, but we hope Jenny Sullivan will assist there.' Bronson glanced up to the door, there was still no sign of food! 'We have a tail on her. Troone, the local guy, let's hope that he's not noticed. I think when you have deposited your parcel, you should get some rest and then report to Moorhead first thing. If we're going to wrap this up, it's going to have to be tomorrow. I have a feeling that some, if not all of the birds will attempt to fly the coop.' She quickly told him of the plans she'd put in place and hung up. She went back to the table, picking out the files of Jongejan and Sullivan. She spread them out, quickly reading the notes, then sifting through several of the photographs. The same pattern, the same people, only this time she found that she had missed something, another person that she hadn't expected to see. Miranda Sullivan, standing in close discussion with Jongejan, Blanchard was watching them in the background.

'How the fuck did I not see that before! That's two damned people, in the last bloody half hour that I've missed, my brain is overloaded – or something is.' Marguriette went back to the phone, taking the photo with her, just as Rory came into the room. He was carrying two plates and another bottle of wine was tucked under his arm. She looked up at him, and waved in the direction of a table out by the pool. 'I'll just be a minute.' She pressed a button that dialled directly into the Central control room. The duty Constable answered immediately, things had apparently gone quiet. 'Is Chief still in his office?' When told that he was she went on. 'Put me through, it's Bronson.' Her voice terse, impatient.

It was only a moment before the gruff voice was on the line. 'What now Bronson, had another brain wave?' He sounded tired and more than a little fed up.

'Sorry Sir, just had a thought, I've been going through the files again. Have you still got the McGillveray files in front of you? I have a photo here that I'm afraid I hadn't noticed before. It shows Miranda Sullivan with Jongejan, close to him, like very close, and Blanchard is watching from the background. I thought that she had nothing to do with them. This shows a different slant, well it might, not that she's in a position to confirm or deny, but if there was just something in there that might tie up why she's dead, why her father is almost, and who it might point to?'

'Hang on a minute, I'll have a look, but I think we could be clutching at bloody straws. Can you hold or will I call you back?'

She looked out at Rory sitting with a glass in his hand. 'Call me back, yes – of course - I'm not going anywhere am I!'

'Right, I have copies of those files downstairs, I'll be just ten minutes.'

Marguriette frowned 'Why is it downstairs? He was just looking at it! And anyway that one - it should be in his bloody computer! I thought we were working top priority,' She sighed, 'I guess perhaps he is not? And perhaps he is not where he was before – what the hell am I talking about this for?' She put the phone down and went out onto the patio. Calder poured her another glass of the wine 'The food is plenty hot enough, and it's extremely good, thank you, I needed something to put a bit of a spark back in me.'

'Yes, I feel much the same way. I wonder at times, and even more just recently, like, well, over the last few months, as to why I am still doing this work. It doesn't get any easier, and it becomes - more - gruesome, is a word that comes to mind. Remember when in this country that crime was petty, pretty mundane, and murder almost unheard of, now it seems every second day there is some disgruntled bastard knocking someone else off! And they are not usually very pretty either.' She sank into the soft cushions on the chair at the table and picked up her glass.

'Here's to - what - better days, success in crime fighting, peace and serenity. Whatever, no let's toast you Rory, thanks for the help and the acceleration of events, and that you are still alive and in almost one piece. Tell me though, how close did you get to this Jenny Sullivan. I mean did you like her, were you, you know, wanting to get - really close, into knickers type close? Or was it just your job that you were doing.' She eyed him hawkishly. 'You had only been there a couple of days, and I'm still not sure what the truth is about that! Moorhead says one thing – you another – MacDonald something else. And, I know, that you - you rotten teasing bastard, are not going to tell me, are you.'

He shook his head. 'No I'm not, and as far as the girl goes, I was presented with a couple of opportunities, I didn't take them. Nor did I want them - well, maybe part of me did. But right from the beginning - I guess, she was strange - would be a word I would use, and often what she said never made sense to me. Now I know why, there was no sense to it, just mayhem! Come on eat, the food is getting cold, and it's far too good for that.'

The next five minutes they devoted to the wine and the food, he'd already started, and finished well before her. Rory lounged back in the comfort of the cushioned chair, he sipped his wine and watched her eating, waiting until she'd finished her last mouthful, and had pushed her plate away before he spoke again.

'Who do you think killed Serena? Tell me Marguriette, who do you think it was? Or do you take the line of the official enquiry? An accident, the brakes and steering were just unfortunately faulty, hadn't been tampered with - even though I was a suspect in having done that? Strange how suddenly the attitudes changed. Then I was dragged, no that's not right – connively manoeuvred, from Cardiff, and brought into an investigation that's led us to where we are now. Almost bloody nowhere! Very strange wouldn't you say, and all this time you've been caught up in it as well. The Sullivan affair - the documents - Primmer, the supposed contraband, the Political involvement, and the South African Jongejan. Is it all part of the same scene - as it appears - or is there something else, is there something that I'm missing? Maybe all of us are missing?'

Marguriette sat silent, listening to him, - sipping her wine. Her eyes on his face, taking in the confused concerned concentration, that had spread over him in the last few minutes.

'No Rory, you haven't missed any more than anyone else. But, we've all missed something. We, in our trade, pride ourselves on our ability to solve - to delve and solve. But we don't always get it right. We quite often in fact miss something, miss some clue, a vital sign - and head off in the wrong direction. A bit like in our "real lives" - we miss the vital signs and miss the timing, the turning that should take us to the correct destination - the right answers. When we do, we like to cover it up, put something in it's place, make people think we have done the right thing - solved the crime. This time we may have stuffed up more than we know. If we can't locate the McGillverays and Jongejan, as well as stopping Jenny Sullivan connecting with them, then we've lost the game. The pieces that we need complete the puzzle are missing. I feel that they've planned it this way - that everything, suddenly came to a head, quickly, concisely, but perhaps a fraction ahead of the time frame they wanted. That this would have happened whether you were here or not – coincidence? I don't know. The Domino theory? Probably a load of bloody rubbish - but we try to justify, by whatever means we can.'

'You've answered some of my query - but not all, and seem to have nicely avoided the first part - who do you think killed Serena?' He leant forward, his look bored into her, she could see he wanted an answer. His next statement threw her completely. 'The reason that I didn't pursue our relationship any further, was because - I was told that you were involved with a certain Constable. Heavily involved, and that you had - although we were seeing each other virtually continually, been told that I was seeing Serena. That I was more serious about her than you, this was a lie, I'd only met her casually once, during that time.' Rory saw the look on her face, 'Yes, well later, it was a bit more than seeing, sort of wasn't it. But you, evidently – according to this 'rumour' were just waiting, biding your time until you were able to - to quote my sources, "get your claws into him". By the time I found out that it was a load of crap, I was with Serena, and you, well, I don't know what happened. Besides it's a long time ago, and you still haven't answered the question, partly because I keep bloody talking!' He smiled at her for the first time since they had been at the house.

'Well, I guess now you know, you were told was a lot of bloody rubbish and the rumour was spread by the person I was supposed to want to get my claws into. Now as far as "who killed Serena" I could have a guess. But that's all it would be. But I do agree that she was killed, deliberately, so I suppose that she, and the children were murdered. Though I would also suspect it was to make it look like an accident. But if that's true, that she was murdered, then the person who did it was extremely ruthless, and didn't give a damn about anyone or anyone's life.' She saw his face begin to crumple and the tears forming in his eyes. 'I'm sorry, those sorts of wounds don't heal, I would imagine more because of the children than Serena, but then, I'm just being bitchy and harsh - but that's typical isn't it?'

'No, and yes, but I think it's more probably tiredness. I haven't slept for several nights, what with the nights at the Cafe, the storm, then the cottage and barge. Bloody ridiculous! And trying to work out what the hell it's all about -- I think I've had it! I presume you have a spare bedroom, mind if I crash out? I imagine tomorrow will be as bloody difficult if not more so. I really don't think there is any more that can be done right now. You too, you look as if you could be feeling the same, just without the cuts and bruises to body, mind and ego.' He stood up from the chair. 'Point me in the direction that I need to go, I would imagine that if anything happens, crops up or whatever someone will get on to us.'

'You're right Rory, I am beat too. Yes, the last forty-eight hours haven't been bloody easy have they. The bedrooms are upstairs, the one on the left, at the top of the landing is made up, you can use that, there are towels and toiletries you may need, in the en-suite. I'll clean up this stuff, you get going. I think we will be making a very early start, I want you to go down there in the Chopper, you know Primmer, he his going to get a hell of a shock when you turn up with the Squad.'

Marguriette picked up the plates. He took the glasses and bottle and followed her out of the study around into the kitchen, he placed them on the bench. 'Thanks, now go and get some rest, I'll lock up. See you in the morning Rory, five okay?'

He nodded as he left the kitchen and limped up the stairs, the wound in his leg now very stiff and painful, the rest of his body was aching from the bruising. He found the room went in and shut the door. Sitting on the edge of the bed he kicked off his shoes then stripped of his clothes, noticing for the first time their state - torn and filthy. His mind considered a shower, but rejected the notion.

'I think it can wait until morning.' He looked at his watch and realised that it actually not very far away. He pulled back the duvet and looked at the clean cool sheets. Feeling guilty that he was more than grubby, he was filthy, he got up and went to the bathroom and turned on the shower.

* *

Troone's car began to slide sideways through the gravel. He twisted the wheel into the skid and the tail slewed back the other way, then the back tyres gripped the seal again, the car spun twice in a circle, then shot backwards across towards side of the road that dropped down onto the rough rocky shore. He wrestled with the out of control vehicle, his hands wet and useless on the steering wheel. The car hurtled out into mid air, then fell straight down onto the rocks, the impact completely knocking the breath out of him and the recoil of the crash whipping his body against the seat belt and his head smacked into the door pillar.

Fred Troone was unconscious for several minutes, he came round to the stench of petrol fumes and blood. The side of his head and right cheek were stinging painfully from the blow against the side of the car, the sticky fluid flowed down his neck soaking into his shirt and jacket. He clicked open the belt and pushed on the driver's door, it was jammed shut, he leant across to the passenger side, he breathed a sigh of relief, it had sprung open.

Collecting his phone from the floor he struggled across the passenger seat and tumbled out onto the ground. He was badly shaken and shocked.

Each movement seemed to take supreme effort but he gradually gained enough momentum and he was able to crawl, then stagger to his feet. As he reached the bank below the road some fifteen or so yards from the wreck, he felt the blast of air then the heat as the petrol ignited on the hot exhaust pipe. The concussion of the blast threw him against the clay bank in front of him, and as he fell he twisted. The crack of his leg breaking seemed even louder than the explosion. Troone gasped from the pain in his right leg, and from the heat, searing across the rocks towards him. He fell back against the bank and watched the flames devour the place that he had been minutes earlier.

Jenny Sullivan slowed her car. There had been no sign of lights in front of her - or behind now for some time. She pulled over to the far side of the road into a rest area above the beach. This was the last part where the road travelled by the sea, and she was on a long sweeping curve. From where she stopped, she had a good view back the coast road. The girl got out of the car and walked to where the park sloped down to a small sandy bay. She stood taking in the view across the water to the lights of small settlements on the far side of the firth. The evening was windless and perfectly peaceful. The contrast from the last hours struck her, and she began to ponder her position, what lay in store from this moment on. Her reflective mood was suddenly changed and her eyes widened as she saw a huge tower of flame shoot skyward.

'Fucking hell! What was that, it looked a bloody big bang!' She stood watching the flames begin to fall back. She got back into her car, hesitating only briefly before deciding, against her better judgement, to investigate. 'It's probably only five k's back. Perhaps that Cop saw it too, he may be there. No, there are no lights, coming or going, maybe it's him? That would be fun, a cooked coppy!'

She'd been talking aloud, she laughed, at herself, and the thoughts that were flowing in her mind. She drove out of the Rest area, turning left onto the highway, accelerating back in the direction of the fire. It took less than ten minutes to where she'd seen the fiery explosion. There was no-one else around. Jenny pulled her car into the metal shoulder and got out, at the top of the bank she looked down onto the rocks where she could now see that it was, or had been, a car.

The flames were subsiding and she could see that the wreck was completely burnt out - gutted.

'Whoever the poor bastard was in that, sure ain't going nowhere now. It looks like it may be Troone's car. But I can't be worried about who it was, or him, just makes things a bit easier if it is.' Then she saw the number plate, her mouth twisted cynically, this time her laughter was maniacal!

As he lay against the bank watching his car disintegrate, Troone thought, 'That was bloody stupid, and I'm bloody lucky to still be here.' He wasn't for the moment thinking that he should be calling in to MacDonald. The pain from the his broken leg, the shock of that and the accident, had dulled his senses away from the immediate needs to call for help. What brought him back to his reality was the sound of a car pulling into the side of the road above his head, he heard the door open and the footsteps coming over to the top of the bank above him.

Initial instinct told him to call out, but something stopped him, he held his breath and sat very still.

'Tough shit copper,' she laughed again - it was now a crazed hysterical sound, it echoed over the top of him, mingling with the crash of the waves on the stony shore. 'You might be more careful in future who you're chasing - not.' He heard her footsteps moving away, then a car door slam, the engine starting, allowed him to exhale. He listened as it left, then he picked up his phone, pressing the numbers for the Station, he hoped someone was still on duty. It was Mackay who answered.

'Troone here,' He didn't give Mackay a chance to reply. 'I've cocked things up a bit, I'm lying on the rocks about fifteen minutes from town, got into a spin in loose metal, went over onto the rocks and the car exploded.' His tone through the pain was strained. 'I'm sort of okay, but shaken, and I think, broken my right leg. The girl - she came back to see what had happened, but didn't see me. Can you get someone out here to help? And get some road blocks - three - one on the one way bridge, one to the main road south of that, and the other on the gorge.' Mackay asked a stupid question. 'Of course I've no idea where she's headed, but we should stop her. She was very pleased to see the wreck, and I think she thought I was dead.'

'Yes right – a stupid question, but for an injured man you can still bloody talk a lot, give me a better location as to where you are. I'll get MacDonald to get one of his men out to you, I'll call the Ambulance from town as well.'

'No, don't do that, if she sees that she might twig that I'm alive and kicking, and that the cavalry are on the way. She thinks - to quote the voice on top of the bank - "I'm a cooked coppy" - What a pleasant caring lady - I don't think! I'll be okay, for half an hour, just get organised. And – call Jocelyn please, I didn't tell her I was going out on a chase case! You might be able to keep her calmer than me if I call her from my bed of rocks!'

'You're a cheeky sod Troone, for a man with a broken leg and a wrecked car. Who do you think you're talking to, the Office girl? But okay, you could well be right about the Ambulance alerting Jenny Sullivan, and - we'll get organised. Get the road blocks into place.' Mackay frowned as he hung up. He sat back in his chair tapping his pen on his leg, then stood and went to the window. He looked across to Bland's house. 'I wonder what's going on over there?' He mused. After a few minutes he sat down and began to doodle on the blotter. He didn't pick up the phone.

Troone leant back on the clay. He took several deep breaths, then closed his eyes, shutting out the sight of his car. He focused on being thankful the whole thing hadn't been worse, and he had been a "cooked cop". He was brought back to the situation within minutes as the sound of another vehicle approached at high speed down the road. He could here it slowing and the gears changing down as it came across to the seaside of the highway and slid to a halt in the gravel above him. The flames were now almost out but the smoke still choked the area around him. He heard first the running feet, then saw the figure jump down the bank and began to scramble across the rocks towards the car.

Whoever it was, was carrying a fire extinguisher. Troone shouted, as they began to spray foam at the burning wreck.

'I'm over here, there is no one else in the car, I need help. Please, over here!' He felt relief that at least it wasn't Jenny Sullivan come back to gather souvenirs.

*   *

Marguriette cleared up the kitchen, and came back to the study. For some time she looked at the photographs, concentrating on Jenny Sullivan, and the people that she'd been with. There was something nagging at the back of her mind. What had happened with Rory with this girl over the last few days? But there appeared no clue that could help her in the file, or the photographs. She switched to the photo with Serena Calder in it. She turned it over, checking the date that it was taken. It was over a year ago, before she had become involved with James Peterson, and well before she went to England. Marguriette pondered whether or not, to talk to Rory about this. Would it put his mind to rest that she wasn't involved with the criminal side of these men? But then, how do we know that she hadn't been caught up in Sullivan's dark sticky web? That she'd tried to escape with the 'influential' James Peterson? Get clear away and break the bonds? No answers were forthcoming, everything was supposition. She went back to the files on Jenny Wilson.

'There has to be some way she found out about Cheryl – Helen, and Rory. If she's really behind her death, and the attempt on Rory.' She tossed the files back on the table. 'Of course she bloody well is – who else would it be! We just have to get hold of the conniving bitch – and find out why?' Marguriette secured the sliding glass doors, and left the office..

'Bugger him, he may be tired and battered, but I need some answers! So coffee, cognac, and wake up Rory! We're going to continue our chat!' Bronson made a strong brew in a plunger, grabbed mugs, and glasses, then propped a bottle of Cognac under her arm.

'To bloody bad if he suddenly decides he wants sugar and milk - and sleep, he's getting neither, until I see if I can get even an inkling of what tipped her off.' At the top of the stairs she put everything on a long iron and glass table and went to his door, pushed it open, collecting the mugs and glasses, she took them in putting them on the dressing table, then collected the bottle and Coffee. As she back, Marguriette pushed the light switch down with her elbow. The room leapt into light. The bed was empty. But, there was a voice behind her.

'What the hell are you doing? It can't be bloody five o'clock already!' He looked at his watch. It was eleven thirty. 'What's all this! What are you doing you crazy woman. I was about to try to get some sleep for the first time for days!' Rory was standing in the doorway of the bathroom a towel wrapped around his waist, water dripping from his hair.

'Hmm – at least you look a bit cleaner. Need to talk. There's more than one missing "tile" in my game. It may only be a tiny one, but I want to know how Jenny Sullivan was tipped to know who you were. No, rather not who - what, and who Cheryl Brown was. It may not change anything, but if she knew, and then passed on the information to others, then it may help us work out what they plan to do next. Or not – but I have to try – I am getting bloody frustrated with this whole thing!'

'How - if I may be so bold as to ask, is it going to help you work that out, and anyway, Primmer could have possibly worked it out.' As he came further into the bedroom Rory glanced at the bottle of Cognac and the coffee. May I dry myself and put on a gown or something – my immodesty if I drop the towel, may offend you.'

Marguriette grinned at him. 'I don't think so – but I shall spare you. Get yourself sorted while I pour us coffee and evil spirits'. She went to the closet and pulled out a cotton robe and threw it to him

As Rory retreated to the bathroom, he pulled the towel off and began drying his hair, he went on. 'If he'd been thinking along the lines that he appears to have been for some time, he knew what I did, before, you know at the University, what I was doing there. Well, some of it, not all by any means.' He thought for a moment. 'Don't you think, that perhaps it's more important that we figure out where the hell Jongejan, Euan and Maxine are? What they're doing? Then how and when, if this Jenny creature is connecting up with them?'

'You suddenly seem very "wide awake". Are you sure that you were feeling tired and needed sleep, you don't even look it now.' Rory had come back into the room hair done robe on. 'Anyway, would Primmer have really worked it out without some other help, would he really have suspected that you were here working on something, did he ever know that you had been - how shall we say - "brought in". Given the Research Fellowship and Lecturing position – yes he had been there for a long time – but – well – yes I suppose he could have. What did you talk to him about? You know – when you weren't working?'

'I was tired and yes I need sleep, but thank you – now I am afraid that I have the same problem as you, too many, far too many loose ends and unanswered questions. I was standing in the shower thinking about it all, and I was going to call out to you to come in and talk again.' He smiled at her quizzical look. No – not in the shower – though – ? Just wanted you to feel guilty that you might have been waking me up, mind you a fat chance of you feeling guilty about anything like that, you always were quite good at waking people up in the middle of the night -.'

Marguriette was standing by the bed, with the coffee and Cognac. She didn't react to his last comment and went on. 'This is possibly a very bad idea, but I don't really care,' she handed him the drink, and put the mug of coffee on the bedside table, then collected her own and sat on the edge of the bed. She lifted her glass and touched his. 'To the final solution - whatever that may be - but let's find the bloody thing!'

* *

Hans Jongejan poured the Bollinger, then placed the bottle back in the silver cooler. He raised his glass, the others followed and they touched over the centre of the table. 'To our future prosperity, and the success of this and many other of our ventures, and adventures that are still to come.'

They all drank, each draining their glasses to the last drop. It was a ritual they had invented for themselves some years ago - like a lucky talisman. They replaced them on the table and he filled them again. This time they sat back in the comfort of the deep cushioned alcove and sipped the bubbling nectar.

Hans put his glass carefully on the table then sat back again, folding his large chubby fingers over his stomach. He was a short solid man, not yet run to fat, but he was verging on it, but there was a powerfulness, a toughness, about him, not just a physical one, but a mental one. He spoke quietly, but his voice penetrated their minds with its tone.

'I will have to admit to you, that when we started our association ten years ago, I had quite grave doubts about you two. Whether you would make the grade, whether you would be hard enough. Oh yes, you had the basics, the intelligence, the avarice, and you will note, I would think, that I often tested you. Tested your abilities, your loyalty and your resolve to carry on. We have at last reached the end of that passage in our work, and that from now on I consider you equal partners with me. You have passed the test. You have graduated. So,' he reached over and picked up his glass again and raised it to them. 'So this toast is to you - my partners - in crime - and in the future.'

Euan and Maxine smiled, murmuring their thanks. Both feeling, relief, for they had always wondered - "what if he took a dislike to them" they had seen too many times the results of that. They had put in the hard yards and now it had paid off.

'Now - after we have eaten we will go and study our new selves and check over between us that we understand what we have to do, the responses that we will need from each other in the next twenty four hours until we are well out of this place. There is of course quite a lot to do, and we will have to secure some of our trophies, particularly the ones that Mr. Blanchard was so kind to deliver to us.' He waved again to one of the staff that was wandering around clearing tables.

'Another of this is fine wine please, and could we have a look at the menu for tonight. We would like to eat within the next hour, but if we could sort out our meals now we would be grateful, perhaps you could pop back shortly and get our orders, would save us time later, if that is alright.' Jongejan smiled ingratiatingly at the young man.

He agreed that it would not be a problem, smiled politely, went away and returned within minutes with the new bottle, fresh glasses and the menus, placed them on the table, and took the room number for the account. They spent the next ten minutes perusing them and continuing to enjoy the Champagne.

* *

Jenny Sullivan smiled to herself as she drove, now at a much more sedate pace than before. There was no real hurry, all she had to do was get a place to stay for the rest of the night and then meet the pick up in the morning - she had been instructed to wait at dawn at the sports ground down by the old harbour.

'I will check it out now before I get some rest, it may have changed since I was there last, unlikely but it may have, there may be better cover or there may be less.' Talking aloud, then singing to herself, as she swung the car off the main street as she entered the coastal town, she headed down a side road then into another that ran parallel to the main street. At the end were the sports grounds. She turned into the parking area behind the pavilion and wooden grandstand. Jenny switched off the motor and sat in the silence, stretching her neck and arms relieving the stiff tense muscles. She got out and walked between the two buildings, and out onto the flat wide grass area. There was no shelter, no trees around the perimeter, the area exposed to the wind and salt spray of the Firth when the strong westerlies blew in. It was exactly as it had been the last time she was here - playing hockey for the school nearly seventeen years ago, nothing had changed, except the paint work on the buildings was flaking and cracking, bare boards testimony to the lack of use and maintenance.

There was plenty of space for the helicopter. It could come in low and fast over the water, there were no obstacles, the only thing that was visible above the ground were the power pylons at the north west corner that carried high tension cable to the factories a kilometre away.

Jenny went back to the car and opened the hatch, she would place her marker now, the indicator that she had received the instructions to place in the ground so that the crew of the chopper would know that she was there and ready. She took out the small stake and the bright orange flag, taking them out to twenty metres from the buildings she pushed the spike into the hard ground and attached the flag. Then she got back into the car and drove back to the main street.

It had been a mining town back over a hundred years ago and many of the old Hotels were still there, now turned into tourist attractions with boutique accommodation, trendy cafes and restaurants. She selected one on the left hand side that had a view towards the sea and river. It wasn't that late and there were still a few patrons drinking in the bar that opened onto the street. Jenny parked at the curb and grabbed the small overnighter that had been put in for her. She locked the car and went into the reception. The girl behind the desk looked up from the magazine she was reading. 'Yeah, what can I do for you at this time of night.' She was chewing gum and smelt of cheap perfume and alcohol. She did not seem pleased to be disturbed.

'I would like a room for the night please, at the front facing the road. I have to be up early for an appointment, so could I also have a wakeup call at five o'clock please.' Jenny was polite, and commented on the girls watch and bracelet.

The receptionist responded to the flattery, and set about organising the room with a smile and thank you for the compliment. She gave her the key and the directions as to how to find the stairs and the room, also apologising that there was no bathroom attached and that it was two doors down the corridor. There was no one else staying tonight, the Restaurant and bar were closing in half an hour, so she would not be disturbed by any noise from there.

Jenny took the key, asked if a large whisky, with some Ginger ale, could be sent up, to her room, and went up the ornate curved stair case, a reminder of the more affluent days of the town. The rest of the decor was beginning to look tired and she was beginning to feel the same, she thought briefly of going down and having a drink and something to eat, then rejected the idea. She would still need to be on top of things in the morning.

The room was clean and tidy, the bed large, with old oak head and end boards, a deep feather and kapok mattress covered with crisp white sheets, soft feather pillows and a huge quilt. She tossed the bag on the chair and opened the sash window, pulling the drapes across, then folded down the bed.

There was a knock on the door. Jenny opened it and found the receptionist there with her drink, also on the tray with two miniatures and a small bottle of Dry Ginger ale, she took it, thanked the girl and shut the door, she set the tray on a table at the end of the room and picked up the glass. After taking a long pull at the strong amber liquid almost emptying the glass. She put it on the bedside table, slipped off her jeans, shirt and underwear and fell onto the softness of the mattress, feeling the cool luxury of the linen on her tanned skin. Within minutes she was asleep.

* *

Maxine excused herself from the table and went out to the Toilets. She was beginning to feel the effects of the four glasses of Champagne, both in her head and her bladder. As she crossed the room Maxine was aware of the eyes following her. Those of her husband, Hans Jongejan, and several other men in the bar. She felt flattered by the attention on one hand, and degraded on the other, she loved being admired, and loved her husband, even though she had not always been as honest as she should have with him, and she knew that was the same with him.

There was something on her mind tonight that worried and confused her - in fact more than one thing, in particular their daughter - they hadn't ever let her know what they did - and were going to do – they had always been just Mum and Dad the Law firm - and now they were going to leave. Yes, they had her well looked after - but she was their daughter, their flesh - their blood, well almost, "were they doing the right thing - by her - by themselves".

Maxine went into the toilets and looked at herself in the mirror. Her mind flashed across it all, all the ten years of deceit, and she knew that there was no way to turn back.

* *

Troone called out to the figure by the car – 'Help me – over here – I'm over here – I'm not in the car!' He realised what a stupid statement that was, and he saw that it was Sergeant Smith!

Roger Smith turned at the sound of the voice. 'What the hell happened to you, do you often park in strange places and have beach bonfires.'

'Very funny, get me out of here. I've a broken leg, apart from that a bit scorched and a few cuts, but generally I think I'll live!. What the hell are you doing here anyway? I just called Mackay, he was going to get MacDonald to get someone down here, I didn't expect express treatment.'

'No, I haven't heard from either of them, but I've got one of our earlier accidents with me, Andrea Jones, we've moved her out - safety precaution. We need to talk to her and the way things have been going in the last twenty four hours it seems that people are rather expendable.' Smith knelt by Troone, inspecting the damage. 'It's not going to be that easy to get you up the bank, let's have a look at that leg.' He carefully tore the leg of the slacks off the injured right leg. Above and below the knee was already blackening from bleeding and bruising – and the knee was badly swollen, but there was no broken skin or bones protruding. 'It looks a bit on the nasty side but I can't tell if there's any serious damage.' Smith searched quickly around the area and came up with a flat piece of drift wood. He ripped the rest of the trouser leg away and tore it into strips, binding the splint to the leg.

'It may only be badly sprained or cracked, that may help to give it some support, right let's get you out of here.'

There was a part of the bank just along from their right that had crumbled away to a slight ramp, they were able to slowly manoeuvre their way up and onto the roadside. At the car, he was able to move the passenger seat far enough back for Troone to stretch out. Andrea Jones was still in her drug induced sleep on the back seat. Once he had strapped Troone in, Smith called MacDonald, relating the situation. The conversation was brief, with MacDonald firstly surprised, then disturbed that he hadn't heard from Mackay. He suggested that Smith keep a good eye out for the blue hatch, and that road blocks should be in place by now, but they had been on his initiative, not from information from Mackay, or from Bronson.. He would be checking in the next few minutes to see that they were, and inform Mackay that Troone had been picked up. He would be asking a few pertinent questions about the lack of communication regarding several matters.

Smith was about to tell him the Marguriette had also ordered blocks, and though he shouldn't have neglected to relay the information, thought what the hell, let's see who does what, and if it works! Twenty minutes later Smith drove into the main road of the next town, the last of the Hotels and Restaurants were closing, and there were few people on the street, a few slightly intoxicated young people poured onto the footpath from a Bar, their raucous voices caught his attention. Outside the same building was parked the dark blue hatchback. It was the only car on the street.

Smith called MacDonald. 'She's here, her cars parked outside a Hotel, will I get the local guys to pick her up, or what, do we actually have anything on her? I mean the incident with Rory – could have just been an unfortunate accident? No, I'm being bloody stupid – there's also the matter of Cheryl Brown – sorry, not thinking.' He hadn't seen the information Bronson had, nor been kept up to date with the present situation. Jenny Sullivan and Jim Bland being at Primmer's Lodge.

MacDonald became indecisive. 'Can you get your patients to the Hospital, get them looked at and kept under watch, see the local men, get their assistance, they know about the road blocks. Then just watch her car, see what happens, whether she is staying there or just stopped for a meal and a drink. I'll call Bronson, check with her, see what she wants done. I also have been unable to raise Mackay, or anyone else at the station - seems a bit strange.'

'They've probably gone home for the night – left the hard yards to us, nothing unusual. Though Trooney here, was obviously being helpful.' Then Smith acknowledged that he would see what he could do. MacDonald would call back when he'd spoken to Bronson.

* *

Marguriette was about to drink her Cognac, when the phone rang. She went out of the room and picked up an extension on the landing. She listened for a few minutes.

Rory could see out the door of the bedroom and saw the frown of concern on her face. She turned away from him and began to speak to the caller, he couldn't make out who she was talking to, or saying. He could see however, from the look of her body language, it was important.

Bronson slowly put the receiver back on the cradle. She stood for a moment, as if reflecting on what had been talked about.

'What's the matter, was that good news or bad news?' Rory queried from the bedroom but he could see in her eyes as she came back - it was bad news.

Marguriette picked up her Cognac, drained the glass, and poured another. She sat on the edge of the bed beside him, but still didn't say anything. Rory decided not to probe, just to wait, it was plain that she was mulling over something important.

'I really am getting tired of all this, I think I'm getting past all this crap. Why the shit some people cannot make decisions when they know the situation, is quite beyond me.' Her tone was sharp, irritated. Her comment brought a look of surprise to Rory's face, his eyebrows shot up and he shifted up the bed so he was leaning against the wall..

'What the hell are you going on about, who was that on the phone - what's gone wrong now.' He looked at her intently.

'They know where Jenny Sullivan is, they want to know what to do, they have road blocks in place, or so they say - she can't go anywhere - unless there is another - yes that's it, she's stopped for a reason. She might want a rest but there is something else - I'll bet on it. Not only that, Fred Troone's car went off the road, and he lost her. It could've been very nasty for him. It was by luck I guess, that Smith had left later with Andrea Jones. He fortunately came across the wreck and picked him up. He thinks Troone might have a broken leg, he's got bad bruising, a few cuts – some, well, several deep, he's lost a bit of the red stuff. You know, bit of blood and gore – and a rather charred car! How are you feeling? I mean, apart from the stiffness and the cut leg, how are you - mentally - alert - dull – dim witted - not with it?'

'I am, believe it or not feeling alright, I'm still tired, but then - that I think applies to both of us. What have you in mind. We've had a bit to drink, you're not thinking that we should head out tonight. Are you?'

'No, not really, but I think that we should have a slight change of plan, we both go down in the chopper, and go into where she is, they will be watching her, and if she moves they will know, and she can't get out by road. Then when we have dealt with that, then we both go up and pick up Primmer, Bland and co.'

'Wouldn't it be more to the point if we stayed up here and tried to track down the other three. They could be on their way to God knows where by now or planning something - oh I don't know, maybe I am too bloody tired to think about it right now.' He held out his brandy balloon. 'I shouldn't but I will - more please.' As she poured it he drank some of the coffee, which was now getting cold. 'I mean it's just one damn girl, surely they can handle that. How many have we got down there, by all means send the backup there first, but I really don't feel that we are necessary, I think that we could be over-reacting.'

Marguriette ran her hand through her luxurious hair. Her body sagged, she breathed a long deep rattling sigh.

'You're right, if we are going to play Superman and Supergirl, we should concentrate on where these others are. Then hope like hell they don't have a bag of Kryptonite!' She half laughed at her idea, then swung herself around and leant against the bed head next to him. She swung her long legs up, and poured herself another shot of Cognac. 'And, yes we've had too much to drink, and it's been a long bloody day, after several other long bloody days. Shall I go and heat the coffee up, it's gone cold.'

'No, don't worry about it, it's not important, there are other matters that are.'

'You know, this whole thing really just seems to be out of control. I mean, well, we seemed to be on top of it, but we are in fact not. What have we really got - nothing. We don't even know who exactly, or where these ring leaders, for want of a better word, are - or why - despite all the guff in the files and the supposes and the supposes nots - what are we doing! - Have we really got a case against them. I mean really - is it a crime to be seen with people that live near you in the same town, or at a party – a pub – whatever? He looked at her intently. 'Small town folk socialise - they do things together. Some of the information gathered in their files, does in a way, point to some sort of collusion, but some of it is pretty bloody sketchy.

Perhaps we can pin something on Jenny Sullivan, perhaps we can't. The file that you say has the linchpin is with your boss, or is it - have you actually seen it, and read it?'

'No.' Her reply.' No – I said that I had and – well I have had a quick glance at it – but no nothing in depth. Which bloody well reminds me – where the hell is 'Clarke Kent Moorhead'! He should have called back damned ages ago – he said ten minutes! Should I call him?'

'I don't think it matters whether you call him or wait. Anyway - well what use is it, and why didn't you see it, you said that you had seen some of it - I thought you were the big cheese in this?'

'No - I lied and I don't know why I did, and, no I'm not the big cheese in this.' her voice had become very quiet. 'But that's another story. But one thing I do know and I have told you – these people – shit you know this – they are evil and they are dealing in some very nasty stuff never mind the diamonds and the gold – it's the drugs and the prostitution! That is the worst part and they are getting away with it – aren't they.'

They lapsed into silence. As they sipped their drinks, their shoulders touched. Marguriette tilted her head, resting it on Rorys, her hair fell, brushing his face.

SEVENTEEN

T he wind blew the short wrap skirt around her thighs, it ruffled her hair and cooled the smear of perspiration from her forehead. She looked down into the shadows below and watched the swelling waves pour through the broken hull, rocking the body back and forth in the dirty water. The blood from the head wound spread from the tangled hair, staining the sea and what had been clean white clothing. She dropped the heavy piece of timber, it fell, bouncing off the jutting tangled jaws of the barges broken ribs, before it splashed into the water by the body. A larger wave came through the gaping hole in the side of the wrecked hull, lifting the lifeless form, rolling it over. The dead eyes stared up at her. She felt their accusation. 'What have you done to me? Why have you done this to me? I loved you - I loved you!'

Jenny Sullivan sat up in the bed. She was drenched in sweat, her breathing fast, ragged, her heart pounding. She stared around the room, disorientated! Then the breeze through the open window rustled the curtains apart, letting in the mornings soft grey light.

Realising where she was, her breathing slowed. She threw back the cover and stepped from the big soft bed. Padding across to the window she peered out the crack in the drapes. She took hold of them, stopping their movement, holding them on either side of her face, framing it, as she looked out into the beginning of the day, out over the town, the buildings across the street to the spread of open land that bordered the old river port.

The dream had deeply disturbed her, taking her back to the times that

433

she had been alone with Cheryl, alone, wanted and wanting. The thought of the passion of those moments brought a rush of blood, it coursed through her, warming her body, colouring her cheeks. Though they had only been "moments" for her, they'd not been for the other woman, who had become aggressively passionate and obsessive about her.

But then Cheryl had been aggressively passionate and obsessive about a number of people. Particularly Jenny's father Peter Sullivan.

Feeling the cool breeze eased the heat of the dream, and the other feelings in her body. Goose bumps formed on her taut smooth skin. She shivered, from that, and the memories. Below the street was deserted, she looked at her watch, it was four thirty. Jenny turned from the window, picked up a sheet from the bed and wound it around her, took the towel off the end the bed, went out of the room, and down two doors to the bathroom. She turned on the taps to the shower - an ancient brass affair, over a large chipped enamel tray. When it was hot enough she stepped in and let the heavy tumble of water flow over her, but for only a few minutes, she didn't have time to linger.

Refreshed, and now very wide awake, she towelled herself vigorously, did her hair and quickly cleaned her teeth and applied her make-up, wrapped herself in the sheet again and went back to the room. From her bag, she took clean underwear a fresh shirt, and jeans, and dressed. Jenny stuffed all the clothes she he'd been wearing, and her personal items, including her wallet and passport into the bag and pushed it into a back corner of the deep wardrobe, she knew they would be found – but that wouldn't matter. She would be replacing everything, very shortly. After she'd connected with Jongejan and the McGillveray. By the time they were discovered she would be well gone.

Jenny closed the door of her room and went down stairs, she turned away from the main door and down a corridor that lead to the back of the building. At the end it branched off to the left and right, she checked both directions. To the right another short passage led out to an alleyway. It was, as far as she could see, empty. Back in the other direction, another door went out onto a side street. She went back to the main foyer, pausing to see if she could be seen coming out from the back instead of down the stairs.

At the reception desk the early morning staff was facing away from her. She came out of the passage and came crossed the lobby, as she went passed the desk she gave a cheery wave and good morning. The man behind the counter, responded with a smile and "Off for a walk?" She nodded and went out into the main street.

As she opened the car door, she peered up and down the street, there were a few people gathering near a lonely, early morning Takeaway Caravan. Across the other side, a drunk was asleep in a doorway, two delivery trucks were outside some shops about two hundred metres away. She could see the clock tower, it was nearly five am, she had about thirty minutes.

*   *

Maxine came back into the Bar, the two men had their heads close together. 'Talking together like conspirators,' she muttered to herself, 'But that is of course exactly what they are, we all are.' She thought again about the knowledge that there was no turning back, and she thought of the note that she should have left for their daughter. She thought of the way in which they had deceived so many people - in particular right at this moment - one - someone that they had allowed so close - Rory Calder. Then she remembered how Euan had feelings, very deep feelings, for Rory's wife, Serena. That she had known, and never ever told him, or Rory, that she knew. The despising and loathing of herself grew and knotted in her stomach.

The two men looked up as she came back to the table. 'We have selected our meals, and as you were not here we organised you as well, I hope you don't mind – but I have an idea what you would like.' Euan smiled at her. 'Shall we go through, we have a lot to do yet, and I am getting hungry.'

Maxine nodded vaguely. 'Yes, alright - yes I am a bit too, got a bit of a head ache as well, must be too many bubbles, need food.' She attempted a smile but it somehow didn't work.

Euan came and put his arm around her shoulder. He was now in one of his good expansive moods. The wine had taken some of the earlier tension out of him.

'Come along you'll be fine, get some good solid food into you. I ordered the Roast beef and Yorkshire pudding for you. Hans is having a New York cut steak with blue vein and garlic butter, and I'm having Pork fillets with Camembert and Spiced apricots, all sounds very appetising, should keep us going for a while.'

Maxine said nothing, she was not sure why, having just said that perhaps she needed to eat, but the sound of that food right that second, made her feel nauseous. 'Could I have a double brandy please, little ice a little dry?'

Hans had been standing near by listening. 'I'll organise that, and some Red, you two get to the table.' He disappeared towards the secluded bar in the corner.

They walked into the dining area, to a table that had been prepared for them. It was well away from anyone else in the room. As they sat down, she spoke quietly to Euan.

'Why are we having so much to drink? Everyone of us is saying that we've a lot to get through, a lot to learn, yet we're acting as if we are on a damned holiday jaunt!' She sighed, looking up into his eyes. 'Sorry, I'm tired, and not seeing things in my usual way. I have always liked a good time and fun, but this somehow, isn't, is it? This is very very serious!. Oh what the hell, I'll probably feel better after the brandy and some food. I guess I'm being melodramatic.'

Jongejan came back to the table. The waiter followed, carrying a tray with the brandy, four wine glasses and a bottle of one of Hans' favourite South African reds. The waiter put it all on the table and opened the wine. As the men sipped the wine, Maxine took a good gulp of the brandy, it burned down her throat and quickly warmed the uneasy feelings.

Hans was about to begin another toast, when two waitress's in Olde English costume, arrived with their meals.

That was forgotten as they set about the meal. The conversation lapsed, as they started eating and drinking. Maxine picked at her food, the flavours although good, made no impression on her pallet. After five minutes she excused herself. 'My headache hasn't improved, I'll just pop up to the room and get some aspirin, I won't be long. Perhaps you could ask the waitress if they could cover my meal and keep it warm for me?' She started to walk away from the table, then stopped and came back. 'I know this is stupid, but what number room was it, and did they get our bags and take them - up, I know I have been there but with everything that's been going through my mind I seem to have suddenly become very absent-minded.'

Hans looked up from his meal. 'They didn't say? I'm sure that I did ask them to collect our overnight bags, to take them up, which surely you saw when you were there freshening up. But, I forgot to ask the numbers of the rooms. Sorry Maxine, you will have to ask at the desk.' He gave her a look as if to say "your brain is befuddled with booze you silly cow". He returned to his meal, his large bald head, hovering over his plate.

'I didn't go up to the room just now, I was in the toilets.' She scowled at Hans then left them, going out to the reception she asked about their rooms. The clerk was very helpful, that she would take her up and show her exactly where things were.

The rooms were situated at the back of the Inn, the girl explained that although they were over the kitchen and dining area they were well sound proofed and afforded the best and quietest, with views out over the river and the farm land beyond. She laughed at her explanation. 'Of course not that it matters at the moment it's dark, and you can only see a few lights of houses and the motorway.' She smiled at the older woman and as she left her, she turned momentarily. 'Are you okay, you look, - kind of exhausted?'

Maxine assured her that she would be fine. When she had gone she found her bag and toiletries, rummaged and found the packet of aspirin. She poured a glass of water from the jug on top of mini bar and swallowed the tabs. She sat on the bed letting her head fall forward, stretching the taut tense muscles of her neck. Maxine reached over and picked up the phone by the bed. She sat momentarily with it held half way to her ear, she almost replaced the receiver, then suddenly she reached over, pressed the button to reconnect the dial tone and dialled for an outside line, when the dial tone came on she began to press the numbers.

* *

The grey of the dawn crept across the flat water and mud of the bay, it's cold fingers stretched out touching the town as the tide too crept over the last of the mud. The water slithered across creeping up to, and beginning it's cling to the piles of the wharf.

MacDonald and Thomas sat huddled into the seats of the police car. They'd moved out of the direct sight of Bland's house. But they could see if there was any movement, in or out. There hadn't been any, since the lights had come on again, just before midnight when Bland arrived home from Primmers Lodge. They decided not to approach him now until the morning – unless, there were further developments.

The report from Eton and Clooney, was the same. They reported that there was no sign of anyone coming to or leaving the house since Jenny Sullivan. They'd seen Bland arrive, but they hadn't seen him leave. He must have been able to get out a door that they were unable to watch, or they had had a momentary lapse in their concentration. However, MacDonald felt that it didn't matter, they knew where they were now. He decided that there was no point in continuing the present status of their watch. He called them again.

'You guys may as well get back down here, I don't think that anything will happen now, I think they will all play very low key and hope that we disappear into the morning mist, they will of course be very much mistaken about that. They may start to have thoughts about it when they hear the chopper, but by then it will be too late. Besides, we will need to liaise with the Squad when they get here, it will be their call as how it is to be handled, and they will want to deploy their men and us as they see fit. 'After we have briefed them.' MacDonald thought of calling Bronson, then decided, "To hell with it and her" there's nothing she can do, or contribute, that'll be of any use.

It was a cool morning and they were all uncomfortable and hungry. 'Come on down and we'll try to dig up some coffee and something to eat. Anyway, if they try to leave the house, they have to come down the road over the back there and we can see it clearly.' He got out of the car and stretched, feeling irritable and tired. He had always hated doing long nights of surveillance, even more than he disliked his colleague Bronson.

Eton and Clooney arrived back five minutes after MacDonald had spoken to them. They looked even more tired than he and Thomas, at least they had been able to sit in the comfort and warmth of the car. Both men as they came up across to them, looked as if they had been dragged through a gorse bush backwards and then wet down with a fine spray from a garden hose. Their hair and clothing, was damp from the morning dew.

'Is there somewhere that we can get coffee and some food?' MacDonald asked Clooney,

'I think you are being rather optimistic, this place doesn't open until nine o'clock, and then you would be pushing your luck. Besides it's seven thirty five now, I'll call my wife and see if she can rustle up something. Though my guess would be that she wont be terribly impressed. What time are we expecting the storm troopers?'

'They should be here within an hour. According to the oracle organiser.' As he finished talking the sound of the helicopter could be heard echoing off the cliffs around the bay, the four men turned to see it come around the point to the north. It was flying very low, almost touching the water, and within minutes it was hovering then lowering onto the recreation area. The blades slowed and six men tumbled out, but they could see that there were still four men, plus the pilot on board, the chopper took off again immediately.

'Well bugger me, I'm wrong about the timing. Bronson – or Moorhead at last, must have decided to be more decisive! I guess there goes our opportunity for an early breakfast. I wonder where the rest of them are off to?' MacDonald watched the Helicopter swirl up and away from the village. MacDonald stirred himself into action and drove across to the field, he got out and approached to the six men. 'What's the guts guys where are the rest going? You're far earlier than I expected! Sorry we weren't right here, Johnny on the spot, but we've been on night watch! And nothing much has come out to watch – yet.'

'They're headed back down the coast, we were all going there first to arrest the girl. But Moorhead changed the plans.' It was a young constable who spoke, he was tall, fair headed, confident. 'I've been given charge of this lot, I'm Senior Constable Williams - under your instructions of course Sir. We were a bit thin on the ground this morning, something to do with the busy city weekend crime scene I guess. Right, what's the lay of the land here?'

MacDonald quickly explained the situation and where the people were that they needed to have an intense chat with. It was agreed that most of the squad would go up to the Lodge, it was more likely people could get away from there, easier than Blands.

Eton, and Clooney, with their men, got under way. They crossed the field to the road. Then Eton, with one, went to the Gondola, and Clooney with the other, up through the bush track.

MacDonald sent Thomas with the remaining men to the back of the Bland house, to move as wide and far as possible around the adjoining property and keep well out of sight. He and the last man would go to the front door. As he gave the instructions, and the need for keeping out of sight, a low profile he thought – 'What the hell – they will, along with everyone else in the fucking place, have all seen and heard the bloody chopper – they'll know exactly what's going on!'

He continued the instructions - that no-one was to make any move until all had reported that they were in position. He gave the men going to the Lodge ten minutes, and while he waited he called Mackay to inform him, and to ask for his assistance. He realised as he made the call that he was well out of line and should have brought the man in on this earlier, he just hoped that this oversight would not be mentioned to certain people later. MacDonald sighed with resignation as he made the call.

Mackay was his usual surly unhelpful self when he heard what MacDonald had to say. It was plain he felt he should have been called into this much earlier and been part of the operation. MacDonald gritted his teeth and apologised. 'It's just a silly mistake, an oversight, something that slipped my mind in the heat of the moment'. It was clear from the tone of Mackay's reply, and his foul language, that assured MacDonald that it wouldn't go "unmentioned"! There would be repercussions. MacDonald swore under his breath and berated himself for his stupidity. Bronson was going to love this, and Moorhead would enjoy it even more! He switched off his phone and leant back against the bonnet of the car, the other officer stood apart from him, his eyes intent on the house and the surrounding area.

*   *

Marguriette moved down the bed, snuggling in, until her head was resting on Rory's chest. 'A little bit like old times, when we used to sit up late and talk in front of the fire, the rain sleeting down and the wind rattling the windows of the house. God it caught everything from all directions, that place perched up there above the harbour, the views may have been spectacular, and the house may have been solid, but it sure did make a racket with both the southerly and the northerly. But we had some good times there Rory. So I guess when I say this is a bit like old times, I mean the sitting and talking and enjoying good cognac - there sure ain't any wind here! Never get any it's so sheltered, you can hear it in the trees sometimes, but I'm so tucked away and private sometimes you can almost forget that there is another world out there.' She snuggled down further and wrapped an arm over his chest. 'Unfortunately - tonight there are other matters that are disturbing the peace!'

Rory turned his head slightly towards her and looked at her. Her eyes were closed and her face for the first time since they had met again was relaxed. 'Whether it's my company or the Cognac, I'll never know,' he thought to himself. Then aloud.

'Yes, they were, weren't they. Funny how things change so much, just small but significant misunderstandings - people not wanting to face the truth - interfering - destroying - it seems that almost everything from that time has been like that, and here it is again, different but still things being destroyed. I think when this is over I'll take a break, a real holiday, get away and evaluate where I am. I don't think that I want to carry on the way things are, or have been.' Rory stopped talking and tried to look at her. Her breathing had become very even and quiet, she had fallen asleep. 'Fuck – well that was a waste of time- or was it – at least I said something and maybe something of value? Maybe?' He was about to move her gently and get her into a more comfortable position when the phone shrilled, giving them both a hell of a fright. Bronson sat up with a jerk and jumped off the bed.

'Who - what the hell is that, who's ringing at this time of the night!' She looked at her watch, it was nearly twelve thirty. Marguriette stumbled out and picked up the phone, she barked irritably into it. The tranquil mood, lost. 'Yes! What!'

'Moorhead here, it took me a bit longer than I expected to sort this out. However, you are on duty, and call, while we try to wrap this thing up. So shut up and listen, and don't be so bloody short and grumpy with me! Sorry, but we've made a decision - you two are staying put to see what develops up here.'

But Marguriette interrupted. 'Who the hell is this 'we' that have made a decision? It's supposed to be you and me!' She was tired and angry.

'It doesn't damned well matter who the 'we' is and I said to shut up and listen – do just that – please.' The end of the statement was softer. 'Now, a Squad will go down at first light, but we can only spare ten. Six will work with MacDonald and four will look after the Sullivan girl, provided of course she hasn't slipped away again! Smith is hopefully keeping an eye on her, with a couple of men from the town. He's also arranged things at the Hospital for the Jones woman and Troone,' Moorhead stopped talking. There was the rustling of paper, and tapping on a key board, then he started again.

'Now, according to our records, that I'm looking at here, and these are on my computer – not from your funny files! Your friend and ours, Mr Rory Calder, knows the McGillverays very well. Although plainly not as well as he may now have liked, with the information that he now has! They have a daughter - where is she? Is she in on this deal? My gut feeling that she knows nothing about it, she doesn't appear in any of our investigations, photographs, files - nothing - we have no record on her apart that she worked in their office as their secretary. She may well be the key to their whereabouts.'

'We'll look into it, Rory is of course still here, he's still a bit shocked and sore but he's a resilient bastard, and after he gets a bit of sleep we will make an early start. I'll have a word with him now.' Bronson hung up and went back to the bedroom. Rory had finished his drink and was leaning against the headboard his eyes closed. She tiptoed over to the bed to see if he was asleep.

'No I'm not - and what now? Who was that toad that decided to disturb us. Mr. bloody Moorhead again?' He opened one eye – he had a silly grin on his face.

'Yes, it was the Sacred Bull, just updated a couple of things. He thinks he has a new slant on things. Maxine McGillveray's daughter could well be the link to finding them. Why the hell didn't you think of that before, you know her well, well at least I presume you still do. He doesn't, for some reason, feel that she is a part of it.' Marguriette sat on the bed, her face pensive, her hand strayed to Rory's chest, then slid down over his stomach. She sat silent for a few moments. Her fingers caressing his taught skin. 'Colin doesn't think, from what he's got on file, points to her knowing anything. Would that be right, do you think that they would, or could keep her out of it, in the dark about their activities?'

'Sarah? Sarah!' Rory sat bolt upright. 'Shit - of course – he might well be right! Why hadn't I thought of her before, yet, why should I? Until a few hours ago. I didn't even know that they were even part of it – this – this whatever 'it' is!. God, I'm a blind fuckwit. Maybe that's a bit harsh on myself, but they certainly must be having a bloody good laugh at me.' He thought for a few seconds. 'She may not know anything, she's a sort of innocent type, reclusive, prone to depression. They always kept her sheltered from most of the people they dealt with. She was okay as their helper – reception and so on, though I have a feeling that she may have had another life – one they did not know about at all. I spent quite a lot of time with her when I got back – after Serena and the children.' He hesitated. 'I got on well with her, I thought of myself as a pseudo Uncle. I have a funny feeling she did not want to see me quite that way. She lives in a flat on her own. Have you got a telephone book handy - let's see if we can track her down – now!'

Bronson went and collected the phone book. Rory thumbed quickly through and found what he thought was the number. 'Does that phone reach in here?'

'No, but you could try the one beside the bed there,' she waved at the far side of the room. 'I think that'll work fine.' She grinned at him. 'I could have answered on that, but I may have had to crawl across that fine body of yours, and you may not have approved. You may have thought of me as a wanton wench only interested in the delights of sex and sin.'

Rory gave her an old fashioned look, and reached for the receiver. It was cordless , he tapped out the number on the hand piece.

The phone didn't ring but went straight into answer phone. 'I'm sorry, Sarah is not here right now, please leave your name and number and I'll call you back as soon as I can.'

'It's her number alright. Right name, right voice, but not there.' He put the hand piece back on its cradle.

'Why didn't you leave a message?' She looked at him quizzically.

'Oh famous detective sleuth - I wonder why? I've never rung the girl at her home before, and why the hell would I be ringing at this time of the morning? If she does know anything about what they are doing, she would certainly be alerted wouldn't she, she may be there, she may not. I don't even know whether or not she has a boy friend - some Uncle. I don't know much about her life outside that of her family at all. But we could pay her a visit at their office - first thing, she is usually always there early - like very early, conscientious little beast - often as early as six!'

Marguriette stood by the bed, her eyes softened. Her annoyance from the call had gone. 'I'm glad you said in the morning, I'm rather liking it here! I'd suddenly had visions of us traipsing across town in search of her - when you already know that she's probably not home!'

*   *

Jenny Sullivan began her drive around to the sports ground. She went through different streets than when she had arrived in the town. She watched her mirror constantly and stopped at different places, two dairies – where she bought a paper in one and milk in another – then at two other stops she went into houses that appeared empty – taking the paper to one and the milk to another. She hadn't been followed as far as she could make out. She arrived – twenty minutes later at the Sports ground, parking the car between the buildings as she had before. After turning off the motor she watched the area for a short time, when she was sure that there was no-one around she got out and opened the hatch. She took out the cartons placing them in the dark shadows of the Grandstand. It was a risk, but she would be back in less than ten minutes.

* *

Roger Smith had watched the front of the hotel from a Lunch Bar across the road. Although it was closed and had been for the weekend, one of the local Constables knew the owner and had been able to arrange for him to get in, it was that sort of town – favours for favours.

The same constable was sitting in an unmarked car in an alley at the back of the Hotel, where he had a good yet concealed view of any rear exits. Then unfortunately, he had decided that he needed to go to the toilet. It was in those few minutes that Sullivan left the building.

When he returned those moments later, her car was gone. He called the Officer watching the rear. 'Bugger! - I needed a leak and the bitch scarpered! But - she can't have known I was here! Have you seen any movement any sign of her, where the hell has she gone. Alert the "blocks" at the south end, she may be on her way out.' He was about to ring off when the blue hatch appeared, coming back down the street from the northern end of the main street.

'Hang on, she's bloody well back!' He watched the girl get out of the car, and go back into the Hotel. 'Okay, seems a false alarm, but I wonder where she's been at this time of the morning. Right let's get back to it, she seems a slippery little critter, we'd better not take our eyes off her.'

As Jenny parked back in the front of the Hotel, she looked at her watch. It was now twenty minutes past five, she would have to move quickly, but cautiously. There was a feeling in her stomach, a feeling of excitement, a feeling of fear and expectation, and a feeling that there was always the possibility that she was being watched. She glanced around the street, there was a bit more activity than fifteen minutes ago. It would take her ten minutes to walk back. She went into the hotel, not bothering to lock the car, as if she would come back shortly.

Jenny ran up the stairs to her room - it was just an off chance act, one stirred from the fear that there could be someone watching her. She was far to close to getting what she wanted - wealth - and freedom from the past she had bound around herself. She went over to the window and peered through the crack in the curtains, down into the street. Time was running short, but she stayed - searching for anything that may not be that which she wished to see.

Finally, she decided it was clear. Then, as she pushed the drapes open she saw the movement in the window of the shop opposite. The light was sufficient through the window for her to see clearly who it was, and she recognised the Sergeant, Roger Smith, she had seen him in the village, she knew she was not mistaken, he was looking straight up at the window of her room.

*   *

Maxine listened to the phone ring, then the click as it went into answer phone. She often didn't know where or what her daughter was doing, but she was twenty five, why should she, but outside of the office Sarah led strictly her own life and although her feelings for her family were strong she rarely let them into her private world. She listened to the message, she had been holding her breath with the tension of what she was doing. They had been over this many times - "*we must keep Sarah out of it*". But this was her baby, and she was leaving her, abandoning her, and in a way she would have to face the consequences of their actions.

'Sarah - it's me - of course, your mother. Dad and I are - well, we're going away - for quite a while, overseas. Um, some work with Uncle Hans. We may be gone longer than we originally thought, planned, and, we won't be in contact for sometime, please forgive us for not telling you, but we can't, and I don't want you, to tell anyone - but - yes - please just one - say to Uncle Rory - sorry - just that. He may understand, he may not - but tell him - sorry. We love you very very much, but we have to do this - work. Take care of yourself". She was reaching across to hang up the phone, when the door opened. Euan came into the room.

'What the hell are you doing, I thought you were only going to be a few minutes - who the hell are you talking to!' He was shouting, agitated, angry. 'We're not to talk to anyone - what do you bloody well think you are doing you stupid bitch!' He stood menacingly in front of her.

The tears began to flow down Maxine's face, heavy sobs began to shake her.

'I can't, I won't go without at least - a message for Sarah. For God's sake, she's our daughter! Surely - surely we can just say goodbye? Anyway, all I said was that we have to go overseas on business, and we are not sure how long we will be. She's supposed to work for us, how is she going to live, what is she going to do when she goes into work tomorrow? We're abandoning her for our own greed - and yes I suppose protection, if she knows nothing, she can't tell anybody anything can she?'

Euan's expression changed, the harshness left his voice, he sat on the bed with her. 'No, I guess you're right. Anyway, I haven't told you, but I left a letter on her desk, no explanation, just to close the office for the time being. There's a message on the answer phone for any clients that call, vague, no specifics, and I've told her to use the Number three account for her own needs, until we get back. There's enough in it to keep her going for at least ten years, by then it won't matter. Come on, let's get back to dinner. Hans will be wondering what we're up to, and we will I'm sure, have plenty of time to recriminate over our actions in the years to come, whether we want to or not.'

Maxine got up off the bed and leant on him momentarily then stepped back and looked into her husband's eyes. 'We don't have a choice anyway. We have put our hand to the wheel and it's now - this - this vehicle, is leading us. We are not doing the steering any more, at least not now - right at this moment - if ever again.'

They went back to the Restaurant. Hans was deep in conversation with one of the waitress's. They would both take a private bet with themselves that it wasn't about the food. They glanced at each other and shrugged.

Jongejan had his hand touching the young woman's thigh, his lecherous eyes boring into her.

It was the waitress who'd taken Maxine's meal to keep warm. She had seen them coming and was able to release herself, and go and get her meal.

The pair sat back at the table, and Hans turned the conversation back to their main task of the evening.

*   *

A call came through from Eton. They were all in position, there appeared to be no movement in the house, he presumed that they were all still asleep.

MacDonald suddenly realised that he had overlooked a rather important detail, they had no cars in place, only the men on foot.

'You stupid bastard, how could you be so bloody incompetent.' He said it aloud, and the men standing nearby turned and looked at him.

'What's the problem?' It was Senior Constable Williams.

'Uh, nothing, I just have to make a call.' He called Eton back. 'Hold your positions, don't move in yet.' Then Mackay. This was a call that he was not going to enjoy, Mackay may, but he would not!

'Hello, Sergeant Mackay? MacDonald, sorry, but we need your assistance, urgently. Get two patrol cars up to the lodge immediately.' He listened to the reply, then. 'I know, – yes - I know I should have, I guess, - well I'm sorry, but I'm actually not asking, I'm bloody ordering, you! Report it if you like, I don't at this moment give a monkey's bugger. Just get two up here, and park in the driveway, back from the house, block it. Don't approach anybody, until you get the okay from Eton.' He cut off his phone, his face red with the embarrassment at his incompetence, and it being observed by the young Officer. He called Eton again, and told him what he'd arranged with Mackay. He tried to keep his voice calm, as if the oversight was of little significance, but wasn't successful - the strain was beginning to tell.

He looked back at the town, and saw two cars leave the local station house.

'Okay, they're on their way, three minutes should be enough, then move in.' He clipped his phone to his belt and waved to the tall blonde man to follow him. They jogged across the road. Thomas and his man saw them, they moved around to the rear of Bland's house.

Constable Eton directed his men in to three different positions. Two to go to the front door, one to the French doors that led out the far side, and he and the last Constable went to the back door. He pressed the bell, there was no response, He tried again also knocking solidly on the door. He waited another minute, he banged it hard with his fist, calling out as he pushed the bell for at least thirty seconds. His patience was getting short! Then he heard a dog barking and movement inside the house. Through the sheer curtains he could see someone come into the kitchen with a large black labrador dog. He knocked again, this time, without quite the same vigour.

The door opened a few inches, to the extent the heavy safety chain would allow.

'Yes, what is it, is there something wrong? Can I help you, it's very early. We don't have any vacancies.'

Eton looked at the woman peering at him, he'd never seen her before! She was small, very pretty with short curly red hair, she was wearing in a long white satin dressing gown. And plainly had just woken up. He was positive she hadn't been there earlier, when they'd been watching Jenny Sullivan, the Primmers and Bland.

'I would like to speak with Mr. Franklin Primmer and Mrs Amelia Primmer. Would you ask them to come down please?' He flipped open his ID.

The woman looked at it, completely non-plussed, she shrugged. 'I'm sorry, but there's definitely no-one of that name here. My husband Michael and I own and run this place.'

Eton was completely perplexed by this. 'What? Look, I'm sorry, but I'm sure, positive, this property is owned by the Primmers, Frank and Amelia Primmer! I saw them here earlier, I've talked to them, they've lived here in the village for some years, at least four or five I've been told. What's your name?'

'Jane Flint, and I don't like your tone Officer.' Her faced had flushed and her eyes were flashing – angry. 'I just told you that my husband and I have owned, and run the Lodge, for more than five years, we have never heard of anyone by the name of Primmer. What do you want with them, you have obviously got the wrong place, and the wrong people. Perhaps you had better come in and discuss this ridiculous accusation!' She pulled the door open, as a voice came from behind her, from the other side of the kitchen.

'What's the matter Jane, who is it.' A man came across the room and stood beside her. He too, looked as if he had just got out of bed, and was wearing a tartan night shirt and bare feet, he was tall – lean - dark tight curly hair, and had at least two days growth of beard.

Eton looked from one to the other. 'Look I don't know what you're up to, but this place is owned by Franklin and Amelia Primmer, and earlier - last night, they were visited by their friends, Jim Bland and a girl - Jenny Sullivan. I need to talk to them - urgently!' His voice took on a frustrated edge.

'It's bloody early for a visit from the Police or anyone else, what really is the trouble officer?' The man sighed a tired expression. 'Look, we've been away on holiday for four weeks. Got back a couple of days ago, we know old Jim, and Jenny – yes of course we do, haven't seen them though since we arrived home. But people named Primmer? Never heard of them.' He glanced at his wife. 'Come in and we will try to sort this out. Perhaps you could make some coffee Jane.'

Eton turned to his companion. 'Go and get the others, I want a word before I talk to these people.' He looked back to the "Flints". 'Thank you, under the circumstances, that's very kind of you. I just need to have a chat to some colleagues, then would you mind if my fellow officers and I, had a look around, the house, the grounds?'

'Not at all,' replied Michael Flint, 'we have nothing to hide. We'll just be here in the kitchen when you're ready.'

Eton turned to his men, they were standing a few yards back from the door.

'I'm damned if I know what has happened here or what is going on, but there is sure as hell something that's just not right! Have a really good search of the grounds and out buildings. Look for any vehicles, tracks - footprints - anything that may point to something or someone that has left. For there sure as hell is something funny going on here. Or I, and the rest of us, are going fucking barmy!' He saw the questioning eye of one of the Constables. 'Yes – I know we haven't got a warrant – bring that up with MacDonald later! Now do what I said!'

Eton was about to go into the house when he stopped. Coming up the path at the other side of the house, was Mackay with three men.

Then his phone rang. It was MacDonald.

*   *

Smith stepped back from the window, he wasn't sure whether she had seen him or not. He clicked on his radio and called his backup in the car behind the Hotel.

'She's back in her room, she must just have been out for - well - I have no damned idea what she went out for, but she is back. Keep your eyes peeled, her car is at the front, but that doesn't mean she will use it. If she comes out this way I'll call you and you had better move fast and pick me up.'

The Constable acknowledged and eased himself forward in the seat so he could look up at the top level of the building. He could see that there were two fire escapes, one from the roof level at the far end, and one from some windows about half way across, both seemed to drop into the alley. He got out of the car and walked down to the corner, there was another coming down the side of the building into the street adjacent to where he was parked, and also a the side door. She had five alternatives, not including the front door out to her car. He shook his head.

'This could be tricky,' He muttered, 'I haven't got enough clear sight of any of the exits.' He jogged back to the car and looked around where he was parked. 'If I leave the car here, and position myself near the far corner of the building I may have a better chance of seeing which way she may leave, if she leaves at all, shit why in these situations are we always short of man power!' He took his phone and called Smith, telling him of what he was doing.

Jenny stood at the window in the shadows of the room. She looked at her watch. If the pick up was on time, she had less than ten minutes. There wasn't time to walk, or run to the rendezvous, and when the chopper arrived they would only have a minute or so to load the cartons and get away. Her determination grew. She was not going to let these bastards stop her, not after what she had been through, all that was planned. 'Can I distract him and get out to my car. Or will I just risk and run for it, but try to look as if I am not aware of him, or any others he may have with him - I was careless. I should have parked the car elsewhere.' Her musing at her situation frustrated her more, she looked out over the buildings opposite.

In the distance out over the waters of the harbour she could see a helicopter.

Roger Smith's radio buzzed. He picked it up but he kept his eyes on the window of the Hotel where he had seen Sullivan.

'Flight Lieutenant Manston, we're on our way! I believe you have suspect under surveillance - any movement - or update to report? We should be with you in under ten minutes - will land at sports grounds - Over.'

'She is still in the hotel, we have a watch on the back and the front, if she moves we will know - how many in the Squad, we are a bit thin on the ground here with most at the road-blocks. We could call them in, but that could seem premature, but she has proved a little elusive - over.'

Roger turned slightly away from the window, there was a noise from the back of the shop. He stood up and peered into the shadows.

'No, I wouldn't worry about that, if they are in place and even if she makes a run for it, we will be able to cover her, and there are five of us - we will - hang on. There's another whirly coming in towards the old port. We can see him about three or four k's to our south west, travelling very low, fast - wave top, a black Robinson, can hardly see him, bit of mist and he's so low he's churning up spray! We'll be with you shortly. Meet us at the sports ground, over and out.'

Jenny Sullivan saw the movement but she couldn't tell how much he had moved, or why. She seized the moment and ran out of the room and down stairs, at the front door she hesitated a second, she couldn't see him, she ran out to the car and thanked her brain for telling her not to lock it. She flicked the keys in the ignition and as the motor caught she swung the car in a tight turn and headed back up the main street.

As Smith turned to see what the noise was, he stepped back from the window. It was the owner of the business coming in to start work. He held up his hand to warn the man he was there. But the sound of a car engine brought him whirling back to the window. 'Bugger,' he snapped to himself, he ran to the door, pushing the proprietor out of the way and calling on the radio at the same time to his man at the back of the hotel. 'Get the car, she's taken off, I only took my eyes off her for a second - get around here, pick me up at the corner.' He switched back to the Iroquois frequency. The Pilot answered immediately.

'She's mobile, small blue hatch, heading south – I think. Bugger, now I've lost sight of her! I can hear that other chopper, seems to be in at the back of these buildings - can you see it yet, is that where the sports grounds are?'

'Affirmative, yes can see it. It's already hovering ready to land, he must have been travelling fast, bloody fast and was closer than I thought, can see the main road, no sign of any blue hatch - our quarry could be headed there to the grounds and that chopper - we are approx two minutes from destination – over.'

Smith could now here the sound of the Iroquois, as well as the Robinson.

'Will head there. My car is coming round now, he will know the way - will rendezvous less than two minutes - over and out.'

The Police car skidded to a halt and before Smith had the door closed the driver was pulling away from the curb. 'Heard your talk to the Pilot, I think that may be right, she could get away from there easily.' He threw the car around the corners, it's tyres screeching on the tarmac. Then he was accelerating down the narrow access road that led straight to the grounds

The two men could see the Grandstand and Pavilion, Sullivan's car was parked between them. The girl was out on the grounds passing cartons up into the Helicopter, as she passed the last one she swung herself onto the skid and someone inside hauled her in. The pilot accelerated the rotors and the machine rose rapidly swinging away from the buildings.

They were still a hundred metres from the grounds, but they could see the Police chopper racing in from the north. It was coming in at grass top at a hell of a speed, the black Robinson banked away at the end of the grounds and was lost from sight behind the buildings. They skidded to a stop on the edge of the field as the Police chopper swung past them.

* *

MacDonald knocked on the door and called out, 'Mr Bland - it's John MacDonald, sorry to disturb so early but we would like a word please, very important.' He the knocking and listened as he had the last time he had tried to get into see Bland. There was no response. 'Mr. Bland, it's really important, we have information about your Granddaughters, and your son-in-law.' MacDonald muttered under his breath. 'That might get the old coot moving.' There was still no movement. He tried to look in through the windows into the lounge where a light was still burning, but the sun now starting to brighten the landscape, and was reflecting off the window and the arrangement of the curtains screened the room.

'Oh to hell with it and him.' MacDonald's patience was wearing extremely thin, he put his hand on the door handle and turned it, the door wasn't locked, he pushed it open and stood staring into the dimly lit hall way, a singular bulb hung surrounded by an ornate Tiffany shade. He called again, but there was no reply. He waved to his companion. 'Okay let's have a look. He may still be out, or has slipped away again. Or he may be asleep - or drunk. With what I have seen lately, and heard of him.'

The two Officers went into the passage. 'You go through there and check, let the others in the back, then do a wander through each room, I'll start in the living rooms.'

Williams went down the hall and through the door on the right, into the kitchen, as he reached the back door and opened it he heard MacDonald call out.

'You lot get back here, back here in the living room - fast.'

MacDonald stood in the door way of the lounge, in the chair at the far side of the room was Jim Bland, he was sitting in the old leather arm chair, his head was slumped forward, and his arms hung loosely over the sides. A cut crystal glass lay on the floor below his right hand, its contents had spilt and soaked into the carpet, a half empty bottle of whisky sat on the small round table to his left.

The Inspector didn't move into the room until the other three men were with him. Then when they had all entered the room he went over and spoke to the man in the chair. 'Mr. Bland - Jim, are you alright?' When there was no response, he shook his shoulder, thinking he was sleeping drunk. His head lolled back, the cold eyes of the old man stared into the room. He was very dead. Blood oozed from the back of Bland's head staining the chair.

MacDonald jumped back, he had seen plenty of deceased people, but it was the way that the body flopped and the head had moved. Then there was the look in his eyes - there was still the look of shock, and fear in them. He swallowed, coughing nervously as he regained some composure.

'Well that explains why we couldn't get him to answer the door. Thomas - call the Ambulance, and the Hospital, there'll be someone on duty, I guess. At least a night porter and a nurse or two. I'll call Eton. Jesus! What the hell sort of mess will he have found up there!' He pulled out the Mobile and pressed in the numbers. The Detective Constable answered the call immediately. Eton stood on the steps listening to MacDonald, as Sergeant Dougal MacKay arrived. He waited, with his men, standing apart from the rest. The group looked uncomfortable, very unhappy at having been dragged out at the early hour.

After Eton heard MacDonald's story about Bland, he quickly told him the situation that they'd come across at the Lodge. 'Mackay has just arrived as well, perhaps he can shed some light on this, he must surely know the truth of who owns this place. Anyway, we will have a bloody good look around, I think too that you should get up here - I don't like the feelings that I am getting about all of this.'

MacDonald agreed. 'No - I don't either. I'll get there as soon as possible, as soon as the Ambulance gets here, I'll leave Thomas and Williams here to keep an eye.'

*   *

Marguriette picked up her glass, pouring herself more Cognac, then sat on the edge of the bed. She still had the bottle in her hand and indicated towards his empty glass.

'No thanks, I think I've had more than enough. Especially on top of what's happened today, as much as I could be tempted though, I will not. Are you okay?'

'You're not going to disapprove of me having my fourth cognac though are you Rory!' Bronson put on a mock scowl. - It was not a question, it was a light hearted "don't you dare", and she was strangely, extremely sober.

'I wouldn't dream of it, I learnt my lesson a long time ago about that, and if I remember rightly - so did you, neither of us particularly like "being told" - do we?'

She smiled down at him, and then swung herself back onto the bed, drank the rest of the glass in one gulp, put it on the bedside table and cuddled into his side, draping her arm over his bare chest. 'I'd be much warmer and more comfortable if I was under the covers.' She muttered into his shoulder. 'Would you really object if I slept here with you? I can keep my knickers on and I won't molest you - too much anyway.'

'Do I have a choice in this matter, or are you just pretending to be polite and ask, and do what you really want to anyway?' Rory despite the years gone, still had deep affection for her – and until a few moments ago hadn't realised just how deep those feelings were.

She sat up and stared into his eyes. 'You know sometimes Rory Calder, you can be the most off putting boring bastard - of course you don't have a choice.' Marguriette stood up and stripped off her clothes, except for her black lacy knickers. She threw them in a heap beside his clothes that lay crumpled on the floor, then slipped into the sheets beside him and lay her firm lean body against him, twisting her long slim legs around his.

'See - I did leave the knickers on. Remember the first time we went to bed together? We both kept them on, thought we could be strong and not indulge in the evils of sex on our first night together! Well we managed that until the early hours of the morning, then all hell broke loose!' She reached out and flicked the switch above the bed, as the room went into darkness she kissed him lightly on the mouth. 'Don't forget to wake us very very early - we have a lot to achieve in the morning.' Then a second kiss – this time not lightly, but with a passionate urgency, but not lingering. She broke it off, and before Rory could respond she snuggled down under the bed clothes. Now, as well as her legs, she wrapped her arms across him as well, within seconds her breathing was quiet and even. She was asleep.

Rory lay awake, his mind over the events of the last days. It still seemed too far fetched - too coincidental. And, after all these years, what on earth was he doing in this bed with Marguriette? Someone he'd loved and cared for very deeply. But that was before. When he fell into sleep - it was filled with nightmares. Clinging mud, wrecked cars wrecked barges, burning buildings – the faces of too many dead - far too many dead.

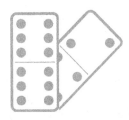

EIGHTEEN

Hans and Euan had finished their meals. Maxine continued to pick at hers, her appetite gone. She did drink the wine, in fact several glasses, a mellowness began to flow through her.

She was glad she had made the call to Sarah. And began to think about - "Mother's saw things differently from Father's". Although she was not his biological daughter, she knew that he deeply loved Sarah, but he wouldn't admit that it was right to at least tell her they were going away, and they would not be back! He'd done so much for her - as if she were his own. What had they done? But – maybe – just maybe, if and when it had all settled down, they could call her? From wherever, and maybe then, she could join them? Of course they would still have to be very careful. She did not realise she had been murmuring her thoughts to – she thought only to herself.

'Who are you talking to?' Euan smiled at Maxine, 'Or are you just muttering away to yourself, or someone we can't see?' He took her hand, a partly amused, partly worried expression on his face. 'You okay Max? You seemed to be miles away, and you were talking to yourself.'

'Sorry - was I - must be too much to drink and not enough food.' She began to pick at the meal.

'You may be right about the amount we've drunk Maxine. I think we should go up to the rooms, sort out the final and fine details. We've all had quite a bit of wine, not to mention the Brandy! Are you going to finish your meal, or can we get under way?' McGillveray became serious.

458

'No, I really don't feel like the rest of it - it was very nice, I'm just not - hungry. Coffee might be nice though - if that's okay?' Maxine's voice was flat – toneless. She wasn't focusing.

Hans broke in. 'That's a fine idea, but not here, I'll see if they will have a pot of coffee sent up to the room for us, I'm sure that they will oblige.' Hans' voice for a change, was more conciliatory than demanding. 'You two go on ahead, I'll get this organised, and our accounts, as we will be leaving pretty early. I'll only be a few minutes. My room is next to yours, of course, just go on in. In the large brown satchel that'll be with my other bags there are the papers and all the documents that we need to go over - you have your new passports, make a start. Start matching yourselves to your future.' Hans went to the Reception desk.

As Euan and Maxine left the Restaurant he took her hand, and they went up to the room in silence, each caught up in their own thoughts of what was to come. At the door of Hans' room they stopped. Euan put his arm around his wife, and gave her a gentle hug. 'You go in and find this satchel thing, I just want to get the briefcase that our friend Mr. Blanchard delivered so kindly to us, we'll need to deal with that as well.'

Maxine's expression revealed her thoughts about what had happened to Blanchard, what they'd done to him. 'Don't, please Euan, don't be so flippant - so cold and bloody callous! If we're ever connected to that! And Peter and Mangus! If it is found out - you know what it will mean. We have been lucky so far, let's hope that it doesn't run out.' Her frown was severe and the tears were close to flowing. She opened the door, and went into Jongejan's room.

McGillveray went into theirs. Going to the bathroom, he washed his hands and face, he stared at himself in the mirror, noting the lines of strain and tiredness around his eyes and mouth. He sighed brushed his hair back, went back into the bedroom and picked up the black case. He joined his wife just as Hans arrived. He came in and closed the door.

'They will send coffee and brandy up in about half an hour, that will give us time to make some progress.' Hans went to the window and drew the curtains. 'We are all intelligent, quick learning people. I don't think that it will take us long to memorise the first part, then it's simply to go over our plans, our movements for the next few days.' He took the satchel from Maxine who had just retrieved it from the floor by his bags. There was a table near the window with four chairs. They arranged themselves around it, he opened the bag, taking out four large brown envelopes. He handed one to each, and placed one in front of himself. The other he set aside. 'That's for our young lady Jenny Sullivan. She wont get quite the same opportunity to study - but that shouldn't matter too much, she wont be on the same flight as myself – or you, we are all on separate airlines, so she will not have to interact with us until we are well clear of the country. Right, open them, we'll spend ten minutes going over the contents, then we will discuss them.'

Those next minutes seemed an eternity as they found their new selves laid out in detail front of them. Their names, new birth dates and certificates, they already had seen their passports, this was all the detail to go with them, and summaries of their new 'past history'.

Hans was the first to put the papers down and stand up. He walked to the window pulled the curtain partly aside, and looked into the darkness. The McGillverays continued to read for another few minutes, then pushed their papers aside.

The South African turned to them. 'So, that's what and who we are. You will also have noted that you two are in the sense of those documents, no longer married, and that your occupations are vastly different from that of before. It will be of no matter, as where we will be - we will not be working - at least, not in the sense of our pasts. You will also have seen that we are all travelling, as I said a few minutes ago, as individuals, on different Airlines and to different destinations, our second flights will bring us back together again in two days. All accommodation of course as you saw is organised. It's not foolproof, and there could be hitches, but the way that my partner - our "English lady" has arranged things - with other "associates" it should all run smoothly. Provided we keep to the new "characters" and their characteristics.'

'Now let us go over those details.' He looked at his watch. 'We still have twenty minutes before our coffee will arrive. Not that we are in any rush – no – hopefully we will not be rushing for a long long time!'

* *

Eton organised Clooney to take some men, to do a thorough search of the grounds, and all the out buildings. After that was set in place, he asked Sergeant Mackay to accompany him, with the other two officers to come into the house.

Jane Flint was in the kitchen making the coffee and thawing some muffins from the freezer, she seemed quite unperturbed by the presence of the Police.

Michael Flint came through the door from another part of the house, he also appeared cool and laid back about the Police being there. 'It all seems a bit strange, you say there were people here, living here, and they said that they owned the place - what did you say their names were again?'

Eton told him a little of the background, as he knew and understood it. Which wasn't a great deal, in either direction! He described the Primmers, Bland and the Sullivan girl.

The Flint's looked completely blank and baffled. Michael Flint turned to Mackay. 'Look I know what Jim and Jenny look like – and I sure as hell would have noticed if they'd been here last night! This all seems a bit bloody far fetched. Dougal, do you know anything about this? These people - these 'Primmers', unusual name that - being here, living in our home? Sounds all completely ridiculous! We told you that we'd be away, and you said you'd keep an eye - so what's this fellow here going on about?'

Mackay seemed for a moment to be taken off guard by Flint's question. His reply was slightly stammered. 'Well um I - ah this - investigation has - actually I think, Constable Eton knows more, I really don't, it's not been my - ah - investigation, really city's CIB thing. We're just on the side - to help if - we - ah - can. I've only just been told of some of the bits and pieces, but, no - no I haven't seen anything strange, nothing unusual going on at all - anywhere in the Village. Oh, a couple of holiday makers - nothing more. I could ask old Bland if what Eton here says is correct. That he and these people - strangers were here, with Jenny from the Crazy Cow? All seems rather far fetched, as you say - and ah - um - no I can't understand it either.'

Eton could see Mackay's discomfort. He hadn't said anything of his conversation with MacDonald, and the voice behind them, meant he wouldn't have to.

'Bland is dead, I have men with him and have arranged the hospital to deal with what needs to be done. It does look like he's been dead for a number of hours, more than likely a heart attack.' He did not mention the other factors that they had seen. 'I'm sure that you are all probably upset by this news, but now we want to know who and what you are - and surely - Sergeant Mackay, surely you know what goes on on your patch?' MacDonald's tone indicated that he had enjoyed seeing the local man suddenly out of his depth, and he could see there was considerable shock of his statement, registering on all of the people present.

He went on. 'Now Mr. Flint, I know we don't have a warrant, but would you mind if we had a look around inside the house, I'm sure that if you have nothing to hide and all is as you say it is - it should not be a problem.'

'No - absolutely - go ahead, Constable Eton has already had a bit of a look, but – no, by all means, not at all - feel free. Now Jane, are the muffins and coffee ready, I think by the bleary eyed look of all present, and this shocking news about Jim, that we need that, and probably something even stronger? Would you like that before you have a look around or after. I've got some excellent brandy, or you might prefer a Malt?' Flint's casual manner was a surprise to MacDonald and his men, and they filed his attitude to discuss later.

'That can wait.' MacDonald though tempted, declined and ordered his men. 'Eton, you go with these two and have a really close look, a good nosy around - all of the house, every room, thorough! Mackay and I, will have a little chat. Where's Clooney with his men?' The Inspectors tone was icy.

'Doing the ground and surrounding area, it's quite a large place, so they may be a little while. Okay, we'll get on with this, do you want to accompany us this time Mr. Flint?'

Michael Flint shook his head. 'No I am sure that you will be fine on your own, and anyway, then I can't be accused of influencing where you look and what you look at.'

Mackay watched as the three men went out of the room. Then he turned to MacDonald. 'Don't you think that this has gone far enough - you city lot come in here with your bloody ideas that there is a conspiracy of some sort going on, when it's more than likely a few goons from your area are down here vandalising the place. I think you all watch far too TV and too many ridiculous crime movies! Probably read too many thrillers as well - all your minds are warped! You invent things to think about, you let your imaginations run bloody wild! You should be concentrating on the real fucking world! It's damned well time you left, and I want that as soon as you've finished you stupid unnecessary search! And, what's this ridiculous nonsense about Bland, he was fine this morning, and I saw him out this afternoon!'

MacDonald listened to him impassively, inwardly enjoying the other man's discomfort, and wondering just what this local man was up to. He didn't answer the question about Bland. But he made no comment.

Jane Flint poured the coffee, put out a jug of cream, and sugar, and the plate of hot muffins.

MacDonald watched each move she made and noted her extreme familiarity with her surroundings.

It was twenty minutes before Eton and his officers came back to the kitchen, a few minutes later Clooney and his men also returned. Their reports were the same.

'There's no evidence of any kind, that remotely suggests that there's ever been anyone else living here. Particularly anyone resembling the Primmers, ever being in the house, there's - just - nothing - no evidence, no photos, clothes, nothing, not even an old sock! And also, no evidence or anything to indicate that Rory Calder has been here either!

Clooney shrugged and held his hands out, and shook his head, indicating he too, had come up empty handed. Re-iterating that there was no evidence of any vehicles or of anyone having left the property or area in any form that he could see. The only other vehicle that he had any knowledge of was Calder's Chev! Though of course, they'd seen the Blue Hatch arrive and leave!

Michael Flint broke in, 'For God's sake, what bloody next! That Chev is actually mine! Who the hell is this person Calder? Another one of your phantom people that lurk in the shadows? Never heard of him either! The papers for the old bus are in my desk, would you like to see them too?' Now he had an edge to his voice, as if he too was losing patience.

MacDonald finished chewing a muffin and swallowed the last of his coffee, he thought for a moment before he answered. 'Okay, I guess then Sergeant Mackay, the patch is back to you. There appears that for the moment, there is nothing else we can do. I will leave it all in your capable hands to deal with the final arrangements for Mr. Jim Bland. The ambulance should by now have him at the local mortuary. But I wouldn't be at all surprised if you were to hear from us and see us again, very soon. No, not at all surprised.' He waved at Eton to follow him. They thanked the Flints, and the other officers for their assistance and left the house. At the door he stopped. 'Oh yes there is one other thing, this Calder fellow, he was in the village, but he like Bland, is dead. Think we'd better have a few more CIB down here to have a chat Sergeant Mackay.'

At the car Eton turned to MacDonald. 'I don't like it, and I don't understand it. Whatever's gone on, and whoever planned it, has certainly done an exceptional intricate cover up job, and I'm buggered if I know how? The whole scene is quite fucking unbelievable! But unfortunately on what we've found – or more to the point - haven't found, we have for the time being - to believe it, well no not believe it, live with it! But like you, I think we'll be back, and I don't think that Sergeant Dougal Mackay has been overly forthcoming with his knowledge - or help. Though he certainly spins a good line with the Flint's - or whoever the hell they are. He sems to know them – how the hell does that happen? And they're damned convincing too! But that would be a horse of another colour wouldn't it?' He shook his head, plainly bewildered. And what do we do about this business of Rory's old bomb? He's not going to be impressed!'

MacDonald nodded. 'Yes indeed I think it would be. He's definitely hiding something – he knows more than he wants to let on. I don't like it or him - at all! And, I also don't like to think what is going to be said to us when we present our report to certain Superior Officers. And as far as Rory's car is concerned, there doesn't seem a bloody thing we can do about that either! Apart from steal it, and that wouldn't be all that bright would it!'

* *

Sarah McGillveray arrived home at her flat. It was nearly one o'clock in the morning. She had been out at a nightclub with several girlfriends from another Law firm. She had been hoping to meet - as she did most nights that she went out - a male that may share her interests, hopes and desires. As well as being someone that she may feel that she would like to take home to bed. Of late, this had not eventuated and she was beginning to feel and realise that the club scene was not where she was going to meet that person. She came into her kitchen and put on the jug to make coffee. The girl leant against the bench and kicked off her shoes, hoisted her skirt and pulled off her panti-hose and knickers, throwing them through the laundry door. She stood staring at the kettle as it started to come to the boil. She had had a considerable amount to drink, but for some reason her head seemed clear.

The girl looked across at her phone and the message machine. It was not her usual habit to check her messaging, at this time of night, but for some reason she went over and turned it on, rewinding the tape and listening to the messages as she prepared her coffee. Two were from members of the local squash club seeking games the following week. Then the message from her mother. Sarah stood listening, the spoonful of coffee held hovering in mid-air over the mug. She put down the spoon, turned off the jug and went back to the machine and rewound the tape, then played it again, listening this time intently to the message and the tone of her mother's voice.

At the end of the message she played it again. 'What do they mean - going away - for work. What the shit is she talking about, and who the hell is Uncle Hans, and why do I have to say sorry to Rory?' Troubled shadows deepened on her face. She played the message again, wondering if she was becoming delusional with tiredness and alcohol. At the end of the third playing she dialled their number, there was only the answer phone. She called their office to see if a message had been left their, again there, but only got the answer phone -- blank, no messages, no explanations.

'Rory - say sorry to Rory, what the hell has he got to do with this, and where would he be anyway at this time of night, he called that other day and I spoke to him – but that was the first time for months!' A panic attack started to grip her and she began to shake, she knew that there was something wrong – very wrong.

There was something "cryptic" in her Mother's message and the way that she had relayed it. She went through her personal phone book, she didn't have Rory's number, but - why should she. Sarah knew where he lived and found the large city telephone directory in a draw near the phone. She flicked through until she found his number - it rang six times before it too clicked into his answering service. She looked at her watch. It was now one fifteen.

'God, if I do track him down, what the hell is he going to think.' She listened to his message, at the end "If you wish to contact me urgently please call me on my Mobile". She listened to it, it was a simple easy number to memorise, but for safety and future reference she wrote it down. She was suddenly feeling very alert and very sober. Sarah heard the long beep and left a quick message that she needed to talk to him urgently, she left her phone number, then she dialled his mobile.

*   *

After the cartons had been thrown into the Robinson, Jenny Sullivan clambered off the skid and staggered across to her seat by the pilot. A man who had helped her in sat behind them. They strapped themselves into their safety harness, as the chopper gained speed and began to climb rapidly.

'Where in the hells name did that thing come from!' Jenny pointed across the pilot. He swivelled his head in the direction that she was pointing, the Police Iroquois was heading straight for them.

'Jesus! Hold onto your hats. I just hope that this souped-up machine can out run the that big bastard! But I doubt it - doubt it very much!

Where did that bastard come from! I don't how I didn't see, or hear him!' He dragged on his controls, hurling their machine sideways banking away from the sea towards the south end of the town. 'But I will bet anything they have backup, and will follow us anyway, but here goes.' The pilot pushed the throttles to full power and they felt the thrust push them back in their seats. All eyes were on the other helicopter - it was closing very quickly.

Then they hit the high-tension wires. Their machine exploded, disintegrating in seconds, it's parts flying out in all directions and scattering over the fields and the edge of the old harbour below.

Smith and his driver jumped from the car and ran out onto the grass playing area in front of the Grandstand. The black helicopter was banking away towards the sea, they could see that the pilot had seen the Police coming in over from the north, he was keeping low and increasing his speed. The two men gaped and almost screamed aloud as they saw the black machine hit the hi-tension power lines. They felt the buffeting force of the concussion from the explosion - and watched horrified as the debris filled the air, and the remains of the torn bodies of the people on board fell with the wreckage to the ground.

The Police helicopter banked away over the top of where the Robinson crashed. Somehow it had not snapped the heavy wire, but they had swung together - touched creating a huge arc - sending a fireworks display over the harbours edge and shorting out the local area. The pilot circled the machine back over the top of the pylons, hovered over the field then landed. The pilot had already alerted all the emergency services and the air began to fill with the sound of fire and Ambulance sirens.

* *

Rory's nightmares dragged him out of the deep sleep, and left him lying restless, disturbed, in and out of the twilight zone. From the dreams though a thought came to him about the incidents at the Cottage – why the explosive device? Why not just hit him on the head – shoot him – stab or poison him? – She had plenty of opportunity to do any of those – why the elaborate set up. Yes, there were plenty of accelerates in that shed to assist with the bombs effectiveness. But why - why did she want to blow the whole thing - and me - sky high? What was in this girl's plainly warped mind? Was it her dramatic paranoia?

As he woke, he could feel Marguriette's legs, wound around his. They had at least restricted his movement to toss and turn, not that he had wanted to move and toss and turn. However - nightmares of the type he often had, tended to make tossing and turning mandatory! But now those lovely long entwining legs, were now producing a claustrophobic effect. And the lack of circulation produced by the pressure on them and accentuated the throbbing in his wound. He put his hands down to try to move them, extricate himself as gently as possible, not to disturb her. Her breathing was peaceful, steady, calm.

The touch of her smooth firm skin on his fingers brought back memories, and not like the nightmares he had just been suffering. He stopped moving and lay still for a second, then twisted his head to see the clock, remembering that they were to make a very early start. It was only one thirty! They'd only been asleep for forty odd minutes, yet it seemed as if it had been hours. His hands were still touching her thighs, she began to stir and press even closer to him. One arm was caught under his neck, now the other snaked across his chest, her face and lips nuzzled into his neck, she was murmuring incoherently..

Then 'Are you awake?' the voice muffled in the pillow and the hollow of his shoulder. She ran her hand down from his chest to his stomach, then down further until she found him, caressed him, held him gently, then she moved away.

But as she released him, she turned and twisted, lifting herself above him. Holding herself up on one hand she brushed her hair away from her face with the other, and looked down at him. They were illuminated only by the fluorescence of the clock. Its red glow tingeing their faces as if they were embarrassed children blushing at their brashness.

Marguriette put her hand down to help, and they removed the last barrier. She lifted herself over him then lowered herself onto his hardness

- she felt his hardness, his strength, begin to slowly enter her, she gripped him inside her – her moisture flowed, and the memories of their long gone past flooded back.

The screeching tune of his cellphone broke their magic. Marguriette fell off him, cursing vehemently. His expletives no less than hers.

Rory rolled over the side of the bed and picked up the phone from his pile of clothes. 'Who on the bloody earth is this?' He felt he should have ignored it, but he knew that it would ring ten times and the mood would have been shattered by it anyway. 'Hello – Calder.' Rory heard the shaking, distraught voice of Sarah McGillveray. He looked over his shoulder to see an exasperated, frustrated look on Marguriette's face. He could see that she was about to speak, but held his hand up. The gesture and his expression stopped her. She realised this was important, and lay back on the pillows watching him as his listened to the caller.

After several minutes of listening he interrupted the caller. 'Okay, Sarah - look calm down. I - we - Marguriette and I, we can help you. She's a Police Super, she's here with me now. We need more information, hang up and I'll call you back, we need to listen to you together and get some information down on paper - now hang up now, I'll call straight back.' He clicked off his cell, swung his legs out and sat on the edge of the bed.

Marguriette couldn't resist, remarking with a grin, about his appearance. 'Haven't seen anything like that for quite some time – you are a big boy aren't you!' Her hand reached for him, but he slapped it away, but gently. They both laughed, taking away the serious note, for a brief moment. Her frown of concern returned as she asked the question. 'I gather that was Sarah McGillveray - what's she got to tell us? Can she shed any light on where they might be? Does she know anything about where they are? And why and how the hell on earth did she know where to call you at this time of the night? You said you didn't leave a message!'

'Grab some paper, I'll get that portable phone in here, I think she may be able to help, but she doesn't know it yet.' He went out into the hall, picked up the phone book, and found her number again. Back in the room as he dialled, Rory signalled for Marguriette to connect on the cordless. Sarah's phone began to ring.

When the girl answered she had calmed to an extent. Rory began questioning her, talking to her quietly, asking - probing - searching – questioning for clues that the girl may have to her parents whereabouts. Trying not to alarm her or indicate that they had other information about them. She could not provide them with anything at all.

Finally - 'What time was the call made to your phone - and do you have any idea where it may have been made from. Was there any background noise, anything that could give you an idea - like were there aircraft sounds, could they have been at an airport, traffic noises, - anything Sarah - think.'

'No Rory, nothing, it was dead quiet. Like she could have been in a booth, or a hotel room, or an office. But there was nothing, not even a radio or TV, no background at all, and her voice was so - well tense, and no I don't know the time it was made, my machine doesn't tell me that.'

'Have you still got the message, if you have can you play it again, or is it one that I would be able to access, with a pin number?' Rory questioned.

'Yes, yes, I kept it, my answer machine is - you know the tape type - you can listen, hang on, I'll play it.'

They heard the click and whirr of the tape, then Maxine McGillveray's voice came through clearly.

As they listened, Marguriette whispered to Rory. - 'We may be able to get a trace on that, it might take a little while, but I think that we should be able to.'

The girl played it again twice. 'Was that, is that any help?'

'Yes, and maybe not, at least we know that she wanted to tell you something, and to get a message to me, even if it was to say sorry. And I am beginning to know why.'

'Why does she want to say sorry to you Rory, that sounds really strange - what's this all about, and who is this "Uncle Hans" I have never ever heard of him.' She was beginning to sound upset again.

'Look Sarah just stay put, go to bed or watch TV, or have another drink, we'll be in touch soon, we think we may be able to get a trace on the call, and any others that may have been made from where she is. Just try to relax - and yes Sarah, I'm sorry but we think that there is something wrong, I shouldn't tell you that, but well now I have. So try to help us by thinking of anything that has happened over the last few weeks – months – even years that point to - shall we say - "things" not being as they should be with Mum and Dad - okay?' He heard the girl mutter a muffled tearful "alright" and he hung up.

Rory looked at Marguriette, they were still standing with absolutely nothing on.

'I think we may work on this better if we get dressed - don't you think?' Despite the new tension of the situation they both grinned. She went into the bedroom and came back with two towelling robes, she threw him one and shrugged on the other.

'Right, now we are respectable and have made some progress be it all slight - see if you can get the office to get a trace on the call to the girl, and I'll wake up Senior and give him a run down. I am sure he'll be thrilled - even at this time of the morning! Oh – and you had better use my name – they probably haven't a clue who you are.' She went down to her office.

Rory spoke with the Duty desk and explained what they needed and that it was needed it quick bloody time. When he had finished that call, he rang Sarah again. He explained what they were doing, and as soon as they had the trace he would call her.

He hung up the phone, over the last time of the call he had felt himself physically and mentally sagging, but then the tension of the sudden change in events made his mind swing back into an operational mode. He went down stairs to the study. He found walking down the stairs difficult, the deep cut in his leg had stiffened, and although during the recent activity he hadn't noticed it, he now did.

Marguriette called Chief Moorhead. The response to the call was tired and irritable, until he heard what she had to say.

'Right, good work, as soon as you get the trace, get back to me, I'll be ready to go with you as soon as you call.'

She sighed and hung up. She turned to Rory who was leaning against the wall near the door watching her as she finished the call.

'Well I guess we had better make ourselves respectable!' She looked at him and began to smile, but suddenly she frowned and came over to him, looking down at his leg. 'Jesus Rory, you're dripping blood all over my floor - when did that start bleeding again?' She knelt down in front of him and pushed aside the gown, the inside of the towelling was red.

'Sit down over at the desk, I'll get some fresh bandages, we are going I hope, to have a busy morning cleaning up another mess, so we had better get this one done first.' She disappeared from the room. Rory sat himself in the chair and looked at the stream of oozing blood coming from under the gauze, he began to unwind the old bandage, just as she returned to the room with a first aid box, the phone rang.

Marguriette picked up. 'Bronson.' She listened to the caller, hung up and immediately dialled another number. As she waited for the call to be answered she held her hand over the mouthpiece. 'They've traced it, bloody amazing whizz kid bastards, from a -.' She stopped talking as the other number was answered.

'Yes, I already know. I asked them to contact me before you, I've a squad on the way - it's an Inn, Hotel - small boutique – whatever - about twenty five minutes from the airport, we've also put extra men there as well. So Mummy slipped up, we should send her a thank you card.' Moorhead's tone dripped acid, as he gave Bronson the exact location.

'Right from home it should only take you twenty straight down the Motorway if you plant it and use all your bells and whistles. We'll rendezvous half a kilometre north, on the old main road south, there's a park on the right near a Supermarket.' Moorhead hung up.

Bronson related the information to Rory, as she rapidly re-bandaged his leg, first placing a pressure pad over the wound, before binding it tightly, it felt stiff and uncomfortable. They went up stairs to the bedroom and dressed quickly, all thoughts now only directed on what they had to do.

When Rory finished dressing, he went to the phone and called Sarah McGillveray.

*   *

Hans Jongejan went over the documents. The fine details of their plans, their arrangements, three times. Each time he got them to repeat them back to him, then he did the same with their identities, their new backgrounds, then back to arrangements again. 'No mistakes I want NO mistakes, no stone to left unturned – it is crucial to our success - crucial!' He sounded almost fanatical.

The coffee arrived, it was much later than he wanted, but before he could complain the Steward explained the delay. A large group had arrived for a meal and had put everything out of order, by the time they had dealt with them and they'd left, it was realised that their order had been overlooked, therefore wouldn't be any charged. The steward pushed the trolley into the room.

Hans was about to berate the Steward, but decided that it was completely unimportant. He indicated for Maxine to pour the coffee, he dealt with the brandy. There was also a bottle of good port, he pointed from one to other – they opted for the port. As he fixed the drinks and she handed each of the men their coffee, he began again, now using their new identities, and questioning them about their individual families. He stood sipping his brandy and coffee - watching them, listening to them, listening to the intonation of their voices, looking for mistakes and any hint that they were unsure of themselves. He looked at his watch, it was after one thirty, the 'interrogation' had gone on far longer than any of them had realised. They had become so intensely involved in what at first had seemed just simple roll play. They were become their new selves.

'We have done well, very well. We will be leaving in just over three hours, let us have a break and relax for half an hour, let our minds just mull over what we have been doing, place ourselves now as the we are to be, in a general conversation. Is the coffee hot enough, or shall I order more?'

Maxine touched the pot. 'No it's fine.' She poured each another cup, they sat down for the first time in over an hour. They lapsed into silence, suddenly awkward with each other, as if they were strangers.

It was Hans who broke the silence. 'Well as long as we feel comfortable with our new selves, and where we are headed, there is just one more item that we need to deal with.' He pointed to the heavy black leather briefcase on the bed. 'That contains, some very important items. I would have liked them to have been taken out some other way, but Andrea slipped up, excuse the pun, and of course so did our Mr. Blanchard. It's a shame that Peter will not be able to enjoy the fruits of his labours, and how careless to leave them so accessible.' His expression showed his enjoyment of the other man's misfortune.

Maxine inwardly cringed.

Jongejan went on. 'It would be foolish of us to take all of the packages in one container, they should be distributed amongst the luggage of the three of us.'

Hans went over to the bed and lifted the case, he inspected the combination locking. 'Do you have the combination, did you get it from Blanchard?' He eyed them speculatively.

Euan came and stood by him, Maxine stayed seated at the table. 'No, I tried to get him to open it, but he couldn't, or more likely wouldn't. It seemed he was going to take it and do a runner. That's when we decided he needed a bad headache, and to try bungy jumping in a lift shaft, without the rubber rope!'

Maxine grimaced at her husband's flippancy. Sometimes she was shocked and dismayed by his similar attitudes to Hans. Euan saw his wife's look, and turned his back to her. He realised that in her eyes, he'd over stepped the mark of any decency.

Hans tried the levers, they would not move, he moved the numbers on each dial several times, trying different combinations, nothing.

'Andrea may have known what it was before she locked the case, but I would think it unlikely that she remembers now, and anyway we have no way of getting that from her. She would have spun the four disks each side when she locked it as were her instructions.' He tried again, ten more combinations, but with no result. 'The computations are considerable. I think that our only course is to break open the locks, shame it's such a good case. I have unfortunately blundered – I didn't foresee that we would have to be in quite this situation – most unlike me – to trust someone like Blanchard.' Although his comments were meant for his own ears, Jongejan had spoken aloud. There was intense anger in his tone.

The McGillverays looked at each other – surprised at the South African's outburst.

* *

Rory listened as the phone in Sarah's apartment rang five times, before it was answered. His mind travelled the road of "what the hell to say to the girl!". She was aware something was very wrong. Should he tell her the truth or lie? Cover everything up for the moment - tell her they hadn't been able to find them - or anything about where they were, and not to worry, they probably just wanted a ---. No --- the young woman was certainly no fool, she would see through the lie and that would make the situation worse for her. But what was "worse"?

Even at this point did they have, despite all the files and photographs, any really hard evidence against any of these people? The girl could be panicking over nothing. They all could be. Yet, there were people dead, plainly murdered, and Marguriettes files and dossiers, told a vivid story. So, how much did the McGillveray's and this Jongejan have to do with it? He realised he was trying to make excuses, he knew "how much"! He brought back all he'd read – all he'd seen – all that he knew and had experienced. The only thing they didn't have was any hard evidence! What were they involved in? It was all in a sense hearsay. Drugs, gold and diamonds? – Was there any real testimony from the girls that they were using? None of it! And how were they controlling them, where had they "obtained" them from? But Rory knew of course how they were – and his mind and heart hardened.

But still, despite the realisation, he became even more confused. Confused by the people involved in all the events of the last days. Primmer – Euan – Jenny – Bland. The Sullivan's and Helen Greene? Who else was caught in the web? None were as they'd been to him before, particularly the ones that he'd called his friends. The actions and reactions - the files, the evidence. What he wanted to believe and not believe. Then there was Marguriette - how - where did she really fit into all this? But he knew the answer, that was a stupid question, but the other things - resurrected emotions, that had occurred between them was a different matter! How in the hell had she tracked him down? More to the point - why? Was this too just a coincidence – part of her Domino game? Every thought raced at breakneck speed in the seconds he waited for Sarah to answer. It was the first time for months that his brain had actually begun to function the way it had been trained!

Sarah's voice cut into the jumble in his head. 'Hello - is that you Rory, have you heard anything, do you know where they are, what they're doing?' She didn't give him and opportunity to reply or respond, before she burst into sobbing tears. 'I know that something is really really not right. I have listened to Mum's message again and again, then I had to lie down. I just started crying - I don't know what to do, I don't know who this other man "Hans" is, and why are they saying sorry to you?'

'Well you could try calming down and letting me get a word in.' Rory was beginning to feel very tired of emotionally erratic people, and the girl irritated him with her hysteria. 'Look Sarah, you said you had been out and had a lot to drink.' (She hadn't actually told him that - but he had gathered that was the case.) 'Just listen to me - we've been able to find out where they are, they're fine. They are with a business friend, and are working on a very difficult case that requires a great deal of discretion - it also requires that they are out of the country for a time. So just go to bed and get some sleep. I'm sure that they will be in touch as soon as they can.' He had opted for the fabrication, the distortion of the facts and the truth - but what was that anyway? He gambled on her tiredness and the fact that she had been drinking, that she would not, at the moment realise that he had told her a load of rubbish. Under normal circumstances Sarah would have been known about any difficult case.

There was silence on the other end for a short time, then a quiet reply. 'Yes, alright, sorry, you're probably right, I have had a lot to drink, and I was feeling lonely and a bit down. I'm sorry Rory. I'll call you in a couple of days - perhaps you could take me to lunch, perhaps we could talk about it then, and anyway they may have been in touch by then, I am being a childish fool.'

'Okay - um, well I suppose they may be and yes, you are and yes I'll meet you for lunch – whatever - okay?' He was taken off guard, the sudden change again in the mood and the tone reminded him of Jenny Sullivan - and that was not a good memory. He sighed deeply. 'I'll give you a ring in a day or two, and see how you are, just get on with it all, get into work tomorrow and see what turns up.' As he hung up he wondered why he had even said that, but it was all that seemed to come into his mind.

'What's all that about, was that Sarah?' She didn't wait for his reply. 'Come on we have to get moving, I was listening to you, so I have the gist of it. I liked you line of bullshit, but it may turn out to be the truth anyway.'

Out at the car Marguriette slid into the driver's seat. 'I think I had better do this, two reasons - one - you're not supposed to drive these things, even if I did let you before. There may be a few people in the next hour or so who may not approve, and second and even more to the point - you can hardly walk, never mind drive.' She grinned across at him as he levered himself in. 'We were just beginning to get to the interesting, shame about the phone, still another time another place - maybe, anyway, I hope I didn't damage you too much.' She backed the car at speed down the driveway and spun it onto the street. At the top of the hill where it joined the main road she switched on the lights and siren and headed for the motorway. There was little traffic. She swung the big car into the fast lane and accelerated to a hundred and forty. She handled the car in a relaxed and confident manner. Much the way she handled most things, most of the time - but not always.

Fifteen minutes later they were approaching the turn off. They hadn't spoken at all during that time. Marguriette became absorbed in her driving. Rory - with - "if he was to confront the McGillverays", what would his reaction be, and theirs to him? He realised that while he had been taken for a fool - they also had no idea as to what he did, his work - and all that was involved in his life. As he thought through this, he was watching the road. 'That's the exit coming up, you'd better get over to the inside lane.'

They were still travelling at high speed, there were three cars on their left, they began to slow when they saw the flashing lights and heard the Siren. Marguriette braked hard, but too late to cut in behind them, they missed the off ramp. 'Shit! Now we'll have to take the next exit, that's going to add nearly ten minutes! Head beaky will not be pleased!' She was now clear of the other traffic and pulled across into the left lane and sped up

again, they were heading down a long slope and could see the next exit -
well lit and clear of traffic. To their left, across a small river, they could see
groups of buildings, the Hotel. They would have to come back past there,
to get to where Moorhead would be waiting with his squad.

*   *

Hans went to his luggage and found his toilet gear. 'I usually have a pair
of scissors or a nail file in here, that may do the trick, although I think we
may need something stronger - like a screwdriver.' He began to unpack
the small bag, placing the items tidily on the sink bench where the usual
coffee and tea making facilities were.

While Hans was searching, Euan picked up the heavy black case,
turned it over, and began to inspect the locks, hinges and its construction.
It was made of very solid leather and the hinges were tightly bound into
the stitching. He looked again at the locks. He moved all the dials back to
zero, then tried several simple combinations, ones that most people would
think were too easy, and that no one would think of using. As he was about
to try the third of his ideas, Hans came over and stood with him, he had
a pair of long pointed scissors in his hand.

'Okay, shall I try with these - they may be strong enough?'

'Wait just a minute, let me try just two more.' As he completed the
third combination, there was a distinct "click" from the locks.

'What was that? Perhaps that's it! You've done it Euan!' Jongejan's voice
was excited, 'go on - try now!'

Euan pressed his thumbs on the catches, pushing outward. They still
wouldn't move. He shrugged, 'No, I guess that wasn't it. I'll try one more
time. Besides - if we can't open it here, why don't we just take it as is?
Customs may not even take any notice of it, after all it's just hand luggage,
and the other containers won't show up on the X-ray. As you said, it's a fine
piece of luggage, why destroy it, and with more time and the possibility
of a kind Locksmith?'

'We can't take the risk, it they wanted it opened, either, as we leave, or
at a destination, and we can't do it, what are they going to think? I have

seen it before. They just burst them open. That wouldn't be clever to have happen, and another thing, - which one of us would carry it?' He cocked a questioning eye at them both.

Maxine was still by the window, she half turned towards them, she was feeling extremely tired, and was becoming irritated by the whole thing.

'Oh for God's sake, just open the bloody thing, and sort it out - then let's get some rest, it's only a couple of hours or so, before we have to get out of here and be well gone. I need to lie down for a while.'

'Well go back to our room and lie down! I'm sure that Hans and I can manage this. It doesn't take three pairs of hands and brains, it actually only needs one - and that's this one here with the sharp instrument.' He pointed to Jongejan. 'Go on Max – go get some rest, I'll be through with you shortly.'

Maxine went to the door, she opened it to go into the corridor. She looked back at the two men crouched over the briefcase. It was the last time she would see her husband, actually, to be able to see anything ever again. A huge blinding flash and a massive blast of super heated air burnt into her, the skin was seared from her face, her hair lit like a candle as she was flung out over the balustrade of the balcony.

The apartment dissolved, a raging blasting sheet of flame, smashing the windows outwards, the walls between the rooms on either side disintegrated. The two men died instantly, their bodies crushed by the blast and burnt beyond recognition by the intense heat of the fireball.

* *

'That's the hotel there.' Rory pointed across at the buildings. 'Between those trees and a couple of - Jesus fucking Christ in hell! What on earth is that - what's happened there!'

Marguriette's eyes flicked sideways at Rory's loud exclamation, then her head jerked around. Her foot pressed hard into the brakes, the car slewed, as she pulled onto the apron at the side of the motorway. For several minutes they stared at the bright glow three hundred metres away. Bronson's curse was louder and more strongly worded than Rory's. She yanked the car into gear and accelerated off down the highway to the junction.

* *

Rory could feel the pounding thumping surf, tumbling him onto hard sand – screeching gulls echoed in his ears, turbulent winds throwing spray and flotsam over him as he struggled to avoid the smashing waves. The ghosts raged and ran over and through him screaming at him – you are finished you are nothing - somehow he knew why and what the outcome would be - what impact all that swirled around and over him would have. It was the struggle through the pain of his children's death, worse than anything he had experienced, but he didn't know why! He did not have any answers. Was this the mud that was closing over him again? Sucking him down – preparing him for the cold realisation of where his life was? His breakdown all over again but worse?

* *

Superintendent Moorhead assembled the Armed Squad. As they waited for Bronson and Calder to arrive, he summarised the events of the last few days - and the present situation. He looked at his watch several times as he paced about the car park. 'They should have been here by now what the in the hell is keeping them.' He shrugged irritably. 'Oh to hell with it, I think we'll move in without them. They will see that we aren't here and I am sure will realise that we are down the road at the Inn.' He began to walk across the parking area. 'Okay? Right - let's get to it.' As they went to their cars the sound of an explosion rocked the area, he looked up to see the upper level at the back of the Hotel erupt outwards - bright tongues of flame and debris spewed out from the rear of the building, showering the yard below.

'Holy mother of God - the place is disintegrating!' Moorhead ran to his car, as he started the engine, he grabbed the microphone and called Central Headquarters. Demanding in a frantic voice for them to call for as much emergency service as they could muster, and for extra Police back up! Within minutes the air was filled with the wail of sirens, as the Police cars raced the half-mile to the Hotel, then Ambulances and Fire appliances joined the bubbling cauldron of sounds as they were dispatched from the nearby stations. The cacophony drowning out all sense from all the minds that mulled and milled towards the chaos.

*   *

At the off ramp Marguriette slowed enough to negotiate the tight curving road safely. She glanced at Rory – his face was ghostly white, his eyes wide. 'What the hell's the matter – I mean apart from the Hotel being on fire – you look terrible! What is it – tell me before we get there – because there sure as hell wont be time after that!' She wondered why she was asking, but there was something in Rory Calder's expression that frightened her, and she wasn't easily frightened, by anything or anyone.

They were back on the old main road heading towards the fire. 'Nothing - everything – I don't know – I just had this – this vision – a feeling - a premonition. I can't describe it exactly! Like a de ja vue – the past – the present – and maybe the future – sorry – sorry, I must be too bloody tired, my mind's going all over the place, and that's not so bloody strange under the circumstances is it! When I was talking to Sarah, everything seemed clear - momentarily, then it all turned - to - mud! Forget it I'm okay – I'll be okay, just forget what you think you saw.' He glanced across at the Bronson, she was still driving like a person possessed, and staring at him! 'And watch the fucking road or we'll end up in one of those Ambulances I can hear coming this way!'

Marguriette swivelled her eyes back to where they should've been. She was nearly heading up onto the verge on the other side of the road. She pulled the speeding car back and slowed her speed. 'Shit sorry but you scared me – I wondered what was happening to you! Tell me alter what it was – I think we have a number of other things and people to deal with right now!' They were now at the front parking area of the Hotel, it was already alive with Police, Fire trucks and Ambulances.

As she pulled the car to a squealing halt, Moorhead was running towards them. The man's square bulk a silhouette against the glow of the fire. As they got out to meet him, he was puffing, but that did not stop the beginning of his tirade, 'Where the bloody hell have you two been – if you'd been here when you were supposed to be,- -' He stopped, and turned to look at the building.

'Ah – yes – well maybe it is just as well you're late – you would have been in there – and so would the rest of us.' He looked at them, then back at the fire raging on the far side of the building. The staff and guests were being brought out through the front door and a fire exit on the far end of the Hotel. 'It seems to be the season for large violent explosions and we seem to be in the middle of all of them in one way or another. Guy Fawkes would be proud! But I'm not! This is really one helluva mess – and if I can make a wild assumption – I think that the people that we would like to have caught up with may no longer be with us – but there's a large question mark hanging in the air – what the hell has gone on and why?'

Rory was tempted to suggest that that was two questions, but Marguriette guessed what he was thinking and gave him a jolt in the ribs with her elbow. 'I know what you were going to say – I thought the same – but I fear my friend, that this is most certainly not the time for a comment like that. It wouldn't have been at all appreciated.'

It'd been three hours before the fire was brought under complete control, and the Ambulances had taken away ten people with minor injuries – six in extreme shock and several of the staff and three customers for smoke inhalation.

During those three hours the two senior Police Officers and Rory Calder had sat in the Chief's car, there was nothing more that they could do. Senior Sergeant Wilson and his men from the Southern district Division were controlling the onlookers and assisting with the evacuation and the security. The trio's conversation ranged through all of the events of the last seventy two hours – then over the relationships between the people that they thought were involved in whatever it was they were involved in – and this was right that moment speculative – with huge amounts of the imponderable. Bronson began to talk about her Domino theory. Moorhead was not in any mood to listen and commented with exasperation. 'You can theorise all you damned well like Marguriette – but the whole matter is that now we have nothing – unless we find the bloody Primmers, and that's seeming more unlikely by the minute! He shook his head. 'I feel it in my gut, they are the main players, and I think that our friend here – who's been saying bugger all, will agree. Because he has been working on this bloody case for a long time – and has said very little of use over the last few days. And I know why he hasn't.'

'Why?' Both spoke at the same time.

'Because we haven't thought to ask him the fucking right questions! Also, we've all been too full of our own theories, to think that he may actually be a bloody sight brighter, and more insightful than we've given him credit for. But we shall have wait for the official line of inquiry, before any more theories are pontificated. Now I see no point in all of us sitting here looking miserable cold and tired so – why don't you two piss off to wherever you were before.' Moorhead became dismissive of the direction the discussion was taking.

It was Rory who replied.'You may be right on one or two of those ideas, but then you may be wrong on others – so we wait and continue to see – but - we will I think take up the option of the latter suggestion. What sayest you Ms. Bronson?'

'A bloody good idea and if the Chief here feels that we should do so – let's do so!' She looked at her watch. 'It's five o'clock! No wonder the sky's getting lighter – come on Calder let's go home.'

Moorhead watched the pair walk to their car. His thoughts touched on the last few days, and then to his calls to Rory Calder in Cornwall. It seemed so long ago – and now – what had any of them achieved? From his view point right at that moment – very very little. From the evidence that the weekend had unfolded to now – it was likely that they wouldn't achieve a great deal more. But that was now for people a lot more senior than any of them to decide.

Marguriette drove away from the Hotel. Turning right, she headed back to the motorway overpass. As they drove across the bridge to the northbound on ramp, they looked back at the charred back of the Hotel. There was still a good deal of smouldering smoke. There were still three Fire appliances, and the Firemen were still doing the last dampening down. The ambulances had gone, and the only Police cars were Moorheads, and two others. The men from those, had cordoned off the buildings and the parking areas. Wide yellow plastic strip surrounded the entire Hotel site, and six of the armed Constables were quietly walking their patrol of the perimeter. The bystanders who had been drawn by the commotion had been moved away.

Bronson accelerated down the ramp. The morning traffic heading into the city was beginning to build and the sky over to the east was lightening. – The last of the morning stars faded and the few clouds that were scattered, took on a warm pink glow, as the sun began to rise.

Half an hour later she pulled into her driveway, slid the car to a halt in front of the garage doors and turned off the motor. They hadn't spoken the entire journey back. Even now in the silence outside of her house, they sat still and didn't speak. After a minute of the silence she reached over and placed her hand on his leg – careful not to touch the wound, she pressed her fingers gently on his thigh.

'You must be bloody exhausted Rory – I know I am – mentally – physically – emotionally – when did you last get any sleep?' She had turned and was examining his demeanour, he was slumped in the seat, his head kept falling forward, then jerking back – fighting the fatigue.

'I've had about two hours in three days if you really must know. Now can we try again – and this time turn the bloody phones off!'

Marguriette nodded. 'Yes, a damned good idea – come on hop along – let's get ourselves inside and into a bed. It's almost light but the curtains have blackout, so we can hide the day, and ourselves from the whole bloody thing. Maybe - perhaps after a few good hours sleep we could resume some other activities?' She smiled as she clicked a remote button on the key ring, the garage door slid up. Bronson started the car and drove into the garage – closing the door after them – shutting out the early morning traffic hum.

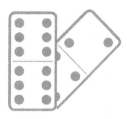

NINETEEN

Rory sat in the car, the large folder he and Bronson had been given, lay on the seat beside him. "The Summary and Conclusions of Events" those that had occurred on that weekend in April 2011. He lifted it onto his knee with the thought of going through it again, but stopped and put above the car's dashboard panel. He'd gone over it – and over it – and found no more sense in it each time he'd done so. Neither had his companion, who'd left the car twenty five minutes ago. She'd walked down to the beach, just as Rory had begun reading for the fourth time.

He looked out the windscreen. Out in front of where they had parked, was the shell edged beach, then dark slippery slimy sea grass - beyond that the mud flats, until last, the spread of broad flat harbour, flat today, there was not a breath of wind, the sky was blue and the sun warm. Far away in the distance, on the far side, the Steel mills tall stacks, belched grey smoke. Behind him the bush covered hills of the West City Ranges. Away to his left a long ancient wharf, where for years harbour steamers had trekked, up from the city, depositing day tripping picnickers, holiday makers, and supplies for residents, farmers, fishermen, eccentrics, artists, potters, writers.

There had been no roads in this part in those days. The farms and the few residents relied on the small ships and barges. To his right a peninsular sheltering three large two storied wooden buildings, that at one time had been very up market boarding houses, beyond them cabins for the not so wealthy, long rows, now run down, rotting.

This had seemed a good place to review and reflect. It had some similarities to other places – the Villages and rugged landscapes contained in the file – just similar - not exactly, just some vague likeness, to the coast in Cornwall. He would ask questions of himself and know that he would probably not get or need the right answers. It was near where he had spent his early years of trying to conquer the mud – and where he had asked so many questions about himself and his dreams - not quite the place - but near enough. And then too, all those years ago he didn't get the answers he sought either.

After five minutes of staring, out at the harbour, and delving the blank mind, Rory picked up the thick folder off the top of the dashboard. He flicked it open and scanned for the fifth time the small type. The final words on the players in the game - the Domino tiles. He ran through everything he could remember, and as he read, he turned the official words and phrases into his own interpretation. He was tired, fed up with it all – but thought – 'One more damned time – this is the last!'

The first analysis of the events of that April weekend, and those prior to it had taken place three days after the explosion at the Hotel. It had firstly been attributed to a gas leak in the kitchen area - despite the fact that the area had only suffered ceiling damage, if compared to that above it – it should have been demolished!

All the persons deceased identities, were kept from the press - not that there was very much left to go on, it was supposition as to who they might be. Maxine McGillveray was unable, because of her extreme physical injuries, and her mental trauma - to confirm - deny - or provide any type of sensible information as to who anyone was, or what had happened.

These initial discussions lasted two days - then the files and thoughts from them were for some inexplicable reason - moved sideways - and no further official talk would take place until a full Commission of Inquiry, an 'Inquest' would formerly investigate the 'events' of that April.

It would be assembled at what the Police Commissioner said would be "the appropriate time". There was a general Press release, very low key.

The Commission was assembled four months later and was held - behind closed doors - ("Of course!" Rory and Marguriette, had both commented sarcastically at the time). It had taken three months to be completed – though not concluded.

After another three weeks had passed, following the first inquiry, another was assembled.

This time the the meeting was called - "The Debriefing" and it lasted just three twelve hour days. Thirty-six hours of waffle, trying to find answers to questions that had never been asked.

It was now eight and a half months since the full, supposed final Inquest had been convened. Enough time for the memories - at least of some people, to become confused - slightly blurred around the edges. It was then that this report had at last been circulated to various "interested and affected parties" The conclusions to become - even more inconclusive.

The whole investigation had been unofficially dubbed - "The Domino Coincidence", after Marguriette Bronson had talked at considerable length, and great detail, about the theories she'd gathered with her files. The people in them, she'd referred to as 'the tiles'. The file though that Marguriette had hoped would've been the lynch pin, the file on the McGillveray's, Euan and Maxine, although numbered as the six - bar – six, wasn't considered at all significant. It was found that the most significant information could be - or should have been, found from the file on Franklin and Amelia Primmer. However, there had been a serious, and it was thought in some circles, not "accidental", but a deliberate omission, of a dozen pages when it was being collated.

Those pages had contained facts, documentation and photographic evidence, that pointed to them as the Heads of the Organisation. The organisations controllers, the brains, but in a close partnership with Hans Jongejan, and the 'woman' in Johannesburg.

Marguriette Bronson was criticised and ridiculed, suffering considerable embarrassment - professional and personal. Her unusual analytical approach to the events that had subsequently taken place on that April weekend, and of the events, that had previously been investigated and documented, hadn't been appreciated - or understood.

She had resigned her Commission from the Force. But after a review
and an apology, she was appointed some weeks later as a "Security Adviser
and Analyst with the Department of Internal Affairs". She would take up
the new position after a few months leave.

Rory closed the folder. The tiles had been placed end on end, they had
been connected into a pattern, the game had been played, but without the
main numbers, the main players - players that this time had slipped away
in the dark. Were they to play another game, or were they not?

The fate and position of the people caught up in, and involved during
the affair, was documented, some briefly others in more detail. But to him
– to them – there seemed no longer any point to it. The damage had been
done and couldn't be undone – it either had to be lived with, forgotten,
or allowed to fester, to eat away like a cancer until it consumed them,
destroying, as it had most involved.

Rory got out of the car and walked over to a large metal rubbish bin,
he took out a box of matches from his pocket. He fanned out the sheaf
of pages and lit the corners of the paper, and the folder. As it caught
he dropped it into the bin. It fell amongst other rubbish, catching that
in the flames as well. He stood and watched it burn for a few minutes,
staring through the smoke at the shore and the incoming creep of the
tide.

When the fire was well alight he walked down onto the shells and
turned towards the wharf. As he walked along that stretch of sand and
shell, he listened to the scrunching beneath his feet, the popping of crab
holes and cockles in the warm early summer sun. The gull calls that echoed
over the soft sound of the ripples of water coming over the mud

As Rory walked towards the jetty, he could see the tall figure of
Marguriette. She was standing back under the rotting decking, about
ten or so yards from the first pylons, near where loading ramps had been
years ago. The tide wash was starting to touch the outer skeletons of the
tall rough timber. Her head was bowed, as she watched the water begin to
swirl into the pools that had been sculptured out of the sand as an earlier
tide had receded. Hands were thrust deep into the pockets of the baggy

denim jacket, her shoulders hunched, as a sudden cool breeze wafted across from the southern side of the harbour.

As he walked between the limpet and mussel encrusted logs she turned, her head lifted, her body straightened, a smile spread on her face, but it didn't hide the sadness behind her eyes.

'I see you've had your bonfire, have you burnt your demons or just the words on the paper?' Marguriette came up to him and slipped her arm through his.

Rory shrugged and shook his head. "I don't know, I may have, I may not have. Burning some paper doesn't actually change anything does it, it doesn't change what has gone before, what happened to all those people, to us. Us – you and I being thrown together in circumstances that possibly neither expected to ever occur in our lives again, and I'm not just talking about our personal re-discovery!'

'No, perhaps it doesn't. And maybe – perhaps they – or we would have? I haven't ever forgotten anything that was between us Rory, and I followed your career – and yes – your personal life. I know – I know that I shouldn't have, because most of it, in fact all of it, was bloody painful!' She lapsed into silence watching him, as he watched the water inching towards them. She reached out and touched his face, turning it to her. 'Let's walk a while, and just not say anything. There's been so much said, and so little achieved. I think we need the silence of this place to cover us, cloak us - take us - well somewhere into another land where there is no mud to suck us down.'

'Then what?' Though it was a question he'd asked. He knew there was no satisfactory answer.

'Then, well, like you - I have no idea either - but I think we should start trying to see the sunlight more, and forget the darkness. Feel the breezes of life on our faces?'

'Is your new work going to let you do that?' His voice soft, expressionless as he looked into her eyes.

Marguriette didn't answer, but pulled in closer to his side. He glanced sideways at her. He noticed the frown that flicked into her face, then deepen.

They walked on, further from his fire, now just a faint wisp of smoke. Further away from the wharf, down the beach, then stopped as they approached some rocky shelves covered with slippery weed, dotted with reflective puddles. He turned to face her, but she was looking out over across the water of the harbour. The deep frown still creasing her face.

'Do you remember the story about the struggle through the mud I told you, and those dreams, that followed over the years?'

'Yes, I remember you telling me.' She didn't look at him immediately. 'And I listened - I listened then, and I listen now.' Marguriette turned and came very close to him. She first rested her hands on his chest, then slid her arms around his neck and shoulders, drawing him into her. 'But what difference does it make. Our paths are going in different directions again anyway - whether we want them to or not. They may cross, they may begin to run along side each others, who knows – maybe like - like railway lines – joined by the sleepers of our experiences and our common interests – maybe even – love? We don't know, they could even run in the same direction? She sighed and clung to him, 'but it's doubtful - isn't it?' She hesitated, pulling back slightly, she looked at him, studying his face, her eyes sad, pleading, asking him to say that they would.

He was about to speak, but she brought her hand up and touched his mouth, then brushed a kiss across it - stopping him.

'But whatever you decide to do, and wherever you decide to go and do it, I think there is one thing that you must do. I think you should wash the mud off, all the mud of the past - scrub yourself as clean as you possibly can. Then put on a new set of clothes, look at where you got the mud from, and pledge yourself never ever to return to it, to try to cross it again, don't ever, please, try to cross it again. Then turn your back on it, and walk away. After that what may happen is up to you, and,' she leant against him and said softly into his chest, 'I must do the same, it's just – a different patch of mud.'

SUMMARISED JOTTINGS FROM THE "DOMINO COINCI-
DENCE" OFFICIAL INQUEST FILES. THESE ARE COMBINED
WITH THOUGHTS AND OBSERVATIONS FROM RORY AND
MARGURIETTE. OTHER INFORMATION RELATING TO THE
FATE OF THE PEOPLE THAT WERE CAUGHT UP IN THIS
'CRIME CONSPIRACY' IS ALSO INCLUDED. BUT SOME OR
ALL OF THAT - MAY POSSIBLY BE JUST - CONJECTURE? AF-
TER ALL – WHAT IS - COINCIDENCE?

When Rory and Marguriette read through all the documentation
regarding the investigations, (and as you know, they did this quite
a number of times), their thoughts were as mine, when I read them.
Confused! I have tried to put some semblance of order to them and to
try to make some sense of it – I'm not sure that I have succeeded.

The Inquest Reports were not clear, concise, and probably nowhere as
accurate as they should have been. Not well written, and nor did they
give a real picture of what the 'events' actually were that April weekend.
Rather a jumble of ideas – mostly vague thoughts and conjecture of
the peoples actions and decisions – and the results.

Rory and Marguriette, had made a number of personal observations,
miscellaneous notes, amongst the reports. They had then made copies
of them, - before Rory burnt the original document supplied to them
by the Judicial Inquest. Why he – they did that, I can only guess.
Make of it what you will.

Miranda Sullivan (Blanchard):
Was deemed to be "an innocent party caught up in a conspiracy that was
completely outside her knowledge and ability to understand".

However, it was their view, that she was either the 'innocent party', - or a very - very clever, manipulator of the 'external' scene in the village. Who had been able to convincingly act out her part in the "play".

But the inquiry couldn't find anything to incriminate her, either in the affairs of her Father, or her husband. That was, apart from her involvement in personal family matters. Nothing of what she appeared to be doing, and seen to be doing, in the photographic evidence could be substantiated. She was at the 'party' as the innocent bystander! But basically, there was no evidence against her, because all of the people who could have been brought to testify – were dead – or couldn't be located – i.e.: Franklin and Amelia Primmer!

The fact that she'd been murdered, was thought to be because she'd discovered, by whatever means, (and that will always remain unclear) the activities that her husband Warren Blanchard, was involved in. And, that he was going to murder her father, and his business partner Mangus Macmillan.

All was very much conjecture and inconclusive – but there could really be no other decision.

Her daughter Suzanne - was adopted by the Headmaster and his wife, from the village's small school.

Peter Sullivan:
Never, despite vague hopes that he might, regained consciousness. Eventually with no relatives - at least that could be found to discuss his condition - the hospital authorities had 'discreetly' turned off his life support. His implication in the affairs and crimes was never entirely proven, as all who had dealings with him, apart from Andrea Jones, were no longer available as either prosecution or defence witness's. Searches of his apartment after the explosion revealed nothing – he had either been very clever, or whatever was there, was destroyed, or he had it in his devious brain, though it was more likely to be in some place that was extraordinarily secure. The DNA and prints from his Mansion also produced little, apart from the fact, that a lot of people had passed through the house at one time or another. His properties and financial affairs were

taken over by the Justice Department and were sold off. The money was distributed to Charities – strangely, Peter Sullivan had somehow been Patron of quite a number of organisations, and they benefited extremely well, – ironical?

Finally - there was no evidence that he was in anyway involved in the death of Serena Calder and her children – and that he had not had any contact with her for well over a year before her death.

Serena Calder:
During the months of her affair with Peter Sullivan, she'd met another man. A Barrister and Solicitor – an Englishman named James Peterson. Over a period of several months she had become very involved with him personally, and his affairs. They'd fallen in love, and had decided that they would move back to Britain, and would set up a Law Firm in Bournemouth, living in nearby Poole. This was all revealed in correspondence, E mails and txts, that were discovered in the on going investigation after her death. Peterson had cooperated fully. Though his name, and 'reputation' had been protected. When the accident occurred, she had been on her way back from visiting friends in Plymouth. None of this information had been given to Rory by the Police during his interviews with them. It appeared that James Peterson had a great many 'friends of considerable influence' in very high places. And was able to be completely overlooked in having any connection in Serena's affairs, and her death - anonymity extraordinary. She had in fact, been running very late for the appointment to meet Peterson. She had been driving very fast and erratically, in a rented vehicle, a Toyota People Mover. A type of vehicle that she would have been very unfamiliar with. These facts, were according to sources who said they had witnessed the accident. But then, if there had been "witnesses" why did it take several days to find the van? Another strange unexplained fact?

Rory only found out some of this information, at a much later time when he clearing out the last of her possessions and was going through private papers that he'd found in in her desk at their home. It now seemed all completely irrelevant.

Jim Bland - the Grandfather:
Had initially appeared to have died of natural causes. A heart attack, coupled with a severe stroke. Approximately an hour, after he had returned to his house, from meeting with the Primmers and Jenny Sullivan.

It was thought that his age, stress, and the amount of alcohol he had consumed that day, and over the previous years, would have contributed to, and accentuated a heart condition that had been diagnosed some years before. However during the autopsy this had been found to be only a minor contributing factor. There was also amount of cyanide in his system. But no report or explanation was ever given with regards to the bullet in the back of his head! (There were a number of suggestive theories as to who would've been able to have shot him, and to whether this had occurred before or after he was poisoned. Mackintosh, Jenny Sullivan, and even Dougal Mackay, all had access to firearms of the calibre that had been used. But of course, there was no proof, and no weapon was ever found to match the bullet.) There was a possibility that the cyanide may have been self administered. However, after a thorough search of his home, there was no evidence to support that theory.

The Inquest found him to be an accomplice, closely involved with the Primmers and his other Granddaughter - Jenny Sullivan. He had played a large part in the operation of the organisation. And he had helped in the arrangements to cover up their departure. But also that he'd been dragged in and out of their affairs at, and for their convenience, when it suited them – and because of his long friendship with Primmer and trusting nature. It seemed to Rory, and Marguriette, that it was convenient for the "Inquests Panel of Judges" to come up with this theory. The missing pages from the Primmer file didn't corroborate any of this at all! But they were the only persons that had ever seen that part of the Primmers file! The question was - "where were those pages?" To them there was much more to the old man's involvement, in the all the affairs of these people and this "Organisation", but there was little use pursuing it. The other old house had been thoroughly searched by the CIB. This occurred a week after Bland's death. Another question mark. Why the delay?

Nothing of any significance was found. The house was filled with memorabilia, old furniture, ornamentation, and paintings, none, according to the authorities, of any significant value. Though there were letters, from his other daughter. Jenny's missing mother - Morag Elizabeth Bland. She was in fact very much alive – living in Cairns in North Queensland, Australia. Jim Bland plainly knew this. Where she was, and how she was living, all her personal details. She was the sole survivor of the family and inherited all of Bland's properties in the village, and his other investment assets. There was also the property of her daughter Jennifer. Morag Bland sold everything in both her Father's and Daughter's Estates through Lawyers and Real Estate agencies. She never returned to the coastal town.

There was also a matter of a particular painting that was found in his home – the signature – R.S.Calder, scrawled in the left corner – almost indecipherable.

Rory was able to identify it. It was a painting he'd done not long after he had married Serena, and he hadn't seen for over ten years. He had never particularly liked it, and had never even wondered where it had disappeared to. Now he knew, and there was a question mark. - How had it arrived in Jim Bland's possession? Though now, after all that he knew, he had a bit of an idea!

Jenny Sullivan:
Alias -Wilson, and the two men in the helicopter - were all killed – buy the Robinson colliding with the Power lines. Their bodies had been only identifiable through dental records. The cargo that the girl had loaded was also destroyed, and nothing was able to be used as evidence against anyone. It was thought in the end, that there wasn't any significance in the contents of the cartons she had been seen loading into the Robinson. It appeared from the investigation into what remained in the wreckage that they may have contained documents, some gems and gold leaf and quantities of class A drugs. This too seemed to be some kind of cover up. Neither Bronson or Calder were able to find any further information regarding this 'supposition'.

Jenny's schizophrenia has developed at an early age. During her time as a foster child she had been abused physically and mentally, and this had contributed to her fear of commitment and getting close to anyone – any sexual or emotional attachment that she had ever formed had been brief, and had usually involved physical and mental violence. She had been institutionalised several times in her teenage years.

Jenny had gone through her life living in a world of fantasy and fiction. Her Grandfather – Jim Bland had brought her back to the Village and attempted to 'normalise' her life, by providing the Cafe's and the Cottage to help her assimilate into a reasonably normal society. She had however discovered the 'secret' lives of her Grandfather, her Father, and the Primmers, and she had exploited all of them expertly for her own ends.

Most of the information, regarding Jenny Sullivan's past life, was discovered amongst Bland's papers, when the Police searched his home after his death.

Jenny along with her sister Miranda, her Grandfather, and her father Peter, were all buried together in the seaside towns Cemetery. Along side other family. Miranda's Mother Katherine, and Jim Bland's wife Molly. No-one apart from the Undertakers and Police, attended the funeral and internment.

Andrea Jones:
Recovered from her accident, when she had slipped and fallen from the spa bath. She stood trial as an accomplice with Peter Sullivan, and to being an accessory in the murder of Mangus and the injuries to Sullivan, which resulted in his subsequent demise. She had played the 'double game' to a high level, but often as in Andrea's case - the dice had been rolled once to often. She was also convicted of conspiracy to withholding evidence and subvert the course of justice. She should have spent five years in Prison, but on appeal, this was reduced to eighteen months, she was release after six!. She left the country – under a good behaviour bond. (This was more than a surprise, to both Rory and Marguriette.) – Jones went to live in Canada. She was killed in a car accident in Quebec twelve months later.

Warren Blanchard:
Found dead at the bottom of the lift shaft - presumably murdered by the McGillverays. He was also assumed, along with two other men, to have murdered his wife Miranda, Peter Sullivan and Mangus MacMillan.

And, was involved in the later killings, of Jongejan and McGillveray. Any association with Andrea Jones was never substantiated, and that he'd arranged for the explosive devices, in collusion with the Franklin and Amelia Primmer, for a considerable financial 'reward'. There was, of course, actually no evidence to corroborate these theories, or to connect any of the three in a conspiracy. And of course, there no-one left to 'confirm or deny' any of this supposition. But remnants of the 'spiders' web will remain.

Cheryl Brown:
(Helen Greene) - had been working undercover in the Village for over two years. She had begun her assignment there, at the same time that Rory had been working on his investigation at the University. Helen had been under orders and 'special' instructions, from Marguriette Bronson and Colin Moorhead. Unfortunately, over time, through the friendship she had developed with Miranda, she had become very involved, and infatuated with Peter Sullivan, and had been caught up with his friends. She had swayed away from her original brief, and became more caught up in the politics of crime. She had then tried to be clever with Jenny Sullivan, and blackmail her. She had, fortunately, continued to feed information, though limited, and sometimes false, to the CIB.

Cheryl's lesbian attachments, her bi-sexuality, drug and alcohol habits, had taken her along paths that she should never have walked. The result of this in the end was her death on the old barge. This may never have occurred – had these "traits" been recognised during her original interviews and psychological assessments. If they were, somehow, they were evidently had never been made known to the Police When this was discovered it had been decided that Rory would be brought back and sent to look further into the affairs of the people in this coastal criminal 'haven'! It is also unfortunate that he never bothered to read the 'brief and instructions' that he had been given when he was assigned to the case!

John Mackintosh:
Was arrested, and charged with possession of stolen property, drug smuggling, and growing cannabis for sale and supply. Further charges

followed, the manufacture of metham-phetamines, conspiracy to commit murder, and an accessory in the murder of Miranda Sullivan. This was based on information supplied by - "an unidentified informant". Though it was thought to be Blanchard, in conjunction with the Primmers, who, it was discovered, had never trusted him, or anyone else for that matter. And had used his naivete to achieve control of the whole of the finances of the Organisation. Mackintosh was imprisoned for a minimum non-parole period, of fifteen years. He attempted to continue his 'trades' while in Prison, and made a number of 'enemies'. He was raped and murdered after serving only three years of his term.

Police Sergeant Dougal Mackay:
Was found to have been in the pay of, and under the influence, the direction, of Bland, Primmer and Sullivan. He was also under instructions to be as obstructive to the CIB as possible. He was convicted, discharged from the force, and given a three year suspended sentence, as much of the evidence was deemed "hearsay". He used some 'legal connections' to assist in the removal of his records. He was able to leave the country, and went to live in North Queensland where he bought, with his 'special redundancy payment' (hush money) a small cattle Ranch. He died of Mel anomic skin cancer eighteen months later.

Troone (when he recovered from his injuries) and Clooney:
Went back to their positions in the Village. Later, the jurisdiction of the Village force was extended to cover a much wider area of the Peninsula. Troone was promoted to Sergeant, and Clooney to Senior Constable. A new Officer was appointed to Senior Sergeant. William (Bill) Williams, who had taken a small, brief part at the tail end of 'Operation Domino'! He fitted into the life on the Coast well. They were all content with their quiet seaside life style with their wives and families. They were advised to never discuss the events of those few with anyone. But on occasions the three men that they would go out on hunting trips, or fishing expeditions, and during the evenings by the camp fire, they would discuss the events of that April.

Superintendent John MacDonald:
Was reprimanded for incompetence in his initial, and final handling of the investigation. He was demoted to Senior Sergeant, and transferred to a Provincial town in the far North. He did not fit in with the local force or community. After four months, dispirited and unhappy, and a marriage break up, he resigned from the force. He went to live in the South Island of New Zealand. where he set up a Private Security firm. He lives there today, has a new partner, and has been very successful.

Constables Eton and Thomas:
Resumed their normal duties with the CIB. They were commended for their 'level headed and sensible approach' to the work on the 'three day case'. After six months, they were both promoted to Detective Senior Sergeants, and transferred to the new positions in different districts. They keep contact and maintain their friendship.

Maxine McGillveray:
Was blinded and crippled. She suffered severe burns, vertebrae damage, multiple broken bones in her legs, ribs and pelvis, and brain damage, from the explosion, and her subsequent fall from the balcony outside their rooms, to the lobby floor. Weeks later, there were attempts to question her. She was unable to remember anything of the events of the previous ten years, and continually shook her head at the Police and Psychiatrists queries. Even though she was able, in a limited way, to communicate. She could speak very slowly and with great difficulty, and could write some words. Maxine would spend the rest of her life in a wheel chair in an institution. After eighteen months though it was apparent that she had lost all will to live, refused food and drink and began to waste away. Three months later she died of pneumonia.

Sarah McGillveray:
Had assisted in the initial identification of her mother's broken burnt body. She had told the Police, and later the inquiry, of the calls from the Hotel and produced the tape from her answer machine. Also the letter her Father

had left in their office for her. She began suffering from severe manic-depression, gradually she became more reclusive, and resisted contact with almost everyone, except the staff of the Hospital where her Mother was. Eight months after the final Commissions report came out - she stepped off the platform and fell in front of a train that was coming into the city station - she was killed instantly. Rory had tried to keep contact with her but never took her to lunch, or went to see her as he had promised. Rory with Marguriette Bronson attended her funeral.

Euan McGillveray and Hans Jongejan.

There were no physical identifiable remains found of either of these men. And - for some unknown reason, not even Dental records could provide substantial enough evidence of the identity of the burnt disfigured bodies found in the shattered remains of the Hotel room. But there was evidence from their old passports, then other documents found in the rental car. This, coupled with photographs that Detective Superintendent Bronson had in her files, and the descriptions supplied by the staff at the Inn, was considered sufficient. It was thought that it could've been an individual – or a conspiracy. Peter Sullivan, Warren Blanchard, the Primmers, or perhaps even Andrea Jones, all could have booby trapped the briefcase. But the question remained - 'Why would any of them----?' It was, as so often in these instances, that 'there was no honour or trust amongst thieves'. The type of explosive used was unknown to any of the experts available. There was much conjecture and disagreement - but in the end it was thought it could've been some new type of previously unknown Plastique. All very wishy washy. The report filled with pages of complete inconclusive, unbelievable waffle.

Although others were also under suspicion, of being closely tied in to the murders – Bland – Jenny Sullivan (who obviously somehow, had knowledge of explosives) - who plainly was no longer available to give evidence, and Andrea Jones.

However, her "unconscious state" when the brief case had been removed by Blanchard helped her alibi. Again, for some unexplained reason, it was decided that it was irrelevant and would not be pursued.

It was wondered in some circles how much the 'Profession were protecting the Professions'? And both the Police and the Justice system were under the spot light!

There was – a few months later, after the final Inquest, an interview with a former Senior Police Detective, regarding 'The Culture of Corruption' in the Police Force. Moorhead of course, denied this accusation vehemently, that there was absolutely no truth in the allegations, and threatened legal action. The intervention of the Minister, who with the Commissioner, and the Police association set up an 'Internal Inquiry' this achieved nothing further, and the Investigation was closed. Rumours of course remained - but nothing eventuated or nothing changed.

Michael and Jane - The Flints:
Were investigated "thoroughly" and "proven" to be the rightful lawful owners of Wisteria Lodge. Council records – rates – Legal purchase agreements – and all papers and accounts pertaining to the property going back over five years were in their names and appeared correct. Nothing could be found to incriminate them in any of the illegal affairs in the district. Or, to have had any connection with the Primmers.

They continued throughout, to plead ignorance of any knowledge of the them, and the activities that had gone on at the house over the last weeks prior to the "drastic conclusions". They were able to produce evidence of their holiday, this was corroborated by Travel agents - the owners of the Island resorts where they had stayed, and the Airlines that they had travelled on.

This is not, of course to say that they were not involved, it just couldn't be proved. To Rory and Marguriette, they were too squeaky clean, but there didn't seem any way that an investigation would go any further with them. Unless it was from a much higher "Authority" - or a lower one - and they employed Private Investigators. The Local population was particularly cooperative in their corroboration of the Flints and their story. Whoever had devised that part of the operation had been extraordinary in their planning, extremely thorough. They must also have paid a considerable number of people, considerable amounts of money for their assistance and evidential "assistance".

Cooperative and corroborative. But not overly forthcoming with the fine factual detail.

Their story, regarding the "missing" Chev Coupe was as follows. "In the middle of one night, a day or so ago, they'd heard some strange, unusual sounds, movements in the bush, around the gardens. No, not the sound of an old V8 motor starting! In the morning they had discovered that the car was gone. When asked why they (the Flints) didn't investigate themselves - their answer was - 'Often get animals - you know - dogs, possums – they make an unholy noise – and even the odd deer, or boar, roaming through. So – well – we just thought – that was what it might be?' They had reported it to the Local Police, Sergeant Dougal Mackay had investigated.

Wisteria Lodge:
The sign advertising the Bed and Breakfast was removed in the following months. The property placed on the market, and was sold several months later for an undisclosed sum to an English woman. She had, by "coincidence", moved from South Africa, some months earlier. She had been resident in the Republic for five years. Her name was Susan Smythe. She most of the time, kept to herself, and was seen rarely in the village, and spend the majority of her time travelling overseas. It appeared that she was an extremely wealthy woman, and that she didn't have a husband or partner – at least not with her, whenever she was in residence.

Franklin and Amelia Primmer:
Had completely vanished. The manner of how they had done so, was a complete enigma. After exactly a month following the April event and their disappearance, persons 'approximately' fitting their description were seen on an Airport surveillance camera. By "coincidence" of course, boarding a Japan Airlines 747 bound for Tokyo. Police were alerted in Japan. That couple never arrived. It was thought they must have disembarked at a stop over in Singapore or Taiwan, and transferred to a flight to - who knows where?

They were never seen again. The missing Domino tiles from the incomplete game - the incomplete and fabricated file? Was dubbed "Bronson's Folly - The Phantom Primmers"! It was also found that extremely sensitive and important documents had recently been removed from the Departments of Internal, and External affairs. No-one had any idea how, or by whom. Despite persistent questioning from the Media, the Government and the SIS made no comment.

There was only one very small shred of evidence that may have been linked to the Primmers getting away from the Lodge, it wasn't exactly over looked, but was never able to be substantiated. Like a lot of it! But an Old Chev Coupe that appeared to be extremely similar to Rory Calders, minus registration plates, engine and chassis numbers, found burned out, about fifty k's, on the other side of the Peninsula, near a private airfield.

The Country Inn:
The explosion and fire had by some "miracle", and a recent upgraded sprinkler system had limited the damage to the three upstairs rooms. The outer back walls of these rooms, the ceiling of and part of the kitchen and storage areas below. More than half of the roof and that side of the building had collapsed. The fire had been contained, by the new sprinkler system, and the extremely rapid response, of the Fire services.

Although these areas were extensively damaged no-one else, was injured. Several of the staff were treated for shock, but with the late hour, only a few staff had still been on the premises. The solid reinforced double cavity brick construction of the internal and external walls of the building had prevented anything further. It was able to reopen for limited trade ten days later and it was hoped that it would be fully restored in two to three months. That work had now been completed, but it had taken, as these things do, considerably longer than anticipated. The up side of the explosion and the intrigue and rumours surrounding it, have made the Inn a tourist destination!

* *

Whoever wrote the reports originally, plainly thought -----

"When nothing is as it seems – it seems there is nothing that makes any sense. Nothing leads to nothing. And all is as an empty can – it makes the most noise – about nothing"

* *

FOOT NOTE (2):

Rory and Marguriette allowed themselves to have some time together in the subsequent weeks after the end of the Inquest.

The past was discussed at length – the present and future were left alone – apart from many walks on long beaches and through bush tracks when little was spoken. A considerable number of evening were spent together, and in the darkness of the night they relived what they had had years before. The fires were rekindled, and the flames burnt high, bright and very hot!

They knew though that this sojourn was not to last, their paths had been set by the circumstances of those three days in April.

Six weeks later, after his document bonfire, Rory returned to Britain. He took up a new Lecturing position at the University in Glasgow, he had wanted to return to Cardiff, but had been advised it would be 'inappropriate' and they had recommended him to the Scottish University.

Marguriette, spent a short period working with the Department of Internal affairs. Unhappy with her work and lifestyle, she asked to be transferred to External Affairs, and a posting overseas. This was granted. She was appointed to a Senior position at the New Zealand Embassy in Brussels.

They kept in contact – close contact, by phone and E mail. Again, neither were settled and were unhappy with where their lives were, and their employment. They resigned from their respective positions, on exactly the same day.

Thirteen months after the 'three days of insanity' Inquest concluded, in early May 2012 they met in Dublin.

They now live in Dun Laoghaire on the coast south of Dublin. They own and run a small Pub, and go sailing. Rory has as yet, not gone back to his idea of advancing his Art, writing, and getting away from 'it all'.

And yes – they're happy with their lives together. But are they content with what they know – or more precisely, what they do not?

Roger Weston is a writer and artist. Formerly a Teacher, Educational motivator; Farmer: and Restaurateur. He studied Education, Psychology and English at Massey University. Previously he has had three books published. Two collections of Poetry -"The Words of an Artist" and "Magpies", and his first Novel, a psychological thriller - "The Backgammon Syndrome." He now lives in Dunedin, New Zealand.